FAERIE TALES

from the

WHITE FOREST

Brigitta of the White Forest
The Ruins of Noe
Ondelle of Grioth

ISBN 978-0-9890828-5-3

Cover art: Copyright © Julie Fain
http://juliefainart.com/

Book 1 chapter heading art: Copyright © Larry Ho

Books 2 & 3 chapter heading art, maps, and illustrations: © Alison Woodward
alisonannwoodward.blogspot.com

Omnibus cover design: Christian Fink-Jensen
finkjensen.com

Published by:

Hydra House
2850 SW Yancy St. #106
Seattle, WA 98126
www.hydrahousebooks.com

These are works of fiction. Names, characters, places, and incidents are either the products of the author's imagination or are used fictitiously. Any resemblance to actual events, locales, situations, faeries, Nhords, Saari, or persons, living or dead, is purely coincidental.

Printed through CreateSpace.

Introduction

Faerie Tales from the White Forest
OMNIBUS Edition

I am pleased to present to you a collection of the first three books in my *Faerie Tales from the White Forest* fantasy series for young readers (and for the young at heart). What a thrill to have these books in one collection. The adventures are far from over, though, and I hope that you will continue along with Brigitta and her friends as they face greater and greater challenges in their quest to unite their world.

I would like to thank my publisher (Tod McCoy) for the suggestion for such an omnibus, my writing group (Chris Fink-Jensen, Tony Ollivier, Lois Peterson, Esther Sarlo) and critique partners (Sara Nickerson, Natalie Smith) for their support, my various focus group readers over the years (Ivaly Cline, Heron and Liz Collins, Lilly Era, Kate Fink-Jensen, Kelly and Karen Hoskins, Emma Kahn, Darline Sanderson, Ella Shaw, Andy Smallman, Angelica Taggart, and Jeremy Zimmerman) for their input, and my Sweetwood Tribe for making it all worthwhile.

Danika Dinsmore

BRIGITTA

of the

WHITE
FOREST

Faerie Tales from the White Forest
Book One

Danika Dinsmore

Hydra House ❖ Seattle, Washington

For my father, Stanley Dinsmore,
who introduced me to my first imaginary worlds
(1929 – 2006)

Chapter One

Brigitta leaned out the window of Auntie Ferna's cottage and balanced on her stomach in the sill. She spread her arms wide open and slowly lifted her legs. Her balance shifted forward and she dove, head first, out the window.

She somersaulted through the air and caught herself just above the large rock burrowed partway up Fernatta's ancient tree. She fluttered the rest of the way down to the rock and looked back up at the window.

Not bad, she thought.

She turned and sat down, facing north, so that the entire village-nest of Gyllenhale was spread before her. She tucked the loose strands of her dark auburn hair back into her hair bands and settled into a patch of moss, listening to the children's voices drifting out the window. Brigitta's little sister Himalette shrieked from somewhere inside the cottage and Brigitta cringed.

"All eyes up front!" called Auntie Ferna from inside and the voices quieted. "Today's lesson will be on the history of the Festival of the Elements."

Brigitta groaned and pulled her knees to her chin. She narrowed her olive eyes and watched the flow of faeries zipping in and out of the busy marketplace below.

Several high-pitched squeals pierced the air and Brigitta turned her attention toward the sound. Two male Elder Apprentices hovered at the top of a very tall tree. Suddenly, they dropped, free-falling until they caught themselves in the air directly in front of the excited faces of three Water Faerie girls sitting on a long branch at the bottom of the tree. Brigitta recognized them; they were from Rioscrea, the village-nest southeast of her own home. The girls applauded and squealed some more as the two boys took a few bows.

"Big deal," muttered Brigitta.

Sliding from the branch, the girls took to the air, playfully circling each other as they made their way through the trees. Brigitta caught sight of the shiny new markings at the ends of their wings.

"They've been changed!" she gasped.

She glanced over her shoulder at her own dull green and yellow wings, then back at the young faeries who disappeared into the busy marketplace.

Brigitta leapt from the rock and flew down past Fernatta's garden arranged like an enormous leafy welcome mat in front of her tree. She glided over the path that led down through the village-nest and descended to Spring River. She landed on the shore at the edge of the marketplace, which was alive with dancing and singing and shouting and laughing under a hundred woven tents pitched on both sides of the river. Dozens of Water Gardeners bobbed in their reed boats, flitting their wings and calling out the names of their crops. *Sharmock! Gundlebean! Dragon flower!*

Brigitta took a deep breath and entered.

Busy stalls crammed the riverbank where Water Faeries offered weather spell ingredients, Fire Faeries displayed feather paints, Air Faeries bartered with bolts of cloth, and Earth Faeries spun delicate candle webs. Brigitta caught a whiff of baking pipberries and her stomach growled in response.

She spotted the three girls as they passed the pink and green tingermint tent, their fresh destiny markings taunting her as she buzzed along behind them. Tilan, the eldest, proudly sported wings marked with a blue moon and three silver shooting stars, the symbols for a Star Teller.

"That wouldn't be so bad, staring up at the sky each night," thought Brigitta as she dodged a family of burly Earth Faeries.

Tilan and her two friends stopped at a tent where a wispy Air Faerie woman was weaving white lyllium flowers into a basket. Brigitta landed behind them, stumbled on a tent peg, and knocked into the weaver. The girls laughed as Brigitta apologized to the Air Faerie.

"Brigitta of Tiragarrow!" said Kyllia, a radiant golden-hued faerie whose wings bore the markings of a Village-Nest Caretaker.

"Running errands for your momma and poppa?" asked Tilan.

"No . . . I . . . " Brigitta stepped back and tucked in her immature wings.

"Where's Himalette? You're not babysitting today?" Tilan looked around the marketplace.

"No . . . well . . . "

"Why don't you come with us then?" teased Dinnae, pink and plump with a wide smile. She leaned closer. "We're going to the Center Realm to watch the festival preparations." She fluttered her rosy wings, freshly colored with an inner eye glyph and two radiating lines at the tip of each.

"You've got your destiny markings," said Brigitta, pointing at Dinnae's wings.

"Well, nothing gets past you, does it?" said Dinnae. "You must get your smarts from your poppa."

The other two burst out laughing.

The two male Center Realm faeries emerged from the crowd and presented Tilan, Kyllia, and Dinnae with yellow flutterscarves. Brigitta stood quietly as they all turned to leave.

"Aren't you coming along?" asked Tilan, waving her new flutterscarf.

Brigitta wondered how many gundlebeans her momma would ask her to shell if she ditched Himalette in Gyllenhale. "Sure, I'll . . . first . . . I have to . . . " Brigitta motioned vaguely behind her.

"Get permission from your Auntie?" suggested Dinnae.

The three girls batted their eyelashes at Brigitta, who said nothing.

"Come on, let's go," said one of the Elder Apprentices.

They left Brigitta standing there without a good-bye, laughter trailing after them like their scarves.

Brigitta landed on Fernatta's porch and entered the cottage. She could hear her Auntie in the gathering room, deep into her lesson.

"Auntie, I was just wondering—" began Brigitta as she stepped into the room.

"Do not interrupt, child." Fernatta glanced up from her Chronicler's book, her silvery hair dancing like fire.

Sitting on the floor in front of her, a dozen large-eyed faerie boys and girls burst into giggles. Himalette sat in the front row playfully shaking her finger at her older sister. Brigitta glared at her.

"Yes, Auntie." Brigitta slid down to the floor.

Fernatta turned back to her students. Although all teachers in the White Forest were called Auntie and Uncle, Auntie Ferna really was Brigitta's Auntie. She was her Great Auntie, her poppa's mother's sister, and Brigitta often flew between their two village-nests trading objects back and forth for them. She didn't mind flying errands so much, as long as her momma didn't make her drag Himalette along with her.

Like every other teacher in the White Forest, the ends of Fernatta's wings were marked with two circles, one inside the other, resembling the two moons or the inner part of an eye, and two radiating lines. The direction of the radiating lines, downwards toward water and earth, meant she was a Chronicler, and was in charge of teaching the children faerie lore and history.

"It is important to remember," Fernatta addressed the children, "that the Festival of Elements is not all fun and games. Our forest depends upon the magic of the festival. The exact combination of elements protects the forest from the beasts who would love access to our home.

"As long as the Elders balance the elements at the end of each growing season, the forest is protected," Fernatta continued. Brigitta mouthed the rest of the familiar words as Fernatta spoke them aloud, "And those nasty beasts can only dream of getting inside."

Folding her arms over her knees, she sighed and stared at a patch of light streaming in through the window. She pictured Dinnae's new destiny markings: inner eye circles with lines radiating toward fire and earth. So, she was to become a Cooking Teacher, thought Brigitta. How terribly dull.

A fluttery shadow appeared and danced in the light. Another shadow joined it and Brigitta watched as the two shadowflies flitted around each other. Up and down and around, the shadows made their way across the floor and onto a set of old books in a bookshelf made of interlocking tree branches.

The shadows danced a moment more, then disappeared from the light. Brigitta stared at the spines of the books on the bottom shelf. She turned her head sideways so she could read the titles: *Faerie Lore*

& Lineage . . . Songs & Dances . . . Potions & Recipes . . . Maps & Passages . . .

Brigitta glanced up at Auntie Ferna, still absorbed in her lesson, then slipped *Maps & Passages* from the shelf and opened the book. The first page contained a map of the entire White Forest. The Earth Realm was spread across the top, the Air Realm to the east, the Fire Realm to the south, and the Water Realm in the west.

She flipped through the pages. There were detailed maps of each village-nest, starting with the Earth Realm: Dmvyle, Grobjahar, Ithcommon, Gyllenhale . . . She flipped past them all until she got to her home, the village-nest of Tiragarrow in the Water Realm.

A blue line marking Spring River flowed east of Tiragarrow. She followed the line down to where Spring River ended at Precipice Falls and the water tumbled down into a series of underground caverns running the length of the White Forest. Dozens of dotted lines spread out from the falls across the page. She traced the dotted lines with her finger, then stopped. The dotted blue lines . . . the underground caverns . . . someone had mapped them! Someone, at some point in time, had explored the caverns and drawn up this map.

She turned back through the pages and took a closer look at each one. There were dotted lines running through every single village-nest. Some branched off of others, and some seemed to start and stop at random. She wondered who had mapped them all and how come she had never heard anyone mention it before. All faerie children were told the caverns were water channels that kept the forest lush and fertile. She hadn't even considered that it was possible to explore them.

Auntie Ferna's voice cut into Brigitta's thoughts: "The Great Hourglass of Protection was a gift from the Ancient Ones when they brought us north to this land long ago. It sits in the Center Realm where the High Priestess and Council of Elders preside."

The Center Realm! Brigitta searched through the book until she came to a map of the Center Realm. In the middle of the page, the Hourglass of Protection was labeled in dark silver. Off to the side, a dotted line led from the drawing of a tree stump into the Elder Chambers, fondly referred to as the Hive.

She looked up from the book. Who else knows about this passage, she wondered, staring out over the heads of the young faeries. Turning back to the map, she re-examined the dotted lines. Then, with her heart pounding in her chest, Brigitta carefully and quietly began to rip the page out of the ancient text.

"Ever since the Great World Cry many seasons ago, Faweh, the world outside the White Forest, has been in complete elemental chaos."

Fernatta paused and Brigitta's fingers froze in mid-tear. She peered up at her Auntie, who was leaning in close to her huddled students. "There exist dangerous beasts with hideous hearts and haphazard magic. No place for faeries."

Brigitta gave one last quick tug and the page came loose. She folded it twice and tucked it into her tunic pocket.

"This is why we must set the Hourglass of Protection just right every season-cycle, so that our forest remains protected. Brigitta?"

Brigitta whipped her head up and slammed the book shut. "Yes, Auntie!"

"You had a question?"

"Uh . . ."

The faerie children laughed as Fernatta studied her great niece. Her mouth was stern, but her eyes twinkled. She removed a small turquoise keronium glass from the shelf.

"I have something for your poppa." She handed the glass to Brigitta, who got up off the floor and took the fragile object from her Auntie. "Be careful with it. This one had to be melted down and reblown four times to get it right."

Brigitta imagined being shut inside a furnace room for many moons and shivered at the idea of being destiny-marked as a Keronium Glass-Blower.

"Why don't you take it to him? I'll bring Himalette home after her lesson." Fernatta winked at Brigitta.

"Of course!" Brigitta called, sailing out the door.

Chapter Two

Brigitta sped through the forest to the Center Realm. She dodged the festival organizers and headed to the top of the Water Faerie grandstand. Dozens of faeries had erected booths outside the immense festival grounds and were preparing them for displays of arts and crafts and inventions. She scanned the booths and then turned her attention inside the festival grounds. In three suns time, every faerie in the White Forest would be gathered in the grandstands to watch the resetting of the Hourglass.

The grandstands were divided into four sections, one for each elemental realm, forming a "U" around a large silver oval platform. Five ornate wooden seats were positioned in front of the platform for the Elders and High Priestess. Suspended above the platform was the gigantic Hourglass of Protection, held in place by a twisted mass of tree branches emerging from two enormous uul trees on either side of the festival grounds.

Brigitta spotted Tilan, Kyllia, and Dinnae at the top of the Air Faerie grandstand, peering over the backside. She fluttered across the arena and landed next to them.

"Well, look who's here!" said Tilan in mock amaze-ment.

"Where are the boys?" asked Brigitta.

"They had important work to do for the Elders," said Dinnae.

"The festival's in three suns time, after all," Kyllia pointed out.

They turned to watch four faeries hauling decorations out of a carved trunk. Brigitta examined Kyllia's wings. Two deep green wisps adorned the ends.

"Are you sure you want to be a Village-Nest Caretaker?" Brigitta finally asked.

"It's my Life Task," Kyllia said, shrugging her shoulders. "Ooh, look!" She pointed as the decorators began to string shadowfly lanterns in the trees.

"But it's just one thing. What if you stop liking to do it? What if . . . ?" Brigitta couldn't think of a single thing she liked enough to do for the rest of her seasons.

A dark-haired sprite zipped past, disturbing Brigitta's thoughts as it narrowly missed her head with the large seed pod it was carrying. Brigitta steadied herself and watched as the sprite dashed off like a mad thunder-bug toward the uul trees.

"Did you see that?" she asked, pointing toward the unapologetic sprite.

The three girls looked up at Brigitta.

"That sprite. It nearly knocked me over with a—with a—big ugly seed pod!"

The girls stared at her blankly.

"Oh Brigitta," sighed Tilan, "who cares about *fringe faeries* at a time like this?"

"I know you're probably a little jealous of our new wing markings and have to make up stories for attention." Dinnae patted Brigitta's arm as if she were a child.

Brigitta fumed. "I'm not jealous. It's just that—Look, it makes complete sense that my poppa has the markings of an Inventor and my momma has the markings of a Feast Master. They like those things. They're *good* at those things."

"Oh, right. The only thing Brigitta's good at is daydreaming," said Tilan, winking at the other girls.

"I've never heard of destiny markings for a Day Dreamer," Kyllia teased.

"Maybe she'll be the first!" Dinnae chimed in.

This sent the three faeries into fits of laughter. Brigitta's ears began to burn.

"I'm good at plenty of things . . . " Brigitta grumbled. She felt the folded piece of paper in her pocket. "I'm good at . . . I'm good at . . . reading maps!"

"What's that got to do with anything?" asked Tilan.

"Follow me and I'll show you," said Brigitta.

"Are we done playing around in the brush?" asked Dinnae, examining her hands. She wiped them on a leaf. "Let's go to the river and lie on the sundreaming rocks."

Brigitta and the others were searching through the trees behind the Fire Faerie grandstand. Brigitta gripped the map in her pocket as if that would magically lead them to the hidden entrance.

"Yes, let's," agreed Tilan. "I've had enough treasure hunting."

"Here it is!" Brigitta shouted and fluttered her wings. She pointed to an old tree stump, covered in vines. She dropped down and pulled the vines away to reveal a large hole at the base. The others drew in around her. Brigitta poked her head inside and felt a cool breeze. "This way."

The entrance was tight. They had to crawl through one at a time until it opened up into an underground passageway carved into the earth. Her friends stumbled and giggled in the dark.

"Shhhhh!" Brigitta hushed them.

The girls pushed each other along and after several twists in the passageway they saw a dim light streaming in from the stone wall. They gathered around and peered through the gap.

On the other side of the wall was an entryway and past the entryway was a chamber. On the far side of the chamber, illuminated by dozens of long silver candles, High Priestess Ondelle of Grioth was leading the Elders through their spell rehearsals. Ondelle stood tall on her dark frame. Her fiery red wings quivered. Both were marked with a large golden eye and four golden lines radiating in four directions, the destiny markings of a High Priestess.

Each Elder held a miniature hourglass in one hand and a yellow keronium glass in the other. One at a time, Ondelle faced the Elders and waved her hands over the objects. Brigitta held her breath, mesmerized by Ondelle's long slender fingers dancing so effortlessly, as if supported by the air itself. Ondelle's deep black eyes glimmered in the candlelight. She turned and pulled her scepter down from a nook in the wall.

Brigitta moved closer to the gap as the Elders gathered around Ondelle and raised their arms. Ondelle turned around in a circle, pointing her scepter toward the Elders.

"By the authority of the Eternal Dragon, by the wisdom of the Ancients, by the power of faerie Blue Spell—we charge these sands."

"You'd think they'd be sick of practicing by now, they've been at it for moons," whispered Dinnae.

"They have to get it right. They have to practice because of Hrathgar," Brigitta whispered. "A long time ago she tried to steal the power of the Hourglass and was banished from the White Forest."

"Everyone knows that," said Kyllia.

The Elders and Ondelle all closed their eyes and began to chant. Brigitta could feel the reverberations of their voices inside her body. Losing herself in the rhythm of the words, she leaned toward the Elders.

"Brigitta, move back, we can't see," shot Dinnae, tugging on Brigitta's pack.

Ondelle suddenly stopped chanting and opened her eyes. She stared across the room to where the four faerie girls were hiding. Brigitta's three friends gasped and leapt to their feet, but Brigitta was frozen in place by Ondelle's black moon eyes. They grew wide and her face stiffened.

"Come on!" Tilan pulled Brigitta up by her pack straps.

The others fled down the passageway and Brigitta followed. As they emerged from the tree stump, the girls squealed with the delight that mischief brings. Brigitta pretended to laugh with them, looking back over her shoulder, expecting at any moment for Ondelle to come flying out after them.

Chapter Three

Brigitta left her friends in the Center Realm and flew through the forest until she came to Spring River. She headed south with the river, racing the leaves caught in its current. The trees broke away and she turned west into the lyllium field that bordered the Water Realm. The smell of the flowers comforted her, and she slowed down to touch the tops of their white petals. She plucked one and stared into its dark center, picturing Ondelle's face and her black moon eyes.

She hadn't dared tell the other girls how that stare had penetrated her. They would have laughed and accused her of trying to draw attention to herself. How easily they had dismissed the entire incident, caring more about which boys they would dance with at the festival. But Brigitta couldn't shake the feeling that Ondelle had known it was her behind the wall, and that Ondelle's look had meant something.

Brigitta hovered in the middle of the field and stared across the dreamy whiteness. She thought about flying down to Precipice Falls to see if she could find another secret passageway, but then remembered the delivery she had for her poppa. Instead, she blew a kiss to the lylliums and headed toward Tiragarrow.

Brigitta's cottage was on the southern edge of the village-nest above a moss glade. The trees in back of their cottage were covered in tangled vines on which the girls could swing into the downy green.

She arrived home to find Auntie Ferna and Himalette sitting on the front porch shelling gundlebeans and singing one of Himalette's made-up songs. Brigitta's momma, Pippet of Rioscrea, emerged from the cottage, followed by the aroma of familiar spices used in her famous goldenfew. The fermented gundlebean stew was a festival favorite.

"Just in time," her momma laughed, handing Brigitta a glass of iced frommafin. She handed drinks to Himalette and Fernatta. "Like your poppa," she added, holding up a fourth glass for Mousha as his ruddy face appeared in the doorway.

"So, Mousha of Grobjahar, you haven't disappeared into the ether after all?" Fernatta teased her nephew.

Mousha pouted as he handed a well-worn potion book to Fernatta. "If I'd known you were going to collect your book today . . . "

"You may borrow it back again after the festival," said Fernatta.

"Hey, Poppa, here." Brigitta pulled the turquoise keronium glass from her pack.

Mousha's eyes lit up and he clapped his hands in approval. He ran back to his cluttered laboratory to search for a proper gift in trade.

Fernatta examined the bright pink liquid in her glass and then sniffed it. Pippet paused at the door. Her golden hair was swept into a haphazard pile on her round faerie head. Loose curls stuck to her face and the backs of her dusty coral wings.

Fernatta took a slow sip, swirling it around in her mouth before swallowing. "Ahhh!" she exclaimed. "How do you make such a perfect refreshment every time?"

Pippit only smiled as she made her way back to the kitchen, taking Himalette and the shelled gundlebeans with her.

Mousha re-emerged and presented Fernatta with a tiny red spout snake which she accepted with a gracious smile. Brigitta waved good-bye to the snake as Fernatta tucked it into her tunic pocket. She bid them good-bye and swooped off the porch, leaving her signature cloud of crotia flower scent behind. Mousha patted

Brigitta's head and retreated to his laboratory with the keronium glass, his little yellow wings tapping together like contemplative fingers.

Brigitta followed him into the lab and sank down into her favorite mushroom chair, watching his round body bounce about the room. His right wing was stubbornly twisted where he had injured it collecting thunderbugs as a boy. The brown marks on the ends of his wings looked like dot-less question marks.

"Poppa, Ondelle's a deodyte . . ." said Brigitta.

Mousha held his new keronium glass up to the light. "Magnificent."

"She has two elements, Air and Fire."

"What's that? Oh, yes, two elements. Very rare. Rare indeed." He set the glass down and pulled a jar from the shelf.

"But what's that feel like? Is it like having another faerie inside of you?"

"Three glassfuls?" Mousha asked himself. "No, four." He reached into the jar and began to scoop keronium glassfuls of a powder into a large beaker of liquid. The liquid turned deep purple. He gave the beaker a little shake.

Brigitta sighed and got up from the chair. She fluttered to the door. The frame was wrapped with a gundlebean vine on which Mousha strung his thunderbug symphony during special occasions. Brigitta stroked the leaves of the vine. They resembled enormous green dewdrops. One of them began to vibrate.

"Poppa, are you going to string the symphony?" she asked hopefully, opening the vibrating leaf.

Mousha grumbled from inside the lab and Brigitta looked up as a sad poof of purple smoke fell off the table and landed on the floor. "Bog stench!" he swore.

Brigitta turned back to the vine just as an orange thunderbug darted up from the opened leaves. It weaved through the air and into Mousha's lab. It flew about his head and he absentmindedly swatted it away as he examined a large vial of smoke-colored liquid.

Brigitta watched, amused, as the bug explored the room. Mousha poured the smoky liquid into a tube of pink liquid. It immediately bubbled over. He lifted the vial up to the light and gave a satisfied nod. The thunderbug buzzed over and landed on his hand.

"Ahhh!" Mousha shrieked and fumbled the vial, spattering pink liquid across his face and chest. The vial fell to the ground and shattered.

"You . . . you!" he sputtered pink bubbles from his lips. He searched the room for the intruder as it hovered high above his head.

Brigitta put her hand over her mouth to keep from laughing.

Mousha looked up. "Aha!"

He picked up a crystal atomizer and squeezed it at the thunderbug, missing it entirely. The bug zigzagged around the room as Mousha chased it with his bug stunner, flinging pink spots across every wall. The thunderbug landed on a shelf above his work table.

Mousha fluttered up to the shelf on his little wings. "I've got you now!"

"Brigitta!" her momma's voice called.

Brigitta turned toward the kitchen. Pippet stood in the doorway with a spoon in one hand and a handful of gundlebeans in the other. Himalette peered out from behind her.

"You know your poppa is working very hard and—"

There was a CRASH from the laboratory. Pippet and Himalette rushed to the door. Pippet tried not to laugh as she caught sight of Mousha, bug stunner in one hand, shelf in the other, pink liquid dripping from his chin. In the window sill, the thunderbug sat cleaning itself, emitting low drum beats of annoyance.

"I won't be working on anything at all," Mousha said, frowning at the floor, "until I get this mess cleaned up."

They all looked at the broken shards on the ground.

"Sorry, Poppa," said Brigitta sincerely as Mousha stared weepy eyed at the remains. His yellow wings tapped together.

"Come on, then," said Pippet, rolling up her sleeves. "Let's help him out."

They cleaned up the lab, caught the thunderbug, and put it in a jar for Himalette. When they were done, Pippet gave a satisfied nod. Then her face fell. "My stew!"

Pippet and the girls flew to the kitchen, where the fermented gundlebeans blurped away. Pippet took one whiff and shook her head. "Well, this won't do."

"I'll get rid of it for you, Momma," said Brigitta.

"Take Himalette with you," said Pippet as she doused the fire. "I've got a lot of chopping to do."

"My friends don't have to take their little sisters with them everywhere they go!"

"Please, Brigitta, just take your sister and dump the stew." Pippet eyed Brigitta sternly. "No shenanigans and no trips to the Center Realm."

"I could do it faster on my own," said Brigitta.

"That's enough."

Brigitta grumbled to herself as she poked a stick at the dying embers beneath the hot vat. Suddenly inspired, she turned to her sister, "Himmy, make yourself useful. Grab Poppa's bug stunner and his globelight and the vine from the doorway. We're going to fix up his symphony."

Brigitta and Himalette peered over the northern edge of Tiragarrow. The warm vat of goldenfew sat between them. Together they tipped it and spilled the stewy contents over the side. Himalette squealed as it sloshed over the trees and bushes and onto the ground below. Brigitta crouched down at the edge of the village-nest and Himalette crawled up beside her.

"Maybe they won't come?" she said. "Maybe they don't like goldenfew anymore. Or maybe it's a specially bad batch."

"Shhhh," Brigitta silenced her sister.

Himalette leaned her chin out over the forest. She made soft popping sounds with her lips for a few moments and then rolled over onto her back and stared at the patches of sky through the tree branches. A loud buzz careened past and they both sat up. They watched and listened as hisses came in swarms from the river, sparkles came in flocks from the lyllium field, and buzzes came in bursts from every other direction. A silent formation of tiny shadows flitted through the trees and landed on a stew-covered branch.

"Shadowflies!" Himalette floated up on excited wings.

Brigitta yanked her back down. "We're waiting for the thunderbugs."

On cue, there was a burst of little clashing beats. Ricocheting off the trunks of the trees, vibrating beasts of all different sizes, shapes, and colors made their way to the steamy mess below. All the other flying, blinking, and zipping beasts abandoned the meal and slipped back into the forest.

Once the thunderbugs had polished off the stew, they settled into the branches to digest it, emitting a steady stream of drunken hiccups as they lazed and swayed. The faerie sisters leapt off the edge of the village-nest and glided to the ground. Brigitta examined four thunderbugs wobbling across a branch while Himalette plucked a tiny yellow beast from a leaf and placed it in a jar.

"Only the biggest and loudest ones, Himmy." Brigitta pulled out the atomizer and sprayed a vivid pink bug with an enormous vibrating bottom.

"I'm going to make up a song for the thunderbugs!" declared Himalette. *"Thunderbugs, how you twinkle and shine, how you twinkle and shine . . ."*

"Thunderbugs don't twinkle. Or shine." Brigitta sprayed and plucked a drunken thunderbug from a branch and placed it in a jar, doing her best to pretend that Himalette was in another world, one that was so far away she couldn't be heard.

She practiced her favorite ignoring technique, a hum that radiated from the space between her eyes. "Hmmmmmmmmmmmnnnnnnnnn . . ." she hummed as she continued through the trees, spraying and plucking thunderbugs until she reached the lyllium field. She placed the jars of bugs inside her pack and turned back toward Tiragarrow.

"Himalette?" Brigitta called. Then louder, "Hima-lette!"

Her voice echoed through the trees.

"Himmy!" she growled.

The faint sound of laughter danced in the air.

Brigitta followed the laughter into the trees until she came across a large fallen log that sounded suspiciously like a giggling young faerie.

"Himalette, come out of there," Brigitta commanded.

"I found a sprite! I found a sprite!" Himalette called back from inside the log.

"Leave it alone."

"She's pretty."

"Don't touch it!" Brigitta climbed into the long, narrow log. She could see Himalette farther down, illuminated by a blue light. Himalette squealed, and then the light vanished.

Brigitta removed her pack and dug out her poppa's globelight. She rubbed the globe a few times to charge it. After it lit up, she made her way through the log, scrunching down as it narrowed. She held the light up to Himalette and gasped. The globelight flickered.

Himalette was blue from her face to her feet. Even her pink wings and blonde hair had blue tints to them. She waved her blue fingers in front of her eyes.

"Aw, Himalette, I told you not to touch it." Brigitta shook her head. "You know sprites are full of stupid tricks."

"She gave me her blue," Himalette said, checking the underside of her arms.

"What do you mean she gave you her blue?"

"She gave me her blue. Then she went up there." Himalette pointed to a hole in the top of the log. Brigitta squinted up at it and saw nothing but forest and sky.

"Come on, twerp. Maybe Poppa can turn you back." Brigitta smirked. "Maybe," she said under her breath. She turned to exit the log.

Himalette pouted and rubbed her shoulder against the rough interior of the log.

"Brigitta, it itches," she whined.

"Serves you right."

Brigitta grabbed Himalette's hand. The warm blue instantly shot from Himalette's hand up Brigitta's arm all the way to her face. She could feel it spreading down her body and legs and finally her toes.

"Oh, great. I should have left you tied to a tree," Brigitta moaned as she pulled Himalette toward the opening of the log.

There was a bright flash from somewhere outside and a loud, low hum. The log trembled; the globelight went out. A moment later everything was dark and still.

"What was that?" asked Himalette, frozen mid-scratch.

"I don't know."

They quietly felt their way through the log. They emerged from the end and peered through the trees. Nothing looked any different, but there was something odd about the forest, something Brigitta couldn't quite place. Out of Water Faerie instinct, they both looked to the sky. The sun was out, there were very few clouds, and Brigitta could feel no storm on the horizon.

"I'm scared," whispered Himalette.

"Shhhhhhh," said Brigitta.

"I want to go home."

"Stay here."

Himalette sat in the mouth of the log, scratching her itchy blue face, while Brigitta made her way back toward the lyllium field. When she got there, it looked the same as it had before, but something was definitely wrong. After a moment, she realized what it was. The field was too still. There were no buzzing or flying beasts anywhere.

"Not one shadowfly," Brigitta muttered as she looked across the field to the other side. "Not one—"

Himalette's screaming cut the silence and Brigitta raced back to the log to find her sister pressed up against it.

"What?" Brigitta shook Himalette. "What!?!"

Himalette pointed to the ground with a trembling finger.

The sprite lay there, motionless and gray.

Brigitta picked up a stick and poked at the sprite. It didn't budge. Brigitta bent down and touched it, then retracted her blue hand in horror.

"It's turned to stone!" she exclaimed.

Himalette began to cry.

"Stop that!" Brigitta scolded, more harshly than she had intended.

She opened her pack and pulled out one of the jars. Three stone thunderbugs sat inside. It was definitely some sort of sprite trickery, Brigitta tried to convince herself, she'd make a complaint to the Elders. She dropped the jar back into her pack and put it on so that it swung from the front. "Come on, lola, I'll carry you home."

Himalette sniffled as she climbed onto her sister's back and snuggled between her wings. She folded her own wings flat along her backside. As soon as Brigitta was airborne and heading toward Tiragarrow, the image of Ondelle's face interrupted her thoughts. That expression Ondelle had made, she suddenly realized what it meant. It was the look of someone who had just been warned.

Chapter Four

Himalette's head bobbed up and down as Brigitta wove around the rocks and branches. The eerie stillness followed them. No buzzing. No chirping. No fluttering.

Brigitta stopped and gazed up at their village-nest. No sounds echoed from the trees. "Himmy, I have to put you down, all right?"

Himalette stepped down from her sister's back.

"Stay behind me," Brigitta warned, "and don't touch anything."

They flew up to the edge of the village-nest. It was completely still. No faeries flew in or out of the nest on festival errands. The nearest cottage belonged to Orl and Edl Featherkind. Orl was Tiragarrow's Caretaker and Edl harvested tingermint in neat little rows in front of their home, which resembled a giant yellow squash stuffed inside a tree with a porch bursting outward from the front door.

Edl Featherkind sat near the doorway with a pile of tingermint sprigs in her lap. She wasn't paying attention to the sprigs, however, she was squinting into the forest.

"Edl Featherkind?" Brigitta called. Edl didn't move. Not an eyebrow. Not a wingtwitch.

Brigitta and Himalette crept closer until they noticed a peculiar grayness to Edl's skin. They gasped as they realized she had turned to stone.

They leapt back in fear, knocking into Orl Featherkind who dangled by his foot from a vine, his eyes wide in alarm. They stared as he swung back and forth. The trees creaked above them.

Brigitta reached out to stop him from swinging. The creaking ceased and a moment later, Orl plunged to the ground and landed with a loud crack as his right arm broke off.

Himalette shrieked, piercing the stillness. Brigitta grabbed her and pulled her close.

"Be quiet, Himmy. Shhhh." Brigitta scanned the surrounding trees.

"But you killed him, Briggy, you killed him!" cried Himalette.

"I didn't kill him," Brigitta insisted, feeling sick to her stomach.

"You broke him!"

"I—I didn't—he can be—fixed."

They looked down at Orl Featherkind. He was definitely broken. They looked back up at each other in panic.

"Momma and Poppa!" the sisters cried.

⬤ ⬤ ⬤

The young faeries entered their cottage and made their way to the kitchen. Pippet's stone body leaned over her new pot of bubbling goldenfew. Her head was turned toward the window, a startled look upon her face.

"Momma!" Himalette ran toward her mother, but Brigitta yanked her back.

Brigitta nodded in the direction of the broken faerie outside. Himalette stood there shaking and whimpering as Brigitta tip-toed to the counter and picked up a pitcher of water. She leaned over and doused the fire underneath the pot.

"Don't go anywhere," Brigitta whispered. "I need to check on Poppa."

Himalette nodded gravely as Brigitta made her way to Mousha's laboratory. She froze in the doorway.

Mousha was balanced in the window sill on his hands and knees.

Himalette entered behind her, crying into a pillow.

"Shhhhh! Be careful," Brigitta warned. "We have to get Poppa down."

She took a cautious step toward him. Then another, and another.

She slowly reached out for his left wing. Himalette drew in her breath. Mousha's balance shifted and he plummeted over the side of the window.

"No!" The girls screamed as they heard his stone body crashing through the branches below.

Brigitta zoomed out the window faster than she'd ever flown before. She dove after Mousha as he fell through the trees. She grabbed a hold of his leg and flapped her wings as hard as she could, but she could barely slow him down. She felt movement above her, and then Himalette was there, grabbing her leg.

As they rapidly approached the ground, they became tangled in the dangling tree vines. The vines wrapped around their legs and bodies and pulled them back, catching their fall just before they hit the ground. They hung there, frozen in disbelief.

Brigitta finally let out her breath. "Can you untangle yourself?"

"I think so," whispered Himalette.

"Be careful."

Himalette unwrapped herself from the vines and fluttered to the earth. She dragged a large clump of moss from the glade and they lowered Mousha onto it.

They dropped down beside him and inspected him from head to toe.

"I think he's okay," Brigitta sighed, "other than . . ." She glanced over at Himalette, who was stroking their poppa's stone head. Brigitta felt a storm of tears gathering inside of her. She immediately swallowed them and tightened her jaw.

Himalette looked up at her sister. Her cheeks were stained with blue-tinted tears. Brigitta wiped them with her sleeve. "Come on," she coaxed, "we'll go to the Elders. They'll know what to do."

The sun was sinking over the forest by the time Brigitta and Himalette arrived at the Center Realm. They were exhausted and Brigitta was worried about her sister. Himalette had never been so quiet in all her life. Under different circumstances, Brigitta would have been overjoyed by the absence of silly songs and annoying questions.

As soon as Brigitta and Himalette landed, they knew all the faeries in the Center Realm were turned to stone as well. They held each other, trembling, as they passed two faeries frozen in the middle of raising a banner. Another three were assembling booths. Brigitta swiftly herded Himalette away from a faerie whose leg had broken off when it fell to the ground, and past another whose wings lay shattered beneath her. There were frozen faeries in mid-taste of food, showing plans to festival organizers, and sitting in the trees holding decorations. All of the faeries' faces were turned in the direction of the Hourglass.

Brigitta and Himalette made their way past the grandstands and into the arena. They surveyed what looked like a battle scene, or at least what Brigitta imagined a battle scene looked like, as she had never witnessed one. Everywhere she looked there were frightened stone faeries: some in the stands, some on the ground, some hanging in the giant uul trees, some whole, some broken. Himalette gripped Brigitta's hand as they stepped through the arena toward the platform.

They had never been this close to the Hourglass. No one was allowed on the platform without an Elder. They climbed the silver stairs and gazed, dejected, at the figure of Ondelle, their High Priestess. She stood overlooking the festival grounds with a determined expression. Her scepter lay on the platform in front of her. Himalette reached down to pick it up, then stopped herself before Brigitta could scold her. She scratched her blue shoulders as they stared at Ondelle's stone face. Brigitta could no longer hold her tears. They streamed down her cheeks as she choked on her sobs.

"Briggy?"

Brigitta didn't respond. She wiped her tears away with quivering fingers and did her best to compose herself. She studied Ondelle's eyes, no longer intense pools of black, but hard and gray. Even turned to stone, Brigitta thought she was the most beautiful faerie in the White Forest.

She turned and looked in the direction Ondelle was looking. Every other faerie Brigitta could see was facing the Hourglass, but Ondelle had her back to the Hourglass, and was looking out over her faeries. Brigitta gazed down at the scepter.

She had the look of someone who had just been warned.

She stared back up at Ondelle, willing her eyes to tell her something. What had she been trying to do?

"Priestess Ondelle . . . it's Brigitta . . . of Tiragarrow   . . . Please . . . help us."

She reached out and touched Ondelle's hand. The coldness of her fingers shocked Brigitta and she leapt back. Her foot hit the scepter, knocking it from the platform, down the steps, and into the dirt below.

Horrified, Brigitta flew down to retrieve it. Next to the scepter was an open black seed pod, the same kind the rude sprite had been carrying earlier that day.

She picked up the seed pod and examined it. It was surprisingly light, but firm. She knocked on it with her knuckles and turned it over in her hand.

"Hey Briggy, watch!" called Himalette from the platform.

Brigitta placed the seed pod in her pack, retrieved the scepter, and flew back up to the platform. She found Himalette pressed up against the branches that cradled the Hourglass, watching the sands inside fall like a heavy, rainbow-colored rain.

Himalette reached out to touch the glass.

"No!" cried Brigitta.

"It's okay," Himalette insisted and she tapped on the glass. As she did, little blue sparks flew off her finger. "See? It likes me!"

Brigitta pulled Himalette's finger away. "That's enough."

Brigitta turned to survey the scene once more. She went back to Ondelle and carefully placed the scepter in her hand. Then she looked out to the frightened faeries on the festival grounds. "What were they all looking at?"

"Maybe this is where the bright light came from?" Himalette

offered, "before everyone became . . . " Her voice trailed off and her eyes filled with tears.

"But the Hourglass protects the White Forest," Brigitta insisted, gazing up at it. The top half was nearly empty. The bottom half held a mountain of multi-colored sands.

"Briggy, what happens when the Hourglass runs out?"

Chapter Five

For the first time in her young life, Brigitta wished she had paid more attention to her Auntie Ferna's lessons. Being able to string a thunder-bug symphony wasn't going to help them now. She didn't know exactly what would happen when the Hourglass ran out since no living faerie knew a time when the Hourglass hadn't protected the forest by keeping the elements balanced and harmful beasts at bay. And even though she couldn't remember the details, she did know that without the Hourglass there would be no White Forest. It was how the Ancients had protected them long ago and how it had been ever since.

Brigitta began to suspect that she and Himalette were the only two unchanged faeries left in the forest. Their spirits sank lower and lower with each stone faerie they passed. Eventually, it dawned on them that all the other beasts were stone as well: the snakes, the birds, the beetles, the grovens. The grovens were especially pitiful, with sad wide stone eyes and clownish stone lips. Himalette patted the top of a groven's head as she passed, then reached down and gave it a careful squeeze. Its bulbous toad-like face didn't respond.

There was only one faerie left in the entire forest who Brigitta thought might be able to help them. This was truly her last hope, and she didn't have much hope at that, but she didn't say this to Himalette as they flew northwest toward Gyllenhale.

When their wings grew weak, they ran. When they could no longer run, they plodded along until Himalette tripped over a root and collapsed into tears. She climbed onto Brigitta's back. With aching arms she held Himalette steady with one hand and the flickering globelight with the other. She hummed along the way to keep them both company.

Himalette was falling asleep by the time they arrived. Brigitta roused her, for she was far too tired to carry Himalette up to Auntie Ferna's cottage. With the last of their energy, they fluttered up to their auntie's porch.

Brigitta handed Himalette the globelight.

"You stay here, lola," Brigitta said, "I'm going to see if Auntie Ferna is home. If she's—"

"Broken?" Himalette asked.

"Just stay here," Brigitta instructed.

"Briggy, how come everyone turned to stone except us?"

"I don't know."

"What are we going to do?" Himalette was too tired to cry.

"We'll stay the night here and decide in the morning."

Brigitta entered the dark cottage and waited for her eyes to adjust. She eased her way toward the kitchen. "Auntie Ferna?" she called as she picked up a breath-lantern. Brigitta blew into it and a small orange flame appeared inside.

"Auntie Fer—" she stopped herself as she entered the den and spotted Fernatta, who stood immobile over a potion book on a pedestal. She lifted the lantern and craned her neck. It was the same book Fernatta had retrieved from Mousha earlier that day.

She looked up at her Auntie's face as every last bit of hope drained from her body. Fernatta was looking anxiously out the window, no doubt just as surprised as everyone else by the strange and sudden flash of light.

Himalette screamed from outside. Brigitta flew through the cottage smack into Himalette in the doorway.

"I saw something!" Himalette cried. "Something moved in the forest."

"It was just the wind in the trees," Brigitta said.

They both listened. The night was completely still.

"Come inside," Brigitta said, guiding Himalette into the cottage. "Let's see if we can find a way to change our skin back."

Himalette scratched her blue face as she entered. Brigitta glanced out into the trees one last time before closing the door.

After placing a scarf over Fernatta's head to cover her face, Brigitta set Himalette in front of a warm fire in the den and grabbed the potion book from the pedestal. "Sorry, Auntie," she said.

She looked down and spotted her poppa's tiny red spout snake peering up at her from inside Fernatta's pocket.

"Hey there," cooed Brigitta. She grabbed a small vile and slipped the spout snake into it. She capped the vile and held it up to her face. "You're lucky you're an invention, or I bet you'd be turned to stone, too."

She warmed some gundlebeans and made a pot of tingermint tea. She served up the modest meal in the den. Himalette ate quietly by the fire, scratching her legs between spoonfuls, while Brigitta perched at a high table surrounded by pots and jars. She placed Fernatta's potion book on the table.

"I should have paid more attention to my lessons," moaned Brigitta, searching through the book. She located a color changing potion and hoped it would work. She wasn't sure if it was meant for faeries, but it was the only thing she could find. She didn't understand how Fernatta's book was organized and there weren't many illustrations.

"Dragon Flower dew . . . " Brigitta read the labels off all the jars. "Aha." She grabbed the jar, opened the lid, and sniffed, "Hmmm . . . " She poured a yellow keronium glassful into a bowl.

Himalette picked a stick out of the woodbox and poked at a stone spider on the hearth. "Even the spiders are turned to stone," Himalette sighed.

"Dried sharmock root . . . " Brigitta counted three sand-petals full of the dark orange shrivels and added them to the mix. Then she added a few drops of a dark brown syrup simply labeled *alterings*.

"I wonder if the worms underground are stone, too?" continued Himalette.

"Mix with licotia nectar . . . " Brigitta poured the various liquids into a large beaker. "Allow bubbles to settle to the bottom . . . "

"And little baby birds inside of eggs."

"Done," Brigitta declared, "I think." She peered suspiciously at the dark mixture, then sniffed it. "Only one way to find out." She retrieved two chalices from the cupboard.

Himalette threw the stick into the fire and crawled over to the stone spider. She tapped it with her finger.

"But he doesn't turn blue, like when I touched you," she murmured. She got up from the floor and smiled. "I made a rhyme."

Brigitta poured the liquid into the two chalices.

Himalette moved to the table and examined the seed pod sitting on top of Brigitta's pack. She grabbed the pod and shook it, then placed it on the table and spun it around.

Brigitta lifted one of the chalices to her lips.

"*He doesn't turn blue, like when I touched you . . .* " Himalette sang as the seed pod whirled around and around and around.

Brigitta spat out the mixture and dropped the chalice. "Himmy, that's it!" She slammed her hand down on the seed pod.

Startled, Himalette jumped back from the table. "What's it?"

Brigitta ran out of the den and into the gathering room. She rushed to the dusty bookshelf by the window and searched the lower shelf. She retrieved the thick manuscript called *Faerie Lore and Lineage*. She ran back to the den and pulled Himalette to the floor with her.

"A History of the White Forest as Chronicled by Fernatta of Gyllenhale, Eighth Faerie Lorekeeper," read Brigitta. She flipped through the pages until she came to an entry for Blue Spell. She remembered the Elders' spell rehearsals. "By the wisdom of the Ancients, by the power of Blue Spell . . . "

"Blue Spell?" asked Himalette.

"It's the most powerful of all faerie magic." Brigitta showed Himalette a passage in the book.

"What's it say?"

"Blue Spell may only be conjured by the acting High Priest or Priestess upon consensus of the Faerie Elders or by authority of the Ethereals themselves."

"What are consenses?" yawned Himalette as she slid closer to the fire.

"It means they have to agree." Brigitta continued reading aloud. "Faerie Blue Spell is reserved for rebalancing the Hourglass of Protection every season cycle or for rare circumstances when extraordinary force is required. Other than to rebalance the Hourglass, there are only three known occasions in which Blue Spell has been conjured in the past: to move the elemental faeries north during the Great World Cry, to create the Hourglass and its protective field over the White Forest, and to expel Hrathgar of Bobbercurxy to Dead Mountain after she attempted to steal the power from the Hourglass itself." Brigitta looked up from the book and stared into the fire.

Himalette picked up the stone spider and walked it up Brigitta's leg. "Are you going to turn us back?" she finally asked.

"I don't think I can." Brigitta brushed the spider away.

"But it itches horribly," complained Himalette, scratching around the top of her wings to demonstrate. "I'd rather be turned to stone." She stopped scratching and cradled the spider in her hands.

"Don't say that." Brigitta snapped out of her trance. "Listen, I don't know how she did it, because it says it's for Elders and Ethereals only, but I think it's *because* the sprite gave you her blue that we didn't turn to stone."

"So it was good I touched the sprite!" Himalette said.

Brigitta examined the blue skin of her arms and legs. "We have to find a faerie who knows about Blue Spell. If the sprite figured out how use it, maybe someone else has, too. Then we can use it to turn the Elders back to normal so they can reset the Hourglass." She carefully tore out the pages referring to Blue Spell.

"But everyone else is stone. There aren't any faeries left."

"There's still one left," Brigitta held out the manu-script pages and pointed to the passage she had been reading. Her finger landed on the word *Hrathgar*.

Chapter Six

Troubled by nightmares of what they had witnessed that day and visions of what might lie ahead, Brigitta and Himalette spent a restless night huddled near the fire despite their exhaustion. Brigitta did not feel refreshed the next morning, and certainly not ready for the long journey. But she knew they had no choice. They had to get help.

With a fresh pack of supplies on her back, Brigitta paused on the porch overlooking Fernatta's meticulous garden. She looked down at Himalette and straightened her sister's canteen strap, then put on a determined face and grabbed her hand. She felt a hard object in her palm. Brigitta opened Himalette's hand. It was the stone spider.

"Leave it here," Brigitta instructed.

Himalette pouted and set the spider down on the porch.

A little wobbly from the previous day's travels, Brigitta and Himalette flew from the porch down to the river. Doing her best to ignore the hundreds of faeries scattered about in the grass, in the trees, under the tents, and along the river, Brigitta wondered if stone faeries could drown, but quickly put the thought from her mind. They didn't have time for rescuing stone faeries. The only way to save the forest was to turn the Elders and Ondelle back so they could reset the Hourglass.

They followed the river north to the spring and filled their canteens, then headed northeast out of the Earth Faerie Realm toward The Shift. They flew close to the ground navigating through the trees, passing dozens of stone faeries and other forest beasts. All of the frozen faerie faces were turned in the same direction.

They reached a small pond where three faerie boys had been interrupted in the middle of teasing a groven. Brigitta noticed that even the groven's stone eyes were looking through the woods toward the Center Realm. Further on, they encountered a young faerie couple camped out on a giant mushroom. Then, there were no more faeries.

The forest grew thicker and wilder and darker as they traveled. Brigitta thought about flying up and over the trees, like the Air Faerie Perimeter Guards, but the guards' wings were strong and mature and they were talented flyers. Brigitta and Himalette were likely to get tossed back into the trees by a strong wind and tear their wings.

After a lengthy silence, Himalette landed on the ground and folded her arms across her chest. "I'm hungry," she declared.

"Not yet, Himmy," Brigitta answered, landing near a very old and twisted tree.

"You're going too fast," Himalette complained.

Brigitta flew back to Himalette and knelt in front of her. "Listen, we don't have much time and I can't leave you behind. You're going to have to—"

Himalette wasn't listening. She was staring over Brigitta's shoulder. Brigitta turned to see what had caught her attention.

A stone faun sat on a rock with a wooden flute to his lips. Brigitta and Himalette approached him. If he hadn't been frozen, they could never have gotten so close. Once, many seasons before, Brigitta had spotted three fauns hiding behind some trees watching faerie festival games. This one's eyes were closed in a stone reverie.

"He looks happy," murmured Himalette, doing her best not to pet him.

Brigitta peered through the forest. They were very far from the Center Realm and the Hourglass of Protection. "Didn't see what hit him," she said.

"I've never been this far from home," Himalette observed.

Brigitta looked down at her little sister and wiped a dirt smudge from her blue cheek. She opened her pack and pulled out a slice of sweet pipberry bread.

"Here," she offered, "But that's it until supper. Come on."

🌰 🌰 🌰

Eventually, the vines became so dense that the girls could no longer fly without getting tangled in them. They pushed their way through the forest, passing occasional songless stone birds perched in the trees. Brigitta was long past humming and concentrated on a breathing rhythm to keep herself moving.

They were both so focused on putting one foot in front of the other that they were completely startled when the forest ended and they found themselves standing before an immense river of dry earth that stretched around the perimeter of the White Forest as far as their eyes could see. Ahead of them, across the shifting dirt moat, was the rest of the world, beginning with the edge of the Dark Forest.

"The Shift," said Brigitta, holding Himalette back with one arm. They stood listening for a moment. There were no trees or plants or beasts of any kind across the large expanse of land. They could hear nothing but the strange sound of the slowly churning earth.

"Are you sure?" Himalette whispered.

Brigitta nodded and moved forward. There was nothing else it could have been. She had heard it described many times by the Air Faerie Perimeter Guards, but this was more endless and empty than she had ever imagined. There was nothing to protect them, and nowhere to hide.

"Is it safe?" asked Himalette.

Brigitta took a few tentative steps into The Shift. She could feel the dirt moving beneath her, carrying her along on its sluggish journey. She fluttered back to her sister.

"Where's the magic field?" asked Himalette.

"Wait here." Brigitta picked up a small rock and stepped back into The Shift.

There was a light breeze, and a strange scent rode in on it.

"What's that smell?" Himalette called, wrinkling her nose.

"The other side." Brigitta threw the rock as hard as she could. Half-way across The Shift, it passed through a watery barrier and continued out the other side. It landed with a soft thud on the outskirts of the Dark Forest. Brigitta returned to Himalette, who quickly hid her hands behind her back.

"What's that? What have you got?" Brigitta demanded.

"Nothing."

Brigitta reached behind Himalette and grabbed her arm. Himalette opened her hand to reveal a stone bird.

"It's just a bird," admitted Himalette. "It was on the ground. It was lonely."

"Himmy, you have to stop taking everything all the time." Brigitta grabbed the bird from Himalette and contemplated where to put it.

"I'll keep it in my pocket," Himalette pleaded. "You won't even see it." Her frightened face softened Brigitta's heart just a little.

"No more, Himmy." Brigitta handed the bird back to her. "Stay close to me and don't touch anything else. Do you understand?"

Himalette nodded and put the bird back into her pocket.

"Will the magic field let us back in?" asked Himalette.

"Anything originally from the White Forest can get back across," said Brigitta. "Anything that comes from the other side has to be escorted by a Perimeter Guard. Like this."

Brigitta took Himalette's hand and carefully led her over the rough earth river until they were half-way across. They hesitated in front of the force-field, a little bewildered to be standing still and moving at the same time. Brigitta took a deep breath and walked forward.

She felt streams of coldness, not completely unpleasant, like walking through an invisible waterfall. A moment later, they had passed through to the other side. They shivered and paused to look back at the White Forest. Himalette's free hand went into her pocket.

Brigitta looked down at Himalette, whose face was contorted in horror. "What? What is it?"

Himalette pulled her hand out of her pocket and opened it. Instead of a stone bird, there was a pile of gray dust. She looked up with frightened eyes as the dust fell through her fingers.

Chapter Seven

The girls half flew, half hiked through the thick forest in silence for several moon-beats. Brigitta led the way, holding branches back, pointing at tricky areas of twisted roots or vines. Himalette followed, at first cautiously, then curiously, and then finally with no more dread than exploring the forest around her home.

It wasn't so long ago that the past and future could escape Brigitta's mind. She wished she could be more like Himalette and simply forget to worry. But right now, someone had to keep them focused on their task.

"Is this Faweh?" asked Himalette.

"Of course," Brigitta answered while removing a sticky spider web from her hair. "Everything outside the White Forest is Faweh."

"How big is it?"

"Big."

"How do you know?" Himalette ran to keep up with Brigitta.

"Because . . . because . . . I just do." Brigitta held back a thorny branch for Himalette and pricked her finger as she let it go. She looked down at the trickle of blood on her finger, only mildly surprised to discover that it, too, was tinted blue. She wiped her finger on her tunic. "Don't you listen to Auntie Ferna's lessons?"

"Sometimes," Himalette said, "but other times I just watch the shadowflies outside her window."

Brigitta smirked to herself. She had watched the shadowflies so many times she could sometimes figure out what they were saying. They mostly danced about the weather or where flowers were in bloom.

Once Brigitta spent half a morning interpreting a dance about a patch of ripe pipberries. After their lesson, she and Kyllia had found the bush at the top of a steep bank. They had poked at the ripe red berries, which burst with a "pip" and spilled sweet juice. The riper the berry was, the redder and fuller with juice, and the bigger the "pip" sound it made.

Brigitta shook her head out of her daydream. It was making her crave her momma's iced frommafin. She thought about her momma's nickname, Pippet, and how she always locked up her pipberry supply to keep Brigitta and Himalette from eating them before she could make her specialty drink.

Brigitta's mouth felt dry. She didn't know if there were any pipberries around, but she wouldn't eat off a pipberry bush in the Dark Forest no matter how thirsty she was. She wasn't taking any chances.

She paused for a moment to concentrate. She wanted to stay heading east, but it was much harder to read the air in the Dark Forest, even though Brigitta had been at the top of her class in sensing directions. The elements were just not as cooperative outside the protected realm. The moisture in the air was heavy and stank of mold.

Himalette moved closer to her sister. "Briggy?"

"Shhhh." Brigitta closed her eyes and visualized separating the water from the air as she had been taught in her Elemental Elements class. It was always a matter of balance. When she could feel the balance, she let the foul Dark Forest water fall away and held the air. East, she thought, and the air began to pull. She could only hope it was pulling in the right direction.

She opened her eyes and resumed pushing her way through the trees. Himalette trotted along behind her.

"Briggy?" Himalette tried again.

"Yes?"

"How come faeries aren't allowed to leave the White Forest?"

"A very, very long time ago," Brigitta began in her best Auntie Ferna impression, turning to point her finger at Himalette.

Himalette giggled as Brigitta continued, "There were more faeries than you could possibly imagine. All the elemental faeries lived in beautiful villages surrounding Lake Indago in the Valley of Noe. They were taken care of by the Ethereals—"

"The Ancient Ones?"

"Do not interrupt, young faerie," Brigitta scolded. She picked up a stick and used it like an orchestra baton. "Yes, the Ancient Ones, the oldest and wisest of all faeries. They looked after everybody else."

Brigitta assumed an Auntie Ferna stride while she waved her baton to the beat of her lecture. "In those days, Faweh was peaceful, and the Five Civilizations of the world were strong. There were four Sages, each representing a civilization and an element, and a fifth Tender of the Elements. This High Sage was an Ancient One, an Ethereal Faerie, and he was very, very wise—"

"Like our poppa!"

Brigitta snapped around and pointed her baton at Himalette who jumped back and laughed. Brigitta turned and launched herself over a moss-ridden log. "The powers of the four elements were housed in Lake Indago, which was the entry point to the Center of the World, from which all Faweh's energy comes. The World Sages would gather at a great palace in the Valley of Noe and the High Sage would call forth the energy from the Center World."

Brigitta sped up her baton rhythm. "One day, the World Sages had a bad argument. The High Sage tried to stop them, but the other Sages turned on him. They didn't see why the Ethereal Faeries got to be Tenders of the Elements. They wanted access to the Center World, too. During their argument, too much magic was cast, and the High Sage was accidentally killed. The World Sages threw his body into Lake Indago and fled to their homelands."

"I don't like this story anymore," said Himalette.

"The balance of the elements was lost. The lake evaporated. In order to protect their faerie kin, the Ancient Ones gathered every grain of balanced sand from the dry lakebed, placed them in an hourglass, and moved it to the far north, where it was safer."

"The Hourglass of Protection!" Himalette interrupted.

"Around the Hourglass, they created the White Forest and moved all the elemental faeries there, where they have been protected for thousands of seasons. And when the last drop of water evaporated from Lake Indago, the Center of the World gave a Great Cry, and out sprung The River That Runs Backwards, which starts from the old lakebed, travels north all the way up the land, and goes back into the earth at Dead Mountain," Brigitta paused, dropping her Auntie Ferna impression and flinging her baton into the trees, "which is where Hrathgar lives."

"But what about the Ancient Ones? What happened to them?"

There was a long silence as Brigitta searched for the best path through the trees. The plants and flowers and buzzing beasts were growing more and more unfamiliar. Everything was engulfed in a gloom. The forest choked on undergrowth. Vines wrapped menacingly around trees like thick spiky snakes. There were no silvery hues in the forest leaves, no sudden fields of lyllium, and no thrumming thunder-bugs. Even a groven stench-bog would have been a welcome sight, thought Brigitta.

"They're gone."

"Oh."

It wasn't entirely true, but Brigitta didn't feel like explaining how the Ethereals could only be felt, not seen, and that they only visited a faerie twice, once at birth to mark her destiny and once at the end of life to disperse her spirit.

Auntie Ferna said that the Ethereals still protected all the elemental faeries, but Brigitta had doubts about that. Her mind filled with images of frozen faces and broken wings, of Ondelle's cold gray eyes, and of her poppa's stone body lying in the moss.

Brigitta coughed. She was having trouble breathing because the air was so dank. As she slipped past a tree with a leggy orange blob cradled in one of its branches, the blob's two black eyes popped open. She hurried along, although it was difficult to go any faster than they were already going. Her body ached and she was terribly hot. Her immature wings felt inadequate. She had never used them so much in her life, not even during festival games. Himalette struggled to keep up with her.

"How do we get to Hrathgar's?" Himalette ran to Brigitta as a high whining cry pierced the air.

Brigitta glanced over her shoulder. "Auntie's book said go east until you get to The River That Runs Backwards, then follow it straight north to Dead Mountain."

"Which way is east?"

Brigitta stopped and pointed, "East!" she declared before moving on again. "You're a Water Faerie, Himmy, it's time you learned how to interpret the clouds and the air. Being a Water Faerie is good for some things, like sensing direction and weather."

"I like Fire Faeries," said Himalette, ignoring her sister's sharp tone. "I wish I could be a Fire Faerie. They get to dance and play with shimmery things. They get to—Hey, look, a caterpillar!"

Himalette stopped. Caterpillars were one of her favorite crawling beasts. She spent many moon-beats watching the ones outside Tiragarrow spin fuzzy pink cocoons which hung from the tree branches in the Gray Months.

Brigitta tolerated the Gray Months by helping her poppa in his laboratory. After the Gray Months came the Grow Months. The Festival of Elements started on the last day of the Grow Months and continued for two days into the Green Months, Brigitta's favorite season. She wondered if there would be Green Months if the Hourglass wasn't turned. And if there were no Green Months, the caterpillars wouldn't know when to spin their cocoons. And if they didn't spin their cocoons, there would be no butterflies in the Grow Months. And if there were no butterflies, there would be no more caterpillars.

"Leave it alone," Brigitta warned.

"It's just a caterpillar," Himalette mumbled to herself. She paused for a moment, then flew to catch up with Brigitta. "Are Dark Forest caterpillars very noisy?"

"How should I know?"

"Maybe they're like our caterpillars and they're only noisy when they're hungry."

"And maybe they eat little faerie girls who talk too much," Brigitta shot back. Her blue skin itched and she burned all over, especially across her wings.

"I was just—"

"Wait. Listen." Brigitta held up her arm.

There was a rustling sound in the bushes, then a muffled whimper.

Brigitta motioned for Himalette to stay back. She silently fluttered up and over to the shaking bush. She lifted a large leaf. A brown object, almost as tall as Himalette, tumbled from the brush, startling the girls. They flew up to the safety of a near-by tree branch.

The object wriggled around on the ground. Something pushed at it from the inside.

"What is it?" asked Himalette as she yanked on Brigitta's tunic.

"It looks like a big cocoon," answered Brigitta.

"It's not like our cocoons at all!"

"Shhhh!"

"Is it going to hatch?" Himalette whispered.

"I don't know," Brigitta whispered back.

"It's saying something."

They listened for a moment, then dropped to a lower branch and watched the cocoon bouncing and rolling around on the ground. "Hurmmmmmmmmp!" came its muffled cry.

Brigitta snapped off a long twig and poked at it a few times.

"Heeeerrrrmmmmmmmp!"

"It's saying 'help,'" Himalette determined. "It wants us to help it."

"Help it what to what? Stand on end?" Brigitta dropped from the tree to the ground and Himalette landed beside her.

Brigitta poked at the cocoon again. It bounced up and down and wriggled some more. She wondered what kind of beast could possibly be inside. She reached out to touch it. The brown strands were sticky. As she pulled her finger back several strands came with it.

"C-c-c-caterpillar . . . " Himalette stammered from behind Brigitta.

"I said leave it alone, Himmy." Brigitta struggled to break the strands off by winding them around and around her stick. "Bog buggers, this stuff is strong."

"B-B-B-Briggy . . . " Himalette's voice was barely audible.

"What!" Brigitta snapped around.

She had been so distracted she hadn't noticed an immense leafy tunnel in the trees. Staring down at them from the entrance was a gigantic, wrinkled, mossy-colored caterpillar with legs the size of tree branches. Himalette stood frozen in terror as it snarled, flexing the hard pinchers of its mouth. Brigitta's heart dropped to her stomach. She opened her lips to speak, but nothing came out.

"Himmy . . . " she finally managed, "back up slowly. Come to me."

Himalette stood there trembling.

"Himmy," Brigitta called again. She inched toward her sister.

The giant caterpillar stretched up into the air and stood on its hind legs, doubling its height. Its arms flailed and its pinchers gnashed the air.

"Himalette . . . " Brigitta moved closer to her. She could almost touch her right shoulder..

Himalette's hand shook as she reached into her pocket. She pulled it out and opened it. Inside sat a little caterpillar. Brigitta looked from the wee beast to the enormous one flailing above them. Himalette slowly set the tiny caterpillar on a leaf and it crept away.

The giant caterpillar maneuvered toward them. Brigitta lunged for Himalette and pulled her back by the strap of her canteen. The great beast moved forward again. Brigitta searched for an escape route and noticed that the trees were slightly thinner behind them. She pulled Himalette close and leaned into her ear.

"Listen to me," Brigitta whispered to Himalette. "On the count of three, fly straight up as high as you can. Whatever you do, don't stop, Himmy, okay? Okay?"

Himalette nodded.

"One—two—THREE!"

Brigitta flew straight up, pushing through thick vines and webs, scraping her arms and wings. Branches snapped out of her way as she climbed through the air. When she was out of strength, she landed on a sturdy branch and held onto the trunk of the tree, gasping for breath. She looked back down for Himalette and her heart skipped a beat. She wasn't there.

"Himmy?" she called. "Himmy!"

Himalette was still on the ground, caught in the strands of the cocoon. She tried to fly, but her legs and wings were tangled in the sticky mess.

"Brigitta!" Himalette struggled, tangling herself further, as the giant caterpillar approached. She screamed as the terrifying beast descended.

Brigitta leapt from the branch and plummeted head first toward Himalette. She felt a sudden jolt of pain as a branch tore into her right wing with a sickening ripping sound.

The giant caterpillar lunged after the cocoon and grabbed it in its mouth. It turned back around and crawled off through the trees, its branch-like legs kicking up the earth and ripping vines. Himalette dangled from the cocoon, screaming in terror. She fluttered about trying to get unstuck.

Brigitta darted after them, "No! Let go of her, you stupid worm!"

The caterpillar dove into a tunnel underneath an enormous blood-red tree. Brigitta collapsed at the entrance to the hole, her right wing throbbing.

"Hold on, Himmy!" she gasped into the darkness. She heard the distant sound of scurrying and felt a draught of cold air on her skin. She pulled herself to a sitting position and removed her pack. She dug through it, her hands shaking, trying to locate the globelight.

A very small caterpillar crawled across the ground toward the hole. Brigitta pulled the globelight out of her pack and, in a fit of despair, smashed the caterpillar into the ground.

Chapter Eight

The globelight wasn't working. Brigitta panicked. What if she had broken it with her impulsive behavior? She rubbed it furiously with her hand and it remained unlit.

"Poppa," she cried out, "make it work!" She took a breath, counted to three, and tried again. She exhaled in relief as it started to glow

She rolled the globelight into the tunnel, which curved downward so that Brigitta had to fly to keep up with the light. Her torn wing ached so badly she didn't know how long she could go on. The tunnel floor finally evened out and the globelight stopped rolling. She landed and picked it up, listening for any movement. Brigitta rolled the globelight again and ran after it. She rolled and followed, rolled and followed, venturing deeper and deeper into the tunnel until she came to a division.

Himalette's cries echoed from the dark passageway on the left. Following the sound, Brigitta turned left, then right, then left again. The tunnel opened up into a larger, brighter cavern. At the far end of the cavern, the giant caterpillar stood with its back to Brigitta. She slipped into the room, ducked behind a rock, and hid the globelight in her pack.

As her eyes adjusted, she noticed that the brightness in the cave was not stationary, but coming from thousands of tiny shifting lights. Brigitta watched the lights crawling around and realized they weren't lights at all. They were small glowing worms. The little beasts covered the surface of the walls and most of the ceiling, crawling under and over each other, filling the cave with a strange scuttling sound. Several dozen large cocoons were spread about the cave, including the wriggling cocoon she had found in the forest. Beside it, the giant caterpillar was bent over Himalette, her feet struggling beneath it.

Brigitta covered her own mouth to stifle a scream. A moment later the giant caterpillar moved away and Himalette sat there cocooned up to her nose in silky threads. She spied Brigitta and her eyes grew wider. She cried out, but the sound was muffled by the cocoon. Brigitta motioned for Himalette to shush.

The giant caterpillar disappeared through another tunnel. Brigitta crawled over to Himalette and pulled at the cocoon threads, which stuck to her fingers as soon as she touched them.

"Hagspit!" Brigitta swore.

The cocoon next to them began to whine and bounce up and down. Brigitta ignored it and struggled to unstick herself from Himalette. She wiped her hands on her tunic and became stuck to it. Himalette whimpered, her eyes panic-stricken.

Something large scurried through one of the tunnels. Brigitta, Himalette, and the cocoon all froze, listening.

The sound passed and they all continued struggling. The cocoon bounced its way over to Brigitta.

"Grwwwwwww wrrrrrrrmmmms!" its muffled voice cried.

Brigitta managed to loosen the threads around Himalette's mouth. Himalette inhaled deeply.

"It's . . . trying . . . to tell . . . us something," Himalette gasped, nodding toward the cocoon, which bounced up and down a few times.

"Yes, it's telling us to hurry up!" Brigitta took the globelight out of her pack so she could search for something with which to cut the threads. "I have to get you out of this thing, Himmy." She looked back at her injured wing. "I can't drag you through all these tunnels. Not faster than a giant caterpillar."

"Grrrrrrrrrrrr wrrrrrrrrrms!" insisted the cocoon.

"But what about him?" Himalette cried. "We can't leave him behind!"

"We don't have time!"

"Glrrrrrrrr wrrrrrrrrrrrrrrrrms!" the cocoon insisted again.

"Glow worms!" Himalette jiggled up and down along with the cocoon.

"Shhhhh!" Brigitta hissed at Himalette, nodding to the tunnels.

"It's saying glow worms," Himalette whispered.

The cocoon nodded frantically and fell forward.

Brigitta stared at the lights crawling across the cave. She moved to the wall and plucked off the nearest glow worm. Pain shot through in her finger. "Ow!" she yelped and dropped the worm.

She bent down and held the globelight up to it. Its feisty oversized jaws clamped at the air with razor sharp teeth. She carefully picked up the wiggling worm between her finger and thumb and followed along the wall until she came to a pile of half-devoured cocoons. She peered inside one of them. It was infested with glow worms. Whatever had been wrapped up for dinner was long gone.

She moved back over to Himalette and set the glow worm on top of her encased legs. It began to chomp its way through the threads. Himalette squirmed.

"Don't let it eat me," Himalette pleaded.

"I won't," Brigitta assured her. "Just enough to get you out of there."

The cocoon wiggled over to Brigitta and started to whimper.

Brigitta plucked two more glow worms from the walls and placed them on top of the helpful cocoon. The worms began to munch. She gathered two more and dropped them on the cocoon's bottom half. Brigitta turned back to Himalette and placed a few more glow worms on Himalette's front and two on her back.

There was more scurrying through the tunnels as Brigitta pulled the atomizer from her pack.

"Poppa's bug-stunner," Brigitta said. "When they bite through the cocoon, I'll spray them with this."

"How will I know when—OWWWW!" Himalette cried out as one of her wings burst through the loosened threads. A glow worm was clamped onto her wing with its teeth. Brigitta sprayed it with the atomizer and, stunned, it dropped to the ground.

Tears streamed down Himalette's face as her left arm burst through the threads with a glow worm attached. When Brigitta sprayed the little beast, it released its grip and fell from her arm.

"I don't like this!" moaned Himalette. "It hurts! It hurts!"

"Shush!" Brigitta sprayed another glow worm with the atomizer.

Sensing movement behind them, they looked up as the giant caterpillar crawled from the tunnel. Brigitta stood up, guarding Himalette and the cocoon with her wings and arms. The enormous beast reared up and waved its black legs just as two long pale ears burst through the top of the cocoon and flailed around, trying to shake the biting glow worms off. Brigitta sprayed them with the bug stunner and they dropped to the ground.

Himalette's second wing burst through the threads. Brigitta grabbed her sister by the hand and yanked her away just as the giant caterpillar lunged at them, knocking the eared cocoon aside. She towed a screaming Himalette to the top of the cavern, still partially encased in sticky threads. The giant caterpillar roared and they dodged its arms and jaws. Brigitta flew in circles about its head and it twisted itself around after them.

Brigitta heard a ripping sound as two legs burst through the bottom of the cocoon and it jumped to attention. She swooped down and grabbed the cocoon by the ears as the giant caterpillar crashed into the wall of the cave.

Brigitta flew from the cavern and into the tunnels with Himalette by the hand and the cocoon by the ears. Glow worms dangled in lingering threads illuminating the way. They turned a corner and turned again. It got darker and darker as the glow worms dropped away until they could no longer see.

"The globelight!" said Himalette.

"Too late." Brigitta landed in the dirt.

"Owwwweee—" yelped Himalette. Brigitta clamped her hand over Himalette's mouth and removed the last glow worm from her leg. She tossed it onto the ground and the cocoon stomped on it.

The tunnel went pitch black.

There was scurrying in the distance. Himalette whimpered as Brigitta removed her hand from her sister's face.

"We have to get out of here," said Brigitta.

"This way," said the cocoon. "I hear in dark."

Brigitta, Himalette, and the cocoon emerged from the ground in a completely different part of the forest, with fewer trees. The ones that were there were balder or broken in half. The ground was covered in giant caterpillar tracks and remnants of sticky thread.

Brigitta took several deep breaths, relieved to be out in the open air, even if it was moldy. She was so grateful to be outside that it took her a moment to realize that the cocoon was no longer a cocoon. It was a pale brown hairless creature with the face of a frightened rodent and droopy ears that were as long as Brigitta's arms. It trotted up to a tree and rubbed itself free of the remaining cocoon threads, purring in relief.

"I hate caterpillars," said Himalette, frowning at two tiny beasts inching away from the mouth of the tunnel.

Brigitta pulled Himalette from the dark hole in the ground and spun her around, checking for lingering threads and caterpillar damage. Himalette's wings and legs had some nasty glow worm bites and her skin was torn and bleeding. Brigitta ripped a sleeve off her tunic and wiped the bluish blood away. Satisfied Himalette was in no immediate danger, she turned to the curious creature they had rescued who was using his large ears to brush himself off.

"Who are you?" Brigitta asked.

"I Minq!" he said, thrusting his ears straight out from the sides of his head and taking a bow.

"What are you?" Himalette asked.

"I Minq," he said. "What you?"

"We're faeries, silly," said Himalette.

Minq trotted up to Himalette. On all fours the top of his head came up to her waist. He stroked one of her soft wings with his left ear. She giggled in return. Minq turned to touch Brigitta's wings, but she pulled away. Her right wing was torn near the top and bleeding.

"Wing hurt," he said, frowning. He gestured with his ear. "Come. Be safe."

"We're in a very big hurry," explained Brigitta. "We can't stay."

"Come," he insisted. "Come, come." He took Himalette's hand and pulled.

A deep vibrating growl emerged from the caterpillar tunnel along with a gust of cold air. Himalette gasped and wrapped herself around Brigitta. She studied her sister's wounds and the remaining threads stuck to her filthy tunic. She looked up at the sky. The light was fading.

"Fine," she sighed, "lead the way."

Chapter Nine

Minq led the girls through the forest and before long they came to an ancient wall composed of very tall, thick stones and covered with greenish-purple vines. Minq glanced left, paused, then right. He stretched his ears in both directions.

"What are—" started Brigitta.

Minq hushed her with his right ear and continued to listen with his left. He gave a satisfied nod and pulled up a loose mat of grass. Underneath was a miniature version of one of the large vertical stones. He picked it up and placed it into a hole in the wall like a key. He pushed forward into the wall and a door-shaped section of it gave way. He gestured inside with his ear.

"Inside," he whispered, "quick, quick!"

The girls crept in and Minq closed the door behind them. They were inside a tall circular wall of stones. Along the walls, vines smothered crumbling rock structures. The center of the fortress was bare except for the remains of a campfire, some scraps of forest vegetation, and a small pile of wood.

"What is this place? Did someone used to live here?" asked Brigitta, noting how Minq placed the stone key inside a hole in the ground and covered it with a dried bush.

"We safe here," said Minq, his ears darting about. "We stay night. Rest please. I fix wing."

He reached for Brigitta's injured wing and she pulled away.

"Not so fast." Brigitta eyed Minq. "How do we know you won't eat us during the night?"

"Yeah!" said Himalette.

Minq looked aghast. "Why I eat you?"

"Or trade us to a . . . a . . . " Brigitta started.

"A monster," suggested Himalette. Brigitta nodded in agreement and pulled Himalette close.

"You save life. I yours," offered Minq. "I do what you say always." He bowed deeply to demonstrate his loyalty, glancing up at them with a wide smile that looked more like a grimace.

Himalette smiled back and tugged on Brigitta's tunic. "Can we keep him?"

"We're not going to keep him, Himmy. He's not a bird or a butterfly. He's a—he's—uh—"

"Minq!" he stood up and gestured toward them with his ears. "I yours!"

"See?" Himalette pleaded. "He's ours!"

"Excuse us for a moment. Minq." Brigitta pulled Himalette to the other side of the camp and they huddled up. Brigitta glanced back to make sure Minq wasn't following them. Still smiling like crazy toward them, he moved over to the campfire pit and began clearing out some burnt wood.

"Remember what I said about taking things," Brigitta whispered to Himalette.

"He wants to come with us," Himalette begged.

"He'll slow us down. He can't even fly."

"He can help," Himalette pointed out.

"The only one who can help us now is Hrathgar."

Minq's ears, then the rest of him, appeared at Brigitta's side. "Hrathgar?" he gulped. "You not go Hrathgar?"

"Why?" Brigitta asked.

"If you say go Dead Mountain, I go," he said, ears drooping down to the ground. "You save life. I yours."

Himalette squealed and hugged him. He patted her back with his ears.

"But why we go Hrathgar? Much worse than caterpillar. She

only look you, turn you stone." He peered around the campsite as if Hrathgar would magically appear by simply mentioning this fact.

"Turn to stone!" Himalette cried. "Brigitta, she can turn things to stone!" Minq and Himalette shivered at the thought.

"Then maybe she can turn them back," Brigitta said.

Minq built an impressive fire and the girls moved to the pit and sank to the ground. Brigitta divided up some gundlebeans and all three of them sighed as the warm food hit their bellies. After filling themselves almost to satisfaction, Minq excused himself to gather some medicinal plants from outside the wall. Brigitta picked leaves and cocoon threads from Himalette's blue-tinted hair while they waited for him to return.

Himalette scratched at her arms. "It still itches."

"I know. Try not to think about it," said Brigitta.

"Briggy, what if we can't find Hrathgar? What if she won't help us?"

"Shhhhh." Brigitta kissed Himalette's head. "Don't worry, lola." The same questions plagued Brigitta's mind. Himalette's soft hair and the warmth of the fire comforted her a little, but her head felt woozy and her torn wing ached. She wasn't even sure if she would be able to fly in the morning.

Minq returned with an armful of petals, leaves, roots, and an earful of uul tree sap. He mixed a sticky concoction in a cup over the fire.

"See wing?" He held out his ear to Brigitta.

She turned around and Minq slathered the mixture over the tear. She winced from the sharp sting, but the pain quickly melted into a numbing warmth.

"Does it hurt?" Himalette peered at the salve on Brigitta's wing.

"Only at first. Now it feels kind of tingly."

Minq spread some of the mixture on Himalette's glow worm bites. She squirmed with the first sting, then slowly relaxed. She smiled a sleepy thank you up at Minq.

"This learn from Gola," Minq said. "We go her tomorrow. She Drutan."

"What's that?" asked Himalette.

"Tree-woman. Very old." Minq put the mixture down and began fanning their injuries with his ears.

"She can help us?" Brigitta asked.

"She see."

"Have you ever been to Hrathgar's?" Brigitta asked Minq.

"If I go Hrathgar, not be here now. Everyone go Dead Mountain never come back." Minq stopped fanning and wrapped Brigitta's wing with a large soft leaf. "Sleep now. Stay close fire."

Minq trotted over to the pile of extra wood, and from behind it, pulled out some brown furry blankets. He handed them to Brigitta, who took them, wondering what had originally worn the fur. She and Himalette snuggled close on one side of the fire as Minq settled down on the opposite side.

Brigitta whispered into Himalette's ear, "When we reach The River That Runs Backwards, we'll fly north and leave Minq behind."

"But I like him," Himalette whispered back into Brigitta's ear.

"We have to, Himmy. Think about our forest and our momma and poppa." Brigitta squirmed closer to Himalette. "Listen to me. Don't make friends, don't make enemies, and never take anything from anybody unless I say it's okay. Do you hear me?"

"Yeah."

"Himmy?"

"Yes, yes, I hear you. No friends."

"We can't trust anyone, not even him." Brigitta glanced over at Minq on the other side of the fire pit.

Minq shifted his ears and opened one of his eyes. He quickly shut his eye again.

Brigitta held Himalette tightly as they drifted to sleep.

Chapter Ten

The next morning Brigitta and Himalette woke early to find Minq preparing a breakfast porridge of mixed roots and the remaining uul tree sap. Their momma was the best Feast Master in Tiragarrow, perhaps even the whole Water Faerie Realm, so they knew what good porridge tasted like. Minq caught their sour expressions as they took their first bites and then put down their bowls.

"You not like?" he gazed at them sadly.

"It tastes like—" Himalette started.

"It tastes just fine," said Brigitta, quivering her wings at Himalette. "It's just a little hot."

Brigitta knew any breakfast was better than no breakfast. There were few rations in her pack and any lessons she'd had on edible plants did not include Dark Forest flora. She picked up the bowl and gave Himalette a steely glare as she took another spoonful. Himalette pouted and did the same.

Minq removed the leafy bandage from Brigitta's wing and inspected her injury. He patted the herbal goo with his ears.

"Heal good," said Minq with a satisfied nod, "but no fly today." He returned the bandage to Brigitta's wound and cleaned up around the campsite. "We go now."

* * *

They set off into the woods with Minq leading the way over twisted roots, around snapping plants, and under protruding limbs. The forest grew more and more menacing as they traveled. Branches and vines reached out for them as they passed. The girls jumped at every rustle, every throaty growl, and every flying beast that crossed their path. The trees grew thicker and taller, until they could no longer see the sky.

Himalette followed Minq, half walking, half flying, with her arms tucked close to her body. Brigitta picked up the rear, twisting around and walking backwards every time she sensed any movement behind them.

"How come there are no birds in the Dark Forest?" Himalette asked.

"What mean?" returned Minq. "Birds everywhere. They watch now."

Himalette stopped and listened. Brigitta shot her a warning look.

"I'm not touching anything," said Himalette. She stuck her hands in her pockets to demonstrate.

"Good."

"I'm not even looking at anything I might want to touch."

They came to a break in the trees where a small and surprisingly picturesque waterfall dropped into a green pool. Minq took a right at the pool and continued on. Himalette gave the tranquil scene a longing gaze before turning and following Minq. Removing her pack, Brigitta dropped behind and knelt on the moist bank.

She paused for a moment. There was something strange about the pool. Then she realized that even though water flowed into it from the waterfall, the pool didn't appear to lead anywhere. There were no streams from it heading uphill or downhill. And the waterfall wasn't splashing over any rocks into deep caverns, like at Precipice Falls south of Tiragarrow.

The water was completely clear. The pool's color came from the little feathery green plants dotting the bottom. Brigitta stared at her reflection on the water's surface. A strange blue-faced young faerie with tangled hair stared back. She removed her canteen from her pack and reached down. Minq was suddenly at her side, snatching her hand away just before it touched the surface of the water. She gasped and dropped the canteen.

"Pond vile." Minq picked up Brigitta's canteen and handed it to her. He then picked up a stick and touched the water with it. As soon as it hit the surface, one of the green plants stretched out and seized it, dragging it underwater. The stick shook a bit before another plant grabbed hold of the other end and snapped it in two. The little plants let go of it and the broken pieces floated to the surface.

"Don't touch anything, right?" Himalette said from behind them.

"Right." Brigitta rummaged through her knapsack while Minq peered over her shoulder. She pulled her pack to the side, out of his view, and removed the tiny bottle she had found at Auntie Ferna's. "Poppa's spout snake." She smirked as she uncorked it.

She set the bottle on the bank of the pool and out slithered the miniscule red snake. At the edge of the water, it paused, sniffed with its triple forked tongue, then dove into the water, streaking through the pool faster than she could see and faster than Minq's ears could hear. The pond vile snapped at the snake as it propelled itself out of the water and onto the ground in front of them with a wet thud. It was as long and thick as Brigitta's arm.

Brigitta picked up the snake and gave it a test squeeze. A stream of water shot out from its mouth. She held the snake over her canteen and squeezed snake-water into it. When her canteen was full, she pinched the snake's mouth shut, flung it over her shoulder, and corked her canteen.

Brigitta gestured to Himalette who handed her own canteen over. Himalette clapped as Brigitta squirted water into it, then squealed as Brigitta sprayed her face.

Minq approached and examined the snake. Brigitta offered it to him. He shrugged and opened his mouth. She released a stream of snake-water down his throat.

"Poppa's spout snake took third place in New Creations at last year's festival." Brigitta rolled the snake up from the bottom to squeeze out the remaining drops.

"It was supposed to be a fountain," said Himalette.

"It was supposed to work more than once, too," added Brigitta.

"Now snake broken?" asked Minq.

"Not broken," said Brigitta, "just used."

She gave one last little squirt into her own mouth, then released the snake into the grass. It lay there, not knowing what to do.

"Snake be eaten," Minq warned, "you leave here."

"I doubt it." Brigitta gave it a little nudge and it slithered forward. "It wouldn't taste very good."

They watched as a prickly flower leaned over and sniffed the snake as it passed. The flower turned away in disgust as the squishy red snake disappeared into the forest forever.

Minq and the two young faeries trudged through the trees. Brigitta swore to herself that if she could make things right, she would never complain about the long flight to Auntie Ferna's cottage ever again.

Minq had done a decent job on her injured wing, but the severe tear still pained her with every step. She was frustrated they weren't able to fly and was haunted by the image of sand falling through the Hourglass. They were running out of time.

For a land beast, Minq was surprisingly quick and agile. He would trot ahead and return with news of swampy ground or prickly trees, or simply to encourage them. "Listen! Listen! Hear?" he would say excitedly and then bound off.

"Hear what?" Brigitta and Himalette would call out as he disappeared again.

Far past their usual lunchtime, Brigitta began to hear a great rushing of water in the distance. The roar grew louder and louder until the trees finally opened up and they found themselves standing near the edge of a steep embankment, confronted by a menacing river. The water was dark brownish-green and moved like a storm, churning and fighting against itself as it flowed uphill. Brigitta could feel its pull, even from a distance. She steadied her feet and grabbed Himalette's shoulder to stop her from getting too close.

Their eyes followed the river's path uphill and the girls gasped as they caught sight of an enormous, rugged dark lump of earth surrounded by a dirty haze. Two-thirds of the way up, twisted into the barren rocks, was a foreboding castle.

"Dead Mountain." Minq pointed toward the castle and shivered. "Hrathgar live there. You sure we go?"

"Our forest depends on it." Brigitta swallowed at the lump that had formed in her throat.

"And our momma and poppa," said Himalette, reaching for Brigitta's arm.

Brigitta broke away and stepped a little closer to the embankment for a better view. The river-wind pulled at her, whipping at her hair and tunic. She was drenched in the heavy mist that the river spat out and sucked back in. She grabbed hold of a tree branch for safety. The forest grew right up to the edge and it was a long drop to the river below.

"Careful," warned Minq, holding her back with an ear, "too close edge!"

She scrambled back and glanced over her shoulder at her bandaged wing. She tested it a few times and winced as a sharp pain shot through to her shoulder. "We'll have to fly over the river to the mountain."

"No good," Minq explained. "Bad river-wind. Take you down. Bones come out there." He pointed to Dead Mountain with his ear. He wrapped his other ear around a trunk, picked up a leaf, stretched out, and dropped the leaf over the embankment. The unsuspecting leaf immediately disappeared, sucked into the river-wind. "Best go Gola. Not far. Stay night. Go mountain tomorrow if still want."

"Gola will help?" Brigitta was skeptical.

"Gola see."

"Will there be food?" Himalette held her stomach as it emitted a gurgle to punctuate her question.

Brigitta looked back up at the castle and back down at the river. She removed her pack, dug out the last piece of squished pipberry bread, and handed it to Himalette.

A tiny yellow light emerged from the forest and floated on the breeze toward them. It bumped up against Himalette's nose. "Hey!" she laughed with her mouth full of bread.

The floating light swirled away from Himalette and bumped into Brigitta's forehead. It was fuzzy, as if spun from soft web. It made a hissing noise as it bombarded her face.

"Minq, you don't understand." Brigitta swatted at the light. "The Hourglass of Protection runs out when tomorrow ends. It's supposed to be turned by the Elders or else . . . or else . . . " Brigitta didn't have time to explain. "We have to get to Hrathgar's *today*."

"No time. No time before dark," he insisted. "Come. Gola see."

Himalette held up her hand to the yellow light, letting it dance on her fingers. She grabbed at it as it drifted away, caught in the river-wind.

"It's whispering to me!" Himalette exclaimed as the yellow light picked up speed and spun toward the river.

"Sorry, Minq." Brigitta was adamant. "We really have to leave you now. Thank you very much for all your help. I release you of . . . of . . . I mean . . . you don't have to be ours.

"Come on, Himmy." Brigitta slung her pack over one shoulder and turned to retrieve her little sister. "Himalette!"

Himalette was dangerously close to the embankment. She stood there, blue-tinted hair and dirty tunic whipping wildly as the yellow light flew over the edge and was sucked out of sight.

Himalette pouted. As she turned back toward Brigitta, the ground beneath her gave way. She screamed as she slipped and the river-wind pulled her down toward the mad water. She beat her little wings against the wind and grabbed hold of a long tree root. Her legs flailed behind her as she struggled, unable to fly out of the current.

"Hold on!" cried Brigitta.

Minq wrapped his forearms around a tree, braced his legs against two sturdy roots, and held his right ear out to Brigitta. She took hold of it, surprised by its strength as it wrapped itself around her wrist. She inched her way out until she could almost touch Himalette.

"Grab my hand!" she called.

"I can't!" cried Himalette. "I can't reach it!"

"Yes, you can." Brigitta slid a little more toward Himalette and stretched downwards. Her pack slipped from her shoulder and down her arm. The ground moved beneath them and the river-wind pulled as if the world had opened up and was trying to swallow them. Brigitta reached for her pack a second too late. It slipped off her arm, dropped to the ground, and disappeared over the embankment.

She stretched out, grabbed her sister, and held on to Minq as he pulled them out of danger. They collapsed under the tree and caught their breaths.

After her heart had stopped racing, Brigitta smacked at the leaves above her. "I can't believe you, Himmy!"

"Sorry," said Himalette weakly.

"Why can't you leave things alone? You're going to get us both killed!"

"I'm sorry! I'm sorry!"

Brigitta sat up. "You couldn't keep your hands off that stupid flying beast, could you?"

"Whisper light," said Minq as if this cleared up the matter.

"Now all our supplies are gone—including the pages from Auntie Ferna's book!" Brigitta stared hard at Himalette. "And all our food."

"I didn't know!" Himalette sobbed.

"I knew you would get us into trouble." Brigitta stood up and brushed herself off. "I should have left you back home in a groven stench-bog!"

Himalette collapsed to the ground in tears. Minq wrapped his ears around her and patted her gently.

"Stop it, you big baby!" Brigitta turned away.

"No cry, little faerie." Minq lifted Himalette off the ground and addressed Brigitta. "Follow Minq, please. We get new supply and food."

"From Gola?" Brigitta turned back around.

"She'll help?" Himalette lifted her head and wiped her nose with her sleeve.

"Gola see." Minq gestured with an ear toward a rough path into the forest. It was the first real path Brigitta had seen since they had left the Giant Caterpillar realm.

Without food or supplies, they had little choice but to follow Minq to Gola's. Brigitta signaled for Minq to lead the way and for Himalette to follow. Avoiding her big sister's glare, Himalette stumbled after him.

Brigitta glanced once more at Dead Mountain and sighed heavily, then turned to follow them down the path.

Chapter Eleven

As the forest grew darker, sleepy pairs of eyes appeared in the trees, watching them as they traveled. Himalette stopped to check out a wide split down the middle of a trunk. A growl from inside startled her and she ran to Brigitta, who shrugged her off, still fuming about the river incident.

Minq leapt over a fallen log. Himalette sullenly floated over it, then Brigitta flew over it, wincing as her injured wing knocked against a branch. She tumbled to the ground.

"Are you all right?" asked Himalette.

"I'm fine," Brigitta grunted. She picked herself up and motioned them along with a wave. They continued in silence. Brigitta cringed as her wing banged against another branch.

"Oh, no!" Himalette pointed into the trees. A fuzzy yellow light floated alongside them. It bumped into a tree branch and then danced over it.

"It all right, only whisper light." Minq motioned with his ear. "Come, come, very soon. Almost there."

Himalette caught Brigitta's eyes to let her know that she wasn't going to go running after the light. Brigitta took Himalette's hand just in case and led her after Minq, who bounded ahead with a whooping bark.

Brigitta heard a soft hissing noise. She glanced around and through the trees. There was another hiss, slightly louder. Someone was whispering. She looked down at her sister.

"Stop it."

"Stop what?"

"That hissing. That whispering. Stop it."

"I wasn't whispering, honest." Himalette looked out into the forest. "I hear something, too."

Pssssss bssssss fsssss . . .

Two more fuzzy yellow lights appeared near her right ear. "Leave us alone," Brigitta growled and pulled Himalette away.

The rough path grew wider, more defined. It curved to the left, then the right, and then opened into a field of ochre colored flowers. It was brighter in the open field, but not much, as the sky was thick with muddy clouds. On the other side of the field, at the end of the path, stood an immense tree with an old knotted wood door and two small windows with faded curtains. Half-way up the trunk a tree-hole emitted a fine curl of smoke. Two more paths led off into the forest on either side of the tree.

Minq hopped up and down in front of the field. He motioned to them wildly and Brigitta had to smile. The tree looked homey and warm. She could smell something cooking, and she was more than famished.

As Minq stepped into the field, his leg glanced one of the flowers. It shivered a moment, then its petals dropped away, releasing the center of the flower into the air. The flower center caught the breeze and began to glow, first white, then yellow, like a little star. It drifted up and away.

Brigitta, still grasping Himalette's hand, made her way across the field. Minq trotted backwards shouting, "Come! Come!"

When Brigitta and Himalette were half-way across the field, a gust of wind sent flower petals whirling about. Dozens of fuzzy white star-lights floated from their stems. They turned from white to yellow as they drifted about. Himalette squealed with delight. Brigitta gripped Himalette's hand tighter and proceeded through the field.

"Ow!" complained Himalette.

Pssssst vssst . . . Brigitta could hear the whispers again. The yellow lights were everywhere, bombarding her. She shooed them away with her hand. The whispers grew more and more intense until the air was thick with them.

Psssst vrsst whhhhyyyuuu . . . stupid girl . . .

She could see them swirling across the length of the field. It sounded as if they were whispering directly into her ears. Her head began to thrum with sound. She wondered why Minq was still jumping up and down at the edge of the field. Could he not hear the whispers?

"Minq, stop them!" Brigitta finally pleaded.

"Come. Come. They say nothing." Minq gestured toward the tree. "Almost there."

Psssst vrsst whhhhyyyuuu stupid, stupid girl . . . all your friends are laughing at your empty wings . . .

"Brigitta, please!" Himalette yanked on her hand. "You're hurting me!"

Brigitta looked down at her hand; it was white from gripping Himalette's so hard. "Himmy, can't you hear them?"

"Yes, they're pretty. Like laughing."

She let go of Himalette, put both hands to her ears, and shut her eyes tight. "No, they're horrible and nasty!"

"They say nothing, please, come," Minq insisted.

Your momma turned to stone . . . your poppa turned to stone . . . Ondelle turned to stone . . . broken faeries everywhere . . .

"What do you mean? They're saying terrible things to me. You tricked me! You tricked us!" Brigitta's head echoed with the sound of the whispers, even with her hands over both her ears.

Minq grabbed Brigitta's arm and hauled her through the field. She stumbled along, arms flailing. He released her and she fell forward into the dirt. She opened her eyes to find she was staring at a twisted wooden cane. She followed the cane up.

A tall, thin being stooped over Brigitta. She was dressed in numerous folds of cloth and a tattered brown hooded cape. She removed her hood. Her skin was bark-like and her eye sockets were so sunken that Brigitta couldn't see any eyes. She tapped at the top of her cane with fingers of long, jagged twigs.

Himalette hid behind Brigitta who was still shaking the whispers out of her head.

The tree-woman stopped tapping and leaned into her cane. "What the ground creature means," she said in a gravelly voice, "is that the whispers indicate nothing."

"But—but," stammered Brigitta, "they knew things."

"Your mind will tell you what you want to hear."

Brigitta said nothing. She was certain those were not things she wanted to hear.

"Minq," the woman continued, "bring your . . . faeries inside." She hobbled over to the tree and slipped in through the door.

Minq's grimace-like smile appeared once again and he gestured toward Gola's home. Brigitta looked back at the field as the whisper lights drifted away, zigzagging against the darkening sky. She and Himalette made their way toward the tree while two pairs of wide eyes watched them from the forest.

A row of cauldrons filled with plants and herbs lined the path to Gola's door. As Brigitta and Himalette passed the cauldrons, several tiny violet flowers reached out and sniffed them.

"Chatterbuds. No hurt you. No say bad things," said Minq.

The plants greeted them in a tinny chorus, "Hello! Hello! Hello!" and eagerly waved their leaves.

Himalette reached out to touch one of them, then pulled her hand back and sulked. "I'm not allowed to make any friends," she said, nodding her head toward Brigitta.

"Sound advice in these forests," Gola's husky voice came from inside the tree.

Minq nudged the girls along with his ears, smiling to encourage them. Brigitta entered first with Himalette clinging to her from behind.

Gola's tree was surprisingly roomy. There was an unmade bed, a messy kitchen, and a laboratory piled with ancient books, vials of dark liquids, strange prickly plants, and jars of fermenting beasts. Dark splotches covered the inside walls of the trunk.

A small blue-gray pool of water, lined with stones, sat in the center of the floor. Gola tapped her way to the pool with her cane. Minq gestured for Brigitta and Himalette to sit down on the smooth stones and he sat down next to them, curling his long ears around himself like a shawl.

"What have you brought for me?" Gola addressed Minq as she faced the pool.

"Find sharmock root near caterpillar nest."

"Sharmock roots?" She turned toward him. "Very nice."

"But caterpillar catch me." Minq indicated Brigitta and Himalette. "Faeries save life."

"So no roots?" she inquired.

Minq shook his head sadly.

A pair of dark spots on the wall next to Himalette sprang open. It was a pair of Eyes. She shrieked and slipped off her rock. Brigitta pulled Himalette to her side.

The pair of Eyes flew from the wall on little bat wings and hovered in front of Minq. His face appeared in the blue-gray pool, wavering on the water as the Eyes fluttered about his face.

"Speak up, ground creature; I cannot hear you," said Gola.

Minq looked into the hovering Eyes and smiled nervously. "No roots."

"Bah!" She waved her hand at the pool.

Another pair of Eyes flew off the wall and joined the first pair. They swung around to examine the young faeries whose blue faces appeared in the pool. The Eyes studied Brigitta and Himalette's blue arms and legs and these images, too, materialized in the pool.

"What kind of faeries are you?" Gola asked.

"Please, your . . . tree-ness . . . we're Water Faeries," Brigitta's voice quivered. She held up her arm. "We're not usually, um, blue."

"What have I to do with Water Faeries?" Gola frowned and

turned to the pool. The Eyes bobbed closer to the girls. "Have you run away from your forest?"

"Everyone in the White Forest is turned to stone," burst out Himalette, "and we have to go to Hrathgar's to find Blue Spell—"

"Himmy!" Brigitta hissed.

Gola spun around to face Brigitta and Himalette. "Blue Spell? Hrathgar has access to faerie Blue Spell?"

"You know about Blue Spell?" Brigitta asked.

The two pairs of Eyes flew up and landed on each of Gola's shoulders. "I have heard of it."

"Well," Brigitta paused, choosing her words carefully, "we don't know if she has it. We just know the White Forest has been cursed and, besides us, she's the only other faerie left."

"What makes you so certain Hrathgar will assist you?"

"She's kin! Faeries always help their kin. She's had such a long punishment. Maybe she's lonely and misses the White Forest? Maybe . . . maybe . . . she feels bad about what she did?"

Gola grunted. "Of that I doubt. She is one who only serves herself."

"She's our only hope." Brigitta was on the verge of tears. "We have nowhere else to go. If we don't reverse the curse—if we don't turn everyone back soon—there won't be a White Forest."

Gola stood in silence, her two pairs of Eyes staring blankly ahead.

"It is a foolish idea," she finally said. She waved her hand and the Eyes returned to the wall. The images disappeared from the pool.

"Whether you help us or not," Brigitta said, "we're going to Dead Mountain."

Gola shuffled to her kitchen and felt her way to a large kettle that hung on a bar across a fire pit. A pair of Eyes dropped away from the kitchen wall and searched the jars of various herbs and roots until they found a glass container filled with shiny red stones.

Gola reached for the jar and removed one of the stones. She threw it into the fire pit and it burst into flames. The smoke danced and curled up the sides of the kettle and slipped through a crack in the tree-wall. Gola replaced the lid on the jar and the Eyes settled on top of it. They stared into the wisp of smoke as it escaped through the crack and Gola's barky brow wrinkled in thought.

"Hrathgar cannot be trusted," she said. The Eyes hopped over to the top of a jar of brown paste and peered into the kettle as Gola stirred its contents with a long spoon. "However, she is highly skilled and may indeed possess a way of undoing this curse."

Brigitta stood up and moved to the kitchen. Himalette slid off her stone and curled up against Minq who wrapped one of his long ears around her shoulders.

A second pair of Eyes flew from the wall and across the counter until they came to a row of wooden cups. Gola grabbed one of the cups and sampled the brew from the kettle.

"You do not have the strength or knowledge to subdue Hrathgar. The only way would be to find her source of power and use it against her," she said.

"Can you help us, please?"

"I can see." Gola grabbed another cup and dipped it into the kettle. "But only on one condition." The second pair of Eyes landed on Gola's shoulder and blinked down at Brigitta. Gola handed the cup to her. "This land is too harsh for an old Drutan. I would prefer to live in your White Forest."

"But only the Elders can decide that," Brigitta said, taking the cup.

Gola gave a throaty chuckle. "Little faerie, if you succeed in tricking Hrathgar, than you are more than clever enough to convince your Elders to allow me passage into your forest."

Chapter Twelve

$\mathcal{B}$rigitta and Himalette sat by the blue-gray pool watching Minq and Gola huddled in the entrance of her tree. Pointing a knobby finger into the forest, Gola dismissed a pair of Eyes from her shoulder and they flew off like a drunken bird. She held out her hand and Minq placed an ear in her palm. She whispered into his ear and he gave a nervous nod.

Everyone gathered around the pool. Several pairs of Eyes dropped from the walls and landed next to the murky water.

"Look here and see as I see." Gola pointed to the pool.

A wavering image appeared in the water. It was a bird's-eye view of The River That Runs Backwards. Avoiding its deadly pull, the Eyes flew high above the river which grew increasingly dark and tumultuous as it fought its way up the craggy mountain like a snaking storm. The river climbed up and up and then was sucked into the side of the mountain through an enormous cave.

"Where does the river come back out again?" asked Brigitta.

"Some say it goes to the Center of the World. Some say it emerges on the other side."

The pool reflected the mouth of the cave, then the inside, and then it grew dark.

"How strong are your wings?" Gola inquired, a pair of Eyes fluttering from the wall to examine Brigitta's blue-tinted wings.

Brigitta stretched them out, then winced. "One of them is torn."

Himalette fluttered her wings. "I have good wings!"

"I will take care of your injury and give you something for

your strength," Gola said to Brigitta. She pointed at the image, indicating the mouth of the cave. "You will need to enter the cave here, otherwise, you will be attacked by Hrathgar's rock guards as you ascend the mountain or inhale some poison cloud. The river wind cleanses the air."

"I no have wings," Minq reminded her.

"The older faerie will carry you."

"We don't need Minq," Brigitta said.

"Minq will go."

A hazy greenish light appeared in the pool. As the Eyes moved deeper into the cave, the light grew brighter and soon they could see a much larger cavern with glowing crystals dotting the ceiling.

"When you reach the room of green zynthias," said Gola pointing to the green crystals, "you must quickly locate the entrance to the castle courtyard." Gola turned to Brigitta, and all the Eyes perched at the edge of the pool did the same. "Do not linger in this room or look directly into any of the crystals. They have an hypnotic effect and you may find yourself falling into a dream state from which you might never awake."

The pool reflected a dark cavity in the ceiling between two large crystals. Everyone watched as the Eyes entered the cavity, flew through a tunnel, and propelled themselves out of an opening in the ground. The water reflected a crumbling courtyard overgrown with thorny brush. Above the brush loomed the walls of Hrathgar's castle, greasy with slime and age.

The wavering image held for a moment, then suddenly vanished. Brigitta, Himalette, and Minq pulled back from the pool. The water returned to its original blue-gray state. All the Eyes around the pool shuddered.

"What happened?" Brigitta turned to Gola.

"Each time that is as far as I have seen." Gola motioned for the Eyes to lead her to her laboratory. "Perhaps you will fare better. The Eyes can see for me, but all alone they are defenseless."

"I've changed my mind. I want Minq to come with me.

Himalette will stay here."

"But I want to come," said Himalette. "I want to help Momma and Poppa!"

"You wouldn't get past the zynthias, Himmy. You'd want to touch them or put them in your pockets."

"I won't. I promise I won't," she pleaded. "I'll show you. I'll be good from now on."

"You'll be good from now on and you'll stay here with Gola."

"Please don't leave me here!" Himalette looked up at Brigitta with large, watery eyes. "I want to go with you and Minq!"

"Your sister is right, little one." Gola motioned for Minq to get up. "It is far too dangerous."

Himalette sulked by the pool, dragging her hand through the water as Minq and Gola worked in the kitchen. A pair of Eyes landed on a jar and another landed on a stone measuring spoon. Minq gathered both items and presented them to Gola.

Brigitta wandered over to a shelf on the far wall piled with dusty books and broken pieces of red pottery. The books were a hodgepodge of shapes and sizes with strange symbols on their spines. She absent-mindedly scratched her blue neck as she followed the books to the end of the shelf. Next to the shelf, hanging on a tarnished silver hook in the wall, was a large stained and yellowed parchment with faded symbols.

It was a map of a continent, but its name was too worn to read. The continent was bordered on the west by a body of water labeled Sea of Tzajeek with a silvery spiny-backed serpent weaving through the letters.

Brigitta peered closer. On the southern part of the continent she could just make out the words Valley of Noe, the home of her ancestors and the Ancient Ones. She was looking at Foraglenn, the continent upon which they lived.

She looked to the northern end of Foraglenn and found the

Dark Forest. A bare spot in the middle of the Dark Forest was labeled White Forest. In the middle of the bare spot was a miniscule hourglass no bigger than her pinkie fingernail.

To the east of the White Forest, a meandering line caught her attention. She guessed it to be The River That Runs Backwards. She followed it up to Dead Mountain where the line became dotted. The dotted line briefly went up, then turned sharply down and disappeared. It must be the river cavern, she thought.

Brigitta put her hand to her tunic pocket. Miraculously, the map she had stolen from her Auntie's book was still there. Without even looking at it, she knew the two maps had the same patterns and symbols. Gola's map must have been drawn by faeries.

Had Gola stolen it?

Brigitta poked at the map on the wall. "Where did you . . . " She stopped poking. There was nothing behind the map.

She lifted the map and it slipped from its hook on the wall revealing a hidden nook. Inside the nook sat four small red clay pots and an empty space where a fifth pot had previously been. Brigitta tipped the first pot and peeked inside. A round glassy object sat at the bottom. She reached in and took it out. It was like a piece of night sky.

She turned the dark stone around and around in her hand. Miniscule stars glimmered inside of it. As she stared into it, she felt her mind being pulled into the stars, drifting away . . .

Gola's gnarly hand swiped the stone away. Brigitta looked up to find several pairs of accusing Eyes hovering beside Gola's shadowy face.

"You will leave my possessions alone!" spat Gola returning the stone to the red pot and rehooking the map on the wall. She and the Eyes turned their attention back to Brigitta. Gola's empty wooden eye-sockets bore into her.

Brigitta opened her mouth to speak, but changed her mind. She scooted away from the map and Gola shuffled back to her kitchen with all her pairs of Eyes except one, which stayed behind and sat themselves upon the dusty bookshelf.

Brigitta caught Minq giving her a strange look from the kitchen, but he recovered with one of his nervous toothy grins. She fluttered over to Gola's massive bed and dropped down onto it.

She closed her eyes and thought of her cottage in Tiragarrow, how light and warm it was compared to Gola's drafty tree. The wind outside made low musical sounds as it blew through the old, hollow branches. She imagined these to be the sounds of a new musical invention of her poppa's. A hollow tree that could sing. As she drifted off to sleep, she pictured his excited face as he proudly revealed his new creation.

Someone nudged the bed and Brigitta opened her eyes. Gola placed two large wrinkled black seed pods beside her. Brigitta sat upright and stared at the pods.

"What are those?" she asked.

"They are spell-seeds." Gola leaned on her cane as a pair of Eyes looked down from her shoulder. "For carrying potions and spells long distances." She patted a seed. "The contents are undetectable from the outside."

Brigitta took one of the seed pods from Gola and examined it. It was exactly like the one the White Forest sprite had been carrying— the one Brigitta had found later on the ground near the Hourglass and was now possibly traveling to the Center of the World inside of her pack.

"Just before you enter the cave, open the spell-seed and drink the root potion. It will give you enough strength to carry Minq through the cave and up to the courtyard," Gola said. "Do not drink it prematurely. Its effects are temporary. You will return to your own strength within four moon-beats, perhaps less."

"How do I open it?"

"Spin it exactly three times in the same direction as the sun and moons travel, then balance it on end and release three drops of water onto it. Tears will also work. Saliva will not, as it is impure."

"*Three turns . . . three tears . . . three turns . . . three tears . . . of wa-ter . . .*" Himalette sang as she appeared beneath them, craning her neck to get a better look.

"Be warned," said Gola, motioning for Minq, who brought Brigitta a woven pack, "when the effects of the mixture have completely subsided, there is a short period of paralysis, less than a moon-beat, but you will be helpless. Find somewhere safe to hide until the paralysis has worn off."

"What's pa-ral-sis?" asked Himalette, crawling up beside Brigitta. "Hey, Briggy, that's just like—"

"It means you can't move by yourself," Brigitta interrupted her sister with a glare. She placed the seed inside the pack. "Gola, do sprites use spell-seeds?"

"Sprites?" Gola looked surprised. She leaned forward. "I am the only one who knows how to construct a spell-seed. They are my specialty."

Gola thrust the second spell-seed at Brigitta.

"What's this one for?"

"You will require it for your return." The Eyes flew back toward the kitchen and Gola followed. "You will leave with first light. Now we will tend to your wing."

Brigitta placed the second seed in the pack and jumped down off the bed. She caught Himalette's attention and put her finger to her lips. Himalette nodded in response.

As Gola straightened up her kitchen and prepared for bed, Minq took the girls outside to what he called his Dream Tree. "Night or day," he said, "good sleep in Dream Tree."

Ten steps from Gola's door, his Dream Tree was a smaller, squatter tree with a hollow L-shaped curve lined with soft beast fur. As they approached, its thick, crisp leaves rustled together in the wind. It sounded like the pitter-patter of rain. Himalette gasped in delight when she heard the rain-music of the tree and tugged on Brigitta's tunic. Brigitta was deep in thought.

"Sleep here." Minq patted the fur with his ear. "Be safe. Be warm."

Himalette climbed into the tree, curled up in the fur, and let out a tremendous sigh.

Brigitta set her new pack inside the tree. "What did Gola whisper in your ear earlier this evening by the door?"

"Not concern you." Minq looked her squarely in the eyes. "No matter."

Brigitta placed one foot into the tree and paused. "And what's with those dark stones behind the map?"

"Shhhhh!" Minq took Brigitta by the shoulders and steered her into the tree. He leaned inside. "No touch Gola's moonstone. Only Drutan use. Very dangerous. Split your mind up." He tapped the side of his head with his ear.

"Well, I . . . " Brigitta paused. Himalette had stopped rolling in the fur and was listening to them.

"You sleep now," Minq said, and trotted back to Gola's tree.

The sisters curled up together in the warm fur.

"I don't trust her, not at all," said Brigitta. "Nor Minq."

"She scares me, Briggy," said Himalette. "I don't want to stay here."

Brigitta shifted so that the bandage on her wing was not directly under her shoulder. "We don't have a choice, do we?"

"I could go with you instead."

"No, Himmy, I might not be able to protect you up there."

"I can take care of myself," Himalette murmured.

Brigitta was quiet. She thought of her momma and poppa, of her auntie and her friends, and of Ondelle's beautiful cold stone face. She watched as the Great Blue Moon escaped from the clouds and the orange Lola Moon chased after it. She sank deeper into the layers of fur, lulled by the sounds of the gentle rain-music above.

Chapter Thirteen

Brigitta awoke to the yawning and chirping of the chatterbuds lining the path to Gola's door. It took a moment for her to realize where she was and that she was alone inside Minq's Dream Tree. She leapt out of the tree, raced to Gola's door, and burst inside.

"Himalette?"

Gola was startled out of bed. Winged Eyes dropped from the walls around her, hovering and blinking in a sleepy daze. Minq's head jerked up from the floor, his giant ears knocking a fluttering pair of Eyes across the room.

Gola snatched a shawl from the bedpost and threw it over her barky shoulders. "She is not with you?" she asked, all Eyes focused on Brigitta.

The three of them rushed outside and Gola sent a flock of Eyes into the forest. She stood there, concentrating, as Brigitta raced back to the blue-gray pool in the middle of the floor. There were too many images for her to sort out as the Eyes rushed past trees, down paths, out to the river. Branches and leaves and rocks sailed past at a dizzying speed.

"I can't see her! I can't see anything!" She rushed back to the door.

Minq stepped outside and spread out his ears. He rotated east, south, west, and north then shook his head. "No hear her either."

Brigitta zipped back to the Dream Tree to retrieve Gola's woven pack. She dumped out the contents. "She took one of the spell-seeds!" Brigitta cried. "She's gone to Hrathgar's on her own!"

"Then you must leave at once." Gola's flock of Eyes returned from the forest and everyone moved back inside. All of the Eyes flew to the wall except for one that landed on Gola's shoulder and blinked down at Brigitta. Gola removed a small pendant off a hook on the wall and placed it around Brigitta's neck. "Do not worry young faerie, you are much faster than she."

Brigitta glanced at the pendant. It was a small watery mirror. The pair of Eyes on Gola's shoulder hopped down to Brigitta's head and looked back up at Gola, whose face appeared in the pendant.

"And you will have my Eyes," Gola said.

Brigitta and Minq gathered their supplies and sped through the door. They were equipped with only a few essentials: food and water, healing bandages, branches treated with a flare spell, and the seed pod containing the strength potion. They did not want anything to slow them down.

Following a path leading away from the field of whisper lights, they tore through the forest as fast as they could. Brigitta's wings were much stronger than the day before, and she could fly swiftly when the path was wide enough. Minq leapt over logs and roots to keep up, using his ears to pull himself around trees. The Eyes followed them from above.

"It's all my fault." Brigitta ducked under a branch. "I was too mean."

"You only want keep safe," Minq panted back.

"She's just a little girl."

"We find her," Minq reassured Brigitta.

"Momma and Poppa will never forgive me if something happens to Himmy. Oh, lola!" Brigitta fought back her tears. What good would it do to save the White Forest if she had to go back and tell her momma and poppa she had lost Himalette? She thought about which horrible fates might befall her little sister. Sucked into the river-wind? Drowned in the cave? Eaten by Hrathgar's guards?

They broke through the forest onto an outcropping of rock and dropped into stunned silence as the massive shape of Dead

Mountain loomed before them. The mountain was steep and jagged and barren. There weren't many places to hide from blood-thirsty beasts. Below them churned the unforgiving waters of The River That Runs Backwards. The river climbed the face of the mountain and disappeared. Farther up the mountain, she could just make out Hrathgar's castle camouflaged in the rocks and filthy air. The Eyes looked apprehensively at Brigitta and Minq.

Brigitta reached into her satchel and removed the spell-seed.

"Minq, if we use this one up, how will we get back?"

"Bigger problem first get *into* castle," Minq pointed out.

Brigitta nodded and placed the spell-seed on the ground. She was about to spin it when Minq stopped her with an ear.

"No, too early."

"But I want to carry you up the mountain. You'll take too long without wings."

"Wait for cave," Minq insisted.

"Himalette could be in danger."

"If you paralyze in cave, we fall and drown. No help Himalette we dead."

Brigitta knew he was right. She put the spell-seed back into her pack and they began the steep ascent. There were no shadows to speak of, even though it was the middle of the day. It was too dark to cast shadows, but it wasn't clouds overhead that blocked out the daylight. The air itself was thick and dark. The darkness stuck to them as they made their way higher and higher. Brigitta's blue skin turned progressively gray, and her wings turned a sickly green. Minq looked as though he had been rolling in ashes and the Eyes had to keep blinking to shake the darkness off.

Brigitta sent the Eyes back and forth several times to check the distance to the cave. As they continued up the mountain, Minq slipped and slid on the rock slime and fell further and further behind. He's wasting time, Brigitta thought as she flew ahead. She could go much faster alone. Or even with Himalette, for that matter.

The top of the massive cave appeared over the rocks. The

entrance to the cave was taller than the tallest tree Brigitta could imagine and as wide as the lyllium field outside of Tiragarrow. She could feel the pull of the river-wind as the water was sucked into the cave, inhaling the river like a giant mouth. She stopped short of getting caught in the suction and braced herself against a rock.

She looked out over what should have been a valley. She was high enough, she figured, to see the White Forest. But the darkness was too thick. The River That Runs Backwards shot out of it, toward the mountain, at a frightening speed.

She peered into the mirror necklace Gola had given her and panicked. The image was completely black. Then she realized this was simply because it was covered with a layer of soot. She looked up and spied the Eyes hovering high in the air in the entrance to the cave. Brigitta wiped off the mirror as the Eyes returned to her. They landed behind a rock and proceeded to clean themselves off with their little bat wings. When they were done preening, they sat and looked fixedly at Brigitta.

"Maybe she got scared and hid?" Brigitta regarded the Eyes. She knew Gola could only see her and not hear her, but she didn't know how much the Eyes themselves understood.

The Eyes blinked back at her.

Brigitta pointed out over the craggy mountain. "Go look for Himalette!"

The Eyes begrudgingly took off and fluttered in and out of the rocks while Brigitta watched in the mirror. Dark images flew past as the Eyes darted around, and then Minq's face appeared. She looked back up to see the Eyes fluttering toward her, followed by an exhausted Minq. He crawled up to her and collapsed on the ground.

"We can't stop now!" Brigitta cried. "What if she's gone inside? We have to find her!"

Minq rolled over onto his back and groaned. "Why not see with Eyes?"

"Search the cave!" Brigitta pointed and the Eyes flew up high and into the cave. She watched the image of the menacing river churning and then saw cavern walls drenched with filthy water. It quickly grew dark, and there were a few harrowing moments of complete blackness before the strange glow of the green zynthias appeared.

"She'd want to touch the crystals. I know she would," Brigitta murmured.

Minq dragged himself over to Brigitta and peered into the necklace as the Eyes searched the cave walls and the angry water below.

"I don't see her. She's drowned!" Brigitta felt faint and dizzy.

"You not know she drown." Minq steadied her by the shoulders with his ears.

"Or fallen and hurt herself or been eaten by a—" Brigitta didn't even know what kind of beasts inhabited this place.

"Maybe she just turned to stone?" Minq offered.

Brigitta gasped and began to cry.

Minq wrapped an ear around her shoulder and she cast it off. She grabbed her pack and dumped out the remaining spell-seed. She placed it on the ground and spun it, counting as it turned, and stopping it after three revolutions. She stood it on end and collected the tears from her cheeks. She dropped them, one at a time, from her fingers onto the spell-seed.

"One for Momma . . . one for Poppa . . . and one for Himmy."

The spell-seed crackled. The top of it split open. Brigitta put it to her lips and drank the contents in one long gulp. She threw the wrinkled spell-seed into the river, where it was sucked away by the turbulent stream of water. With fierce determination, Brigitta pulled a flare branch from her pack, handed it to Minq, slung her pack over her front side, and leapt up.

"Get on."

Minq climbed aboard Brigitta's back and held on for dear life as she shot straight up, then into the cave. She flew near the top so Minq could strike the end of the branch on the ceiling of the cave. The ceiling was as sopping wet as the soggy walls. He struck it several times before the end of the branch lit up, cutting through the murky darkness. Brigitta's wings sliced through the air effortlessly.

"You strong," called Minq over the noise.

She scanned the water below. It was loud and mad, and no place for any beast, faerie or otherwise. She shuddered and concentrated on flying.

"No look down," Minq warned. "Make dizzy."

"Hold on, Himmy. We're coming."

They flew into a thick blackness so dark it absorbed everything save a disembodied flame on the end of the flare branch. If it weren't for the crashing of the water below, she wouldn't even have known which way was up.

She flew carefully until she could see the green glow of the zynthia cavern ahead. Looking for any sign of her sister, she focused her gaze on the walls of the cave. When they entered the zynthia cavern, the wind grew even more fierce as the river suddenly plummeted into an eternity of darkness. No doubt, Brigitta thought, on its way to the Center of the World.

She took a deep breath and sped toward the top of the cave. She hovered there, scanning the walls, as gusts of river-wind tossed them around.

"No look into crystals," Minq reminded Brigitta.

She couldn't stay still long enough to get a good look at anything. "I can't see her anywhere!" Brigitta shouted over the roar of the river.

"Maybe she find tunnel to castle! We look!" Minq shouted back.

She flew to the far side of the cavern and combed the ceiling, careful never to look a green zynthia straight on. One of her wings faltered and she caught herself. "Minq!"

"What wrong?"

"You're starting to get heavy."

A fierce wind caught them and they dropped down toward the water.

"Must fly higher!"

"I can't! I can't!"

As they fell, Brigitta spotted a ledge in the rock wall. She maneuvered to it and landed to rest. Minq climbed down from her back.

She spit as the foul water from the walls splashed her face. "Where did the Eyes go?" She pulled out the mirror necklace and they both gazed into it.

Himalette's anguished face appeared in the mirror, crying out to them.

"Himmy!" Brigitta called and scanned the cavern. "Where are they? I can't hear her!"

"River too loud." Minq thrust out his ears and closed his eyes to concentrate. He twisted his ears in every direction. He opened his eyes again and pointed, "That way!"

Minq jumped up on Brigitta's back and she leapt into the air. Minq felt heavier than before, and her hands and feet were tingling. She mustered as much energy as she could and followed Minq's ear as it pointed the way to the far side of the cavern. Tucked behind some rocks, Brigitta could see Himalette waving to them frantically as the Eyes fluttered about her head. Brigitta landed behind the rocks and wrapped her arms around her sobbing sister.

"You're alive! Oh, Himmy!" She grasped Himalette tightly. She let go and drew back. "What were you thinking! How did you get here!"

"I—hid—in the forest—and followed you—I just —I wanted to—" Himalette managed to blurt out through her tears. "I can't feel my feet!" she cried.

Brigitta's own feet were now going numb. She shook them out.

"You lose strength, paralyze." Minq poked at Brigitta, "Must get out of cave."

"Minq, stay here," Brigitta commanded. "I'm going to get Himmy safe and then come back for you."

Himalette jumped on Brigitta's back. With a burst of strength, Brigitta leapt from the ledge and flew toward the ceiling.

"Close your eyes, Himmy."

Brigitta quickly scanned for the image she had seen in Gola's pool, keeping her eyes slightly closed and out of focus so the zynthia hypnosis couldn't take hold. She felt for the cold spot in the ceiling Gola spoke of. She reached three zynthias the size of large mushrooms hanging in a triangle around a dark hole.

"I feel it! It's cold here!"

Brigitta flew through an opening just big enough for the two of them to slip inside. She felt her strength waning as she darted up the hole in the earth.

"Himmy, can you fly on your own now?" she asked.

Himalette slipped off her back and Brigitta took her hand. They flew up the crevasse until they were well out of the river-wind. Brigitta stopped and looked up. She could just barely make out the other side of the crevasse, a pin prick of sky in the distance.

"Himmy, listen to me," Brigitta said sternly, "you must get out of here."

"I can't," Himalette moaned. "I'm so tired."

Brigitta looked around. There were no hand or footholds in the crevasse, nowhere for Himalette to go when the paralysis took over.

"I have to go back for Minq before I lose all my strength," said Brigitta. The tingling sensation had crawled up to her knees and elbows. "Do you remember the image of the castle in Gola's pool?"

"Yes, I remember."

"Good girl. I want you to fly as hard and fast as you can out of this tunnel and in through one of those castle windows."

"I'm too scared!"

Brigitta knew she didn't have the energy to take Himalette to the castle and go back for Minq. And she couldn't risk going into the zynthia cavern without a strength potion. She shook her hands to relieve the tingling.

"Let's play a game. You like games, right?"

"Yes . . . " Himalette eyed Brigitta suspiciously.

"Pretend you're the fastest faerie in the White Forest. Fly into the castle as quick as you can and then hide. I'll find you with Gola's Eyes! Okay? What are you going to do?"

"Go fast then hide."

"You can do this," said Brigitta. "Sing yourself a flying fast song. And find a really good hiding spot. Remember, you won't be able to move for a bit. But that's just part of the game."

"I'll sing about shadowflies. They're fast."

"Minq and I will be there soon. I promise. Go, now, quick!"

Himalette headed up the crevasse and Brigitta dove back into the cave for Minq. "If you're really there, somewhere," Brigitta said out loud to the Ethereals, "please protect my little sister. That's all I ask."

The tingling sensation had reached her hips and shoulders by the time she returned to the ledge. Minq jumped on her back and the exhausted Eyes gripped her right shoulder as she made one last journey to the ceiling. Minq pointed the flaring branch toward the crevasse. As she was about to enter, she felt Minq slump over on her back.

"Hmm . . . pretty," Minq sighed in her ear.

"What? Minq, you're slipping!"

"Pretty . . . pretty green." Minq began to laugh as Brigitta struggled to keep him balanced. The Eyes leapt from Brigitta's shoulder and batted Minq's face with their wings. He laughed harder and dropped the flaring branch. It tumbled to the water below and vanished. Brigitta felt Minq's body slip from her back.

"No!"

"Whee!" he cried as he plummeted toward the water.

Brigitta dove after him with lightning speed and grabbed him by the ears. She flew back up toward the crevasse, the Eyes leading the way. She fought to keep her energy and focus as they disappeared inside.

Chapter Fourteen

With the delirious Minq weighing her down, Brigitta struggled after Gola's Eyes, hoping the strength potion would last long enough to get them up the narrow opening. Lit with a hazy green light from the zynthias below, it was less a tunnel than a large crack in the earth that had grown wide from the seasons of river rumblings below.

Before she knew it, they had burst through into the open air and were hovering in the middle of a decaying courtyard. The lawn and garden had long turned to dust and the only remnants of more fertile days were a few dry, thorny bushes along two sides of the walled courtyard. The third side looked out over the wall, thick with slime, onto the darkness below. The courtyard stood at the base of an imposing stone castle coated in layers of sludge.

Brigitta dropped to the ground in relief and Minq tumbled away from her. The Eyes fluttered around Brigitta's head and she waved her hand to let Gola know they had made it safely out of the cave. As she started to get up, the Eyes were yanked from the air and Brigitta watched in horror as they vanished into a gigantic frog's open mouth.

She jumped to her feet and stumbled. She could no longer feel her left foot. The bulbous frog cocked its head toward her. It took a leap in her direction and she backed up, tripping over Minq.

"So that what happen Gola's Eyes," mused Minq dreamily, still under the spell of the green zynthias. He laughed and pointed at the approaching frog. "She feeding frogs."

"Minq! Come on!" Brigitta grabbed one of Minq's ears and pulled.

The frog leapt closer and opened its mouth. Its tongue shot out and wrapped itself around Minq's leg. The frog yanked Minq and Brigitta forward.

"Oh, no you don't, you oversized tadpole!" Brigitta yanked back and beat her wings with all her might. Minq continued to laugh as she and the frog fought their deadly a tug-of-war.

"Tongue prickly. Tickles!" He squirmed around on the ground.

Three more frogs appeared from the dark corners of the courtyard and hopped toward them. Brigitta pulled as hard as she could, but her strength was draining. Minq started to slip from her grasp. "Snap out of it, Minq!"

"I frog food!" Minq howled with laughter.

Brigitta gripped his ear desperately as they were dragged closer and closer to the giant frog's mouth. Minq's other ear swatted Brigitta in the face as he squirmed.

"Cut it out!"

"Wheeee!"

Brigitta grabbed a hold of his free ear and pulled both ears toward her face. "Miiiiiiiiinq!!!" She screamed as loud as she could into them.

He snapped out of his daze and shook his head. He looked up into the googly-eyed frog face. "Ahhhhhhh!" he shrieked and dug his paws into the earth.

Together they pulled against the frog's grasp, gaining a little ground. Another frog tongue shot out toward them, the first frog let go, and they toppled backwards. They leapt up again and Minq jumped onto Brigitta's back. She flew unsteadily toward the castle, dodging oncoming frog tongues.

Brigitta spotted a small window in the castle wall, high off the ground. She flew through the window and they spilled onto the cold hard floor. Minq sprang up on his hind legs, positioning himself for an attack. Brigitta struggled to get up, but her body was frozen. She lay on the floor unable to move.

Minq tried to lift her from under the arms. "You heavy like stone."

"Don't say stone," she winced.

"You heavy like . . . big rock."

"How long will I be paralyzed?" Brigitta could barely turn her head. The rest of her body felt like clay. She gazed across the ancient floor. She could see to the end of the dark, empty hallway and nothing else.

"Not know. At least frog too big come in window."

Voices echoed from somewhere inside the castle. They heard the shuffling of footsteps as a shadow appeared at the end of the hall. Minq gasped and frantically pulled at Brigitta from behind. His paws skidded and slipped on the floor. He ran around and grabbed her hands. He heaved and managed to pull her into a sitting position, but she couldn't move her legs. They weighed her down like two sacks of uul tree sap.

The shadow grew larger on the wall. Minq moved behind Brigitta and cowered under her wings, whimpering. He held onto her and covered his eyes with his ears. "No watch. Tell Hrathgar kill us quick."

Himalette's face appeared from around the corner and she squealed, "Briggy!"

"Himalette!" Brigitta was overcome with joy. "Oh, lola, I knew you could do it!"

Himalette flew into Brigitta, knocking her back over on top of Minq. She hugged Brigitta as Minq crawled out from under her. When Himalette pulled away, Brigitta examined her for injuries, noting a dozen cuts and bruises on her arms and legs. She motioned weakly for Himalette to lean down and she kissed her little sister on the cheek.

"You're not mad at me, Briggy?"

"I should be!" Brigitta scolded. She looked around and lowered her voice to a harsh whisper. "What were you thinking following us up here? You could have been killed."

"You were going to leave me all alone with Gola," Himalette said meekly.

"We'll talk about this later." Brigitta glanced down the hall. "Right now, you have to help Minq get me up."

"It's all right. The same thing happened to me," Himalette said proudly and then burst into tears. "Oh, Briggy, I was so scared of the river. I remembered to make myself strong and I didn't look at the green lights, but I got tired and my feet paralyzed . . . and then you saved me . . . " Himalette sniffed and wiped her eyes on her sleeves. "I went fast, like you said, and I landed in here and I was so cold and scared . . . and then Hrathgar—"

"Hrathgar?!?" gasped Brigitta and Minq.

Himalette grinned as a figure appeared at the end of the hallway and shuffled toward them. Minq wrapped one ear around Brigitta and the other around Himalette and growled. Brigitta stretched her head up from behind his ear and saw a kind-faced old faerie woman with shriveled wings. Whatever destiny markings she had been given as a youth had faded away. She wore a long red tunic woven with flowers. Her wild gray hair was piled on top of her head and her green eyes twinkled out from the crevices in her face. She bent over and examined Brigitta and Minq.

"This must be Brigitta. My goodness, you're as blue as your sister." Hrathgar reached out to touch Brigitta's face. Minq leapt forward and bared his teeth. Hrathgar took her hand away. "Oh, such a charming beast. And so protective."

"It's all right, Minq," said Himalette.

"Yes, yes," said Hrathgar. "You have nothing to worry about now. The frogs can't hurt you in here. Let me help you." She reached down to lift Brigitta from the floor. "Oh, you poor lolas."

"You're Hrathgar?" Brigitta studied the elderly faerie's face for signs of evilness.

Hrathgar smiled and assisted Brigitta to her feet. Minq moved to Brigitta's other side and assisted with his ears, watching Hrathgar's every move. Brigitta steadied herself with one hand on his head and one arm around Hrathgar. Himalette flew and danced around them as they shuffled down the corridor.

"Not only that, she says she'll help us!" cheered Himalette.

"Really?" Brigitta was astounded. "You can help us?

"Well, I don't know, " Hrathgar replied humbly. "I'll do what I can."

"She's going to help us save the White Forest!" cried Himalette. "We're going home!"

🍂 🍂 🍂

Hrathgar's kitchen was filled with herbs and roots and vegetables. It reminded Brigitta of her momma's kitchen and she was immediately comforted by the familiar smells. Once Hrathgar had Brigitta settled at the large wooden table, she went about making something to eat.

Brigitta's arms and wings were working again, but her legs were still numb. She and Himalette rubbed them briskly to get the feeling back. Brigitta tickled Himalette and they laughed together. It felt like a million moons since Brigitta had laughed.

They patted Minq on the head and played with his ears as he sat there like a guard, silently watching Hrathgar puttering about the kitchen. He ignored their teasing, even when Himalette called him "boggy breath" and "gundle toes," which sent the girls into new fits of giggles.

Brigitta felt warm and dreamy as Hrathgar returned to the table and dished out four healthy portions of root stew and four cups of tingermint tea. Brigitta and Himalette devoured their food. Minq sniffed at his dish and pushed it aside.

Hrathgar sat down with her guests. "It's so nice to have visitors who enjoy traditional faerie cooking."

"Do you get many visitors?" asked Brigitta, blowing on her hot tea.

"I don't think so. I—no." Hrathgar stopped eating and put down her spoon. Her eyes welled up with tears.

Brigitta stared at Hrathgar and the warm, dreamy feeling started to drain from her body.

Himalette kept slurping away at her stew. "I told her all about how we turned blue and about the broken faeries and the stone grovens and the Hourglass," Himalette said with her mouth full. "And how we need special faerie magic to turn everyone back."

"The only magic I know involves food and gar-dening," Hrathgar said, smiling weakly at Himalette and stroking her hair. "I have a wonderful potted crotia. And an entire row of gundlebeans."

"Your stew's delicious," commented Himalette, licking her bowl clean. "Almost as good as our momma's."

"I don't understand," Brigitta said finally.

Hrathgar turned toward Brigitta. Her eyes bore seasons of sadness.

"Why you not monster?" demanded Minq, startling the others.

"A monster? Oh, dear," said Hrathgar. "As far as I know I've always been a faerie." She looked over her shoulder and flapped her withered wings. "But as you can see, my wings are useless."

Brigitta examined them. It was true. They looked like old dried up leaves. Auntie Ferna had said Hrathgar had been marked for Elderhood and that was her path before she was banished. But where were her markings? Brigitta had never heard of any faerie straying from her Life Task. But there Hrathgar was, far away from the Council of Elders.

"Why did you have to leave the White Forest?" asked Himalette.

"Honestly, I don't remember much at all," Hrathgar sighed. "I know I did a very bad thing and was sent to live here. I know I've been here, alone in this castle, for a long, long time. But ask me the details of how I have spent my time? I do not know."

Brigitta thought about the faerie tales of Hrathgar's attempt to steal the power from the Hourglass. It was a very long time ago. Brigitta couldn't imagine this kindly faerie committing such a horrible act. Had they banished the wrong faerie? Brigitta knew Ondelle had been an Elder at the time. Surely the wise and just Ondelle would never have banished anyone unless it had been absolutely necessary.

"How we know you tell truth?" Minq pointed an accusing ear at Hrathgar.

"How do I know you're telling the truth?" Hrathgar pointed her spoon back at him.

"What do you remember?" asked Brigitta.

"My garden and kitchen." She gestured and smiled proudly at her roots and vegetables. "I know how to tend plants and herbs. That seems important."

"If you help us, maybe the Elders will forgive you and let you live in the White Forest again," suggested Himalette.

"I would like that very much." Hrathgar took Himalette's hand and gave it a squeeze.

They finished up their meal. Minq succumbed and took a few laps of stew. Brigitta gave him a smirk.

"Test make sure not poison." Minq lapped at the cup of tea a few times as well.

They withdrew to the castle's spell-chamber. It was crammed with potions and plants and dead beasts and dried powders and jars of strange liquids. Everyone, even Hrathgar, stood in the center of the room, not touching anything. Hrathgar moved to a podium on the far side of the room. She removed a massive, ancient book and brought it to the others. Everyone except Minq sat on the floor and gathered around the book. Minq wandered around, poking his nose into drawers and behind cabinets, keeping one ear cocked backwards and listening.

"I found this here this morning," said Hrathgar. "It looks useful. And several potions were brewing. I don't remember what they're for, though."

"You can make magic potions?" asked Himalette.

"I don't know." Hrathgar shook her head sadly.

"So you don't know anything about faerie Blue Spell?" Brigitta opened the book to the first page. The title was handwritten in a language she didn't recognize. The page was splattered with green and purple stains.

"Faerie Blue Spell?" Hrathgar gasped.

"Isn't that why we look this way? Isn't that how the sprite

protected us from the curse?"

"You were most definitely protected by strong magic." Hrathgar studied Brigitta's blue skin. "But, I've never seen anything like this before. At least, not that I remember."

Brigitta's heart sank. "If we can't use Blue Spell, we'll have to find something in this book to reverse the stone curse. If we can get the Elders back to normal, they can reset the Hourglass."

Brigitta flipped through the pages of the book. The writing wasn't at all familiar. There were squiggly lines and small symbols similar to the ones on the spines of Gola's books. "I can't read this, any of it." Brigitta turned to the end of the book. "What is it? What does it say?"

"I have no idea," said Hrathgar as she pondered the book.

"You lie!" Minq was at Brigitta's side. "Someone wrote book. Someone make potions. You say you only one here!"

"I wish I were lying, Minq." Hrathgar pointed to one of the pages. "I wish I did know what this said. How do you think it feels to wake up in a room and not recognize the things around you?"

Minq tapped the book. "This Dark Forest language." Minq looked Hrathgar squarely in the eyes and scowled at her. "Someone teach you."

"I don't know!" She cried and then dropped her head into her hands. "I don't remember."

"Perhaps forgetting is part of your punishment?" Brigitta suggested. "So you wouldn't be able to . . . you know . . . do your very bad thing again?"

"Yes," Hrathgar said solemnly. "That's it. I'm sure you're right. I'm being punished."

"If we can't read this, we'll never be able to save the White Forest." Brigitta slammed the book shut in despair. "The Hourglass runs out at night's end!" Brigitta leapt up and flew to the window. "As soon as the moons have left the sky," she murmured. She could just make out a faint glow behind the dingy air and clouds. How much time did they have? Less than twenty moon-beats; she was sure of it.

"Momma and Poppa," whimpered Himalette.

"I'm so sorry." Hrathgar put her arm around Himalette, who started to cry. "Isn't there anyone else we can go to for assistance?"

"There aren't any other faeries left. We're the only—" Brigitta slapped her forehead. "Wait! Minq, you said this was Dark Forest language. Do you think Gola could read this spell book?"

Minq twitched at the mention of Gola's name. "It possible." He eyed Hrathgar as her brow wrinkled in thought.

"Then I'll take it to her."

"No strength potion," he pointed out. "River wind too strong in cave."

"I'll fly outside, down the mountain."

"Too dangerous," said Hrathgar. "The frogs are not the only beasts guarding this castle."

"We have to do something!" exclaimed Brigitta. "We're running out of time."

The room went silent. Minq paced back and forth while Hrathgar rocked Himalette in her arms and Brigitta tapped her wings together, like her poppa.

"If only Gola could see," said Brigitta.

"Briggy, the Eyes can see!" Himalette suddenly perked up. "Where did they go?"

Brigitta pulled out her mirror necklace and peered into it. It was completely black. "Frog food," she muttered.

Minq's ears darted into the air. "You have sharp knife?" he asked Hrathgar.

"Yes, in the kitchen."

"Give me. Have idea."

Chapter Fifteen

Brigitta, Himalette, Minq, and Hrathgar stood at the edge of the courtyard. Shrubs lined the stone walls like dark, disfigured skeletons. The sky above was bleak, and the last light on the horizon was smothered by a dreary haze.

As her eyes adjusted to the dimness, Brigitta caught sight of several large bulbous frogs sitting in the weeds. The frogs cocked their heads toward them. Hrathgar pulled Himalette to her side. Minq held out the large sharp knife he had retrieved from Hrathgar's kitchen.

"How can we tell which frog it was?" Brigitta scanned the courtyard. "They all look the same to me."

"Will know." Minq's ears shot out toward one frog, then another, as they hopped toward them. "He sound mean."

"They all sound the same, too," muttered Brigitta.

"Shhhh." Minq's ears stopped moving. "There, see," he said, "next to tunnel in ground."

Mean Frog hopped closer into a square patch of faint light drifting down from the castle. His slimy face was briefly illuminated before he hopped out of the light again. Brigitta had no idea how to tell the difference between the sounds of frog hops, but she had to admit that its face looked familiar, and mean, with its large bloodshot eyes and snotty nostrils.

"Ready?" she whispered to Minq.

Minq nodded. Brigitta flew through the air zig-zagging toward the frog. It stopped hopping and its eyes rolled around as she zipped past it. It opened its mouth and zapped its tongue at her, missing by a wing's length.

"Missed me, bog-breath. Ha-ha!" Brigitta circled back again.

Two more frogs joined Mean Frog. Their tongues flew out at her and she dodged them both, heading straight for the first frog. As she turned, its tongue darted past her ear.

The smallest of the three frogs suddenly stopped and turned back toward the castle.

"Hey! Up here!" Brigitta called. "Up here you slimy, green—"

"Haaaaaaaayaaaaaaaaaa!" Minq leapt through the air. He landed on Mean Frog's bumpy back and wrapped his ears around its belly to secure himself. He lifted the knife over his head . . . ZAP! a frog tongue wrapped around his arm. The tongue belonged to an extremely fat frog with spindly front legs that had joined the other three.

Before Minq could brace himself, he was yanked off of Mean Frog's back and dragged across the courtyard toward Fat Frog's mouth.

Himalette and Hrathgar cried out from the edge of the courtyard. Brigitta looked up as Himalette tried to fly out of Hrathgar's grasp.

"Stay there, Himmy!" yelled Brigitta as she dodged another tongue.

"Heeeeeelp!" shrieked Minq as he dug his back paws and ears into the dirt.

Himalette wriggled out of Hrathgar's grasp and flew into the courtyard.

"Himalette, no!" Hrathgar pleaded. She flapped her useless wings and ran after Himalette. Three menacing frogs leapt toward her. She retreated back to the castle, wringing her hands together as she watched the frightening scene from behind a pillar.

Himalette dropped down to the ground and picked up a rock. She launched herself over Fat Frog and dropped the rock solidly on its head. It retracted its hold on Minq's arm and Minq went tumbling backward, feet over ears, the knife flying out of his hand.

A purple frog and a brown frog paused at the knife and looked down at it curiously.

"Himmy, get out of here!" Brigitta turned and scolded Himalette.

"I'm helping!" Himalette dove down to pick up more rocks. She chucked them at Purple Frog and Brown Frog, stunning them long enough for Brigitta to fly down and pick up the knife.

"Over here, Mean Frog!" Brigitta somersaulted through the air.

Minq pulled himself up and steadied his dizzy head. He spotted Mean Frog and glanced around desperately. Brigitta whistled from above and dropped the knife. He caught it with an ear, took a deep breath, and catapulted himself onto Mean Frog's back. He drove the knife into its back with a sickening crunch. A dark greasy fluid gushed forth. He twisted the knife and the frog sunk to the ground, fouling the air with a nasty belch.

Brigitta joined Himalette, dodging tongues as they picked up rocks. They smashed them over frog heads as they hopped toward Minq. He leapt off of Mean Frog and with great effort, heaved it over onto its back. He jumped onto its stomach and bounced up and down on all fours.

"Hurry, Minq, we can't hold them off!" Brigitta called as two more frogs hopped over the castle wall and cocked their heads.

"Ohhhh!" a voice cried from behind them.

Brigitta glanced toward the castle. The three frogs were still there, but Hrathgar was gone. Brigitta flew across the courtyard. "Hrathgar?" she called.

"Frog stink bad," Minq grumbled.

Hrathgar wasn't behind the pillars. The three frogs turned and leapt toward Himalette. Brigitta dashed toward her sister, grabbing her hand and pulling her higher into the air.

Minq bounced up and down on Mean Frog's stomach. With a whoosh of air the Eyes popped out of the frog's mouth. Brigitta swooped down and caught them, dripping green slime all over herself.

"I've got them!" she cried as a frog tongue wrapped around her leg.

Minq dashed forward, sliced the frog tongue away with the knife, and grabbed a hold of Brigitta's other leg. Himalette joined them and they soared out of the courtyard, Minq clinging to Brigitta's calf. He threw the knife down at the frogs and hit one in the thigh. They flew through a high window as frog tongues blatted against the castle wall.

They fell to the floor with a great thud, with Brigitta on the bottom of the pile and Himalette on top.

"I hate frogs," Himalette said to the floor.

"Think hurt something," said Minq, sandwiched between the girls.

"Yeah, me," Brigitta heaved. "Get off!"

Himalette rolled over, then Minq. Brigitta sat up and handed him the Eyes. He shook them gently. They were limp and lifeless and covered in frog juice. Brigitta looked at them skeptically as she rubbed frog slime from her leg.

"Will work," Minq said, tucking the Eyes into his left ear and scrolling it down to protect them. "Need soak in water with lyllium nectar. Need lyllium blossom."

Brigitta got up and dusted herself off. "Lyllium blossom? Where are we going to find lyllium blossom on this rock heap, let alone figure out how to get nectar from it?"

"You forget, Hrathgar master gardener."

"Hrathgar!" Brigitta exclaimed and rushed to the window. All the frogs below were slowly hopping toward the dead body of Mean Frog.

Hrathgar was nowhere in sight.

Chapter Sixteen

Minq and the faerie sisters raced back to Hrathgar's spell-chamber and in through the door. Brigitta felt a rush of relief. Hrathgar was bent over the podium, her back to them as she examined the spell book.

"Hrathgar!" exclaimed Brigitta collapsing to the ground and catching her breath. "We got the Eyes! All we need is—"

Hrathgar turned around and Brigitta's skin went ice cold. Hrathgar's face was yellow and leathery and her eyes were blood-red. She drew herself up to her full height and grinned at their bewildered faces, teeth rotting inside her shriveled mouth. "Hello, my dear faerie kin."

"Hrathgar, what happened to you?" Himalette's voice shook.

Hrathgar moved to the nearest window and peered out the dingy curtain. "So close to night's end," she sighed. "Such sweet news to a long suffering outcast." Hrathgar flung the curtain back to reveal the two moons, wild and bright, through an opening in the sinister clouds. "When the moons leave the sky the White Forest will lose its protective field." She took a step toward them and pointed a knotted finger. "And I will take over as the new High Priestess."

"What I say?" growled Minq. "She lying whole time."

"But what about—" Brigitta started to say.

"Silence!" Hrathgar commanded as she dropped the curtain back down. She glared at all of them. "Three hundred seasons of this disgraceful existence have allowed me to develop my talents."

"You're the one who turned everyone to stone!" Brigitta gasped. "But how?"

Hrathgar cackled and took two steps toward them. They all took two steps back. "Through a little trick of green zynthia hypnosis on an unfortunate sprite I caught before my frogs got the best of her." She squinted her eyes at the two faerie girls. "Judging by the color of your skin, it seems that someone managed a little trick of their own." Hrathgar reached over to her collection of potions. She selected a beaker of deep crimson liquid and turned back to them, raising her crooked eyebrows. "Tell me, how did you get your blue?"

As Hrathgar leaned forward Brigitta noticed around her neck, hanging on a silver chain, a black stone with glistening stars. Minq stiffened beside her as he spied the amulet, too. Brigitta stared into it, her mind drifting.

"Tell me!" Hrathgar threw the beaker to the ground, startling Brigitta. As it shattered, red liquid splattered across the floor. Each drop began to hiss and fizzle as it burned into the stone.

"Brigitta!" Minq tossed the Eyes to her and rushed at Hrathgar. "Fly! Escape!" he shouted.

Brigitta caught the Eyes and grabbed Himalette by the hand. Minq leapt toward Hrathgar and she snatched him mid-air, wrapping her hand around his neck. His eyes bulged as she squeezed.

"Fool," she grumbled. She called after Brigitta and Himalette as they flew from the room in a flurry of wingbeats. "There is no escape for you!"

Brigitta and Himalette darted down one dark corridor and through another. They turned a third corner and then dropped to the floor and listened. Nothing.

Brigitta held up the lifeless Eyes. She ripped the remaining sleeve from her tunic and carefully wrapped the Eyes in it before tucking them in her pocket.

"Briggy, we can't leave him!" Himalette tugged at her sister.

"I know."

"We have to help him!"

"I know!" Brigitta snapped. "Let me think."

Himalette pulled her legs to her chest and wrapped her arms

tightly around them, singing nervously to herself while Brigitta peeked around the next corner. Not two hops away, sitting at the bottom of a staircase, was a giant frog. Brigitta gasped and pulled back. She pressed Himalette up against the wall and signaled for her to be still.

Nothing happened.

Brigitta waited a few moments, puzzled. She slowly peeked around the corner again. The frog hadn't moved. Brigitta waved her hand and the frog just sat there. She squinted up the dark hallway, breathing a sigh of relief as she realized the frog had been turned to stone. As her eyes adjusted to the darkness, Brigitta saw that stone beasts of every kind were sitting on nearly every step. There were ro- dent-like creatures, bird-like creatures, little horned creatures, more frogs, and a smattering of beasts that were half stone, half decaying skeleton.

"All stone . . ." she murmured.

Himalette peered around the corner and gave a little cry. "Why, Briggy?"

"Practice." Brigitta grabbed Himalette's hand and they wandered up the staircase, past the stone beasts standing at attention. Half- way up, they came to a window.

"Maybe I can fly around the back of the castle and in through her spell-chamber window?" Brigitta mused. It was a dangerous plan, she thought, but a surprise attack would be best. Perhaps Hrathgar would leave the room in search of them with Minq locked inside? She could fly in through the window and grab him.

"You'll have to come with me. I can't leave you here by yourself." Brigitta studied her little sister's tear-streaked face. "You must do exactly as I say, when I say it, without any questions."

Himalette agreed as she wiped her dirty nose with her sleeve.

They flew out the window into the cold night. They were much farther from the ground than they had anticipated, and the sheer drop startled them both. Large jagged rocks rose from the ground below.

They flew high along the castle close to the walls. When they turned to fly along the back side of the castle, butting up against the sheer mountainside, they were greeted by several colorful gardens built on immense stone terraces jutting out from the castle walls. The plants and flowers were the only things outside the castle that remained unsullied by sticky darkness. As they rounded the next corner, they slowed and dropped down past the first darkened window.

Brigitta stopped and pointed toward the second window, which cast a yellow glow out into the gloom. She motioned for Himalette to stay back and keep quiet. Himalette nodded and hovered in the air.

Brigitta's heart pounded in her chest as she inched her way toward the second window. Steadying herself with carefully placed wingbeats, she maneuvered below the window and grabbed hold of its crumbling rock frame.

"Ha!" came Hrathgar's voice from inside the castle, startling Brigitta. Her hand slipped and she fluttered her wings to catch her balance. She pulled herself close to the wall.

"You are in no position to bargain with me," Hrathgar continued.

"It not belong you first place," came Minq's hoarse voice. "No good do you. No need."

"Perhaps I have grown used to it," Hrathgar snorted.

"It valuable only Gola."

"How valuable?" Hrathgar's voice grew serious.

"Her life depend on it."

"Then I am sure it is worth the Blue Spell magic of your two young faeries."

The wind suddenly picked up and Brigitta was blown away from the window frame. She heard a muffled cry from Himalette and looked down to see her sister picked up by a strong gust and sent tumbling toward the rocks. Brigitta fought the wind and sped toward Himalette. She caught up with her and they were both thrust into the castle wall. They spun against the hard stone, the wind whipping and howling around them.

As Brigitta and Himalette struggled to steady themselves, one of the immense rocks stretched up and opened its eyes. It lifted its long, rocky tail and craned its head toward them for a closer look. Himalette opened her mouth to scream, but Brigitta stifled it with her hand. The rock creature snorted and a storm of pebbles rained down on them.

Brigitta yanked her sister by the arm and they flew along the side of the castle as close to the ground as they dared. They turned the corner and there stood another rock beast, stretching its neck and yawning loudly. Its sharp silver teeth glinted in the moonslight.

"Briggy!" screamed Himalette over the howl of the wind.

Brigitta dove down and maneuvered between the beast's legs with Himalette fluttering madly behind her. She spied a small opening in the wall at the base of the castle and zipped toward it. The rock guard bounded after them and with each heavy step the jarring sound of rock hitting rock echoed off the mountain. Brigitta and Himalette dove through the opening in the wall. The rock guard rushed at the entrance, banging its head against the castle and blowing hot angry dust from its nostrils.

Just inside the castle, huddled in a dark tunnel, Brigitta and Himalette caught their breaths. The beast smashed against the castle wall once more and then shuffled away with one final snort. After it was gone, the only sounds were the wind whipping through the tunnel and the water dripping from the slimy walls. They exhaled in relief.

"Wha—what—was that?" Himalette asked in a shaky voice.

Brigitta seized Himalette's hand and pulled her along the wet passageway.

"Where are we going?" whispered Himalette.

"I don't know," answered Brigitta through clenched teeth.

"What are we going to do?"

"I don't know!"

"I'm scared," Himalette whined as she struggled to keep up with Brigitta.

"Himmy!" Brigitta glared down at her sister.

Himalette started to cry. She gave a great heaving sob and yanked her hand from Brigitta's. Brigitta turned away and marched up the passageway. I'm a bog-brain, she thought to herself. Minq was a traitor! Gola had sent him to Hrathgar's to trade them for a stupid black rock!

Brigitta slowed her pace. It all made sense now, she thought. Why would Gola help them, after all? She had sent her Eyes many times to find her precious moonstone and they had failed. She must have been thrilled when Brigitta told her she wanted to go to Dead Mountain. Minq might belong to them, but he had belonged to Gola first.

Brigitta stopped and twitched her wings. How had Hrathgar gotten the moonstone in the first place? And what about the spell seed she had given the hypnotized sprite to get a curse into the White Forest? Gola had said she was the only one who could make spell-seeds. Had Gola given Hrathgar the spell-seed? What if they had planned to curse the White Forest together and Hrathgar had double-crossed her?

Himalette's sobs grew fainter behind her. Serves her right, Brigitta fumed. They wouldn't be in this mess if Himalette hadn't made her lose all their supplies in the river. And if Himalette had been paying attention, she wouldn't have gotten caught by the caterpillar. She couldn't leave anything alone! Brigitta started up the tunnel again. Her sister's cries grew more desperate. Brigitta kicked the cavern wall.

Pippet's disapproving face appeared in her mind. She thought of her momma and poppa turned to stone in the White Forest and that she might never see them again. They would want her to take care of her little sister. They would want her to comfort her. They would be ashamed of her for leaving her behind. Himalette was just a child and she couldn't help herself. It wasn't her fault their home had been cursed.

"I'm sorry, Momma. I'm sorry, Poppa." Brigitta rushed back to

Himalette, who was lying on the floor of the cold, damp tunnel with her head in her arms.

"Come on. Get up." She tugged at her sister.

Himalette sniffed and allowed herself to be picked up. "Where—"

Brigitta placed her hands on Himalette's shoulders and looked into her eyes. "Just come on. I'll figure something out."

They moved down the passageway toward a pale light and emerged in a large cold room. There were several metal cages in the middle of the floor, with spiky bars, and four prison cells lining the walls. Fur and bones of long-dead beasts rotted in two of the cages. The cells held the remains of half-stone beasts; one with a small stone head and a body with decaying limbs, another with a skull stuck on a stone neck with stone legs and one stone arm. The smell of rotting flesh hung like fog in the dungeon room. Brigitta turned away from the dead beasts. "Don't look, Himmy."

A few large rodents scurried about, with menacing front teeth, long black tails, and matted brown fur. Brigitta threw a rock at one of them and it looked at her dully before skulking off. The girls tiptoed across the dungeon floor. As they passed the last cell a figure moved in the dark. They jumped back as Hrathgar emerged from the shadows.

Chapter Seventeen

Hrathgar's eyes lit up when she saw them, her face kind and soft again. "My dear girls! I am so glad to see you!" She clasped her hands together.

"Hrathgar!" exclaimed Brigitta and Himalette.

One of the mangy prison rodents scuttled toward them. Himalette squealed as Brigitta picked up a rock and threw it at the beast.

"Ignore the bone-dwellers. They are only interested in what is already dead."

Himalette stepped closer to the cell. "Hrathgar, how did—"

Brigitta placed her hand on the top of Himalette's wing to stop her. "Stay back, Himmy, it's a trick."

"It is a trick indeed," Hrathgar nodded. "But you needn't fear me."

"Who are you?" Brigitta demanded, keeping her distance.

"I am Hrathgar Good."

"There are two Hrathgars?" Himalette asked.

"We are one, split in two. Pure good and pure evil. Between night and day and day and night, we exchange places."

"Briggy, we have to let her out." Himalette moved toward the cell bars.

"Stay back!" commanded Brigitta.

"Where is your friend?" Hrathgar peered around the room.

"He was captured by the mean Hrathgar!" exclaimed Himalette.

"Minq is no longer our friend," spat Brigitta.

"No!" Himalette turned and looked incredulously at Brigitta. "He's our friend. We have to help him."

"Himalette, listen to me." Brigitta pulled her from Hrathgar's cell. "When I was at the castle window I heard Minq and the other Hrathgar arguing about Gola's moonstone. He wants to trade us for it."

"No!" insisted Himalette. "He's ours! He wouldn't let anybody hurt us."

"That's enough! You didn't see it at Gola's. Her moonstone is really valuable. She couldn't find it with her Eyes, so she sent Minq up here with us to get it back."

Himalette shook her head.

Hrathgar Good slumped to the ground and groaned. "Oh no. Oh no, no. It is all my fault. Brigitta, listen, please . . . Gola would not trade you for her moonstone."

"So, you admit it. You know about Gola and her moonstones."

"Yes, yes," moaned Hrathgar Good. "I was the one who stole it from her. Among other things."

"Like her spell-seeds?" Brigitta accused Hrathgar.

Hrathgar nodded sadly.

"Why?" Himalette asked.

"Selfish reasons." Hrathgar Good's eyes filled with tears. "I was young and full of myself. I was going to show the Elders how clever I was. I ran away from the White Forest, but didn't make it far before I had to be rescued by Gola."

"Three hundred seasons ago?" asked Brigitta.

"Yes. Gola was so pleased to have saved a faerie. She nursed me back to health and I lived with her for quite some time. She taught me many things about plants and potions.

"But she held things back. She said I was not ready. So I stole several of her belongings, including one of her moonstones, and returned to the White Forest."

"Minq says the moonstones are dangerous," said Brigitta as she moved closer to Hrathgar Good's cell.

"Dangerous for anyone other than their rightful owner," said Hrathgar. "It split my mind up. My mind became two minds. Two voices, good and evil, fought in my head until my evil mind tried to put a spell on the Hourglass of Protection."

"What happened?" asked Himalette.

"The Hourglass defended itself! Since I was wearing the moonstone, I was divided into two Hrathgars. The Elders banished us both here to Dead Mountain."

"That's terrible!" cried Himalette. "They should've kept the good you!"

"They had no choice."

"Auntie Ferna never told us the whole story," Brigitta murmured to herself.

"Fernatta of Gyllenhale?" Hrathgar Good smiled. "How is my old friend?"

"She's turned to stone!"

Hrathgar Good slumped again. "Oh, I am so sorry."

"You said you didn't remember anything except your garden," Brigitta accused.

"That is the doing of Hrathgar Evil. She imprisoned me, but as we exchange places when the day transitions, she is imprisoned half of the time as well. She cast a spell so that by day I would not remember anything except how to cook and garden. She did not want me to try to harm her or myself. And as she and I are one, she spends her days in this cell, dreaming of sharmock roots and wondering why she is behind bars."

Hrathgar Good's eyes widened. "But when she roams the castle at night, and I am here, we remember everything. She seeks a way to destroy me that will not destroy her along with it."

"Oh no!" Himalette gasped.

Brigitta stood there contemplating Hrathgar's story.

"You can count on Gola, I swear upon the Hourglass." Hrathgar moved forward, an intense look upon her face. "Of course she wants her moonstone back. When I stole it, I stole her destiny. She is a solitary being, but not cruel-hearted. She most likely found it difficult to trust you."

"I don't know." Brigitta stepped closer and examined Hrathgar Good carefully.

Hrathgar gazed into Brigitta's eyes. "Be careful of the bars. They will burn you."

Brigitta reached out and lightly touched a bar. She drew back as the bar singed her finger and gave off a little puff of black smoke. She sucked on her finger and eyed Hrathgar suspiciously.

"Don't you believe her?" Himalette asked.

"There's only one way to find out," decided Brigitta, pulling the wrapped up Eyes gently from her pocket. "Hrathgar, do you know where we can get lyllium blossoms?"

Chapter Eighteen

Brigitta made her way back through the passageway. When she reached the entrance, she poked her head out to see if the coast was clear of nasty beasts. She quickly reached outside and grabbed two rocks.

"Take two rocks and knock them together in a slow, steady beat," Hrathgar had told her. "It is a lullaby to the rock dragons."

Brigitta clicked her rocks together a few times to steady her rhythm. Rock dragons, she thought, so that's what they were. She hoped when all this was over she'd never have to see one again. Not even in a dream.

She flew slowly along the castle wall, knocking her rocks together and singing a traditional faerie lullaby to help keep tempo:

Lola Moon you've come too soon
My eyes are not yet tired
Great Blue Moon I ask of you
Please chase your sister away

A sleepy rock dragon lifted its head, snorted, and then lay back down with a small avalanche of pebbles. Brigitta slipped past the massive beast and continued around until she reached the back side of the castle where one of the large terraces jutted out half-way up the side.

The garden path lead right up to the mountain and overlooked the endless rock dragon fields on either side. It was an oasis in the gray, with dozens of rows of plants and flowers of all shapes and sizes illuminating the sooty air. In front of the garden was a work station of stone shelves stacked with pots and piled with soil. A few gardening tools hung from a wooden plank.

Brigitta fluttered over and poked around the shelves until she found a spell-seed tucked into a nook where Hrathgar Good said one would be. Something scurried across the garden, and she froze for a moment.

"It's just a little garden beastie," she told herself and placed the spell-seed into a sack hanging next to the tools. She wrapped it with some twine and pulled it tight.

She slipped down the right side of the garden, counting as she went. "Three rows down, one, two, three." She turned and moved along the third row. "Four plots over . . . "

Relief rushed over her as she spotted the leafy lylliums with their delicate white blossoms.

If it weren't for the urgency of her task, Brigitta might have enjoyed pulling the blossoms off the lyllium plants, allowing them to soothe her into a daydream. She smelled the blossoms carefully to see which ones were ready. Hrathgar had said that as lylliums grew less fragrant on the outside they grew more potent on the inside, and that the best lylliums for potions had no scent whatsoever.

As Brigitta was about to collect an odorless blossom, the sleeping thorny plants in the next plot over woke up and shook their leaves. "HEEEELP! Thief! HEEEEEELP!" they shouted from their large-lipped purple bulbs.

"Shhhhh!" she scolded, "I'm not a thief. Hrathgar Good sent me."

"HEEEEEEEEEEEELP! Somebody HEEEEELP!" they screeched.

Brigitta grabbed one of the shrieking plants by the stem and pricked herself on a thorn. "Ow!"

"Hee-hee-hee!" they squealed in delight. "Serves you right, thief. Heeeeeeelp!"

"Stop it! Be quiet!"

"Heeeeeeeeeeeeeeeeelp!" they cried out as they bounced up and down.

"Hush! You'll wake the rock dragons!" she kneeled down in front of them. "What do you want? Tell me whatever it is. I'll do it."

"Heeeell—" they stopped and turned to her slyly. "Really?"

"Yes, anything to shut you up," Brigitta hissed.

The bulbs huddled together and whispered among themselves. "Please hurry!"

They stopped whispering and sang out in a chorus, "Gwenefire!" Then they began to whistle and hoot loudly and rustle their leaves. "Oooooowooooo!" they called like a pack of wild beasts.

"Gwenefire?" Brigitta searched her gardening lesson memory bank. "Oh, please stop that racket," she cried to the annoying things as they continued to howl.

She got up and hunted through the rows of plants and flowers. "Gwenefire, gwenefire," she mumbled over and over, nearly in tears by the time she reached the eighth row.

Then she heard a soft giggling. That was it! *Giggling Gwenefires* her mother sometimes called them when she and Himalette had an unstoppable fit of laughter. She ran through the next row and there they were, with long lavender flowers and lashes and spots of pink on what could have been cheeks, giggling like a group of faerie girls.

Quickly and carefully, Brigitta dug up and transferred the gwenefires. She patted the ground around them as the purple bulbs purred. "Sweet gwenefire!" they sighed.

The gwenefires giggled and batted their lashes. The plants snuggled up against each other. "Ooh!" the gwenefires squealed as the prickly plants groped them.

"Everybody happy?" asked Brigitta. The plants ignored her and continued nuzzling. She returned to the lyllium blossoms and searched for odorless flowers. When she had collected a dozen of them, she tied them together with twine and tip-toed out of the garden.

Hoping she had collected everything Hrathgar Good needed, Brigitta rushed through the passageway toward the dungeon. She stopped when she spotted Himalette trembling up against the stone wall grasping a metal bowl.

She moved silently to her sister and wrenched the bowl from her grip. Water from the cavern wall trickled down Himalette's back, soaking her clothes. She stood there shivering as her terrified eyes told Brigitta not to make a sound.

Brigitta's skin froze when she heard the cackling voice of Hrathgar Evil. "All these seasons, you have been working so hard for me, helping to perfect my stone spell ingredients with your fine gardening skills." There was the sound of metal clanking against metal as Hrathgar Evil traveled the length of her dungeon, rapping on the bars. "Even so, I still could not penetrate the White Forest's protective field, let alone leave our castle grounds, due to those filthy Elders' curse on us!"

"So you managed to enter the forest by hypnotizing one of their kin!" exclaimed Hrathgar Good. "You had that poor sprite perform your terrible magic from the inside!"

"What luck that I caught her spying on us!" Hrathgar Evil was positively giddy. "We have had so few visitors. And now it seems that our young Water Faeries have been touched by Blue Spell. What a delightful surprise!" She gave a maniacal laugh. "I'll split them open to find its magic!"

Himalette looked down at her blue arms and then back up at Brigitta, who wrapped herself around Himalette to keep her from shivering.

"You mustn't! They are only children!"

"Children who possess the secret of the greatest faerie magic! They will be mine, for when the Hourglass of Protection runs out at night's end, its hold on us will be relinquished. We will be two . . . and you will still be behind those bars."

"Then I will kill myself before the moons leave the sky," said Hrathgar Good bitterly, "so that you will die along with me."

A large bone-dweller scuttled by, its tail brushing against Himalette's leg. Brigitta covered her sister's mouth with one hand to keep her from crying out.

"In your position, I find that highly unlikely."

They heard Hrathgar Evil shuffle away and then the clank as she shut the front bars of the prison. When they were sure Hrathgar Evil was out of hearing range, Brigitta and Himalette poked their heads into the dungeon. Himalette gasped. A stone Minq sat in front of Hrathgar Good's cell with wide frozen eyes and mouth.

"Minq!" Himalette ran over and hugged him.

"You do not know how sorry I am." Hrathgar Good's face hung with sadness.

"We'll turn him back, Himmy, I promise."

"And she wants to take our blue!" wailed Himalette.

"We won't let her, do you hear?" Brigitta handed Himalette the metal bowl. "Quickly now, go fill this bowl with water from the passageway walls."

"That's what I was doing when Hrathgar Evil—"

"It's okay, Himmy, she won't come back. She'll be looking for us someplace else." Brigitta turned to Hrathgar Good. She removed the blossoms and the spell-seed and placed them on the floor in front of the cell. She retrieved the Eyes from behind a rock.

"I forgot to warn you about the prickly munshmins," said Hrathgar as she rolled up her sleeves. "They are a noisy bunch, but they remember everything. Ask a munshmin, I always say." Hrathgar Good reached carefully through the bars for the flowers and spell-seed. "They did not give you any trouble?"

"Not at all," said Brigitta, smiling to herself.

🌿 🌿 🌿

Brigitta, Himalette and Hrathgar stared at the metal bowl filled with the lyllium nectar potion. The submerged Eyes didn't look any more alert. Himalette bent down on her hands and knees for a closer look.

"It's not working," she said.

"It has to work." Brigitta examined the bowl.

"You are certain he said lyllium blossom nectar, not pollen or essence?" asked Hrathgar in a faraway voice.

"Yes, yes." Brigitta stood up and paced back and forth.

"If this plan does not work, I have another." Hrathgar picked up the spell-seed.

"What's in it?" Brigitta asked.

"A gardener's weapon. An extremely poisonous root tincture."

"We'll poison Hrathgar Evil?"

"I am sure you could not get close enough to give it to her." Hrathgar placed the spell-seed on the ground and spun it three times. "No, no . . . I will poison myself."

"What?" gasped Himalette.

"If I do so before night's end, Hrathgar Evil will die along with me."

"No!" Himalette cried. "You can't!"

"This will work," Brigitta said, kneeling back down to look at the Eyes. She gave the bowl a little shake.

"Brigitta, even if the Eyes do resuscitate, how will you ever get them past the Evil One to view her spell book?" Hrathgar Good looked at the girls tenderly. "I am sorry to have made you an accomplice, Brigitta, but it is my choice." She wiped a tear from her cheek.

"That was your plan all along, wasn't it? When you sent me for the lyllium and asked me to get the spell-seed?" Brigitta looked at Hrathgar in disbelief.

"You are a wise faerie." Hrathgar dabbed the tear on the top of the spell-seed. Then dabbed a second one.

"No, no! We won't let you," Himalette cried in despair.

Hrathgar Good looked intently at Brigitta and gestured toward Himalette. "I know you understand."

Himalette shook her head back and forth, tears streaming down her face, "No, no, please!"

"Unfortunately," Hrathgar said, lifting her finger and placing the third tear on the spell-seed, "if the Evil One is destroyed, you might never be able to break the stone curse." The spell seed crackled in Hrathgar's hands. "But at least we will have saved your faerie kin from being ruled by a monster. It is the very least I can do for all the suffering I have caused."

The Eyes twitched in the bowl. Brigitta and Himalette let out a simultaneous cry as the Eyes rose unsteadily into the air and shook themselves off. Momentarily distracted, Hrathgar paused long enough for Brigitta to snatch the spell-seed, burning both her arms as she pulled it out of Hrathgar's reach.

The Eyes fluttered about the room and bounced against the far wall, then turned around and flew back. Himalette jumped in front of them, waving frantically. "Gola!" she called happily. The Eyes blinked at Himalette several times and bobbed in the air.

When the Eyes turned and saw the stone Minq, they looked back at Brigitta and Himalette with concern. They continued examining the room, approaching Hrathgar and hovering in the air to get a good look at her face.

"Hello, Gola." Hrathgar blinked back at the Eyes. "It has been a long time."

"The necklace!" Brigitta exclaimed. She set the spell-seed down and pulled the mirrored locket from inside her tunic to see Hrathgar's face reflected back at her. She smiled. "Gola will see."

"Yes, but I fear the next step is nearly impossible." Hrathgar looked away from the Eyes and stared at the spell-seed on the floor.

"And we haven't much time," Brigitta realized, tucking the mirrored necklace back into her tunic. She tapped her wings together.

Hrathgar paced in her cell. "We must think of a way to distract the Evil One so you can get to her book."

"Briggy?" Himalette asked.

"I could use myself as a distraction," Brigitta suggested.

"Too dangerous."

"Briggy!" Himalette called.

"In a moment, Himmy . . ."

Himalette folded her arms in front of her chest and gave an exaggerated sigh.

"Yes, Himalette?" Hrathgar stopped pacing and looked at the young faerie.

"Hrathgar Evil said she hypnotized the sprite using green zynthias."

Hrathgar Good turned to Brigitta in wide-eyed wonder. "I see cleverness runs in your family."

Clicking her two stones together in a slow rhythm, Brigitta lead the way past the sleeping rock guards.

"I hate rock dragons," muttered Himalette, twisting the gardener's bag in her hands.

"Shhh," hushed Brigitta. She nodded to the Eyes to lead the way and when they were out of rock dragon reach, she pulled out her mirror necklace. She sent the Eyes up and over the wall of the castle. She and Himalette peered into the mirror as the Eyes made their way to the courtyard and settled behind a bush. Brigitta and Himalette flew up over the side.

They immediately hid themselves under the bush and spied on the frogs. Most of the frogs were still gathered around the slain frog on the other side of the courtyard looking puzzled by its lack of movement. None of the frogs were guarding the entrance to the cavern below the castle.

"You stay here," Brigitta instructed the Eyes. "I don't want to fetch you out of another frog belly."

The Eyes bobbed in agreement.

Brigitta and Himalette hunted around under the bush and gathered as many stones as Brigitta could carry in the sack, remembering that they would need to save two in order to keep the rock dragons away. They streaked toward the cave entrance as close to the ground as possible and zoomed inside. They were immediately enveloped in the darkness, but it was easy enough to follow the crack in the earth. In a few moments the green glow of the zynthias appeared beneath them.

They emerged from the earth and looked away from the crystals, hovering high above the fierce river. Brigitta reached inside the sack and drew out several stones. She handed the sack to Himalette. "Whatever you do—"

"I know, I know, don't look at the crystals." Himalette flew below Brigitta and steadied herself. She opened the sack, turned her face away and squeezed her eyes shut. "Ready!" she hollered.

Facing the opposite direction, Brigitta blindly threw one of the stones toward the crystals. It bounced off the ceiling and plummeted to the river. She threw a second stone and missed again. She adjusted her position and threw a third stone, knocking several crystals from the ceiling.

"Did you catch any?" shouted Brigitta over the roar of the river.

"No. Do it again!" yelled Himalette.

"Move farther to your right."

Himalette followed the instructions, squeezed her eyes tighter and opened the bag. Brigitta took a deep breath and threw a fourth stone. Crystals came raining down from the ceiling.

"I got some! I got some!" Himalette said gleefully. "I can feel them in my sack!"

"Let's try again, just in case," said Brigitta, "and Himmy?"

"What?"

"You're doing great."

* * *

When they were sure they had more than enough zynthias in the bag, they returned to the cold crack in the earth and made their way back up the crevasse. Just before they reached the opening, Brigitta felt around in the bag, gathered a few crystals, and launched them into the courtyard. Himalette giggled and Brigitta hushed her. They waited a little while, then emerged from the tunnel to find four hypnotized frogs gathered around the zynthias.

Brigitta and Himalette muffled their laughter as they flew back to the waiting Eyes. The Eyes looked at them quizzically from under the bush.

"I wonder why the Eyes aren't hypnotized by the crystals?" Himalette said.

Brigitta shrugged, pointed to her own head, then pointed to the Eyes. "No brains?"

The Eyes blinked back at them. Brigitta gestured to the courtyard wall, and the Eyes turned and made their way back down the side of the castle.

Brigitta handed the sack to Himalette. "Can you carry that all right?"

Himalette nodded confidently. Brigitta picked up her two lullaby stones and they slipped over the wall.

Chapter Nineteen

Hrathgar Good was astounded when Brigitta held up the bulging sack of green zynthias. "Well," she said as they maneuvered the sack through the prison bars, "you two are full of surprises."

Brigitta pulled her hand away, grazing her fingers on the hot metal. She blew on her fingers to cool the sting.

"You're sure this will work?" she asked Hrathgar.

"We are connected, two as one." Hrathgar Good pulled up her sleeve, revealing a long scar. "This is where Hrathgar Evil burned herself several moons ago."

"Will we be able to unhypnotize you afterwards?" asked Himalette suddenly.

"It does not matter." Hrathgar rolled down her sleeve and gripped the sack tightly. "Brigitta, remember, if this does not work, if Gola cannot undo the curse, you must promise to give me the poison before night's end."

"No!" pronounced Himalette, checking to see that the spell-seed was well out of Hrathgar's reach.

Brigitta, too, glanced at the spell-seed leaning up against a rock, then over to the stone Minq. "I can't . . ."

"I am old. Think of your sister." She dropped her voice, "Brigitta, the Evil One would do anything to find the secret of Blue Spell. And she is most unsympathetic."

Brigitta nodded and fluttered to Himalette. She looked into her troubled eyes and took her hand. "Gola will see."

Hrathgar Good wrapped the edges of the sack tightly around her wrists and gripped it so hard her fingers turned white. "I hope so, my faeries, for all our sakes." She opened the sack and looked inside. Her eyes glazed over as the zynthia hypnosis set in.

Brigitta and Himalette hid outside the doorway of Hrathgar's spell chamber. Brigitta sent the Eyes into the room and peered into her mirror necklace.

Himalette craned her neck to look. "Did it work?"

Brigitta lowered the mirror so Himalette could see the image of Hrathgar Evil's ugly frozen face. They smirked at each other and entered the chambers. The Eyes hovered in front of Hrathgar Evil, who stood perfectly still in the center of the room. The Eyes fluttered about her face, bumped up against her forehead a few times, then gave a satisfied nod.

Brigitta and Himalette slowly approached Hrathgar and studied her immobile form. She wasn't frozen like the stone faeries, all lifeless and gray. Her wrinkled yellow hands looked as if they might dart, fingernails first, to one of their throats at any moment. Brigitta's eyes were drawn to the moonstone around her neck, but she caught herself before she could be pulled into its mind-distorting darkness.

Brigitta tugged on her sister. "Careful, Himmy, not too close."

Himalette stuck her tongue out at Hrathgar as Brigitta turned her attention to the spell book, open on the podium.

"How will we know if Gola can read it?" asked Himalette as they dashed across the room.

"We'll just have to hope she can." Brigitta turned the book to the first page and looked at the foreign forest language. She whistled softly for the Eyes. The Eyes slapped Hrathgar upside the head with a wing before making their way over to the spell book. "Okay, do your thing," said Brigitta, pointing to the page.

The Eyes puffed themselves up as if taking a deep breath, then proceeded to scan each page as quickly and thoroughly as possible, pausing every so often to study something further. Brigitta turned the pages as the Eyes scanned. Himalette pulled up a stool to watch. The only sound in the room was the quiet flick of each page.

🍂 🍂 🍂

Brigitta and the Eyes had a good rhythm going. She turned the pages and the Eyes scanned each line and then nodded when they were ready for the next page. The Eyes began to wobble, dizzy from the movement. Brigitta gave them words of encouragement.

She flipped another page. "Good work! More than half-way now."

Himalette got down from her stool and stretched her arms and wings. She wandered around the room, glaring at Hrathgar Evil. Suddenly Himalette gasped and flew back to Brigitta.

"Brigitta, she moved! I saw her move!"

Brigitta whirled around and studied Hrathgar Evil, who remained still. "It's all right," she said, and turned back around, flipping the page quickly.

"Hurry, Briggy, hurry!" Himalette yanked on Brigitta's tunic.

The Eyes picked up their pace, but exhaustion was setting in. They were bloodshot, their lids drooped, and their wings fluttered erratically. Himalette approached the book and fingered the remaining pages. "Almost done," she breathed.

"Interesting reading?" a chilling voice inquired from behind them.

Brigitta, Himalette, and the Eyes whirled around in terror. Hrathgar Evil rubbed her hands together and stretched her limbs. A wicked smile broke out across her sallow face.

The Eyes turned back to the book and started scanning in double-time. They turned the pages with their own wings and kept scanning. Brigitta and Himalette fell away as Hrathgar Evil stormed over to the book and knocked the Eyes aside. They slammed into the wall, dropped to the floor, and lay there motionless.

Brigitta and Himalette flew to the door. Hrathgar picked up

a round, dark green object from her shelf and hurled it across the room. It landed in front of them and grew rapidly into a thorny vine, blocking the doorway. The girls backed away from the plant as it grew and grew, stretching out toward them with menacing speed.

Brigitta held her sister and they trembled together, caught between Hrathgar and the twisting vines, which lashed out and grabbed them by the ankles. The girls shrieked as the vines crawled up their legs and squeezed them in a thorny hug.

"Nice try," growled Hrathgar.

Hrathgar Evil pushed Brigitta and Himalette into the dungeon. Chained to each other by the ankles, they lost their balance and fell to the cold stone floor. They looked over as Hrathgar Good groaned from her cell. She picked herself up and shook herself awake. Underneath her lay the bag of green zynthias. She steadied herself, and then leaned over to pick up the bag.

"Do not think of it, dear sister." Hrathgar Evil yanked the girls up and thrust them toward Hrathgar Good's cell. She reached her gnarled hand around Himalette's throat.

Hrathgar Good looked into Himalette's desperate eyes. She looked back down at the bag of zynthias. "The bag—it must have slipped from my grasp."

Hrathgar Evil snapped her fingers. A small bone-dweller scurried across the floor and into Hrathgar Good's cell where it nabbed the bag of zynthias in its teeth and dragged it out between the bars. It squeaked as the bars singed its fur, and the acrid smell of burning bone-dweller hair filled the air.

"I am afraid the night is coming to an end," the Evil One said. "In a few moon-beats, your forest will be completely unprotected."

She dug her nails into Brigitta's shoulder and leaned closer to the frightened faeries. "The Center Realm will make a lovely stone garden. I will line your Council of Elders around your precious

Hourglass and your High Priest will guard my front door."

Brigitta yanked herself from Hrathgar Evil's grip. "You'll never even touch High *Priestess* Ondelle!"

"Ondelle!" Both Hrathgars turned to Brigitta.

Hrathgar Evil's grip loosened around Himalette's neck. Himalette turned and kicked at her ankles, and she knocked both girls to the ground.

"That traitor Ondelle of Grioth is now High Priestess? Ha! Even better! I will enjoy eating my breakfast while I gaze upon her sorry stone face." Hrathgar Evil picked up the ends of the heavy chain and pulled the faerie girls across the floor. "Now, how would you like to watch as my sister's forgotten body is consumed by bone-dwellers?"

She shoved Brigitta and Himalette toward the next cell with a rough kick. She laughed and lifted her leg again. Himalette cowered, but Brigitta looked up at Hrathgar defiantly, until the empty space in front of Hrathgar Good's cell caught her attention.

"Where's Minq?"

"What?" Hrathgar Evil whipped around.

Himalette looked out from behind her hands and Hrathgar Good began to chuckle.

Hrathgar Evil picked up the two faeries by the hair and dragged them back to Hrathgar Good's cell as they shrieked in pain. "What did you do with him?" she demanded. "Where is he?"

"I did nothing," responded Hrathgar Good.

"Gola did it!" cried Himalette.

"She read the book and broke your curse!" snarled Brigitta at Hrathgar Evil.

"No!" Hrathgar Evil lost her grip on the girls' hair and they dropped to the ground. "No. Impossible."

Like a lightning bolt, Minq sprang from the tunnel and headed for Hrathgar Evil, teeth bared. He leapt into the air and slammed a spiky stone into the back of Hrathgar Evil's head. Both Hrathgars cried out and grasped their skulls. Both pulled their bloody hands back and stared at the thick red liquid in shock.

Hrathgar Evil whirled around and smacked Minq solidly with her arm. He fell against the cell bars, crying out as they burned into his back. Hrathgar Evil swiped the spiky stone from the ground, picked Minq up by the ears, and held the weapon to his face. She glared down at the frightened faeries huddled together on the floor. "You will all suffer greatly for this."

Himalette cried hysterically. "Please, no!"

The Evil One lifted the stone and stared into Minq's dazed eyes. "The little faerie will be next."

Brigitta looked frantically from her little sister to Hrathgar Good, then back to her sister. "I don't think so!" Brigitta grabbed Himalette's hand and with all the strength she could muster took a flying leap, chains and all, landing next to the spell-seed.

Hrathgar Evil spun around. Brigitta snatched the open spell-seed from the ground. Hrathgar Good reached through the bars, scorching her arms. Hrathgar Evil gasped as her flesh was burned and she dropped Minq from her powerful grasp.

Brigitta hesitated.

"You must. She will kill you all!" Hrathgar Good pleaded, reaching farther, baring the pain as gray-green smoke drifted from her burning arms.

Hrathgar Evil screamed and lunged toward Himalette.

"No!" Himalette shrieked and jumped backwards.

Brigitta tossed the spell-seed to Hrathgar Good's waiting hands. In one swift motion, she pulled it to her lips and downed the poison.

Hrathgar Evil took one more heavy step toward them, then wobbled slightly on her feet. Regaining her balance, she zigzagged across the floor and reached for the bars of Good Hrathgar's cell. Her hands sizzled as she started to choke. Both Hrathgars clutched at their throats and fell to the ground.

Brigitta, Himalette, and Minq rushed to the cell. Brigitta reached through the bars, ignoring the burn, to take Hrathgar Good's hand. Hrathgar coughed and smiled.

"Isn't there anything we can do?" pleaded Brigitta. "A potion? A spell?"

"No, our suns and moons are over," Hrathgar smiled weakly.

Himalette held onto Brigitta. Minq wrapped his ears around them both.

"Please, tell the Elders that I am so very sorry for our transgressions." Hrathgar squeezed Brigitta's hand. "But I hope now, at least, I have made amends for them."

"I will tell them how kind you were," Brigitta managed to say through her tears. "How brave."

"And tell Ondelle of Grioth . . . " Hrathgar closed her eyes, "I am so pleased to have finally met you."

Hrathgar's grip loosened from Brigitta's hand, and before she could ask Hrathgar what she had meant, both Hrathgars coughed a few more times and then were still. Brigitta, Himalette, and Minq stared at the two Hrathgars in silence.

The moonstone amulet around Hrathgar Evil's neck began to glow. Minq pulled the girls back with his ears. They watched as the white-blue light grew brighter and warmer.

"No look," commanded Minq, shading the sisters' eyes with his ears.

As the light reached them, Brigitta began to tingle, as if being enveloped in thousands of miniature stars. The sensation spread from the outside of her body inwards until she felt her whole being would burst with joy. Himalette laughed next to her. Brigitta took her hand.

Then the warmth and tingling receded and Minq removed his ears from around their eyes.

There was only one Hrathgar lying on the ground outside of the cell.

Brigitta kneeled in front of her. Hrathgar's skin was soft and rosy and her eyes were crystal white. Her mustard wings were spread beneath her, and in a deeper shade, the destiny markings of an Elder colored the tips of each: eyes with four radiating lines in four directions.

Himalette crawled to Brigitta's side and peered into Hrathgar's face. "Her eyes! What happened to them?"

"The Ethereals," said Brigitta, closing Hrathgar's eyelids, "they have dispersed her energy."

"They were here? They came back?"

"Yes, they came back." Brigitta wiped Himalette's soiled blue nose with her finger. She pulled it back and examined her blue hand, wondering if the Ethereals had been protecting them all along.

Brigitta reached over and gently kissed Hrathgar's cheek. "Thank you," she whispered. She removed the moonstone amulet from Hrathgar's neck and handed it to Minq.

Minq gave a little bow to Brigitta and accepted it. He picked up the open spell-seed and placed the amulet inside. The spell-seed made a little kissing sound as it sealed itself up again.

Chapter Twenty

Hearts torn from their loss, Brigitta, Himalette, and Minq dragged their weary bodies up the castle stairs and through several passageways until they found themselves in the courtyard. Four hypnotized frogs sat around the zynthias. The rest were perched on top of the shortest stone wall, staring out over the forest. As the trio tentatively entered the courtyard, the frogs glanced at them, then turned their attention back to the forest. They went on ignoring them as Brigitta took a few steps toward the wall.

Brigitta shrugged. "I guess it's okay now."

"We should help those ones," said Himalette, pointing to the hypnotized beasts.

Unfurling his great ears, Minq picked up the zynthias with them and scrolled the crystals up inside. The four frogs wobbled a bit and then collapsed. "They okay." Minq examined them. "Be in shock."

He trotted over to the crack in the earth and peered into the great darkness that led down to The River That Runs Backwards. He lifted his ear to drop them inside.

"Wait!" Brigitta fluttered over to Minq. "Better save one just in case. Might come in handy someday."

Minq dropped all the zynthias save one into the crevasse. Brigitta looked at her torn tunic and laughed. "I'm all out of sleeves."

Himalette ripped one of her own sleeves off and handed it to Brigitta, who wrapped the zynthia inside. As she slid it into her pocket, Himalette squealed and pointed over the wall. "Briggy, look!"

In the far distance, a shimmering blue light cut through the dark air.

"It's coming from the White Forest!" Brigitta cried, and without thinking, ran the rest of the way to the wall. She stood between two frogs, who looked down at her indifferently.

"Hooray!" cheered Himalette, pulling Minq to the wall with her.

As the three travelers watched, the blue light grew brighter and brighter.

"What mean?" asked Minq.

"They've reset the hourglass," said Brigitta, beaming down at her sister. "Everyone is safe. We can go home."

The blue light rose from the darkness and slowly faded to mist. The mist floated up into the sky and dis-appeared into the night.

"That's my favorite part of the ceremony," said Brigitta, "when the mist disappears. I used to think the Ancients lived among the stars."

"I like the singing and dancing best," said Himalette.

"Of course you do," teased Brigitta.

After the light show had completely faded, the frogs turned toward Brigitta, Himalette, and Minq. Brigitta quickly counted twelve of them, plus four more dizzy frogs in the courtyard.

"Uh-oh," Minq said under his breath.

Suddenly, one of the frogs hopped from the wall, landed on the other side, and blinked several times as if seeing the world for the first time. Another frog followed, then another and another, until they were all hopping down the mountain.

"I guess their mean spell was broken," said Brigitta, putting her arm around Himalette.

"I still hate frogs," muttered Himalette, waving good-bye to them as they hopped away. When the last frog had leapt from the wall, even the four dizzy ones, Brigitta, Minq, and Himalette turned back toward the castle. A small shape fluttered out of one of the windows.

"Gola's Eyes!" whooped Minq, holding out his free ear.

The Eyes wobbled about as they examined Minq's offered ear, then they fumbled toward Brigitta. She held out her arm and they landed on it, staring into Brigitta's face, and blinking in weary pleasure.

"Thank you, Gola," Brigitta said. She pulled out the mirror necklace and held it up. Her own smiling face shone back at her.

Himalette craned her neck to look into the mirror. Brigitta scratched her nose. A layer of grime came off, revealing her blue skin underneath.

"Hey," said Himalette, suddenly getting itchy herself. She scratched her right shoulder. "We're still blue."

"Yeah," Brigitta said as she poked Himalette in the stomach playfully. "But I bet there's someone back home who can fix it."

Without Hrathgar Evil's presence, the castle now only exuded an ancient sadness as if it knew it had once been beautiful. Brigitta, Himalette, and Minq trudged in silence back down through the castle and retrieved Hrathgar's body. They carried it to her garden and laid it to rest next to the lylliums, covering it with soil and blossoms. The munshmins and gwenefires were silent out of respect for the faerie who had nurtured them.

When Hrathgar's body was concealed and they had each said a few words of gratitude, Brigitta turned and stared down at the prickly plants. "Ask a munshmin," she murmured to herself.

"What!" they growled.

"How do we get down the mountain through the poison clouds?"

"Hmmmmm . . . heh-heh-heh," laughed the munshmins.

Brigitta was in no mood to be teased. She lifted her foot above the munshmins as if to stomp on them, but they only howled with laughter. "Tell me!" Brigitta commanded.

The gwenefires shook their leaves at the munshmins and they grumbled amongst themselves until the gwenefires turned their flower faces away and folded their leaves.

"Fine, fine, fine," chattered the munshmins, thrusting their bulbs forward. "Delia grass. Chew, chew, chew it. Delia grass." They gestured toward a patch of grass, then turned and tickled the gwenefires. "And breathe through your mouth. Yes, breathe through your mouth."

Brigitta plucked a handful of sticky green grass and handed some to Himalette and Minq. They each popped a blade into their mouths and immediately spat it back out. "It's awful!" Brigitta grimaced.

The munshmins nearly split their stalks laughing. Minq growled back at the flowers as he and the faeries left the garden. As worn out as they were, Brigitta and Himalette couldn't help giggling themselves. They stuffed flower petals in their noses, placed the delia blades back in their mouths, and chewed.

With two rocks each, they descended the mountain, taking turns banging out a lullaby to keep the rock dragons at bay. Brigitta was too tired to fly, and too tired to speak, but there was a lightness within her. She knew the Hourglass had been turned and that her momma and poppa, Auntie Ferna, and High Priestess Ondelle were safe.

As the day broke and scattered morning sunlight through the valley below, they continued as if sleepwalking, barely conscious. Nothing could penetrate Brigitta's haze. Even the wild sound of The River That Runs Backwards was like a distant dream. She put one foot in front of the other, again and again. She knew Himalette must be exhausted, but her little sister didn't complain, not once the entire way down the mountain. Not even when Minq and Brigitta had to pull thorns from her arm or when she tangled herself up in a vine.

The sun was leaving the sky again by the time they reached Gola's tree. Brigitta thought they would all surely collapse before they could get inside. Gola stood in the doorway, looking down at them with her empty eye sockets, a pair of Eyes on each shoulder.

Brigitta stumbled into her and hugged her strange barky body, which smelled of earth and moss. Gola hesitated for a moment, then wrapped her arms around Brigitta in return.

"It is time to rest," she said.

◖ ◖ ◖

Brigitta sat up with a start and looked around. She was in Gola's bed. She heard a familiar laugh and caught sight of Himalette in the kitchen, stirring a pot under Gola's supervision. Several pairs of bored Eyes watched as the spoon went around and around.

Minq burst through the door with an earful of firewood and noticed Brigitta on the bed. "You wake!" He dropped the wood and trotted to Brigitta. "Help you down. Sleep long time."

Himalette gave an excited squeal and Brigitta didn't even cringe. "We're going home! We're going home! And Minq and Gola are coming with us!"

Minq gave a shy smile as Gola shuffled into the room. It was so hard to read any expression on her ancient face, but Brigitta sensed that she was smiling, so she smiled back.

"Yes, Himmy, yes." Brigitta hugged her sister. "But first, I'm hungry! Is there anything to eat?"

Gola laughed. "Your sister has made you a healing stew."

Brigitta ate four bowls of Himalette's stew before her hunger was satisfied. As their momma and poppa would be very worried, they decided they would leave the following morning, and spent the rest of the day helping Gola gather her belongings and replant her flowers in the forest.

No longer suspicious of her every move, Brigitta watched Gola shuffling about her tree home. She was older and more feeble than Brigitta had realized. Her clothes were horribly tattered, which made Brigitta feel sorry for her. She thought perhaps a White Forest faerie could make her a new tunic, something warm and soft against her jagged skin.

Gola was also one of few words, carefully chosen. Brigitta

imagined it was the effect of many moons of solitude and suspicion. There was something about her way that made Brigitta respect that silence. Himalette, however, chatted on enough for the both of them about birds and caterpillars and grovens and, of course, their momma and poppa. Brigitta thought Gola showed magnificent restraint in not knocking Himalette on the head with a spoon.

After Gola had packed her books, she took the ancient map down from the wall. Behind it was a spell seed. She brought it to Brigitta. "Your zynthia. Safe for traveling."

Gola's moonstone shone from around her neck, and Brigitta noticed tiny cracks in the stone, among the stars, that she hadn't seen before. She pulled her gaze away from its lure.

"The moonstone," she said, "it's where it's meant to be."

As she watched Gola roll up her map for the trip, Brigitta couldn't hold back her questions any longer. "Gola, your map, where did it come from?"

"Long ago, I received it as a gift from one of your Ancients." Gola placed the map into a beast skin and tied it.

"But . . ." Brigitta was astonished. "That means . . . before the Great World Cry?"

"Shortly thereafter," said Gola, placing the map with her growing pile of personal items.

"How can that be?" asked Brigitta. "You must be . . . I mean you're . . ."

"Very old." Gola patted Brigitta on her head.

Brigitta wanted to ask Gola so many more questions, like what the Ethereals had been like and how she met them. She wanted to know what Faweh had been like before the Great World Cry. But then she thought about Hrathgar, and how her pursuit of knowledge had ended badly. Gola was wise and must have kept information back for a reason.

Maybe, Brigitta thought, knowing too much before one is ready can be a bad thing. Like having strong wings or access to potion magic before you knew what to do with them.

"Aren't you going to miss your tree?" asked Himalette, interrupting Brigitta's thoughts. She sat by the pool brushing her blue-tinted hair, clean and shiny from a recent wash.

"It was my destiny to live here," said Gola, "and now it is my destiny to leave."

Gola, Minq, and the faerie sisters stood in front of Gola's tree with packs lashed to their backs. Gola had a small wheeled box for her heavy books and jars. They watched as Gola's Eyes flew from the windows in a jagged black stream and fluttered about excitedly. Himalette danced around them in the air.

"The Eyes are flying home with us," sang Himalette as they made their way across the field of whisper lights. *"The Eyes are flying home."*

A dozen flowers shivered as they passed, releasing their centers. They began to glow, first white, then yellow. As the whisper lights drifted around their heads. Brigitta heard their shiny voices in her ears.

"They're laughing," said Himalette, "Right, Briggy?"

"Yes, they're laughing." Brigitta raced across the field, releasing more flower centers, laughing along with them.

Chapter Twenty-One

Even with Gola, Minq, and all the Eyes along for the journey, the Dark Forest was still a frightening place, and Brigitta couldn't wait to get home as soon as possible. Gola may have had every magical item she owned with them, but she was no match for a giant caterpillar. She was slow, and her Eyes were sometimes temperamental and lazy. Brigitta noted how much concentration it took for Gola to walk, although she was pretty handy with her cane, which was so strong it could practically lift her over fallen logs.

They spent the first night in a shallow cave. Brigitta thought it was a good spot, until Gola woke them before the sun had risen to tell them they must leave immediately before the vicious occupant of the cave returned for his daylight sleep.

The second night they spent in the rock fortress Minq had taken them to after they had escaped the caterpillar. It seemed like seasons ago, Brigitta mused as they entered, then smiled, realizing they would be home by the next moonsrise.

Minq and Himalette snuggled together by the fire and were fast asleep before the first log burned. Brigitta sat next to Gola and stared at the row of sleepy Eyes perched on a rock. She counted them a few times and was sure there were less pairs of Eyes than when they had started.

"Gola, your Eyes!" She craned her neck to search the shadows. "I think some are missing."

"Yes," responded Gola, looking wearily into the fire.

"What happened? Where are they?"

"There have been predators along the way."

Brigitta realized why Gola's concentration had been so fierce as they had journeyed through the forest. It wasn't just because of her elderly limbs; she had been using the Eyes to keep the danger away. She could see danger coming through her Eyes and even lure it from them.

"Thank you," murmured Brigitta, then she shud-dered. She felt terrible about Gola sacrificing her Eyes for them. They were not just her creations, they were her companions. "And thank you for reading Hrathgar's book and lifting the curse on the White Forest. Thank you for saving my momma and poppa."

"I did not lift the curse on your forest," said Gola. "I could only lift the curse on Minq because he is my familiar. The rest was your doing."

"What do you mean?"

"I am not versed in faerie magic. I could not undo a curse cast from within your own forest any more than I could undo the spell that protected you from that curse." Gola poked at the fire with her cane. "It was Hrathgar's death that undid the curse."

"I didn't mean to . . . I didn't want to . . . " Brigitta lay her head down in Gola's lap. There were no words for how sorry she was for her part in Hrathgar Good's demise. She began to cry, softly at first, and then in great heaving sobs.

"It was your destiny." Gola stroked Brigitta's face with her long, jagged fingers. "What is done is done."

❧ ❧ ❧

Brigitta, Himalette, Gola, and Minq stumbled out of the Dark Forest into The Shift. Gola had seen the way through her Eyes, but until Brigitta could touch the earth on the other side of the protective field, she wouldn't feel safe.

As soon as they saw that wide expanse of bare land, Brigitta and Himalette cried with joy. As they crossed The Shift and jettisoned through the watery field, they were met by an Air Faerie male with long teal wings and an Air Faerie female with translucent lavender ones. They both had three darker bands on the ends of their wings, the destiny markings of White Forest Perimeter Guards.

Brigitta explained to the Air Faeries that Gola and Minq had saved their lives and wanted to meet with the Elders.

"You have to go with them," Brigitta called to Gola and Minq. "It's the only way for you to cross."

As the Perimeter Guards retrieved Gola and Minq, they shuddered as they passed through the field. No faerie, thought Brigitta, not even a Perimeter Guard, likes to be outside the White Forest.

After they were all safely inside, the female Air Faerie sped ahead to bring the news of their arrival, and the rest of the party made its way to the Center Realm.

◆ ◆ ◆

Pippet's shrieks filled the air as she zipped toward her daughters, nearly knocking them over with the force of her embrace. Mousha followed as quickly as his small wings could carry him and together they cried tears of relief and joy, thoroughly examining their strange blue children. After rubbing at their skin in disbelief, they exclaimed at each bump, bruise, and cut they found. Brigitta and Himalette swore again and again that they were fine as they kissed their parents' faces.

"But your skin!" exclaimed Pippet.

Remembering that they still itched, Brigitta and Himalette both began to scratch.

"I rather like it," said Mousha. "No one else has ever had blue daughters!"

Faeries swarmed them, fussing and asking questions. Minq and Gola shied away, not used to so much attention. The younger faeries were fascinated by Gola's Eyes and tried to play with them. Brigitta had to shoo the children away for fear of Gola getting dizzy from their over-excitement.

As more and more faeries crowded around them, Minq knocked over a table, catapulting pipberry pies and tingermint teacakes into the crowd. The whole celebration was far too overwhelming for Brigitta, and she guessed for her sister as well, so she grabbed Himalette's hand and they escaped during the commotion. They hid themselves behind a large uul tree to wait for the official ceremony marking their return.

They watched as Mousha led Minq into the festival grounds to view the new inventions, and Ondelle took Gola into The Hive, the Elder chambers, to speak with her privately. Although Brigitta was tempted to spy on them through the secret passageway, that would mean leaving the safety of the tree, and Brigitta wanted to be left alone until the last possible moment.

Several moon-beats later, Ondelle and Gola re-turned, and all of the faeries from each of the four realms assembled in the festival fairgrounds. Flowers of every color imaginable fell from the trees and dancing shadowflies pulled bright streams of paper through the air. Cheering faeries packed the stands, and Pippet, Mousha, and Auntie Ferna grinned proudly from the front row of the Water Realm seats. To Brigitta's great relief, wearing an immense leafy bandage on his arm, Orl Featherkind sat to Pippet's right. Edl Featherkind sat next to him, applauding.

The Elders sat down in their council chairs in front of the steps that led to the great Hourglass. Brigitta, Himalette, Minq, and Gola were guided up the steps of the silver platform by four Elder Apprentices, a male and female from the Fire Realm and a male and female from the Earth Realm, bearing shimmering hourglasses encircled by the four elemental symbols on their silver tunics.

Brigitta and Himalette held hands and gazed up at the Hourglass, smiling as the colored sands trickled silently through the narrow crystal tube. High Priestess Ondelle made her way across the platform to the four guests of honor and stared down at Brigitta and Himalette, who scratched her nose nervously as Brigitta squeezed her hand.

Ondelle quieted the cheers and applause with a wave of her scepter and addressed Gola. "Gola, for your generous assistance, if you so desire, I invite you to live with us in our protected land, partaking in all our customs. As well, we would be honored to have you serve as an advisor to our Council of Elders."

A pair of Eyes hovered in front of Ondelle's face. They gave an awkward bow and flew away again. "Thank you," Gola said solemnly as the Eyes landed on her shoulder and surveyed the crowd. "I would like that very much."

Ondelle's amused gaze landed on Minq. The High Priestess motioned to the two male Elder Apprentices and they flew onto the stage carrying a glass box with a pair of translucent wings inside.

"Minq, for risking your life to save our beloved kin, I present you with your own faerie wings."

She waved her scepter and the two faerie men opened the delicate box and held up the wings. Minq gazed at them, too stunned to speak. At Ondelle's urging, he slipped into them and grinned in his strange toothy way. Ondelle pointed her scepter at him, a stream of colored beams spilled out over the wings, and they began to flap. Minq tested them a few times, then flew up, knocking into the two faerie men, who nearly dropped the glass box.

"They may take a bit of getting used to," Ondelle pointed out as Minq landed with a sheepish smile.

"And Minq can stay, too?" asked Himalette.

"And Minq can stay, too," said Ondelle as Minq took off once again, bumping into her and knocking her scepter from her hand. The audience tittered as she gave him an unconvincing frown and picked it up.

She moved in front of Himalette and held out her hand. One of the female Elder Apprentices placed a necklace in her palm, which she fastened around Himalette's neck. It held a glowing, disc-shaped amulet.

"Himalette, for your quick thinking, aiding your sister in saving our dear home, I present you with the element of fire, which will serve you well on your next grand adventure."

"I'm a Fire Faerie now?" Himalette examined the disc excitedly.

Ondelle laughed. "Not exactly."

Himalette considered this. "That's okay . . . it's not so bad being a Water Faerie." Himalette beamed up at Brigitta. "But I'd like to keep it all the same. It's pretty."

Ondelle gestured to the second female Apprentice who brought her a clear shallow dish of sparkling liquid. She dipped her hands in the liquid, then turned and caressed Himalette's face with them. Himalette's face turned back to its regular pinkish hue and the color spread through her body and out across her wings. Himalette gave a loud sigh of relief and the crowd burst into laughter.

Ondelle leaned down and gave Himalette a hug. Himalette blushed and looked out at her momma and poppa as they wiped proud tears from their cheeks.

Ondelle then moved to Brigitta. Her black eyes turned serious. Brigitta held her breath as her heart pounded in her chest.

"Brigitta of Tiragarrow, for bravery under extreme circumstances, I present you with our highest honor, Protector of the Forest."

The crowd sat in stunned silence as Ondelle removed her own hourglass necklace from around her neck and placed it over Brigitta's head.

The Elders gasped. Air Elder Fozk of Fhorsa stood up from his chair. "Ondelle!" he cautioned.

"This necklace contains sands charged with each of the four elements," continued Ondelle, ignoring Fozk's outburst. Fozk sat back down, and the Elders whispered amongst themselves.

Ondelle slipped her hands into the shallow dish once again, closing her eyes as they soaked in the liquid. "With time, you will learn how to cultivate its power." She opened her eyes, turned to Brigitta, and paused.

Their eyes connected. Brigitta felt a rush of anticipation.

Ondelle reached down and took Brigitta's face in her hands. Relief spread through her skin, and she sighed as she watched the blue fade away from her arms. There was a collective gasp from the crowd and Brigitta looked up. She found her momma's and poppa's wide-eyed expressions in the front row. Pippet's hands darted to her open mouth.

Brigitta looked up at Ondelle. "What? What's wrong?"

"Nothing is wrong, my dear one," said Ondelle with a smile so beautiful it broke Brigitta's heart. "Look at your wings."

Brigitta craned her neck and stretched out her wings. Her mind went numb and her stomach lurched as she stared in awe. At the top of each velvety wing, in a stunning deep green, were the unmistakable markings of an Elder.

At the top of the Water Faerie grandstand, Brigitta sat alone, watching as all the White Forest faeries celebrated below. A pair of sprites played lively music on a glass flute made for two, accompanied by three Earth Faeries drumming on carved tree stumps. Air Faeries led games of cloud-tossing around dancing faerie couples. Festival decorators lit candle webs stretched across tree branches to carry the festivities into the evening.

Catching Brigitta's eye, Pippet waved between feverishly dishing out cups of iced frommafin to thirsty families. Brigitta waved back and searched the festival grounds for the rest of her family. She watched as Mousha showed Minq how to use his new wings, Gola and Fernatta huddled together in deep discussion of who knows what, and Himalette chased pairs of Eyes around the trees with four other faerie children.

As Brigitta observed the festival activities, she felt distant and numb, like she was on the outside of something looking in. She noticed her three Water Faerie friends, with the markings of a Cooking Teacher, a Village-Nest Caretaker, and a Star Teller. They are so carefree, Brigitta thought as a young Fire Faerie boy zipped between two of them, tousling Dinnae's hair. Giggling like gwenefires, the trio dashed after him into the crowd.

Gwenefires, munshmins, rock dragons, Hrathgar Good and Evil . . . Brigitta shook her head, wanting to leave those images behind for a few suns, to pretend, for a short while, it had all been a bad dream. Her chest tingled where the miniature hourglass lay, and its warmth penetrated her skin, comforting her even though it spoke to her heart in a language she didn't understand.

"You are not going to join your friends?" Ondelle landed beside Brigitta and sat down.

"I don't know." Brigitta looked at all the cheerful faeries below. She felt small and awkward with Ondelle's powerful presence beside her.

"You are concerned with the markings on your wings."

"How can I not be?" Brigitta burst out, looking up into Ondelle's black moon eyes, holding back her tears. "It's got to be a mistake."

"Why would you think that?" Ondelle asked.

"I can't—I don't know how—I'm not qualified!"

"There is much to learn, of course. You will apprentice for many seasons."

"But Elders are so wise." Brigitta felt defeated. She would certainly be laughed at when everyone realized how completely wrong she was for this Life Task.

"Tell me," asked Ondelle gesturing out toward all the celebrating faeries, "what kind of faerie would think of traveling to Hrathgar's castle for assistance? And what kind of faerie would have taken on such a brave mission?"

"An Elder, I suppose." Brigitta sighed. "But we had to do something. We were desperate! And I wasn't marked as an Elder when I left the White Forest."

"Would your choice have been any different if you had known your markings?"

"I don't know." Brigitta was lost in confusion. "Was I marked as an Elder because I saved the forest or did I save the forest because I was destined to be an Elder?"

"That sounds like the question of a very wise faerie."

Ondelle led Brigitta into the Elder chambers and pointed to the chair meant for the Water Faerie Elder, a post currently held by the jovial Jorris of Rioscrea. Brigitta nervously sat down in the plush seat of the high-backed chair and felt a rush of dizziness. Ondelle placed her hand on Brigitta's arm and the dizziness vanished.

"It is the previous Water Faerie Elders speaking to you all at once. It takes several seasons to learn how to separate their voices."

"It felt like a swarm of butterflies in my head."

The High Priestess laughed and her dark eyes twinkled. Brigitta stared at them. They were so happy and so sad at the same time. She glanced across the room, through the entry way, at the wall where she and her friends had been hiding. Ondelle's gaze followed hers, but she said nothing.

Instead, she turned and sat down in her own chair and studied Brigitta for a moment before speaking again. "On the day the stone curse took our forest, I noticed our sprite, Vivilia, with the black spell-seed. Moments later, I noticed her again without the spell-seed. I was reminded of the night Hrathgar tried to steal the power of the Hourglass three hundred seasons ago." She leaned back in her chair. "She had used a similar seed."

"She stole that from Gola."

"Yes." Ondelle's eyes drifted away from Brigitta and back to the entrance of the chambers.

"Priestess Ondelle," said Brigitta quietly, "on that day, we were hiding . . . Did you know?"

"I sensed your presence."

"And later, the sprite came to us. She protected us. Did you know that, too?"

Ondelle stood again and slowly paced back and forth in front of her chair. "Brigitta, sometimes, as Elders, we possess information of which other faeries are not aware. For instance, Fernatta of Gyllenhale and I are the only remaining faeries who know what truly happened on the night Hrathgar attempted to steal the power of the Hourglass."

"All I know is that Gola's moonstone split Hrathgar in two."

"Yes, and I am afraid the rest of the Elders and I, as well as the High Priest at the time, had not the knowledge to return her to her single self. I am ashamed to admit that we hid both Hrathgars away and then conjured Blue Spell to imprison her in the ancient castle on Dead Mountain."

"Nobody else knew about the two Hrathgars?"

"It was too painful to admit that we were banishing Hrathgar Good, a faerie so dear and innocent. She herself agreed it was the only way to keep Hrathgar Evil from accessing the White Forest." Ondelle sat back down. "Mind you, this decision weighed heavily upon all of us. Particularly on Fernatta of Gyllenhale, who resigned as an Elder due to her sorrow."

"But, Auntie Ferna isn't an Elder. She has the markings of a Chronicler."

"She was only an Elder for a few seasons before the incident. Most have forgotten as her markings have faded and only the inner circle of the eye glyph remains. Look closer and you will see."

"How can destiny markings change? Aren't we all marked for life?"

"Each one's destiny unfolds differently. Fernatta's markings changed because it was her destiny for them to change."

"Gola said it was her destiny to leave her home, but where would she have gone if we hadn't met her?"

"What do you know of a Drutan's moonstones?" asked Ondelle.

"I know they are bad for anyone except their rightful owner."

"A Drutan, a Tree Being, may receive several moon-stones at birth. Each reveals a new path along her life. Without fulfilling them, she will never take her final root in the earth. She will decay instead, slowly and painfully."

Brigitta shivered at the thought.

"The moonstone Hrathgar stole contained her final destiny."

"What did it tell her?"

"That it was her destiny to help save the White Forest where she would spend her final days."

"That doesn't make any sense." Brigitta was more puzzled than ever. "What if Hrathgar hadn't stolen it? Then Gola's destiny wouldn't have been fulfilled!"

"And here is something else." Ondelle's eyes nar-rowed. "I was the one who sent our sprite to Hrathgar's castle. She was to report back to the Elders on Hrathgar's health and status. Does this mean I was the one who brought the curse upon our forest that served in fulfilling Gola's destiny?"

Brigitta shook her head. "Destiny is a confusing thing. I don't know if I'll ever understand it."

"One thing I have learned," said Ondelle, "is to allow all des-tinies to unfold as they should. This becomes challenging if one . . . " Ondelle glanced briefly toward the spot where Brigitta and her friends had been hiding, " . . . knows things that others do not."

Brigitta suddenly recalled Hrathgar's final words in the dungeon. "Hrathgar said something odd. She said to tell you she was glad to have finally met me."

Brigitta detected the faintest twitch in Ondelle's face, so faint she could almost convince herself it didn't happen.

"Yes, that is an odd thing to say."

She waited for Ondelle to elaborate, but when she didn't, Brigitta wasn't surprised. "It must be very lonely having to keep so many secrets," she said softly.

Ondelle only smiled. "Your mind is quite inquisitive, Brigitta. You will make a fine Elder some day."

Brigitta was doubtful but didn't argue with the High Priestess.

"Right now, however, there is a celebration to attend." Ondelle stood once more and gestured toward the chamber entrance. "It is time for you to remember that you are still a young faerie and not too old for games."

Three suns later, just after breakfast, Brigitta stepped into the lyllium meadow, followed by Pippet, Mousha, Gola, and Auntie Ferna. Tiny white flowers greeted them under a warm sun. Himalette zipped over their heads, followed by Minq on his unsteady wings.

"Lower to ground, Himalette!" Minq cried. "Lower to ground!"

Himalette dropped down closer to the ground and joined the others as they made their way to a simple memory-marking of interlocking silver tree branches. Set into the branches, bright yellow crystals spelled out: HRATHGAR THE GOOD. Brigitta placed a purple keronium glass below the branches. Himalette landed, stuck a few fragrant crotias in the glass, and took Brigitta's hand.

"I wish she could have returned," said Brigitta as she wiped a tear from her sister's cheek.

"We will forever be in her debt." Pippet put her arms around her daughters.

"Yes," Brigitta agreed, although her mind was busy replaying Ondelle's words. Destiny was so confusing. If Hrathgar hadn't cast the spell in the first place, her Evil half at least, there wouldn't have been anything to save. But still, deep in her heart, she knew that the Good Hrathgar was the real Hrathgar, and she was more than grateful for her sacrifice.

"She's not gone, you know." Mousha gestured out-ward. "She's simply merged with the elements. The Ancient Ones will look after her now, as they have always done."

Brigitta looked closely at her poppa's destiny mar-kings, the brownish question marks, the symbols of an Inventor. She looked at her momma's wings, a beautiful dusty pink with swirls of darker pink dots marking her as a Feast Master.

Auntie Ferna kneeled down beside Hrathgar's memory-marking. Her eyes were moist despite her smile. Brigitta noticed that the dark circles on her ginger wings were outlined by very faint eye-shapes and two even fainter lines radiating up toward air and fire. Ondelle was right. Brigitta couldn't believe she hadn't noticed this before. She wondered what other details she had failed to perceive.

Gola's Eyes fluttered to the memory-marking, examining the keronium glass and the flowers. From out of the woods, a large orange butterfly flew past and the Eyes followed it. The butterfly flew around them a few times, then landed on the top of the silver branches. The Eyes landed next to it.

There was a small spitting sound and the butterfly transformed into the Center Realm's sprite. Brigitta put out her finger. The Sprite touched it and bowed delicately.

"Vivilia," Brigitta murmured. She was lovely to look at, Brigitta decided, and silently thanked her for being part of the destiny she still didn't understand.

"Can I touch her, too, Briggy?" asked Himalette, holding herself back with great restraint.

"Yes, lola, you can touch her, too."

As Himalette reached out, the sprite flew away, laughing. She returned to her butterfly form and crossed the meadow, with the Eyes fluttering after her.

Himalette pouted. Everyone else laughed. Brigitta reached down and hugged her little sister, wondering what destiny markings would appear on her wings when the time came.

White Forest Lexicon

Ancient Ones
Another name for the **Ethereal Faeries**. They brought the **elemental faeries** north during the **Great World Cry** and created the protected realm known as the White Forest. Bound to the fifth element (ether), they are the keepers of **Blue Spell**, the highest form of faerie magic. The White Forest faeries believe the Ancients no longer exist in the material realm, but "visit" each elemental faerie on two occasions: to mark their destiny at birth and disperse their energy at death. They also impart knowledge to the new High Priest or Priestess through the **Eternal Dragon**. (see also **elemental faeries**)

beasts
Faerie term for all animals (there are flying beasts, buzzing beasts, swimming beasts, burrowing beasts, hopping beasts, etc.). Some faeries consider themselves to be beasts, others don't.

Blue Spell
The highest form of faerie magic, the secrets of which are passed down by the **Ethereals** (or **Ancient Ones**) to each new High Priest or Priestess during a visit with the **Eternal Dragon**. The Ethereals used Blue Spell to create the protected realm of the White Forest and "charge" the sands of the **Hourglass of Protection**. It is so powerful to the **elemental faeries** that it is reserved for rare and extreme circumstances. Only the High Priest or Priestess has the authority to conjure it via consensus of the White Forest Elders, or by the approval of the Ethereals themselves. These precautionary measures were necessary after the tragedies of the **Great World Cry**.

bone-dwellers
A large rodent that lives off of dead flesh and bones. Somewhat blind and deaf, they are not very skittish. They are also not dangerous to

living beasts, just ugly and foul-smelling, with long, wiry whiskers, bald pink heads and tails, and thick matted brown fur on the rest of their bodies. If any are around, there is something dead close by.

breath-lantern
An Air Faerie specialty made of wood and translucent fabric. Inside the lantern is a small cloud treated with a fire spell. When a faerie blows into it, the cloud glows bright orange. Quite beautiful and surprisingly sturdy.

candle webs
A very special decorative candle that is spun, just like a web. There is no wick. Any portion of it may be lit, including the entire web, which is often done during festive occasions.

carnivorous caterpillars
Caterpillars in the dark forests of **Foraglenn** can grow to be quite large and vicious. They cocoon other living animals and suffocate them. Their offspring (see **glow worms**) chew through the cocoons and eat the remains. Carnivorous caterpillars do not turn into butterflies.

NOTE: There are also ordinary caterpillars that turn into butterflies across **Foraglenn** (as well as on **Pariglenn** and **Storlglenn**). They are harmless distant cousins to the carnivorous kind. Carnivorous caterpillars do not eat regular caterpillars. They don't like the taste.

The Change
The Change is a time between childhood and adulthood, lasting several seasons. It is a time of introspection. Young faeries are moody during this time as they contemplate their Life's Task, which is revealed as a symbol on their wings that marks the "official" onset of their change. During this time their wings also grow longer and stronger, shedding once, twice, or sometimes three times and emerging brighter and more colorful. It is said by the adults that children wouldn't know what to do with such wings unless they had a purpose.

chatterbuds
One of Gola the Drutan's numerous creations. Her chatterbuds were created, more for pleasure than practicality, from a potion watered over

them when they were seedlings. They grew up in the cauldrons lining her walkway, keeping her company with their friendly chatter. Gola prefers solitude, but she is wise enough to know that a being needs others to talk to in order to stay sane.

chroniclers

Earth Faeries have always been destiny-marked as chroniclers and they keep track of everything in books. Once a Chronicler disperses with the elements, her books are moved to the lower levels of **the Hive**. Any faerie may request access to these books, although very rarely do they bother. Faeries aren't known for being that interested in reading. Faerie Lorekeepers keep track of the history of the White Forest. Fernatta of Gyllenhale is the 8th Faerie Lorekeeper.

Continents: Araglenn, Carraiglenn, Pariglenn, and Storlglenn
(See **Foraglenn**)

crotia

A distinct plant with yellow-green leaves and extremely fragrant multi-colored petals. Used for perfumes, candles, oils, bath salts, and other pleasant smelling items. Has warming properties. Not recommended for eating as it would taste like perfume and might make one sick.

Dead Mountain

The castle on Dead Mountain is where Hrathgar was banished. Before the **Great World Cry**, when **Faweh** was balanced, and the five civilizations flourished together, the castle on the mountain was used as a retreat for the Sages and their guests. It was a sacred place. At that time the mountain was referred to as Dragon Mountain, and on a clear day one could see all the way down the continent to the mountains surrounding the **Valley of Noe**. (See **Lake Indago**.)

delia grass

Delia means faith. Delia was also the name of the High Sage from **Storlglenn** who created the grass before the **Great World Cry**. The only place it exists outside of Storlglenn is **Dead Mountain**, because she planted some in the castle garden while visiting there. The grass grows from a spell that allows the chewer of the grass to resist harm or to rapidly heal, but only if the chewer believes they will. It has no power if the chewer does not have faith in the magic of the grass.

deodyte

Faeries may procreate with faeries bound by other elements. As when giving birth to a boy or a girl, there is a dominant element. For instance, an earth faerie and a fire faerie may give birth to a fire girl, fire boy, earth girl, or earth boy. Once every great while, a **deodyte** will be born. This is a faerie of duel elements. These faeries are respected, though slightly feared. Their Life Tasks are usually something self-directed and less social.

dragon flower (or dragon egg flower)

The center of the enormous red and green flower is a speckled white bulb that looks like an egg in its mouth, so it is often referred to as a "dragon egg flower." Dragon flower grows sporadically in very wet areas. It takes the dew from four or five "eggs" to fill even the smallest **keronium glass**. It is used as a binding and activating agent in potions.

Drutan

A "Tree Being." There are several scattered about the continent of **Foraglenn**. They live a very long time (longer than faeries) and are solitary beings. They have faerie-like body features (such as hands, fingers, arms, toes, knees, ears, etc.) except that they are much taller and their skin grows progressively more fibrous and bark-like as they age and lose their facial features. They are quite good with magic, especially dealing with plants. When they die, and if they have properly fulfilled their destiny, they simply stop where they are and take root, almost indistinguishable from the actual trees. (see also **moonstones**)

elemental faeries

The faeries of the White Forest are bound by one of four elements: earth, air, fire, water. This affects their appearance (i.e. skin and hair tone, body shape), talents, and temperament. Faeries tend to live in the realm associated with their element, but there is no law that keeps them there and many faeries find mates of another element. For the most part faeries celebrate, respect, and appreciate each other's differences. Although they sometimes become impatient when dealing with each other, they are happy to allow other elemental faeries to do the tasks they aren't interested in, which keeps everything in balance. (see also **Ancient Ones**)

Eternal Dragon (Tzajeek)

When the Elders work spells, they call forth the power of the Eternal Dragon, Tzajeek, a sea serpent with the ability to absorb elements. Instead of a fire-breather you might say It's a fire-eater . . . and an earth, water, and air eater. It is Faweh's true Keeper of the Elements and the only one of its kind. Its origin is unknown.

Before a High Priest or Priestess takes position, he or she must journey, alone, to the Sea of Tzajeek to receive private wisdom from the Eternal Dragon. When the faeries lived in the Valley of Noe, Tzajeek would appear in Lake Indago to counsel with the High Sage once every season cycle. But after the **Great World Cry**, Tzajeek became a traveler of the open seas.

Most elemental faeries only think of Tzajeek as a mythical creature from ancient tales.

Ethereal Faeries
(see **Ancient Ones**)

The Eyes
Gola, a gifted **Drutan**, developed a special breed of eyes with wings that can see for her. Drutans are not known for their eyesight and as they grow older, their own eyes sink further and further into their barky skin until they disappear completely. Gola's Eyes allow her to continue to see in her old age. She also has a shallow pool in the center of the floor of her home that allows others to see what her Eyes see.

Faweh
The planet is called many things by many beings, but the White Forest faeries simply refer to the outer world beyond the White Forest as Faweh, which literally translates to "house of elements."

feather paints

Feather paints are used on the decorative feathers of festival costumes. The thin and delicate paint is specially made to coat feathers. It dries very fast, so one can dip the feathers in multiple colors. Fire Faeries are expert feather paint makers and are extremely competitive when it comes to making the best paint. The colors are seemingly endless and the most popular are the sparkled and metallic versions.

Festival of Elements

Faeries love festivals. They love singing and dancing and eating and games. The Festival of Elements is the most important festival in the White Forest due to the rotating of the **Hourglass of Protection**. The Ethereals designed the White Forest so that it would be protected against incident or intruder by the magic of the Hourglass, which contains sands empowered by **Blue Spell**. As a preventative measure, however, the sands' Blue Spell power runs out every **season cycle** to prevent any possible evil-minded being or intruder from having access to too much power. (see also **Blue Spell** and **Hourglass of Protection**)

flutterscarves

Scarves created primarily for dance and entertainment. They are so light and airy they can be directed by even the slightest breeze. They jump about in the air if a faerie so much as waves her hand past them.

Foraglenn

Beyond the White Forest, the elemental faeries have mapped very little. They have a general idea of the continent upon which they live and the four smaller continents beyond. They refer to their continent, the largest, as **Foraglenn**, and the other continents (in order of size): **Pariglenn**, **Araglenn**, **Carraiglenn**, and **Storlglenn**. Each continent has its own distinct geography, history, flora, fauna, myths, and magic. There are no other known faerie realms on the other continents.

frogs (giant)

In addition to a variety of regular-sized frogs, there are giant frogs on the continents of **Foraglenn**, **Pariglenn**, and **Storlglenn**, but they are fairly harmless. They are also not the smartest hopping beasts in the forest. They do eat small flying beasts, but faeries are generally not on their menu. Hrathgar Evil's frogs were cast with a spell to be especially aggressive.

frommafin
A bubbly refreshment served iced or hot. Usually reserved for festive occasions as it takes a long time to prepare. Made with **tingermint** and **pipberries**.

globelight
A faerie's flashlight. Not difficult to make, but tricky to make well. If one has a good mold and can read a cookbook, one can make a globelight. However, it takes a skilled faerie to make one that stays charged for any length of time. Globelights are round, fit in the palm of one's hand, and give off light from any part that is rubbed. Use a thumb to make a spotlight, swipe the whole thing and hang it for a night dance.

glow worms
Glow worms are the offspring of **carnivorous caterpillars.** When young, they feed on the flesh of beasts cocooned by the caterpillars. They lose their glow after eight to ten suns, then enter an extraordinary growth spurt, after which they are able to make cocoons of their own. They are quite vulnerable in the between time, however, and are susceptible to the elements and predators. Most never make it to their full size. When they die, they are also cocooned and eaten.

goldenfew
A very traditional festival stew made from fermented **gundlebeans**. Sort of like lentil soup for faeries, but more tangy. It warms one up inside when eaten. It is not uncommon for various forest creatures to gather around the bases of village trees during festival preparation, hoping for an inferior batch to be discarded. Buzzing beasts are particularly fond of goldenfew as it makes them tipsy.

Great Moon

The larger and bluer of the two moons of **Faweh**. It travels across the sky more slowly than the smaller moon. Sometimes referred to as the Great Blue Moon or just Blue Moon.

Great World Cry

A pivotal moment in Faweh's history, when the energies that kept the planet peaceful became unstable and threw the world into elemental chaos. This happened when the World Sages misused the power of **Blue Spell** and the High Sage (one of the **Ancient Ones**) was killed. They threw his body into **Lake Indago**, a sacred lake that was the elemental entryway for the planet. The lake dried up and out sprung the **River That Runs Backwards**, a symbol of the chaos of energetic forces now inhabiting the planet. Although the chaos has settled over time, the word remains a dangerous place for many beasts, including faeries.

green zynthias

A crystal with hypnotic properties, very common inside the caves beneath **Dead Mountain**. Also found in caves in many parts of the continent of **Araglenn** (one of plenty of reasons not to visit).

grovens

A furry purple toad-like creature with very large eyes and fat lips. They are slow and not very bright. Sometimes faerie children keep them as pets, but they aren't very exciting. They aren't sad, but their expressions might lead one to believe they are. Playing with them is harmless, but it's best not to follow them home, as they live in a slimy bog filled with **stench-mold**, where they gather to mate, give birth, and raise their young. They spend the rest of their time wandering around the forest, eating creepy-crawly beasts and sleeping in damp places. They have no sense of smell and poor eyesight, but their hearing is pretty good.

gundlebeans

A hearty, extremely versatile faerie staple. "Eat your gundlebeans" is probably the most common phrase out of a mother faerie's mouth at the dinner table. Plump, meaty brown beans that grow in great clumps on vines all over the White Forest. One can eat them straight off the vine or cooked in a variety of dishes such as pie or stew.

gwenefire
Used for love potions, hypnotic potions, dream potions, and seduction potions. Long lavender and pink flowers with lashes. Very fragrant. Very potent.

the Hive
The Hive is what the White Forest faeries fondly call the Elders' enclave underground in the Center Realm. It consists of spell chambers, living quarters for Elders and Apprentices, libraries, storage for all sorts of magical items, and access to many of the underground passageways of the forest.

Hourglass of Protection
An enormous hourglass located in the Center Realm of the White Forest shaped from the branches of two immense **uul trees** and inlaid with transparent crystal that only the **Ethereals** know how to form. Its protective magic (see **Blue Spell**) keeps the forest safe from the outside world. Once every **season cycle**, during the **Festival of Elements**, the hourglass is turned, the elemental sands are rebalanced, and the protective shield is renewed. Only the acting High Priest or Priestess has the knowledge to rotate the Hourglass, and can only do so with the assistance of at least two White Forest Elders.

keronium glass
A very delicate hand-blown instrument used for measuring ingredients for potions and spells. Each glass must be blown to perfection and have the right amount of element. The sizes from smallest to largest are: yellow, orange, red, turquoise, and purple. There are 20 different kinds of keronium glassware (i.e. earth orange, fire orange, water orange, etc.)

Lake Indago
Many, many seasons ago there were several sophisticated civilizations on **Faweh**. There was also a very large faerie population, centered in the Valley of Noe, in the southern region of **Foraglenn**. The valley

housed a great quantity of faerie villages, which are now in ruins, many completely vanished forever. These villages peppered the shores of the enormous Lake Indago, the former entryway for all elements, which now births **The River that Runs Backwards** into this world.

licotia nectar

Licotia nectar is really only used to make nasty tasting potions go down better. It comes from a deep purple flower that grows in the tops of the trees only in the White Forest. It's challenging to gather not only due to the height at which it grows, but because the nectar bulbs are slippery and difficult to remove. Luckily, it only takes a few drops to flavor a potion as it is very strong and no faerie would ever drink it without diluting it first. Also used in a soothing faerie treat called "triple lyllium suclaid."

Lola Moon

The smaller, oranger of **Faweh**'s two moons. Lola means "small one" or "little one." Sometimes older sisters call their little sisters "lola" or parents use it as a term of endearment. Also referred to as Sister Moon, especially in faerie lullabies.

lyllium

Non-descript, leafy plant with delicate white flowers. Inside each flower is a small nectar pouch. Lyllium is used for its restorative properties. It isn't capable of bringing a full-sized beast back to life, but it could cheer it up if it were unhappy. The nectar must be drained and needs to be prepared for use in potions. Eating the flower alone has very little effect. The flowers are quite fragrant when they first bloom and as they lose their scent, the nectar becomes more potent.

Minq

Minq is a pale brown, hairless cross between a fox and rodent with exceptionally long and useful ears, which he uses like a spare set of front legs. He latches on to others for safety, pledging allegiance if necessary. He has never met another of his kind. Many **Drutans** have animal "familiars" and Minq is Gola's. If a forest beast accidentally devours a piece of a Drutan's rooted parent, mistaking them for a tree, destiny draws them together and the connection is understood at once. Gola rescued Minq from a large bird when he was a young pup and he has been with her ever since, although she is not possessive and encourages his independence.

moon-beat

A way of measuring the passing of time using the traveling speed of the **Great Moon**. One moon-beat is approximately 15 minutes. The smaller **Lola Moon** travels faster than the Great Moon, so that it always appears to be chasing it, or running from it, across the sky. If a faerie is in a hurry, one might say to her, "What's your rush, Lola Moon?"

moonstone

A **Drutan**'s most prized possession. Drutans are always born at night. When a female Drutan is ready to give birth, she passes the baby through her bark-skin to a pouch in the male. The male "plants" the baby in an open area under the moonslight and then continues on. The mother, father, and child might never see each other ever again. When the child awakens, its first tears, mingled with the two moons' light, form moonstones, which the Drutan will use for the rest of his or her life. Each stone is unique and reveals a portion of the Drutan's destiny. Moonstones formed under two moons are more powerful than when formed under one moon. A Drutan born under no moon light receives no moonstones and therefore perishes quickly. Moonstones are particular to their owners and have mind-altering effects on others who attempt to use them: they become separated from rational thought and suffer from a division of personalities.

munshmins

Extremely annoying, precocious, and loud-mouthed plant. Dark purple, thorny, with large-lipped bulbs. They make great burglar alarms and are also used in potions that involve making inanimate objects speak. They have an excellent genetic memory, and can often remember information overheard many seasons in the past. Although they don't ever share information unless they feel like it, they are not known to lie.

pipberries

Named after the small "pip" sound they make when a ripe one is poked and breaks open, spilling its delicious juice. The riper they are, the sweeter they taste. They are so tempting that when they start to get plump and red it takes a very disciplined faerie to wait for them to fully ripen.

Precipice Waterfall

The largest waterfall in the White Forest, located southwest of the Water Realm. **Spring River** (which begins northeast of the Earth Realm) ends at Precipice Waterfall, where the water runs over numerous rocks and crags and falls back into the earth and through a series of caverns running the length of the White Forest, leaving it lush and fertile. When the **Ethereals** first moved the lesser (**elemental**) faeries to the White Forest, several Earth Faeries charted maps of the caverns. The books are kept deep in **The Hive**'s library and most faeries have forgotten about them. Young faeries are not allowed into the caverns, and very few adult faeries have bothered to venture there.

pond vile

A nasty, carnivorous plant that lives at the bottom of some fresh water pools in the Dark Forest that don't get enough moonslight. It's easy to be fooled by the innocent looking little green feathery plants, but they can snag a beast quickly and pull it underwater with their little bulbs, which open up into barbed fingers.

River That Runs Backwards

(see **Great World Cry**)

rock dragons

Leftover beasts from an ancient time. Usually pretty lazy unless provoked, and being woken up from one of their numerous naps will provoke them. They only live in the vicinity of the castle at **Dead Mountain** (previously **Dragon Mountain**, since that's where the rock dragons lived). The ancient Sages had conjured them up to keep curious beasts away from the castle. There are about two dozen of them left. They do not procreate.

sand petals

Another measuring tool, like **keronium glass**. Sand petals are just that, petals made from crystallized sand. They aren't real petals from plants, it's simply a shape faeries are fond of that makes for a good spoon-like tool. They come in ½, full, and double sizes.

season cycle

There are three seasons: Grow Months, Green Months, Gray Months. Generally things are planted in the Grow Months, inventions are revealed, new recipes tried, new songs and dances shared. During the Green Months, there is a lot of activity and each village-nest and elemental realm hosts festivals and community events. The Gray Months are a time of learning, studying, harvesting, and developing new feats, inventions, recipes, songs, and other projects. Instruments are built for songmaking in the Gray Months. The Elders work on their spells. It is a more serious time . . . although most faeries don't stay serious for long.

shadowfly

Shadowflies are quiet flying beasts that perform patterned dances in the sunlight in order to communicate. Lots of faerie children daydream while watching them as they are quite mesmerizing. If a faerie studies the shadows long enough, they can figure out what the shadowflies are saying. The messages are usually reports about the weather or where certain flowers are in bloom.

sharmock roots

A common ingredient in a variety of faerie stews, herbal medicines and spells. They are extremely versatile and pleasant enough tasting on their own (raw or cooked). The roots are bright orange and round, but they are difficult to spot on the forest floor because the top of the root looks like a common moss. However, they usually grow in large clumps, like crabgrass, so when a faerie finds one, she just pulls and she's in business. They grow well in the White Forest due to its particular balance of water and light. They are much less common in the Dark Forest.

The Shift

A moat of earth that stretches around the perimeter of the White Forest, keeping it separated and safe from the rest of the world. Through the middle of The Shift is a force-field that no one but White Forest residents may cross. Anyone who does not belong in the White Forest must be escorted across by a Perimeter Guard.

spell-seed

Another specialty of Gola the **Drutan**. Used for transporting potions or magical items. It is large, hard, wrinkled, and black and when closed it is vacuum-sealed and nearly impossible to penetrate. It is easily opened, however, by spinning it three times in the same direction the sun and moons travel, then balancing it on end and releasing three drops of water on it. It is odorless.

Spring River

Spring River is quite unique as it begins and ends in the White Forest. It bubbles from the ground in the Earth Faerie Realm, where is runs slow and wide. It narrows as it heads south west through the Water Faerie Realm, where it ends at **Precipice Falls** and is swallowed back into the earth through an endless series of underground caverns. This intricate web of catacombs distributes the water throughout the forest, making it extremely fertile land.

sprites

Sprites have been peripheral companions to the faeries for thousands of seasons. They were also brought to the White Forest by the **Ancient Ones** after the **Great World Cry**. They are much smaller, less communal, are not bound by an element, and have no destiny markings on their wings. They have a variety of skin and hair tones, but a uniform body type. There is no such thing as a chubby sprite. They are temperamental, prone to playing tricks on the elemental faeries, and consider themselves to be superior beings. They live in the **uul trees** surrounding the Center Realm, but mostly keep out of sight. There is always one designated as the Center Realm Sprite and he or she is a liaison to the White Forest Elders.

Star Teller

Star Tellers can tell what time of year it is by looking at the night sky. They keep track of the names of stars and create stories about them. They are often called to parties to tell Star Tales, which they do with great enthusiasm. The names of the stars and their stories tend to change, because not many Star Tellers bother to read old star charts. They prefer to make up their own, although there are a few favorite stories that have been passed down for several generations.

stench-mold

Not a fun thing for a faerie to get into. It's a slimy mold that smells like rotting eggs and is very difficult to get off. The only beasts it doesn't bother are **grovens**. It glides right off their slick fur. Grovens also lack a sense of smell.

thunderbug

Thunderbugs cling to branches and shake their back ends to make rhythmic, percussive sounds. They each have their own rhythm, so a swarm of them can be quite dizzying. When thunderbugs are drunk on discarded **goldenfew** or lazy on **lyllium nectar,** faerie children like to catch them and put them in jars.

tingermint

A dusty-lavender flower that has a nectar used for flavoring. The nectar is earthy and sweet, with a tiny spicy zing when it hits the tongue.

uul tree

An ancient tree that oozes a light flavorless sap used for making spreadable tinctures or pastes. A very sturdy tree due to its thick trunk and twisting branches, which grow toward and into other uul trees creating canopies for young faeries to play in. Uul trees have been known to aid other trees by supporting them if they are in danger of falling or by oozing sap over injured bark. The Center Realm is surrounded by uul trees and the **Hourglass of Protection** is hung from the interlocking branches of the two largest ones.

Water Gardeners

Water Gardeners are Water Faeries who primarily work and live in the Earth Realm. They collaborate with the Earth Faerie gardeners to create marsh farms for plants that thrive in a wet environment. Earth Faeries tend to be good with plants and Water Faerie Gardeners are good at empathing (faerie sensing) the needs of water flora. Earth Faeries are also talented reed boat builders, which are used to tend the marsh farm crops.

weather spell

Faeries can't control the weather, but Water Faeries are quite in tune with it and can train themselves to empath (sense) clouds. Not only can they tell if it's going to rain, but if they are really good they can tell what kind of rain, how hard, or how big the drops will be. They can also train themselves to direct the wind. Weather spells can be used to encourage impending rain to come faster, slower, harder, softer, or even change the color of the drops (a favorite weather spell activity).

whisper light

The seed of the whisper grass, carried off by the breeze. The "whisps" glow yellow, which indicates they are ready to plant themselves. If the light is extinguished before it manages to plant itself in the ground the seed loses its fertility. Not only does a whisper light emit light, it also emits sound. The sounds are whispers, hence the name. Although it doesn't actually say anything that makes sense, it can drive one crazy trying to figure out what it is saying, because it sounds like something. In addition, what one hears them whispering is entirely a reflection of what's going on in one's own mind.

The
RUINS
of
NOE

Faerie Tales from the White Forest
Book Two

Danika Dinsmore

Hydra House ❖ Seattle, Washington

For Satori

Do not go where the path may lead, go instead
where there is no path and leave a trail.
Ralph Waldo Emerson

Moonsrise Ridge
Ithcommon
Marsh farm
Gylenhale
Green River
Sprite Realm
Spring River
Green Lake
Dionsdale
Water Realm
Center Realm
Sun Dreaming Rocks
Tiragarrow
Precipice falls
Easyl
Rioscrea
The White Forest
warm ponds
Tintlebar
villagenests
markets

Eternal Spring

Marsh farms

* Grobjahar

Singing Caves

Foradern

Sea of Trojeck

the White Forest ☆

Reed Forest

...th REALM

Iola Spring

E•REALM

Thachreek *

Rivenbow *

Thorsa *

AIR REALM

The Elder Hive

Erriondower *

Bobbercurry

LOLA BASIN RIVER

LITTLE MOON CREEK

Flying Fields

Grioth *

* Dottisdagh

FIRE REALM

...nllebar

No Moons Canyon

Prologue

*T*he female Nhord shuffled to wake her tired feet. It was the end of her shift and her male companion would be replacing her shortly. Their shift changes were the brief moments they had together to enjoy each other's company. It was not a life anyone, even the most steadfast Nhord, would wish for themselves. The two long-time friends had accepted their destinies, however, and took fierce pride in their lineage of Purview Sentries.

The male Nhord entered, a wild look in his double-lidded eyes. The female's first thought was that he looked quite handsome, standing in the entrance to the petrified sandcave with the sun setting behind his armored back.

It is time, he whispered.

What do you—you mean THE time?

He nodded and held up his right front flipperpaw. A little fuzzy light danced around inside the webbing between his claws.

The Knowing. She felt it too. It was crisp and clear and eternal. It called them.

This was what six generations of Nhords had been waiting for. She glanced back at the large, ancient ring behind her. She had imagined the great joy or relief that would flood her body at this moment, but she only nodded, tightened the straps of her supply pack, always at the ready, and stepped aside to make room for her friend.

The little light sailed from his flipperpaw, drawn to the ring. Drawn home. It caught on the breeze wafting into the cave from the dry heat of the desert.

The male sentry approached the female and nuzzled her lip horn with his own. She blinked each of her four lids fully and slowly to indicate that she was ready.

Together they stood and watched the little light flutter and bump into the wall of the cave before spinning into the Purview and disappearing from sight. Together they stood and faced the Purview as the vine patterns around its frame began to move.

Chapter One

Brigitta concentrated on the black pebble in her hand. She turned it over and over in her palm, gathering its energy, and then tossed it over the embankment into Precipice Falls. She closed her eyes and visualized the rock falling downward, splashing into the water below, and spinning through the underground caverns of the Water Faerie Realm.

"Be the rock," she murmured to herself. "Follow the energy of the rock."

Brigitta couldn't focus her mind. She opened her eyes and sighed. How should she know what it felt like to be a rock or to travel through the forest's underground caverns? She wasn't even allowed to explore them, not until she was a First Elder Apprentice, which was silly considering she had already been outside the White Forest itself, something none of the other First Apprentices had ever done.

"I'd like to see First Apprentice Flanna fight off a carnivorous caterpillar." She picked up the rest of the pebbles sitting beside her and threw them over the embankment.

"Ow!" came a voice from below.

"Sorry, Minq!" called Brigitta, peeking over the edge as Minq's rodent-like face appeared.

He rubbed his eye with one of his long, droopy ears. "Why you throw rock?" he asked as he fluttered over the embankment.

"Something Elder Dervia cooked up to keep me busy," Brigitta said, immediately wishing she could retract her comment. It was not a fair accusation since every Apprentice was required to learn empathing. What she really needed was to practice being more "Elderlike" and not saying spiteful things. "I'm supposed to learn how to be other things. Like that tree or the water or, someday, even you."

"If you me, who I?" Minq landed awkwardly on the grass and removed his translucent wings, the ones that had been gifted to him by High Priestess Ondelle herself. He had never completely gotten the hang of the wings, nor did he like to wear them in the water or when he slept. But he did enjoy flying to Precipice Falls with Brigitta every few moons to practice flying in the winds of the water's currents.

"You're my best friend," Brigitta said. My only friend, she thought to herself.

They both fell back into the grass and stared up at the clouds, huge and white like dreamy mountains. Clouds were the only things Brigitta was good at empathing. She had a particular affinity with clouds, having spent so many hours watching them while lying on her back in the lyllium fields northwest of Tiragarrow. It seemed natural to become a cloud, slow moving in flight, overlooking the forest.

As she relaxed and focused on cloud energy, letting go of all intrusive thoughts as she had been taught, she was suddenly looking down from a great height, passing over the Water Realm. Tiragarrow appeared below, alive with tiny faeries scurrying around preparing for a party. Watching them zip about, Brigitta grew dizzy and lost her concentration.

She shook her head clear and rolled over onto her stomach, turning her attention to her favorite section of the falls, where the streams of water were like hair billowing over a faerie woman's shoulder. Waterfalls were trickier to empath, even for a Water Faerie. They were more complex and changed too fast. It was easiest to empath things if they were still and most difficult if they had minds of their own. At least that's what she had been told. Empathing a thinking beast was advanced magic and dangerous for an untrained faerie.

Minq's mind might be harmless enough, she thought, glancing over at his pointy pale brown face before turning her attention back to the water. Elder Dervia's low voice echoed in her head. *Dismiss anything that isn't related to the energy of the object. Dismiss your thoughts.*

"Easier said then done," Brigitta murmured. She allowed that thought to drift away, like a flutterscarf on the wind, as she stared into the water, emptying her mind.

For a moment she felt herself rushing downward and a penetrating coolness overcame her. It was brief but exhilarating.

Brigitta shot up in surprise. "I did it!"

"What do?"

"I was the waterfall. Only for a moonsbreath. But I did it!"

Minq clapped his ears together like hands. Then he threw his wings back on and spun his ears around while he flapped, twirling straight up into the air.

Brigitta laughed and it felt good. She hadn't laughed much since moving to the Center Realm two seasons ago to apprentice with the Elders. She missed her momma and poppa and even her little sister Himalette, but whenever she visited them it didn't feel the same. Her momma was over-fussy, her poppa only wanted to know what the Elders were up to, and Himmy had a busy social life that centered around the latest faerie gossip.

Flying with Minq to Precipice Falls was one of Brigitta's few pleasures. That and visiting Gola the Drutan in her tree home just west of Grioth in the Fire Faerie Realm. Gola said she liked the faeries of Grioth best because they left her alone, although she always made time for Brigitta when she came by unannounced.

Something round and white dropped at Brigitta's feet and she picked it up. It was a broodnut. A message was carved into its shell, exposing the red inner meat: *Time to come home—Love, Momma.* Brigitta looked up to see Roucho, her poppa's new featherless delivery bird, flying back in the direction of Tiragarrow. She smiled sadly at the thought of her momma still referring to their cottage as Brigitta's home.

"Hey, Minq," Brigitta pointed to the departing bird. "It's time."

Minq stopped twirling and waved at the bird with one of his lengthy ears. He liked Roucho, the only other bald flying beast in the forest. He landed, closed his eyes, and opened his mouth.

Brigitta laughed again as she cracked the nut open and tossed the meaty center onto his pink tongue.

By the time Brigitta and Minq arrived in Tiragarrow, most of the local faeries, and some not so local ones, had already gathered outside of her family's cottage. Her Great Auntie Ferna, from the village-nest of Gyllenhale, sat on a stump chatting with Edl Featherkind. Himalette's numerous friends dangled from the tree branches in their brightest party-wear as the adult faeries exchanged stories of their own unveilings. Edl gave Brigitta and Minq a friendly wave as they landed on the new moss she and Pippet had planted in front of the cottage for the occasion. Brigitta waved back. Edl had lovely yellow wings with a thick V shape spreading out toward the ends like friendly green smiles, marking her as a Master Gardener. Her specialty was tingermint, but her moss was excellent as well, perfectly spongy and soft.

Edl and her companion Orl Featherkind, Tiragarrow's Caretaker, were among the small number of faeries who treated Brigitta no differently than they had before she had saved the White Forest, and her Elder destiny markings had been revealed. But it didn't really count, since Edl and Orl were friendly toward everyone.

Brigitta looked around for Orl, even though she felt a tinge of guilt whenever she saw him, feeling a bit responsible for his arm breaking after the stone curse hit the forest. He always told her the spell reversal had healed it, that it was better than ever, but she noticed how it had pained him through the Gray Months.

The Gray Months. The last season Brigitta had spent with her family in Tiragarrow before Water Elder Jorris had died, advancing Dervia of Dionsdale to Elder status, Flanna of Rioscrea to First Apprentice, and Brigitta to Second Apprentice. The cottage before her was no longer her home. She had been living in the Center Realm and performing her Second Apprentice duties for almost two seasons.

It was just as well because she was sure most of the faeries in Tiragarrow were suspicious of her. And why shouldn't they be? Hrathgar had become an Elder Apprentice when she returned from the Dark Forest, and she tried to steal the power of the Hourglass. Twice.

"What destiny mark Himalette have?" asked Minq.

"I don't know," replied Brigitta. "She's managed to keep it a secret from everyone. She's been wearing wingmitts for the past few moons."

The crowd hushed as Brigitta's parents, Mousha and Pippet, emerged from the cottage and stood on either side of the doorway. Mousha looked particularly pleased with himself, and Brigitta wondered with what invention he would kick off the unveiling. He nodded to the faeries gathered in front of the cottage and they began to hum and flap their wings in rhythm. Pippet started the traditional celebration song and everyone joined in.

Show your wings little faerie kin
Wings that carry on the wind
Show your wings and hold them high
Share with us your Task in life

Minq struggled to keep the rhythm and remember the words at the same time. Brigitta helped him along by reciting the words in his ear.

Show your wings little faerie kin
You have now grown into them
Show your wings and hold them high
Celebrate your Task in life

As the last notes of the song drifted away, Mousha gestured to the doorway. Sparkling pink and yellow bubbles shot out from the entrance of the cottage and everyone cheered. Children flew from the branches and caught them in their hands, squealing with delight. The bubbles were thick and didn't pop on impact. Instead, they settled in the tree branches, on the moss, and on everyone's heads. A neighbor boy stomped on one. It slipped out from underneath his foot and flew into Auntie Ferna's face. She tumbled backward from her tree stump, laughing and catching her balance with her strong wings. A mound of bubbles gathered at Brigitta's feet. Minq dislodged one from his right ear.

"Poppa!" called Himalette from inside the cottage. She appeared in a filmy lavender gown and held up a small box, out from which the crazed bubbles fired.

Mousha grabbed the box and reached inside. The bubbles stopped and he withdrew his goo-covered hand. The gathered faeries stifled their laughter.

"Go ahead, lola," Pippet urged Himalette forward.

Himalette regained her composure and glided to the edge of the porch, grinning from ear to ear. "Thank you all for coming to my unveiling. Afterwards we will have leaf races, a lantern dance, and Momma has made tingermint tea and pipberry pies."

Brigitta and Minq exchanged glances. Himalette's eyes shone with a child's innocence, but she had grown in the last season. Her hair was darker, her face had lost its roundness, and her wings extended farther from her back.

Minq placed his ear across Brigitta's shoulders and she rubbed her cheek against it. How happy her sister sounded. Had they really taken the same journey through the Dark Forest two season cycles ago? Had Himalette really managed to forget the dangers that lurked outside the White Forest, like a distant dream?

Brigitta grabbed Minq's ear and held it, suddenly overcome by sadness as she recalled Hrathgar Good's teary goodbye on the dungeon floor of the castle on Dead Mountain. His ear squeezed back, as if he were empathing her thoughts.

Himalette's smile danced with excitement as Mousha and Pippet took their places on either side of her. They both grasped a wingmitt and beamed at each other.

"Two moons, two wings, one heart, one destiny!" they called and lifted the wingmitts.

Underneath, Himalette's pink wings shone brightly. On the ends, in a deep rose to match her momma's markings, were two long bars with two filled circles sandwiched between them, like snuggling musical notes. The faeries cheered and fluttered their own wings as Himalette curtsied.

"What marking mean?" asked Minq, flapping his wings along with everyone else.

"She's been marked as a Song Master," said Brigitta. "She'll learn to write songs and arrange music for festivals."

"This important Life Task?"

"It's perfect for Himmy. She'll love it."

Her sister flew up and over everyone's heads, showering the crowd with multi-colored flower petals. She landed in front of her best friends and they hugged her and kissed her cheeks, admiring her markings and pointing to each other's empty wings, describing what signs they thought might appear there some day.

"Friends not have mark. She young for destiny?" asked Minq as Brigitta plucked a yellow petal from his snout.

"Yes, a bit, but if her heart knows what it wants . . ." Brigitta tried to push away her envy. Everyone knew Himmy's heart; she wore it on her sleeve. She'd always loved music. But how did Brigitta's markings reflect her own conflicted heart?

She watched her sister making goofy poses for her friends. How simple life would be to write songs all day and learn to play instruments. Sure, Brigitta would learn to play a durma as an Elder Apprentice, but it was a sacred instrument to be used when honoring the dead. It wasn't anything festive like a hoopflute or light and joyful like blossom bells. Durmas were about as serious as an instrument could get.

"Poppa must be happy. He loves musical inventions." Brigitta couldn't help smiling to herself when she thought about her poppa's thunderbug symphony. She peered into the cottage to see if he had one waiting inside.

Mousha and Pippet caught Brigitta's attention and motioned for her and Minq to join them. They were about to fly over when a short reddish Water Faerie girl with dark yellow wings dropped down in front of them.

"Brigitta! Minq!" The young faerie bounced up and down. She patted Minq on the head and he winced. "I thought maybe you were going to miss everything, Brigitta, because you had important Apprentice things to do."

"Hi Glennis, we were just—" started Brigitta.

"Not as exciting as your unveiling!" Glennis exclaimed, referring to Brigitta's surprise destiny revealing in front of the entire forest. "But how could any faerie beat that? It was the most amazing unveiling ever!"

"It's not like I planned it that way."

"I guess Himalette isn't like you. I thought since she had been to Faweh she would become an Elder Apprentice, too, or at least a Wising, but she didn't. That means another one will be unveiled. Maybe from my own village-nest!"

"Maybe, we haven't had one from Easyl in a—"

"What's it like living in the Hive?" Glennis leaned closer to Brigitta.

"We don't call it that, we—"

"Do you get to sit in on any Elder meetings?" Glennis's eyes grew wide and she lowered her voice. "What's High Priestess Ondelle really like?"

Brigitta took a slow breath to control her annoyance. She was about to tell Glennis it was none of her business when Pippet's strong arm landed on her shoulder.

"Hello, Glennis, nice to see you. I need to borrow Brigitta and

Minq to help me with the refreshments." Pippet steered Brigitta toward the porch, laughing. Minq fluttered behind them.

"Thanks, Momma. Bog buggers, that Glennis is a real—" Brigitta stopped and sighed. "Elder-like, Elder-like," she mumbled to herself.

"Ah, lola, she means well. She looks up to you." Pippet hugged her daughter. "I'm glad you're here. You, too, Minq."

Once inside the kitchen, Pippet handed four trays of little pipberry pies to Minq, who balanced them on his hands and ears. After he had flown from the room, Pippet sat Brigitta down.

"I haven't seen you since Himalette had her change. Let me look at you."

"Aw, Momma, I'm not any different than I was the last time I saw you."

"You are, you've lost weight. And you're not sleeping, I can tell."

"I'm fine. I'm sleeping." Brigitta left out the part about not sleeping well, but that was nothing new. She hadn't slept well since returning from the Dark Forest.

Pippet wasn't listening. She was pulling ingredients off the shelves. "Nothing a little triple lyllium suclaide won't cure. That will fatten you up and bring sweet dreams."

"Momma, you don't have time to make suclaide."

Pippet reached into a jar and pulled out some leaves and white petals. "Hmmm, I'm out of lyllium root."

Brigitta placed her hand on Pippet's shoulder. "Mother, I'm fine. Please. It's Himalette's unveiling party. You have guests."

"So, I'm 'Mother' now?" Pippet touched Brigitta's cheek. Her eyes grew misty. "Guess you don't really need me anymore."

"Don't say that. Of course I need you."

"It was only a matter of time." Pippet dug into her pocket for a bit of cloth and dabbed her eyes with it. "My big lola."

"How can I be big and be a lola at the same time?" Brigitta joked and then hugged Pippet to keep the tears from her own eyes.

As she snuggled against her momma's warm body, Minq burst

in through the door. "More pies! Faerie took all before get to table."

"That's because Momma makes the best pipberry pies in the entire forest."

Pippet gave Brigitta one final squeeze and then turned to pile more pies on the trays. Brigitta grabbed a ladle and started filling cups with the tea brewing in the vat over the fire. She glanced at Pippet's soft pink face and noticed new wrinkles around her eyes.

"And you should try her triple lyllium suclaide," Brigitta added. "It's a secret recipe. Maybe she'll have time to make a batch for us tomorrow."

Pippet beamed at her daughter. "Maybe."

From the porch, Brigitta stared out over the party guests. Mousha and Orl Featherkind were stringing a thunderbug symphony, Minq was fluttering around delivering pies, Edl Featherkind and a skinny Air Faerie with silky sky blue wings were stretching candlewebs across tree holes, and Auntie Ferna sat on a sturdy branch shooting flutterscarves out of a long hollow branch.

The object of a leaf race was to be the first to collect one of each color flutterscarf without touching them with your hands. Faerie children zipped around with giant leaves, trying to catch the elusive scarves that switched direction with the slightest breeze. Laughter filled the air as one boy used his wings to blow a scarf away from the faeries behind him.

Pippet floated past Brigitta with a tray of mugs. "You should join them. Have some fun."

Brigitta did want to join the fun. She wanted to forget about her worries and responsibilities and simply be a Tiragarrow faerie again. She lifted off from the porch, determined to have a good time, then stopped short as she felt an intense buzzing emanating from her chest. She dropped to the ground with a sharp cry, and several faeries turned to stare. Brigitta's hands went to her breast and found her hourglass necklace. It was warm and vibrating.

"Brigitta, what's wrong?" asked Glennis, hurtling herself toward Brigitta.

Fernatta stopped mid-scarf toss. The leaf racers turned to look as well. Pippet and Himalette flew to Brigitta's side.

Brigitta waved everyone off. "It's fine, it's just . . . my hourglass . . . Ondelle's never called me with it before."

"Ondelle's calling you?" Pippet looked astonished.

"Away from my unveiling party?" Himalette pouted and crossed her arms.

Several faeries began to whisper.

"I'm sorry, lola. Maybe she forgot?"

The partygoers slowly resumed their activities, buzzing quietly to each other. Pippet handed the tray of mugs to Glennis and shooed a disgruntled Himalette away. She stood arms akimbo and waited for an explanation.

"I have to go." Brigitta kissed her concerned mother's forehead. "Don't worry, Momma, I'm sure everything's just fine."

Chapter Two

Brigitta sped toward the Center Realm, taking a direct route rather than the roundabout one she usually took to avoid the popular sundreaming rocks along Spring River. The trees parted and she flew over the expanse of warm rocks lining the river, which created a shallow creek with little ponds of water that heated up in the sun.

Luckily, most of the local Water Faeries were gathered at Himalette's party, and the seasonal warmth of the Green Months, the best time for sundreaming, was waning as the Gray Months approached. Two older Earth Faeries floated on their backs in the ponds, an Air Faerie family picnicked on a table-shaped rock, and a Fire Faerie couple cuddled near the creek, so absorbed in each other they wouldn't have noticed if it were day or night. As she buzzed over them unnoticed, Brigitta relaxed.

Before she had been called to her Apprenticeship, Brigitta had spent most of the seasons after her return from the Dark Forest helping her momma around the cottage or in the quiet company of Minq and Gola. Himalette had been declared old enough to travel to her lessons on her own and the White Forest faeries had gone back to their simple pleasures. Even her poppa had returned to the numerous experiments that absorbed his time. Only her momma's concerned glances and the pesky questions from Glennis intruded on her attempt to forget about her troublesome destiny markings.

Then, in the middle of the Grow Months, Jorris had died and Brigitta had been called to the Center Realm. That was when the whispers and nervous teasing began. She was very young for an Elder Second Apprentice and it was easy to draw conclusions about the similarities between her and Hrathgar.

As she zipped through the trees, she reached down to the hourglass dangling from around her neck. It was still vibrating and warm.

Why would Ondelle call her with the hourglass? What could be so important? Brigitta hovered in the air, suddenly realizing it must have been a mistake. The High Priestess was calling the Elders together and had forgotten that Brigitta had her hourglass necklace. But how could Ondelle forget something like that? She let go and continued her journey.

She entered a final long stretch of slender silverwood trees and then burst into the Center Realm, pausing only for a moment to gaze upon the Hourglass of Protection. It was suspended in its usual manner by the many twisted branches of the two immense uul trees on either side of it. It was less than a full season since it had been turned and the protective field around the forest renewed, but checking up on it every day was a habit Brigitta couldn't break.

The sturdy branches cradled the crystal structure as the colorful sands silently tumbled. The only sounds were the chittering birds and a few grawping grovens.

Satisfied that things were in order, Brigitta headed for the Elder Chambers entrance, a tunnel carved into a stone mound surrounded by an unassuming copse of trees. The Hive was the affectionate term many faeries used for the collection of caverns that made up the chambers, the living and training quarters, and the various dens for Elder magic practice and artistic pursuits. The caverns extended far below the ground, farther than Brigitta had ever imagined before her first official visit. And in the depths of the Hive were entrances to tunnels that diverged and spread beneath the entire forest.

When the Ancients created the White Forest to protect the elemental faeries from the outside world, they also created the Hive and its passages as further precaution, though against what Brigitta had no idea. The caverns seemed so counter to faerie nature that she often wondered if the Ancients could see in the dark. Or *hear in dark*, as Minq would put it. She pictured tall elegant Ancients with long ears trailing behind them and snickered at the irreverent thought.

Still smiling at the absurd image, she entered the tunnel and flew straight into First Water Apprentice Flanna of Rioscrea and First Fire Apprentice Thane of Tintlebar. Flanna startled and dropped the red fire flower she was carrying.

Flanna was a large Water Faerie, but well-proportioned and strong. She had bright yellow wings and hair so red it matched the flower. Thane was tall and thin with dark features and lovely cobalt wings that everyone admired, including Thane himself.

"Oh, sorry," Brigitta mumbled as she dropped down to pick up the flower.

Flanna brushed her aside and snatched up the flower. She wiped it off and scowled at Brigitta. "The tunnels are not a racetrack, Apprentice Brigitta."

"Ondelle called me," Brigitta held up her hourglass necklace, immediately regretting doing so.

Thane and Flanna exchanged looks.

"Well," was all Thane said.

"I hope you aren't in any trouble, dear," added Flanna, arranging the petals of her flower. "Your lack of discipline reflects directly on me, you realize."

"I'm sure it's nothing. Excuse me, Apprentice Flanna, Thane." Brigitta turned and flew off, feeling the heat of their stares as she continued through the passageway.

Flanna was nearly as old as her momma, but Brigitta thought she acted more like a spoiled child. And she was definitely never maternal toward Brigitta. One of Flanna's duties was taking all the Seconds to Green Lake north of Dionsdale for water studies, and Brigitta always got the feeling Flanna resented any progress she made.

She rounded a corner and stopped, hovering in the air. Was it just her imagination or did Flanna really think ill of her? She held the hourglass in her hand and closed her eyes, letting her thoughts go, and misting her mind out. Brigitta's mind-mist gravitated to Flanna's energy using the lingering feeling of Flanna's skin brushing against her.

A moonsbreath later Brigitta was looking into Thane's sparkling eyes.

I wonder what that's all about? said Flanna, her voice reverberating inside Brigitta's own head.

Do I detect a hint of jealousy? Thane replied.

Flanna playfully swatted him on the head with the flower. *Jealous of a Second Apprentice?* she replied. *Don't be silly. She's not that bright. Look, she doesn't even know not to pick up someone else's reddened fire flower.* She giggled like a young girl.

Thane laughed. *Is it damaged? I can pick another one.*

"Brigitta!"

Brigitta opened her eyes. Ondelle was traveling toward her through the passageway. Her expression was serious.

"Oh. I was just—"

"Practicing a little empathing?" asked Ondelle.

If Brigitta wasn't in trouble before, as Flanna had suggested, she was now. She let go of the necklace and landed on the ground.

"I just don't like others talking about me behind my back," she mumbled.

"Is that what they were doing?" asked Ondelle, her expression unreadable.

Brigitta only nodded.

Ondelle studied Brigitta with tired eyes. "We've been waiting for you," she finally said. "Come along."

"Waiting for me?" Brigitta asked as she trailed after Ondelle through the tunnel. "You meant to call me away from Himalette's unveiling party?"

Ondelle turned, puzzled for a moment. "Oh. I had forgotten."

She glanced up the passageway and then back to Brigitta. "Do you need to return?"

"It's all right," said Brigitta, trying to read Ondelle's face. She was distracted, that was obvious, but when had Brigitta ever known the High Priestess to forget anything?

Ondelle continued and Brigitta trailed after her. As they drew closer to the Elder Chambers she thought about something else. It dawned on her that without much effort, she had empathed another faerie. Even though she was probably going to get a severe lecture from Water Elder Dervia about invasion of privacy and irresponsible behavior, she couldn't help feeling just a little bit smug.

Ondelle and Brigitta entered the first chamber, a high-ceilinged cavern lit by numerous webs of candles and slices of globelight strung along the walls. Nine wooden chairs and a long wooden table dominated the room. The furniture was as old as the Chambers, having been crafted by the Ancients themselves. The room served as the Elders' primary gathering space and was where they counseled the other White Forest faeries.

Earth Elder Adaire of the village-nest of Dmvyle, Air Elder Fozk of Fhorsa, Fire Elder Hammus of Bobbercurxy, and Water Elder Dervia of Dionsdale were clustered around a woven basket on the table. As Ondelle and Brigitta landed, the Elders turned away from the basket, blocking it from view. Fozk, whose white hair and beard looked as if they were made of clouds and his long blue wings from a piece of sky, nodded to Dervia.

"Really, Priestess," Dervia approached, flitting her forest green wings, their yellow destiny markings shimmering in the candlelight, "my Second Apprentice?" She sent a terse smile to Brigitta and then jerked her gaze back to Ondelle.

The Elders were known to be less cavalier than most other faeries, but the tone of the room was unusually grave. It didn't take any empathing at all to detect the dark mood. Not even Hammus, the smooth-faced socialite fond of playful jokes and festive parties, was smiling. He pulled his tawny wings together as he looked from one Elder to the next.

Ondelle simply gestured to Brigitta, who meekly followed her to the table.

The Elders stepped back. Adaire sat down in her chair, shaking her head. Her black and silver hair spilled out of her bun onto her stocky shoulders.

Ondelle reached into the basket and pulled back a blanket. Sleeping inside was a tiny newborn Earth Faerie with dark features and a square body.

"Brigitta, meet Duna of Dmvyle. Three moons old." Ondelle studied the baby.

"This has nothing to do with Dmvyle." Adaire pointed at the basket. "This has never happened in my village-nest before."

"This has never happened in any village-nest before, Elder Adaire," said Fozk.

"That we know of," added Hammus.

"I'm sure it would have been chronicled," said Dervia, "and Fernatta would have mentioned it. She has studied every journal as far back as they go."

The Elders gave exasperated sighs and paced about the room. Brigitta was very confused. She peered into the basket. The Earth Faerie baby had all her limbs and two honey-colored wings tucked beneath her.

"I don't understand," said Brigitta as the baby yawned and opened her eyes. They were crystal white. "Oh!" she exclaimed.

"She has no destiny." Ondelle reached in, picked the baby up, and cradled it in her arms. "The Ethereals have not visited her. If they had, her eyes would be colored. Green or brown I would imagine by the look of her."

"Maybe they just haven't done it yet?" suggested Brigitta, who had never spent much time around newborn babies.

"Perhaps, though it would be quite unusual," answered Ondelle.

"Unusual?" blurted Fozk with a laugh.

"Unheard of," corrected Dervia.

The baby started to cry. Adaire grabbed a leaf from a bowl on the table and held it on Duna's tongue until she stopped crying.

"Yes, wean her on ceunias leaf." Dervia threw her hands in the air.

"She'll need a tremendous amount of it later to deal with the embarrassment of her village-nest," grunted Hammus.

"Embarrassment!" Adaire spun to face him.

"Enough!" Ondelle placed the baby back in the basket. "Elders, hold your tongues!"

Brigitta looked around the room at the agitated Elders. She had never heard the High Priestess raise her voice to anyone. Not that she had been invited to one of their private gatherings before, but she was pretty sure this wasn't how they usually acted behind closed doors. Was one destiny-less child all that terrible? Surely the White Forest faeries would be kind to her and find something she liked to do.

Just then, the Center Realm sprite, Vivilia, flew into the room. "Ondelle, the baby's parents are getting worried. What shall I tell them?"

If there were such a thing, Brigitta would call Vivilia the Elder Sprite. She knew Vivilia as the sprite who had given her and Himalette the protection of Blue Spell when the forest had been threatened by Hrathgar's stone curse, something that had never made any sense to her according to what she knew about the laws of Blue Spell magic. Then again, there was a growing list of things she didn't understand and a growing list of things she'd learned that the Elders kept to themselves, like the fact that Ondelle had sent Vivilia up to Dead Mountain to check on Hrathgar, who in turn had used the sprite to sneak the stone spell into the White Forest in the first place.

Sometimes Brigitta saw Vivilia flying in or out of Ondelle's private den. She never spoke directly to Brigitta, but whenever their eyes met, the sprite would smile slightly, just enough to remind Brigitta of their shared history.

"Tell them . . . " Ondelle looked to the blank expressions of her Elders, "that they will all stay in the Center Realm tonight and we will have an answer in the morning. And give them anything they require."

Vivilia looked a bit put off by being requested to do the work of an Apprentice, but Brigitta figured none of the other Apprentices had been told about the baby. The sprite simply nodded and left the room.

"The parents, Vivilia, and the six of us are the only ones who know about this situation," said Ondelle, as if empathing Brigitta's thoughts.

"Not for long, I'm afraid," Fozk admitted.

Ondelle looked down at the baby and addressed Brigitta, "A child receives its destiny when the Ethereals visit it through its first dream. This usually happens—"

"Always happens," Dervia muttered.

"—within the first few hours of its birth," continued Ondelle. "So, what suppositions can you make from this?"

Brigitta wrinkled her brow in thought. "Well, maybe the baby hasn't had its first dream yet. Or maybe it can't dream at all?"

"Nothing we haven't covered already," said Dervia. "Simple empathing tells us the child dreams."

"Maybe it needs longer ones?" Brigitta suggested. "Or deeper ones? Have you tried giving it triple lyllium suclaide?"

"Ha!" called Hammus.

Brigitta's cheeks flushed and she clenched her teeth. What were they expecting she could do about any of this?

"We must find a spell for the parents," concluded Dervia. "Something that will make them forget this ever happened."

"I'm sure I can give some color to her eyes," said Adaire, contemplating the small bundle in the basket. "Perhaps a combination of hennabane and—"

"You mean lie to everyone in the forest?" blurted Brigitta in disbelief.

The Elders sank into silence.

"Ondelle, perhaps she isn't old enough to understand the implications," Dervia finally spoke up.

"Then why don't you explain them to her?" proposed Ondelle. Something in her tone stilled Brigitta's breath.

Dervia's jaw twitched. She lowered her voice. "I'd rather she be excused."

"Are you going to give me a forgetting spell, too?" chided Brigitta. She knew she was being insolent, but the words escaped before she could catch them in time.

Ondelle placed a hand on Brigitta's upper back between her wings, immediately calming the young faerie. She turned to look into Ondelle's black moon eyes. The High Priestess's fiery red wings fanned the air behind her.

"Why am I even here?" asked Brigitta. "What can I do that the Elders can't?"

Ondelle gestured with her hands and a kiss of wind flew out from them and into the tunnels. "Elder Adaire, take the child to its parents and make sure they are comfortable," she said.

Adaire picked up the basket and left the room. A moment later, the kiss of air returned, and with it a male Air Faerie with long graceful teal wings and a female Air Faerie with translucent purple ones, both sporting three bold bars of matching darker color on the tops of their wings, marking them as Perimeter Guards. The male carried a jar inside of which floated a fuzzy yellow light.

Brigitta gasped and ran to the jar. "A whisper light!"

"You know what this thing is?" the male guard asked as he landed. "We found it east of Rivenbow."

The three remaining Elders stiffened and their nervous glances returned. Ondelle observed Brigitta, expressionless.

Brigitta tapped on the glass and the whisper light tapped back.

She thought about her first encounter with the floating lights, when Himalette almost followed one right into the River That Runs Backwards. She couldn't hear any whispers now. The glass must muffle the sounds.

"Did it say anything to you?" she asked innocently.

"Oh, uh, some nonsense about me deserving to be Lead Guard." The male cleared his throat. "Although Trease here seems to think it said something else." He indicated his guard partner, whose cheeks turned pink. "Tell them, Trease."

"It told me how elegant my wings are," she said quietly.

Brigitta burst out laughing. The Elders stared at her as she pointed to the jar.

"Whisper lights only tell you what you want to hear," she said, composing herself. "There's a whole field of them outside Gola's old tree in the Dark Forest."

A chill went down Brigitta's spine as she caught the worried looks on everyone's faces. The gravity of what she had just said dawned on her as she watched the fuzzy little light tapping against the inside of the jar.

For the first time in almost one thousand season cycles, something uninvited to the White Forest had gotten in.

Chapter Three

After Brigitta had relayed all of her experiences with whisper lights, Ondelle requested that she wait in her living quarters until further notice. Wait for what, she didn't know, but she was certain her name would come up in whatever heated discussion they had behind their heavy wooden doors. It seemed like everyone in the entire forest was talking about her behind her back.

But everything wasn't about her, she scolded herself. She was being self-absorbed, feeling sorry for herself, yet again.

She spiraled down the tunnel to the second level, where the Apprentices and Wisings lived. Brigitta was still not used to living underground. The air particles were treated with a glow, in much the same manner as a globelight, but on a larger scale, so that the tunnels were surprisingly light. It was being enclosed that Brigitta didn't like, especially in the narrow bits. It reminded her of the carnivorous caterpillar caverns in the Dark Forest.

As she rounded the bend, she nodded at Kiera and Lalam, two Center Realm Wisings, who were headed in the other direction. The Wisings were always more polite than the rest of the Apprentices, perhaps because they were destined to remain Apprentices. Since there were only four Elders at any given time, not every Apprentice would have the opportunity to become one, so there were always a few Wisings in the Center Realm who spent their lives in service to the others.

The Elders were lucky that Air Faerie Perimeter Guards took their Life Task so seriously, Brigitta thought as she entered her room and closed the door. They were honored to keep a secret for the Elders and proud to have discovered something so unique. Perhaps that male guard would get his promotion after all.

They were so proud, though, that they hadn't completely grasped the significance of their find. What lurked in Faweh wasn't all pretty whisper lights. What if something more menacing had gotten in? What if something more menacing *could* get in?

"And what did that whisper light have to do with Duna of Dmvyle?" Brigitta asked out loud. She couldn't see how the two things were connected, but something in Ondelle's distracted gaze told her that they were.

She moved across her small space to the mirror over her desk and gazed at her reflection. Her dark auburn hair had come loose from its bands and she had a pipberry stain above her lips. No wonder none of the Elders had taken her seriously.

"Is it so bad for a faerie to choose her own destiny?" she asked her reflection as she licked her finger and rubbed the pink spot from her face.

"Would you have chosen yours?" her image replied.

Brigitta couldn't answer that. She didn't know.

"Auntie Ferna chose hers," Brigitta reminded herself. "She was an Elder when they had to banish the Hrathgars. Not many faeries know that, and the older ones have forgotten."

She stared into her image's olive eyes.

"I wonder what other secrets the Elders are keeping?" her image asked.

Brigitta had been thinking the same thing. Of course, that was what the Thought Mirror was for, to meditate on one's thoughts. It only spoke the thoughts of the faerie looking into it, and only if the faerie were alone. Brigitta liked being alone with her thoughts, although lying in the lyllium field was a much better place to do it.

She stretched out her wings. The eye glyph and element symbols had grown sharper since they had appeared, revealing her destiny as an Elder, and were a richer shade of green.

"Still there," her image pointed out the obvious, "and not going away."

There was a knock at the door. Her image froze.

"Come in," Brigitta called, moving to her bed and sitting down.

Brigitta startled as Ondelle opened the door and entered the room. She closed the door behind her. Her presence filled the space, as if the Great Moon itself had walked in the door.

"It has been a long time since I have been inside an Apprentice's room." She approached the mirror. Brigitta's frozen image faded away. "I still use my own Thought Mirror," she continued and smiled.

Brigitta sat silently on her bed while Ondelle surveyed the rest of the room. Her gaze landed on the necklace around Brigitta's neck, which was back to its original cool temperature. Brigitta's hand instinctively went to the hourglass.

Ondelle sat down on the bed next to Brigitta and bounced up and down a little. "I believe these are the same beds from when I was an Apprentice."

She stopped bouncing and looked Brigitta straight on. Her deep black eyes conveyed knowledge and experience beyond the faerie realm and a heaviness that suggested she alone bore the weight of her kin.

"Do you like it here in the Hive?" Ondelle suddenly asked. The familiar term sounded strange coming from the High Priestess's lips.

"In the Hive? Oh, well . . . " Brigitta shrugged her wings.

"I had a difficult time making friends when I was your age," Ondelle said, then laughed. "I still do, as a matter of fact."

It had never dawned on Brigitta that Ondelle might need friends or that she cared about being lonely. At least, she assumed Ondelle was lonely. She was an only child, her mother had dispersed when she was quite young, and her father had dispersed just before Brigitta was born.

"About what happened earlier with First Apprentice Flanna." Ondelle stood up and began pacing the small room.

"It won't happen again," blurted Brigitta. "I promise."

"Not in that way," Ondelle agreed. "We will train you to empath others safely." She stopped pacing and looked down at Brigitta. "And wisely."

It was not the response Brigitta had expected to hear, but she waited for Ondelle to continue. She was certain Ondelle was not there to discuss her studies.

"Aside from your sister Himalette, who seems to have recovered from her experience, you, Vivilia, and I are the only living White Forest faeries who have been outside our forest. It sounds incredible, but it's true. The elemental faeries have become, I'm afraid, isolated and . . ."

"Spoiled?" Brigitta suggested.

Ondelle laughed, "I was going to say 'comfortable' but I rather like your choice of words."

"Our faeries don't like anything too out of the ordinary, do they?" said Brigitta.

"No," Ondelle said through a sigh, "and things will get a lot less ordinary unless we do something about it." She drew closer to Brigitta and put her hand on the young faerie's cheek. Her palm felt soft and warm and Brigitta wanted to close her eyes and melt into it. "I just wish we didn't have to ask so much of you."

"Of me?" Brigitta sat up. "What can I do?"

"Come with me." Ondelle offered her hand. "There's something else I need to show you."

Ondelle led her farther into the Hive than Brigitta had ever traveled. As they descended, spiraling through the tunnels, the light grew dimmer and the passage narrower. The third level was where the four Elders and Ondelle lived, the fourth level where they practiced magic in various spell chambers, and the fifth level where they kept Center Realm herbs, potions, and important texts.

They landed in the fifth level in an odd cylindrical library. Between the shelves of books, dark tunnels radiated in four directions. The whisper light hovered in its jar on a wooden pedestal against the far wall. It glowed in the dim light with a kind of intelligence. Brigitta could swear that it was watching her.

"I wonder how it's still yellow," Brigitta wondered aloud, "and alive?"

"It shouldn't be?" asked Ondelle as she opened a cupboard in the wall and removed a book. A hole appeared in the middle of the floor and she dropped down into it.

"Gola said they only last a few suns," said Brigitta as she followed.

They landed in a small antechamber with no tunnels. The light was reduced to an eerie green, thick vines stretched along the walls, and earthy roots met them coming up from the edges of the ceiling and floor.

Elder Dervia stood there looking especially nervous, and another faerie lay on a stone altar in the center of the room. At first Brigitta thought the faerie, a large male with grayish blue wings and matching grayish blue hair, was sleeping. But she couldn't detect an element bound to him. As she stepped closer, she realized it was Jorris of Rioscrea, the Water Faerie Elder Dervia had replaced.

"But . . ." Brigitta gasped, "Elder Jorris! Isn't he—I thought he had—"

"Died, yes," responded Ondelle, who nodded to Dervia.

"Ondelle, must we?" Dervia wrung her hands. "She's still a child."

"We have settled this matter," Ondelle said, alluding to their private meeting while Brigitta waited in her room. "The signs cannot be ignored."

Sighing in resignation, Dervia signaled to Brigitta, who crept closer and leaned over Jorris's body. He hadn't changed much, which Brigitta found astonishing. She remembered him as jovial and kind, and she knew it wasn't fair, but a part of her resented him for dying. His death had pulled her away from her days of shelling gundlebeans with her momma, daydreaming with Minq, and sorting seeds with Gola.

Dervia lifted Jorris's left eyelid with her finger. His glassy brown eye shone back. She let his eyelid drop again.

"When a faerie's destiny is fulfilled, he or she dies, and the Ethereals claim the spirit," said Ondelle. "You're familiar with dispersement, of course."

"His eyes!" Brigitta exclaimed. "I saw it happen to Hrathgar Good. Her eyes returned to crystal white when she died."

"Correct," said Ondelle. "His spirit has not been dispersed."

As soon as Ondelle spoke the words Brigitta felt it. Another presence was in the room like a soft, dark cloud hovering behind Dervia, as if listening in. Its water energy was a faint mist easily overlooked. She sensed it now.

"As with Duna, the Ancients should have visited him. A destiny at birth, a dispersement with death. Until Duna was born, we did not know if Jorris's condition was an isolated incident." Ondelle handed Brigitta the antiquated book she had taken from the library. "Read what it says on the inside cover, please."

Wary of the silent presence now making its way around the room, Brigitta took the book, which was so heavy she nearly dropped it. She opened the faded cover and was surprised to see a poem in bright blue ink, as if it had been written that morning. She cleared her throat and read:

When forest spirits cannot leave home
And babes keep eyes of crystal white
When tongues of Elders start to moan
So will come a guiding light
And she who calls it by its name
Who knows it from its forest kin
Will travel back to times of old
To make the balance right again.

Brigitta's heart dropped into her stomach. "Who wrote that?" she whispered, looking up from the book.

"We're not sure," replied Ondelle gently. "This is the very first White Forest book written by the very first Chronicler, so we suppose it was the Chronicler herself."

"It could be a nursery rhyme for all we know," added Dervia, although she sounded unconvinced of this.

"It's all true. The dead keeping their eyes, the child not getting her destiny . . . " The air in the antechamber suddenly felt very thin to Brigitta, and the walls too close, making her head spin. The book began to slip from her hand.

"And she who calls it by its name . . . I had suspected." Ondelle caught the book and tucked it under her arm. "Now you know why I summoned you."

"No, no I don't," stammered Brigitta. "Why me? Why not Himalette or Gola or . . . or . . . They've seen whisper lights, too!" She looked from Ondelle to Dervia and then dropped her head.

Ondelle took the young faerie by the shoulders. "I think you know the answer to that already." She lifted up Brigitta's chin to look into her eyes. "Brigitta, undispersed spirits do not relinquish their elements to the next generation. When a spirit is dispersed, a new child is born bound to that element. It is a cycle of balance."

Brigitta's eyes welled up with tears. "You mean no more Water Faeries will be born if Jorris isn't dispersed?"

"If this trend continues, no more faeries of any element will be born."

"Duna . . ." Brigitta's thought trailed off. The little destinyless Earth Faerie could be the last one of her kind.

"Also, we have no idea, without the Ancients, if the Hourglass spell will last through the season cycle. But we do know, without the Ancients, it cannot be turned."

Ondelle let go of Brigitta and straightened up, looking at Dervia with a combination of sadness and apology.

"You may be the one to explain everything to her mother and father." Dervia's thin lips trembled. "My Life Task includes protecting my Apprentices, not sending them headlong into situations for which they are unprepared!" With that Dervia flew up through the ceiling.

"I cannot insist you come with me," said Ondelle, ignoring

Dervia's outburst. "I leave it completely up to you. There are dangers I know nothing about."

"Go with you where?" asked Brigitta, sensing Jorris's spirit slumping to the floor in despair.

"To the faerie ruins in the Valley of Noe. I will depart in four suns' time."

Chapter Four

Alone in the ancient library as the other Apprentices went about their duties, Brigitta wondered how her absence would be accounted for. What lies would be piled on top of the growing number of secrets? She glanced at the whisper light, still floating in its jar, still watching her. A choice had to be made about traveling to Noe, and Ondelle insisted Brigitta decide without her influence.

She turned her attention to the passageway on her left. Ondelle had informed her that it led to the Fire Faerie Realm and had granted her permission to use it. Being awarded this kind of privilege would have shocked her that morning, but so much can change between one sun's rising and setting.

The tunnel was dark and still. She didn't have to take this route, but it would mean avoiding any Elders and Apprentices. She rubbed her globelight until it shone brightly in all directions and entered the tunnel.

Sticking to the main passage wasn't easy. There were so many enticing smaller tunnels. She heard water rushing from a few and saw long roots dangling from the ceilings of others, roots so long they created tempting curtains to pass through. At one point there were markings on the walls in silvery-blue: three large circles with squares inside of them and another circle inside each square. Brigitta studied them a moment before moving on.

To her amazement, she wasn't frightened in the underground passageways. She felt rather comforted because no one except Ondelle knew where she was. There was something very delicious about that fact.

After several moonbeats, the main tunnel began to narrow and curve upward until Brigitta emerged from the stump of a large dead tree on the northeast border of the Fire Faerie Realm. Lola Spring River, the smaller of the two White Forest rivers, ran south here, then turned west toward Bobbercurxy, the largest village-nest of the realm. Hrathgar's childhood home.

She flew downriver to the bend, where she could just make out the colorful tents and flags of the Bobbercurxy marketplace, then crossed over the river and slipped into the silverwood trees on the other side. She kept south until she came to the fire flower farm. The flowers were pale pink, as they remained until a faerie's passion deepened the color.

Brigitta shook her head, recalling Flanna's red flower. What a frivolous plant, she thought. It wasn't good for eating and had no healing properties. She plucked a flower from the end of the last row and sniffed it. It was odorless. Who cared if it could stay fresh for many moons after it was picked if one couldn't even use it to scent a room?

The Master Gardener, Trovish of Grioth, was nowhere in sight. This didn't surprise Brigitta, as he was known to spend most of his time north at the Air Faerie marketplace in Rivenbow. For some reason, Air Faeries were especially fond of fire flowers. Perhaps they were the most frivolous faeries of all, she concluded. She stuffed the flower into her tunic pocket as she flew from the farm.

She followed a path southeast until she came to a crooked tree with an enormous burl at the bottom, carved out to make room for Gola's home. It was smaller than her Dark Forest home, but Gola insisted she needed very little and preferred puttering around her expanding gardens to hiding in her tree.

As Brigitta approached, she could see Gola pushing a seed mixture into little holes in the burl. Brigitta and Minq had helped carve out the holes so that Gola could plant mosses and ivies on the outside of her home, something she could never do in the Dark

Forest because the beasts insisted on eating or poisoning the mixture before it could sprout. It seemed to Brigitta that Gola, too, found more trivial things to do living in the White Forest. She had gotten *comfortable*.

As Brigitta approached, the little bat-winged Eyes perched on Gola's shoulder turned around and opened wide. If the Eyes could smile, she figured that's what they were doing, so she smiled back.

"Hello, dear child," Gola said without turning away from her task. Her barky fingers continued their work. "One moment and I'll fetch us some tingermint tea." Gola smoothed the seed mixture down with her thumb and then dropped the remainder of the mixture into a little silver bucket.

She slowly straightened herself to step away from her work, but her left foot was stuck. Brigitta watched in dismay as Gola bent down and ripped her foot away from the ground with her hands. She grunted as the roots of her foot broke free from the earth, and she lost her balance.

"Gola!" exclaimed Brigitta, steadying the old Drutan. "Are you all right?"

Gola gave a harsh chuckle, her empty eye sockets squinting in the direction of Brigitta's voice. "A tree-woman of my age should know better than to stand in one place for so long!"

Her Eyes fluttered to the door and Brigitta followed, helping Gola into her tree-home. She led Gola to a chair and then went to the kitchen to dish out some tea. Gola raised her feet onto some old blankets piled under the table and let out a tremendous sigh.

"The earth calls to me and I find it harder and harder to resist." Her Eyes landed on her shoulder, closed themselves, and leaned into her barky neck.

Brigitta placed the mugs on the table and sat down. She glanced around the walls, at the small shelf holding Gola's moonstone pots, at another shelf of books, and at the fading map of Foraglenn.

"Gola, where are all your other Eyes?"

"Bah! Too much effort to hold all those images in my weary mind.

I released them to the flying fields. The Air Faerie children are looking after them. Or vice versa, perhaps."

Her remaining pair of Eyes blinked open and gazed at Brigitta. Even they looked old and tired.

"Don't you need them?" Brigitta asked.

"You forget, dear, my destiny is complete. I could lie down right now in the fire flowers and root myself if I so desired."

"But you won't, will you?" Brigitta's voice caught in her throat.

"Not yet, child, not yet." Gola reached for her tea and took a sip. "First I must perfect this tea your mother makes so well."

"And there's Minq," Brigitta said quietly. "He would miss you."

"You didn't come here to talk about me rooting myself to the earth," said Gola, always one to get straight to the point. "Spill your thoughts."

Brigitta told Gola, whom Ondelle trusted completely, about the poem inside the ancient book that predicted the white-eyed baby, the non-dispersed Elder, and the naming of the whisper light. Then she relayed the heavy decision she had to make about traveling to Noe.

"Hmmm, I was aware of Elder Jorris's condition, but not the rest."

"You were?" asked Brigitta.

"I was asked to be advisor to your council, remember?" Gola gestured to her door with her tea mug. "Though none but Ondelle ever bothers to visit."

"Ondelle comes here? To your home?"

"You expect me to lug myself to the Center Realm?"

Brigitta didn't know how she felt about the fact that Gola kept things from her as well. As much as she loved Gola, there were seasons and seasons of her life that Brigitta knew nothing about.

Glancing up at the map of Foraglenn on the wall, she asked, "Were you ever in Noe? Is that how you got your map?"

Gola burst out laughing, "Good grovens, it would have taken half my life to get there and back!"

She placed her mug down on the table. The Eyes fixed their gaze on Brigitta. "After the Great World Cry left Faweh in complete chaos, a young Noe faerie named Narine gave me that map and asked me to tend to the whisper lights."

Brigitta choked on her drink. Gola waited patiently while she coughed and caught her breath. "She—who— what?" she managed. "How come you never told me?"

"I am telling you now."

"Who was she?"

"She was an Ancient, daughter to the High Sage of Noe. She saved my life and we became friends."

Brigitta stared at Gola in disbelief and annoyance. Why did Gola, and every other so-called wise being, always leave out the important details?

"Do not let your anger get the best of you," Gola pointed a barky finger in Brigitta's direction. "Listen. My destiny has always been entwined with that of the faeries, but it is not my place to interfere with yours. I answer my own calling, understand?"

"Yes," said Brigitta meekly. She gripped her mug in her lap and waited for Gola to continue.

"The elemental faeries could not hide in the White Forest forever and they were not meant to. It was far too dangerous after the Great World Cry, but the Ancients knew there would come a time when an attempt to heal Faweh was necessary. At that time, the whisper lights would be released and deliver their true messages to the old civilizations."

"What do you mean?" Brigitta could hold her tongue no longer. "What true messages?"

"That is as much as I know."

"But you said whisper lights only tell you what you want to hear," said Brigitta. "How would anyone know if the message they received was true?"

"You would know." Gola lifted a necklace from her tunic. Five black moonstones dangled on the chain and caught the light.

It was the kind of answer that always exasperated Brigitta. How do you know when you know something? She watched as Gola rubbed the glossy surface of the first stone with her thumb.

"I was new to the world when Narine saved my life; I had no destiny yet. My moonstones formed later that night." Gola emitted a soft snort. "It was no surprise when, over time, each one revealed a new service to the faeries. I was never bitter about my destiny, though, until young Hrathgar broke my heart."

Brigitta stared at the last moonstone on the chain. Ondelle had told her Gola's final destiny was to help save the White Forest from Hrathgar's curse. But Hrathgar had stolen the stone, so Gola didn't even know she was supposed to help the faeries until after she already had. Did that mean destiny was destiny no matter what?

As Brigitta pondered this question, invisible tendrils of energy wove out from the moonstone, criss-crossing toward her like twisting fingers reaching through the air. Without thinking, she leaned forward and touched it with her index finger. A cacophony of images swarmed through her mind—

A boy with starry eyes, dark footprints leading up a rocky path, a mossy field encased in vibrating glass, Elder Fozk with panic on his face and beard whipping in the wind, a winding circular metal structure inside a cave, Glennis leaning over the side of a boat with yellow sails—

The images vanished as quickly as they had appeared and she was back in Gola's den, her body tight with tension, her breath still. She gasped for a lungful of air as Gola felt her way around her kitchen, her pair of Eyes on the table, studying Brigitta face.

"I'm sorry," Brigitta said once she had caught her breath, "I didn't mean to touch it. I just . . . "

"Couldn't help it," said Gola as she opened a jar and scooped out some brown powder. Her Eyes fluttered to her shoulder and she dropped the powder into a beaker of clear liquid. She stirred the mixture with her thin wooden pinky. "You are one who always reaches for answers."

Brigitta didn't know if that was a good or bad thing, considering all the trouble Hrathgar had gotten into seeking too many answers for herself. But she was not like Hrathgar. Was she?

"What were all those images I saw?" asked Brigitta, trying to conjure them again.

"Possible choices you will have to make."

The images were unfamiliar. Even the ones of Fozk and Glennis were out of context, and the faeries looked seasons older. It felt as if Brigitta had, in a moment, seen her life spread before her, but that the events had happened many seasons in the past and she could barely recall them. It was discomforting. She made a mental note never to touch Gola's moonstones ever again.

Gola removed a spell seed from her shelf. She spun it around three times, dipped a finger into a jar of water, and added three drops to the top of the seed. It opened and she poured the mixture inside.

The images were not from the White Forest. Did that mean she had no choice but to leave her home again? Were any of the images of Noe or were they other journeys to come? When Gola's Eyes turned to her, she remembered the image of a boy, perhaps her own age. His eyes had been a deep crystal blue.

Gola handed her the spell seed. It weighed about the same as the one she had used on her trip to Dead Mountain.

"For strength?" asked Brigitta, thinking about the burst of energy Gola's potion had provided when she entered the cave of the River That Runs Backwards.

"For courage."

Chapter Five

Brigitta stared into the space just above the green zynthia sitting on the table in the Elder Chambers. Even though it was only one small crystal, the one she had brought back from Dead Mountain, just having it in the same room with her made her nervous. She knew how zynthias made one's mind weak and prone to suggestion. It was through green zynthia hypnosis that Hrathgar had managed to trick Vivilia into bringing the stone curse into the White Forest.

Brigitta took a deep breath and, as she released it, filled her mind with water energy, letting the cool presence settle there. She then imagined the water energy saturating her whole being, making her strong. At last she imagined this strength expanding, forming a protective shield around her, cocooning her inside.

She lowered her gaze. As it landed on the zynthia, she felt the crystal's power pushing through, and she pushed back. It was like pushing against a dark, thick cloud, elusive and unpredictable as it tried to slip past her. She pushed some more, struggling back and forth until the cloud finally enveloped her and her mind went blank.

Brigitta, a voice called from far away. A familiar voice. Where was it coming from? She couldn't see anything. She didn't know where she was.

"Brigitta?" Ondelle's face emerged from the haze.

Slowly, Brigitta grew conscious of her surroundings. She was sitting on the floor of the Elder Chambers as Ondelle held her by the shoulders.

"You did well." She smiled and helped Brigitta up.

A protective glass covered the green zynthia. Brigitta stared at it and nothing happened; she was safe.

"I didn't. The zynthia energy pushed through."

"The trick is never to push back." Ondelle looked into Brigitta's eyes. "It is about balance, always about balance."

"That's what Elder Dervia says."

"That's what all the Elders will tell you during your lessons, no matter which element is your focus."

"But the zynthia energy is different," Brigitta complained. "It doesn't react right with the elements. It's a mean energy. It wants something from me."

"When something is hungry, what do you do?"

"Feed it?"

"Exactly. I feed it my fire and air energy while reserving a balance for myself. There is no one way to do this. Practice will teach you your way."

Practicing with the zynthia had been Ondelle's idea. As promised, she hadn't pushed Brigitta to make a decision about going to Noe, but she wasn't going to delay any training. There were things she'd need to learn sooner or later, Ondelle had said.

"Why are you bringing it along?" asked Brigitta.

"It is a powerful tool. I'm sure it could be of use." Ondelle stared at the zynthia in the jar.

"Um, Ondelle," said Brigitta, "what exactly would you . . . would we be doing down in Noe?"

"We seek an item left behind by the Ancients."

"And this item will heal Faweh?" asked Brigitta.

"I am afraid it is not that simple," replied Ondelle, lost in thought as she contemplated the crystal. "But it is a step in the right direction."

She swept back around. "How did you enter Apprentice Flanna's mind?"

"She was just kind of open." Brigitta shrugged and then thought about it some more. At the time, she hadn't even hesitated. She had just done it. "I remember I held my hourglass and relaxed. I think Flanna was so open because she's in love with Thane."

Ondelle laughed. "I think you may be right." She touched the glass case. "Let us experiment. I will look into the zynthia and then open my mind to you. You will enter my mind and together we will be with the zynthia."

Brigitta's jaw dropped. Enter Ondelle's mind! That was completely absurd. But apparently Ondelle didn't think so, because she was lifting the glass again. Brigitta averted her eyes from the zynthia.

"Take hold of your necklace."

Brigitta's hand moved to her hourglass necklace and a moment later she felt a tickling energy around her, then a gentle prodding of cool air. She relaxed as much as possible and followed the energy back to Ondelle.

There, see? You are doing well.

Ondelle's mind was expansive. Brigitta suddenly felt larger than the entire forest, but completely focused at the same time. She could tell that all of the focus was Ondelle's doing, and that if not for the High Priestess' skill, she would have been scattered like sands in the wind. Through Ondelle's eyes, Brigitta gazed at the zynthia, no longer afraid. She could see its sharp green facets shining like eyes.

The most important thing to remember, Ondelle's mind spoke through her, *is that when you empath a thinking beast, you must stay connected to your own center. Do not forget yourself or become lost in the maze of unfamiliar thought and feeling. Usually one uses a personal item or memory as an anchor. I believe, for you, holding your hourglass has this effect.*

I would have chosen it, Brigitta realized, *if you had asked me to pick something.* The sound of her own thoughts reverberated through her. They mingled with Ondelle's as they admired the zynthia in front of them. *It's beautiful,* Brigitta's voice echoed.

Abruptly, Ondelle's energy slipped, like someone had poked at the fabric of it. She quickly rebalanced her energy and then dropped the glass lid on the zynthia. Just as quickly, Brigitta was back in her own mind in the room. It wasn't like a zynthia hypnosis or moonstone vision, though, which left her dazed and confused. Her senses actually felt sharper, picking up the vibrations of every item in the room.

"Someone else is here," Ondelle said, looking around. "The zynthia reached out to them."

Brigitta sensed it, too, and both of their gazes landed on the wall on the other side of the chamber's entryway.

❦

As Ondelle and Brigitta approached the hiding spot where Brigitta and her friends had spied on the Elders seasons before, they saw a young faerie collapsed on the ground.

She looked in their direction, eyes foggy.

"Glennis!" Brigitta exclaimed, rushing to her side. "She's a friend of Himalette's from Easyl," she told Ondelle.

"Brigitta." Glennis reached out to touch Brigitta's face, as if she didn't quite believe it were real. Her eyes met Ondelle's and she straightened up. "Ondelle!"

"Are you all right?" asked Ondelle.

"Yes, I . . . I think so . . . " stammered Glennis as she shook her head clear of the zynthia hypnosis.

"You shouldn't have been spying!" snapped Brigitta. "That was wrong of you! How did you even know—" Brigitta stopped. Glennis was cousin to Dinnae, who had been in the tunnel with Brigitta when they had spied on the Elders. Dinnae had a big mouth.

"I should have sealed that crack," Ondelle stared through the tunnel, "although, we have not had very many young spies lately."

Ondelle turned her attention back to Glennis, and Brigitta knew what she was thinking. They couldn't allow Glennis to share what she had overheard. The last thing they needed was for the White Forest faeries to start panicking.

Brigitta grimaced. She was just as wrapped up in secrets as the Elders.

Glennis's eyes shone a fear with which Brigitta was familiar. She felt a pang of pity for the young Water Faerie. Once you start to know things that you didn't know before, Brigitta thought, there's no going back. Unless you were young enough to forget about it all, like her sister had.

But Glennis was not so young. She was, Brigitta realized, only slightly younger than Brigitta had been when she had left the forest seven seasons ago.

"Ondelle," she lowered her voice, "please don't put a spell on her, or hypnotize her to make her forget."

Ondelle looked shocked. "No, of course not."

"Let me talk with her. In private."

Glennis fluttered around Brigitta's living quarters. She flew over the bed, looked at the books on her shelves, the beautiful ceremony beads hanging from her cabinet, and then landed in front of the mirror.

"You can really talk to yourself?" Glennis waved at the mirror, and her image waved back.

"Yes, yes," Brigitta was starting to regret inviting Glennis back to her room. Perhaps a forgetting spell would have been easier after all. "Glennis, please, sit down, we need to talk."

Glennis made a face in the mirror and then sat down on a stool, the effects of the zynthia completely worn off. "I can't believe I'm in your room! You must love it here! Do you stay up all night talking with the other Apprentices?"

"I know it seems exciting to you, but it's not like that. There's a lot of responsibility." Brigitta tried to command some of Ondelle's authority in her voice. "We live in a realm where faeries are safe and happy. That's because the Elders keep it that way. Sometimes, the Elders know things that the other faeries don't. Things I don't even know about. But that's why we have Elders, so all the other faeries don't have to worry about anything. So that they can be Song

Masters or Gardeners or Star Tellers—"

"I can keep a secret, Brigitta, if that's what you want to know." Glennis sat down next to Brigitta, who was surprised by her sudden directness. Her round face took on an unexpected seriousness. "You're leaving the White Forest again."

An image of the older Glennis flashed through Brigitta's mind. The Glennis Brigitta had seen when she had touched Gola's moonstone. In the vision, Glennis had looked at her with the same solemn expression. Brigitta noticed there were little flecks of dark yellow in Glennis's eyes that matched her wings.

"Yes," she finally said, realizing it was true, "I am."

"I won't tell anyone our forest is in danger."

"I—we—appreciate it," said Brigitta, believing her. "Oh, and I need a favor."

"Another one?" laughed Glennis, fluttering her wings.

"If anything happens, and I don't return, I need you to be there for Himmy, like a sister. And to fly with Minq and to make sure Gola has help in her garden."

"You'll come back," Glennis insisted, "I know you will. And you'll tell me all about it." Then she was back in the air, zipping around the room.

"Sure, Glennis, I'll tell you everything."

"I don't see why you have to go. It's unreasonable. You're a child!" Pippet paced across the living room as Mousha sat in his favorite mushroom chair, which swallowed him up in its cushy folds.

"I told you, Momma, it's because I've been outside the forest before. It's because of what I've seen and what I know."

She looked to her father for support. His eyes were filled with concern as he tapped his little yellow wings together.

"I'll be with Ondelle, Poppa," she reasoned. "Ondelle is more wise than any other faerie. She won't let anything happen to me."

"But it's so far away, much farther than before . . ." Pippet's eyes teared up and her voice cracked. "And simply to get some old faerie artifact?"

Brigitta swallowed her guilt. If she told them about the rhyme, she'd have to tell them about everything else. If she told them about everything else, she would only frighten them. She did not want to frighten them, Himmy, or anyone else if she could help it. Hopefully, she and Ondelle could fix whatever needed fixing and nobody would know the difference.

"We'll get the artifact and come right back," Brigitta said quietly. "It's important, Momma, I told you. The artifact will help keep the forest safe in the future. It was made by the Ancient Ones. It's *sacred*."

"I suppose it doesn't matter what I think, does it?" Pippet cried. "Oh, you are just like your poppa!"

There was an uncomfortable silence in the room as Pippet continued to pace. Brigitta's heart went out to her mother. Mousha glanced at Pippet and cleared his throat.

"Might others have the opportunity to examine this artifact?" he asked, leaning forward in his chair.

"Mousha!" scolded Pippet.

Himalette burst into the room, carrying a little package. She twirled in the air, showing off her wing markings, and landed in front of Brigitta.

"I made you a going away present!" Himalette thrust the package in front of Brigitta's face.

"Oh!" Pippet exclaimed and rushed from the room, dabbing her teary eyes with her tunic. Mousha struggled out of his chair and followed Pippet into the kitchen.

"It's a song drop!" exclaimed Himalette, oblivious to Pippet's outburst. "Song Master Helvine taught me to make it. I've been helping her since my Change. We released some unfinished songs on Green Lake today. It was amazing, all those notes bobbing on the water."

Brigitta took the package from her sister and opened the lid. Nestled in pink flower petals was a shiny silver teardrop the size of Brigitta's thumb.

"When you want to hear the song just drop it to the ground."

"It's lovely, Himmy. Thanks." She kissed her sister on the top of her head.

"It's my first one, but Helvine says I have a talent for it." Himalette's face lit up. "Tell Ondelle I made it. If she likes my song, maybe she'll let me make an official one for the Twilight Festival or even for the Festival of the Elements!"

"I'll be sure to tell her." Brigitta closed the package and tucked it into her pack. She doubted that Ondelle paid much attention to the choosing of festival songs, but she wasn't about to tell that to Himalette's eager face.

Mousha led Pippet back into the room. Pippet wore a strained smile, although Brigitta got the feeling it was only for Himalette's benefit. She held out a soft bag.

"Your suclaide."

"Thanks, Momma." Brigitta took the bag and squeezed Pippet's hand. "Well, I guess I should –"

"Wait!" exclaimed Mousha, "I've got something, too." He ran into his laboratory and retrieved a flat, green disc. He placed it in Brigitta's hand and crossed his arms.

"Uh . . . thanks . . . Poppa," Brigitta waved the floppy green thing in the air, releasing a faint boggy odor.

"No, not like that!" Mousha took the green disc back from Brigitta and spoke directly into it, "Like this!"

He rolled it up into a ball and flung it through the air. It hit the far wall and stuck with a splat.

"Like this! Like this! Like this!" it called from the wall in Mousha's voice.

"I'm not sure what to call it yet," Mousha tapped his wings together. "Vocal traveler? Throwing voice? Vorple blat?"

"Vorple blat!" laughed Brigitta.

"How about talking stinkball?" suggested Himalette, holding her nose. Brigitta playfully swatted her on the head.

"Fabulous thing and not as difficult as it looks. I ground some of Gola's chatterbud seeds, mixed them with groven saliva . . . "

"Ewwww!" Brigitta and Himalette squealed, looking at each other in disgust.

Mousha fluttered to the wall and peeled the blob off, leaving a round green stain. "It was meant to stay spherical, so you could bounce it or roll it or play catch."

"Who would want to play catch with that?" asked Himalette.

Brigitta flew to her poppa and hugged him. "It's wonderful. I love it!" She retrieved a scarf from the wall of her old bedroom, took the slimy disc between two fingers, and wrapped the scarf around it.

"All you need now is to invent something to clean up after it," said Pippet, examining the stained wall.

Brigitta laughed and hugged Pippet, who let out a heavy sigh and hugged her daughter back. Brigitta was relieved that the tension in the room had finally dissipated, and that she could remember her family like this in the moons to come.

"No, no, Apprentice Brigitta," scolded Elder Dervia, "you're not concentrating!"

Brigitta was tired of concentrating. She had never concentrated so much in her life. She had spent the past few suns in the private company of each Elder, while the other Apprentices prepared the festival grounds for a full forest gathering. Everyone had been told Brigitta and Ondelle were traveling somewhere, but no other details had been revealed. If Brigitta had been bothered by suspicious glares before, the situation was now downright unbearable, so she kept to herself when not in training.

After a transformation lesson from Elder Adaire, a lesson on how to manipulate firepepper from Elder Hammus, and mind-misting practice with Elder Fozk, Elder Dervia had Brigitta working on cloud gathering, which seemed like a waste of time. How would changing the clouds have helped her fight off a giant toad or a rock dragon?

Dervia cleared her throat and stared down her long nose at Brigitta, who braced herself for another lecture on her lack of discipline. "I apologize. You are tired. We are all tired."

An apology from Elder Dervia, Brigitta thought, that's new. She looked into her mentor's eyes and was surprised to detect genuine fear and concern. Elder-like, she told herself and straightened up. "It's all right, Elder Dervia. I'll try again."

Dervia nodded and sat down on a rock. They were on the edge of Green Lake in the northern border of the Water Realm. It was the best place in the forest to work with clouds, which gathered fluffy and white above them.

Taking a breath, Brigitta settled her mind and body, feeling only cloud energy. Slowly and carefully, she tested the weight of each one and found which held the most wetness. Guided by her gentle prodding, the cloud began to reform, graying as it grew denser.

"Yes," Dervia murmured. "Much better."

A subtle movement on the lake's surface drew Brigitta's attention and she lost her concentration. She groaned and was about to apologize when she noticed that the movement was due to raindrops pittering on the water as the cloud she had been working on released a gentle shower. She had done it! She turned to her mentor and smiled as the light rain continued to fall.

Dervia stood and took Brigitta's hands in her own. It was the first time the Elder had ever touched her. Her hands were cool and not unkind. "I am a harsh mentor, I realize. But much harsher tasks lie ahead for you."

Brigitta nodded.

The Elder gave Brigitta's hands a tight squeeze then turned her back around to face the lake. "Now, again."

❦

Back in Brigitta's room, Minq watched as she placed her sister's song drop into a little pouch and placed the pouch, along with her mother's suclaide, into her pack. Saying goodbye to Minq was harder than she had expected, but she wasn't going to cry. Elders-in-training don't cry, she told herself.

"I wish you could come with us," she said as she picked up her father's new invention. The smell alone was enough to leave it behind. "Ondelle says there's limited energy for traveling to Noe and back, and she wouldn't want anyone to get left behind."

"Will not be same forest without you," said Minq.

Brigitta was about to place the "talking stinkball" in her cabinet, but Minq's comment reminded her how much she had missed her family when she was in the Dark Forest. She placed the disc, well wrapped, in her pack along with her other gifts, then added her globelight, two firestones, some herbs from Elder Adaire, and finally Gola's courage potion. Ondelle would carry the zynthia, thank the Dragon.

"If you ask me, I go," Minq told her, touching her arm with the tip of his ear. "You save life. I yours."

Brigitta looked down into his sad rodent face and gave in to her tears. She wrapped her arms around him. "I yours, too, Minq."

He patted her back with an ear. "Do not doubt self."

Brigitta smiled as she pulled away and wiped her face. For a simple ground creature, as Gola called him, he sometimes had surprising insight.

They said their final goodbyes and Minq left to fetch Gola for the forest-wide departure ceremony. Brigitta plopped herself in front of her Thought Mirror.

"And she who calls it by its name, Who knows it from its forest kin, Will travel back to times of old, To make the balance right again," sang the image in the mirror. It had an annoying habit of reminding her of thoughts she'd rather ignore. She supposed that was the whole point.

"And how am I going to make the balance right again?" asked

Brigitta. "I can barely make rain."

"Who else would go with Ondelle?" her image asked. "Would you risk sending an Elder instead?"

"I'm sure we could do without one Elder for a few moons."

"The fate of the forest is at stake. What if no more elemental faeries are born? What if—"

"You're not helping!" Brigitta stomped away from her mirror and flopped onto her bed. She closed her eyes and counted her breaths.

Air Elder Fozk encouraged mind-misting as a meditative practice. Brigitta lay very still and allowed her thoughts to drift away. They misted out of her room and reached through the halls, navigating around the forms of Apprentice faeries.

They spiraled down through the Hive, past doors and furnishings, mingling with the charged particles of air, and slipped through the cracks to the lowest secret chamber, where Elder Jorris lay.

As Brigitta's mind-mist gently explored, she sensed Jorris's undispersed spirit, restless and worried, pacing the room.

Chapter Six

Brigitta stood nervously by Ondelle's side while the crowd of faeries gathered below. She had stood twice before on the silver platform beneath the great Hourglass of Protection. The first time she had looked out over the frozen and broken bodies of hundreds of faeries the day of Hrathgar Evil's stone curse. The second time she had received Ondelle's hourglass necklace and her destiny markings in front of the entire forest. On this day, the White Forest faeries were mingled together rather than grouped by elemental realm. They had no idea what to expect. The gathering was unprecedented in the history of the White Forest, and the air was buzzing with curiosity.

Her momma, poppa, Himalette, and Auntie Ferna stood in the front row, as did Glennis, her shining eyes locked on Brigitta. Brigitta nodded in her direction and Glennis nodded back. With unconvincing smiles on their faces, unconvincing to Brigitta at least, the Elders sat at the base of the platform in their high-backed chairs.

No games or songs or dances had been arranged. It had been difficult enough just to invite them all·on such short notice. Several faeries had brought food, and many had brought instruments. Brigitta was sure a spontaneous party would break out after she and Ondelle left, because that's what faeries did best. That's all they really know how to do, she thought sadly to herself.

She scanned the crowd and spied Gola and Minq at the back near the Fire Faerie grandstand. She was amazed Gola had managed the journey to the Center Realm, even with Minq's assistance. Brigitta's eyes filled with tears as she smiled at her loyal friends.

Gathered in the giant uul trees on either side of the Hourglass, Vivilia and several dozen other sprites observed the faeries pouring into the festival grounds. At the base of one of the trees, looking a bit disgruntled, stood the First and Second Apprentices, and sitting under the tree were Earth Wising Lalam and Fire Wising Kiera. Brigitta had a sudden longing to be sitting there with them.

Ondelle held up her hands to quiet the crowd.

"My White Forest kin," she began and the faeries settled themselves. "Many season cycles ago, my mentor, the wise and respected Oka Kan of Tintlebar, revealed to me that I would one day travel to the ruins of our ancestors in the Valley of Noe. As the moons passed and I became absorbed in the responsibilities of my Life Task as High Priestess, it did not seem likely that premonition would come to pass.

"Recently, however, we received a sign, a message that our ancestors left almost one-thousand season cycles ago. Our old kin sent it to remind us that there had been an important sacred item left behind."

An excited murmur rose from the crowd.

"An artifact," Ondelle continued, after the faeries had quieted down, "that was to be recovered at a later time when we were stronger and wiser and the world outside less chaotic. This artifact was designed to make our world safer in the generations to come."

Ondelle gestured to the two Air Faerie Perimeter Guards. They flitted to the platform and handed her the glass jar containing the bright whisper light. The crowd gasped and buzzed as Ondelle held it up over her head.

"It was written by Chevalde of Grobjahar, our first Chronicler, that we would receive a visitor one day," Ondelle gestured toward the whisper light. "A message would be delivered by this visitor when the time was right. But only one faerie would be able to hear the true message. That faerie would travel with a companion back to the ruins of Noe. That faerie has heard the true message."

Ondelle dropped the glass jar, and it broke neatly in two between them. Brigitta was briefly distracted by the skill it must have taken to create such a jar. The whisper light floated up, and Brigitta got the strange sensation, once again, that it was staring at her.

But it was silent. There were no whispers.

Ondelle pointed her scepter directly at Brigitta's chest. Her eyes narrowed and there was a brief flash that traveled from her face, down her body, and out her scepter, imperceptible to the gathering below, and quick enough to be dismissed by anyone else. Brigitta felt her hourglass necklace vibrate, and her body went numb. A warmth radiated from behind her, from the Great Hourglass itself. Blue waves of energy enveloped her and the scepter and then disappeared in a blink.

The whisper light shot forward, into her necklace, and vanished.

The crowd burst into excited calls. Pippet's jaw dropped open and Mousha fell back, too stunned to steady himself with his wings. The Apprentices' and Wisings' eyes grew wide in astonishment. Even the Elders looked puzzled.

In shock, Brigitta stared up at Ondelle, who smiled and nodded at the crowd. Brigitta's tongue felt heavy in her mouth, and her head spun. What had the High Priestess done to her? She gazed out on the crowd as if in a dream.

Ondelle finished her going away speech, saying something about how precious Blue Spell was and how it was reserved for rare occasions. Brigitta was no longer listening. Her stomach was doing somersaults and her heart pounded in her chest.

Her mind snapped to attention again when the High Priestess pointed at her and bellowed, "Brigitta of Tiragarrow, by the authority granted to me as High Priestess, by the approval of the Council of Elders, and by the blessings of the Eternal Dragon, I grant you permission to leave the White Forest on our behalf and travel by faerie Blue Spell to the ruins in the Valley of Noe."

Securing her scepter into a holder in the front of the platform, so that it stood on its own, she continued, "This scepter, a gift from the Ancients, will stand here as a reminder of this momentous journey. Think of us when you gaze upon it. We look forward to a great celebration upon our return."

She placed her arm around Brigitta's shoulder and leaned close to her ear. "Say goodbye," she whispered.

Brigitta raised her hand without thinking and waved at the crowd. Mousha hugged Pippet as she wiped tears from her eyes.

"Farewell, my kin!" Ondelle called, gripping Brigitta tighter. "May joy fill your every task!"

A moment later, there was a blast from the scepter. Brigitta's entire body was propelled backward, through the air. She panicked in anticipation of ramming straight into the Hourglass. Instead, she was propelled inside a tunnel of wind as images and colors collided around her. She could still feel Ondelle's strong grasp but couldn't turn her body to see her. Faster and faster they were sucked backward, as Brigitta's insides were squashed against her body. Her lungs felt like they would be crushed, and it was impossible to take a breath or swallow. The colors around her blurred by so fast that she could no longer isolate them. They appeared as one continuous stream of brownish-blue.

Expelled of all air, her chest began to ache and her heart pounded desperately. Just as she thought she would suffocate from lack of breath, everything stopped. She collapsed to the ground, too exhausted to open her eyes.

It felt as if she would never be able to move again.

Chapter Seven

When Brigitta did finally open her eyes, she had no concept of how much time had passed, but she knew she was no longer in the White Forest. She lay on the side of a hill in a patch of prickly brown grass. At the base of the lumpy hill, an unfriendly forest threatened to swallow any trespassers. The sky above was a grayish-red with a few grumbling clouds. A sickly haze obscured the sun.

With a dizzy head, Brigitta slowly got to her feet. Her insides ached as if she had been punched all over her body.

"Not the most comfortable way to travel, is it?" Ondelle's pained voice called from above her.

Up the hill, Ondelle sat on the steps of a dilapidated, weed-ridden platform, similar to the one they had just left behind. As Brigitta studied the hillside more carefully, she realized they were standing among the remains of what must have been grandstands, scattered about and camouflaged by the grasses, forming a U around the platform.

"This must have been where their own ceremonies took place," Ondelle said. "Although . . . " Ondelle's voice drifted away as she contemplated the arena. "Whatever used to sit on this platform is missing."

After scanning the entire hillside, Ondelle finally stood up. A little wobbly, she used the steps to steady herself and then stretched her arms, legs, and wings.

"You're sore, too?" asked Brigitta, fumbling her way to the platform.

"I'm bones and blood," laughed Ondelle, wincing. "I have never traveled by Blue Spell before, either."

Weak from the walk uphill, Brigitta was about to sit down when she remembered the ceremony. She grabbed her hourglass. It didn't feel any different.

"You lied to everyone," she accused Ondelle and let go of the necklace.

"In what way?" Ondelle tilted her head, distracted by something.

"I didn't get any true message from the whisper light. It didn't speak to me at all."

"I do not recall saying that you did." Ondelle said and held up her hand before Brigitta could respond. "Quiet."

Confused, Brigitta reached back into her memory of the farewell ceremony. For something that had happened so recently, it felt like seasons in the past. She couldn't reconnect the events. Nauseous from the unfamiliar air, she sat down on the steps.

The winds of her argument scattered. The elements were confused inside her. She tried to locate her water strength, but she was in too much pain and couldn't concentrate. Finally, she muttered, "Well, you tricked them, at least. You led them to believe something that isn't true."

Ondelle shot a stern look at Brigitta. "You would do well to remember that I am your High Priestess. I do not have to explain myself to you or any other Apprentice."

Brigitta closed her mouth tight to keep more words from escaping. Something about the elements in Noe affected her emotions. She could feel them poking around just under her skin. She looked down and counted to ten. When she looked back up, Ondelle's face was turned toward the top of the hill. It took Brigitta a moment to hear the distant rushing sound coming from the other side. Water.

"How are your wings?" asked Ondelle.

Brigitta stretched and fluttered them a few times. They ached, but they worked. She nodded at Ondelle, still angry.

"Come, then."

Brigitta trailed after Ondelle up the hill, although it was difficult to get her wings to function properly. It reminded her of when she flew in the heaviness of the Dark Forest. The elements didn't get along there either. She wondered if the White Forest was the only place left in all of Faweh where the elements cooperated.

Ondelle slowed down, allowing Brigitta to catch up. "The air is unstable. It's affecting our emotions."

Brigitta nodded. "It feels wrong."

"Describe it," suggested Ondelle as they proceeded up the hill, the patches of grass beneath them growing sparser and sparser until the ground was completely bald.

"I have to think about my wings moving through the air, like I'm a toddling faerie again. I can feel it prickling—"

They had reached the top of the hill. On the other side, spread below them at the base of a great valley, was an enormous crater that could fit five Center Realms. Its sides were sloped downward, like a gigantic bowl carved into the rocky earth. From the center of the bowl gushed a thick, violent geyser of water that climbed up the side of the crater, through the valley, and then disappeared into the mountains where Brigitta had met it seasons before.

"The River That Runs Backwards," she whispered.

Mesmerized by the surge of the defiant river, Brigitta and Ondelle stood in awe, staring into the massive crater. On either side of it rose two mountain ranges that toiled north as far as the eye could see. The ranges were inaccessible, with jutting crags above the tree line topped in a strange whiteness Brigitta had never seen before.

Between the mountain ranges stretched the Valley of Noe, a mass of shadows and tangled woods. The River That Runs Backwards sliced the valley, churning itself uphill, where Brigitta knew it would eventually re-enter the earth at Dead Mountain.

She squinted, trying to imagine what the valley had looked like long ago when populated by the Ancients and their kin. She thought about her Auntie Ferna's stories and caught her breath. "Is that where Lake Indago used to be?"

"I believe it is," said Ondelle softly, placing her palms over her heart in reverence. "By the Dragon's breath . . ."

Ondelle suddenly pulled Brigitta behind a fallen pillar strangled with ivy. "Stay here," she said and flew up, hovered above the pillar for a moment, then dropped back down. "Some beasts are moving in the lakebed. It's too far to see what they are."

"What should we do?" asked Brigitta, realizing that they were very much alone against whatever creatures haunted the region, with no idea of where to hide.

"Let's see what kind of beings occupy this land."

They moved down the north side of the hill, close to the ground and as camouflaged into the rocks and debris as possible, until they came to the edge of the crater. They peered down into the bowl. A gust of wind drove a hot, sandy storm into their faces, and they put their hands over their mouths as they squinted.

Dotting the inside of the bowl were dozens of gray-winged creatures. They were pale and skinny and wore ragged tunics with bulky scarves wrapped around their heads to deflect the pelting sands caught in the river-wind. The tops of their heads were oddly flattish and wide. Each one carried some kind of chisel, and a coarse bag hung from a rope around each waist.

The creatures drove their chisels into the lakebed rocks, over and over again, searching for something. One male turned and helped a female stumble back up the side of the crater. When they reached a pile of supplies, the male withdrew a water flask from a pack as the female unwound her scarf. She pulled a wide metal disc from on top of her head. The male poured water into her disc so she could rinse out her eyes. Her face was sallow, her cheekbones sunken, and her eyes crystal white.

"They're faeries!" gasped Ondelle, grabbing hold of Brigitta's arm.

Brigitta stared at them. They couldn't be faeries. They were so small and thin and sickly. Their wings were ragged, papery, and most of all, free from any destiny marks. She stared as they drank, their dull wispy hair blowing in the river-wind.

"But look at them! They're so . . . so . . . awful." Brigitta tried to sense any elemental connection. She shook her head. "They aren't bound to any element. They can't be faeries."

"They have not had the benefits of living in the White Forest. There is no balance here. The poor beasts must not receive an element nor any destiny."

"They were left behind?"

"Or they chose to stay."

Shivers went up Brigitta's spine. She couldn't imagine life without an element. It would be like not being able to touch or taste or see. And what faerie would choose to live like this? They must have been left behind. But why? Had they done something wrong?

The female placed the metal disc back on her head and rewrapped her face. The two turned in unison and chiseled their way back down to the others, digging their tools rhythmically into the rock.

Another smaller female faerie stopped chiseling and called out. Two males knelt down to where she pointed. The river was far too loud to hear what they were saying, but they all nodded in agreement. The two male faeries chiseled beside her until a large portion of rock was loosened. The first faerie dropped the chunk of rock into her pouch, and they patted her on the back.

With a loud cry, a dozen more faeries leapt over the side of the lakebed and shot toward the faerie with the rock. The attacking faeries wore black tunics with circular silver symbols and carried sticks that spat fire. All the chiseler faeries flew to their comrade. They pulled the discs from their heads and held their chisels up, tools now shields and weapons, as another dozen faeries attacked from the other side of the crater.

"Ondelle, do something!" cried Brigitta. "Help them!"

"Which ones? We don't know the cause of this fight."

The chiselers moved into a practiced circular formation, with the rock-holding faerie on the inside and their strongest faeries on the outside.

The attacking faeries shot at them with their firesticks. The chiselers blocked the flames with their shields. A quick flame shot through their defenses to a chiseler faerie's wing. He dropped to the ground and the formation immediately incorporated him into the protected circle.

A female chiseler leapt up, weapon extended, into the attackers. She swerved at the last minute and sliced an attacking faerie's arm. He, too, fell to the ground, but the black tunic faeries left him there, whimpering in pain. The attacking faeries thrust themselves into the chiselers, whose formation broke, and they scattered. The small faerie carrying the rock got caught in the wind.

"Help!" she cried, swimming through the air and flapping her wings. She dropped her pouch, and it was immediately sucked into the river-wind and lost inside the watery mass.

A larger faerie flew to her assistance, reaching out his hands to grasp hers. They struggled against the river-wind, but it was no use, and they were slowly sucked backward. The larger faerie planted his feet against a rock for leverage, but could not hold the weight of the other faerie and was soon torn off his feet. The other chiselers helplessly watched, dodging their attackers as their friends were pulled away.

Without thinking, Brigitta shot over the side. "No!" she cried as she flew toward the struggling faeries.

A moment later, Ondelle zipped past Brigitta and stopped just shy of the two little beasts, wrapping her left arm around an outcropping of rock and reaching out with her right. "Fly to me! You can do it!"

The two faeries, stunned by her imposing presence, stopped fighting the wind and were instantly sucked through the air into the violent spasm of water.

Brigitta caught up with Ondelle and reached forward, not wanting to believe that the faeries were gone. But there was no trace of them. Dust spun about, pelting her skin. She ignored the tiny pricks as she stared into the stormy river, horrified.

"There was nothing you could do," called Ondelle over the noise, holding Brigitta back.

Ondelle steered an astounded Brigitta toward the other faeries. All the fighting had stopped. The black tunic attackers and defending chiselers hovered in mid knife-stroke and fire-blast.

Ondelle held up her hand. "Hello. We mean you no—"

The faeries bolted away in all directions, pulling their wounded through the air. In a moonsbreath, Brigitta and Ondelle were alone in the lakebed with only the sound of the rushing river behind them.

"Are you all right?" asked Ondelle.

Brigitta turned and stared into the river where the two faeries had vanished.

"They . . . they just . . . " stammered Brigitta, her whole body shaking.

"I know," said Ondelle, placing her hands on Brigitta's arms and rubbing some warmth into them as she examined their surroundings. "At least they have stopped fighting. We should leave. It is not safe here."

Once they emerged from the crater that had formerly housed Lake Indago, Ondelle decided they should head west into the forest, as opposed to north or east into the forest. The only other choice was back down the hill of ruins, but she said even the tricky elements could tell her that was the southern border of Noe. The western forest was closest and she wanted to get under cover and set up camp for the night.

So they flew west and were swallowed by the dense leaves, which quickly muffled the sounds of the backward river. Brigitta numbly followed her High Priestess, unable to dislodge the image from her mind of the poor little faeries' surprised faces when they disappeared into the angry water.

After several moonbeats they entered a small clearing. Ondelle landed, studying the trees, which formed a circle around them, and the ground, covered in seasons of wild growth.

She picked a branch up off the ground, rubbed it, and then flicked it at the ivy. The ivy half-heartedly obeyed Ondelle's silent command, dancing a bit before flopping back down on itself.

"We will have to do this the hard way," she said, dropping her pack. "Help me clear these vines."

Together they scraped the vines away until a shallow metallic font appeared on top of a petrified tree stump. The dish was empty but shone as if it had recently been polished. They cleared the overgrown area around the font and uncovered a circular stone floor that stretched out to the trees.

"This will do," said Ondelle. She reached into her pack, removed two firestones, and handed them to Brigitta. "Build a fire in the font, and I will create some protection around us."

"Why don't we stay in the trees?" asked Brigitta.

Ondelle looked up into the dark, twisted leaves, vines, and branches. "I don't trust them." She tapped the stone floor with her foot. "This feels safe. It was a sacred place."

"How can you tell?" Brigitta tapped on the floor as well.

Ondelle pointed to the side of the petrified stump, and Brigitta knelt to have a look at it while Ondelle retrieved a globelight, two thin blankets, and a bottle of dustmist. There was a symbol etched into the stony surface: a circle with a square inside and another circle inside the square.

"I've seen that before," said Brigitta, "in a passageway under the Center Realm. What's it mean?"

"In a passageway under the Center Realm?" asked Ondelle as she shaped a dustmist wall around the perimeter of the stone floor. She stopped working and stood there, hand in mid-wave. "How odd I have never seen it down there before."

Brigitta gathered some dry brush and placed it in the font. She struck the firestones together, but nothing happened. Not a spark.

She struck them several more times but still, nothing. "Stupid rocks," she growled and smashed them together again.

"I believe these symbols lead us to the artifact we seek," continued Ondelle as she finished her wall of dustmist.

"What?" Brigitta dropped one of the stones in the font with a clang, the sound cutting sharply through the forest. Something scurried up a tree and another beast flapped its wings and snarled.

Ondelle placed her hands on Brigitta's shoulders. "Try again."

Taking a deep a breath, Brigitta relaxed and let go of all other thought, concentrating on the weight of the stones in her hands and the fire energy within them. She struck them together again. A flame appeared and caught the brush.

"Thanks," mumbled Brigitta as Ondelle pulled a vial of firepepper from the belt around her tunic.

Tired and hungry and feeling a new weight, Brigitta sat down on a rock with her head in her arms. She pictured, once again, the two little feral faeries being sucked away by the river and how she could do nothing to save them.

"Be careful, I treated the dustmist wall with firepepper." Ondelle spread some moss on the ground and used the last of the dustmist to form a cushion beneath it.

She sat down and opened a container of seasoned gundlebeans. "My own recipe."

For a moment, Brigitta allowed herself to be amused by the image of Ondelle cooking, hair stuck to her face, recipe books scattered, apron stained with trial batches of stew. The image became her own mother, waving her spoon around the kitchen.

Had she really only left the White Forest that morning?

They snacked on the gundlebeans and sucked on some tingermint drops in silence, watching the flames dance inside the font. Brigitta played the events of the day over in her mind, from Ondelle's dramatics in front of everybody in the entire forest, to the painful Blue Spell experience, to that awful attack in the dry lakebed.

"Why didn't you do something to those black tunic faeries?" asked Brigitta. "The little chiseling ones hadn't done anything wrong."

"White Forest faeries are talented healers and artisans. We are not warriors."

"Well, maybe we should teach ourselves to be."

Ondelle didn't argue. She placed the remaining food into her pack and handed Brigitta a blanket. It was surprisingly warm for being so thin. "A gift from Elder Hammus," commented Ondelle. "He has talent with textiles."

It was indeed a well-crafted blanket, and focusing temperature was something she had looked forward to learning, but now it seemed a waste of time. Nothing Apprentices were taught would truly help them survive outside the White Forest.

"Couldn't you have performed some powerful magic to stop them? You're the High Priestess." Brigitta swallowed the lump in her throat that was threatening to turn into tears.

Ondelle handed her a little green leaf. "Have some ceunias. It's been a trying day."

Brigitta took the leaf and eyed Ondelle suspiciously, remembering the controversy about using it on baby Duna. But Ondelle placed a leaf on her own tongue and smiled. Brigitta slipped the leaf into her mouth. Her mind eased and her skin opened to the warmth of the blanket.

"There is no such thing as magic," said Ondelle, packing the remainder of the leaves away. "Not in the sense you imply."

"What do you mean? I've seen plenty of magic. And Hrathgar Evil knew all kinds of terrible sorcery."

Ondelle picked up her globelight and waved her hand across the top to light it. "Was that magic?"

"Of course not. You just lit it with your hand's energy, anyone can do that."

"Yes, but to any beast who has never seen such a thing, who has no knowledge of how globelights work, it is magic."

Ondelle blew onto the sphere and the light disappeared. She handed the globelight to Brigitta, who examined its smooth, round surface. It was flawless. A master craftsfaerie had made it. Brigitta touched it lightly with her pinky, and a tiny perfect dot lit up. She blew it out again.

"One could say that a flower blooming is magic," continued Ondelle, "or that our breathing is magic. Life is magical in that sense, in the absolute miracle of it. But nothing can be conjured without the right conditions, nor can we perform spells that require knowledge we do not have.

"What you call magic is simply knowing how to transform something with that knowledge. You must not become too enamored by so-called sorcery or fear what you do not understand. Anything you witness, you can know."

"Yes, Ondelle."

"You have learned many things these past moons as Second Apprentice, things you did not know before. Things that appeared difficult, perhaps even magical, when you were a child.

"You have become quite the empather, for instance." Ondelle glanced at Brigitta, her signature twinkle in her eyes. "Why don't you lie back and practice on the leaves?"

Brigitta snuggled into the moss, tucking her wings beneath the blanket. She stared up into the trees and watched the leaves flittering in the light wind. One leaf caught her attention. It was greener than the others and whole.

Ondelle lay down next to Brigitta and they listened to the unfamiliar buzzing and howling of the night beasts. Something flew into the firepepper and zapped away with a disgruntled chirp.

"I have kept knowledge from you," murmured Ondelle, as she sucked on her ceunias leaf, "and if this upsets you, I understand." She paused for a moment, gathering her thoughts. "Holding onto knowledge is like holding back a flood. I must feed it to you in trickles to stave off your being drowned."

"You don't think I can handle it," said Brigitta. It wasn't a question;

she knew she had proven herself to be reckless and irresponsible.

"I must protect you." Ondelle closed her eyes. "That is all."

The little green leaf shivered on its branch. Brigitta reached out to it and connected to its water energy. The leaf's energy was weak, like a shaky heartbeat. Life is so delicate, she thought. It can be there, and then gone.

She let those thoughts drift away, breathing steadily until she and the leaf were bound. As the leaf, she looked down at the shapes of two faeries lying below, one large and luminous, the other curled into a ball, cheeks wet with tears.

Chapter Eight

Green light. All she could see and feel was green light. It numbed her. Where was she? What was she supposed to be doing? Somewhere inside herself, she knew she had a task, but she couldn't connect with that part of herself. Brigitta, *a voice echoed through her mind,* come back. *The voice soothed her. It was golden and warm and danced through the green. She wanted to go to it; she wanted more of it. Not sure how she was moving, she did. And as she moved forward, the green became less dense, less confusing. She could see other colors now, browns and yellows. Shapes, too . . .*

"Brigitta?" The golden voice was closer.

Everything snapped into place. She was sitting on her moss bed, next to the font, surrounded by forest in the Valley of Noe. It was morning, and she could just make out the strange red-gray sky through the tops of the trees. She wiggled her fingers and toes.

Ondelle sealed up the larger of the two spell seeds and set it down beside her pack. "Very good," she said, opening a small bottle and vial. She began to undo the dustmist wall. With graceful finger flicks, she separated firepepper from dustmist and directed them into their containers. A puff of dustmist lingered between the trees. She directed it with her index finger and a twist of her wrist, but it stayed, suspended in the air. "I guess the forest is keeping some for itself."

She capped the firepepper and dropped down to the moss beds. Brigitta had not moved.

"The zynthia pushed through," she said.

"Yes," said Ondelle, "but you began to recover before I put it away."

"Only because I could follow your voice."

"It is progress." Ondelle helped Brigitta up and collected the dustmist from the moss. "What was magic to you before, you are now understanding through knowledge."

It was true, Brigitta thought. She never would have imagined she could resist green zynthia hypnosis. All it took was practice, learning how to stay balanced using what she knew about energy. She wondered if she could ever learn the secrets of something even more powerful.

"Ondelle, why did you leave your scepter back in the White Forest?" asked Brigitta, suddenly remembering being caught in its force. "Doesn't it contain powerful energy? Couldn't you have used it against the attacking faeries?"

"The scepter must stay in the White Forest. It was a gift from the Ancients. We would not want it to fall into the wrong hands."

After their morning meal, Ondelle and Brigitta flew east back toward the old lakebed. As they broke through the trees and faced the rocky crater and the raging northbound river, Brigitta was once again reminded of the poor little beasts they had discovered there.

"What are we going to do about those left-behind faeries?" she asked.

"First things first, Brigitta," said Ondelle. "And one thing at a time."

She took off her pack and removed a scroll. She rolled it out on a rock and pinned it in place with some small earthen weights she removed from her belt. It was an ancient map, but the drawings and symbols were familiar to Brigitta.

"Is that Gola's map?" she asked, moving closer.

"No, this map was drawn by Chevalde of Grobjahar. At least we assume it was. It was inside one of her books."

"The one with the rhyme?"

"Yes." Ondelle traced her finger down through the Valley of Noe to Lake Indago, represented by a fading blue-green patch. South of the lake was the hill they had appeared on the day before, labeled Lake Hill, and beneath that lay the Southcoast Forest. There was a symbol on the hill, a circular shape with a square inside it and another circle.

"That's the same symbol as before," said Brigitta, studying the map more carefully.

To the west of Lake Indago was the Valley Forest and past that a mountain range labeled Western Range. To the east was more forest, the Valley Plateau, and then the Eastern Range. The Valley Forest surrounded Lake Indago on the north as well.

"Western Range? Valley Forest? Lake Hill? For such wise beings the Ancients had no imagination."

Ondelle laughed and tapped the round symbol with her finger. "If this symbol is the key, we should go back to the hill and look around. The object could be hidden in all that overgrowth."

"Ondelle," said Brigitta, pointing to the blue-green patch, "Gola's map has the River That Runs Backwards drawn on it. This one has Lake Indago." She pointed to the northern part of the map. "And Gola's has an hourglass symbol in the middle of the White Forest, this one doesn't."

"Brigitta, I am appalled by my own lack of curiosity. I should have studied hers more closely." She stepped aside and motioned with her hand. "Go on. What else?"

"Well, Dead Mountain is called Dragon Mountain on your map. The Sea of Tzajeek has the same serpent running through the name. But that circle and square symbol, Gola's map doesn't have one anywhere on it. I'm positive."

"The maps were drawn on two different occasions . . ." Ondelle furled her brow.

"Before and after the Great World Cry," Brigitta finished Ondelle's thought.

"Before and after the elemental faeries moved to the White Forest," added Ondelle.

"Well, the ones that got moved, anyway," said Brigitta quietly.

She thought about the escape her ancestors had made generations ago. She didn't know why it hadn't occurred to her before, but how exactly did they all get to the White Forest? She had assumed the Ancients were so powerful they had just transported thousands of faeries by Blue Spell. But if they were that powerful, why did they have to abandon their home in the first place?

"I don't think that sacred object is on the hill any longer," decided Brigitta. "I think it was moved. Maybe to keep it safe from—"

Ondelle held up her hand to silence Brigitta, cocked her head, and listened. Her eyes grew wide, but before she could utter a warning, dozens of faeries zipped down from the trees, surrounding them, shields up and daggers drawn. They wore the same ragged tunics as the chiseler faeries.

A young male faerie emerged from the swarm. He was taller than the rest, as tall as Brigitta, with long thin wings, more golden than gray, and deep crystal blue eyes. Brigitta stared. She knew that face.

He wore a blue tunic that matched his eyes. The others hovered behind him as he examined Ondelle and Brigitta, their glares doing nothing to mask their fear.

Ondelle extended her hands, palms up, to show that they were empty. "Hello—"

Before she could finish her sentence, the blue-eyed faerie slapped a long black strap against Ondelle's outstretched arms. The strap immediately wound itself around her wrists and tightened like a thin constricting snake. From behind them, two faeries slapped straps against her wings, and the bands wound themselves around the tips, drawing them together and preventing flight.

Brigitta was so startled that she didn't have a chance to move before they strapped her own wrists and wings. "Hey!" she cried, twisting against the bindings.

The taller faerie boy pulled the straps tight and then snaked them together in the palm of his hand. "A bad-tempered stranglewood vine," he warned. He looked her in the eyes, his dark hair plastered against his forehead. "Don't struggle, and it won't separate your hands from your wrists."

"My faerie kin, there is no need for such bondage." Ondelle's voice was steady.

She looked into his crystal blue eyes, and his composure flittered. Brigitta could tell Ondelle was trying to empath his thoughts, but he shook her off and stared back, his mental walls solid. Ondelle's face brightened in surprise.

He stuffed the map into Ondelle's pack and threw the pack over his shoulder. "Bring them," he said to the smaller white-eyed faeries, whose minds were not as trained as his. Fear emanated from them, made them jittery like dancing flames, which Brigitta knew also made them dangerous.

Chapter Nine

The sickly faeries prodded Brigitta and Ondelle from behind with their shields as they all stumbled down the narrow path. It was overgrown with thorny ivies and roots that burrowed in and out of the ground like rugged sea serpents. Bushy spider nests hung between the thick branches that criss-crossed overhead. The crystal blue-eyed boy flew behind them, barking orders at the scouts in front.

Brigitta's heart pounded so hard it scattered her thoughts. Something washed over them and Ondelle's voice echoed in her head. *Transform your mind. I should not be able to enter this easily.*

"Breathe," Ondelle said out loud. "Remember what you know."

Brigitta had been learning transformation from Elder Adaire; she just needed to alter her thoughts. She allowed them all to appear, the anxious and frightened ones, and then saw them as leaves in a stream. As the thought-leaves floated away, she filled the space left behind with water energy. She glanced at Ondelle, whose expression was one of calm amusement. Brigitta tried her best to imitate that expression.

They traveled for about three moonbeats until they came to a tunnel in a large tree that spanned the path. The tunnel was guarded by a female and male faerie, both slightly taller and more muscular than the other faeries, both wearing dark blue tunics, and both with crystal blue eyes.

The blue-eyed faeries nodded at one another as Brigitta and Ondelle were pushed into the tunnel. The High Priestess had to duck to avoid hitting her forehead against the trunk of the tree. When they emerged from the tunnel, they were standing inside a menacing circle of lifeless trees.

The trunks of the trees were stiff and wide and had grown so closely together they formed an impenetrable wall. The wall grew high around them until it came to a structure at the top that blocked out the sky. Little light filtered through, and it took a moment for Brigitta's eyes to adjust. As they did, she grew more and more ill. Something was horribly wrong with this place. She sensed Ondelle stiffen beside her.

Part way up the tree in front of her, there was a thick metal bar connecting it with the next tree. And where the bar had pierced the skin of each tree, the bark was infected and stained with ooze. She looked from one tree to the next and it was the same. At different heights, the bars held the trees together so that they could not bend or fall. It looked as though someone had thrust the bars into the trees while they were young, imprisoning them, so that they would grow this way.

Brigitta and Ondelle were pushed toward one of the trees. It was cracked up the side, providing an entrance near the base. The crystal blue-eyed faerie boy pointed into the dark opening.

"Inside," he commanded as he hovered beside them.

Ondelle studied his face. "What is your name?"

He stared back at her, trying to match her gaze, but his eyes began to twitch. He glanced down at Brigitta, then back to Ondelle, who smiled.

"Jarlath," he growled. "I am your Watcher."

"And Jarlath, what is this place? Where are we?" Ondelle asked the questions so softly and sweetly that Brigitta could feel his mental wall melting away.

Four older faeries dropped down from the branches, startling Brigitta. She hadn't noticed the numerous cracks in the tree trunks, with a crystal blue-eyed faerie posted at each one. Watching them.

"Queen Mabbe wants to see them as soon as possible," grumbled the largest one, whose wings were less golden than Jarlath's, but longer and thicker.

"Yes, Watcher Dugald," said Jarlath. "You heard him." He shoved Ondelle and Brigitta into the crack.

They stumbled inside and the crack sealed behind them. It was pitch black. Brigitta could only feel Ondelle next to her.

"You're in the Hollows," a voice whispered from beside them.

Brigitta jumped and moved closer to Ondelle.

"Face me," said Ondelle. "Hold up your arms."

Brigitta did so and felt Ondelle rotate her wrists around Brigitta's. The bonds loosened and they both sighed in relief.

"Turn around so I may reach into your pack."

Brigitta turned around and Ondelle rifled through her supplies. A moment later, a light emerged from the center of the trunk, and there was a collective gasp. Ondelle held Brigitta's globelight in a loosely bound hand, illuminating six trembling faeries, four wearing black tunics and two in tattered brown. The faeries' hands and wings were bound with stranglewood vines and their faces were bruised. One black tunic faerie's lip was torn and bleeding. Blood dripped down onto his tunic, staining the silver symbol on the front: a circle with a square inside of it, and another circle.

Brigitta raised her hands to point out the symbol, but Ondelle intercepted the motion and pulled them back down.

"I am High Priestess Ondelle of Grioth and this is Second Elder Apprentice Brigitta of Tiragarrow." Ondelle's voice was soft and warm. "We come from the far north, from a place called the White Forest."

The faeries stood motionless, mesmerized by the purity of the globe's light and stunned by the imposing presence of the woman holding it.

"We are your kin." Ondelle gestured toward them.

The faeries looked at one another.

"Your lip is torn," continued Ondelle, "my healing salve is in my pack, which Watcher Jarlath has taken." She reached out to the injured faerie. "But, if you allow me, I can still ease your pain."

The faerie with the torn lip stepped closer. "So, it's true," he managed with a trembling voice, looking up at Ondelle with wide eyes. She started to speak, but he lurched forward and spat in her face. "The Ancients abandoned us after all!"

Rage fuelled Brigitta and she was about to lash out, but Ondelle held her in place and calmly wiped the bloody spittle from her cheek.

"That is what we would like to find out," she said. "We have lost contact with the Ancient Ones. We were never told that faeries were still living in the Valley of Noe."

"Liar!" Another black tunic faerie stepped forward. She was thin and dirty. Her feet were bare and her left foot was missing two toes. "You have used up all your sorcery and have come to take ours!"

Before Ondelle or Brigitta could respond, there was a loud howling from above. The other faeries seemed unconcerned when the sound came rushing down toward them. They all stood perfectly still with eyes closed.

"Close your eyes!" yelled Ondelle over the noise.

Just as the howling wind hit them, Brigitta shut her eyes tight. The howling spun around the inside of the trunk and became a thick rope of air, winding about them. Brigitta felt herself lifted up off the ground. The band tying her wrist to Ondelle's pulled taut again, cutting into her skin, and she cried out in pain. A moment later the wind stopped.

Brigitta opened her eyes as she was yanked forward by the wrist straps. She stumbled into an enormous burl that twisted wickedly as it rose, growing more and more narrow until it became a dark funnel above them. From the darkness of the funnel, a chain extended on which hung a large chandelier made from thorny branches. The ends of the branches were capped with large bird talons.

Before she had time to ask where they were, she was yanked forward again by a hook on the end of a staff held by Watcher Jarlath. Another Watcher yanked Ondelle forward with his staff hook, and a third shepherded the others out of the trunk.

The burl was large but suffocating, as there was no natural light. The smoke from the candled chandelier snaked through the branches before climbing up the chain and disappearing into the darkness. The rest of the decor looked as though it had been excavated from a ruin. The floor was strewn with faded rugs, and broken pieces of pottery sat in the crevasses of the walls. Two cracked white columns stood across the room. Each column was topped with a rusty cage overflowing with bones. A Watcher holding a hooked staff was posted next to each column.

Between the columns, in a rounded enclave that had been polished smooth, sat three carved chairs with legs that mimicked the burl's twisted design. In the center chair sat the oldest, ugliest faerie woman Brigitta had ever seen. What hair she had left sat like cobwebs on her white scalp. Her face was a maze of wrinkles and spots. Her pupils were clouded over and her nose and ears were stretched long from gravity and time. Her back was stooped and her deformed hands held a scepter topped with more bird talons clutching a black orb. Her wings were ashen and peeling. The only attractive thing about her was her tunic, which was an intense shimmering blue with bold yellow stitching, the brightest thing Brigitta had seen since landing in Noe.

"All honor Queen Mabbe! True leader of Noe!" shouted the Watchers at the pillars.

Two more Watchers moved into the room and sat on either side of the elderly faerie. They wore the standard Watcher garb, except their tunics had bright yellow stitching around the sleeves and neck. One of them was Dugald, the surly male who had been sent down to meet Jarlath. In his lap he held Ondelle's pack. The other Watcher was a female, equally dour, with a large tear in one of her grayish-pink wings. They both looked better fed than any of the other faeries.

The female leaned over and whispered into Mabbe's ear, who nodded, staring out over the burl. She stood up, which didn't alter her height, and rapped her scepter on the floor.

"Just because I'm blind doesn't mean I can't see," she cackled, widening her eyes and sniffing the air like some four-legged beast.

The two captive faeries with brown tunics fell to their knees and bowed. The four black tunic faeries scowled at Mabbe, who snorted, "Your insolence is noted."

"My wise Sister," bowed Ondelle, "we have come—"

"Silence!" Mabbe pointed her staff at Ondelle, the clouds in her eyes darkening like a storm.

A black frog-like tongue shot forth from Mabbe's scepter and into Ondelle's mouth. Just as fast, the black shape retracted from Ondelle's face, struggling and bulging with something in its grasp. It snapped back across the room and into the scepter. Ondelle tried to speak, but no sound came out.

"I will keep your pretty voice while you listen to me." Mabbe reached to her right and the surly male placed Ondelle's pack in her hand. She turned the pack inside out and spilled the contents onto the floor, waving her hands over the items and sniffing the air. "These are items of sorcery." She poked through them with her scepter. "It's against the laws of my Queendom to carry such items."

"One hundred seasons in the Colony!" shouted Dugald, and his female counterpart sniggered.

"I've never sensed you before," said Mabbe, snaking her head through the air. "You've never lived in the Hollows. Were you sent from Croilus?"

"She's not one of ours," spat the torn-lipped faerie.

Mabbe swung her scepter toward him and cocked her head, eyes dotting around as she located him across the room. "Any faerie captured from Croilus's tribe receives life in the Colony for traitorous activity!"

She bobbed her head, and one of the Watchers grabbed the torn-lipped faerie from behind. "I may take pity and lighten your sentence," Mabbe continued, "if you have anything of interest to tell me."

"That large one sent two Hollows faeries into the Mad River yesterday!"

Mabbe's eyes stormed over again, and Brigitta swore she could see lightning bolts behind the gray clouds. "So, that was you who lost my two diggers, was it?"

"No!" exclaimed Brigitta. "We were trying to save them!"

"Liar!" spat the torn-lipped faerie. "The tall one swooped down and sent them to their deaths!"

"She was trying to steal your sorcery sands," another Croilus faerie added, and the rest of them nodded.

"But, but . . . " stammered Brigitta, "they were the ones who attacked your faeries, not us! They had sticks that spat fire."

"I'm afraid you're outnumbered," said Mabbe, "unless there is someone who will speak on your behalf?" She raised her eyebrows and smiled, exposing teeth that had rotted into points.

Brigitta glanced around the room and spotted Jarlath near the entrance to the tree. He gazed back at her, expressionless.

"I thought not." Mabbe gestured, and three Watchers each grabbed a remaining Croilus faerie. "I will consider this information, but you'd better spend your night thinking about what you know of Croilus's activities if you want to impress me."

On his way out of the burl, the torn-lipped faerie shouted back, "She came from the far north! The Ancients left us behind, and now they've come back for our sorcery!"

Mabbe froze with her hand in the air, her gaze softening. For a brief moment, the storm in her eyes slowed, the clouds parted, and a sliver of blue moon flickered in her right eye. A smile spread across her face, and then she cackled, raising the storm in her eyes once again.

"Bring me your pack," Mabbe pointed her scepter at Brigitta, and the strap holding her wrists to Ondelle's loosened and fell to the floor. Brigitta stumbled forward and removed her pack. As she did, her hourglass necklace slipped out from under her tunic. She tucked it back inside as she dropped her pack onto the floor.

"Wait!" Mabbe screeched, hands clawing the air. Brigitta faced the ugly faerie as she stepped closer and pointed at Brigitta's chest. "That necklace, too!"

"No!" Brigitta clenched her hand over the necklace through her tunic.

Mabbe scowled and stung Brigitta in the arm with the tip of her staff, then flicked the hourglass out of Brigitta's tunic again. She lunged for it, then screeched and retracted her hand, smoke rising from her fingers.

She swiftly smacked Brigitta across the head with the stone on the end of her scepter. Pain shot through Brigitta's skull as she fell to the floor. Ondelle rushed to her side and caressed Brigitta's head where the stone had struck her, warming the pain away. Ondelle mouthed an explanation to Mabbe, gesturing at the necklace.

The Queen pointed her scepter at Ondelle and the black tendril shot in and out of her mouth once more, replacing her voice. Ondelle drew her breath.

"The necklace has been spell-cast, she cannot remove it," she said as she helped Brigitta to her feet.

"Perhaps if I remove her head first?" cackled Mabbe. Her Watcher pets guffawed from their chairs.

"It would do you no good. It will deflect the energy of all but the rightful owner." Ondelle tapped the necklace with her pinky finger and a little puff of smoke spat off of it. "You have no need to fear the necklace; there are no harmful uses for it."

"I fear nothing," Mabbe growled, pointing her scepter back at Ondelle. The black tongue extracted her voice once again. The decrepit faerie straightened herself up as far as she was physically able and returned to her chair. "If you are lying, your little companion will be punished."

Legs slung over the armrests of their chairs, the Watchers at her sides lounged as Mabbe contemplated her prisoners. She pointed at Brigitta, "One hundred seasons for your items of sorcery and another one hundred for your unfortunate attitude."

She moved her attention to Ondelle and sent her a vicious smile. "Life in the Colony for murder."

Brigitta was about to protest, but Ondelle held her back and shook her head.

Leaning into her chair, Mabbe put an arm around the female Watcher. She stroked her check affectionately with her bony thumb. "Veena, what of those last two?"

"Found sleeping during harvest time," Veena reported.

"Brand them and let them go with a warning. I'm feeling generous." Mabbe waved her scepter to dismiss them.

The two little Hollows faeries stood up and bowed over and over again. Their Watcher herded them toward the entrance, and they scraped and bowed their way from the burl. "Thank you, Great Mabbe. Long life to the true leader of Noe."

"My faeries love to gossip," said Mabbe after they had disappeared into the trunk of the tree. "News of the murdering and thieving faeries from the North will spread. I'm afraid you won't make many friends during your stay." She mock pouted at them and then cackled. She raised her arms in the air, and the straps snaked up from the floor, wrapped themselves around Brigitta's and Ondelle's wrists, and pulled taut.

Pointing to the items on the floor, Mabbe turned to Dugald, "Bring these to my room." She stood once more and smiled wickedly, "Watcher Jarlath, take our visitors on a tour of the Colony."

Jarlath and the Watcher guard to his right pulled Brigitta and Ondelle backward by the wrist straps with their hooks.

"What about her voice?" asked Brigitta as she stumbled away. "Give her back her voice!"

"She'll get it back," said Mabbe, "after I hear what it has to say." She snickered, petting the black stone that held Ondelle's voice as she shuffled into the alcove and disappeared.

Chapter Ten

The Colony was higher up in the circle of bound trees that made up the Hollows. An opening in each trunk in the circle led to a large mesh prison cell that extended out the back over the forest.

The ground of the Colony was built similarly to a White Forest village-nest, with layers and layers of twigs, bark, earth, and mud. The canopy was thick above, but portions of daylight still shone through and Brigitta was relieved to see the sky again, even if it was reddish-gray.

As Jarlath and the other Watcher led Ondelle and Brigitta through the Colony, faerie prisoners shot them nervous glances while they pounded, sifted, and sorted through piles of rocks similar to the one the chiselers had found in the lakebed. One faerie stood up with some miniscule grains between her forefinger and thumb. She showed them to a Watcher guard and then dropped them into a tube that disappeared into the ground.

A cry came from behind them. Near the entrance to the Colony, one of the Hollow faeries who had been sentenced to branding was lying face down over a log. When a Watcher pulled him up, there was a large X burned into the top of his right wing. The branded faerie glared at Brigitta so viciously that she turned away.

"You will work with the sifters," Jarlath said, "to make up for the sorcery sands you lost in the Mad River."

"You know as well as I do that we didn't lose those sands," growled Brigitta, shifting her strapped wings. "It was the Croilus faeries who attacked your faeries, not us."

The Watcher leading Ondelle was a skinny, pale thing with large hands and muddy-colored wings. He stopped in front of one of the prison trees and before Brigitta realized what was happening, he pushed Ondelle inside. Jarlath continued walking, pulling Brigitta along.

"No, wait," she said, tripping after him, "where are you taking me?"

From the next tree, six bedraggled Croilus faeries emerged, led on a single chain by a straw-haired female Watcher. None of the Croilus faeries had wings. A chill went up Brigitta's spine. Wingless faeries? She had never heard of such an awful thing.

When they reached the following tree, Jarlath pushed Brigitta inside. There were two cages in the near-dark, with a Hollows faerie huddled in each. He opened the door to the cell that extended out the back of the tree and thrust Brigitta forward. He locked the door, poured some water from a pail into a cup, and placed the cup on the floor of her cell.

Brigitta kicked the cup, and water spattered all over Jarlath.

"That was unwise," he said. "That was your daily ration." He put the pail back in the corner.

"Please, Jarlath," pleaded Brigitta, gripping the bars of the cell, "we only came here to find out how to get back in touch with the Ancients. We had no idea there were still faeries left in the old land. We haven't hurt anyone."

"A sentence from Mabbe may only be overturned by Mabbe," he said and left.

The faeries inside the trunk shrunk back in their cages. Brigitta's cell was much bigger than theirs, and she supposed she should be grateful for that.

"Ha!" she shouted and rattled her cage. They'd been two suns in Noe and their situation was already hopeless. She couldn't live in this miserable place for sixty season cycles. This wasn't happening.

A desperate laughter burst from some place inside her. The laughter soon turned to tears and she ran to the back of the cell, stretching as far out as she could to get a glimpse of Ondelle. But she could only see the back of the next cell due to the curve of the trees.

What was wrong with her High Priestess?

"Why haven't you defended us?" she demanded. "I promised my parents you would keep me safe!" Brigitta shook the bars and cried.

She heard a squeak to her right and swung her head in that direction. In the back end of that tree's cell an elderly faerie with an X burned into her right wing and a slash burned into the other clung to mesh bars, holding herself up off the ground. She was a sinewy thing, with short white hair that stood straight up on her head. She gestured toward the floor and Brigitta looked down. Her prison cell floor was one giant trap door with a vine attached to the latch. If anyone pulled the latch, Brigitta, without the use of her wings, would plummet through the trees to the ground far below.

She slowly backed into the trunk as she studied the vine, which stretched out into the trees and terminated at a hut on a small platform where two Watchers stood talking. Not knowing how she could have missed it before, she now saw dozens of these platform huts. They were surrounded by Watchers.

Once she was safely inside the trunk, Brigitta sunk to the ground and pulled her knees up to her chin. She spotted a small stone next to her foot and stared at it for a long while. Then, she took a shaky breath and dropped all thoughts except for stone thoughts. She felt its coolness and let it wash over her. The heat of her anger dissipated as she became still with the stone.

Holding that quiet stoneness, she sent a tendril of energy forth, mind-misting as Elder Fozk had taught. In her mind she moved with the mist out through her prison-tree and down the path. She moved with it through Ondelle's tree to her High Priestess, who sat on the floor against the wall.

As Brigitta's energy settled beside her, she could tell how solid Ondelle's wall of defense was. She knew it was important to prevent any harmful beasts from getting inside, but how come Ondelle wouldn't let Brigitta in?

She felt her balance slipping and she let go of those thoughts and allowed her cool stone energy to drift, waiting for any sliver that could be an opening. Then, she felt it, the slightest crack. Focused and calm, Brigitta slipped into Ondelle's mind.

Mabbe's screams slammed into Brigitta and she felt Ondelle's energy draw them back. Heart pounding, she gasped and opened her eyes. She was back in her own cell.

She slumped down to the floor and lay there. Ondelle was fighting for her thoughts and Brigitta may have just ruined her concentration. But even that thought didn't alarm her as much as what she had just felt while she was in Ondelle's mind.

Her High Priestess was afraid.

Wake up, faerie, a voice called.

Brigitta pulled herself awake. Jarlath was staring down at her with those crystal blue eyes, face up against the cage. She knew those eyes; she knew that face. That was it!

Brigitta leapt up so quickly that Jarlath dropped the tray he was carrying, and it clattered on the floor. He did not bend to pick it up, caught in the intensity of Brigitta's gaze as she moved toward him.

"I know you . . . " she whispered, reaching out through the mesh.

Jarlath, too, moved closer, as if hypnotized.

She cupped the side of his face with the palm of her hand. Both of them breathed together as a thousand voices entered the room, speaking all at once. Jarlath pulled back and the voices stopped. Brigitta blinked, once again aware of the room.

"What was—"

"Shut up!" Jarlath hissed. "Just shut up!" He fumbled as he retrieved the tray and the bits of food scattered on the ground. He threw all the pieces through the bars. "There, that will teach you."

The other two caged faeries watched this display as they gnawed on meager bones.

"Be careful of that one," growled Jarlath, "she has tricky mind sorcery."

The faeries kept staring.

"Look away!" commanded Jarlath, and the faeries grabbed the rest of their food and turned around. He gripped Brigitta's cage and whispered fiercely, "You don't know me. Got it?"

"I saw your face in a vision," insisted Brigitta, voice low.

"Really? And did your vision warn you of this place?" he asked.

Brigitta shook her head.

"Not much good then, was it?"

Before Brigitta could answer, the skinny Watcher who had taken Ondelle stepped into the tree. Jarlath straightened up.

"Mabbe wants to see this one," said the Watcher, pointing to Brigitta.

Brigitta sat on a stool at the front of the burl. The contents of her pack lay on the floor mixed with Ondelle's.

"Leave us, Watcher Jarlath," said Mabbe, hunched in her carved chair. "I will send for you."

Jarlath gave a small bow and left.

"Your companion's voice has been uncooperative. Amusing, but uncooperative."

"Ondelle is a powerful priestess." Brigitta smirked at the cloudy-eyed faerie woman. So, Ondelle had managed to keep Mabbe out of her head after all.

Mabbe laughed. "Obviously not powerful enough. And underprepared, I'm afraid."

She waved her staff at the triple lyllium suclaide. "Bringing sweets on your journey?" Mabbe cackled and pointed to the globelight and herbs. "Some light and some simple remedies?" She gestured over the blankets, firestones, map, the gifts from her poppa and Himalette, and the two spell seeds. "Useless, useless, useless . . . but these are quite interesting. What are they?"

She tapped the two spell seeds with the end of her scepter, then looked up into Brigitta's face and smiled with her pointed teeth. Brigitta could smell her putrid breath, but her smile was also strangely inviting. A glint of light caught Brigitta's attention and she looked up into Mabbe's eyes, where the clouds had parted. The orange Lola Moon appeared in one eye and the Great Blue Moon appeared in the other. They were beautiful, alluring.

"You can tell me, dear," Mabbe's smile broadened. "I can keep a secret."

Brigitta felt herself smiling in response. Yes, she could trust Mabbe. There was no reason to lie. She opened her mouth to speak, but somewhere in the back of her mind she knew it was a trick. She slapped her hand over her mouth.

Whatever she spoke had to be the truth. She knew she couldn't lie. She fought the words back, but they were too strong. Wait, she remembered, don't fight. Relax. Give some up. Let Mabbe think her words were flowing with no resistance. She released her thoughts into her water energy and allowed only a few to emerge, like handing Mabbe a cupful of her momma's tea from a larger vat.

"They are seed pods," said Brigitta. She smiled brightly, impressed with herself.

"Oh, how nice," purred Mabbe. "What kind of seed pods?"

Brigitta allowed another thought to flow from her lips. "Seed pods from Gola," she said, giggling.

"And who is Gola?"

"Gola is an old tree-woman. She's my friend."

"I see," said Mabbe with less patience in her voice. She picked up the smaller of the pods and held it to Brigitta's face. A cloud drifted back over the Lola Moon in her eye. "What's inside the pod?"

"Gola made a potion to give me courage!" exclaimed Brigitta, practically giddy with excitement.

Mabbe dropped the spell seed on the floor. "Useless!" She kicked the other one across the room and into the wall.

Brigitta shook her head. All the giddiness disappeared.

Mabbe rushed at Brigitta, eye clouds storming. She sniffed and pawed the air. "Why are you here?"

"We just came to save our forest," stammered Brigitta.

"The forest of the Ancients!" screeched Mabbe.

"Our forest," Brigitta replied. "The White Forest. The Ancients are gone."

"Gone? Gone! Where did they go?"

"We don't know. That's why we came here."

"Ha! Fools after all!" Mabbe cackled and danced wildly about the room, knocking the globelight across the floor. She suddenly stopped.

"My sweet girl," she approached Brigitta with open hands, "all I want is to rule in peace. But my little faeries are weak, you see, unable to care for themselves." Mabbe tapped on Brigitta's stool with her scepter. "I would like to make you a deal."

"What kind of deal?" asked Brigitta.

"I will allow you and your *powerful* priestess to return home, unharmed, and you will never enter my forest again. But first, you must do something for me."

"What?"

Mabbe made her way back to her chair and sat down. "You have seen how Croilus attacks my defenseless faeries. I need to be able to protect them, do I not?"

"I suppose," said Brigitta. "What can I do about it?"

"You can go to Croilus and retrieve his sorcery sands."

"You mean steal them?"

"It is not stealing to get back that which rightfully belongs to me!" Mabbe struck the ground with her staff, and a lightning bolt shot through the clouds of her left eye. She calmed herself again with a long breath and smiled as she exhaled.

"You will think of some way to acquire them," she continued. "I don't care how. You're a smart one."

"And what if I can't?"

"You don't have much choice, now, do you?" Mabbe's smile broadened. "And if you do not return in three suns' time, I will remove your High Priestess' wings and keep her voice forever."

Remove her wings? Brigitta pictured the wingless Croilus faeries she had seen in the Colony. She clenched her fists. "I'll need my belongings back in order to do so."

Mabbe tapped her scepter against a metallic gong in front of the alcove. Jarlath entered the room, and Mabbe motioned for him to retrieve the items strewn across the floor.

"If you try to trick me in any way," Mabbe sent Brigitta her biggest smile yet, "I promise that your voiceless and wingless High Priestess will be thrown into the Mad River."

❦

Jarlath and Brigitta stepped through a hollow in one of the trees and out onto a platform. He spun her around and removed the lashings on her wings.

She sighed in relief and stretched her body. "Oh, thank the moonbeams!" she exclaimed.

"Can you fly?" asked Jarlath. "Are they all right?"

"I can fly higher and faster than you," said Brigitta.

"But you'll stay with me," he said, "or your friend might lose her wings."

"Yes, of course," said Brigitta.

"Then let's go."

"I need to see Ondelle first."

"We should leave straight away."

"Please, Jarlath," said Brigitta, "she needs to know where I've gone. What if I don't come back? That could happen, right?"

Jarlath narrowed his eyes. "Very well, but make it quick."

They flew up through the trees to the Colony and darted through a split in one of the trunks. They landed inside and startled three malnourished faeries sifting piles of broken rock. All of them had slashes branded on their wings and two had tears in them caked with dried blood.

"I don't know how you can live with yourself," said Brigitta.

"You don't know anything about me or how we've had to live these many seasons," spat Jarlath as he led her to a fenced area.

Inside the pen was a pile of long slender branches. A small group of Hollows and Croilus faeries were stripping fibers from the branches and soaking them in a barrel of thick liquid. More faeries were pulling the strips out of the liquid, setting them in rows to dry, and pulling long thin strands from the dehydrated ones.

"What's this?" asked Brigitta.

"They're making material for clothing," said Jarlath, pointing to the far side of the pen where faeries were weaving the strands into cloth.

Ondelle stood among them.

"Don't you have Clothiers? Faeries born with that talent?"

"They only serve the Queen and her court. The Colony takes care of everyone else. They harvest the folyia branches," Jarlath waved his hand toward the tops of the trees, "make the cloth, and sew the tunics. It's a good system."

"Forced labor is not a system." Brigitta started across the pen, then stopped when she spotted Ondelle's right wing. It was tarnished with a branded line that cut into her golden High Priestess marking. Brigitta's throat constricted with anger.

Huddled over one young weaver, Ondelle was guiding her hands on a loom, showing her how to be in rhythm with the machine. The little faerie looked absolutely terrified by Ondelle but managed a small smile as her hands started to perform on their own. Even under the worst of circumstances, thought Brigitta, Ondelle put herself in the service of others.

Suddenly, Brigitta didn't want to talk with Ondelle any longer.

She was ashamed. All she had been thinking about was how miserable she was when every faerie around her had no other life than this. She contemplated leaving the pen, but it was too late. Ondelle had sensed her. She straightened up as Brigitta and Jarlath approached.

"May we be alone?" asked Brigitta.

Jarlath looked suspiciously from Brigitta to Ondelle, who smiled warmly at him.

"Mabbe has her voice, so she can't even talk to me," said Brigitta.

Jarlath grunted and moved down the fence to speak with another Watcher.

They both kneeled, and Ondelle took Brigitta's hands in her own. Brigitta relaxed her mind as Ondelle's gaze penetrated hers.

"I made a deal. Mabbe is going to let us both return home. I just have to go to the other tribe, to Croilus, and get her stolen sands back."

Ondelle quickly glanced down to where the hourglass lay under Brigitta's tunic. Was she asking Brigitta to empath her? Grabbing hold of the hourglass, Brigitta let go of all her frantic thoughts and allowed them to drift away. They transformed into black feathers on the wind, twisting and dancing. Mesmerized by the feathers, she followed them, further and further until . . .

Brigitta, Ondelle's voice whispered in the vastness of her mind. A protected vastness, as if they were the only two faeries in the world. *You must return to the White Forest.*

No, echoed Brigitta's voice. *I have to get the sands for Mabbe or she'll hurt you.*

It does not matter what happens to me any longer. Do as I say.

But what about the artifact? Don't we need it to save the forest? Maybe there's a way to trade something for it?

Do not chance it. And trust no one about the artifact.

Then we'll find it together, after Mabbe releases you.

Do not fool yourself. Mabbe will never release me, Brigitta, and I am weakened. You must not risk your life. It is too important. You will leave and tell the Elders what you know. That is a direct order—

No! Brigitta snapped back into her own mind, the coldness of the Colony shocking her skin. Ondelle's eyes looked down at her like moist shadows. She looked much older than Brigitta remembered, and tired.

"No!" Brigitta repeated out loud.

Jarlath and the other Watcher turned at the noise. Jarlath patted the Watcher on the arm and headed toward them.

"Even if I could leave you behind," she whispered to Ondelle as Jarlath approached, "I wouldn't know how to return, I don't have the power."

Yes, you do, mouthed Ondelle, dropping her gaze to the hourglass necklace.

Brigitta's hand went to her chest and she recalled the flash from Ondelle's scepter and the blue energy that had enveloped her in front of the Hourglass of Protection. Brigitta now understood what Ondelle had done. Not only had she spell-cast it so no one, not even her, could remove it, but she had also created some kind of spell that could get Brigitta home.

Ondelle let go of Brigitta's hand, leaving something in it. She glanced down at her palm. The words *Blue Spell* were shaped out in strands from the stripped bark.

Jarlath grabbed them both by the arms and hauled them up. Ondelle's message fell apart as it floated to the ground.

Something sliced into Brigitta's thoughts as Jarlath pulled her away. It was Ondelle, forcing her way into her mind. *All you have to do is let me go—*

"No!" Brigitta called, transforming her thoughts to a heavy rain to drown out Ondelle's words. "I won't go back without you!"

"That's enough!" snarled Jarlath. "Don't make it worse for yourselves."

"I'll get their stupid sands and come back. I promise."

Ondelle's eyes misted for a moment and then hardened again as Jarlath pulled Brigitta out of the Colony.

Chapter Eleven

Brigitta glanced at the moody boy flying beside her, his breath heavy, struggling to keep her pace. Even with his larger Watcher's wings, Jarlath was no match for her. She smirked as she slowed down. It might not be wise to demonstrate just how strong she was, even though she was tempted to show off.

He sprung up over a branch and then dropped back down low to the ground. He might be a weaker flyer, but he did have good technique, she admitted to herself. If he had been a White Forest faerie, she guessed he would have been a Fire Faerie. There was definitely a heat about him. His long, slender body was more muscular than his peers. She wondered what his colors would have been, if he had been bound to the element of Fire. Perhaps he'd have wings and skin tinted red and gold.

He was different than the other Watchers in small ways. His hair was thicker and darker, his eyes more intense. He noticed things as well; he paid attention. He would have had the destiny markings for a Life Task requiring cleverness, she thought, like a Potion Master, if he had been visited by the Ancients at birth.

After several moonbeats they broke past the forest perimeter surrounding the old lakebed, and Jarlath stopped. He scanned the landscape in all directions.

"We don't want to be here at night," he said and frowned as he watched the river spouting up from the earth. "There's a nasty pull today."

Brigitta could feel the force of the river-wind from where they stood. It was stronger than the previous day and the waters wilder. "Where I come from, we call it the River That Runs Backwards," she said.

"That name is too kind."

Jarlath set off again, following the tree-line, stopping every few moments to look around and listen. Brigitta looked too. No faerie chiselers from the Hollows were in sight, nor any of the Croilus faeries. They were alone. She wondered if she could overpower Jarlath and leave him tied up somewhere. Then she could go back and rescue Ondelle.

"If you are considering an escape, may I remind you of Mabbe's promise," he said dryly.

"You mean her threat," corrected Brigitta, although she knew he was right. She could not risk Ondelle's life. She had no doubt Mabbe was capable of murder. No, she was going to have to think of a way to trick this Croilus faerie. She wondered how close she could get to him.

"How are we going to get into Croilus's palace?" she asked. "And how will he receive me when I show up?"

"Shhh. Not here."

Jarlath stopped near a fallen tree, and Brigitta stopped behind him. He took a few more nervous looks around and then whistled.

There was a rustling from inside the tree, and a female Watcher appeared. She was about Himalette's age and thin, but muscular, like Jarlath. Her eyes were the telltale crystal blue of a Watcher, and her wings, though not as golden as Jarlath's, were unblemished. She had a kind face, pink from the cold, and braided sand-colored hair.

"Any sign of Croilus's brood?" asked Jarlath.

"Not today," the young faerie said, approaching Brigitta. "It's been unusually quiet."

"Thistle," Jarlath gestured, "this is Brigitta . . . of the White Forest."

"Wow," breathed Thistle, and she bowed slightly.

Brigitta looked from Thistle to Jarlath and back to Thistle again.

Could there possibly be a friendly faerie in these woods?

"Let's go, then," said Jarlath. "We're running out of light."

Brigitta followed the faeries silently as they flew through the woods northwest of the river. The forest was much thinner than around the Hollows, but the trees were covered in a moist sludge from the constant mist. The branches had mossy stalactites, some as long as Brigitta's arm, from seasons of dripping cold river water. As they dove around the hanging forms, Thistle reached out and broke one off. A tinkling of smaller icicle shapes dropped from above and landed, almost musically, on the branches below.

"We call this the Greencicle Forest," she said, waving her mossy cone.

"*You* call this the Greencicle Forest," Jarlath said as he rounded a slick boulder and turned uphill. "To everyone else it's called the Rivermist."

Greencicle Forest, mouthed Thistle, and Brigitta had to laugh.

"Is this the way to Croilus?" Brigitta asked Jarlath.

"Not exactly."

"Then let's go *exactly*! I don't have much time to get those sands." Brigitta stopped flying and hovered in the air.

"You are not in charge." Jarlath stopped and crossed his arms across his chest. A greencicle broke off from a branch above him and nailed him on the shoulder. "Ow!" he cried as it dropped to the ground. "Blasted birdsong!"

"Language!" Thistle cried, then began to giggle. "Oh, Jarlath," she reprimanded him, "don't be such a mossbottom."

She fluttered to Brigitta, "You can't go to Croilus right now. You'd never make it at night. It's not safe." She broke her greencicle in two, handed the bottom half to Brigitta, and then licked her own a few times before biting off the tip. Brigitta gave hers a tentative lick. It tasted like cold, salty moss.

They continued until the trees broke away, and they were faced with a sheer cliff that extended west and disappeared into the mist. It looked as if the foot of the valley had sunk in some violent cataclysm, perhaps when the River That Runs Backwards was born. To the east, the cliff continued for several moonbeats until it crumbled into another part of the forest. Dividing the cliff, the River That Runs Backwards chugged uphill, spraying moisture across the entire valley, creating fleeting rainbows in the setting sun.

"It's beautiful," Brigitta murmured.

"Yeah, until it sucks you down into it. Come on." Jarlath moved along the side of the cliff.

Thistle grabbed Brigitta's greencicle-free hand and led her along. "Be careful of falling rocks," she said. "The Mad River sometimes makes an earthshake." She wiggled her body to demonstrate what shaking earth might look like, which made Brigitta laugh once again. The laugh echoed strangely off the cliff, as if mocking her, and Jarlath turned to glower at them both.

They came to a large portion of the cliff that had broken away and slid down, leaving a mass of boulders and scree at the base of the slump. They stopped for a moment and Jarlath examined a log that had six pits carved into the top. Four pits had white stones in them, and Jarlath placed two more white stones in the empty pits before disappearing into a crevasse that had been created by the slide.

Thistle pulled Brigitta into the crevasse, which was barely wide enough for them to open their wings. They flew up until they reached the top of the area that had broken free, then turned right, flitting over the fallen boulders littering the split in the mountain. They dropped down, soaring between the rocks, until they came to the entrance of a natural stone fortress created by fallen boulders that had gotten stuck between the cliff and the slump. The inside was completely hidden from above.

Thistle made a grand gesture into the cave. "We call it the Secret Palace."

"*You* call it the Secret Palace," said Jarlath. "The rest of us call it the Gathering Place." He continued into the rock cavern.

Thistle whispered to Brigitta, "Secret Palace."

Brigitta decided she liked this young faerie and, to spite Jarlath, would call the forest and the fortress anything Thistle wanted.

A moment later they came to a flat rock near a fire pit with several smaller rock seats around it. A fire burned in the pit, casting haphazard shadows around the cavern. The roof and floor were entirely made of fallen rocks. It looked like something had purposefully laid the boulders in this manner to make a home for rock dragons.

"Is it safe?" Brigitta asked Thistle.

"Oh, no one else in the Hollows or at Croilus knows of this place. We're certain of that, otherwise . . . "

"No, I meant," Brigitta gestured at the boulders balanced around them.

"Oh, um—mostly safe, I think. No sliverleaves or nightwalkers at least."

Before Brigitta could ask what sliverleaves and nightwalkers were, four more Watchers emerged from the rocks and joined them at the fire pit. Two males wore black tunics with the round symbol of Croilus and another female and a small boy wore the blue tunics of Mabbe's Watchers.

"Brigitta, this is Ferris and Jarlath's brother Roane," said Thistle, pointing to the girl and small boy. "They're from the Hollows." She motioned to the other males, "And Devin and Zhay from Croilus."

All together they were a strange band of beasts. Zhay was slightly smaller than Jarlath, with much paler crystal blue eyes, long ragged white hair, and jaundiced skin that was so papery it looked as if one could poke a hole through it with a finger. His muddy green wings were tough and calloused compared to the rest of him.

The other Croilus faerie, Devin, was a little younger and more pleasant to look at. He had darker features, with brown tones to his wings and skin. His hair and eyebrows were more gray than brown, but a neglectful gray, not the wizened gray of old age. The top half of his left ear was missing.

Slightly taller than Devin, Ferris stood protectively at his side.

She had peculiar green-tinted skin covered with dozens of tiny straight scars that shone silver where the skin had healed. Three of these scars marked her face, one across a brow that left a small silver streak of eyebrow hair.

Ferris's green-gray wings were oversized for her small body and also covered in strange silver scars, almost like destiny markings, and what looked to be a large bite off the end of her right wing. She had striking hair, like the burst of a sunset, all reds and yellows and oranges.

The smallest faerie of the bunch, Roane, hid behind Thistle, wrapping his fists in the back of her tunic. He had the palest eyes of them all, with just a hint of blue, but they were too large for his baby face. His dark hair was soft like a girl's, with long lashes to match. His skin and wings carried gold tones like Jarlath's, and as he turned shyly away, Brigitta noticed a branded X on the end of his left wing that made her heart ache.

They all mumbled nervous greetings to her. Thistle, oblivious to the tension in the air, broke her greencicle once again and handed half to Roane. They sat down in front of the fire.

Brigitta dropped next to them and tossed the rest of her greencicle in the dirt beside the fire. As it melted, the faeries continued to stare at her until she could not stand it any longer.

"Why are you all here together?" she asked. "Aren't you sworn enemies?"

Devin, Ferris, and Zhay took seats around the pit.

"We are of like minds," said Jarlath, gathering up a pile of twigs stacked against the rock wall.

"Mostly like minds," said Zhay, correcting Jarlath. "But none of us believes either tribe is ruled fairly." He placed some dry leaves into the fire.

"So, what, you're some kind of rebels?"

They looked around at each other. Even Thistle's friendly face turned anxious.

"Something like that," said Jarlath, carrying the twigs to the pit.

"If you're afraid I'm going to give you away, don't be," said Brigitta. "I have no loyalties to either tribe."

Brigitta wasn't sure how much her word meant to these so called rebel faeries, but she felt the tension in the cavern dissipate as Jarlath and Zhay built up the fire.

"Is it true you come from the home of the Ancients?" asked Devin.

"Well, this is really the home of the Ancients," Brigitta pointed out. "At least it was a long time ago."

"I've never seen one," said Ferris, crossing her scarred arms across her chest. "What are they like?"

"I've never seen one either," admitted Brigitta. "They're ethereal. And they don't live with us elemental faeries in the White Forest."

"Where do they live?" asked Thistle.

"They live in the ethers, bound to the fifth element," Brigitta automatically repeated from her numerous lessons. "At least that's what I've been told. I've never actually spoken with one."

Zhay snickered. "Sounds like a pile of bird drop to me."

Brigitta turned on him, "What do you know? You've never been to the White Forest. You haven't seen how they've protected us all these seasons." She didn't know why she felt the need to protect the Ancients, since she had her own doubts, but she didn't like his accusatory tone.

"Why are you here, then?" asked Zhay.

"Because we've lost touch with them," confessed Brigitta, "which puts us in danger."

"They deserted you just like they deserted us," snorted Jarlath, snapping a twig in two and flinging both halves into the fire.

"You don't know if they deserted us," said Thistle as she hugged Roane to her chest.

"Then why are we still here and not in this amazing White Forest?" asked Jarlath.

"I don't know, but we can't trust what Mabbe tells us," reasoned Thistle.

"If you've never seen an Ancient," yawned Devin, snuggling himself into Ferris, "how do you know they exist?"

"Because of my element and my destiny markings," Brigitta pointed to the dark green symbols on her wings. "Only an Ethereal, an Ancient One, can create a destiny marking."

"So the Ancients brand you with your tribe symbols?" asked Zhay.

"They're not brands," she said. "The destiny markings mean that some day I will sit on the Council of Elders. But right now I'm just a Second Apprentice."

"And everyone in your tribe has an element?" asked Thistle.

"Everyone is bound to one, yes, but every once in a while some are born with two elements, like Ondelle. Everything about the White Forest, the Great Hourglass, the bound elements and destiny markings, has been designed by the Ancients to keep it safe and in balance." Brigitta looked around at all the rebel Watchers. "Haven't you ever been told the story of the Great World Cry?"

The faeries stared out at her blankly. Thistle shook her head.

"You know what I think?" asked Jarlath. "I think these Ancients stole all those elements from Noe, took a bunch of traitorous faeries north, and left us here to rot."

"You can't believe that's true," said Brigitta.

"Too bad we can't ask one to find out."

"They didn't desert you and they haven't deserted us," Brigitta insisted. "They'd never do that. We just have to figure out why they've stopped giving destiny marks and dispersing the spirits of the dead."

Everyone froze and stared at each other. Roane moved over to Jarlath and he took him into his lap.

"Dispersing your spirits?" whispered Thistle, breaking the silence. "You mean ascending the dead?"

"I guess so," said Brigitta, confused as to why they suddenly looked so frightened. "What happens here when a faerie dies? Is their spirit *ascended* as you say?"

"They used to be," said Jarlath, choosing his words carefully, "according to the older members of the Hollows. But now . . ."

"We throw them into the river," finished Ferris.

"You what?" exclaimed Brigitta, horrified. "What happens to their spirits?"

"Usually the spirits go after them into the Mad River," said Devin. "But sometimes, well, they stick around."

"Nightwalkers," said Thistle, and everyone shivered.

"But how can you just throw the bodies into the river?" asked Brigitta.

"You'd rather we let the birds tear them apart and leave us the remains?" spat Ferris. Devin put his arm around her shoulders and squeezed.

Roane began to whimper and buried his face in Jarlath's tunic. Jarlath shot Ferris an angry look.

"Sorry, Roane," said Ferris quietly.

Everyone grew silent and sullen. Brigitta didn't think she was getting anywhere with these rebel faeries. At least, nothing was getting her closer to stealing Mabbe's sands back . . . or finding the sacred item.

"So, this Croilus faerie," said Brigitta, changing the subject, "he named the palace and his lands after himself? Isn't that a little conceited?"

"That's the kind of ruler he is," said Zhay.

"And that's his symbol on your tunic?" she asked Devin, trying to sound casual.

"More like an obsession of his," said Devin, looking down at the front of his tunic and tracing the symbol with a finger. "The Purview, he calls it. It's supposed to be some great tool of sorcery."

"Yeah, and it's probably just as much mythic bird drop," laughed Zhay.

"No, I bet the Ancients took that with them, too," Jarlath pointed out.

"It's not in our forest," said Brigitta. "I'm sure we'd have seen it."

"Is that why you're going to Croilus?" Devin asked. "To find this Purview?"

Brigitta paused. Ondelle had said to trust no one about the artifact. But that was before they knew there was anyone to trust.

"No, she's going to steal all of Croilus's sands," said Jarlath before Brigitta could answer. "She has to," he added quickly, "or Mabbe will kill her High Priestess if she doesn't."

"Mabbe will kill her High Priestess anyway!" shouted Zhay. "You can't leave Croilus defenseless!"

"Defenseless?" Ferris stood up and poked Zhay in the chest. "Whose tribe is attacking whose? Besides, where did he get all those sands in the first place?"

Zhay pointed to Brigitta. "She's going to ruin all our plans."

"What plans?" asked Jarlath. "All we do is argue."

"Yeah, and besides," added Thistle, "maybe she can help us?"

They all turned their crystal blue eyes to Brigitta, and she saw their hopes and their fears reflected there. Could she help them? Could she even help herself?

Brigitta stared into the fire, mind and body numb, as Thistle prepared a meal of strange looking roots inside a battered pot. Roane handed her ingredients as he sucked on the remains of his greencicle.

"Tell us about the White Forest," said Thistle, looking up from her stew.

Brigitta's home and her family seemed so far away. Any description would be muddled, like trying to piece together a dream. Her eyes lit up and she reached into her bag. She pulled out the little pouch containing Himalette's song drop.

"I think this will tell you better."

Brigitta backed away from the fire. She removed the silvery droplet from the pouch and dangled it between her finger and thumb. All the Watchers, even Jarlath and Zhay, admired it as it sparkled in the firelight.

"It's so pretty," said Thistle.

"What's it do?" asked Ferris.

Brigitta let the song drop fall to the rocky floor. It tinkled as the tiny silver object shattered. She felt a slight breeze as her sister's voice flew through the air around them:

> My home is in the trees of white
> They keep us safe both day and night
> Where faeries play and sing and dance
> And eat suclaide at every chance
> So they can dream of clouds above
> And pick blossoms to their heart's delight

Softer and sweeter than Brigitta remembered, Himmy's voice floated through the air around them. Roane played at trying to catch it. Everyone else cocked their heads as they listened.

> When I was young I wished I would
> Have the very best gift I could
> Like Momma makes the finest stew
> And Poppa invents a thing or two
> As Briggy is marked to lead our kin
> I will sing throughout our wood.

"Do you have any more?" asked Thistle as the final quiver of Himalette's little voice faded. Roane nodded with excitement.

"I'm afraid not," said Brigitta. She swept the little silver pieces into her hands and placed them into the front pocket of her tunic. "That was my sister's voice. She was destiny-marked as a Song Master. It was her first song drop." She sniffed back tears of pride as she pictured Himalette gleefully casting the drop with her song.

"When you say marked," asked Jarlath, "you mean you must do what the Ancients command?"

"It's not a command; it's a destiny."

"But you have no choice," said Jarlath. "You must perform this destiny."

"The Ancients are wise, the destiny is . . . " Brigitta searched for the right words to explain, "the destiny is appropriate."

Jarlath folded his arms across his chest, unconvinced.

"You heard the song. Himalette wished to be a Song Master and she became one. She's happy."

"Are you happy?" asked Devin. "With your destiny, I mean."

"My destiny—I'm," struggled Brigitta, "I'm different. I can't explain."

"Sounds just like having to be a Watcher," said Jarlath. "I didn't choose to be bigger and have blue eyes and hear—"

The others looked fiercely at Jarlath.

"I didn't pick to be this, and I'd rather not have anyone, especially not some invisible Ancient, telling me what to do." Jarlath sat down and scowled into the fire.

Roane turned to Brigitta, pointed to her pocket, and then held out his hand. She retrieved a piece of Himalette's song drop and placed it in his palm. He stroked it with a finger and then looked up at her with teary eyes.

"What?" asked Brigitta. "What's wrong?"

"Roane doesn't speak," said Ferris.

"Mabbe took his voice away," said Thistle.

"Oh, yeah," said Brigitta, "I could see why you'd think life here is much better than in the White Forest."

"I didn't say it was better," argued Jarlath.

Brigitta reached into her bag and took out a piece of triple lyllium suclaide. "This will help," she said to Roane. "You eat it. My momma made it. It's the best suclaide in all our forest."

Roane put the treat in his mouth and shut his eyes as he savored it. Brigitta handed out pieces to everyone. Jarlath reluctantly took one and nodded as he sucked on it.

Brigitta popped one into her own mouth. "We'll all have sweet dreams tonight," she said, though she doubted any of them even knew what a good dream was.

Zhay took first watch as the rest of them settled into sleep. Brigitta found herself nestled between Thistle and Roane, who had suddenly decided not to leave her side.

Devin and Ferris retired farther away, snuggled under one of Brigitta's White Forest blankets and sighing as they stroked the soft material. Jarlath tended the fire, ready to take second watch when Zhay's shift was done.

"Are you scared about going to Croilus?" asked Thistle.

"Right now, I don't know how to feel," said Brigitta. "The thing is, I need a plan. I don't know enough about this Croilus faerie."

"Devin will help."

"And Zhay?"

"He's all right," said Thistle. "He and Jarlath are kinda bitter. They've both lost family in the Sorcery Sand Wars. Jarlath's sister . . . Well, she didn't have enough Watcher blood according to Mabbe, so she was made to dig at the Mad River. Then one day . . . "

Roane squirmed uncomfortably at Brigitta's side.

"Oh, I'm sorry Roane," said Thistle. "He doesn't like to hear about what happened to her."

"It must be hard growing up in such a dangerous place," said Brigitta, fingering the pieces of Himmy's song drop in her pocket.

"But you and Ondelle know magic, right?" asked Thistle. "You can help us?"

"There's no such thing as magic," Brigitta murmured to herself.

Chapter Twelve

Brigitta awoke early the next morning and ventured out of the fortress to where Ferris stood guard. They sat next to each other on top of a boulder, facing into the valley, where they could see down into the old lakebed. The valley mist glowed in the morning light and slowly breathed in and out, caught in the changing winds of the River the Runs Backwards. They sat in silence, listening to the buzzing morning beasts. A small brown scaly creature slithered across the broken cliff wall. Its two long tails twitched as it spied the faerie girls.

"Scat!" cried Ferris, throwing a rock at the beast.

The creature hissed, then opened its maw and spat a black substance onto the boulder beneath their feet before disappearing into a crack.

"You can eat them in a pinch," said Ferris. "Except the head. It's poisonous."

"Thanks for the tip." The thought of eating any creature in Rivermist did not appeal to Brigitta. She doubted even her mother could make the creepy thing appetizing.

"How did there get to be two kinds of faeries? How come there are Watchers and the other ones?"

"Lesser faeries, Mabbe and Croilus call them," said Ferris. "According to Mabbe, she created Watchers."

"How?"

"Using the sorcery sands." Ferris picked up a stone and chucked it against the wall. It clattered on the rocks as it bounced down through the crevasse. "A long time ago, she wanted to create a band of stronger and wiser faeries. She used up a bunch of the sorcery sands to do it. She sometimes calls us her *children*." Ferris laughed at this idea.

"Then one of them, Croilus, rose up against her. About fifty season cycles ago he stole her sands and took some faeries with him. We've been in the Sand Wars ever since."

"Croilus is a Watcher, like you?"

"Croilus is mad, like the river."

The strange scaly creature stuck its head out of the crack, and Ferris threw another rock at it. "He's the reason we can't ascend our dead any longer and are trained from birth to keep our minds closed. He was always listening to the—" Ferris stopped and tucked her knees under her chin.

"The what?" Brigitta asked.

"Shhh!" Ferris hissed, looking behind them at the entrance to the fortress. "It's nothing. Forget it."

Brigitta lowered her voice. "If you want me to stop him, you've got to tell me."

Ferris gripped Brigitta's arm so tightly it hurt. "They drove him mad, the voices that spoke to Croilus," she whispered fiercely. "Every Watcher can hear the voices, and before Croilus rebelled they somehow used the voices to ascend the dead. But now we're all trained to block out mind sorcery. We are put to death if we even speak of the voices." Ferris dropped Brigitta's arm.

"But your friends wouldn't tell anyone, would they?"

Ferris only shut her mouth and shook her head.

Brigitta thought about when she touched Jarlath's face back in the Colony. She had heard the voices, too, and had almost given him away. She had almost gotten them both killed.

And now she had to somehow trick this "mad" Croilus into giving her his sands. If Watchers could block out empathing, getting close to him wasn't going to do any good. She had to find something more powerful to use against him.

Just then, a ray of sun broke through the gray, sending a flash sparking over the horizon. It danced on Ferris's greenish skin, the hard silvery scars catching the light.

Ferris saw her looking and wiggled her arm. "Devin thinks it's pretty how they shine. He says it's hypnotic."

Hypnotic. Brigitta stopped Ferris's arm. "Have you ever heard of green zynthias?"

🌷

Thistle dished out a red berry mash for breakfast. Roane fluttered about, topping each bowl of mash with some of Ondelle's herbs.

Meanwhile, Brigitta displayed her supplies on the boulders, and the others gathered around to examine the items.

"Such sorcery!" exclaimed Devin.

"Hardly," said Brigitta. She pointed to two small canisters. "The firepepper and dustmist may come in handy, but this," she picked up the larger spell seed containing the zynthia, "this is our strongest weapon."

"Your zyntha's inside there?" asked Ferris.

"Zynthia, yes. And if they've never seen one before, neither Mabbe nor Croilus could fight its hypnotic power. That takes training to do."

"So Zhay and I pretend to have captured you," said Devin, taking his bowl of mash from Roane, "and you offer this zynthia as a gift to Croilus and use it on him?"

"Exactly."

"And then what?" asked Jarlath.

"Then we take his sands. Mabbe has promised to release Ondelle if I bring them to her."

Zhay burst out laughing. "Yes, and you can trust what Mabbe says."

"I didn't say that," said Brigitta, "but she thinks I believe her. That gives us some time."

"For what?" asked Zhay.

"To figure out how to deal with her. I haven't gotten that far yet." Brigitta looked around at their skeptical faces. "But at least Croilus will be out of the way."

Zhay muttered to himself as he extinguished the fire.

"Do you have a better plan, Zhay?" Jarlath asked.

"Isn't this why we're here?" said Ferris. "To get rid of Croilus and Mabbe."

As Zhay continued to putter around the fire pit, everyone else grew excited about the prospect of leaving Croilus incapacitated. Brigitta packed the spell seed with the green zynthia, along with the firepepper, dustmist, and globelight. She left the rest of her belongings behind a rock, making sure the suclaide was well-hidden from Roane.

"Ready," she said to Devin and Zhay.

They said their goodbyes and flew from the fortress, over the fallen boulders, and back down into the crevasse. When they reached the bottom, Zhay dropped to the log with the pits.

"Hey, there's seven log stones," he said.

"Yeah," Devin said, grinning, "I added a pit for Brigitta this morning."

"What is that?" she asked.

"A message system." Devin pointed at the log. "If you're in the Gathering Place, you put a white stone in your spot. When you leave, if you don't know when you'll be back, you leave it empty. If you plan to be back within a sun or two, put a black stone. If there's trouble, put red. Don't go to the Gathering Place if there's a red stone in your spot."

He pointed to the pit on the far right. "That one's for you."

Brigitta picked up a black stone and placed it in the seventh pit. Devin laughed and placed one in his pit as well.

Zhay shook his head. "Come on."

The three faeries traveled east until they arrived at the River That Runs Backwards, then turned south to follow it, keeping a safe enough distance to avoid its pull. A moonbeat later the banks of the river were high enough that they could cross.

"Don't look down," advised Devin. "And be quick."

As they crossed over, Brigitta focused on the far bank and not the dizzying waters that threatened to suck them under. She was more than relieved when they reached the other side.

With Zhay in the lead, Devin and Brigitta followed him southeast until the forest broke away, and he landed on a bald hill overlooking an enormous overgrown arena. Toppled statues and pillars littered the landscape along with crumbling walls and fountains. Everything was covered in a thorny purple ivy.

In the middle of the ruins stood a plateau supporting a stone palace, gray and crumbling but for the shimmering center structure topped with an immense dome. The brightness of it contrasted with the dull shades of the valley.

There were no other faeries in sight.

Zhay examined the sky. The clouds were thicker and darker than the previous day. He held out his hand for a moment. "Think it's going to rain?" he asked Devin.

Brigitta looked at him, puzzled, but Devin wrinkled his brow and studied the sky. She glanced up as well. The clouds were heavier than White Forest clouds and unfamiliar. She wondered if she could even empath them. "Why does it matter?" she asked.

"If it starts to rain, even a little bit, fly to whichever side of the arena is closest and do not stop," said Devin. "The warwumps come out whenever it rains."

"What's a warwump?"

"You don't want to find out," said Zhay. "Give me your pack."

"Why?"

"Because Croilus will punish us for allowing you inside with it."

Devin nodded in agreement, and Brigitta handed her pack to Zhay.

He gestured to Devin, "Make it look like we're escorting her, one ahead and one behind."

Devin leapt into the air and began to fly over the ruins. Brigitta followed across the littered landscape.

"Don't touch the ivy," Devin warned. "The thorns are vicious and the vines unpredictable." He pointed to a few larger pillars only half smothered by the nasty plant. "If you need to rest, do it as high as possible."

She looked down as they flew. The land was tiered, so that it descended slowly as they flew toward the center, and crumbling buildings poked out under dirt, debris, and writhing ivy.

Devin turned and hovered, gesturing to the ruins below them. "A long time ago, this is where all the Ancients lived."

"Not in the trees?"

"Croilus says they had visitors from all over Faweh and had to host them here."

She contemplated the enormity of the ruins. There must have been thousands of visitors to fill this arena. It was obvious no one had occupied the space for a very long time. "And the palace up there?"

"Where the High Sages and their families lived. Where the World Sages met."

Zhay snorted and gestured over his shoulder. "Yeah, and all the lesser faeries had to live in the Hollows."

"In the dead trees?" said Brigitta. "Why would they live in that horrible place?"

"I guess they weren't good enough to stay with the Ancients," said Zhay.

"Who told you all this?"

"Croilus," Devin said, then shrugged.

"I don't believe him," said Brigitta. "The Ancients exist to protect us."

"Then why did they leave so many of us behind?" Zhay asked and then waved them toward the plateau.

There were at least a dozen Croilus Watchers patrolling the base of the plateau. As they approached, Devin and Zhay took positions on either side of Brigitta and held her arms. Watchers observed them curiously as they made their way to an opening in the plateau, but no one confronted them. A silver staircase ran up through the opening. At the base, the staircase was about as wide as her cottage in Tiragarrow, and it grew narrower and narrower as it reached the top.

The thorny ivy had crawled partway up the stairs. A Watcher sat on the steps above three lesser Croilus faeries, supervising as they pushed the ivy back with firesticks. The lesser faeries stopped and gaped at Brigitta as she passed overhead. A tendril of ivy grabbed one's leg as he was distracted, and he cried out in pain. The others stabbed at the ivy with their sticks, fighting it off as it dragged him down the stairs, thorns caught in his skin. The Watcher stood up but did nothing to assist.

"The ivy!" Brigitta called out and turned to help.

"Leave them!" hissed Zhay, pulling her along.

"But—"

"We can't interfere with another's task," whispered Devin. "It's not allowed."

"But that's ridiculous!" Brigitta said as she watched helplessly from the air.

"It's Croilus's way." Zhay pulled at her again.

Brigitta glanced over her shoulder as they flew up the length of stairs, relieved when the faeries managed to pull their friend free. They reached the top and glided through the crumbling sections of the palace. Frightened lesser faerie eyes watched them from windows and doorways, pulling into the shadows as Brigitta fluttered by.

Past the ruined walls, they entered a courtyard and landed in front of the most beautiful structure Brigitta had ever seen. It shone into the dark air like a star. A dozen columns supported the center structure, on top of which stood a giant dome. The building was pure white and opened like arms from its domed center.

"How come . . . " Brigitta's voice trailed off as she noticed several little white figures darting about the columns. The longer she watched, the more of them she saw flitting in and around the palace. "What are those things doing?"

"Who, the sprites?" asked Zhay.

"Sprites?" Brigitta was dumbfounded. She stepped closer, and sure enough, the little pale-haired, pale-skinned, white-clothed flying beasts were sprites. They were smaller than the ones in her forest, and she'd never seen such ghostly ones before, but they were definitely sprites. "How in Faweh did you get them to—to—*work?*"

"What do you mean?" asked Devin. "They don't do anything else. They never stop."

"I think they've always been here." Zhay looked at the sprites as if for the first time.

It didn't make any sense to Brigitta, but there wasn't much about Noe that made sense, she thought, as they flew up to the center building. She passed a little sprite methodically polishing a column as if under some kind of green zynthia hypnosis. For a moment, Brigitta swore she could see through the wispy beast. Its eyes never left its task.

Everything was painfully clean in the courtyard. Brigitta was afraid she'd leave dirty footprints on the beautiful surface and was surprised when she turned to look and there were none. The open arms of the structure were corridors that led up to the center dome. The corridors had ceilings, but no walls, and were supported by more columns. Along the corridors, silver benches invited non-existent guests to relax, and in the middle of the courtyard sat a dry silver fountain.

Something poked at her side, and she turned to find Devin with a grim expression. He nodded to an older Watcher entering the courtyard.

"Stay here," said Zhay, who fluttered over to the guard, showed him Brigitta's pack, and pointed to her. The guard and Zhay slipped around the side of the building.

It was strangely quiet. The only movements were the eerie sprites, polishing and polishing. It was far too lovely to be so empty. The loneliness of it stung Brigitta's heart.

"Why didn't Mabbe choose to live here?" she whispered.

"Because Mabbe is clever," Devin whispered back, "and Croilus is vain."

There was a metal clang, and Zhay pushed open a pair of enormous silver doors between the centermost columns. Devin flew Brigitta to the entrance and they stepped inside. Zhay shut the door behind them and everything went dark.

As they stood there, shapes slowly appeared. It was dingier inside the domed structure. There were rotting tapestries, dusty floors, and scavenged shelves. They moved through a curved passageway until it opened up into a cavernous room with four sections of stone seats. It was shaped like the Center Realm grandstands, but was not at all festive. The dome above was covered with seasons of grime, so that little light shone through.

In front of the tiers of seats sat another silver platform with five carved chairs of varying size and shape. On the far right was the largest chair, which was squat and wide. Next to it sat a chair that was slightly larger than an Elder's chair. On the far left was a tall slender one, and next to that, one with a high seat and an attached footstool. In the middle was a high-backed chair carved in, of course, more silver.

Brigitta gasped and clutched Devin. "This must be where the High Sages—"

"Quiet!" snarled Zhay, startling Brigitta, who had forgotten for a moment that she was their prisoner.

The older Watcher stood at the base of the platform.

"Here, hold this," said Zhay, handing Brigitta's pack to Devin. Instead of flying to meet the other Watcher, he climbed down on foot, the steps spaced too far apart to do so with any grace.

As they waited for Zhay to reach the other Watcher, Devin squeezed her hand and pulled away. A chill went up Brigitta's spine as she suddenly grew nervous. Her heart pounded in her chest for a moment before she could calm herself again.

When Zhay made it to the bottom, the older Watcher gestured

and Zhay cleared his throat. "Oh, great leader Croilus," he called. "We have captured a faerie who claims to have a gift for you."

They stared up at the domed ceiling.

"She says it is a magical gift, Croilus of Noe," he continued, "and requests your presence."

The cavernous room was still and quiet as if holding its breath.

"Guess he's not interested," grunted the older Watcher, cracking the silence. He twirled his firestick. "Bind her wings and take her to the—"

"The Ancient Ones wish to bestow a gift worthy of you!" yelled Brigitta up at the dome. Croilus was vain, Devin had said.

A moment later, there was a flash, and a large Watcher appeared above them in the air. He dropped down and settled into the silver high-backed chair. He was wearing the most ridiculous robe Brigitta had ever seen. It was thick and purple and longer than his body. The arms flared out into huge poofs of delicately spun lace. Brigitta would have burst out laughing if it weren't for his maniacal crystal blue eyes upon her. The rest of his face was pale and sharp and firm. He wore a silver wreath around his bald head.

Zhay and the older Watcher kneeled in front of him.

"Oh, great leader Croilus," said Devin, voice wavering. "We were patrolling the lakebed and found this faerie." He nudged Brigitta down the steps.

"I knew it!" cried Croilus gleefully. "You've finally come!"

"I'm not sure what you mean, sir," said Brigitta as she descended. "I am Brigitta of the White Forest. I came here on a mission of peace to bring you greetings and a gift from the Ancients."

"Enough! I know why you are here!" wailed Croilus, standing and getting caught in his robe. "You have come to steal my sorcery sands!"

"Why would I do that, sir?" laughed Brigitta. "We have a gigantic hourglass full of sand in the White Forest. We have so much sand we dance around it in celebration."

Croilus stared down at her as she approached the platform. His gaze did not affect her. He had no power to enter her mind. Perhaps she could fool him after all.

"As a matter of fact," she pulled her hourglass necklace from inside her tunic, "I have some right here in this miniature hourglass. Every faerie born in the White Forest is given their own hourglass full of sand, there is so much of it."

"You never told us that," accused Zhay.

Croilus flashed a staff at Zhay and a bolt of red shot out and hit him in the chest, knocking him off his feet. "I did not say you could speak."

Zhay writhed in pain and struggled for breath. "Many . . . apologies . . . sir."

Croilus pointed his staff at Brigitta and smiled wickedly. "You can have the sands. I won't be needing them anymore."

Devin and Zhay exchanged confused glances.

"Now where is this gift?" he asked, pounding the floor with his staff.

"Watcher Devin has it, sir," Zhay pointed to Devin, who held up Brigitta's pack.

"Bring it to me!" Croilus ordered.

Devin stepped up to the platform and held up the pack to Croilus, who snatched it away. Devin dropped to his knees and bowed his head.

Croilus reached hungrily into the pack and pulled out Brigitta's globelight.

"That's just a light to guide my way," said Brigitta.

He dropped the globelight to the floor and dove into the pack again, pulling out the firepepper and dustmist.

"Those are spices," said Brigitta. "It's the large seed pod."

Brigitta approached and Croilus readied his staff. "Stay back, faerie," he said.

He stuck his hand into the pack once more and pulled out the bottom of the bag. "There's nothing else! What's the meaning of this?"

"No, it can't be!" she cried. "There was a sorcery seed! It was a gift from the . . . from the Ancients."

"It's true, there was a sorcery seed. She showed it to us," said Zhay, crawling to his knees.

"Yes!" exclaimed Brigitta. "They both saw it."

"Then Watcher Devin must have stolen it for himself." Zhay pointed at Devin.

Both Devin and Brigitta whirled around to face Zhay.

"No . . . no . . ." stammered Devin, waving his arms in defense. "I didn't take it!" He turned to Brigitta. "It wasn't me!"

"He had her pack, sir," said Zhay, getting to his feet, "and she showed us the pod inside it."

Croilus sent such a flare out to Devin from his staff that it knocked him across the floor and into the first set of stone seats, where he smacked his head and was still.

"Devin!" cried Brigitta, and she turned to run to him.

Croilus jumped from the platform and landed in front of Brigitta, staff pointed in her face.

"But he's lying!" Brigitta pointed to Zhay.

"Silence!" he seethed. "If Watcher Devin wakes, he will bring me this sorcery seed. If he doesn't wake, you'd better hope that you can find it. I've waited far too long for this."

Croilus motioned to Zhay, who grabbed Brigitta by the arm. Before she had a chance to struggle, Croilus flung his staff in her direction. A fiery force struck her in the legs, and they buckled under her. She fell forward to the floor, legs burning. For a second, she thought she would fall flat on her face, but Zhay stopped her just in time and set her down.

She wanted to strike out at him, but her legs pained her so badly that she couldn't speak. The pain intensified, as if a fire grew inside of them, making her dizzy. Immobilized, she lay on the floor, wondering if Devin was still alive.

Chapter Thirteen

A pulse of pain beat through her legs as Brigitta awoke next to Devin on the cold floor under the dome. She didn't remember passing out. She tried to stretch out, but her arms, legs, and wings were restrained. It was quiet except for the sound of Devin breathing. So, he was alive.

Wondering if they were alone, Brigitta relaxed and tentatively misted her mind out, shaky at first, but finding balance quickly. She was getting better at it; Elder Fozk would be proud.

She sensed someone at the back of the room, but she couldn't tell who. Reaching farther, she felt the tattered fabrics and cold stone furniture. After a breath, her mind continued across the room, up the stairs, through the rounded passageway, and out into the courtyard. She could sense the fluttering of the sprites, but what she felt was like the opposite of energy, as if the essence of the sprites had been drained, leaving unconscious and empty shells.

She drifted among their steady rhythms, misting higher and higher, floating up into the sky. The thick fullness of the clouds met her and pulled her in. She faltered for a moonsbreath, surprised at their strength, but relaxed further into her breath and allowed her mind-mist to mingle there. Steady and focused, her vision shifted, and she was gazing down onto the ruins. Something impossibly large shifted under the ivy deep inside the earth.

Zhay crouched down in front of her, and her mind snapped back. "Tell me how to open the spell seed, and I'll help you escape," he whispered.

"What do you want with it?" growled Brigitta.

"The same thing you do. To stop Croilus."

"So you can take his place?"

Zhay moved closer to Brigitta's face and took her chin in his hands. "My father died in the ivy, my mother was swallowed by the Mad River, and my sister taken by the warwumps. Croilus does nothing to better our lives."

"So then help us," Brigitta said, "for them."

"And set everyone free, like Devin and the rest want?"

"Of course!"

"What do you think would happen if these faeries were left to rule themselves? They've never been free. It would be a complete mess. There would be six warring tribes instead of two. More faeries would die." Zhay let go of her face. "But they will follow the one who defeats Croilus."

"And why should you be the one to lead them?" asked Brigitta.

"They couldn't have worse than Croilus." Zhay leaned back and shook his head. "That's the crazy thing. Everyone hates him, but they fear losing their leader more than they fear for their own lives."

"Watcher Zhay!" a voice called from across the room, and Zhay's eyes grew panicked. "Croilus wants to know if you have any knowledge of this faerie light or these spices. One appears to have burned his skin."

"Get my pack back for me and I'll think about helping you," Brigitta hissed.

Zhay stepped over Brigitta. A moment later she heard him and the older Watcher talking in low voices behind her. Devin's eyes fluttered and opened. He stared at Brigitta, confused.

"Shhh. Don't let them know you're awake," whispered Brigitta. "Close your eyes and keep still."

Devin closed his eyes, and Brigitta scooted a little closer. "Zhay took the spell seed but blamed you. Croilus wants you to lead us to it."

"How can I do that?" whispered Devin.

"I want you to pretend to know where it is," she said. "Now, tell me about these warwumps."

Brigitta and Devin hovered in the air, facing the ivy-ridden arena surrounding the plateau. They were linked together by a silver chain. Zhay and five more Watchers hovered in the air behind them with firesticks.

As part of Brigitta's plan, Devin had told the older Watcher the sorcery seed was hidden in the arena. Zhay had tried to protest, but more Watchers had entered with orders from Croilus to find the seed. He had no choice but to go along with them.

Zhay moved closer and spoke quietly to Brigitta. "I don't know what you're up to, but you'll only get yourselves hurt."

"Don't talk to us, you traitor," growled Devin. "I should have known you couldn't be trusted."

"I only want what's best for all of us," replied Zhay. "Don't say I didn't give you a chance. You can't blame me for this."

Zhay moved back into the Watcher formation, taking position in the half circle around Devin and Brigitta.

"Well?" she turned to Devin. "Show us where you hid the seed!"

Devin gave Brigitta an uneasy glance. "This way," he said softly before flying off across the ivy.

As she took off, Brigitta made note on which shoulder Zhay carried her pack. Getting it would be tricky, but she had the element of surprise. And fear. She looked up at the sky and was pleased to see the Watchers do the same. The clouds were thick and dark in the red-gray sky. Manipulating them would be difficult to do while flying.

She pointed to a tall pillar sticking out of the ivy. "Can we land there please?"

"What's wrong?" demanded Zhay.

"I'm feeling weak from Croilus's attack," said Brigitta. "I just need a moonsbreath to rest."

She wavered in the air and Devin took hold of her, but his wings were not strong enough to support them both. He led her to the pillar, and she pretended to catch her breath. Zhay and the other Watchers buzzed around them.

"What's going on?" whispered Devin.

"I'm fine," whispered Brigitta, "just be ready."

Brigitta took a deep breath and stretched out her arms and wings. She settled her mind and body, letting go of everything but cloud energy. Just like at Green Lake, she said to herself, then let that thought go, slowly and carefully drifting up. She bounced around a bit and then was looking down from a great height, passing over the arena. Everything was far below her as she drifted. Once she was balanced, she swam along with the clouds, feeling for moisture, feeling—there! A wide expanse of heaviness, like a bladder about to burst.

"All right, that's enough!" barked Zhay, nudging Brigitta with his stick. "Let's go."

With her eyes, Brigitta directed Devin toward the rain clouds. The color drained from his face as they flew, and Brigitta pulled on the chain to keep him going in the right direction.

Zhay, weary himself, flew around and stopped in front of them. "We didn't fly this way today. This can't be the right place."

Brigitta and Devin hovered in the air, silver chain swaying between them. She gave Zhay a big smile. "Oh, this is exactly the right place."

Gripping her hourglass necklace, Brigitta concentrated with every bit of water energy she could muster. Zhay's voice dropped away. Someone prodded her back, but she ignored it and held her necklace as the clouds reformed, graying as they grew denser.

"We're going back!" Zhay's voice cut into her concentration.

She opened her eyes and looked at Devin, whose face was so terrified she felt guilty for what she had asked him to do.

"I've had enough." Zhay turned to the other Watchers. "Let Croilus deal with them."

The Watchers gathered around the other side of Devin and Brigitta as she touched Devin's arm and nodded. He nodded back, shaking with fear.

"What was that?" one of the Watchers cried out.

"Did you feel that?" called another.

Brigitta felt a drop on her head. A large, wet, oily drop.

"Rain!" cried Zhay. "It's going to rain!"

There was another drop and another and before they knew it, the clouds had opened up, and it was pouring down on them.

"It worked!" laughed Brigitta over the torrent of water.

Zhay and all the other Watchers buzzed around in a panic. Brigitta snagged her pack from Zhay's shoulder. He turned to take it back, but she flew out of reach, dragging Devin with her as the rain pounded harder.

With an anguished cry, Zhay sped toward the outer edge, and the other Watchers took off toward the plateau, leaving Devin and Brigitta alone in the middle of the ruins. As the rain came down, she felt heavier and heavier. Her wings were soaked in oily wetness. The rain was like mucus.

"Follow me," she said to the wet and trembling Devin.

The ground rumbled beneath them, the ivy shook, and the earth caved in. Brigitta grabbed Devin's arm and flew up as hard and fast as she could. The rain had coated her wings so that they slipped in the air. She struggled with him as she flew.

Devin snapped out of his daze and began to pump his wings as well. They flew up together, away from the thunderous sounds. "I—I—I can't fly this high," panted Devin. "I'll never make it."

"Just do it!"

Brigitta glanced down as an enormous black beast burst up through the earth. It was limbless and hairless, like a worm, but with a hard shell and a beakish mouth that took up a quarter of its body. Another sprung through the ground, and they both opened their mouths and flung themselves about wildly. Their screams were deafening. Brigitta and Devin hovered just out of reach. Four more warwumps burst through the ruins, their mouths wide enough to swallow a cottage.

"Can you hover by yourself for a moment?" yelled Brigitta over the sound of the rain and screams.

She let go of Devin and removed the dustmist and the firepepper from her pack. She poured out the dustmist so that it settled beneath them, like a thick floating carpet, and sprinkled the firepepper into it. It was a sloppy job, with holes in the pattern, but it would have to do.

She floated up a little higher, pulling Devin with her. She made another thick carpet of dustmist and sprinkled the remainder of the firepepper inside of it.

They hovered together, Brigitta supporting Devin as best she could, watching as warwump after warwump burst through the earth. One stretched up toward them, and Devin closed his eyes and cringed. The warwump hit the firepepper cloud and immediately shrank back down.

"We're safe up here!" Brigitta squeezed Devin, who opened his eyes, surprised he had not been swallowed.

They watched as the beasts thrashed about beneath them, jaws open wide. Their enormous bodies undulated as the rain streamed down into their mouths. There was a desperation about them, and Brigitta slowed her thoughts to catch a hint of warwump energy. Instead of feeling anger or meanness, as she would expect, she felt only relief.

"They're thirsty, that's all!" exclaimed Brigitta, and then she laughed. "They don't eat faeries. At least not on purpose. They just come for the rain."

"Brigitta," said Devin, as he began to falter. "I can't . . . "

Brigitta refocused on the clouds as she held her hourglass necklace. She pulled and pulled on the water energy, gathering it back up. Slowly, the rain began to subside, and the warwumps became less frantic. As the rain stopped, the gigantic worms retreated back into the earth.

Devin, sopping wet with oily rain, fluttered about erratically while Brigitta gathered the dustmist and firepepper. The air was not cooperating and kept holding back. The chain yanked at her waist as Devin slipped lower. Fearing he would completely exhaust his energy, she gave up on collecting the rest and pulled Devin away from the pepper heat. They descended back down to the arena. The earth and ivy were already closing in over the warwump holes.

There was synchronicity in the Valley of Noe after all, she thought, even if it was a dangerous place for faeries. She led Devin toward the outer side of the arena, away from the directions that Zhay and the other Watchers had sped.

By the time Brigitta and Devin reached the edge of the lakebed, Mabbe's afternoon chiselers were packing up to return to the Hollows. They watched from a safe distance behind an outcropping, pounding a rock on the silver chain that bound them. They had decided to take the long way around the lakebed to the Gathering Place, hoping to surprise Zhay, assuming that's where he had gone. They didn't know what else to do.

"How did you end up with Mabbe's rebel Watchers?" asked Brigitta as she pounded on the chain.

"I was on duty, making my rounds, when I spotted Ferris," said Devin. "She was poking through some ruins on the other side of the hill."

"But weren't you sworn enemies?"

"Mabbe and Croilus are enemies, and we fight for them to survive," said Devin, "but when I saw Ferris, I just sort of forgot who I was. I didn't even bother to hide. I just stood there, staring at her like an idiot."

"Was she, you know, scarred like that?" asked Brigitta.

"Yeah, they were like silver jewels glinting in the light." Devin smiled at the memory, then turned to Brigitta and grinned. "Of course, she gave me an earful that first time. Then we started meeting every few moons in secret. She told me of a Watcher named Jarlath who had once saved a Croilus faerie from a gargan."

"A what?"

"Big ugly spider."

"Don't you have any nice furry animals in Noe?" asked Brigitta, breaking through one of the chain links. "Or perhaps some dimwitted grovens? I haven't even seen any birds."

"We have birds," Devin shuddered.

"As pets?"

Devin looked at Brigitta as if she were insane.

"Never mind." Brigitta watched as the last of the Hollows faeries left the lakebed.

"We do have chygpallas," said Devin. "Children like them. I'll show you one sometime."

"What about Zhay, when did he join up?" asked Brigitta.

"He tracked me out to the Gathering Place. I thought we were as good as dead, but he swore he was on our side. Jarlath never trusted him. I shouldn't have either."

"I think they're all in the woods," said Brigitta. She pulled apart the mangled chain. "Let's go."

As Devin stood up and brushed himself off, Brigitta took hold of his arm. "I don't know what we'll find at your Secret Palace. We need to be ready to fight or fly."

"Yeah," Devin said grimly and leapt into the air. "I know."

It was nearly dark when Brigitta and Devin made it to the slump in the cliff. The message log was no help; every pit was empty. Brigitta pulled out her globelight and rubbed it, and Devin was momentarily mesmerized by the purity of the light. She honed the light down by rubbing it again so that it shone a narrow path in front of them.

The two faeries made their way through the crevasse in silence. They flew around to the back of the slump, over the boulders that hid the entrance to the fortress, and slipped inside. It was empty and there were no embers in the fire pit.

"No one's here," Brigitta whispered, shining her light into the cracks and corners. She pulled her belongings from behind the rock where she had hidden them. "Zhay didn't bother with my things."

"Maybe he was in a hurry?" Devin knelt down by the fire pit and sniffed the air. "It hasn't been lit today."

There was movement and something heavy flew at them. Devin grunted as he was knocked backward onto the ground.

"Show yourself!" called a voice from the rocks.

"It's us, Brigitta and Devin!" said Brigitta, shining her globelight on her face.

"Brigitta!" Thistle came flying out from the darkness and careened into Brigitta, hugging her tightly and knocking the globelight from her hand.

"Thistle!" Jarlath emerged, shading his eyes as the beam of light hit his face. "It could have been a trick."

Roane leapt out and scooped up the globelight, shining it about the cavern. The light landed on Devin as he groaned from the floor.

"Jarlath, you idiot!" cried Brigitta, escaping from Thistle and fluttering to Devin. "You could have hurt him."

"Leave him alone!" commanded Jarlath. "He's a traitor!"

"For the Blue Moon, he's not a traitor." Brigitta eased Devin up off the ground. "He helped me escape."

"We were fooled by Zhay," growled Jarlath. "How do you know he's not fooling us as well?"

"I know," said Brigitta.

Thistle moved to help her set Devin on a rock. They both checked him for damage.

"Zhay was here. He took Ferris," said Thistle.

"What?" cried Devin, wobbling to his feet. Thistle gently pushed him back down onto the rock.

"We couldn't stop him. He had one of those firesticks in her face," said Thistle. "He pretended to be injured, said something about you being captured, so naturally Ferris went to ask him what happened."

"No!" Devin grabbed Brigitta's tunic. "We have to go back for her!"

"We can't risk it," said Jarlath.

"He said he'll give her back if Brigitta tells him how to open the sorcery seed," said Thistle.

"See?" Jarlath said. "Ferris is safe for now. He needs that seed to defeat Croilus."

"We need to get the seed *and* Ferris back," said Brigitta as she watched Roane flashing the globelight on the rocks, casting shadows on the rugged walls. She glanced at the four weary faeries. "We need to get help."

"We've got to get out of here, too," said Jarlath. "It's not safe."

"I'm not going anywhere without Ferris," said Devin.

"Ferris is gone," said Jarlath.

"But if she escapes, she'll come here," Devin pointed out. "This is the only place she knows where to find me."

Jarlath was about to protest, but Brigitta stopped him. "He can't go back to Croilus, and he can't go with us to the Hollows."

"Who says we're going back to the Hollows?" asked Jarlath.

"I'm going back to the Hollows," corrected Brigitta. She gathered up her remaining belongings and reached out for the globelight. "I'm going to rescue Ondelle."

Roane reluctantly handed her the light, and she motioned for him to step back. She slammed the globe onto a rock and it broke into six even pieces, like little slices of the Great Moon. She rubbed one of the slices with two fingers and handed the bright shard to Roane.

Brigitta, Thistle, Jarlath, and Roane flew silently through the crevasse, each carrying a shard of glowing globelight.

"I don't feel right about leaving Devin back there alone," said Thistle.

"What if Ferris does manage to escape?" said Brigitta. "It's better that someone's left to meet her."

As they exited the slump and approached the trees, Brigitta dropped down to the message log. She placed red stones in her own and Devin's spots. "That way Zhay will think we never made it back," she reasoned.

Jarlath nodded at her cleverness as she rose. "Stay behind me," he warned. "There are reasons we don't go into the forest at night."

They flew carefully through the trees, Jarlath and Thistle with shields up, Brigitta and Roane between them. Annoyed with their slow progress, Brigitta was about to ask if they could pick up the pace when Jarlath stopped and hovered in the air.

"Shhhh!" he commanded, even though no one was talking. "Hide your lights!"

They all hid their shards in their tunics and listened. A moment later, there was a rustling, then what sounded like hundreds of little humming beasts.

Brigitta peered into the trees. "What is—"

"To the ground!" Jarlath dropped to the forest floor, and Roane and Thistle followed with frightened squeals.

Brigitta hesitated and several small dark shapes darted past. A moment later something seared her right wing and another stabbed the back of her hand. She dropped to the ground and Jarlath pushed her down, covering her with his own body. Roane whimpered beside her where Thistle was protecting him with her arms.

The humming increased as a swarm of the small creatures flew overhead. Brigitta tried to see what was going on, but Jarlath firmly held her in place. He lowered his own head to the ground next to Brigitta's. "Keep your face down," he said, so close she could feel his breath in her ear.

After a while, the forest grew quiet again, but the faeries remained still, listening. Brigitta turned to face Jarlath and caught his crystal blue eyes off guard. They stared at each other and in that moment a thousand voices began to whip through the air. Jarlath leapt up and wiped himself off. The voices disappeared.

Brigitta stood, pondering what had just happened. It reminded her of the first time she had sat in an Elder's chair. She had been overwhelmed by voices.

She reached out to Jarlath and a sharp sting coursed from her right wing to her shoulder, down her arm, and into her hand. She cried out and grabbed her hand. It was marked with a thin slice of blood. Looking over her shoulder, she saw a thin slit in her wing that went right through the center of the eye glyph. Both cuts were the same size and shape as the numerous scars that dotted Ferris's face and body.

Thistle got up and helped a frightened Roane to his feet. "They'll heal right away," she said, "but the poison stings for a few moons."

Brigitta nodded and thanked Faweh that she had only been sliced twice by the nasty things. "Sliverleaves," she murmured staring into the darkness. "Poor Ferris."

They stayed close to the ground the rest of the way to the lakebed. When they burst through the trees, a glowing landscape greeted them. Through an opening in the thick clouds, the two moons shone down, the little orange moon tagging after her big blue sister.

"It's lovely," said Thistle. "I had no idea."

They landed and stared in awe. The moons were bright and nearly full, but still could not penetrate the dense clouds. They could only shine through the opening, casting an eerie beam down on the valley, spotlighting the lakebed. The River That Runs Backwards churned madly in the light, more ominous than in the day. And in the crater, scattered around the bowl, tiny sparkles danced, caught in the moon rays.

"Those sparkles. It's the sorcery sands!" Thistle pointed into the enormous bowl. "The moons could lead us right to them!"

Brigitta moved forward and Jarlath grabbed her arm. "It's too dangerous."

Thistle nodded and Brigitta sighed. They all looked on, hungrily, as the ancient sands twinkled.

As they stood there, the clouds closed up and the moonslight disappeared, along with the sparkling sands. If it weren't for the little slices of globelight, it would have been pitch black.

Exhausted, they decided to rest against some fallen logs. It was bitterly cold. Brigitta pulled out her two White Forest blankets. Thistle cuddled up to Brigitta, and she wrapped a blanket around them both. Jarlath and Roane did the same. Night beasts croaked and buzzed, and the rushing of the river continued in the background.

"We have to figure out how to get in and out of the Hollows," said Brigitta.

Jarlath snorted. "I'm not convinced we should go back at all."

"I'll make you a deal," said Brigitta. "You help me rescue Ondelle, and we'll make sure Mabbe never harms anyone ever again."

"Don't make promises you can't keep."

"Jarlath, what else can we do?" asked Thistle. "Isn't this what we've been waiting for? Isn't this what the voices meant when you—"

Jarlath grabbed Thistle's arm so forcefully she gasped. "No, it isn't," he hissed. "They didn't mean anything."

She lowered her eyes. "I'm sorry."

Brigitta glared at Jarlath, and Roane stared up at him with his big sad eyes. He let go of Thistle and placed his hand on Roane's head.

"No, Thistle, I'm sorry," he said. "I shouldn't have listened to them, and you shouldn't have listened to me."

He pulled Roane close and gave his little brother a hug. "I got us all in over our heads."

They sat in silence and huddled into the blankets for warmth.

"How many more of your secret clan are there?" asked Brigitta.

"Thistle's mother is servant to Mabbe," said Jarlath.

"Who else?"

"There are no others," admitted Jarlath.

"Not yet," added Thistle.

"The seven of you were planning to overthrow Mabbe and Croilus yourselves?"

"Six. Zhay was a traitor," Jarlath reminded her.

"So, there's no one else who can help us?"

"Brigitta, you have to understand," said Jarlath, "what we're doing, even mentioned in jest, is punishable by death."

"The Watchers are too scared; the lesser faeries are too weak," said Thistle.

"How many Watchers are there?" asked Brigitta.

"A hundred and fifty, maybe more," said Jarlath.

"Do you know them all by face and name?" asked Brigitta.

"Not entirely. Some I see every few moons, some I see once a season, if at all." Jarlath leaned forward into his beam of light. "Why?"

The clouds broke open again, and the moonslight cascaded down into the lakebed. The glittering sorcery sands taunted them.

Brigitta's gaze went from the lakebed to Jarlath's hip, where he wore his dagger. Was it sharp enough to chisel petrified sands?

"Don't even think about it," muttered Jarlath, leaning back against the log. "You'd be invaded by nightwalkers before you even reached the sands."

"I thought nightwalkers were just your non-ascended spirits?" she asked, remembering the sensation of Jorris's undispersed energy in the lower chamber of the Hive. Skin-tingling and unpleasant, yes, but not dangerous.

"Nightwalkers can invade your mind!" said Thistle. "And take over your body!"

"Who told you that?" laughed Brigitta. "Do you know anyone whose mind was taken over by a nightwalker?"

"Well, no," said Thistle, "but Mabbe says . . ." She trailed off, as if contemplating the likelihood that Mabbe ever told them the truth.

Brigitta grabbed her dustmist canister and stood up, tucking the blanket around Thistle. "You know what I think?" She emptied the dustmist into the air and spread a tight, thin wall around the curious faeries, the best she could manage, having lost much of it in the sky above the warwumps. "I think you Watchers have your own kind of sorcery, but Mabbe is so threatened by it that she makes you fear it."

"Or punishes us for talking about it," offered Thistle.

Brigitta stepped back and held her hands in the mist. Using a mirroring technique, she focused on the reflectivity of the water energy, creating a makeshift cloak. It was almost effortless, and she was impressed by her own skill. Maybe she was getting used to how the elements worked in Noe. She slowly twirled her fingers to finish the job, until her right hand stiffened and pain shot up her arm to the tear in her wing. She gritted her teeth as she stepped through.

"That will keep you mostly hidden," she said to the others, trying to shake off the pain. "Douse your globelights if you hear trouble. The light shines through a bit."

"Wait! Where are you going?" cried Thistle.

"Mabbe wants sorcery sands; I'm getting sorcery sands. Jarlath, loan me your knife."

Chapter Fourteen

Against Thistle's pleading, Brigitta struck out alone across the stretch of land that led to the dry lakebed, telling the others that if she did not return before sunbreak to go back to the Hollows without her. The moonslight guided her to the edge of the bowl. She studied the River That Runs Backwards, feeling its powerful draw. No slipups, she told herself. Not this time.

She fluttered over the edge and down the inside of the bowl. The pull of the river-wind increased. Jarlath was right; at night the river was stronger. But she knew water, she told herself. She and water had an understanding.

"Remember me, Mad River?" said Brigitta. "You almost ate my sister once."

She dropped down closer to the lakebed where the air was calmer. She'd have to walk, as her wings weren't strong enough to fight the river's pull. The inner bowl was steeper than she remembered. She grabbed onto an old root sticking out of the side, but it broke away in her hand, throwing her off balance. She steadied herself before continuing, vowing to be more careful.

As she descended, she scanned the lakebed for balanced sands. Sorcery sands, she corrected herself and almost laughed out loud. These naive faeries thought everything was magical.

Hush, she scolded herself. She wasn't any better than they were, Ondelle would say. She pictured her High Priestess assisting the little weavers in the Colony. She was going to save Ondelle, find the Purview, and leave this place. Except she had promised she would help get rid of Mabbe. And rescue Ferris.

"First things first," she muttered. "And one thing at a time."

Most of the sands at the top of the bowl had been gathered, as there were few sparkles remaining in the moonslight. The rest were closer down into the bowl, closer to the river, where fewer faeries had tread.

She spied a little vein of shimmering sands down to her right. She looked up at the moons, nearly across the break in the clouds. As fast as she could, she raced around the side of the bowl, flitting her wings to help her scramble across the rough surface. When she was directly above the sparkling sands, she descended, keeping an eye on the shifting river.

As she clambered down, the wind pulled harder and harder. It picked her up by her wings, and she skidded down until her feet hit a protrusion in the rocky bed. She pulled her wings in tightly and dropped all the way to the ground, grabbing hold of the outcropping until she could get her bearings. The vein of sorcery sands was only a few steps away.

She crawled toward the bright specks, her right arm and wing stinging with the poison of the sliverleaf cuts.

"Hagspit," she swore. The sorcery sands were too scattered about. With the knife in her left hand, she carefully chiseled around one cluster of sands, hoping the vein was deep. As she chiseled, her hourglass necklace began to warm.

"What?" Brigitta asked her hourglass sands. "Do you recognize your kin?"

Her skin prickled as a dark shape shifted in the periphery of her vision, and she glanced up from her work. Nothing was there.

"Just the spirits of the dead," she murmured to herself and went back to her task. "Nothing to get excited about."

She chiseled as quickly as she could around the vein. It was a good sized chunk of rock, but she had no idea if it contained enough balanced sands to appease, or at least fool, Mabbe. She tucked the knife away and pulled at the loosened rock. Just as it broke free from the lakebed, the moons disappeared in the clouds, and the world went black.

She held the rock in her left hand and reached into her pocket for her shard of globelight with her right. Pain shot from the wound in her wing to her fingertips, and the shard slipped from her hand. She reached after it, but it was gone.

The river sounded louder than ever in the dark, and she could feel its pull. She looked up and the sky was utterly black. Maybe she could move the clouds herself. She tried to feel the cloud energy, but she was too disoriented. As she sat there, unable to see an arm's length away, she felt a movement, then another, on either side of her. She couldn't tell how far away the beasts were, but she could tell that they were large. She began to wonder if undispersed spirits really could invade her mind and body in Noe.

Suddenly very afraid, she turned to go back up the way she came. Using the incline of the lakebed as her guide, she crawled as fast as she could while holding onto the rock. Then she realized she had left the knife behind, but there was no going back.

Her hand landed on something scaly. It slid out from under her and she felt a claw strike out against her arm. She shrieked and leapt up, fluttering away from the beast. She tried to fly forward, but the river-wind was too strong. She fought to keep control of her wings. The rock slipped from her hand and tumbled into the darkness.

Brigitta struggled with all her might, but the wind was too strong. She felt herself weakening, her strength used up.

"No!" she cried into the darkness, tumbling backward.

A moment later, her body, then her head, struck something solid. The impact knocked the breath out of her, and everything blurred.

The object moved.

"I've got you now," a deep voice growled.

The hulking beast began to trudge forward as Brigitta blacked out.

Brigitta felt the warmth of a fire and smelled the comforting aroma of toasted mushrooms. It must be a new recipe of her momma's, she thought, smiling to herself.

She opened her eyes to dancing flames and snuggled into the blanket wrapped around her. The thickness and weight of it were unfamiliar. It smelled like wet sand.

"You're awake," a low female voice broke the silence.

Brigitta turned her head to find a large gray beast kneeling over her. A baby rock dragon! She gasped and tried to sit up, but her head was too dizzy.

"It's all right, little faerie," said the beast, blinking her double eyelids, "you're safe."

Brigitta froze in confusion, her memory scattered. Where was she and how did she get here?

The beast tilted her head, concern in her eyes. No, she wasn't a rock dragon at all. Her skin was like armor and covered only with a few brown straps that held a large pack across her back. Her body was thick and round, with sturdy pillars for legs that ended in webbed claws. Her head was small for the rest of her body, flattish and triangular, narrowing into a single horn above her lip.

"I'm Abdira," she said and nodded her head toward another beast on the other side of the fire. "He's Uwain."

Brigitta slowly righted herself and looked at Uwain, a darker, slightly larger version of Abdira. He had two horns, one above his lip and one above and between his eyes. He grunted at Brigitta.

"He's much friendlier than he looks," said Abdira. "Are you hungry?"

Brigitta sat up, trying to remember what had happened and how she had gotten from—where had she last been? "Where—how—" she began.

"There, there." Abdira handed her a wooden bowl of steaming mushrooms. "Have some hrooshka. It'll warm your insides. This place is horribly chilly."

Brigitta took the bowl and stared into the steamy mushrooms.

Her head was so fuzzy she didn't know if she had come from a dream or was having one now, but she did have a sense that she was supposed to be doing something important.

"You smacked yourself pretty good. We're sorry about that." Abdira smiled, and even though there was something a bit beastly about it, it was a trustworthy smile.

Brigitta nipped tentatively at a spoonful of mushrooms. They were meaty and soft and cooked perfectly. As she lifted her spoon again, pain shot through her hand and up to her wing. She dropped the spoon and stared at the back of her hand. A shiny silver scar shone on her skin. She looked up at her wing. In the middle of the dark green destiny marking, through the center of the eye glyph, was another thin silver scar. The haze lifted and she remembered where she was, and that before she lost consciousness, she was hurtling toward the River That Runs Backwards.

"The sorcery sands!" she exclaimed. "Ondelle!"

The two beasts exchanged looks.

Brigitta handed the bowl back to Abdira. "I have to get back to my friends."

Abdira pushed the bowl back again. "There is time. You need strength. Eat first."

Uwain grunted again, and Brigitta looked back and forth at the gray beasts. Abdira nodded at Uwain, and he slowly sat forward and cleared his throat.

"When you are called by whisper light," he began in his low gruff voice, "and know it through the fate of kin, you'll travel back to times of old, and serve to balance all again."

Brigitta nearly dropped the bowl of mushrooms. "Where did you— how did you— that's a faerie prophecy!"

"It's a Nhord prophecy as well," Abdira said.

"It's no prophecy," corrected Uwain, "it's a promise. A promise from the Nhords to the Ancient Ones."

"To the Ancients?" stammered Brigitta. "But who are you? Are you from Noe?"

"No," Uwain said and waved his webbed paws vaguely to the

north. "We're from far away."

Abdira leaned in closer. "We're here to serve."

Uwain stood up. He wasn't much taller this way, with his stumpy pillar-legs. "Born to serve the destiny that awaits."

"That's right," agreed Abdira. "Service is our highest endeavor."

Brigitta's head was spinning, and not just from her injury. What in Faweh did these Nhord beasts have to do with any of this?

"But why did you come here?" she asked.

"For you, dear." Abdira smiled down at her. "We came here for you."

Uwain placed a web-clawed foot over the fire and stamped it out, saving one long stick as a torchlight, which he secured to his harness. Abdira hauled her large frame off the ground, and the three of them began their journey across the edge of the crater. The River That Runs Backwards spouted wildly in the distance. The moons were long gone, and the clouds were blacker than ever.

Brigitta mulled over what she had learned from the Nhords. For hundreds of seasons, passing the promise from generation to generation, two Nhords had always served as Sentries, waiting for a whisper light to open the Purview and give them what they called a "knowing" of where to go.

"Go forward, into the Purview, your destiny awaits?" asked Brigitta and the two Nhords grunted. "That's the only instruction you were given?"

"Simple words are best," said Abdira.

"Well, it's not much to go on."

"We're here to serve," Uwain repeated for the umpteenth time.

"And this Purview brought you here?" Brigitta asked. "You stepped into it and appeared here?"

"Yes," confirmed Abdira, "and, hopplebuggers, it was a strange sensation!"

"Strange and uncomfortable," agreed Uwain.

"You didn't use Blue Spell to get here? No other magic?"

"Nhords have no magic," Uwain said. "Wisdom prevails over magic," he added, as if automatically repeating some Nhord adage.

"We did have our rings," Abdira added, pulling a ring from a small pouch on her strap. The crystal gem sparkled off of Uwain's torch. "A gift from the Ancients."

If this Purview was some quick way to travel, Brigitta thought, admiring the shimmering jewel, could anyone use it? Did she have to have this "knowing" or just the whisper light?

Brigitta stopped and the Nhords stopped with her. She had thought Ondelle simply made the whisper light disappear, but she had really put it into her necklace. Ondelle had hidden the whisper light and then protected it with that spell. Which meant she hadn't trusted Brigitta with this knowledge, but more importantly, it meant Ondelle must have known they could get through with it. Did this mean they could both get back home? Could the rebel faeries come with them?

Her excitement grew as the seeds of a new plan were planted in her mind. She rushed forward as a dark thought passed. Once the Purview was open, would Croilus or Mabbe be able to use it as well?

🌷

As Brigitta approached the dustmist wall, fading in places so that there were moments of light and shadow, she made a decision. She would tell the rebels all about the Purview. They trusted her, and she needed to trust them.

She passed through and found Roane asleep under a blanket. Jarlath and Thistle were whispering so intensely over their shards of globelight that Brigitta's entrance startled them.

"Brigitta!" Thistle flew to her and hugged her. "We were so worried. I was about to go search for you. Where did you get that blanket?"

Brigitta looked down at Abdira's blanket just as the two Nhords appeared. Jarlath and Thistle shrieked in surprise.

"It's all right," Brigitta assured them. "They're friendly. Abdira and Uwain, this is Jarlath, Thistle, and the sleeping boy is Roane."

"We're here to serve," said Abdira and Uwain, bowing slightly.

"They say that a lot," Brigitta said as she sat down.

Jarlath and Thistle stood with mouths gaping as the two Nhords plopped themselves down behind Brigitta.

"They saved me from getting sucked into the river," said Brigitta. "They came from across the ocean." She leaned forward. "They came through a Purview."

Thistle and Jarlath slowly sank back down to the ground, eyes wide with disbelief, as Brigitta explained all that had happened at the river. Thistle wrapped her arms around herself as she listened, and Jarlath, for once, was stunned into silence.

"I think it could be our way home." Brigitta took Thistle's hand. "A way you could come with me. And I think I know how to open it."

"You think?" Jarlath crossed his arms over his chest.

"Jarlath!" exclaimed Thistle. "We could take my momma and Roane and Ferris and Devin and leave this place!"

"Don't get your hopes up," Jarlath warned. "If it doesn't work she can go back to the White Forest and forget all about us, but we'd be traitors. We'd have to fly away, and you wouldn't last three nights out there." Jarlath gestured to the world around them.

"We came through a Purview," said Abdira matter-of-factly.

"We don't even know where it is!" cried Jarlath. "We don't even know where to look for it. Croilus has been searching for seasons and hasn't found it yet."

"First, we rescue Ondelle. If anyone can find it, she can."

Brigitta took hold of her necklace as everyone sank into silence, contemplating this new information. She had to think of a way to sneak into the Hollows. Ondelle had said to leave without her, but she wouldn't. She hadn't even let Ondelle tell her how. And even if she had Blue Spell in her necklace, Brigitta didn't know how to use it. Only Ondelle and the Elders and the Ancients knew—

The Ancients!

She looked into Jarlath's eyes. She remembered her idea about the voices.

"Give me your hands," she said to Jarlath.

Jarlath hesitated, and then held out his hands, palms up. She took them, and a shock of warmth shot up her arms and rested there.

"You've spent your entire life blocking out these so called mad voices," said Brigitta. "I don't think they're mad voices at all. I think what you hear are echoes of the voices of the Ancients."

Jarlath pulled his hands back, but Brigitta held them firmly in place. "Listen to me, it makes sense," she explained. "It's the only way Croilus would know so much. Because he listened to the voices. It's why Mabbe stopped the ascensions, because she was afraid you'd listen too.

"And I think it's part of why I'm here," said Brigitta. "Finding you, bringing you back with us through this Purview, reconnecting with the Ancients . . . "

"I don't know," Jarlath murmured.

"I think Mabbe has made you distrust the Ancients so you wouldn't leave."

"We are loyal to the Ancients," Uwain added in his gruff voice. "Many sand cycles ago, long before our grandparents' memories, we Nhords visited with them in the Valley of Noe."

"And how did their ancestors get here?" Brigitta asked. "Look at them, they couldn't have flown or swum. It must have been through these Purviews."

Jarlath's eyes softened as he contemplated Brigitta's logic.

"The Ancients left a message with the Nhords. They were sent here to help—to *serve* us. If the Ancients were as bad as Mabbe says, why would they do this?"

She concentrated on his crystal blue eyes. "Please, you have to let your mind go. I need to get inside."

Jarlath looked, for the first time since she had met him, truly frightened. Thistle encouraged him with a smile.

He nodded and took a deep breath. When he exhaled, his body heaved relief, as if it had been carrying a heavy burden for a long time and had finally set it down. His grip loosened and the energy flowed between their hands until they were connected with a band of it, warm and vibrating.

Voices ghosted around them. Thousands of echoes filled an eternity of space. She felt Jarlath withdrawing, but Brigitta held him in place.

"It's all right," she murmured. "Just keep looking at me."

She concentrated on her hourglass and let go of all thought that this idea of hers wouldn't work. That it was too dangerous. That she would lose her way back. Shhhhh, she thought, focus and use everything you know.

She was going to get to the Ancients through empathing Jarlath.

You are mad, she thought, and let that go. She watched the thought float away on a wave of blue light. The voices seemed to emanate from the light. She glided into the wave of light, and it lifted her.

Her body felt electrified by the voices. Then they were resonating within her and around her at the same time. She was part of them and it was beautiful. It was safe. She had never felt so at peace. She could stay there. Yes, stay there forever.

Do not forget yourself, Ondelle's warning broke in from somewhere inside her. *Anchor yourself.*

An anchor. She had used her hourglass. But she wasn't holding her hourglass. She was holding Jarlath's hands. And his hands were holding –

She was looking back on herself, through his eyes. She felt an unfamiliar mixture of feelings. There was fear and hope. There was anger and sadness.

Now what? Jarlath's thoughts reverberated in her mind.

She concentrated on the wave of voices. They were weak, she

realized, pulling away. There were so many of them that they sounded loud and powerful, but they weren't. She got the sense that if she used their energy, it would weaken them still. But she had no choice.

From the part of her that was now one with Jarlath, she concentrated on her hourglass. She had no idea how much energy it would take; this wasn't anything she had been taught. She let go of that thought as she invited the Ancients to join her. All connected—the hourglass, Brigitta, Jarlath, and the Ancients—she stated her intention: transformation. She wanted to become like one of them.

For a brief moment, her body went numb and her mind blank. Then, as quickly as it had happened, everything returned to normal. She let go of Jarlath's hands.

Thistle's mouth dropped open and her hands went to her own face. "Your eyes," she whispered.

Brigitta looked over her shoulders to her wings. The destiny markings were gone, and her wings were now a grayish green, but the silver scar remained at the top of her right one.

"I don't believe it," said Jarlath.

"You look just like a Watcher!" exclaimed Thistle.

"Exactly," Brigitta said and lay back, completely exhausted, onto Abdira's foreleg.

Chapter Fifteen

The Nhords left just before dawn. It had been decided that they would stay on the south side of the hill overlooking the lakebed, above the area where Ondelle and Brigitta had appeared. They were a bit too obvious to travel through the forest with the band of faeries.

"We will hide ourselves," agreed Uwain, "until we are needed."

"Hide yourselves?" laughed Brigitta. "That I'd like to see."

"So you shall," said Abdira as the two beasts trudged away without so much as a goodbye.

"Your new friends are a little strange," pondered Thistle, "but I like them. I'm going to call them the Huggabeasts."

Jarlath groaned. "The Huggabeasts?"

"Yeah," said Thistle, "they're beastly, but you still want to hug them."

"Why do you always have to rename everything?" he asked.

Thistle shrugged. "We have to make some kind of fun in this world, Mossbottom."

"I agree," said Brigitta. "Mossbottom."

Roane awoke confused, yet amused, by Brigitta's disguise. After a meager breakfast, they all discussed their plan. They had to get Ondelle away from the Colony and into the Hollows where Thistle's mother could hide them all until nightfall, when they would escape. Jarlath would distract Mabbe by giving her a detailed report as to what had happened with Croilus, including a lengthy story about how he had been captured and had only escaped because of the rain calling forth the warwumps.

"I'll tell her I left you there with a reminder of your deal," he concluded. "Technically, you still have another sun to bring back the sands, Brigitta."

"You shouldn't call me that," Brigitta said. She thought for a moment. "Call me Narine."

They waited until the first shift of chiselers had gone down into the lakebed, and then they made their way to the Hollows. They found a hiding place behind an uprooted tree, where they could spy on the entrance.

"Wait here until the last chiselers get back," Jarlath whispered. "I should be able to speak with Mabbe before then." Jarlath put his arm around Roane's shoulders. "If anything goes wrong, Roane will come out instead, and you will leave immediately."

Brigitta resisted the urge to say that Jarlath couldn't tell her what to do.

"How will you get a message to my mother?" asked Thistle.

"Bird drops," swore Jarlath, "that's right."

"You won't be able to speak with her?" asked Brigitta.

"Not likely. Mabbe doesn't like her guards to socialize with the servants. It makes her suspicious."

"I'll go up and talk with her," suggested Thistle.

"No," insisted Jarlath, "I don't want to leave Brigitta alone out here."

"Can Roane get to her? He's not suspicious."

"Sure, but—" he gestured to Roane's silent face.

Brigitta reached into her pack, pulled out Mousha's greenish-brown disc, and waggled it. "Use this."

Roane screwed up his face at the smell.

"What is it?" Thistle asked, holding her nose.

"It's a, uh . . . vorple blat. An invention of my poppa's," said Brigitta. "Where will we meet her?"

"In the Kitchen Cozy," said Thistle. Off Jarlath's look, she added, "She'll know what that means."

Brigitta held up the vorple blat and whispered into it, "Meet

Thistle in the Kitchen Cozy after dinner." She balled up the rubbery disc and handed it to Jarlath. "Have him throw it at her."

"Throw it?" Jarlath asked as he took the stinkball.

"Make sure she's alone and near a wall. When it hits the wall, it will repeat my message three times, but that's it."

"Your poppa is a genius," said Thistle as Jarlath wrapped up the ball and placed it in Roane's pocket.

"Yes, he is."

Brigitta and Thistle flew high into the trees toward the Colony. Thistle was much stronger than she looked and wasn't even breathing heavily when they reached the top. They were about to step into the nest-like grounds when Thistle put her arm out.

"Your disguise," whispered Thistle. "You're too . . . grand."

A full head and shoulders taller than Thistle, and definitely better fed, Brigitta hunched down and pulled her wings and stomach in.

They didn't see Ondelle on the grounds, so they marched over to her prison tree. There were two Watchers posted outside.

"Watcher Thistle and I have been instructed to bring the large faerie woman to Mabbe for questioning," said Brigitta, giving her iciest glare to the smaller Watcher.

"We need her there in a moonbeat or she'll have all our wings," growled Thistle, and Brigitta nearly laughed, surprised at the ferocity of the little faerie's voice.

The two Watchers looked at each other.

"I've never seen you before," said the larger of the two.

"We've been transferred from patrol to Mabbe's guard," said Brigitta.

"From night patrol," added Thistle, gesturing to Brigitta's scarred wing.

"Is she well-restrained?" asked Brigitta. "I hear she knows powerful magic."

"I checked the bindings myself," the Watcher said.

"We'll see about that!" spat Thistle. "Hand me the key and step aside."

He handed Thistle a key, and she and Brigitta stepped inside. In the mesh cage, Ondelle sat alone, cross-legged, against the inside of the tree. She appeared to be asleep, but Brigitta knew better. She opened her intense eyes as Brigitta approached.

"Ondelle of Grioth," whispered Brigitta, "this is Thistle of Noe."

Thistle gave a small bow as Ondelle rose. The little Watcher looked up in awe at the incredibly tall faerie with black eyes and bright gold markings on her fiery wings.

"We're here to rescue you," Thistle said.

Ondelle reached through the cage and touched Brigitta's face with her bound hands. Brigitta wasn't entirely sure Ondelle was glad to see her, but she could sense her High Priestess wasn't at all surprised.

She could also sense something else. Ondelle's energy was weak.

Thistle unlocked the cell and unbound her feet. "We'll have to leave the hand and wing bindings for now."

They led Ondelle past the Watcher guards and into one of the transport trees. This time, Brigitta was prepared for the journey through the trunk. She closed her eyes as the howling began. The wind surged around her and wrapped her in a blanket of air, tightening and pulling. A moment later, all was still again.

"This way," whispered Thistle.

She guided them out of the trunk and right into another Watcher. Thistle gasped and then recovered. "Watch where you're going!" she growled and pushed past, yanking Ondelle with her.

They continued through the passageway and then slipped silently around a corner. They stopped and listened for a moment.

"You're like two people," whispered Brigitta. "I didn't know you had it in you, Thistle."

"It's easy. I just pretend I'm Jarlath," she said, giggling.

"Where are we?" asked Brigitta.

"Near the servants' burl." Thistle turned and removed the rest of Ondelle's restraints.

Ondelle heaved a sigh and stretched out her wings. They were enormous, reaching across the entire passageway. She pulled them back in and thanked Thistle with a pat on her arm.

They continued quickly, turning another corner, until Thistle held up her hand for them to stop. She looked both ways, twice, down the passageway.

"In here," she finally said, moving a chunk of wood aside and slipping into a narrow crack in the burl.

Brigitta struggled into the crack and was surprised that Ondelle could fit at all. Ondelle replaced the wood behind her, and they squeezed themselves through the gap.

"We're both going to get stuck," Brigitta said.

"Just a little farther," Thistle replied.

A moment later the crack opened up into a mini-burl, a small natural chamber. There was just enough room in the dimly lit space for the three of them to sit down. As Brigitta's eyes adjusted to the darkness, she noticed drawings on the inside of the walls. Seasons and seasons' worth of a child's artwork, faded with time.

"Momma hid me in here to keep me out of trouble," whispered Thistle. "I used to ask too many questions."

"I know someone like that," said Brigitta.

There was a scraping noise as something heavy was dragged across a floor. The wall began to move. A large piece of the burl fell away, and standing in the light was a round faerie woman.

"Oh, lola!" she cried, and for a moment, silhouetted in the light, Brigitta thought she saw her own mother standing there in her cooking tunic.

Granae reached into the wall for her daughter. She was an older version of Thistle, a little paler, much larger, but unmistakably kin. Her crystal blue eyes were faded but shone with delight as she held her daughter.

Brigitta choked back tears, hearing Granae use the familiar pet name. She recovered by stepping out of the chamber and helping Ondelle do the same. When Ondelle emerged, Granae gave a deep bow.

"Momma, this is Ondelle, High Priestess of the White Forest, and Brigitta, Second Elder Apprentice."

"I heard stories of stunning visitors from the north."

Ondelle smiled sweetly and gestured to her mouth.

"Yes, a shame," said Granae, "a vile practice of Mabbe's."

Brigitta looked around the kitchen. It wasn't nearly as homey as her momma's, but it was large and functional. The handle of the heavy wooden door was barred with a sturdy chair. There were jars of strange roots and herbs, mostly green-gray, pots and bowls in rows along the wall, a large vat bubbling away, and a table in the middle piled with an odd assortment of vegetables. She looked back at the hole in the burl and the shelving that had been pushed aside to expose it.

"You got our message," said Thistle.

Granae pulled the vorple blat out of her pocket. "Roane nearly scared me out of my skin when he threw this thing at me."

The stench of the vorple blat was not disguised by the aroma of the food. Brigitta took it from Granae and quickly wrapped it up in a cloth and tucked it into her bag.

"And no one else heard it?" asked Brigitta.

Granae shook her head as Brigitta's stomach growled.

"Oh, shame on me," cooed Granae, "you must be famished."

Granae piled some meaty nuts onto a tray, as well as three steaming bowls of the stew she had brewing, while Thistle and Brigitta relayed their recent adventures. Granae nearly dropped the bowl of stew when Brigitta mentioned the warwumps.

"You called the rain?" she asked, amazed. "You called the warwumps?"

Ondelle's eyes communicated the pride she had in Brigitta, and Brigitta shrugged, cheeks red under her gaze.

Granae touched Brigitta's wings. "And you used magic to transform yourself?"

"She called the voices," Thistle whispered.

"Shhhhh!" Granae hissed, eyes panicked. She looked behind her as if someone might be listening.

"We're all going to sneak away tonight along with Jarlath and Roane," said Thistle. "Gather your things, Momma."

"Oh, no, lola, the outer realm is no place for an old faerie like me." Granae lifted the tray and carried it to the chamber in the wall.

"Then we'll come back for you," said Brigitta, "when we've figured out a way to get home."

"Please," said Granae turning to Ondelle, desperation in her voice. "Please, just take my Thistle and go back to your forest. Don't risk your lives for me. You may know sorcery, but Mabbe has too many guards and no mercy."

"I won't leave you, Momma," said Thistle, tears forming in her eyes.

"You're too sweet for this dark world," Granae said. "I need you to have a better life than this."

Thistle buried her face in her mother's tunic. "We'll get rid of Mabbe, you'll see."

"You know, I've thought of poisoning Mabbe many times," said Granae, putting her arms around Thistle, "but if I failed and she found out, she'd get to me through my daughter. That's how she works."

Ondelle nodded and took Granae's hand. Something knowing passed between them. If Thistle would be punished for Granae's rebellion, surely Granae would be punished for Thistle's.

Like I would have been, thought Brigitta, if Ondelle had attacked Mabbe. She looked at her High Priestess with a new understanding.

Granae ushered them back into the mini-burl. "I'll let you know when it's all right to emerge. For now, you'd better stow away."

The three scooted into the nook, Thistle giving her mother a tearful hug before climbing back inside. They sat down to eat as Granae closed up the hole and pushed the shelving back in front of it.

After their meal, the three faeries spent a cramped evening in the Kitchen Cozy as Thistle alternated between crying about leaving her momma and swearing to return for her. Brigitta offered up the last few pieces of suclaide to help calm the young faerie. Eventually, they drifted off to sleep with the comforting aromas of Granae's kitchen seeping through cracks in the burl.

In the middle of the night they were awoken by the sound of the shelves being slid away. They blinked their eyes into the light when the burl opened. It was Jarlath and Roane. Roane looked up at Ondelle with such wide eyes Brigitta thought they would pop right out of his head. Jarlath signaled for them all to keep quiet as he led them from the kitchen into the passageway.

"What happened with Mabbe?" whispered Brigitta.

"My report seemed to appease her," Jarlath whispered, "although she doubts your success with Croilus."

"Has anyone reported Ondelle missing?"

"I haven't heard a word about it," Jarlath responded.

"Mabbe either doesn't know or doesn't want anyone to think there's been an escape," said Brigitta. "We have to get out of here regardless."

"We'll stick to the servants' burl and exit out the north window," whispered Jarlath. "We'll have to slip past the Watchers posted around the Hollows, which wouldn't be so difficult except for . . ." Jarlath glanced at Ondelle.

Ondelle stood out from the rest of them like the shining Palace at Croilus. She would never blend in with the Watchers, even with gray skin and crystal blue eyes.

"We'll just have to be quick," whispered Brigitta.

"And stick to the shadows," added Thistle.

They made it to the end of the passageway and flew out a small window. It was cold outside. Only a few lanterns shone from the dark like yellow eyes. Jarlath turned and handed a vine to Roane, who handed it to Brigitta.

"We can't risk any lights. Take hold of the vine so we can stick together," said Jarlath.

Brigitta passed the vine to Ondelle and Thistle. Jarlath dropped straight down through the trees, and Roane followed. Brigitta felt the tug of the vine and fell in after them. She let the vine lead her down and around several trees, branches tugging at her hair and tunic.

They landed at the base of an ancient tree. Jarlath pulled on a branch and the bark parted, leaving an opening in the trunk.

"This leads to one of the sky farms." Jarlath gestured for the others to enter the tree. "No one will be there at night."

"Jarlath," said Thistle, "we're not flying above the forest, are we?"

"It's the only way to avoid the night patrols." Jarlath closed the trunk, and all light disappeared.

"But, Jarlath!"

A slice of globelight lit up in Jarlath's hand, illuminating Thistle's frightened face. Brigitta lit another shard and handed it to Ondelle, then lit another for herself.

"What's wrong with flying above the forest?" asked Brigitta.

"The birds," Thistle shuddered. "They feed at night."

Roane frantically pulled on Jarlath's tunic.

"It'll be fine!" growled Jarlath to Roane.

Thistle and Roane looked unconvinced.

"Would you rather be taken back to the Hollows?" he asked. "Because we all know how that will end."

He flew up through the tree, and the vine yanked Roane from his feet. Brigitta followed, then Ondelle and Thistle. As they fluttered up, the trunk grew narrower but still left plenty of room to fly. Brigitta let her finger slide along the inside of the trunk, thinking that finally something was going right and that maybe they would all be safe in the White Forest soon.

They broke through an opening in the top of the tree and into the night air. The clouds were scattered above, and the stars shone down reassuringly. Everyone let go of the vine, and Jarlath wound it in his hands. They landed on a solid field spread across the tops of the trees.

"Wow," said Brigitta, "I've never seen such a thing."

"The sky farms are the only way our crops can get enough light . . . " Thistle's voice trailed off as a *craw* sounded in the distance.

The field stretched out for a great expanse in front of them, row upon row of grasses and herbs and roots and vegetables. There were even whole fruit trees. Brigitta reached down and touched the field. It was earth.

"Dirt!" she exclaimed, letting it slip through her fingers.

"What else would we grow things in?" asked Jarlath. "I suppose in your forest everything grows in the air itself?"

There were two more *craws*, this time closer. Roane grabbed Brigitta's hand, and Thistle held her breath.

"This way." Jarlath took off over the field as two shadows darted from the trees.

Everyone followed silently, the *craws* growing more distant as the faeries flew past the farms.

"We'll stay over the forest, then drop down outside the lakebed and meet up with your friends."

"The Huggabeasts," said Brigitta.

Thistle laughed nervously.

The air that high was strangely light, very different from below. Below the trees, Brigitta's wings felt as if they were slogging through stew. Up above the trees, it felt like the air wasn't heavy enough, and she had to flutter her wings twice as fast to stay afloat. She watched as Thistle and Roane struggled to fly.

"They need to rest, Jarlath," said Brigitta, rushing to catch up with him.

"There's no place to land now," said Jarlath through labored breath. "The branches are too weak."

Roane started to tremble, his wings working frantically. Ondelle slipped under Roane and caught him on her back. He held on and pulled in his wings.

"Not much farther," huffed Jarlath. "Keep—"

There was a loud cry, and a dozen black-winged creatures erupted from the trees, *craw-crawing* in a frenzy. Their red eyes gleamed in the moonlight as they descended upon the faeries, talons extended. Thistle screamed as one attacked her wing, pulling at it with its long beak.

Brigitta swatted at the bird with her shard of globelight, striking the back of its solid head. It let go of Thistle and turned in the air, screeching. It was almost as big as Roane, with mottled black feathers, and as it opened its beak in distress, Brigitta saw that the ugly creature had teeth.

Two more shot after Jarlath. He dropped into the trees and yanked off a branch, swatting at the beasts. Three attacked Ondelle, and she managed to strike one with her fist, sending it plummeting into the trees. With her wing injured, Thistle collided into Ondelle, and Roane slipped off her back, falling through the air. He tried to catch himself, but he was too tired and the air too thin.

"Nooo!" cried Jarlath as he dove after him.

The other three followed, and Brigitta managed to grab Roane's arm just before he hit a thick branch. They tumbled through the air, catching on the trees as they fell. Jarlath grabbed Roane's other arm, and they all steadied themselves. Ondelle swooped down beside them, leading a whimpering Thistle, whose left wing was torn across the top.

The faeries quickly descended and landed heavily on the ground. They all sat there, catching their breaths. Ondelle placed her hands on Thistle's wing, and she stopped crying. Brigitta scowled at Jarlath as he checked Roane for damage. His arms were scraped and his tunic ripped, but he was not seriously hurt. Jarlath gave a satisfied nod.

"Well, we're past the guard perimeter of the Hollows," he said. "We can stick to the forest from here."

Ondelle let go of Thistle's wing and the tear was partially mended. A jagged line remained.

"We're not going anywhere until Thistle and Roane are rested," said Brigitta.

"We're not safe here," said Jarlath.

"Do you want to get us all killed!" hissed Brigitta.

"Not as much as you want us all to get caught!"

"Don't be an idiot!" shot Brigitta.

Ondelle placed one hand on each of the faeries' shoulders and shook her head.

"Stop it, you two," said Thistle. "It's fine. I'm fine."

Jarlath's crystal blue eyes narrowed, and Brigitta glared back at him. She and Ondelle turned to double check on Roane, who was staring past them with terror in his eyes.

They all followed his gaze. A sickly colored Watcher stood between two trees, grinning at them. He gestured at Jarlath with a dagger. "I see traitors run in your family, Watcher Jarlath."

Jarlath straightened up to his full height and drew his own dagger. "I see ugliness runs in yours."

The Watcher snorted and pulled out a shield. He gestured to Ondelle. "There's a big reward for this one's wings, you know."

Jarlath stepped forward with his shield up. "Is there now?"

"Thought we wouldn't realize she was missing?"

"I was betting you were as stupid as you were repulsive."

Just as Jarlath stepped forward for a fight, eight more Watchers descended from the trees with an immense net, knocking them all to the ground and ensnaring them. The ugly Watcher looked down at Jarlath and raised his dagger over his head.

"No!" cried Brigitta as she struggled to free herself.

The Watcher plunged the knife into the ground next to Jarlath's face. "You're lucky the reward is doubled if I bring you traitors back alive."

Chapter Sixteen

It seemed like every Hollows Watcher was stuffed into Mabbe's burl, glaring at the captured faeries with their crystal blue eyes. From along the walls, three rows deep, they surrounded the prisoners, who sat together in a circle in the center of the floor, hands and feet bound. Mabbe meant to make examples out of them.

With Ondelle behind her, Brigitta could not see her High Priestess. She leaned back to feel her warmth, to get some kind of strength, but in her despair, she could no longer focus her energy. She remembered Gola's courage potion, but there was no way she could reach it, since her pack now lay at the foot of Mabbe's chair.

It didn't matter any more, she thought, all was lost.

"So!" Mabbe exclaimed, her gruesome face appearing in front of Brigitta, wrinkles wrapped around her sharp-toothed grin, cloudy eyes wild. She cocked her head and sniffed the air so close to Brigitta's face she could see the dark pores on the end of her nose.

"I underestimated you, faerie. How do you like being a Watcher? Are you interested in joining my clan?" Mabbe cackled and gestured to Dugald and Veena, who howled along with her.

"You're crafty, but not very smart." Mabbe turned serious and the clouds of her eyes slowed. "You don't keep promises very well, do you?"

"Only promises to my High Priestess and the Ancients." Brigitta stuck her chin out defiantly.

"Yes, the Ancients, who abandoned you." Mabbe gave an exaggerated pout. "Just like they abandoned all the others." She waved her scepter to the faeries around the room. "The Ancients promised to protect us all, and what did they do? They forgot about us!"

Mabbe nodded for her two companions to approach. They stepped down from their chairs and glided to Ondelle, lifting her away from the others. In one fluid motion, Dugald sliced Ondelle's hand bonds, pushed her to her knees in front of Brigitta, and held her in place.

Mabbe held out her hand, and Veena placed a long white dagger in it. She reached down and placed the tip of it against Brigitta's cheek. It was ice cold.

"One thing you'll learn about me, Watcher Brigitta, is that I always keep my promises."

Mabbe twisted around and brought the dagger down. Brigitta screamed as one of Ondelle's beautiful red wings dropped to the floor.

In shock, Ondelle swooned as Brigitta struggled with her bonds. The hourglass necklace burned into her chest, her head grew dizzy, eyes burning with tears. No, no, no, this couldn't be happening! She could feel Roane trembling on one side of her and Thistle gasping for breath on the other.

Mabbe picked Ondelle's wing up off the ground and fanned the air with it a few times. "A fine addition to my collection!" She shrieked with delight and tossed it to the crowd.

Despair flooded Brigitta as Ondelle collapsed in a heap at Mabbe's feet. She forced herself to look at the injury, but Ondelle wasn't bleeding.

"No blood," she whispered.

"It's a frore dagger," Jarlath said. "It freezes the wound."

"Pick her up," Mabbe directed her two Watcher companions. They dragged Ondelle up off the floor and placed her in front of Brigitta again.

Ondelle lifted her head, her black eyes as wild as Mabbe's. The look pierced straight to Brigitta's heart, and something stirred deep within her.

"Shall I spare her life?" pondered Mabbe, tapping the dagger against her own lips. The clouds of her eyes parted, revealing a full orange and a full blue moon.

"Death to the sorceress!" called a male Watcher from the back of the room, and the other Watchers shouted agreement.

Gathering her strength, Ondelle straightened up to her full height. Wings or no wings, she was the tallest faerie in the room. She looked around and the room grew silent as each Watcher came under her gaze. Then, she dropped down and grabbed hold of Brigitta's hourglass necklace.

Smoke rose from between Ondelle's fingers. The smell of burning flesh filled Brigitta's nostrils as Ondelle held her in place with her black moon eyes.

A whoosh of air burst from Brigitta's lungs, forcing her mouth open. *"And she who calls it by its name, who knows it by its forest kin, will travel back to times of old, and make the balance right again."*

Brigitta had no idea how the words formed in her mouth. Somehow, someone was speaking through her, as her, but the energy felt as if it belonged to her. Belonged, and didn't belong, like a long lost part of herself had returned.

"Treachery!" screamed Mabbe. "Myths from those Ancient fools!"

Brigitta's body and wings began to tingle. She looked down at her arm and saw its natural color return. She arched her head and witnessed the Elder symbol reemerge, the eye with four markings representing the four elements, a silver scar marring the glyph on her right wing. The markings shone brighter than ever before in the dusky burl.

The air whooshed back inside her, spreading throughout her body and limbs as if they were hollow branches. She felt a surge of new energy, and everything around her grew crisp and clear. Dull colors had more sharpness to them, and she could sense every faerie holding his or her breath. She could even see the specks of dust floating in the air.

Ondelle leaned back and opened her burnt and blistered palm. Everyone burst out at once in confusion.

"Quiet, all of you!" demanded Mabbe, lightning flashing in her eyes.

A voice reverberated in Brigitta's head, and she turned to Mabbe, who froze under her gaze. *"I'm back,"* said Brigitta in a voice not her own. And then, without thinking, she laughed.

"No," uttered Mabbe, the clouds of her eyes quieting. "Impossible."

Ondelle bowed to Brigitta, deeply, her hair almost touching the floor.

The scepter and knife fell from Mabbe's hands and clattered on the floor. She reached out, gnarled hands trembling.

"Narine?" she whispered.

Head clear, Brigitta now saw Mabbe as she once was: a frightened Noe Valley faerie girl hiding out in the Hollows. Hiding from the other Ancients after the world burst forth in its Great Cry.

In a sudden rage, Mabbe picked up the frore dagger and attacked Ondelle, slicing off her other wing. Ondelle once again fell to the floor, and Brigitta's heart tore open as she and the other captive faeries watched in horror.

Ondelle's shoulders shook, and a burst of energy darted from her lips and went dancing about the burl. The Watchers dodged it as it came at them. Mabbe screamed in frustration and drove the dagger into Ondelle's side.

Before Brigitta could react, four lesser faeries and two Watchers burst into the burl. "They're coming! They're coming!" they screamed, fluttering about in a panic.

"What's the meaning of this?" demanded Mabbe, catching one of the lesser faeries by the arm as she wove about the room. The tiny faerie was too worked up to speak. She sputtered for a moment, and Mabbe threw her into the crowd.

One of the Watchers landed in front of Mabbe. "Croilus! Croilus faeries! They're here!" He pointed to the entrance.

A dozen Croilus faeries tumbled into the room through the hollow tree. Several more burst from the enclave. They waved their firesticks, shooting flames at the Watchers along the wall, who barely had time to put up their shields and raise their daggers. Mabbe retrieved her scepter and whacked at two of the Croilus faeries with surprising strength.

Brigitta felt movement to her left. Roane had wiggled an arm free. He started to untie the knot in Brigitta's bonds, but his fingers slipped in his panic.

"Hurry, hurry!" Brigitta said as he struggled with the knot. The knot released and she pulled her arm out as Roane turned to work on Jarlath's bonds.

One of the Croilus faeries knocked the frore dagger out of Mabbe's hand and it clattered to the floor, just out of reach. Brigitta stretched her bound feet out but couldn't get to it. From the floor, Ondelle pushed herself up and with the last of her strength, she slid the dagger to Brigitta, who sliced open her remaining straps. She turned and sliced Thistle free.

"There!" came a voice from the tree. Brigitta twisted around to see the Watcher from Croilus's palace. He pointed his stick at Ondelle and Brigitta. "Bring them! Alive! Croilus wants them alive!"

More Croilus faeries streamed into the burl. Four of them scooped up Ondelle as Mabbe's faeries fought off their attackers. Mabbe pointed her scepter at one of the faeries carrying Ondelle, and a thick black stream snaked out, wrapping around his legs. He let go of Ondelle, and another Croilus faerie took his place.

Brigitta, Roane, Thistle, and Jarlath untangled themselves. Jarlath pushed a Croilus faerie out of the way and he tumbled over, dropping his firestick. Roane picked it up and tossed it to Jarlath.

Brigitta raced to save Ondelle, but Mabbe launched another stream of black, and it wrapped itself around Brigitta's neck, yanking her back as Ondelle was dragged from the burl. In a breathless struggle, Brigitta sliced at the snaky blackness with the frore dagger, and it cut through, releasing her. She lifted the dagger and rushed at Mabbe, but Dugald intercepted her, grabbing her by the wrist. Stabs of sliverleaf poison pain shot from her hand, down her arm, to her scarred wing, and she dropped the knife.

"Alive, you say?" he bellowed. In an instant he had the frore dagger at her neck.

Firesticks in mid-strike, the Croilus faeries halted.

Jarlath split from his own fight and slipped in behind Mabbe, who spun around and turned her scepter on him. "Well done, my pet," she cooed to Dugald.

"Then we shall take her alive!" Dugald pushed Brigitta into two Croilus faeries, who placed their firesticks at her chest. "And bring her pack!"

"Dugald?" Mabbe turned to him, the clouds of her eyes gathering in a thick wet mass. "No . . . no, my pet . . . not you."

Dugald saluted Mabbe and grinned. "I'm afraid so, my Queen."

In a flash, Dugald and all of the uninjured Croilus faeries backed away and disappeared through the hollow tree, hauling Brigitta with them. She could hear Mabbe's anguished cries as they dropped into the darkness.

Chapter Seventeen

Ondelle was nowhere in sight. Inside the Croilus faerie formation, Brigitta flew with a heavy desperation. Her world was ripping apart. How could her High Priestess have lost her wings?

She glanced at her captors in the hazy morning light, not a friendly face among them. She had no plan, no hope, and yet something drove her on. Something held her together and charged her energy within.

"Narine," she said under her breath. Friend of Gola's, the Ancient High Sage's daughter. That's what Mabbe had whispered. But was it pure coincidence that Brigitta had chosen Narine as her Watcher name?

Mabbe and Narine must have known each other back in the golden days of Noe, but how was that even possible? That would mean Mabbe was over 900 season cycles old. No faeries, not even Ancients, ever lived that long. Had Mabbe been using the sorcery sands to unnaturally extend her life? Brigitta shivered. Perhaps Mabbe was just an old body held together by bad magic.

The wind felt sharp and cool against every part of her exposed skin. She had thought it was fear that had given her sudden clarity back in Mabbe's burl, but the feeling hadn't left. Or rather, it was like it had always been there and had simply been awoken.

Back in the burl, the air had burst open inside her and forced her to speak. And then . . . Brigitta searched for something to compare it to, a way to describe how it felt. Then she knew. It felt like the air energy had *commingled* with her water energy.

"That's it!" she cried, startling the Croilus faeries.

"Quiet!" commanded Dugald from behind her.

Ondelle had somehow given her all of her air energy. She had no idea how, but she knew it was true. And now that she knew what it was, it seemed obvious. The union of water and air energy coursed inside her. What she had previously thought impossible had been done, and this bit of insight sparked new hope in her heart.

"Why did you betray Mabbe?" Brigitta called to Dugald.

"That old beast plans to live for a long, long time," Dugald snorted. "But someone has to rule Croilus's land when he leaves this place behind."

"Croilus isn't going anywhere until he finds his precious Purview."

Dugald laughed. She could feel the breath of his laughter, she was so in tune with the air now. And she knew what that laugh meant. Croilus had found the Purview.

But he was still here. He couldn't activate it. That's why he was so desperate for the so-called gift Brigitta brought from the Ancients. He thought it would open the Purview. So, Zhay had managed to keep the spell seed hidden from Croilus. Or, Croilus had found it and...

They broke through the trees, and the massive bowl of the empty riverbed was spread before her. On the south side stood a large regimen of Croilus faeries, Watchers and lesser ones, ready for battle. Behind them sat a stage draped with a black cloth. On the stage, lounging on an ornate couch, was Croilus in his ridiculous robe. Ondelle lay on the stage next to him, and Ferris was restrained by Zhay on the other side, a nervous look on his pale face.

Brigitta's captors guided her over the lines of faeries and landed in front of the stage, pushing her forward. A dozen firesticks held her in place as she searched for signs of life from her High Priestess. She sensed Ondelle's breathing, though it was weak.

"Ah, Dugald!" Croilus clasped his hands together and beamed. "I knew you were the Watcher for the job!"

"Is this what you wanted?" Brigitta turned to Zhay. "A war between your kin?"

"There has always been war in the Valley of Noe," said Zhay without emotion.

"Oh, do be quiet," snapped Croilus.

"The Ancients didn't abandon you," Brigitta addressed Zhay. "You've been able to hear them all along. That's how Croilus knows about the—"

"I said be quiet!" Croilus stood up and pointed a jeweled firestick at Brigitta.

Zhay stared at her but said nothing, the muscles in his jaw clenched. With her sharpened senses, she could see beads of sweat forming on his brow.

Croilus stepped down from his stage. "There doesn't have to be any more violence, Brigitta," he said, pulling his robe behind him. "You can have your priestess and your Hollows friend." He lifted Brigitta's chin with his stick. "All I want is that gift from the Ancients."

She quickly glanced at Zhay. No wonder he was so nervous, waiting to see what Brigitta would do. If she would give him away. She tried to sense what Zhay was playing at, but his mind was an impenetrable wall.

"You'll hand Ferris and Ondelle over and let us all go?" Brigitta asked.

"Absolutely," he purred and gestured toward the Hollows. "I am nowhere near as heartless as Mabbe. You are even welcome in Croilus if you'd like to stay, right Dugald?" He spread his arms out to Dugald, his lengthy sleeves dragging on the stage.

Fat chance, thought Brigitta. She had one last trick, but it depended upon Zhay's cooperation. "May I have my pack?" she asked.

Croilus motioned for Dugald to hand it over and went back to sit on his couch.

Brigitta pulled the courage spell seed out of her bag and shot

Zhay a look that she hoped communicated her intention. They could only pull this off together.

"I'll need some water," she said.

Croilus snapped his fingers, and three canteens appeared in front of her. She grabbed the nearest one and set the spell seed on the platform. "Spin three times in the direction the sun and moons travel," she said as if she were remembering some recent instruction. "One, two, three."

She glanced at Zhay once again, dipping her finger into the canteen. She held the seed on end and lifted her finger. "Then three drops of water on the top of the seed."

There was a kissing sound as the seed popped open. Brigitta tried to look pleased and surprised.

Croilus leaned over expectantly. "Well? Let's see it! Bring it here."

Brigitta climbed the platform and showed Croilus the contents of the spell seed.

"What is that? It looks like a seed full of juice."

"Oh, it's a potion," said Brigitta. "Um, someone drinks it and goes through the Purview. That's how it's activated, I guess." She looked up at him innocently.

"Then you drink it!" he snarled.

"I can't." She leaned closer to him and dropped her voice. "It destroys the body when it goes through the Purview. Is there anyone here you don't mind . . . sacrificing?"

Croilus scanned the crowd. "Pick someone, I don't care."

She nodded toward Zhay. "What about him?"

"Fine, fine," Croilus growled impatiently.

Brigitta approached Zhay and handed him the spell seed. "Drink this." She looked into Ferris's eyes to let her know she was up to something. Ferris blinked back at her.

Zhay took the seed pod and looked skeptically into it. "And go through the Purview?"

Brigitta nodded and whispered. "Do you have the zynthia with you?"

Zhay dipped his head ever so slightly.

"Trust me," said Brigitta as she retreated to the edge of the platform.

"Drink!" demanded Croilus.

Zhay tilted the seed to his lips and drank, then coughed a bit. He shook his head as the courage potion took affect. His eyes widened.

"Well?" asked Croilus, leaning forward, every Croilus faerie leaning forward with him.

"I feel . . ." Zhay put his hands to his head, then grinned. "I feel alive!"

"Excellent!" Croilus spun around and struck Brigitta in the chest with his firestick. She fell from the platform into Dugald, knocking him to the ground. He picked himself up and then yanked Brigitta to her feet. Pain soared from her chest to her hand to her wing as she tried to catch her breath.

Dizzy from the bolt of fire, she lifted her head and saw Zhay spinning Gola's seed pod on the platform behind Croilus. Brigitta screamed to distract everyone. "I gave you what you wanted! Now let us go!"

"Of course!" Croilus reached for Ferris, knocking the spell seed away from Zhay. He pushed Ferris out into the gathered faeries, and they caught her and passed her along to the steep edge of the bowl. They held her there, suspended.

Zhay looked helplessly from Brigitta to Croilus to the spell seed on the ground. The only sound was from the river, rushing up the other side of the crater.

Croilus laughed and grabbed Zhay as the faeries holding Ferris threw her back and forth between them, taunting her.

From the forest, a wild call sounded and everyone froze. A moonsbreath later, a horde of Hollows Watchers came streaming out, knives and shields in hand.

The faeries on the edge of the bowl dropped Ferris and picked up their firesticks. With her hands bound, Ferris went tumbling into the lakebed as the Croilus faeries reorganized their regiment.

Brigitta leapt up to fly after Ferris but was swatted back by three Watchers. One shot at her with a firestick, and she dodged it, gliding to the ground. She buzzed around their legs and headed for the edge of the bowl.

When she arrived, she heard someone shouting in the distance. A dark-haired faerie was streaming like a mad thunderbug around the west side of the lakebed. It was Devin.

"Ferris!" He shouted as he got closer.

As Ferris slid toward the River That Runs Backwards, he swooped under her, catching her in his arms. He kept on flying, struggling with the weight of her, around the inside of the bowl and over the edge out of the fray.

Ondelle! The seed pod! Brigitta turned and flew smack into Dugald. He grabbed her right arm, tripping the poison once again as he brought her back to the platform.

Croilus was seated at his couch, with Ondelle and Zhay at his feet. His regimen stood ready and waiting as Mabbe's Watchers emerged from the forest. The last Watcher out was Veena, and then Mabbe herself appeared.

Croilus's faeries backed toward his stage.

"No!" shouted Croilus, shooting his firestick into the ground in front of them, sending two of his own flying. "Stand your ground! She's an old woman! She's no match for us!"

After Mabbe's Watchers landed on the ground in front of the Croilus faeries, they parted down the center, and Mabbe and Veena made their way through. Scepter in hand, Mabbe strode to the front, then stopped. The clouds of her eyes dark and stormy, she sneered and sniffed at the crowd before her. The Croilus faeries shrunk back in fear.

"How dare you attack my home!" Mabbe bellowed, planting her staff in the ground.

"Did my faeries attack you?" Croilus asked in mock alarm.

Mabbe's lips trembled, and the clouds of her eyes twirled like whirlpools. "I gave you everything!" she wailed. "And you betray me over and over again."

Croilus fluttered off the stage and into crowd. They parted for him as he landed, and Dugald pulled Brigitta through the faeries to meet him.

"Yes, you did spoil me, didn't you?" admitted Croilus. "But there is only one thing I want from you now." He stepped closer and pointed to her scepter.

She sniffed, snaking her head in the air, then jerked her scepter out of the ground and pointed it at him.

"I'm willing to forgive you, dear Queen, let bygones be bygones, and never bother you again." He gestured to Dugald, who brought Brigitta forward. "I'll even trade this White Forest faerie for it."

Mabbe raised her wiry eyebrows, the clouds of her eyes slowing their swirls. "Now why would I do that?"

"Because I know something about you no one else does."

"You know nothing!" Mabbe glared at Croilus for a moment and then shot a dark stream from her staff. He held up his hand, and the black stream struck it, dissipating as soon as it touched his skin.

"Really, Mabbe," he snorted, "all those sands I stole from you and you don't think I can concoct a simple repellant?"

Croilus, now smug, stepped close to Mabbe. "I know that you have lived for a very long time. Longer than any single faerie here." He spoke loudly, so every faerie could hear. "I know you use the sands to extend your life."

"As do you." Mabbe scowled.

"I know that you have been around since the Great World Cry."

"What does it matter how old I am?" spat Mabbe. "You will return the girl to me at once! I doubt all your faeries have repelling charms."

The Croilus faeries looked uneasily at each other. Croilus spun around, his robes twirling perfectly as if he had practiced the move in a mirror. "It's not how old you are, dear Queen, it's what you are! You aren't a descendent of the faeries left here by the Ancients. You *are* an Ancient."

All the faeries, both Croilus and Hollows, murmured to each other in bewilderment. A few Hollows faeries stepped away from her.

Mabbe paused for a moment, then the clouds of her eyes parted and the two moons shone out from them. "So what if I am?" She twisted around, scepter pointed out over her Watchers. "They're the ones who abandoned you, not I! I've protected you!"

"No!" shouted Brigitta and she shook herself free. "You weren't abandoned! Mabbe convinced your kin to stay! She's the reason you're still here."

Everyone turned to stare at Brigitta. Mabbe slowly rotated to face her, eyes no longer cloudy, but dark crystal blue. She pulled herself to her full height and stretched her ragged wings. She raised her scepter at Brigitta.

With a primal scream, Zhay lunged from the stage straight for Mabbe, landing on top of her, knocking her staff from her hand. She swiped at him with her long nails and gouged his neck. He fell to the ground bleeding. Several Hollows Watchers surrounded him. Someone shot their firestick toward Veena, and she plunged into Croilus's army. Firesticks went off and daggers flashed. Wings fluttered and screams pierced the air.

Brigitta leaped for the seed pod as both Mabbe and Croilus sprang for her staff. They reached it at the same time and struggled for it, winding themselves up in Croilus's outlandish robes. Brigitta dropped to the ground. Had Zhay already spun it three times? she thought frantically as the chaos closed in on her. What would happen if he had and she spun it again?

Someone fell into her, and the seed was lost in the fray. There were too many fighting bodies to dodge. She glanced up to the platform just as Jarlath, Devin, Thistle, and Ferris landed. Thistle rushed to Ondelle.

"The spell seed, do you see it?" she shouted to them. "It's down here somewhere!"

Jarlath scanned the ground and then leapt from the platform.

He dove into the crowd and came up with the spell seed. Mabbe and Croilus broke through the brawl, still fighting over the scepter. A black stream burst from it and collided with Brigitta's chest, striking her hourglass necklace. There was a popping sound and the whisper light spat forth into the air. It immediately disappeared into the frantic fighting.

"No!" cried Brigitta. "Come back!"

The black stream shot toward her again and she ducked. It lashed out at Jarlath, coiling around him and the spell seed. As Mabbe and Croilus fought, the black stream careened through the air, hauling Jarlath with it.

Dugald charged with the frore dagger and plunged it into Mabbe's back. In her surprise, she let go of the scepter and spun around to strike Dugald. As she did, Croilus nabbed the scepter for himself. The black stream escaped, out of control, wrapping itself around Mabbe. Waves of voices, the ones she had collected over the season cycles, escaped into the air like a cacophony of ghosts. She looked around wildly, the clouds reforming over her crystal eyes as she was yanked from her feet. The crazed black stream shot past the fighting faeries, carrying Jarlath over the embankment and towing a howling Mabbe along with it.

Brigitta sped through the ruckus after them. As she reached the edge, she saw Jarlath tumbling down the bowl, heading toward the fierce river. She would never make it in time. She fought her way downhill, but the wind picked up, tossing her about.

She was slammed into the side of the bowl by a loud gust. The ground beneath her trembled. It was one of those earthshakes! She held onto an outcropping and watched helplessly as Jarlath spun out of control below her.

The ground in front of him broke away. A large gray shape burst through the earth. It wasn't an earthshake; it was Uwain! A moonsbreath later, Jarlath smacked into the Nhord's armored body and stopped falling. Abdira shot up beside him and shook the petrified sand bits from her horn.

"Thank the Dragon!" Brigitta exhaled in relief. The Nhords might not have any magic or much grace, but they were certainly solid.

One of Mabbe's wings broke free from the black stream, then the other, and she landed against a stone. She thrust up her hands, and her end of the black stream split in two, like a snake's tongue. She held onto the two strands and began to pull Jarlath back up the lakebed. The black streams shifted, and the spell seed fell from his grasp. Abdira stopped it with her clawed flipper.

Brigitta plunged down the lakebed, aiming for Abdira. She dove to the ground and grabbed the seed. Mabbe spread her arms wide and ripped the black stream the rest of the way, down the center, into two separate streams. One still held Jarlath, and the other looped around the seed in Brigitta's hand. Brigitta held on, summoning every particle of water and air energy in her being, and yanked back. Mabbe, caught off guard, came tumbling forward.

Released from the tension of the black stream, Jarlath fell backward and somersaulted past Abdira. Uwain shot out his flipperpaw and snagged Jarlath by the tunic. Jarlath grabbed hold of Uwain's foreleg as his feet flew out from under him, pulled by the mad river-wind.

Brigitta fluttered her wings frantically to keep from toppling away. She gripped the spell seed, lassoed by the black stream. For a moment, Brigitta could see Mabbe contemplating letting go of the seed and sending Brigitta down into the river. But her face turned curious and instead, she yanked back. Brigitta fell forward, over Abdira's foreleg.

She held onto the seed as the lasso slithered around her fingers, attempting to open her grasp. "I need water!" she called to Abdira.

Mabbe inched her way toward them, raveling the black stream into the palms of her hands, steadying herself with every step against the power of the increasing wind. Behind her, above the edge of the bowl, faerie wings flashed, firesticks flared, and daggers glinted in the light. But the river's rush drowned out any sound of the battle.

Brigitta's grip slipped on the spell seed as Abdira held her steady with one flipperpaw and searched her back straps with the other. Uwain started creeping backward, up the lakebed, with Jarlath desperately clinging to him.

Mabbe grinned as she approached, now in complete control of the black streams. She cackled as she danced her hand around in the air, winding the stream around Abdira's neck.

With a heave, Abdira fumbled a flask from her belt.

The storms of Mabbe's eyes flashed lightning as she approached.

Brigitta flung herself onto the rocky ground in front of Abdira and crouched, using the choking Nhord as a shield.

She hoped for all of Faweh's sake that Zhay had spun the seed completely. She uncorked the canteen, thrust her finger inside and spilled three drops onto the end of the pod. It hissed open.

Mabbe shot her hands toward Brigitta, and the stream wrapped itself around her wings. Poison pain wracked Brigitta's body and paralyzed her right arm. With her left arm, she grasped her hourglass and forced herself to stare directly into the tempest of Mabbe's eyes.

She let go of all thought, all fear, and drifted into the storm.

There was no air! How could there be no air within a beast? How could a thing live and breathe? She inhaled deeply and exhaled, filling the endless space with her own breath. Balancing it for a precarious moment. And with the exhale—

Take the crystal from the seed, her mind spoke inside Mabbe's. *Take the crystal from the seed.*

Mabbe's eyes calmed as she looked down. She reached into the seed and drew out the green zynthia.

"Look away, everyone!" Brigitta called to her friends.

Mabbe gazed into her clawed hands, her cloudy eyes caught by the green light.

The black streams fell from her hands and slithered down the lakebed like slippery worms. Abdira gasped for breath, and Uwain wrapped his whole right foreleg around Jarlath, dragging him out of the river's pull.

Brigitta struggled to keep her focus away from the zynthia. Her own hand began to tremble; her eyes began to drop despite her efforts. They slowly landed on the crystal as Mabbe's fingers stroked it.

The world around Brigitta began to fade as the zynthia drew her into its spell. *No,* she thought to herself. *Resist!*

Clutching the crystal, Mabbe had frozen in place. Brigitta tried to move, but her body wouldn't respond. The zynthia haze enveloped her, searching for something. Hungry. *No,* something remembered inside her . . . *don't resist. Feed.* She poured forth her water energy like a potion from her poppa's beaker. She poured forth her air energy like a Growing Season breeze.

Brigitta! called a familiar female voice, *Brigitta!*

Where are you? Brigitta's voice echoed in her own mind.

"Brigitta!" It was Abdira, calling to her above the river-wind. "We're sliding backward!"

Brigitta felt Abdira shifting behind her, and she steadied herself with her wings. Mabbe stood in front of her, lost in a trance. Brigitta snatched the zynthia from Mabbe's gnarled fingers and threw it toward the river. Before she could snap her mind clear, Mabbe stumbled after it. Her wings caught in the river-wind and she went tumbling through the air, tossed like a leaf, and was gone.

Uwain and Jarlath humphed themselves to where Brigitta and Adaire sat speechless, staring into the frothy waters. Jarlath reached for Brigitta's hand, and he pulled her to her feet. Together, they lugged their weary bodies up the side of the lakebed, Abdira and Uwain lumbering behind.

Chapter Eighteen

Whhen they reached the top they found injured faeries lying about and dozens still fighting in the air above.

Thistle was tending to Ondelle. Devin and Ferris were fighting side by side. Croilus and Zhay were nowhere in sight.

And neither was the whisper light.

Jarlath and Brigitta flew to the platform as Abdira and Uwain nosed their way through faeries. Brigitta sped to Ondelle, where she lay with her head in Thistle's lap. Her body seemed smaller without her magnificent wings and dual elements. Brigitta put a hand on her cold cheek.

"Mabbe is dead!" shouted Jarlath over the battle. "Do you hear!? Croilus has deserted you and Mabbe is dead!"

Several faeries heard Jarlath and looked around. Word spread quickly and the fighting slowed. With bloodied arm and cheek, Dugald fluttered up and scanned the scene. He spotted Abdira and Uwain and backed away.

"Where? How?"

"Taken by the river!" Jarlath pointed to lakebed. "She is gone!"

As the truth settled on each faerie, Dugald's disbelief turned into wicked laughter. He thrust his frore dagger in the air. "To the Hollows!" he commanded.

With only a moment's hesitation, the Hollows Watchers retreated from the battlefield, pulling their injured tribemates with them. The Croilus faeries dropped to the ground in exhaustion and began to gather their kin.

The color was draining from Ondelle's face. As painful as it was, Brigitta examined the space where Ondelle's wings should have been. Jarlath was right. No blood escaped from the wounds; there were just two smooth scars. She checked Ondelle's side where Mabbe had thrust the dagger. Again, there was nothing but a long white gash.

Jarlath, Ferris, and Devin landed on the platform next to them.

"What's happening?" cried Brigitta. "Why is she shivering like that?"

Thistle touched the gash in Ondelle's side. "It's the frore dagger. She's freezing on the inside. When the cold reaches her heart . . ." Thistle lowered her eyes.

"No! Make it stop!"

"I don't know how," said Thistle sadly.

"Ondelle," Brigitta pleaded, "you still have fire energy left. Fight the cold and stay with me!"

Ondelle pulled at Brigitta's arm and shook her head. Brigitta could barely bring herself to look into her High Priestess' watery eyes.

Ondelle broke into the smallest of smiles. "Brigitta of the White Forest . . ."

Without warning, a well burst and Brigitta was crying. Ondelle looked at her tenderly and Thistle rubbed her back. She cried for her wingless High Priestess. She cried for her exiled new friends. She cried for her destiny-less White Forest kin. And she cried for herself, because she had failed them all.

As confused Croilus faeries tended to each other and murmured amongst themselves, someone brought Brigitta a canteen of water and she helped Ondelle sit up and drink. Jarlath, Devin, Ferris, Thistle, and the two Nhords stood watch over them.

"There must be a way," sniffed Brigitta, "to get us home."

"You will go . . . when I do . . ." heaved Ondelle, clutching Brigitta's sleeve.

"What do you mean?"

"The spell . . . when we left," Ondelle took a deep breath so she could get her entire thought out. "I cast it so that when I died in Noe you would be sent back safely, and the whisper light would remain to do its work."

"If you died!" cried Brigitta.

Jarlath clenched his jaw, and Thistle's lips trembled. Brigitta had given them hope and Ondelle had just taken it away. How long did she have to live?

"What about that Purview?" Ferris asked.

"That's where Croilus went with Zhay," said Devin.

"The whisper light! The Purview!" Brigitta's despair grew. She turned to Abdira and Uwain. "Can Croilus get through?"

The Nhords thought about this for a moment. "Does he have a ring?" Abdira asked, pulling hers from the small pocket on her strap and handing it to Brigitta.

She examined the large dark crystal in its setting. "You say the Ancients left this for you?"

"May I?" asked Ondelle, and Brigitta brought it closer for her to see. She examined it and then fell back. "It's from a scepter . . . "

"Yes!" agreed Abdira. "Split in two, one for each, through generations."

"We guarded them and waited," added Uwain.

Ondelle coughed a few times. "Every Ancient had a scepter . . . like ours . . . infused with the fifth element."

Mabbe was an Ancient. Croilus had her scepter.

"If the whisper light made it to the Purview and activated it," said Brigitta, "Croilus can use the scepter to enter. But where would he go?"

They didn't have time to figure it out. Ondelle was dying and Brigitta had to get her home. There was no way she could move Ondelle without harming her. She'd have to find the Purview and bring it here. If it was moved once, it could be moved again.

She held up the Nhord ring. "If Ondelle and I each wear one of these, we can get back home?"

Uwain removed his ring from a pouch and handed it to Brigitta. "We came to serve," he said with a bow.

<hr/>

Brigitta, Devin, and Jarlath left Thistle and Ferris with Ondelle, who had lost consciousness but was still breathing as Brigitta laid her on the platform's floor.

With her new deodyte strength, Brigitta could cut through the air and easily flew twice as fast as the boys. Her own strength startled her. And yet, the energy felt so comfortable, as if it had always belonged to her.

But she would not keep this air energy, she said to herself. It belonged to Ondelle. She wished she knew how to give it back. Its absence surely had weakened her.

Jarlath and Devin paused when they reached the ruins, habitually checking clouds for rain.

"Come on!" Brigitta insisted. "I'll keep the rain away!"

The two Watchers didn't look convinced, but they proceeded just the same.

As they arrived at the plateau, only a few frightened lesser faeries, but no Watchers, crouched weaponless on the staircase.

Brigitta slowed. "Which way did Croilus go?" she asked. They silently pointed up the stairs, exchanging looks as to why a Croilus faerie, a Hollows faerie, and a stranger would arrive together.

"The battle is over," sang Devin over his shoulder as they flew up the stairs. "Croilus faeries are free!"

<hr/>

The three faeries entered the domed palace quietly and listened.

"If Croilus believed me and took Zhay to the Purview," Brigitta whispered, "then Zhay knows where it is. We just have to find him."

"If Croilus didn't kill him," Devin pointed out.

"Zhay is a traitor," Jarlath growled. "Why would he help us?"

"So we can all get what we want," Brigitta said. "He's not evil, Jarlath, he was just doing what he thought best for his tribe."

"Look!" Devin called.

On the floor of the great hall where Croilus had met them were scattered shards of glass. They fluttered into the room and examined the pieces.

"What happened?" asked Brigitta, looking around the room for an object that could have produced so much glass.

"The Purview?" asked Devin.

Brigitta and Jarlath exchanged looks. Had Croilus destroyed it when he entered?

A tiny *tip tip tip* drew Brigitta's attention. To her left, drops of bright red were methodically hitting the first tier of seats. She tracked the drops to the ceiling, where one of the glass panels in the dome was shattered, and Zhay's body lay bleeding across it.

Brigitta dashed to the ceiling, with Devin and Jarlath close behind. It was higher, and more detailed, than it appeared from the floor. Holding the glass in place were numerous strips of glazed silverwood, entwined to form strong beams.

Zhay groaned as they reached him, the cut on his arm much less severe than Brigitta had anticipated. They all pushed him through to the outside and then took turns slipping past the broken pane.

A room stood before them, jutting up behind the dome.

It was only accessible from the outside, and only if one thought of checking the backside of the dome. It was small and the outer walls were camouflaged so that no matter where one stood, it looked like a piece of sky or part of the palace. Except for the wall facing the dome, it wasn't a wall at all. It was a large white door, and it was open.

In the center of the room was a round silver hoop, wide enough for two faeries to walk though. Inside the hoop was a decorative square, and then another hoop. Brigitta slowly entered the room and circled the hoop. On its other side, the center wavered like water but reflected like a mirror.

"The Purview," she whispered.

Jarlath and Devin set Zhay down and joined Brigitta. They all stared into the Purview, and their watery images shone back.

"What happened?" she called to Zhay. "Tell me what happened!"

Zhay moaned, "I couldn't go through. I was too scared."

"But it was just a trick we played on Croilus," said Brigitta.

"I didn't know that!" he cried. "Croilus picked me up and sent me through it!" Zhay slumped down in the doorway, shaking. "I went straight through and shattered the dome glass."

"What's wrong with him!" said Jarlath. "Is he mad?"

"No, it's from the courage potion wearing off. He'll be back to his cheerful self in no time."

Zhay wobbled to his feet. "He came after me— but then— he just disappeared!"

"Keep an eye on him," Brigitta said, and Jarlath went to steady him. "I have to figure out a way to get this Purview out to Ondelle."

The silver ring stood perfectly balanced in the center of the room. It had vine-patterned etchings that moved slowly around the perimeter. They wove in and out of each other, mesmerizing her with their silent steady rhythms.

She was so focused on the silver ring that she didn't notice Devin wandering around the room.

"What is all this?" he asked.

Awakened from her reverie, Brigitta examined her surroundings. Each of three walls was painted with a detailed mural.

To her right, the mural depicted five beings sitting in five carved chairs. On the far right, just like in the great hall below them, was the largest chair. In it sat a hulking armored beast with two horns on its face. In spite of her distress, Brigitta had to smile when she recognized the Nhord Sage.

Next to it sat a hairless creature that was a bit faerie-like in the body and limbs, but its skin was pinky-gray, like an earthworm.

Enormous black eyes popped from its bald head, which was capped in shiny purple skin. On the far left was a beast with four arms that came straight down from its neck. It was all limbs and head and looked like it had come from the bottom of Green Lake. Next to that, some kind of maned faun-woman sat with her hooves perched on a stool. All the Sages pointed to Brigitta's right.

In the middle of the Council of Sages was an empty, high-backed, silver chair.

"Where is the High Sage—" Brigitta started to ask, and then she knew. "It's telling us a story."

Jarlath leaned in and Brigitta grabbed Devin. "Look here. The World Sages betrayed the High Sage, who was an Ancient, and he was killed. So no High Sage in the mural. And the other Sages, they're all pointing away to—" Brigitta followed the path of their fingers, or, she thought, whatever you call them. They were directed toward the second panel, to a young faerie girl with green wings bordered in gold. Her arms were lifted and from them flew five fuzzy lights.

"Narine," said Brigitta. She touched the young faerie's wings. "She created the whisper lights that would unlock the Purviews. She asked Gola to watch over them."

In the girl's right hand, she held a scepter. One of the whisper lights had separated from the others and was drifting in front of her scepter, as if flying toward the third wall.

Five silver-blue rings filled the final wall: one in the center, one above and below it, one on either side.

"Five," Brigitta murmured, tugging at Devin. "There are five Purviews."

The rings were drawn just like the symbols in the underground passageway, the map, and the font. A scepter had been painted inside the center one. Inside the other four were two interlocking finger rings with dark gems.

"Just like Abdira and Uwain's," Devin said.

Brigitta snapped back to attention, remembering that she could disappear at any time if Ondelle let herself die. She turned back to the Purview.

"Should we even touch it?"

Jarlath, Devin, and Brigitta contemplated the giant circle of silver.

"I wonder how heavy it is?" Jarlath asked.

Zhay entered, yanked his tunic straight, and cleared his throat. He grasped the ring with both hands and lifted.

"Actually," he said, "it's really light."

Chapter Nineteen

Brigitta and the Watcher boys flew the Purview back through the ruins and placed it on the platform on the side of the hill where Ondelle and Brigitta had appeared in Noe. There it stood on end as it had in the hidden room, vine shapes twisting along its curves.

Now that she had secured the Purview, all her fears returned like a cold rain. Where exactly had Croilus gone? Would traveling through the Purview be too dangerous for Ondelle? What choice did she have, though? Ondelle would die without healing magic, and Brigitta would be drawn home without her.

They returned to the battle scene and the dejected faces of their faerie and Nhord allies. Granae had brought Roane from the Hollows, as well as a full jar of sands she had lifted from Mabbe's chambers while all the Watchers were fighting. A few straggling Croilus faeries spied on them from a distance.

Home. Brigitta and Ondelle were going home.

"I'll come back as soon as I can. We used Blue Spell once, we can use it again. I'll bring the scepter and rings and—"

"Not possible," Ondelle said hoarsely.

Brigitta dropped to her side. "Please, Ondelle, save your strength."

"There are things . . . " breathed Ondelle.

"Shhh, you can tell me after you are well," said Brigitta

"You must know!" Ondelle said with such force that they all stared. "You cannot return . . . "

"What do you mean?"

She lay down again and took a labored breath. "When the Eternal Dragon bestows the fifth element upon the High Priest or Priestess . . . it is limited . . . to the destiny span of that faerie. Once the fifth element is depleted from a High Priestess' scepter . . . the destiny of that faerie is complete."

Ondelle shut her eyes. "The last of the Dragon's gift is in that spell in your necklace."

"What are you saying?" Brigitta cried. "No, no, your destiny is not complete!"

"Brigitta, what I have done to you . . . " Ondelle lifted a finger and traced Brigitta's cheek. "Please, forgive me."

Ondelle's hand dropped to the platform as she lost consciousness.

"Ondelle!" Brigitta buried her face in her High Priestess' hair.

It suddenly made sense. How Ondelle's energy had weakened once they landed in Noe. She had known as soon as she cast that last Blue Spell magic that her life would be over and she would die in Noe. She had paid that price to protect Brigitta. And she had kept this knowledge to herself, because she knew Brigitta would have protested it.

And now, Brigitta was able to go back through the Purview, but she'd have to leave everyone else behind. If she stayed with her friends, Ondelle would die and she'd be spell-cast back to the White Forest alone.

Thistle touched Brigitta's hand, trembling. "It's not your fault."

Devin put his arm around her shoulder. "We know you tried."

She looked up at the Purview, then to the faeries before her. Zhay sat on the edge of the stage with his head in his hands. Both Ferris and Jarlath stood with their arms crossed, not angry, just resigned. Ferris's sliverleaf scars glinted in the fading light. Brigitta looked down at the silver scar on her own hand.

Granae held up the jar of sorcery sands to Brigitta. Abdira and Uwain waited patiently behind her, even after stranding themselves an ocean away from their home by giving up their rings.

A faint *craw craw* sounded in the distance, and Roane grabbed Jarlath's arm. Brigitta looked into Jarlath's bright eyes and held his gaze. Her heart skipped a beat. It was the exact moment, the image from her vision when she had touched Gola's moonstones.

A boy with starry eyes . . . a decision she had to make.

It's not fair, thought Brigitta. I can't leave them! If she took the rings and the sands and left them to fend for themselves, she would be no better than Croilus. But if Croilus had sent himself to the White Forest, would anyone there be able to defend it? *We are not warriors,* Ondelle had told her.

There had to be another way.

"Brigitta?" whispered Granae, holding up the jar. "You'd better leave. It's getting dark."

The straggling Croilus faeries moved closer to the platform. There were only three left, two male and one female, all lesser faeries, and all growing more terrified as the light of day waned.

Roane ran to Brigitta and hugged her waist. She petted his head, and he held her harder. Jarlath reached over and pulled him back. "Come on, Roane." He smiled sadly at Brigitta as they moved away.

"Oh, no," Devin whispered, pointing toward the lakebed.

On the edge of the lakebed, a few shadowy figures wavered. Brigitta could see the river struggling up the valley right through them. She could feel their presence more than anything, and for a moment she could only see the two of them. Then she saw the rest, seven more, coming closer.

"Nightwalkers!" hissed Jarlath.

Everyone huddled together. Abdira and Uwain stood their ground and growled.

"We must fly!" cried Ferris.

The nightwalkers approached, smooth and silent, yet noboy moved. They all looked to Brigitta, and she was about to tell them to flee, when she noticed glints of blue in the shadowy figures. She stepped closer to the Nightwalkers.

They were the spirits of dead Watchers.

"What are you doing? Brigitta, no!" called Granae.

Brigitta waved the faeries back. "It's all right. Trust me."

When the shadows were a moonsbreath away, Brigitta closed her eyes and took hold of her necklace. None of her mentors had ever mentioned how to empath an undispersed spirit, and none had probably ever tried.

Letting go of all thought and fear, Brigitta allowed herself to sit inside her new dual energy. She drifted on a river of wind, which became a tunnel that opened into a fog. The fog was moist but not cold. Nor was it warm. She opened herself to it and it enveloped her.

All echoes of the ether must be called back again, the fog spoke.

What do you mean? Brigitta's voice reverberated through the fog.

We must be dispersed; we are losing touch with the Ancients.

You, too? Brigitta's focus wavered at her surprise, and she rebalanced herself.

If we lose touch with the Ancients, the nightwalkers continued, *we will remain here forever. You must disperse us.*

But how?

A bright light flashed, and Brigitta was looking back at herself and the Watchers behind her on the stage. For that moment, she could not breathe, but before panic hit, she was back in the fog again.

The Watchers can disperse you, Brigitta remembered. *How have Watchers done this? I thought only Ancients could disperse faerie spirits?*

Watchers are descendants of Ancients. Ancients and lesser faeries.

They—what? This sudden insight wreaked too much havoc in Brigitta's thoughts, and she jerked alert in her own body. The Watcher spirits waited in front of her, fading in and out of shadow. Echoes of the ether, they had said. Half-breeds of the Ancients— keepers of the fifth element.

The Watchers weren't created by Mabbe from sorcery sands, they were *descendants* of Mabbe. Her children, she had called them.

Brigitta turned and smiled.

"Oh, thank the moons," cried Thistle, pulling Brigitta forward by the hand, "we thought they'd taken over your mind."

"They haven't moved," said Devin, lips trembling.

"What do they want?" asked Jarlath.

"Our help," said Brigitta. She gestured from her bewildered friends to the nightwalkers. "Everyone, meet our way home."

"It will be a strange journey, but quick," said Brigitta. "Kind of like going up in one of your trees. Hold on tight to Ondelle, Jarlath. And when you get through, you must immediately ask for Gola. She will know what to do. Granae?"

Granae stepped forward. "I was just a girl when ascending the dead was abolished. But I aided my mother in ascending my grandfather. So I hope I've told you all you need."

"Are you sure this will work?" Jarlath looked skeptically at the Watcher spirits, now congregated beside the Purview with them.

"The dispersement, yes," said Brigitta, "my theory about the Purview? No."

"But I guess we'll find out, right?" He smirked at her.

"I could throw you through like Croilus did to me," joked Zhay, but nobody laughed.

Brigitta helped Jarlath and Thistle pick up Ondelle. She checked the Nhord ring around Ondelle's finger. She turned to Abdira and Uwain, a sob stuck in her throat. "There are no words to thank you enough."

The two Nhords bowed slightly.

"It is us who thank you, Brigitta of the White Forest," said Abdira. "Six generations of waiting, and we have the honor of serving you!"

"Born to serve the destiny that awaits," added Uwain gruffly. Thistle was right; they did make her want to hug them.

Jarlath and Thistle stepped up to the Purview with Ondelle. Two Watcher spirits glided up to them, and the color drained from Jarlath's face. Brigitta's theory was that if a Watcher entered the

Purview exactly when they dispersed, there would be enough of the fifth element called to send them through.

"If it doesn't work, we'll just step through the ring," Thistle pointed out.

"That's not the part that worries me," muttered Jarlath.

"Remember," said Abdira, "it can only take you where you know to go, so you must know of Brigitta's home as she has described it."

"Picture this," Brigitta held up her hourglass necklace, "only many sizes larger, so large it must be hung between two uul trees."

"Gotcha," said Jarlath.

"Oh, and these," Brigitta pulled the shards of Himmy's song drop from her pocket. "Think about her song. If you can remember it."

"I can," said Thistle, smiling.

Thistle and Jarlath each took a deep breath, the spirits entered them, and they stepped though.

And disappeared.

"It worked!" cried Granae. Brigitta let out a tremendous sigh of relief.

Granae took Roane's hand. "Just like them, okay?"

She and Roane stepped up to the Purview, waited to absorb two spirits, and then they were gone, too. For a moonsbreath, Brigitta saw the lights of the White Forest reflected back at her.

They were safe.

Suddenly, Brigitta felt the full weight of her exhaustion. She motioned weakly to Zhay, Ferris, and Devin. "You first," said Brigitta. "I'll follow after I say goodbye to the Nhords and return the Purview to its hiding place."

In all that had happened, Brigitta had forgotten about the three lesser Croilus faeries now curled up with their arms around their knees on the corner of the platform. Zhay was observing them.

He turned back to Brigitta and shook his head. "I'm staying here."

"What? No, you mustn't!"

"I'm staying."

"It's all right Zhay, you can come."

Devin and Ferris stepped forward. "We're staying, too," said Ferris, putting her arm around Devin.

"Croilus is gone," said Zhay, gesturing to the lesser faeries. "Perhaps I can do some good at the Palace."

"And what if Dugald makes trouble?" asked Ferris. "We can't have that."

"Plus we can make sure every single spirit left in Noe is ascended," said Devin, "before they get stuck here."

Brigitta looked into the faces of her new friends. They were serious. "You're sure you want to do this?" asked Brigitta.

"We're sure," said Ferris.

"We've created our own destinies," said Zhay with a grin. "We are now the Watchers of the Purview."

"It's an important Life Task," said Brigitta as tears welled up in her eyes.

A moment later, two Watcher spirits thrust themselves into Zhay. His eyes bulged and he opened his mouth to speak but only gagged.

"What's wrong?" cried Ferris. "What's happening? They're killing him!"

"No, I don't think so," said Brigitta.

Zhay fell forward onto his hands and knees and began to shake. His body radiated a heat so intense it warmed them all. They watched, stunned, as bright silver symbols appeared on the ends of his wings. Large round shapes within squares within circles, like miniature Purviews.

When Zhay stopped trembling, Brigitta helped him to his feet and turned his head so that he could see his new markings. "I think those spirits just gave you your entire Change all at once."

"Next time," said Zhay, still shaken up, "perhaps they'll warn me first,"

Brigitta hugged Ferris, trying not to cry. Devin and Zhay kissed her on each cheek. Abdira and Uwain stepped forward, lowered their heads, and touched Brigitta gently on the forehead with their lip horns.

"You know where to find us if you change your mind," said Brigitta.

She stepped closer to the Purview and looked down at the ring around her finger. She was about to step through, then stopped and removed her pack. She took out the jar of sorcery sands and handed them to Zhay.

"You should take these. Study them and maybe you'll learn some new tricks to defend against Dugald. You are part Ancient, after all."

She turned and gazed into the Purview. She concentrated on her home, on the White Forest, on the faces of her momma and poppa and Himmy. She pictured the Great Hourglass and the High Council seated in front of it. She pictured Auntie Ferna and Gola and Minq and Glennis. She pictured Ondelle and stepped through.

Chapter Twenty

Brigitta's body was ripped forward through the air. Images and colors collided, and she saw both worlds simultaneously. There was nothing to hold onto, yet she felt held in place as she traveled, faster and faster, unable to breathe. She let go, knowing breath would come again.

Everything stopped moving. She collapsed to the ground and lay there in the dark, waiting for her vision to clear. The tops of the trees came into focus and the Great Blue Moon beyond. A loud hum filled her head, blocking out any other sounds.

The hum faded, and hushed faerie voices drifted in the air. Flashes of light bombarded the leaves above.

Someone touched her, and wetness landed on her cheeks. Where was she?

A face came into focus, Thistle's, grinning through her tears.

Brigitta sat up on her elbows and looked around. She was sprawled in the festival arena before the Great Hourglass of Protection. Elder Dervia headed her way, wringing her hands as she jetted through the air. Behind her, Earth Elder Adaire was tending to Jarlath's battle wounds. Roane hid in the folds of Granae's tunic as she spoke with Elders Hammus and Fozk.

"What's wrong?" Brigitta managed a hoarse whisper. "Why are you crying?"

"Oh, Brigitta!" Thistle wrapped her arms around Brigitta's neck, almost choking her. "Wait," she said and looked around, "where are the rest?"

"They stayed behind to—" Brigitta started, then grabbed Thistle's arm, "Ondelle!"

"That's what I've come to tell you," said Dervia, landing next to them. She helped Brigitta up and hugged her forcefully. Brigitta's surprised eyes nearly bulged out of their sockets.

"The Perimeter Guards took her to Gola's." Dervia pulled back, looked her square in the eyes. "Her wings . . ." She shook her head. "Well, there's nothing that can be done about that. But Gola is a master healer and I'm sure—"

Brigitta tried to speak the dreadful truth to Dervia, but she couldn't get her mouth to make the words.

Dervia's own mouth dropped open as she sensed the elemental change in Brigitta, and she let go of her. "By the Dragon's breath . . ."

It was obvious by her knitted brow and murmured bewilderment that Elder Dervia had never heard of a faerie transferring one of her elements to another faerie. But then again, deodytes were rare, so few faeries would have ever had a second element to transfer to anyone.

"Who would have taught Ondelle such a thing?" asked Brigitta after she had related her story about receiving the element of air in Mabbe's burl.

Globelights in hand, she and Dervia flew southeast through the forest on the main throughway, skirting the northeastern tip of Bobbercurxy. A few young faerie couples sat on the edge of the village-nest in its popular tree park, which was strung with breathlanterns and candlewebs. They looked up as Dervia and Brigitta flew past.

"One isn't always taught," said Dervia. "Sometimes one just learns, intuitively, if she is inquisitive at heart."

Brigitta nodded. This was something she definitely understood.

When Brigitta and Dervia landed at Gola's tree, Minq was sitting among the chatterbuds at her door waiting for them. The chatterbuds didn't greet Brigitta with their usual joyful chorus, but instead drooped against each other sadly.

"She inside," said Minq softly, touching Brigitta's arm with his ear. Brigitta squeezed it back with her hand.

Minq stayed outside while Brigitta and Dervia ventured through the door. It was dark, and as Brigitta's eye's adjusted, she saw Ondelle lying in Gola's bed under layers of blankets. Gola was puttering about her kitchen, Eyes perched on her shoulder. The Eyes hopped around as Gola continued mixing whatever concoction she was making.

"There is nothing I can do for her," came Gola's gravelly voice, "other than keep her comfortable until the end."

"No!" Brigitta rushed to Ondelle's side. "There must be something. Please, Gola!"

Ondelle looked many season cycles older than when they had left the White Forest. Wrinkles Brigitta had never noticed before lined the High Priestess' mouth and forehead. Her black hair was woven with gray. And without her air energy, she appeared more ordinary.

Still, Brigitta thought, she was stunning. It seemed impossible that such beauty could die.

"Why?" asked Gola as she shuffled back to the bed. "Her life is complete." Gola placed an herbal compress on Ondelle's forehead. "More complete than most."

Elder Dervia squeezed Brigitta's shoulder as they gazed upon their dying priestess. The Eyes hopped from Gola's shoulder to the headboard and blinked.

"Ondelle . . . I'm so sorry . . . " sobbed Brigitta.

Ondelle's eyes fluttered open and she managed a smile. "Why are you sorry, my child?"

"I don't know if I made the right choices."

"There are no right or wrong choices, only the choices themselves . . . We must make them, that is the important thing, and go on."

"I choose for you not to go!" Brigitta cried. "I choose to give you back all your air so you can heal yourself."

"I do not think you could." She nodded to Gola and closed her eyes again. "Goodbye, Brigitta of the White Forest."

"No!"

Gola was suddenly in front of Ondelle, an unfamiliar object in her twig-like fingers. It was round and opaque, about the size of Brigitta's fist, and made of something similar to Gola's moonstones.

"You must take her outside," Gola instructed Dervia as she leaned over Ondelle.

Bewildered, Brigitta allowed herself to be led from the cottage. As she stepped through the door, she heard Ondelle shriek out in pain.

Brigitta looked back at the bed. Gola stooped over Ondelle's body as it relaxed, and she expelled a long, final breath.

As they emerged from the tree Brigitta was enveloped in a tearful group hug. Someone had retrieved Pippet, Mousha, Himalette, and Auntie Ferna when Brigitta had arrived. Even Roucho, her poppa's featherless delivery bird, was there solemnly perched in Gola's tree with a pack of broodnuts on his back.

"Ondelle of Grioth has completed her Life's Task in this world," said Dervia. "I will inform the Center Realm."

Her parents and sister wailed in disbelief as Dervia flitted into the trees. Pippet rocked Brigitta back and forth in her arms. She suddenly stopped and let go.

"You . . . you're . . . " she stammered.

"Yeah, I know."

"But how?" Mousha examined Brigitta all over, as if being a deodyte would include some outward physical change. When he saw the sliverleaf scar on her wing he reached out and touched it. Brigitta braced herself for the shock of poison pain, but there was none.

Mind and body spent, she dropped to the ground. "I guess we'll never know," she said softly as everyone gathered around her.

"Oh, lola," said Pippet, enveloping Brigitta in her plump arms once again.

What should have been a welcome home celebration turned into a strangely melancholy gathering as, one by one, each village-nest's residents drifted into the Center Realm the following morning. Even when faeries dispersed, there was generally celebration. But the appearance of the Watchers, the unexpected death of their High Priestess, and Brigitta's unprecedented change into a deodyte disquieted everyone.

Fear or no fear, the White Forest faeries deserved to hear the truth. At least as much as Brigitta knew of it. Some of it, she had a feeling, was lost forever.

As everyone gathered beneath the Great Hourglass, a realization struck Brigitta, and she wondered how she could have forgotten. She pulled Jarlath aside as the Elders took their seats.

"Jarlath," whispered Brigitta, "has there been any sign of Croilus?"

"No," he replied, "I'd almost forgotten about him in all of this."

"Me, too." She looked around. "And no one mentioned anyone emerging from Noe before you got here with Ondelle."

"Maybe he couldn't do it? Maybe Zhay was wrong."

"Either he never left or he landed somewhere else."

Both options troubled her. There was no way to go back to warn the others. "We got here by knowing the White Forest. If Croilus couldn't know it, maybe he couldn't appear here."

"So, where is he, then?"

"Lost in some between world, I hope."

"Wherever he is, he has Mabbe's staff," Jarlath reminded her.

Brigitta nodded and thought about Zhay, Ferris, and Devin. She suddenly wished she had convinced them to come.

They made their choice, she thought. We must go on.

Brigitta climbed the stairs to the dais. When she got to the top, she bowed to Ondelle, who lay in a glass box in a fiery red gown that would have matched her wings. This was the final time she and Ondelle would share this platform together. She felt older and younger at the same time. A child who knew too much. A child who wanted to crawl into her momma's lap and listen to an old faerie tale. One with a happy ending.

Ondelle's scepter stood in the center of the platform, just as she had left it. Brigitta stepped up to it and cleared her throat.

"My dear kin."

The White Forest faeries looked at her warily, most likely wondering how she had acquired Ondelle's element. For Brigitta, the two elements had interwoven and moved like long-lost parts of each other, so familiar that she marveled how she had lived with only one element before.

Was that what Ondelle had meant when she said, *I do not think you could?*

"We are here to celebrate the life of our dear High Priestess," spoke Brigitta. "It's because of her protection and wisdom that I stand here now. I'm afraid I can't offer you what she could have, but I think the gift of her air element was so that a part of her would remain."

The crowd murmured and the Elders stared up at her strangely. For them, she realized, everything about this was unfamiliar territory. The transference of an element, a Second Apprentice speaking for a dead High Priestess, losing touch with the Ancients. She almost felt sorry for them.

Welcome to my world, she thought grimly.

"The best I can do is offer the truth, because at this point, not knowing it might do more harm." Brigitta took a deep breath and gestured to the Noe Watchers gathered behind the Elders' chairs. "We traveled to Noe, where we met all these faeries, the Watchers. Their kin had somehow been tricked into staying behind after the Great World Cry. The Ancient who tricked them is now gone, but there are others, dangerous faeries who have caused a lot of misery in Noe.

"We will have to learn to defend ourselves, because—" a frantic buzz went up from the crowd, and she waited for them to quiet down again. "Because the truth is . . . " Brigitta peered down at the Elders, who now looked particularly panic-stricken. Adaire stood up from her chair, but Fozk took her arm and shook his head. She sat back down, and he nodded for Brigitta to continue.

"The truth is that the White Forest is falling into imbalance, because we have lost touch with the Ancients."

The crowd gasped and once again broke into excited chatter. Brigitta once again raised her hands to silence everyone.

"That's why Ondelle and I traveled to Noe. We had hoped the sacred artifact would help reconnect us with the Ancients, and in some ways it did. It reconnected us with our past and these Ancient descendants, so at least our elemental faerie line will continue. But sacrifices were also made and there will be more to come." She took a breath and gazed upon Ondelle's remarkable face.

"No faeries will be given destinies at birth. When these new children grow up, they will have to decide their Life's Task on their own. We will have to decide for ourselves who our next leaders will be."

"Brigitta of Tiragarrow!" someone shouted from the crowd, and a few faeries cheered. Brigitta blushed.

Dervia made her way to the stage, and the rest of the Elders Followed.

"I'm afraid she's not ready," Dervia said, placing her arm around Brigitta's shoulders.

Brigitta tightened her fists and felt anger rising up from her stomach. None of the Elders had ever faced a warwump or even so much as glimpsed the River That Runs Backwards. She glared at Dervia but then caught sight of Ondelle in her glass box and quickly calmed her energy.

She looked back at her mentor, but instead of the disdain she expected, she saw only concern. In her own way, Dervia was trying to protect Brigitta, too. She felt ashamed. If she could not control her emotions, then they were right. She wasn't ready.

Besides, she thought, looking out over the crowd, she was tired.

She needed to rest for a while and show her new friends around their adopted home.

Her eyes locked with Glennis's, who stood next to Himalette beside the Water Faerie stands. New markings graced her wings: four yellow-orange lines in four directions. Glennis had gone through her Change while Brigitta was away. She had the markings of a Wising.

Poor Glennis, Brigitta thought, destined to serve. Then she recalled Uwain and Abdira's steadfast pledge: *service is our highest endeavor.* No, not poor Glennis. She was exactly what she was meant to be.

❧

Once the Elders had said a few words, the ceremony ended, and all the faeries began to feast. The festival grounds were still more solemn than usual, but filling their bellies helped to relieve some of the anxiety.

Brigitta sat with her family and the Watchers, who were to disperse Ondelle's spirit later that evening in a private ceremony. Roane sat next to Brigitta on the grass and leaned into her. She poked his nose and he smiled.

Jarlath sat down opposite them with a plate piled ridiculously high with faerie specialties. He had a pink frommafin mustache. "Here," she laughed and wiped his lip with a napkin. Their eyes locked and he smiled.

"Thanks," he murmured, and she knew he meant for everything.

Suddenly shy, she changed the subject. "How come Roane's voice hasn't come back? Didn't all the voices get released during the battle?"

Jarlath playfully messed with Roane's hair. "Mabbe didn't take his voice," he said. "It was just easier to tell everyone that she did. I didn't want the Watchers to think there was something wrong with him and lock him up."

He looked down at his little brother. Roane nodded that it was okay to go on. "He stopped speaking when our parents were killed.

They managed one of the sky farms. He was messing around, hiding from them, and it grew dark. The birds got them." He swallowed hard.

"Mabbe was going to sentence him to chiseling for his behavior, so I became one of her guards in exchange for a lighter sentence." He indicated the burn marks on Roane's wing. "I was already involved with the rebels, so we thought it might help the cause, you know, to be on the inside."

Brigitta didn't know which impressed her more, that Roane had kept himself quiet all these moons, or that Jarlath had taken so many risks.

"Thistle mentioned that you started the rebels because of the voices," said Brigitta. "What did they say to you?"

"To lead the faeries to a new land," he said, drifting off at the memory. "But I was afraid to listen. I didn't want to become like Croilus, mad and vain."

Brigitta shot him a wicked grin. "Well, at least you're not mad."

"Ha ha," Jarlath poked her arm and leapt up, grabbing Roane by the hands. He spun him around until they were both off the ground. Roane kicked his feet playfully and began to laugh, at first raspy and quiet, and then heartier as his body remembered how.

Brigitta started laughing, too. She watched as Jarlath twirled, taller and stronger than he had seemed to her in Noe. His skin would grow redder in the White Forest sun, she decided. And as it darkened, his eyes would shine more brightly than ever before.

❧

Brigitta dashed toward the Apprentices' chambers to prepare for Ondelle's dispersement. All the First Apprentices— Flanna, Thane, Na Tam, and Mora—were waiting for her at the end of the hall beside her door. Thane cleared his throat and held out his hand, palm up. Brigitta hesitated before brushing it with her own. This was a gesture reserved for the senior Apprentices.

"I—" began Flanna. The others nodded for her to go on, which was obviously difficult for her. "I have been unfair to you."

Brigitta didn't respond for fear she would be less than gracious.

"After tonight, you may be one of us," added Mora, a sinewy Air Faerie with deep aqua wings and a pale, angular face. "Well, if Dervia is revealed as the new High Priestess."

Brigitta hadn't even thought of this. If Dervia became High Priestess, then Flanna would become an Elder and Brigitta would move to First Apprentice. Flanna didn't look particularly happy about the idea.

"It won't be Dervia," said Brigitta to Flanna.

"How do you know?" asked Flanna, forgetting her dislike for Brigitta and grabbing her arm. "Are you sure?"

"Pretty sure," said Brigitta, then she smiled. "She's not ready."

The rest of them laughed.

"Thanks," said Brigitta, not quite to Flanna. "I need to prepare." She turned to open her door.

"Apprentice Brigitta," asked Mora, "what is it like being a deodyte?"

"It feels," Brigitta thought for a moment, "like having someone else with you. Someone you know really well."

When Brigitta was finally alone in her room, she climbed onto her bed, curled up into the tightest ball she could, and began to sob.

How could any of this be her destiny? How could Ondelle leave her with such a mess? She caught a wisp of a shadow close to her bed. She sniffed and lifted her head up.

"Ondelle?" she called.

The shadow shifted in the air, and then it was beside Brigitta. It gave off no elemental energy. She looked into it, held her hourglass, and relaxed her mind. Nothing happened. She could not get through.

Granae had been chosen to disperse Ondelle's spirit, since she essentially had the most experience. The Elders also agreed that using the eldest member of the Watchers would be more respectful.

They first supervised Jarlath in dispersing Jorris's spirit in the Elders' ceremony chambers, and then Granae stepped forward to receive Ondelle's. Jorris's body was given to the earth outside of Rioscrea, and Ondelle's was taken to her childhood home, Grioth, the smallest village-nest in the Fire Faerie realm.

Before dawn, Air Elder Fozk of Fhorsa's markings had already turned gold.

That's that, thought Brigitta, staring into her Thought Mirror the next day. Destiny was still alive in the White Forest. For now.

Maybe there's an Apprentice already with gold High Priestess markings under her Elder symbols, waiting to be revealed, the image in her mirror said.

She turned away from her mirror. She didn't want to think about that.

Brigitta didn't attend Ondelle's burial. She had already said her goodbyes. But she did watch from afar, perched in a tree, as the faeries Ondelle had grown up with lowered her body into the ground. Her Auntie Ferna was there. Brigitta had almost forgotten that she and Ondelle had served on the Council of Elders together for a short time. That they had even been friends.

Only a moonbeat from Gola's place and Brigitta had never been to Grioth before. Some day she would ask the Grioth faeries to tell her about the Ondelle they had known.

After the ceremony she snuck away and headed west until she found the Lola Spring River. She flew above its tranquil surface until it sunk into the warm ponds, where several Fire Faeries were floating, contemplating the sky.

She meandered for most of the morning, following whatever path opened for her, skirting the village-nest of Rioscrea, as she did not want to make conversation. Midday she found herself at Precipice Falls. She dropped to the soft ground and stared at the glistening streams, so tame compared to the River That Runs Backwards. The Mad River, she corrected herself.

She lay on her stomach, staring into the water as it splashed over the rocks into the caverns below. She didn't try to empath the water or rocks or trees or anything. After awhile, she rolled over onto her back to stare in the other direction.

She put her hands in her tunic pockets. There was something soft at the bottom of one. She pulled out a pink fire flower, the one she had stolen from the garden on her way to visit Gola before she left for the Ruins of Noe. She straightened the petals and marveled at the flower's tenacity.

There was a rustle from the trees. Brigitta sat up. Jarlath stood a few feet away with a sheepish grin. Minq fluttered around him a few times before landing next to Brigitta.

"I show him waterfall," he said, proudly stretching out his ears. "Favorite place to be alone."

"Yeah, exactly," Brigitta scolded, then laughed as she caught Jarlath's sparkling crystal blue eyes.

Minq sniggered and pulled his special move, twirling up and then diving down over the edge into the falls. Brigitta scooted over and sat with her legs dangling off the embankment. Jarlath sat down next to her.

"Everyone seems to be settling in," he said.

"I hear Momma and Poppa will look after Roane?" Brigitta twirled the flower.

"Yes, and Granae and Thistle decided to live in Grobjahar, near the marsh farms."

"It's strange . . . all these destinyless faeries . . . "

"They all managed to find something to do," teased Jarlath.

"Our destiny markings really only reveal what we already know," said Brigitta.

He looked up at her wings and squinted. "You know, that sliverleaf scar looks like it's supposed to be there."

She twisted around to look at her right wing. The silver scar did look like it was melting into the eye glyph, and the edges of the scar were taking on some of her mark's deep green coloring.

"Everything is as it's supposed to be," she murmured.

The White Forest is good for him, she thought, studying his own wings. They were actually quite brilliant in the right light. She caught herself staring and quickly looked away again.

"What about you?" she asked, watching Minq fluttering about the falls.

"Minq took me to meet Gola," he said. "She's amazing."

"Mmmm, she is." Brigitta traced her lips with the flower.

"I might apprentice with her," he added.

"Wheeeeeeee!" Minq called as he flew up and sprayed them with an earful of water.

Jarlath leaned hard into Brigitta's right shoulder. A strange sensation shot up her arm, but this time, it didn't sting.

Brigitta blushed as he pulled away, and she handed him the fire flower. He took it without thinking, and before their eyes, as he held it, the flower grew a deeper shade of red.

White Forest Lexicon

blossom bells
Hanging chimes, shaped like flower buds, used during many faerie festivals and a favorite of the Twilight Festival, which takes place at the end of the **Green Months**.

broodnut
Its "shell" is soft and thin, so that when carved into, the red meat of it is exposed. Named "broodnut" because love-sick faeries often use it to carve messages to their heartthrobs (and the evidence can be eaten). Also sometimes used in faerie games because it is light and soft so it doesn't hurt to catch one. The meat of it is plain, but when cooked and spiced makes a great party snack. Broodnut trees grow best in the forest between the Earth and Water Realms near Green Lake (see White Forest map).

ceunias leaf
It takes a Master Gardener to grow ceunias. It must be frequently trimmed, and meditation is essential while it sprouts. There is no blossom, the leaves are shiny and waxy, and when placed on the tongue the "wax" melts and gives a calming effect. The more peaceful the meditations while caring for the plant, the better the calming effect, as it essentially carries this meditation within. The leaves are slightly fragrant, but not used for cooking.

chygpallas
Found primarily in southeastern Foraglenn (see Foraglenn map), they are a bit like big, fat mice but without ears or tails. They are completely deaf and have large round eyes and tiny mouths with long tongues for catching tiny beasts inside hollow branches. Noe Valley children like them as pets because they are docile, although a bit skittish, and have soft fur. If you keep a steady supply of buggy beasts, they'll stick around.

Croilus

Croilus refers to both the male Watcher who rebelled against Mabbe and the palace lands. Croilus named the area after himself when he retreated there with his rebel force. The land was originally home to the Ancients and lesser faeries and the palace was the seat of the World Sages. At that time the area was called Noe, part of the larger Noe Valley. (See Foraglenn map)

Dragon's breath / by the Dragon

Whenever faeries use the term Dragon in reverence, they are referring to the Eternal Dragon, Tzajeek, a sea serpent with the ability to absorb elements. Tzajeek is **Faweh's** true Keeper of the Elements and the only one of its kind. Its origin is unknown. When exclaiming something in great awe and wonder, faeries often say, "by the Dragon" or "by the Dragon's breath."

When a new High Priest or Priestess takes their position, he or she must journey, alone, to the Sea of Tzajeek to seek audience with the Eternal Dragon. The serpent imparts private wisdom, often things that must never be shared with another being. In addition, Tzajeek infuses the White Forest scepter (a gift from the Ancients) with the fifth element, essentially giving the High Priest or Priestess the ability to conjure Blue Spell and therefore reset the hourglass each season cycle.

durma

The only somber instrument in the White Forest. Used in Elder ceremonies, in particular ceremonies celebrating the life of a deceased faerie. A thick **silverwood** branch is used, but it must have fallen naturally, symbolizing the branch having fulfilled its first destiny. It is hollowed out and one end encased in sunbleached strips from the Reed Forest (see White Forest map) of the Air Faerie Realm. It resembles a drum, but the durma is rubbed with the palm of the hand, rather than beaten. Each instrument has a unique sound somewhat like a low wind.

dustmist

A diverse and useful tool (created most often by a talented Air Faerie) used to spread spells, aromas, sounds, or any other light item through the air or to make it stick or stay in one place. Can also be used to conceal things. With a great deal of practice, one can learn to send messages using dustmist. Mothers can leave lullabies in the air above their babies. Festival grounds can be sprinkled with dustmist to keep sparkles or musical notes in the air.

empathing

A skill developed during Elder Apprenticeships. Water Faeries are particularly adept in this area, so the task of teaching it generally lies with the Water Faerie Elder. It is the ability to enter the "mind" or "body" of other things with one's own mind. Inanimate objects are easier because of the lack of messy thoughts and resistance getting in the way. One can "be" a cloud because the cloud doesn't care one way or the other.

Eternal Dragon (Tzajeek)
(see **Dragon's breath**)

Faweh

What the faeries call the world outside the White Forest and the world in general. There are five continents on Faweh, and the White Forest is on Foraglenn. The remaining continents are Pariglenn, Araglenn, Carraiglenn, and Storlglenn. The Nhords are from Araglenn.

Featherkind, Orl and Edl

Most faeries go by their first name and the name of their birth village-nest (Brigitta of Tiragarrow, Ondelle of Grioth, Mousha of Grobjahar). There is no need for any further naming, but some couples take on a joint name of their choosing, particularly if they do not have children. There is, of course, a name-revealing party to go along with the choosing. Edl and Orl, both of Tiragarrow, chose Featherkind as a second name because they thought it sounded friendly.

firepepper

A Fire Faerie specialty, of course. Fine spell-treated granules used to make something hot to touch. It can really burn, so it's not often used full-strength. More generally it is diluted and used in anything you'd want warm, like a compress, blanket, or water to bathe in. Some Master Gardeners use it to keep beasties from getting into their gardens.

folyia tree
A tall, thin tree found throughout Foraglenn and Pariglenn, with fibrous bark that can be pulled apart and used to bind or weave. If you soak the fibers, they can be woven into cloth.

font
A metal bowl on a pedestal used by the Ancients for both ceremonial and practical purposes. Every element, and combinations thereof, can be called into a font if one knows how to do so. For instance, if one were thirsty or wanted to wash one's hands, water could be filled in the font. If warmth were needed, then fire could be called.

frore dagger
An ice-cold dagger that immediately heals the cut it makes. Originally used by the Ancients on anything that needed to be trimmed. For instance, if a tree had a sick limb, it could be cut off with a frore dagger and not leave a wound. Mabbe has a few frore daggers, but she uses them for nasty business, like slicing off wings without killing the faerie.

gargan
A big ugly spider. The only thing the birds of Noe are afraid of. Luckily for Noe faeries, they primarily stick to the mountains away from the mist, because the moisture makes their hairs heavy. Every once in a while, one will venture down and build a web in the forest around the valley. You do not want to get caught in a gargan web.

green zynthia
Before the Great World Cry, the zynthia crystals found inside the caves beneath Dead Mountain, and in parts of Araglenn, were harmless. They were never harvested but were sometimes meditated upon. They were mesmerizing even before the Great World Cry. After the Great World Cry, and the subsequent elemental chaos, they became strongly hypnotic and dangerous. Few have had a chance to study them and fewer still have developed a way to resist their effects.

Grow, Green, and Gray Months
These are the three seasons in the White Forest that make up a **season**

cycle. Each season, all birth celebrations take place at the same time in each village-nest (otherwise there would be nothing but celebrations every day). For instance, everyone in Tiragarrow who was born in the Green Months (like Brigitta) is honored on the same day. The Festival of Elements takes place as Grow transitions to Green, the Twilight Festival takes place as Green gives way to Gray, and the Festival of Moons (also called The Masquerade) takes place as Gray moves into Grow.

hennabane

A plant grown in the shadow of Moonsrise Ridge east of the Earth Realm (see White Forest map) used for dying items different colors, mostly shades of red (from light pinks to dark browns and everything in between). With the right combination of ingredients, one could color almost anything, even grass or clouds.

Hive, the

The Hive was created by the Ancients to house the Apprentices, Elders, High Priest or Priestess and give them privacy for their magical practices. No one knows when faeries started calling it the Hive, as this was not its original name. It is a curiosity in that it is mostly underground, which seems counter to faeries' attraction to light and air. The Elders know it was meant as a protective fortress in case of a forest invasion, though none think this likely. One can get to any village-nest through the underground tunnels that start beneath the Hive, but almost everyone prefers to fly above ground.

Hollows, the

Contrary to what many of **Croilus's** and Mabbe's faeries think, the Hollows were not where the "lesser" faeries lived during Ancient times, although they did spend plenty of time there and some of the younger ones might have wanted to live there had their parents allowed it. The trees were not bound mercilessly by poles, but rather grew in natural circular formations, which were perfect for parties, camping, games, dances, concerts, and theatrical presentations. The Hollows that Mabbe bound together were an attempt to recreate this environment for the faeries that she convinced to stay behind.

hoopflute

Just like it sounds, a flute in the shape of a hoop. Different sizes can be made from different types of tree branches, but the branches must be harvested while still green, then formed, hardened, and lacquered with uul tree sap. Very talented musicians can fly or dance while using multiple hoopflutes.

hopplebugs

Tiny annoying sand beasts that get under the Nhords' armor-like skin and make them itch. Not fun.

hrooshka

Like gundlebeans are to White Forest faeries, hrooshka are to **Nhords**. They are meaty sand mushrooms, grown in the oases of the Araglenn deserts. When they are picked, they shrivel, but when cooked, they take in moisture and plump back up. Really quite satisfying.

mind-misting

Mind-misting is a way of "reaching out" to things around you without physically touching them. Elders use it as a meditative practice and encourage Apprentices to use it as well. The faerie closes her eyes, relaxes into her breath, and sends her mind out to feel the energy of objects or sentient beings. Very talented mind-misters can identify other faeries and species of plants and beasts. One can mind-mist without **empathing**, but one cannot empath if she has no talent for mind-misting.

moons / moonbeats / moonsbreath

Faeries use the term "moons" and "suns" interchangeably, depending upon the occasion and their own personal preference. When being more specific they typically use suns, as in, "The festival is in three suns' time!" When being vague, they use the term "moons" to represent the passing of time, as in, "it's been many moons since your unveiling." A "moonbeat" is specific, however. It equals just under 15 minutes. They use it when measuring time or distance. For instance, Brigitta's village-nest is about half a moonbeat long, meaning it takes an average faerie about 7.5 minutes to fly across. If you are a less than average flyer, take that into consideration. An unspecified short moment in time is a **moonsbreath.**

Nhords

Araglenn is the second smallest continent on Faweh. After the Great World Cry, it was overridden by the element of air, which produced a harsh, arid climate. Its ancient civilization consists of the Nhords, who have developed rhino-like skin, multiple-eyelids, and flat, aerodynamic limbs and heads. They can navigate through sand and have buried their homes in the earth.

The Nhords are a very proud, very communal culture. They believe in doing things democratically, so there is much discussion before anything changes. They were the last civilization to join the World Council at Noe but were considered the most loyal.

sand cycles

Since the **Nhords** live in the desert, there is very little to indicate seasons. They tell time by sand cycles. The winds move the sand like clockwork across the desert. Four sand cycles (North, South, East, West) are equivalent to a season cycle in the White Forest.

seasons / season cycle
(See Grow, Green, and Gray months)

silverwood

Don't confuse silverwood and **sliverleaf** (although it would be hard to do so for any competent faerie). Silverwood is the most common type of tree in the White Forest. Its bark is sturdy, its branches and leaves numerous, and it looks like someone's dusted it with a silver powder. Even though the White Forest looks white from a great height or distance, up close, it is actually silver hued. The myth around the forest is that there used to be three moons in the sky and one of them fell to Faweh, littering the trees with moondust.

sliverleaves

Only found in the mountains around the Valley of Noe, razor sharp sliverleaves travel in flocks at night. When they drop from the sliverleaf tree they are immediately drawn to the River that Runs Backwards like metal to magnets. The only warning a faerie gets is the rustle as they drop and the humming sound as they fly through the air. They can slice through a faerie's wings and leave gashes on the skin. The wounds heal extremely fast, trapping poison inside, which can sting for many suns afterward. The more sliverleaf scars, the more poison, and the more pain.

stranglewood vine
Stranglewood grows throughout Foraglenn (except in the White Forest). The ivy loves to wrap around things and squeeze. Hrathgar spellcast some, adding her special thorny touch, and captured Brigitta and Himalette in her spell chamber. Mabbe used stranglewood as shackles. Stranglewood vine is quite willing to cooperate if one has knowledge of how to use it.

thought mirror
Thought mirrors have been used by Apprentices and Elders alike since the elemental faeries came to the White Forest. They were actually invented by the Saarin of Pariglenn and brought to the Ancients of Noe as gifts. They allow gazers to meditate on one's thoughts, basically having a conversation with oneself, but they only work when no one else is around. Extremely helpful when working a problem out. No other faeries in the White Forest use them as there are only enough for the residents of **the Hive**.

transformation
A practice of many learned Ancients through which they could reshape objects with their thoughts. The White Forest Elders aren't as knowledgeable, but they can perform some basic transformations as well as change the state of their own mind by transforming their thoughts. Elder Adaire is the best "transformationist" on the Elder Council. She's so talented that, if she chose to do so, she could change the state of another faerie's mind by transforming their thoughts.

triple lyllium suclaide
A specialty of several Feast Masters, though many would agree Brigitta's

mother Pippet holds the best recipe, which has won much recognition. Suclaide is a sweet that melts in the mouth. It's sort of fudgy, but not as rich, and usually has a hint of mint or fruit. Triple lyllium suclaide is known to bring happy and healing dreams from the use of lyllium roots, leaves, and petals in the mix.

wingmitts

An item of clothing that no faerie would ever wear on her wings unless she didn't want her destiny markings to be seen before her unveiling ceremony. Faeries can't fly very well in them unless the mitts are especially thin and tailored exactly to that faerie's wing measurements, which no Clothier wants to do since they are only worn once by any faerie. The material is fairly light and dyed with **hennabane** to hide the wing markings from curious eyes.

Wising

There are always one High Priest or Priestess, four Elders, and a combination of at least eight Apprentices and Wisings in the Center Realm. Elder Apprentices are mentored far longer than any other faerie apprentice in the White Forest and have greater and greater responsibility as they advance in their craft. Some magical skills take many season cycles to master. First Apprentices generally assume Eldership later in life, but not all Apprentices become Elders. These servants of the Center Realm are called "Wisings" and live to be of service to the Elders, the other Apprentices, and the community. Their markings are different—they have the four directional symbols, but no center eye glyph. This is not a shameful position. It is a sacred calling, just like any other destiny, and the Wisings consider it an honor.

ONDELLE

of

GRIOTH

Faerie Tales from the White Forest
Book Three

Danika Dinsmore

Hydra House ❖ Seattle, Washington

To all the Connies, in all the CoZi cafes,
who feed the hungry writers.

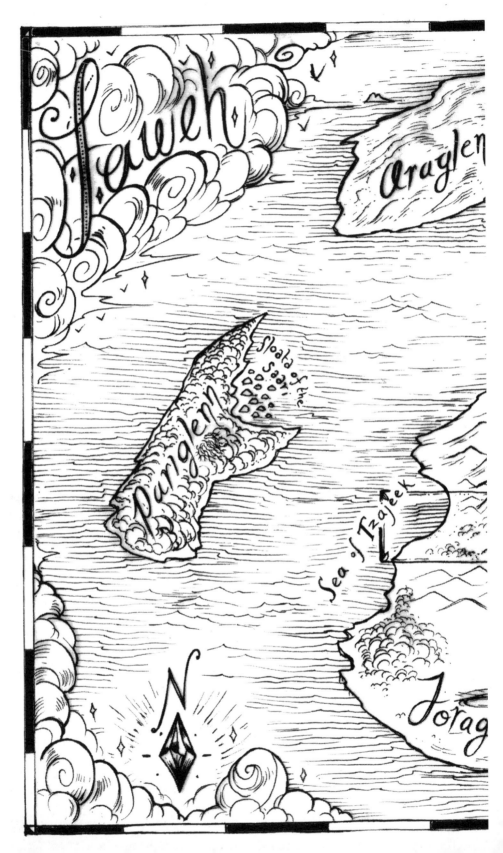

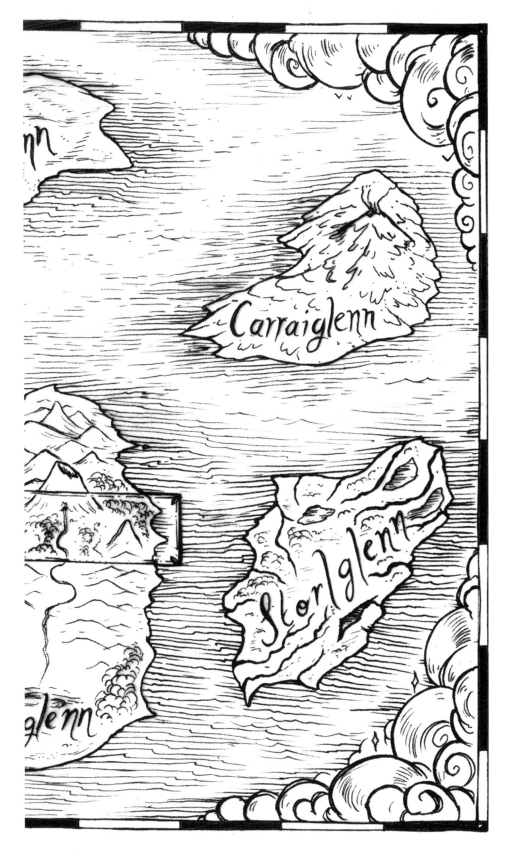

Dead Mountain

To Pariglenn

The Standing Stones

White Forest

Sea of Tzajeek

Forever Beach

The Dark Fo

North Central Foraglenn

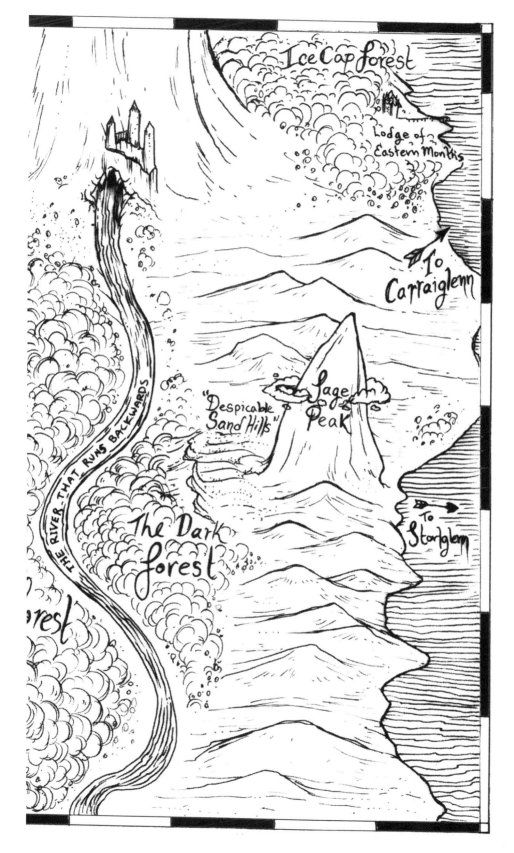

Chapter One

Ondelle and Hrathgar poked through the brush, giggling while they pulled branches away to spy on Cam, a sun-kissed and muscular Air Faerie Perimeter Guard. Cam stood before The Shift as the rocky river crumbled over itself in an infinite loop around the White Forest. He picked up a stick and tossed it into the protective field, which rippled with the impact before the stick continued out the other side. He listened for a moment, then nodded to no one, and leapt into the air to finish his rounds.

When he was a speck in the distance, Ondelle pulled herself out of the dense foliage and gazed after him. As she wiped herself off, Hrathgar fluttered out of the bush toward The Shift. At the final tree before the dirt moat began, she paused to pluck a broodnut from its branches.

"What are you doing?" asked Ondelle, red wings quivering.

Hrathgar didn't answer, only pulled her arm back and catapulted the nut into The Shift. It skipped once on a rock before flipping through the field.

"Come on, Gar." Ondelle flitted over to her friend, who hovered in the air as she stared after the nut. "We should get back. Auntie Parmaline will wonder where we've gotten off to."

"One of these days . . ." Hrathgar murmured toward the Dark Forest, then turned to face Ondelle, tears stippling the corners of her green eyes. "I'm going through that field."

Before Ondelle could respond, another faerie streamed out of the brush toward them.

"Hrathgar, no!" she cried. It was young Fernatta of Gyllenhale. The fresh Earth Elder glyphs on her laurel wings appeared wet in the warm sunlight.

"Oh, for the Dragon, Ferna," scolded Hrathgar, dropping to the ground and placing her hands on her hips. "What are you doing out this far on your own?"

"I'm not on my own," Fernatta pointed out, stepping past the edge of the forest as Hrathgar slowly drifted away, riding along on the immense rocky river. "I followed the two of you."

"That was unwise," said Ondelle from above them.

Hrathgar and Fernatta regarded each other and then burst out laughing.

"That was unwise," Hrathgar repeated, imitating Ondelle's serious tone. She leapt back up into the air. "You're not even an Apprentice yet and you sound just like Earth Elder Grish Ba."

"You said you were going to leave the forest!" said Fernatta. "You mustn't! There are horrible beasts out there just waiting to rip off your wings."

"Fernatta's right," said Ondelle. "It's unthinkable." She turned to escort the younger faerie back into the forest as Hrathgar stewed over The Shift.

"Do you know what's unthinkable?" asked Hrathgar, catching up with Ondelle and grabbing her arm. "That I won't be an Apprentice for ages. That I'll be wasting my time collecting eggshells for Auntie Parmaline's festival masks. That I'll have one wing in the ethers by the time I'm an Elder."

"You don't know that," said Ondelle.

"You were marked first," Hrathgar pointed out. "You'll be the next Fire Apprentice even though we were born only a few seasons apart."

"Just because I was born in Grioth doesn't mean I'll apprentice with a Fire Elder," Ondelle responded. "I could just as easily become an Air Apprentice."

"Fozk of Fhorsa is already marked for Air Eldership, Ondelle," said Hrathgar, anger rising in her voice. "You know that perfectly well."

She let go of Ondelle's arm and looked intently into her black moon eyes. "And let's just say that you live a long and healthy life—which I wish for you because you're my friend—but as I do, I'm wishing for my own pointless existence."

"Unless Ondelle becomes High Priestess," Fernatta interjected. "Then you would take her place as Fire Elder on the council."

"I would never presume such a thing," said Ondelle.

"Exactly," said Hrathgar, "so we must assume you will remain an Elder, which means I will not become an Elder until you disperse."

"And you can't wait that long?" Ondelle half-heartedly teased.

"It's not that." Hrathgar twisted in the air to face the Dark Forest. "I'm afraid that a part of me will always hope something bad happens to you. I don't want to live being pulled in two directions like that, always fighting off some resentment." She gestured across The Shift. "I'd rather take my chances out there. At least I could have my own adventure."

Tears sprung to Hrathgar's eyes once more and Ondelle wrapped an arm around her friend. As she searched herself for words of comfort, the clouds above The Shift rippled, then drifted open. She dropped her arm and stared up at them.

"What's wrong?" asked Fernatta, turning to glance at the sky.

"Ondelle?" asked Hrathgar. "Are you all right?"

Overhead, a flock of bright flecks spun through the opening in the clouds like tiny luminescent birds. Bewildered, Ondelle pointed toward the strange, sparkling swarm.

"What are those?" she asked.

"What are what?" Hrathgar squinted up at the clouds.

"You can't see them?"

"No, do you see anything, Ferna?"

Fernatta shook her head and shrugged.

"They're . . . so beautiful . . . and . . . " Ondelle felt a tug from somewhere deep within her heart, and she shivered as the flecks twisted into a funnel, spinning faster and faster until, all at once, they bolted into the trees.

"Freena!" Brigitta cried out and leapt to her feet.

Around her, Air Faeries paused in their relay practice and hovered over the flying fields, staring at her poised on the edge of the plateau.

"Uh," Jarlath stood up next to her, "Brigitta?"

She spun around to face him, taking a moment to recall where she was. The Air Faeries remained curious until a momentary glare from Jarlath sent them back to their practice relays.

He stepped closer to Brigitta so as not to be heard. "Another vision?" he whispered.

Brigitta tried to shake the images away, but they were now a part of her, as if she had lived those moments herself. It was always the same.

"They're not visions, Jarlath," she snapped back, then collected her emotions as she reminded herself she was speaking to one of the few faeries she truly trusted. "They're memories. Ondelle's memories. And they're getting worse."

"Or getting better," Jarlath offered, trying to make light of the situation.

Brigitta groaned and turned back to watch the Air Faeries flying in and out of an intricate loop system made from connected tree branches. Higher up, three faeries were experimenting with a wind-winder, a new contraption created by an Air Faerie Inventor, a large bubble-shaped net that could hold pockets of conjured air.

The memories, as Brigitta insisted they be called, had started as vague whispers. Snippets of waking dreams. Brief lapses ending in dull headaches Auntie Ferna had treated with warm ceunias compresses and lyllium tea.

Over time, the headaches had subsided, but the memories had grown sharper and more elaborate.

"Auntie Ferna," Brigitta murmured.

"You need to see your Auntie?" asked Jarlath.

"No." Brigitta stared into his starry eyes. "The memory was of Ondelle with Auntie Ferna and Hrathgar. Before she left the forest." She dropped her voice to a whisper. "And something else."

"You cried out," said Jarlath. "What's Freena?"

"Not what," said Brigitta. "Who. Freena was High Priestess a long time ago. When she dispersed, Grish Ba became High Priest." She paused, sorting through her new knowledge. "But why would Ondelle feel so intensely for Freena? She was too young to have mentored with her. She wasn't even an Apprentice yet. She mentored with Fire Elder Oka Kan . . ."

"You've lost me," said Jarlath, easing her back down to the rock she had been sitting on before her outburst.

"The lineage doesn't matter," said Brigitta, "but what I saw, I mean, what I *remembered* was seeing the Ethereal energy coming to disperse Freena's spirit." She grabbed onto Jarlath's arm. "Ondelle saw the Ethereal energy, but Hrathgar and Auntie Ferna couldn't. She saw the energy and knew it had come for Freena's spirit."

Jarlath glanced down to where Brigitta gripped his bicep, and a slight pink bloomed on his cheeks. His muscle tensed and warmed beneath her fingers. She pulled her hand away and gestured to the air fields.

"We should finish up here."

"Are you sure?" asked Jarlath, sitting down beside her.

"The sooner the better," she said. "They don't like me being here."

She gestured for Jarlath to continue his observations. He had the task of making recommendations to the Elders and the Master of the Perimeter Guard, having served on Mabbe's guard for several seasons, as well as having first-hand knowledge of what went on in the outside world. For the first time in the history of the White Forest, the Elders were stepping up their security.

All around them the Air Faeries completed their relays, flying up and over and through the obstacle course of tall grasses, formed branches, and sculpted rocks, shooting nervous glances at Brigitta and Jarlath as they observed their movements. Blown off course, the wind-winder had climbed higher into the air where the three Air Faeries struggled to keep the net in its optimum globe shape. An older Air Faerie buzzed up to help them, hands slightly apart, palms facing each other, brewing up thick patches of air.

"What use is that thing if it takes four faeries to control it?" Jarlath laughed and crossed his arms.

"Poppa's Inventor friend says it's meant to help weaker flyers go higher," responded Brigitta skeptically. She wondered about the maximum height one could travel within it. Could a faerie drift through the clouds? Disappear from sight?

A part of Brigitta dearly wanted to escape from view and hide among the clouds, yet another part of her yearned to embrace the Air Faeries as her new kin. Ever since Ondelle had gifted her with her Air element, there was something inside Brigitta longing to express itself. That part wanted to join in the relays, plummet from the trees, listen to her ancestors on the wind. But the Elders had postponed her Air element lessons "until further notice," and none of the Air Faeries showed any interest in helping her develop her new talents because they were afraid of her.

At least that was her assumption. It's not like she had empathed them for this information. She wouldn't even practice mind-misting around anyone anymore. She didn't want to do anything that would make her seem suspicious. It was bad enough that her body mysteriously housed the Air energy of a dead High Priestess, continually reminding them of their loss. What had saved her in the Valley of Noe, she now tucked back as much as possible. But it took so much effort to restrain it that it exhausted Brigitta, and she found herself crawling into bed each night.

She rubbed at her temples as she contemplated the group of candidates before them. Jarlath stood next to her, scrunching up his mouth and drumming on the end of his chin with his fingers.

"What do you think?" she asked him. "Have you decided?"

"Yeah." He nodded. "I've got about a dozen candidates."

He watched the relays for another moonsbreath and then snapped his fingers in front of Brigitta's face. "Race you back to the Center Realm!"

He sprung up from the Flying Field plateau before she could even answer and hovered in the air wearing a mischievous grin. She managed a laugh and flew after him, feeling the stares of the Air Faeries behind them.

"Please, please!" called High Priest Fozk into the crowded chamber. "If you cannot find a seat, just try to get comfortable."

"These meetings are drawing more and more faeries each time," said Water Elder Dervia, tapping her fingers against the armrest of her Elder chair, which had been pushed back to make room for everyone.

At the carved wooden table sat twelve Village-Nest Caretakers, including Orl Featherkind from Tiragarrow. Four more Caretakers sat on wooden chests lining the wall. Reykia of Rivenbow, the tall Master of the Air Faerie Perimeter Guards, stood on one side of the door with her bold purple wings at attention, as if ready to act at a moment's notice. Gaowen of Thachreek, the Guard who had caught the whisper light Brigitta and Ondelle brought to the Valley of Noe, stood on the other. He was Reykia's Lead Guard.

The First Apprentices were forced to sit on the ground, and they grumbled as they lowered themselves onto the woven mats that the Wisings—Kiera, Lalam, and Bastian, the newest Wising—brought in for them. Seated on the floor next to Dervia's chair, Brigitta was the only Second Apprentice present, and Jarlath, the only White Forest outsider among them, stood behind her protectively. She leaned into his legs for support, moral and otherwise, exhausted from digesting Ondelle's memory that morning and aching from holding back her Air energy all day. She was not in the mood for this gathering of anxious faeries.

"The lack of accommodation in this room should indicate that what we are doing is counter to the Ancients' intentions," muttered Adaire.

"Or," Fozk looked sternly at her, "that the Ancients did not prepare us for all possibilities."

The room quickly hushed. If it had not been High Priest Fozk speaking, Brigitta thought someone would have surely called him out on such blasphemy.

"Now that I have your attention," said Fozk, sitting down in his chair, "Elder Adaire?" He gestured to the sturdy Earth Faerie on his left.

Elder Adaire stood and addressed the Village-Nest Caretakers. "Thank you all for being here in these questionable times. As you may have heard, we are assigning Air Faerie Guards to each village-nest."

A collective grumbling issued from the assembled faeries.

"As there are not enough faeries destiny-marked for such a task," continued Adaire, raising her voice over their murmurs, "we have taken volunteers, who have been participating in relays for our training team: Reykia, Gaowen, and Jarlath of Noe—"

"Pardon, Elder Adaire," spoke Bailen, Caretaker of Ithcommon, "but isn't he a bit young?"

Brigitta felt Jarlath's body stiffen behind her, poised to defend himself, and she bristled as well.

"And not even from the White Forest," added Plinth of Erriondower, avoiding Jarlath's eyes. "How can—"

Adaire put her hand up to interrupt Plinth before Jarlath, or Brigitta, could interject. "If any of you have more experience dealing with the threats of the outside world, you are welcome to replace him," she said, scanning the room for any takers.

"What outside threats?" asked Bailen. He turned to the Air Faerie Perimeter Guards at the door. "Has something entered the forest again? What is it? What have you seen?"

The faeries buzzed excitedly until Fozk could quiet them again. He nodded to Reykia.

"Nothing has entered the forest that we know of," she said carefully, "but the beasts do seem to be braving The Shift more often."

"And it's only a matter of time before Croilus makes himself known," added Jarlath.

"You don't know that," countered Plinth. "You don't even know if he's alive, let alone what his intentions are. You've said so yourself."

"My kin," Fozk's soothing voice encircled the room, "we are merely taking precautions while we contemplate our long-term objectives."

"Long-term objectives?" piped up Violetta, Caretaker of Dmvyle. "Like what to do with all the destinyless children? We'll have a nursery full in Dmvyle before long."

Several other Caretakers nodded in response.

"Just make them all Perimeter Guards," grumbled Bailen.

"There'll be nothing to guard if the Hourglass isn't turned," said Plinth. He turned to address Fozk. "The scepter needs to be taken to the Eternal Dragon."

"If we haven't lost touch with It as well," added Caretaker Violetta softly.

All of the faeries exploded in new conversation until Fozk stood, clapped his hands twice, and the cacophony of sound was swept up in a blanket of wind and hung above them, muffling the din.

"How do you expect me to take such a journey if I cannot rely on you to manage yourselves while I'm away?" he asked, his voice on edge.

As Fozk waited for the faeries to settle down, Brigitta examined his face. In the season she had been home from her journey to Noe, his skin had paled, his hair thinned, and deep circles now haunted his eyes. She did not envy High Priest Fozk's position, although she had trouble sympathizing with him since he had disallowed her to resume her lessons. Plus, as much as she hated to admit it, she agreed with Plinth. The Eternal Dragon was their connection to Blue Spell, which was required to turn the Hourglass and renew the protective field around their forest.

He clapped his hands again, the blanket of air dropped, and the voices dissipated in the room.

"Now," he continued, sitting back down and motioning to Adaire.

"If you have questions," she said, "please raise your hand and I'll—"

Nine Caretaker hands, two First Apprentice hands, and Reykia's hand all shot into the air. Adaire pointed to Orl Featherkind, whose dark russet hair was streaked with more gray than Brigitta remembered, and looked as if it had not been combed in many moons.

"What if something *does* get into the forest?" he asked, yellow eyes darting to each Elder's face. "What then?"

"That is why we have Jarlath working with the perimeter team," answered Adaire. "He can prepare us for that event. As can Brigitta . . . when she is ready." The Elder glanced quickly in Brigitta's direction.

"I'm ready now!" she burst out, and then cringed as an assortment of unnerved faces turned to stare at her. Only Earth Wising Lalam of Ithcommon, with his shaggy brown hair and ruddy boyish cheeks, cast a smile of encouragement her way.

"Yes, Reykia?" asked Adaire, redirecting everyone's attention.

Reykia pulled down her hand. "What about Gola?"

"What do you mean what about Gola?" shot Brigitta again before she could stop herself.

"Please, Brigitta," said Water Elder Dervia, placing a hand on her shoulder.

"Well," continued Reykia, "how do we know we can trust her? She's from the outside, and she knows Dark Forest magic."

"I can vouch for Gola's intentions," put in Jarlath. "I've been working closely with her since I arrived."

"She's quite unsocial," said Caretaker Grindel of Grioth. "She never attends Fire Realm festivities and barely visits the marketplace any more." He gestured to Jarlath. "She sends him or that Minq beast instead."

The rest of the Fire Faerie Caretakers nodded their heads.

"That's because she's an old Drutan," explained Brigitta. "She's practically rooted to the earth."

Grindel addressed Fire Elder Hammus. "You're not going to let her root in the Fire Realm, are you? Who knows what effect that will have on our forest."

"Let's save that for a later discussion," replied Hammus. "Right now we need to—"

Brigitta fluttered to her feet. "For a later discussion?!"

"Sit down, Apprentice Brigitta," said Adaire. "We need to stay focused."

Brigitta turned to Grindel, ignoring Elder Adaire's request. "How can you even say such a thing!" She turned to the rest of the faeries. "There wouldn't even be a Fire Realm, let alone a White Forest, if it weren't for Gola!"

"Brigitta, I will not ask again," warned Adaire, hands on hips and gray hair springing loose from the wiry bun on her head.

Jarlath reached for Brigitta's arm, but she shook him off, overcome by her anger and frustration. "Gola's place in this forest would never have been questioned by Ondelle!"

"That is enough," said Water Elder Dervia, rising to meet her. "You cannot presume what our departed High Priestess would say or do at a time like this."

"Yes, I can!" cried Brigitta, fatigue overtaking all caution. Tears sprung to her eyes without warning.

"I can!" she cried again. "I can, I can. I carry her here." Brigitta pounded on her chest. She burst into sobs and Dervia wrapped her arms around her, pulling her into her bosom.

As Brigitta wept, she relinquished the insufferable hold she had on her Air energy, and it radiated forth, whipping the hair and tunics of every faerie in the room.

It grew frighteningly still; the only sound was Fozk's deep inhale before he spoke.

"Second Apprentice Brigitta," he said, his own typically steady voice wavering as he rose, "please follow me into the corridor."

Dervia handed a teary Brigitta off to Wising Lalam, who had appeared with an herbal compress, which he applied to the back of her neck. Jarlath stepped forth to assist him, but Dervia shook her head.

Before she knew it, Brigitta was alone in the cool and quiet corridor. The comforting compress was still at her neck, but Lalam had slipped back into the room, quiet as a shadowfly, before she could thank him.

"Ondelle was a wise leader," Fozk said gently from behind her.

She turned to catch his watery eyes of sky as he approached.

"We all miss her dearly," he continued, folding his hands together, "but she may have done a disservice to you, and for that, I am truly sorry."

He took a long, steadying breath and Brigitta found herself taking a breath and exhaling along with him. "I believe that your experience in Noe and this transference of energy have distressed you beyond our original assessment."

Brigitta simply sniffed and nodded, too upset to speak.

"It is with deep regret," said Fozk, looking very regretful indeed, "and due to no wrongdoing on your behalf, that I must relieve you of all Apprentice and Center Realm duties for the time being."

"But—"

He placed a hand on her shoulder. "You will return to Tiragarrow until further notice."

Chapter Two

Ondelle sucked at her thumb as she scooted farther into the cupboard. It was her favorite place to hide. It smelled of earth and wood. Wood from her Momma's leftover carvings. Half-done, or half-undone, depending upon how one looked at it. Ondelle could sense the livingness of the uncarved wood. The wanting of it to be something new to the world. She wished she knew how to carve. Perhaps then, she could make her Momma happy.

She could hear voices in the gathering room. Her Poppa's hushed and calming. Her Momma's strained, tired, afraid.

"You weren't there, Sade," her Momma said, all color dropping from her words.

"Yes, Runida," he said, soothing as ever, "I was lying right next to you."

"Asleep."

Ondelle's Poppa sighed and then she could sense him pacing the room. Could picture the way he scrunched his thin, dark eyebrows in concern. "Perhaps if you started carving again? We've had many requests for—"

"It won't help," said Runida.

"You could try," Sade responded. "Just try for my sake. For our sake. It will give you something to occupy yourself while I'm away."

"Please don't leave me alone with her."

"I'll only be gone for a few suns, five at most. Our team must finish the Moonrise Amphitheater before the Ithcommon faeries lose their patience."

Runida was quiet as the rocking chair creaked beneath her.

"Others are talking," said Sade. "You're making them nervous."

"They should be nervous."

"Runida . . ."

The creaking chair halted. "What reason is there for her to have both Air and Fire?"

"It's not impossible," said Sade. "It's a wonder, yes, but not impossible. We must have Air ancestors somewhere along—"

"She's not mine."

"She is our child!" Sade yelled, and Ondelle's foot slipped, startled by her Poppa's sudden outburst, and knocked over a block of wood with a dull thud.

A moment later and the cupboard door opened. Light streamed in and Ondelle blinked. Her Poppa didn't look angry, as she had expected; he looked very sad as he pushed aside the blocks of uncarved wood and reached in for his daughter. He pulled her out and looked deep into her eyes with his own large, black ones. He always said she had his eyes, and that should mean something.

He pulled her to him and she dropped her chin onto his shoulder, absorbing the warmth of him. As he lifted her up, she could see her Momma in her worn wooden rocking chair, staring into the fire. She never looked at Ondelle anymore. She never spoke to Ondelle anymore. She never left the cottage.

Brigitta sobbed in Gola's barky arms. Ondelle's memory had come upon her so suddenly and painfully that she had dropped to the ground as soon as she had reached the old Drutan's door. She had awoken in Gola's bed and quickly related everything that had happened that day, relieved to tell someone who understood.

"They don't believe me about Ondelle's memories," murmured Brigitta as Gola rocked her back and forth.

The sorrow she felt had as much to do with her dismissal from the Center Realm as it had to do with the memory of Ondelle's mother. That feeling of rejection had settled in Brigitta, and Ondelle's heartbreak had melded with her own. So pervasive was it that she was having trouble remembering that her own mother loved her very much.

She shifted in Gola's lap as she tried to conjure images of her mother's kindly face. Gola's body wasn't the most comfortable place to lay oneself, but at the moment, Brigitta didn't care. She had done nothing wrong; Fozk had said so himself.

"Several faeries at the gathering even questioned your right to be here," she said.

Gola sat quietly for a moment as she stroked Brigitta's hair. "It is not my forest; it is not my place to disagree."

Brigitta pulled back in surprise to gaze at the blind tree woman. "But that's so unfair! You helped save our forest. And, and . . . you're old! You wouldn't survive being thrown back into the Dark Forest."

Gola's familiar throaty chuckle tickled the air, and her only remaining pair of winged Eyes gazed at Brigitta from their perch on the back of her chair. "My child, I am not going to survive anywhere for much longer. Not even in the protected realm."

She eased Brigitta off her lap and onto the floor, stood and stretched, and then shuffled to her small kitchen to fetch Brigitta a cup of tingermint tea. The Eyes reluctantly leapt from the chair and puttered after her.

"If I'm quick about it," Gola said as she ladled the brew into a mug, "maybe I can root myself in your forest before they drive me away."

"How can you even joke like that?"

The old Drutan returned, handed the mug to Brigitta, and settled back into her chair, Eyes dropping down onto her shoulder and tucking in their leathery wings. She hefted her feet onto the worn pillows beneath her, the ones she used to keep herself from rooting right there in her cottage.

"So, the memories have grown stronger," she said.

Brigitta held the warm mug between her hands and studied the thick little fibers growing from the bottoms of Gola's feet. A few of them quivered and twisted in the air, as if searching for a place to bury themselves.

"It's not little jolts of images and emotions any longer," she said, looking away from the growing tendrils and staring down into her drink. "I see more detail now. And when I look out onto the world from her eyes, I feel just as she felt." She traced the rim of her mug with a finger, then dipped it into her tea. She pulled it out and tasted it: a perfect combination of warmth and mint, with just a hint of earthiness. Gola had done it; she had mastered a faultless brew.

"Ondelle could sense things others couldn't," Brigitta continued. "Even when she was young. It made her different and lonely, and now I carry her loneliness inside of me."

"And it's too much of a burden in addition to your own?"

"Maybe. I don't know . . . I'm just wondering why she saw these things? Was it her deodyte nature? Am I going to start seeing things, too?"

"I imagine it is more about the original owner of the energies than the dual nature of them."

"Original owner?" Brigitta looked up from her cup. "What are you talking about?"

"Where do you believe the elemental energies originally came from?" asked Gola.

"Gifted by the Ancients," Brigitta recited dutifully.

"Yes, gifted by the Ancients," agreed Gola, "from their own energies. The Ancients were bound by all four of your elements, plus the fifth element, which bound them to the ethers."

Brigitta stared at Gola, incredulous. "You mean our elements, the elements of all the White Forest faeries, were originally bound to the Ancients themselves?"

"I do."

"Save for Ether, they divided their own elemental energies up among us, and we've been carrying them over and over through generations?"

"Yes."

A little storm of water and air brewed in Brigitta's veins. It grew until her heart and head pounded with it. "Why do you always do that!" she exclaimed, slamming her mug of tea down on the floor, steamy liquid sloshing over the side. "No wonder the other faeries don't trust you. You hold onto information about us, keep it a secret until . . . until . . . you decide when it's right for us to know!"

"It is not a decision I make," said Gola. "It is information that surfaces when the time for the question to be answered arrives. "

"Hagspit!" Brigitta swore as she stood, wings flung wide.

"I have told you before," said Gola, her own voice on edge, "it is not my place—"

"You know things that could help me understand what's happening to me!" Brigitta's voice echoed through the small tree-home. "You know things that could help save our forest! And you're just going to hold onto it all until I ask the exact right questions at the exact right time?"

Brigitta glared down at Gola, breath heavy. The Drutan's mouth grew stern. Her barky eyebrows knit and the winged Eyes imitated her expression from her shoulder. "Are you quite finished with your tantrum?" she asked.

"Our forest is in danger and you don't care!" Brigitta continued and kicked her cup across the floor, splattering the tea about the room. "You could help yourself and help us, and you don't care!"

"Are you now presuming to know what I feel?"

"Maybe all your secrets are what drove Hrathgar mad!" spat Brigitta, immediately wishing she could withdraw her comment. She had gone too far. The air grew thick around her accusation.

"I am beginning to think High Priest Fozk's decision was a wise one," Gola said slowly. "At least until you can sort through your emotions."

Furious, Brigitta tore from Gola's tree-home without looking back. She sped toward Tiragarrow, paying no attention to the hard smacks of branches against her skin and wings. She could not believe how Gola picked and chose the knowledge she shared, while Brigitta struggled and their forest sat on the brink of danger. She had trusted Gola with all of her own secrets. How could the old Drutan she loved so dearly not return that trust?

Since Brigitta had been cast out of the Center Realm, and she wasn't in the mood to visit with any of her Noe friends, she was forced to return to her family's cottage for the night. She dreaded having to explain to them what had happened, though the news had probably spread to her village-nest already, since Orl Featherkind, Tiragarrow's Caretaker, had been at the gathering when she was banished.

Not banished, Brigitta reminded herself, *relieved of duty until you are sufficiently recovered.*

She ignored the furtive looks that followed her as she criss-crossed through Tiragarrow and landed on her parents' porch. As soon as she had done so, the door opened and Minq's pointy face poked out, the ends of his long ears clasped together like two worrying hands.

"Heard news," he said, shaking his head.

Her foul mood had subsided into a dull ache along the journey home, and she allowed her dear friend to wrap himself around her in a heartfelt embrace. When he looked up at her with his sad rodent-like eyes, she nearly burst into tears again. But she was not going to cry. It seemed all she could manage these days was anger or sadness, with nothing in between.

"Your Momma and Poppa away," said Minq.

She patted him on the head and entered the cottage to wait for Pippet and Mousha.

Himalette was entertaining Roane in the gathering room, working on a song that she had suspended in the air. As she pointed to each of eight variously colored pebblenotes, a different glassy sound vibrated, and she and Roane hummed along with the melody.

As Brigitta fluttered into the room, Roane squealed and tackled her with a hug.

"Brigitta!" he called, cheeks flush with excitement. He leapt back over to her sister before she could even return the hug. "Listen to what Himalette can do now."

"It's called a song flight." Himalette turned to demonstrate her new talent. She collected the pebblenotes from the air and, one by one, hummed a note into each, releasing them back into the air where they hovered and vibrated harmoniously.

"Song Master Helvine loaned me her pebblenotes," Himalette admitted. "I can't make any myself yet, but isn't it beautiful?"

"Yeah, great," Brigitta mumbled and fell into a cushiony mushroom chair. "When Croilus attacks we can song flight him out of the forest."

The little pebblenotes dropped to the floor, tinkling as they scattered in all directions, and Himalette crossed her arms. "Just because I can't be one of your precious Village Guards doesn't mean you have to be such a mossbottom to me."

"Mossbottom?" Brigitta snorted. "You've been hanging around Thistle too much."

Himalette stuck her tongue out at her sister as she and Roane gathered the notes. Then she grabbed Roane's hand and stomped off to her room.

Brigitta sank into the chair. "I can't seem to do anything right anymore. I can't even open my mouth without offending someone. And now, other than Hrathgar, I'm the only faerie who has ever been banned from her apprenticeship."

"Many hardship in Noe," Minq responded. "Need time to heal."

"Not you, too!" said Brigitta, sitting up in the chair. "You know, I would be perfectly fine if everyone would just listen to me."

"I listen," Minq said, perking up his long ears. "That my specialty."

Brigitta closed her eyes and released the Air energy she had been suppressing since the incident in the Hive. It relieved her head of so much tension she was surprised she didn't spark the room again. She breathed in and out, allowing her Water and Air energies to mingle, like a morning fog on Green Lake.

Her eyes were still closed when Minq spoke. "You want me leave you alone?"

"No, no," murmured Brigitta, "just give me a moonsbreath."

Relaxing into her breathing, her body began to calm itself. The fact that she had refrained from any empathing or mind mist practice for so long might have something to do with her unsteady emotions. On the other hand, she'd been in no condition for concentrated mind work. That kind of skill took balance, and she had been neither balanced nor relaxed since Ondelle's memories started.

That was what she found so frustrating. Everyone thought she was reeling from the loss of Ondelle, when she was truly plagued by her increasing presence, which they interpreted as her inability to let go.

How does one let go of something that is a part of her? Could any faerie let go of her sight or hearing?

Brigitta continued to breathe and relax, breathe and relax, until she could conjure a light mind mist. A few moments later, she felt balanced enough, more balanced than she had felt in moons, and misted her mind out, touching the familiar energies of the objects in her old home. Her mist meandered through the hall and into her old bedroom, and she was slightly charmed to find that the room felt the same. She wondered if her parents had changed it at all.

Feeling stronger, she drifted to the wall to see how well she could identify the objects in the room and found that she could almost make out an old thunderbug symphony vine that was strung across her walls. It was easier to mind mist at home than it had been in Noe, and she impressed herself when the soft woven blankets that occupied her bed popped into view. And then a reed painting on her dresser that Himalette had made for her seasons ago.

More and more distinct images appeared as she roamed her room before misting to the window and coming to a halt. Outside, it felt pitch dark, which she knew to be impossible. Curious, she misted closer to the window, and then she moved through.

Chapter Three

Ondelle stood on the edge of a dense forest before a wide expanse of sand, cold wind stinging her arms and face. It was daytime, yet the sky was dark and thick with slate green clouds. Along the beach, little whirlwinds of sand spun crazily in and out of each other like mad dance partners. Past the beach, a dark sea stretched into the distance, strangely calm. Rhythmic waves lapped the pebbly sand, pulling shells and rocks with them as they receded.

Wind snipped at her tunic as she scanned the edge of the forest. To the north, the enormous dark plateau she had skirted to get to the beach. To the south, wind-bedraggled trees stretched into the sand. And submerged a few wingbeats ahead of her was a large solitary rock. She flitted toward it, pausing only to shield her face when the sands stormed up around her.

What had first appeared as one stone was in fact two long, flat stones that came together at the top of the beach and opened up to the sea in an immense V. Between the stones, where they met at the apex of the V, was just enough room for a few fingers. Ondelle removed a cloth bundle from her back and unraveled the scepter within. She gripped it in both hands, stepped back, and in one swift motion lifted the scepter up and slammed the bottom end into the sand between the rocks.

She pulled away and waited, hugging herself against the chill.

The stones began to shake, loosening themselves from the sand and knocking Ondelle backward. She scrambled down the beach to the edge of the water as the stones rose and expanded, stretching up and out, extending into the sea, with her imprisoned between them. Up the beach, her scepter was now a mere speck in the apex of the V.

When she was certain the stones had grown to their full size, she flew back to where the rocks met and hefted her scepter out of the sand, lighting it with a concentrated breath. With her other hand she held onto her hourglass necklace and returned her gaze to the great sea, only then becoming conscious of the silenced winds.

"Stay sharp, Ondelle," she cautioned herself.

She fluttered to the shoreline, cliffs looming above her malevolently, and dipped her scepter into the water. The glowing orb atop it shattered, scattering its brilliance into the dark sea like a school of frightened fish.

She pulled back and waited, watching the thick green clouds accumulate around the tops of the cliffs, enclosing her within. When she turned her attention back to the sea, she caught a glimpse of silver in the distance. A moment later, a series of sharp silver fins arced up and over so gracefully they could have been mistaken for a trick of light on the waves. She waited, transfixed, as the silvery movement swirled and arced and then finally surfaced.

A long neck rose from the darkness, glistening as if fashioned from the Great Moon's beams. Atop the neck was a slender earless head that ended in a black snout into which its eyes perfectly slanted. When its eyes opened, Ondelle gasped, for they didn't bulge outward as one would expect, but fell inward, pulling her into their abyss.

The Eternal Dragon.

Ondelle was afraid, not of the dragon itself, but of the feeling of complete insignificance in an eternity of eternities. The dragon's head stretched toward her. It inhaled through its great nostrils and then blew, a bubble breezing forth from its mouth enveloping Ondelle before she could move. The feeling of falling into a void ceased as she was cocooned inside. The dragon's head dropped back down into the water.

"Wait!" Ondelle cried, reaching forward only to be confronted by the thick, mucousy bubble-wall.

A moonsbreath later, and the bubble was inhaled by the sea itself, and Ondelle along with it. She panicked and tried to resist, but it was no use. As she was dragged into the ocean, she closed her eyes and braced herself for the icy impact.

But there was no impact. She was encased safely in the dragon's breath bubble as it was drawn farther and farther down the ocean floor. Dark and murky green, it was impossible to see where she was headed. Her hand flew to her scepter, having forgotten that the orb was now gone. When the bubble jolted to a halt, she stood, heart pounding, on the bottom of the sea.

The dragon sped past in a silver streak and the water cleared. In front of her was another bubble, just like her own, and a young faerie was trapped inside.

"Brigitta?" a faraway voice called to her. "Lola?" A warm hand settled on her cheek.

"Minq, what happened?" another voice asked. A familiar voice. Anxious.

Brigitta blinked open her eyes. She was lying on the floor with her parents, Minq, Himalette, and Roane gathered around her.

"Oh, thank the Dragon," her mother Pippet cooed, helping Brigitta to sit up.

"The Dragon . . ." Brigitta looked around at her family as if they were the vision. She grabbed her mother's arm, startling her. "I have to get back!"

"Get back where?" Pippet asked, concern etched on her rosy face. "You haven't been anywhere."

"You under meditation," Minq said. "Me wait and you cry out. Fall to floor. Not know what to do."

"We were in discussion with Orl Featherkind," said Mousha carefully, placing his hand on Brigitta's back to steady her.

Pippet hushed him with a look. "We can talk about that later."

She turned to her younger daughter. "Himalette, please go fetch a ceunias compress from the marketplace."

"Aw, Momma," Himalette pouted, pink wings quivering, "I have to practice for the Masquerade."

"It's not a suggestion, Himalette."

"I'll do it," said Roane.

"No," Brigitta said, getting to her feet. She wobbled and Mousha caught her. Pain shot through her skull and she grimaced. "Don't bother; I'm fine. I just need some water."

Pippet and Mousha looked skeptically at Brigitta as she tried her best to appear "fine." She did not want Himmy or Roane talking about her at the Dionsdale marketplace, not after what had happened in the Hive that morning. There would be enough gossip around the Water Faerie Realm.

"I can get water," Himalette said and headed toward the kitchen before her mother could argue. As Himalette disappeared around the corner she called over her shoulder, "Even though you were a stinky bog bug earlier."

"Himalette!" Pippet scolded her.

Brigitta forced a laugh. "It's all right, Momma, I was a stinky bog bug earlier."

"And a mossbottom!" Himalette shouted from the kitchen.

Roane giggled, and Brigitta reached down to tickle his sides. He fell into her lap in a fit of laughter.

"Let's at least get you something warm to eat," said Pippet. "That will help."

Food, Brigitta thought, tussling Roane's hair, her Momma's answer to everything.

It was not easy to hide how unnerved she was by Ondelle's memory, but after a light snack, Brigitta managed to convince her momma that a trip to the lyllium field with Minq would be the best thing for her. Outside of their cottage, she grabbed Roucho, her Poppa's featherless delivery bird, from his roost, hastily scratched a message into a broodnut, and sent the bird to find Jarlath. As it flutter-wobbled into the trees, she thought of Gola, and supposed she should send a message of apology when Roucho returned. First things first, though. She needed to figure out a way back to Ondelle's memory of the Eternal Dragon.

She and Minq settled quietly in the lyllium field to wait for Jarlath. Removing her booties, she stretched her feet into the flowers and it did actually calm her, as it always had. It had been ages since she had lain in the field, soaking up the warmth. They lay there side by side in the hazy Gray Season sun, and she assured Minq she was all right.

"I just need to figure some things out," she said, picking one of the small white flowers from above her head and chewing on the end of its sweet stem.

"What figure?" Minq asked.

"Well, for one thing, how to purposely connect with Ondelle's memories. I don't know exactly how they're triggered or have any control over which ones I see."

"Why need control?"

"Because I need to remember something." Brigitta rolled onto her side and leaned up on her elbow, facing Minq. "I saw the Eternal Dragon."

Her stomach plummeted with the mention of Its name. As if the memory were her own, she could recall the eternity in Its eyes, the feeling of falling forward into an abyss.

A whistling noise escaped from Minq's whiskered mouth.

"It took Ondelle to see a girl, an Ancient faerie, I'm sure of it. She was trapped at the bottom of the sea. And when I looked at her through Ondelle's eyes . . ." Brigitta paused. Not having an element, she wasn't sure Minq would understand. "I felt me."

"Felt you?" Minq scratched his back where his wings were attached when he wore them.

"My Water energy. This Ancient faerie girl had my energy."

"You sure this not dream?"

"I know the difference between dreaming and a memory, Minq." She flopped onto her back, cushioned by the mass of flowers beneath her. She watched the innocent clouds as they dawdled over the forest, forming and reforming in a slow orchestra of light and shadow.

"You remember when we met, right?"

"How I forget?" Minq said. "Almost eaten by giant caterpillar."

"Right. It's just like remembering that, only mixed up with these other things now. I remember Hrathgar as a child, but then I remember her at Dead Mountain with us. I also remember High Priestess Freena and Elder Grish Ba and others who died before I was even born."

Minq thought about this while Brigitta thumped on the ground with her fists. "I need to figure out how to control the memories so I can get to that specific one," she finally said. "I need to go back to that faerie."

They settled back into the flowers and had nearly dozed off when Jarlath buzzed into the lyllium field on his shimmering wings. Himalette always called them "sunbrown," because they resembled light glancing off of wet late-season leaves. His crystal blue eyes were bright with mischief.

"I'm meant to be back at the Air Fields, but they can wait."

Brigitta and Minq sat up as he landed and plopped himself down in front of them.

"I'm sorry, Brigitta," he said, eyes turning serious. "It's really unfair. And I would've come earlier, but the Elders—"

"No," she said quickly, "you need to stay in their good graces. We can't both get released from our duties. Promise me you won't cause trouble over this."

Jarlath nodded grimly.

Brigitta recounted her visit with Gola, and how she'd learned that all the White Forest faeries had been carrying the energies of

the Ancients all these seasons. Then she related the memory of the
Ancient girl under the sea with her own Water energy, who she
intended to reach again. She wanted Minq to stand guard, which he
did grumbling, and Jarlath to help her stay focused.

"I'll try," he said. "You know I'm not good at this kind of thing.
I have no element to work with."

"You used your connection to the Ancients to help me in Noe."

"Yeah, it's just . . ." He paused and shook his head. "Never mind,
let's concentrate on you."

Brigitta looked at him quizzically as he sat up straighter. "Well?"
he asked and held out his hand as if he were asking her to dance.
"Shall we?"

She laughed and took his hand, which had lost much of its
roughness since moving to the White Forest and didn't startle her
with buzzing voices anymore. Not since she had contacted the
Ancients through him in Noe. Comforted by his willingness, she
closed her eyes. She appreciated him more than anything at that
moment, the way he never dismissed her ideas as absurd.

Focusing on the image of the Ancient faerie girl on the bottom
of the sea, she let her mind mist out across the field, tickling the
tops of the flowers. It was tricky accessing her emotions about the
girl without upsetting her own balance. She allowed Jarlath to be
an anchor for her, an extension, losing the distinction between her
hand and his.

Slowly and carefully, she misted around the perimeter of the
field, pausing at Minq's nervous energy, and then she misted up and
up, over the tops of the trees to the clouds and back down again, but
nothing triggered the memory. And what was left of it was already
growing vague, as memories did after time had muddled them.

Finally, she dropped Jarlath's hand. "It's no use," she said.

"Maybe you're trying too hard?" he suggested. "Or maybe you're
not meant to control them?"

"What's the point of Ondelle giving me her memories if I can't
use them when I want to!" Brigitta picked up a small rock and

chucked it across the field, disturbing a flock of shadowflies.

From the edge of the meadow, Minq turned his immense ears toward them. Brigitta waved to indicate that she was fine, and then turned to stare after the shadowflies flitting and weaving over the field.

"What if," Jarlath said after a few moments, "it's not time to have them yet?"

One by one, the shadowflies disappeared into the trees. Brigitta gazed after them until she could no longer see their flutterings.

"Wait," she swung around to meet Jarlath's eyes, "what did you just say?"

"That maybe you're not supposed to have all the memories yet? Maybe they only come when you're ready for them?"

She stared past him to where Minq stood, ears stretched to capacity. "It's not a decision I make . . ." she said slowly. "It's information that surfaces when the time for the question arrives."

"Uh, sure."

"No, that's what Gola said!" Brigitta's thoughts raced. Had Gola meant that she literally could not give Brigitta any information before it was time? Was she under some kind of spell that only allowed this information to surface when the time was right? And if so, why hadn't she just told her so? Or was that part of the spell, too?

"Brigitta?"

What if Ondelle's memories were triggered, like clues, specifically when she needed them? What if they were leading her to something or somewhere?

An idea struck her. A terrible idea. An *unthinkable* one.

"I have to go there myself," she said.

"Go where?" asked Jarlath.

"To visit the Eternal Dragon."

Minq's ears, and then the rest of him, were quickly beside Brigitta. "Now you talk nonsense," he said, hands on hips, standing above her.

He shook his head as Brigitta explained that it made perfect sense. And the more she thought about it, the more positive she was that she was meant to go. The Elders didn't believe her, Fozk had postponed the ritual journey each High Priest or Priestess took to Forever Beach, and in the meantime, the White Forest was probably losing its only connection to the Ancients. She was sure that the memory of this girl was triggered to help her, just like Gola's information was always triggered to assist her in some way.

Gola . . . she had behaved horribly to the Drutan. What she had said about her driving Hrathgar mad was cruel. Gola had shared what she could with Hrathgar, and her heart had been broken. Now Brigitta was shattering it all over again.

She shook herself into the present. She would make things right with Gola before she left. But for now, she had to think about the leaving part.

"The Festival of the Moons is approaching. Everyone will be preoccupied with the Masquerade. It's the perfect time to go."

"I'm coming with you," said Jarlath emphatically.

"I was hoping you'd say that," said Brigitta, taking his hand again and giving it a squeeze.

"Bad idea," said Minq. "You been outside. Very dangerous place."

"Yes, I've been outside twice, and Jarlath lived most of his life in Noe. We're the most qualified faeries to make the trip if you ask me."

"Trip based on mind tricks?" asked Minq. "No like idea at all."

"You don't have to, Minq," said Jarlath. "I believe Brigitta. If she says we have to go to this Eternal Dragon, I'm going. I owe my life to her. And so do you."

"Yes," said Minq sadly. "I yours. Still no good idea, but I yours."

Brigitta scratched him behind his ear. "The most difficult part will be getting into the Elder chambers on Masquerade night."

"What for?" asked Jarlath. "I can get anything you need from your Apprentice room."

"It's not my possessions I'm after," said Brigitta, standing up and brushing herself off. "It's Fozk's scepter. We have to take it with us."

Silence descended upon the lyllium field as if the flowers

themselves had hushed the beasts around them. Both Minq and Jarlath stared at Brigitta like she was completely deranged, but she insisted she needed the scepter to call the Dragon and get to the girl. They followed her over the field as she explained.

"I saw it in Ondelle's memory," she said. "Besides, it's useless to them right now. It's empty of power. Maybe I can get it recharged? Then Fozk doesn't even need to go!"

"Steal from Elders and mess with destiny," lamented Minq, fluttering behind her.

"Destiny has already been messed with," said Jarlath. "I don't think it cares."

"Still, big trouble!"

"How much more trouble could I get into?" asked Brigitta. "And anyway, I think you're wrong. I think destiny is calling to us right now."

They definitely needed a plan, but Brigitta wanted to mull it over, so they decided to meet up at Moonsrise Ridge the next morning. No one was to be told what they were up to.

"Not Granae nor Thistle nor even Gola," Brigitta said. "At least not yet."

Jarlath agreed, but Minq shook his head. "What if something go wrong?" he asked. "Need help, protection, spell?"

"That's why you'll stay here in the White Forest, Minq," said Brigitta as they landed in the village-nest. She lowered her voice. "Somebody has to know where we are. Just in case."

"Just in case maybe too late," he said.

She shushed him as three Tiragarrow faeries flitted past. "We'll talk about it tomorrow."

"See you then," said Jarlath, saluting her as he took off.

Inside her parents' cottage, the air was tinged with tension. Brigitta moved into the dining nook to discover High Priest Fozk sitting across the table from her parents. They all looked up as she entered.

Fozk stood and smiled. With his characteristic whites and pale blues, it was like having the sky and clouds inside one's cottage. She was astonished that she'd never realized how tall he was before. His presence dominated the nook.

"Hello, Brigitta. I stopped by to make sure your parents understood the Elders' concerns and to see if they had any questions." His eyes showed sympathy, but Brigitta couldn't help her suspicion. A personal visit from a High Priest was pretty unusual. "How are you feeling?"

"Um, okay," Brigitta managed, glancing at her parents. "I've been relaxing in the lyllium field with Minq." She waved at Minq standing behind her in the doorway. He flashed a nervous grin before waving good-bye with an ear and retreating from the room.

"Your parents tell me you've had another episode?"

Brigitta glanced at them as Pippet fidgeted with the hem of her tunic and Mousha tapped his wings together. She took a deep breath to contain her emotions.

"I did," she answered, sitting down next to Pippet as casually as she could manage, "but the lylliums comforted me."

"I'm glad. I find mind mist meditation beneficial when I'm unsettled." Fozk sat down across from Brigitta and placed a hand on her forearm. His watery eyes urged trust. "I know you will adjust, in time, with the support of your family and friends."

Brigitta nodded. Adjust? Did he mean that she didn't fit in any longer in the White Forest? Or did he mean she would grow used to being a deodyte?

"You are a fine Second Apprentice, Brigitta, both inquisitive and quick to learn. But, it was irresponsible of us to overlook how the events in Noe and the death of Ondelle might have significant and lasting effects on you.

"As well, we are aware of some prejudice against you. We need to ease the minds of other White Forest faeries for your own peace of mind."

"They think I'll turn out like Hrathgar," she blurted out.

"Oh, no, lola," cooed Pippet, reaching over to give Brigitta's shoulders a squeeze. "Of course they don't."

Her Poppa grunted in agreement, but Fozk, Brigitta noted, did not comment. She gazed into his bright sky eyes. There was wisdom there, and an inviting sincerity. It reminded her of when Mabbe forced her to tell the truth with her sincerity spell. She removed her arm from his grasp and stood up.

"Let me fetch you some tea," she said. "Momma's is the best in Tiragarrow."

"Possibly in all the forest," he chuckled and held up an empty mug. "I've already enjoyed one cup while waiting for your return."

Brigitta cocked her head. There was something he wasn't telling her. "You didn't come just to check on me, did you?"

Both of her parents glanced around the room and Mousha's wing taps halted.

"You see?" Fozk said, tapping a finger on his temple. "Perceptive."

Brigitta sat back down with a dreadful knot in her stomach.

"Yes, there is one more thing." He gestured toward her necklace. "As Ondelle has now passed, so her hourglass needs passing."

"What do you mean?"

"He means," said Pippet gently, "that you need to return it to the Elders."

Brigitta's hand automatically went to her necklace. "But it was a gift from Ondelle!"

"I don't think she meant for you to keep it forever."

"She said I was Protector of the Forest," insisted Brigitta, a little less emphatically.

"That was just an honorary title, dear," said Mousha, frowning at the hourglass necklace as if he would miss it, too. "There's no such thing."

"Actually . . ." all eyes flew to Fozk as he spoke, "before I could request the necklace be returned, I had to do some research on the matter. We never take the actions of a High Priest or Priestess lightly and Ondelle knew this of course."

"Are you saying there was more to it?" asked Mousha.

"According to the first Chronicler, Chevalde of Grobjahar, the 'Protector of the Forest' is appointed in case a High Priest or Priestess is incapacitated beyond the ability to perform his or her duties."

"You—you mean," stammered Brigitta, "if Ondelle had been badly injured I would have become the High Priestess?"

"Not exactly," said Fozk. "You would have stood in for her until a new High Priest or Priestess was revealed via his or her destiny markings."

"I've never heard of such a thing!" said Pippet.

"Neither had I," Fozk admitted, "nor had any of the Elders."

"Well," Pippet put a strong arm protectively around her daughter, "I'm sure she never intended such a thing. What a ridiculous idea!"

"I must say," added Mousha, "it does seem irrational."

"Ondelle never did anything without intention."

Brigitta's mother bent close to her daughter's face. "Brigitta, you must give it back," she said earnestly.

Brigitta held the hourglass in her hands, twisting her fingers around it.

"I do realize it has served you well, and you it," said Fozk, "but there are only five necklaces, one for each Elder and one for the High Priest or Priestess."

It was completely selfish of her, she knew, but all she could think about was how it had saved her life in Noe. She had not expected to leave the White Forest without it, but she certainly couldn't use that as a reason to keep it. Really, there was no reason she could give.

"While she was High Priestess, it was her prerogative. Perhaps in her prescience she had known something was going to happen to her in Noe and was preparing us for this emergency. But, we are a full council again, and it must be returned to us or we will not be able to function effectively."

Everyone looked at Brigitta expectantly. What could she do? If she refused his request, it might test the limits of the Elders' patience. What would her punishment be for such a thing? Would it jeopardize her plan to leave the forest?

"Brigitta," said Mousha, "we know how much Ondelle meant to you. We understand the necklace is a comfort. But you must do the right thing, no matter how painful it may be."

She closed her eyes against a storm of tears and pulled the chain over her head. There was a slight bluish crackle in the air as the ownership spell Ondelle had cast was dissolved, the one that allowed only Brigitta to remove it, which she hadn't done since it was first gifted to her almost two season cycles ago.

Immediately, a coldness took over where it had lain, and she felt naked in the room. As she handed the necklace to Fozk, he patted her shoulder.

"Thank you," Fozk's bright sky eyes bore into her, "Brigitta of the White Forest."

He was wise enough not to attempt to console her with words, simply slipping the necklace into his tunic pocket and leaving the table. As Pippet and Mousha escorted him from the cottage, Brigitta burst into tears, flew to her bedroom, and slammed the door.

Chapter Four

Ondelle stepped into Pippet and Mousha's gathering room, and Mousha brushed off his best mushroom chair so she could sit down. The young couple's eyes were bright and curious as Ondelle looked around the room. If she stretched out her enormous fiery wings, she would probably knock the pottery from the shelves. It was a cozy room.

Mousha fidgeted behind Pippet, who eased her very pregnant body down onto a wide pillowed bench across from Ondelle.

"To what do we owe this pleasant surprise?" asked Pippet.

"I was at the Gyllenhale marketplace today and took lunch with Fernatta, who mentioned that you were due soon with a child."

Pippet laughed, her round cheeks rosy with motherhood. "It doesn't take any special kind of insight to know that, does it?"

"I am fond of visiting expectant families. Each birth is a celebration, and I enjoy welcoming new kin into our forest."

"That is very kind of you," beamed Pippet.

Ondelle slipped from her chair, kneeled before a startled Pippet and Mousha, and held up her hands. "Do you mind?" she asked.

Pippet gestured to her overlarge belly, and Ondelle placed her hands on either side of it, while Mousha peered down from behind Pippet's shoulder.

"Oh, silly me," said Pippet, "our manners! Mousha, some honeyroll and pipberry tea for the High Priestess."

As Mousha buzzed to the kitchen, Ondelle looked up from Pippet's belly. "Would you like to know anything about it?" she asked.

The mother-to-be shook her head. "Oh, no. I'm happy not knowing. I want to experience everything as it happens. It's all so new."

A crash sounded from the kitchen and Pippet cringed.

"Mousha?" she called, craning her neck to peer down the hall. "Is everything all right, dear?"

"Fine, fine!" he yelled, and then stuck his head around the corner. "Just be a moonsbreath."

They exchanged smiles as he pulled back into the kitchen. While Pippet was momentarily distracted, Ondelle grabbed her hourglass necklace with her free hand, and with a practiced pull from the depths of the secret corners of her body, she drew the hidden Water energy out and propelled it forth, down her arm, through the palm of her hand, and into Pippet.

Pippet gave a little cry and spun back around.

"Did you do that?"

"Do what?" Ondelle got up off the floor, swiped her hands, and sat back down in the chair with a smile.

"I can feel her Water energy!" cried Pippet. "I couldn't feel it before, but now there it is. It's—it's—it's extraordinary!" She felt her own belly with her hands, tears of joy springing to her eyes. "Mousha! Come quick!"

"I have never been a mother," said Ondelle. "I do not know what it feels like to sense a child's energy for the first time. But I can sense it, too."

"What is it?" Mousha rushed in from the kitchen with a slice of honeyroll on a plate and a cup of steamy brew, dropping them on a stool. The cup toppled into the plate, soaking the bread, and dripping down the stool onto the floor.

"Oh, dear," said Ondelle through a laugh.

Ignoring the mess, Pippet took his hand and placed it on her belly. He smiled a wide, proud poppa-to-be smile as he placed his other hand over hers.

Distracted by the miracle, and by their love, Pippet and Mousha did not see Ondelle take hold of her necklace with both hands, close her eyes, and send a delicate mind mist out in search of the child.

Brigitta's hands shook as she packed a lunch of roasted gundlebeans and ripe pipberries. She grabbed a knife and sliced into a fresh honeyroll. When Pippet stepped into the kitchen with an armful of lyllium roots, Brigitta was staring at the slice as it sat on the counter.

"Lola?" Pippet asked as she set the roots down next to a large bowl on her prep table. "Are you all right?"

"Did Ondelle visit you just before I was born?"

Pippet considered her daughter for a moment and then picked up the first lyllium root. "Of course; she was fond of visiting new families." She stripped the skin off the root and set the exposed portion in a large bowl of water.

"I never knew her to do that," responded Brigitta, wrapping the honeyroll slice in a cloth napkin.

"Well, she probably got so busy she had to stop," Pippet said and picked up the next root.

"Do you know of anyone else she visited who was pregnant? Did she come when you were pregnant with Himalette?"

Pippet stopped shucking her root and frowned at Brigitta. "What are you getting at, lola? That Ondelle knew you were special before you were born? I wouldn't be surprised if she'd known you'd be marked as an Elder, she was quite—"

"No, no," Brigitta shook her head. "I wasn't special, that's my point. Ondelle *made* me special. Ondelle gave me my Water energy. Maybe even my destiny."

Going back to her lyllium roots, Pippet laughed. "Brigitta, there was no possibility of you being any other element. Both your Poppa and I are Water Faeries and so were my parents and Mousha's father . . . I suppose you might have inherited his mother's Earth element, but I can't think of a case where that has happened. It must be rare."

Brigitta shoved her lunch into her pack. "Ondelle was Fire and Air and both her parents were only Air."

Pippet's eyes drifted off in search of this bit of history. "Hmmm. You might be right about that. I never knew her parents."

"High Priestess Freena gave Ondelle her elements when Runida was pregnant. And when you were pregnant with me, Ondelle moved her Water Energy into me, just like she did in Noe when she gave me her Air."

"Ondelle didn't have any Water energy, of that much I'm sure."

"She had it," Brigitta said stubbornly as she threw her pack on her back, "and she gave it to you. You didn't see it happen because Poppa distracted you from the kitchen."

Pippet dropped the root in her hand and turned to her daughter. "Did Mousha tell you this?"

"I saw it in Ondelle's memory. She gave me my Water. That was the moment you felt it for the first time, wasn't it?"

"I don't recall, Brigitta, it was a long time ago."

"After she became High Priestess she went to visit the Eternal Dragon. When she was there—" Brigitta stopped before she gave too much away. That faerie in the memory had Brigitta's Water. She must have given it to Ondelle, and then Ondelle had given it to Brigitta. Did that mean Ondelle's Fire and Air had belonged to this Ancient faerie as well?

And there was something else about that underwater faerie. Something Brigitta had kept to herself. Something she hadn't even told Jarlath.

Pippet wiped her hands on a cloth and took Brigitta's shoulders. "Lola, you must stop with this obsession. It won't do you any good, and it could prolong your suspension from the Center Realm."

"You knew." Brigitta looked into Pippet's hazel eyes. "Deep down, when it happened, you knew, and you won't admit it! Ondelle gave me her Water energy!"

"It was time for the energy to appear," said Pippet. "There was nothing unusual about it."

"Ondelle made me this way!" Brigitta insisted, choking back her tears. "She asked me to forgive her in Noe and I didn't understand! Now I do. She chose me and she made me . . . and then she left me!"

Pippet attempted to pull Brigitta into her arms, but her daughter spun away from her. If her mother held her now, she would surely burst open like a raincloud and give everything away.

"You are in mourning, Brigitta," Pippet said. "You are trying to make connections where there are none. You must let go or else—"

Brigitta sped out of the cottage before her mother could tell her what that imagined "or else" could be.

She flew as hard and fast as she could for Moonsrise Ridge, northwest of Gyllenhale, charging each wingstroke with her sadness and pain. She took the birds' route, as the faeries say, cutting straight through the forest rather than following the river or drawing west and gliding over Green Lake.

Minq was waiting for her at the southern tail of the crescent-shaped ridge on a path that rose up from the forest. He sensed her mood, but simply patted her arm with an ear in greeting before they headed up the trail.

The ridge was open, exposed, a way of hiding in plain sight as anyone approaching would be spotted far before reaching them. The drop was sheer on the eastern side, inside the crescent, and the scree on the outside slope of the crescent was only good for chasing rainbow lizards.

Even though it was a beautiful route between Ithcommon and Gyllenhale, most faeries preferred to fly inside the cool canopy of trees below. And since the Masquerade was in two nights, the White Forest faeries were far too busy for scenery or rainbow lizards, and the ridge was deserted.

"I'm sure none of the Elders can empath our thoughts up here," Brigitta said, calmer now in the open air. She sat on the ledge and pulled the slice of honeyroll from her pack.

"Mind too suspicious," said Minq, pointing to his head with one lengthy ear and wiping off a place to sit with the other.

"Cautious," Brigitta clarified, and waved as Jarlath appeared over the southern curve of the ridge. "Like Jarlath."

She watched his sinewy body sail through the air as nimbly as any faerie who had grown up in the White Forest. Yes, he was healthier and happier inside the protected realm, but he carried within him a wariness she knew he could never shed. It was one of the reasons she trusted him.

"So," she teased as he landed next to them on the ridge, "excited about the Masquerade?"

"I've been planning my costume for moons," he said dryly.

They were agreed that most faerie festivals were frivolous. And at the last Twilight Festival, Roane and Thistle's over-enthusiasm during a hoop flute dance had embarrassed him, and he had lost them on purpose.

"The Festival of Moons is just like any other festival," explained Brigitta. "There's new music and dances and inventions."

"And food!" said Minq, fluttering up on his translucent wings. "Pie and berryroll and tingermint candy and lyllium suclaide."

"Stay focused," said Brigitta, and he fluttered back down.

"Food good," he mumbled, rubbing his belly with an ear.

"This festival, though, starts with the Masquerade," Brigitta continued. "Everyone dresses up in costumes, so it will be hard to tell who is who. If I can figure out how to temper my Water energy, maybe I can disguise myself as an Air Faerie and paint my wings as a Perimeter Guard."

"Is that even possible?" Jarlath asked.

"Well, it will take a lot of effort," she admitted, "but I've been doing it the other way around for moons, tempering my new Air so that only my Water energy is noticeable."

"Is that your only plan?" Jarlath scratched at his chin.

"It's my best plan," Brigitta said. "I'll start practicing right away."

"What about me?" asked Jarlath, kicking at a loose rock in the mountainside.

"You can pretty much be you," she laughed, "you're not the bad influence here."

"What do faeries dress up for anyway?" he asked as the rock broke free and they all watched it tumble down the side of the cliff.

"Why do they do anything? For the fun of it." Brigitta remembered some lesson she had learned in one of Auntie Ferna's Lore and Lineage classes. "A long time ago there was more emphasis on the symbolism of the Gray Months transitioning into the Grow Months. Everyone dressed in gray cloaks with colorful clothes underneath, and halfway through the Masquerade they would strip the cloaks away."

She pulled her knees up to her chin and stared out over the Earth Realm to the Center Realm, where she could just make out the sun glinting off the Hourglass. "But now it's just an excuse to make silly costumes and dance until the sun rises."

"What did you go as last year?" asked Jarlath softly, distracted by something on the horizon.

"Best costume!" Minq hooted. "She rockdragonfly."

"Can we get back to our plan?" Brigitta asked. "We've got less than two suns to figure this out. Jarlath?"

Beside her, Jarlath's breath was still and his eyes vacant. A moment later he shuddered and was fully awake again.

"What was that?" asked Brigitta. "What just happened?"

"Nothing, nothing." He rubbed at his eyes. "All those relays, flying back and forth to the Center Realm, you know." He waved her questions off and took a steadying breath. "Go on."

"Well . . ." She hesitated, now worried she was putting far too much pressure on her friend.

He raised his eyebrows playfully and she laughed.

"I can't go dressed as a Perimeter Guard," she continued, "that's not a costume, so I'll have to disguise myself as a Perimeter Guard *inside* of a costume."

"Disguise inside costume!" Minq said, impressed in spite of his misgivings. "Double disguise."

"Then it's just a matter of sneaking into the Hive," said Brigitta. "Well, that and keeping everyone distracted long enough to steal the scepter and make our escape without notice."

"Yeah," said Jarlath, "there's that."

"Okay, so I'm still working on the how," she said. "But I do know the when."

They stood up and walked south along the ridge, hatching the rest of the plan as they traversed the trail.

"At the end of the evening's events there's a processional," she explained. "It will be High Priest Fozk up front, then Elders, Apprentices, and Wisings. The scepter is kept with the Wisings until the processional, during which the newest Wising lights it and hands it up the processional."

Lost in the memory of her last Festival of the Moons, Brigitta smiled. "Actually, it's quite pretty. The scepter grows in brightness as it goes up the line of faeries. It's like watching a star being born."

"So, you're saying," said Jarlath, looking a bit pale, "this scepter light trick is a big deal and the whole forest is going to fall into a panic when the scepter goes missing?"

"The Elders won't let that happen," Brigitta assured him. "They'll think of something. And if they don't, Minq can go into the Hive with some important question. When he finds them all upset, he can suggest they use Ondelle's hourglass necklace instead and tell everyone the change is a symbol of creating traditions for a new era or something. The point is, if we enter the tunnel just as the main entertainment begins, it gives us four or five moonbeats to trick the Wisings into giving us the scepter and get as far away as possible."

"Huh," said Jarlath, clearly impressed. "You've thought of everything."

"Not everything," she said. "I have no idea what happens after we leave the White Forest." She put a hand to her chest where the hourglass necklace used to lay. "Or how we'll protect ourselves."

"That's why you have me," said Jarlath, flexing his arms. "You're the brains; I'm the muscle."

Below them, a swell of blossom bells sounded from Gyllenhale, their echoes bubbling up to them on the breeze. They stood quietly listening to the soothing chimes surrounding them like a joyful spring. Brigitta closed her eyes and inhaled the sound, gathering strength from the momentary peace.

Since Brigitta had promised Thistle she'd lend a hand with her Masquerade costume, she bade good-bye to Jarlath and Minq and headed for Dmvyle. Thistle had given herself the task of helping out in the little nursery that had sprung up in the home of Dwinn and Cairys, parents of Duna, the little destinyless faerie Brigitta had first met in the Elder chamber before she and Ondelle traveled to Noe.

Duna was no longer the only destinyless child, however. A crystal-eyed Air Faerie boy named Tustin had been born in Thachreek, and the two mothers spent most of their spare time together. Cairys was a nervous little Fire Faerie. Her Earth Faerie spouse, Dwinn, worked in the marsh farms, which was how he had met Granae and Thistle. Tustin's mother, Brea, was a calming presence for Cairys, especially since she could now share her concerns for her child's future with someone who understood.

Thistle, who was technically "destinyless" herself, had taken to the children immediately. And when a pregnant Water Faerie woman from Easyl showed up to the cottage in tears, it was Thistle who had the idea to start a "Destiny Nursery" away from the rest of the faeries, so as not to upset the other parents and children. Thistle and Granae were positive that if they all observed carefully, they would find appropriate Life Tasks for Duna and Tustin. If they could do so in Mabbe's Hollows, Granae reasoned, they could certainly do so in the White Forest.

With time, thought Brigitta as she headed for the nursery, *there will be so many unmarked faeries flying around the forest that it won't matter anymore.* But if it made the families feel better, and gave Thistle something to do, Brigitta was all for it. And it was clear that Thistle loved the crystal-eyed babies without fear or prejudice.

As it turned out, Granae had done a fabulous job costuming her daughter as a baby rainbow lizard and herself as a matching mother rainbow lizard. She had even sewn little bubblebug costumes for Duna and Tustin. The cozy cottage was filled with laughter as Granae snipped at loose threads and adjusted Thistle's striped tail.

"You don't need my help," said Brigitta to Thistle. "Your costumes are better than most. Prize-worthy, even."

"You think?" asked Thistle, eyes sparkling above her pointy lizard lips. She picked up the destinyless Duna and zoomed her around the room, popping her lips like a bubblebug calling to its friends across the lake.

It broke Brigitta's heart to see her so happy. She reminded Brigitta of Himalette, who was already losing that innocence, and Brigitta couldn't help thinking that some day Thistle would lose hers, too.

"You are a masterful, magical Clothier, Granae," said Brigitta, truly impressed.

"No magic," Granae held up her hands, "just seasons and seasons of helping out in Mabbe's Hollows."

Unaware of the misty-eyed melancholy that flickered through Granae's eyes, Cairys and Brea laughed as Thistle swerved and bubbled her way about the cottage. When Granae pulled back from adjusting the hem of Tustin's costume, her hand went to her forehead, and she gazed into the air, stunned. A moment later, and Thistle fell into the same trance. If it weren't for Brigitta's quick reaction, Thistle would have dropped Duna on the floor.

A moonsbreath later, they both shook themselves awake again.

"Okay," said Brigitta, handing little Duna to Cairys. "One of you has to tell me what's going on. Jarlath did the exact same thing today."

"Did what exact same thing?" asked Thistle distractedly.

"That thing you just did, like you weren't there for a moment," explained Brigitta. "How often does that happen?"

"I—" said Granae, looking down at the scissors in her hands as if she didn't know how they had gotten there.

Brigitta removed the scissors from Granae's grip and set the faerie woman down on a stool, while Cairys, balancing Duna on her hip, produced a wet cloth from the kitchen and placed it on Granae's forehead. When Granae looked up, there was something dulled about her eyes, something missing.

"What just happened?" Granae asked, grabbing Brigitta's tunic. "What did you see?"

"I don't know, you just sort of went . . . blank," was the best she could describe it.

"Blank," Granae repeated, nodding. She nabbed Thistle and pulled her to her bosom, stroking her hair. They sat there rocking in silence, staring out at nothing.

"Why won't anyone tell me what's going on?" demanded Brigitta.

Duna burst into tears and Tustin followed suit. The two mothers carried their little bubblebugs into the next room, singing and cooing to quiet them down.

"It's the voices," said Granae in a hushed tone, hugging Thistle tighter as she trembled. "The ones Mabbe trained all of us to tune out."

"The echoes of the Ancients, you mean?" asked Brigitta. "They're speaking to you now?"

"No," said Granae, her face pale with worry. "They've stopped. I mean—I think—they're gone."

"I'm not being selfish," Brigitta told her reflection in her bedroom mirror. "It's for the good of the forest." She leaned in closer, challenging her reflection to disagree. "It's my destiny."

Her reflection imitated her motions, and then both of them sat still, waiting for the other to continue. She missed her Thought Mirror, the one item in her Apprentice chambers she wished she could have taken with her.

"I'm the same faerie who left for Noe with Ondelle," she said to the mirror. "I haven't changed, not really."

She squinted at her reflection and spoke back to herself as the mirror. "Haven't you? Through our actions aren't we defined?"

It was something Ondelle had once said to her. She reviewed her recent actions. The old Brigitta would never have stomped off in anger at Gola. The old Brigitta hadn't been as distrustful of others. The old Brigitta wasn't so full of secrets.

And now she was asking others to keep secrets for her. All because she didn't want anything to interfere with her plans to leave the forest. Although, it hadn't taken much to convince Thistle and Granae to keep silent about losing touch with the Ancient voices. At least for the time being. No one wanted to spoil the festival. Obviously, the Elders had to be told, and Granae agreed to call a meeting with them as soon as the festivities were over.

"After Jarlath and I are long gone," Brigitta said to her reflection.

Jarlath. She needed to see him as soon as possible to find out if he, too, had lost touch with the Ancient voices. Granae had said that hearing the voices was like living near a stream. The sound could be ignored, as it was constantly flowing in the background. Over time, she'd stopped noticing it . . . until it went silent.

Thistle hadn't been as sure. She could tell something was missing, but she had also been trained from a toddling to block it all out, whereas Granae had been Brigitta's age before Mabbe's ruling came down. Brigitta imagined for Thistle it was more like losing the whisper of a forgotten dream.

Roane never said much about what went on in his head. Brigitta had watched him intently during supper, and it could have been her imagination, or Himalette's ability to talk enough for four faeries, but Roane had seemed unusually quiet.

Regardless, it only served to make her departure more crucial. They could live without destiny marks from the Ancients, but the Noe Watchers were the only faeries who could perform dispersements when any faerie died.

She shuddered at the thought of no more dispersements, faerie spirits wandering their forest, unable to let go of their elemental energies for the next generation. No released energy, no new babies. Duna and her crystal-eyed companions would be the last of their kin unless Brigitta could fix things.

Was she mad for thinking that she was the one who was supposed to put everything right? Or that she even could? For taking it upon herself to steal the scepter and visit the dragon?

"You are not like Hrathgar," she whispered.

Her own image looked back at her suspiciously, and rightly so, as she had buried a secret so deep inside she could almost pretend that it wasn't there. She had an ulterior motive for not telling the Elders what had happened to Granae and Thistle. She didn't want Fozk to change his mind and rush off to find the Eternal Dragon. Not now.

She wanted to find the Dragon herself.

She knew for certain that Ondelle had released Water energy into her before she was born. Water energy Ondelle had gotten from that Ancient faerie. She was now convinced that Ondelle's own Fire and Air had been given to her in the same manner, forced upon her by High Priestess Freena. It was why Ondelle's own mother had denied their bond.

It was why Ondelle had detected Brigitta hiding in the passageway when she and Kyllia, Tilan, and Dinnae had spied on the Elders' spell rehearsals all those seasons ago. It was why Brigitta had felt such a connection to Ondelle, why Ondelle's Air energy felt so at home coursing through Brigitta, and why the High Priestess's memories settled inside of her like they belonged there.

And it was why Brigitta knew she had to get to the Eternal Dragon first, so It could take her to the bottom of the sea. She hadn't told anyone yet, not even Jarlath, that there was something else she had felt during Ondelle's memory.

"That faerie trapped inside the bubble?" she said, placing her hand to its reflection. "She has one element left, her Earth, and it belongs with me."

Chapter Five

Ondelle scanned the Center Realm arena, gripping her scepter so hard her knuckles had locked. If the White Forest faeries weren't so preoccupied with their festival preparations, they might have noticed the panic in her eyes. She looked to the ground beneath the platform. The open spell seed was still there. Of course it was still there.

It was exactly the kind of spell seed Hrathgar had used all those seasons ago when she had tried to steal the power of the Hourglass. And a moment earlier Ondelle had seen a resolved Vivilia carrying it toward the platform. As requested, Vivilia had left for Dead Mountain five suns earlier to check on the banished faerie, and now Ondelle cursed herself for her curiosity and concern for her old friend. Concern was only natural, of course, but one faerie's well-being could not eclipse the well-being of the entire White Forest.

Open on the ground in front of her, the spell seed had obviously been used somehow, but to what end she had no idea. Had Hrathgar put a spell on the Hourglass? On Ondelle and the Elders? On all the White Forest faeries?

"By the Dragon, Hrathgar," she hissed, "what have you done?"

She had to find Vivilia, but there was too much activity going on around her, too much energy to separate. She took equal breaths Air and Fire and laced them together into a seamless ring. She held the energy ring steady, readying it for quick action.

Ondelle loosened her anxious grip on the scepter, breathed from her belly, and scanned the arena once again. She felt a fluttering around the inner edge of the Fire Faerie grandstand like a drunken shadowfly. Vivilia! Without hesitation, Ondelle threw her looped energy, the ring expanding out to form a long, round tunnel. When it reached Vivilia, she ensnared her and felt for an opening through which to empath her thoughts.

What Ondelle felt was more than an opening; it was an empty vessel ready to receive. So, Hrathgar had used Vivilia as transportation to get the spell seed into the White Forest. Her old friend was clever, but Ondelle was quick-thinking. She could use Hrathgar's vessel, too.

She raised her hands and closed her eyes, whirling the lasso seductively around Vivilia's mind, preparing a thought-loop. Thought-loops were tricky and usually had to start with the subject's original thought. But, with Vivilia's empty mind, Hrathgar had almost made it too easy for Ondelle. She opened her eyes again and sent a thought forth. *I must find and protect Brigitta.*

In her enchanted state, the sprite repeated through the tunnel of energy, *I must find and protect Brigitta.*

I must take her this spell.

I must take her this spell.

There was no time to consult the Elders about the use of Blue Spell. The Dragon had given her all the permission she needed and the life-long task of protecting the energy's destiny. Ondelle's life was cut shorter with each use, but she couldn't think about that now.

By the power of the Eternal Dragon, Ondelle called as she lifted her scepter, gathered her forces, and shot a Blue Spell message across the arena straight into Vivilia's heart. A look of shock registered on the sprite's face, and then she disappeared in a quick poof of blue.

Lying in bed the next morning, Brigitta practiced forming Air and Water energy rings and stretching them out within her own mind, thought-looping a meditation of silvery scales skating to and fro. The image slid back and forth, circling her thoughts, as she contemplated the latest memory, which had come to her in the early morning hours as she tossed and turned, plagued by her secrets.

This proved the authenticity of the memories, she decided. No one had taught her to thought-loop. It wasn't something a Second Apprentice would ever learn on her own. Yet there she was with the knowledge of how to perform it, and here she was practicing it in her own mind. It didn't feel like she had just learned how to use it, either. She had *remembered* how to use it.

She shivered as she also recalled Ondelle's fear and panic on the day of Hrathgar's curse. She now understood how and why Ondelle had sent the Blue Spell protection through Vivilia, but she didn't understand why Ondelle had never told her about it. She hadn't found that memory.

"When the time is right," she said to her herself, the silver scales still sliding back and forth.

She dropped the thought-looped image and sighed. She couldn't stay in bed practicing spells all morning, so she got dressed and joined her family. Attempting to appear as awake and happy as possible, she spent the morning molding tingermint taffy with her Momma, polishing jars for her Poppa's new moonbeat moths, and feigning interest in Himalette's Masquerade costume: a pink, large-bottomed thunderbug she had designed to chime when she shook her behind. Himalette flew around the front yard, entertaining her family and neighbors with her tumbling, tinkling dance.

"You know, Himmy," Brigitta teased, "with a bottom that big, I would expect more of a big *BONG*."

Himalette smirked and shook her rear in her sister's direction, sending the Tiragarrow children into fits of laughter.

Brigitta looked to the sky. "Well, I should get moving if I'm going to meet up with Jarlath," she said to Pippet, who was handing out samples of taffy to neighbors with Roane quietly tagging along behind her.

"You're certain you feel up to it?" Pippet asked.

Neither of them had mentioned Brigitta's outburst from the other day, but there was a palpable tension now, a tension that saddened Brigitta because there was nothing to be done about it. She couldn't risk letting her guard down. What would her mother say if she found out the truth?

"Yes, I'm certain."

"You can always come find us if you need us," Mousha offered, nabbing his fourth taffy from Pippet's tray. "Orl Featherkind offered to watch my booth if necessary. I don't mind missing anything. Not for you."

"That's sweet, Poppa." She kissed his cheek. "I'll keep that in mind."

She gave Pippet a quick hug, grabbed her bulging pack, and was out of Tiragarrow before anyone could see the tears stinging her eyes. She wiped them away, trying not to think about how much her parents would worry after she went missing, and flew down along the southern tail of Spring River. The rushing of Precipice Falls comforted her and she paused for a moment to watch the waters churn before heading east toward Gola's to meet up with Jarlath and Minq.

As she skirted past Rioscrea, she made up her mind to confide in the old Drutan. To make things right with her and tell her everything. Ondelle had trusted her. Who knew what secrets they had shared? Brigitta grew determined to prove herself worthy of Gola's trust.

Beneath all of these thoughts festered a darker notion. There was a chance Brigitta might not return from her quest, and she did not want those angry words to be the last Gola ever heard from her. She did not want to be remembered as the second faerie to break her heart.

She reached the small clearing in front of Gola's tree, where Minq and Jarlath stood looking more than a little anxious.

"What's wrong?" she asked as she landed.

"We can't find Gola," said Jarlath. "And look."

He pointed to the cauldrons in front of Gola's tree-home, from which her chatterbuds usually greeted them with their tinny chorus. The four cauldrons were empty but for a few handfuls of soil.

"She's probably trading them at the market today," said Brigitta. "She's been talking about doing that for moons." She gazed wistfully at the abandoned cauldrons. Gola had been giving more and more of her possessions away. "I'll fly up and try to catch her on the path. You wait here in case we miss each other."

Before they could suggest otherwise, Brigitta was off, following the narrow trail from Gola's to Bobbercurxy. It was perfect, she thought. She could tell Gola everything on the stroll home. Even the part that she hadn't confessed to anyone else. Gola had already told her it wasn't her place to interfere with faerie destiny, only impart knowledge where, and when, she could.

But Gola was not at the marketplace, and her few friends, an old Fire Faerie Weaver named Krisanna and an Earth Faerie Potter called Valance, had not seen her in several suns. Brigitta streamed back to Gola's tree twice as fast.

"Where else could she be?" she asked Minq and Jarlath upon her return, now as concerned as they were.

Gola was not in the habit of wandering much past her gardens, other than to Bobbercurxy and, every once in a while, to the Center Realm. But someone always traveled along to assist her.

"We've been down to the river and out to the fire flower farm," said Jarlath.

"What about the market at Rivenbow?"

"Too far," said Minq. "Never go by self."

They all turned to consider Gola's tree-home. Under any other circumstances, none of them would have thought about entering it without her permission. Not even Minq. And although Gola had never left a note for them in the past, they decided to check inside to see if she had.

They were met with a dark, chilly room. Nothing had been

brewed or baked in her kitchen that day. The bed was made and the whole space was unusually tidy. As Jarlath opened the curtains, the light caught some stones strung above the hearth.

"Are those her moonstones?" asked Jarlath.

"No, no, they can't be . . ." said Brigitta, moving closer.

There were four of them, and they were shaped exactly like Gola's moonstones, strung along an identical thin black strap. But these stones had no starry shimmers and looked as if they were formed from dark clay rather than the night sky reflected in a pool of water. Brigitta touched one with a pinky finger and its absolute stillness sent a shiver through her heart. She braved a closer look and wrapped her hand around one. Nothing happened. No visions, no energy pulling her in.

"If they are her moonstones, one's missing," she murmured. "Look."

Minq and Jarlath moved to either side of her. With his ear, Minq lifted the strand of stones off the hearth and gazed at them, moisture dotting the edges of his eyes. Drawing in a shaky breath, he placed the strand around Brigitta's neck.

"What are you doing?" she said, fumbling for the stones. "Those are Gola's!"

"She left for you," he said.

"What do you mean *left* for me?" asked Brigitta.

"What are you telling us?" asked Jarlath, seizing Minq's arm.

"She old Drutan," he said, blinking his beady eyes at them. "She gone to root." He waved his ear toward the forest. "Out there."

"No, no . . . no . . ." The room started to spin and Brigitta grabbed onto a chair as Minq and Jarlath both reached out to steady her.

"I . . . I . . . She can't!" Brigitta burst into tears. "I haven't told her I'm sorry!"

Minq hugged her with both ears and Jarlath wrapped himself around his two friends, tears engulfing them all.

"She know," Minq said between sniffles, "she know."

It was horribly wrong, Brigitta thought as she entered the Center Realm, that there could be such celebration with Gola taking root all alone out there in their forest. But there the White Forest faeries were, laughing and singing and dancing along, oblivious to the pain that made Brigitta's insides feel as though they were collapsing in on themselves.

As soon as they landed in the wide sandy path surrounding the grandstands, she, Minq, and Jarlath were drawn into the excited flow of faeries, like leaves into a river. The noise and motion and color were too much for her, and she began to panic, unable to breathe under her costume mask. Jarlath reached out and pulled her to his side, linking his arm through hers. Minq stepped to her other side, placing an ear against the small of her back to guide her along.

With all her heart, she wanted to postpone their journey to Forever Beach, but when would they get another chance to distract nearly every faerie in the forest? No, after the festival, the scepter would be under Fozk's nose again, and Granae would tell him about the Watchers losing touch with . . . the Watchers!

Brigitta spun around to look at Jarlath, his tree head bobbing along in the crowd. His eyes were sunken into the mask, so she couldn't see his expression, and she was too distraught to empath it.

Losing Gola that day made their choice of costumes seem cruel. They were both dressed as trees. Brown fabric wrapped their bodies, leaves and branches criss-crossed their faces, and a nest sat on Brigitta's head. Underneath the Masquerade costume, she was disguised as a Perimeter Guard, the colors and markings on her wings carefully rendered in feather paints, which now appeared to her as too crude to fool anyone.

In her worry and grief over Gola's disappearance, she had forgotten to ask Jarlath about the Ancients. She hadn't even stopped to get a sense of any change in him. She had barely been able to get her costume on and get to the Center Realm. And now she was surrounded and being jostled by faeries pouring into the fairgrounds. The heat was nauseating, and her heart quickened. She had to pull herself together, or they wouldn't be able to get the scepter in time, and they'd never have another chance.

She stopped walking and Minq and Jarlath stopped along with her as faeries jostled them from all sides. Instinctively, Brigitta reached for her hourglass necklace, but instead found the lumps of lifeless moonstone hidden beneath her costume. Still, they were oddly comforting with their absolute absence of energy. Perhaps that was why Gola had left them for her. Maybe she had known all along that Brigitta was going to leave, had perhaps even chosen to root so she could give Brigitta the comfort of her silent stones. That would be just like something Gola would do, protecting Brigitta in her secret and humble way.

She rubbed at the stones through her costume. Gola was still with her. And like Ondelle, she would always be with her. She could find strength in that.

As her heart and breathing slowed, Brigitta became more conscious of her surroundings. Cooking contestants thrust culinary treats into the hands of every reveler, Traders called from tables lining the outer grandstands, and at the entrance to the arena, a hoopflute orchestra played as children held a leaf race overhead, the air from the instruments tossing the flutterscarves about.

"This way," she said to Jarlath and Minq, leading them around the Fire Faerie grandstand. She gazed over faerie heads as she navigated past hundreds of brightly colored tents and peeked into the arena at the costumed aerialists. Her eyes landed on the Hourglass of Protection. It was two-thirds empty. And no one seemed concerned.

They grabbed some taffy off of a passing tray and some tarts off another. Under cover of the chaos, Brigitta led Jarlath and Minq through the crowd, behind the Fire Faerie grandstand, and into the brush, hoping the tunnel entrance in the old tree stump hadn't been blocked off by the Elders.

Luckily, when they arrived, the only difference was that the stump was now covered in more vines.

She dumped an armful of goodies at Minq's feet. "Have at it."

For a moment, it seemed his unruly appetite had been curbed by his sadness, but a moonsbreath later he had downed two pipberry tarts.

Brigitta lit the lower quarter of a globelight and handed the light to Jarlath, who spread open the vines, squeezed through the crack in the stump, and disappeared into the tunnel. The leafy vines shook closed behind him.

She stepped up to the stump, and then turned back to Minq. "Be careful you don't pass out from over-digestion, Minq. Pace yourself."

He waved her off with his right ear while he wiped his hands and mouth with his left.

"And stay away from anything with lyllium in it," she warned, slipping into the trunk.

Hands tracing the dark walls, Brigitta made her way toward the glowing light ahead. When she reached Jarlath she pulled him around and studied his face.

"What?" he whispered.

"Your eyes look different," she said. "Are different."

He shrugged and looked away, up the tunnel. "We need to get going; we don't have a lot of time."

"I know about the Ancient voices, Jarlath," said Brigitta. "Granae told me." She placed a hand on his arm. "Is that what's been going on with you? Is that what you've been keeping from me?"

He whirled back around. "And you have no secrets from me?"

His accusation caught her off guard, and she fell back into the wall of the tunnel, creating a little avalanche of pebbles and dust. They both paused and listened until they were sure no one had heard.

"I'm sorry . . ." he continued and shook his head, "I'm just . . . these past few days . . ." He gestured helplessly.

"Are the voices gone completely?" she asked. "Have you really lost touch with them?"

He let out a sigh. "Maybe. I don't know. Does it matter right now?"

Brigitta thought about this. There would be no more dispersements for the dead if it were true, but what did that matter if they lost their forest entirely? There would also be no empathing him to get to the Ancients as she had done to change her physical form in Noe.

"I get it," he said when she didn't answer. "You only cared about me for my connection to them."

"Ha, ha." Brigitta swatted him.

They considered each other a moment longer. There was nothing to do but trust.

"Give me a chance to cloak my Water and focus my Air," she finally said. "And then . . ."

He nodded. "Yeah. And then."

Two Wisings, Lalam and Bastian, were sitting in the gathering room of the Elder Chamber in simple white tunics streamed with shimmering gold. Their hair flickered gold as well, like the morning light catching on Green Lake. They were passing the time making shadow figures on the wall as Brigitta and Jarlath observed them through the entryway from the crack in the stone wall on the other side of the hallway.

Lalam was about twice Brigitta's age and slender for an Earth Faerie, but solid. His wings were a barky brown, and his sun-warmed skin housed a subtle strength. Bastian had the lighter tones of an Air Faerie, slender teal wings, and eager yellow eyes.

Elder Mora and First Air Apprentice Na Tam were putting the final touches on the crystal box that held the scepter. They were not costumed at all yet. Na Tam wiped away some small speck of dirt on the surface of the box while Elder Mora added a touch of light to the air surrounding it. They stepped back to admire their work.

"I like it," Elder Mora said. "Subtle, yet . . . enchanting."

"Your first Masquerade as Air Elder." Na Tam nudged Elder Mora.

Mora emitted a very un-Elderlike giggle and nudged Na Tam back. "And yours as First Apprentice."

Arm in arm, Mora and Na Tam left the chamber and Brigitta and Jarlath pulled away from the crack, slipping up against the wall. It was almost too easy, Brigitta thought. Bastian, the young Air Wising, had little mind training at all. And Earth Wising Lalam was a sweet and gentle man whom she judged open to suggestion. She just had to create the right thought-loop to keep their minds occupied. To make a thought-looping between two people without their consent, the thoughts would have to be verbalized, and the loop would have to make sense.

Because of what she now knew through Ondelle's memories, she was confident she could do it, but the whole idea made her uneasy. It will be a harmless trick, she told herself as they made their way downward, through the passageway, to an exit between two bookcases outside the Apprentice chambers. No one will get hurt.

They spiraled upward through the main passageway, and just before they rounded the curve that led to the Elder Chamber, Jarlath pulled back, but it was a moment too late. Perimeter Guard Master Reykia of Rivenbow flew toward them. Brigitta almost let her Water energy slip, but caught it back again carefully, like closing the gap between a pair of cupped hands.

"What are you doing here?" Reykia asked Jarlath. "And who are you?" she demanded of Brigitta.

"Ferris of Erriondower." Brigitta bowed slightly. She peeked through the costume leaves around her face, hoping her Watcher friend's name would bring her luck.

"The Elders approved her to join the guard," said Jarlath. "Dervia spell-cast the marking on her wings so she'd be recognized as one."

"Why wasn't I told?" barked Reykia. "We agreed on a system for guard selection."

"She was ready," he said, "and they figured you'd need the help tonight."

Conjuring Ondelle's benevolence, Brigitta emanated a hint of warm calming Air. Just a slight change in energy, not enough to cause suspicion.

Reykia composed herself and studied Brigitta. "Well, yes, I suppose I could use you on the periphery tonight."

"She's here to serve," encouraged Jarlath.

"Service is my highest endeavor," added Brigitta.

Jarlath coughed to cover a laugh.

"Fine," Reykia said, eyeing them one last time. "Follow me."

As she turned back around, Jarlath reached up with balled fists and struck her on the back of the head. She immediately crumpled to the ground.

Brigitta's surprised eyes shot to Jarlath's, and she clamped her own hand over her mouth to stifle a scream. This was not part of the plan.

"She'll be okay," he said. "*I promise.*"

Slipping her hands away from her lips, Brigitta stood there in shock.

"I'm sorry," he said. "Old habits. I didn't know what else to do."

"Well, don't do it again," said Brigitta, bending down to make sure Reykia was all right. She was still breathing at least.

"It's a good trick, though," he said. "You should learn it."

She fired him an irritated look from beneath the bird's nest in her tree branches. "Let's just do this."

Jarlath nodded as she stood up, closed her eyes, and took a deep breath. On the exhale, she let her Water energy go, swirling and mixing it evenly with the Air, creating the end of the loop, a ring that could be stretched out to form a tunnel. When the end of the loop felt sturdy enough, she opened her eyes.

"Just get the Wisings talking so I can set the loop."

They fluttered the rest of the way up the passage to the Elder Chamber. The two Wisings stood up to greet them as they entered the main room. Lalam's brow knit in confusion, but Bastian remained happily ready to assist.

"Perimeter Guard Ferris," Jarlath gestured vaguely at Brigitta, "and I have been sent to escort the scepter into the procession."

Wising Bastian smiled and turned to gather the box, but Lalam held him back with an arm. "I thought Reykia was to do it?"

"Reykia had to go out to the perimeter," said Jarlath. "I'm sure it's nothing to worry about, though." He turned to Bastian. "Which side of the box do you wish to stand on for the procession, left or right?"

Bastian turned to the older Wising and asked him, "Right or left?"

As soon as Bastian asked his question of Lalam, Brigitta's mind sprang into action. "Left or right?" she repeated to Bastian, tenderly looping the end of the energy ring around his mind. She stretched the ring into a tunnel and looped Lalam's thoughts, "Right or left?"

"Left or right?" repeated Bastian cheerfully.

Lalam hesitated, as if trying to remember what he was about to say. "Right or left?" he said, turning his eyes from Brigitta to the other Wising.

"Left or right?" asked Bastian.

They repeated the questions to each other, over and over, caught in the thought-loop. Jarlath crossed his arms and eyed Brigitta suspiciously.

"They'll be okay," she said. "I promise."

"Seems a conk on the head is easier," Jarlath muttered.

"Any of the Elders can easily stop the loop if it doesn't wear off on its own," she said, stepping back to marvel at her handiwork.

They retrieved Reykia from the passageway and hid her behind a wooden chest. Brigitta removed the scepter from its crystal case, pulled the soft cord that held the fabric of her tree costume on, and wrapped the scepter up in the cloth. With the cord, she tied up the bundle and slung it across her back.

"We've got about three moonbeats before the Elders come looking for the scepter," she said, straightening the branches across her face.

There was a groan from behind the chest.

Jarlath pulled Brigitta by the arm. "We've got less time than that."

The two of them swooped down the passageway back toward the tunnel entrance. As they turned to duck between the bookshelves, someone emerged from within the tunnel and they all startled to a halt.

An amber-toned sprite hovered in front of them. It was Vivilia. She glanced back and forth at Brigitta and Jarlath as voices echoed behind her in the tunnel. She turned to call to the voices.

"Wait!" Brigitta whispered sharply, parting the leaves in front of her face.

Vivilia smiled, the corners of her eyes curving up like ribbons.

More voices called from the direction of the Elder Chamber. It sounded like Reykia was conscious and the thought-loop broken. Brigitta pleaded to the sprite with her eyes.

Vivilia nodded and pointed upward. The two faeries followed the path of her finger. At first, Brigitta didn't notice anything but rocky ceiling. Then, Vivilia took a deep breath and blew. As the little breeze hit the ceiling, a portion of the rock wavered. It was some kind of hidden space in the roof of the cave spellcast to appear solid. In a moonsbreath, Brigitta was up and through the hole with Jarlath right behind.

It was dark and tight, with just enough room to open her wings. Plenty of room for a sprite, she thought as she felt her way with her hands, not wanting to risk using the globelight. Muffled voices sounded from beneath them. Then, unmistakably, the high whine of Minq's voice. Brigitta cringed and hoped he could manage to keep their plan a secret. She didn't know if someone had found him dozing and he had squealed, if their plan was still in effect and he was playing his part, or if somehow the Elders had gotten wind of what she and Jarlath were up to.

The shape of the sprite tunnel was odd. First it shot straight up and then angled sharply. Several wingbeats later, it angled down again, as if they had flown up and over something. Maybe another tunnel or the entrance to the Hive. It curved once more and Brigitta was sure they were now flying parallel to the ground. She stopped and crouched on her knees, the tunnel too shallow to stand. She removed the tree branches and nest from her head and misted her mind out, working through the cracks and minuscule spaces within the rock, then the dirt, to the open air.

"We're about twelve hands deep," she said, relighting the globelight. The tunnel stretched out in both directions. Roots had been cut or tied back to keep them out of the way. "Have you felt any other passages breaking off?"

"No," said Jarlath, crouching next to her and removing his own headpiece. "It's more like a channel then a tunnel."

Brigitta tightened the straps of the bundle on her back, making sure the scepter was secure. "I guess we just follow it," she said.

"Do you trust her?" asked Jarlath.

"Ondelle did."

They continued along and in a few wingbeats the tunnel ended at a wall of stone. They pushed at it together, but it wouldn't budge. Confused, they looked back in the other direction to see if they had missed something. Then Brigitta looked up and smirked. She blew at the ceiling and it wavered.

"This way," she said, flying up through the spellcast image. As soon as she did so, her globelight went out. She rubbed her hand over it and nothing happened.

They climbed and climbed until Brigitta was more than sure they were above ground level, yet they still climbed. She stopped for a moment and hovered in the air.

"We should have emerged already," she said.

"I was thinking the same thing," said Jarlath.

There was movement beneath them, and light. Brigitta sucked in her breath and shielded her eyes. A moment later, Vivilia scurried past, glowing like a torch.

"Follow me," she said in her small sprite voice.

It was a world within a world, nestled in the widest section of an enormous uul tree. All Brigitta could say while she gazed upon the sprite village was, "How is this possible? How can this be?"

Jarlath patted her shoulder. "Now you know how I felt when I landed in the White Forest."

There were fissures crafted into the trunk that let in natural light. The lines worked with the tree's natural shape, along and between its winding fibers. The light inside was a celestial blue, as if the night sky itself had found its way into the trunk. And what first appeared to be stars above were simply slowly dancing specks of brightness that floated overhead.

There were a few hundred sprites, male and female, who were hard to tell apart. They had reddish and yellowish tones to their skin, and eyes and hair of shifting colors, deep reds and earthy browns and mossy greens. Even Vivilia's hair had grown tawnier since entering the tree, and her eyes grew darker and darker with every moonsbreath.

The sprites didn't seem to have individual homes; they just sat about wherever it was convenient. Some worked crafts, some puzzled over solitary games, some played music or read or drew. It looked like a giant playspace, only there were no children. And Brigitta wondered, had she ever seen a sprite child?

There was a patience about them, as if they were all waiting for something. Nothing was particularly organized, but neither was it disorganized. Everything just was.

All of it was counter to the impish nature she had assumed of them. That most of the White Forest faeries assumed of them. It dawned on Brigitta that perhaps they didn't know anything about the sprites after all.

For instance, the sprites didn't even seem concerned that Brigitta and Jarlath were standing there gawping at them. As a matter of fact, other than several curious glances, they pretty much ignored the two intruders.

"Um," Brigitta turned to Vivilia, "they don't seem surprised about us being here."

"No," was all Vivilia said.

She led them to what Brigitta assumed was the main entrance, as it was the widest trunk hollow leading out of the village. Even at that, there wasn't room enough for Brigitta or Jarlath to open their wings, so they scrabbled and hauled themselves up through the thick branches that formed another kind of tunnel.

When they emerged from the uul tree, they followed Vivilia up and through the canopy to a small wooden bench secured to a branch by vines strung into the trees. As they sat, Brigitta got her bearings. It was dark to the north, but to the south she could make out the twinkling lights of the festival through the leaves and hear the faint cheers and laughter of celebrating faeries. Apparently, news of the stolen scepter hadn't reached them yet.

"Thank you," Brigitta said to Vivilia.

"I don't know why you did it," added Jarlath, "but, yeah, thanks."

The sprite touched the top of Brigitta's hand with her own and smiled. There was a devotion in that touch, a loyalty, something so sincere that Brigitta was nearly overcome. But before she could say anything further, Vivilia had slipped away from the bench.

"Three dusk owl hoots means all clear," she said and disappeared into the leaves.

They settled in to wait for the sprite's signal, anxiety brewing in Brigitta's stomach. She didn't want to think about what lay ahead. What she had gotten them *both* into. And now Vivilia was caught up in her schemes. Or had she been caught in them since the beginning? Brigitta's arms prickled in the cool air as unanswered questions filled her mind.

Something about Ondelle's memory of the day the stone curse hit the White Forest nagged at her. Ondelle had used Vivilia to transport her own spell, just like Hrathgar had, probably *because* Hrathgar had, to protect Brigitta. But if Ondelle had given the Water energy to a different faerie, then Ondelle would have protected *that* faerie and sent *her* into danger. Brigitta would have been turned to stone like all the rest.

The problem was, Brigitta didn't know whether she was the way she was because Ondelle had made her that way, or if Ondelle had entrusted her with the Water energy because she had *known* Brigitta was destined to have it. But how could she have known when Brigitta hadn't even been born yet? And if it wasn't her destiny, what did that say about her attraction to that faerie's Earth energy, waiting, at the bottom of the sea?

What was so special about that faerie's energy anyway?

Three dusk owl hoots sounded beneath them. Brigitta shook her head clear and pain shot through her temples. She grabbed the sides of her head, wondering if living with Ondelle's memories would ever cease to hurt so much.

"Are you all right?" asked Jarlath.

"Yeah, it's just . . ."

"It's just what?" Jarlath was still waiting for Brigitta to finish her thought when three additional hoots, slightly more adamant, sounded from below.

"We gotta go," she said and took to the air. She flew ahead of him, cutting the air efficiently, curving northeast out of the trees and heading toward the reed forest where no faeries would be this time of night, especially during the Masquerade. But just because the Masquerade had continued, it didn't mean no one was searching for them. And why shouldn't they be, after what Jarlath and Brigitta had just done?

"Jarlath," she finally spoke up as the tall reeds enveloped them in a grassy sound barrier. "Am I doing the right thing?"

He buzzed through the blades and disappeared, then poked his head back through them. "I don't know, but you're doing something."

"But am I being selfish?" She felt for the scepter on her back, a reminder of the reality of what she had done.

Jarlath fluttered toward her and looked her in the eyes. "You're being very brave, that's what."

"But there's more," she confessed. "You were right. I haven't told you everything about why I need to go—"

He put his hand up. "It doesn't matter. I trust your decision."

Something Ondelle once said sprang to her mind. *There are no right and wrong choices, only the choices themselves. We must make them and go on.*

She nodded and they continued, making a beeline through the reed forest. They skimmed quickly through the soft lowland brush that was the far eastern side of the Earth Realm and jetted toward the dense trees that acted as a buffer between their homeland and The Shift. A waning Great Moon sat low on the horizon, the smaller Lola Moon crescent chasing after her.

This far from the Center Realm, Brigitta and Jarlath could no longer hear the festivities. It was quiet but for the low exhales of the Singing Caves. In the moonslight, their dark mouths spouted from rocky mounds, calling to each other with every breeze, like earthy ghosts. It was impossible not to stop and listen to them.

"It sounds like dream songs coming from the center of the world," said Jarlath.

Brigitta murmured assent before taking off again. Jarlath followed as she flitted back into the trees and kept a steady pace for several moonbeats. This was the third time she was leaving home. Only this time, she didn't know if she'd be welcomed back.

They made The Shift in good time and scouted the area for Perimeter Guards. There were none, and the Great Moon had disappeared, leaving the smaller crescent to light their way. They stepped into the rocky moat under the Lola Moon's eerie orange glow.

Jarlath shook his head as he looked back and forth across the expanse of earth. "We would never have gotten away with leaving our perimeter so unguarded in Noe."

"It's not their fault they've never known real danger," said Brigitta, feeling the need to defend her kin.

"Well, tonight," he said, "I'm grateful for their ignorance."

Brigitta stopped in front of the protective field and Jarlath nearly ran into her.

She turned around. "You're sure about this? You don't have to come, you know. You can say I spellcast you to do my bidding."

"No, I can't." He smiled, and for a moment, even without their starry-ness, his eyes reflected their signature mischievous spark. "That would mean admitting you could overpower me."

"Ha, ha."

Jarlath suddenly turned serious. "You do need to promise me one thing, though."

"What's that?"

"Whatever happens, you stick to your plan. If for some reason I can't go on, or . . . or . . . just promise you'll go on without me."

"Don't say that. We're in this together."

"This is bigger than me, Brigitta," insisted Jarlath. "Don't ever let me hold you back. Promise me, that's all. Please."

"All right," said Brigitta. "Fine."

Jarlath eyed her skeptically.

"I promise," she said, hand on her heart. "But it won't come to that. It won't."

He wrapped his left hand around her right and they turned toward the wavering field. Each took a deep breath, and they stepped through.

It only took a moment to cross the cool streams of the field. And then it was done. They were on the other side: slightly darker, definitely chillier, and spoiled by a foul odor that made Brigitta scowl.

"I forgot about the smell," she said, gazing the rest of the way across the dirt moat.

"Huh," said Jarlath. He turned back to look at the White Forest with its shimmering leaves punctuating the night. "That was undramatic."

Brigitta laughed and then realized they were still holding hands. She let go and busied herself by straightening her pack and the scepter strapped alongside it.

Jarlath placed both his hands against the field and pushed. He bounced and wobbled against it.

"It feels like pushing against a wall of water." He pulled his hands out and examined them. "But it's not wet."

"You can't get back inside without a White Forest Perimeter Guard. Not as long as the Hourglass spell holds, at least."

"Well," said Jarlath, puffing up his chest, "since you're the only White Forest faerie I know who can go in and fetch one, I'd better take good care of you."

"You'd better be nice to me, too," Brigitta pointed out. A movement in the distance, on the periphery of the White Forest, caught her eye. "We'd better get going."

They hastened into the Dark Forest and were quickly swallowed into its thickness. Brigitta halved her globelight and gave one side to Jarlath, which he tucked away in his pack. She lit hers and they were on their way. She preferred not to travel at night, but she didn't want to stop until they found a safe spot to sleep either. Something far enough from the White Forest so they couldn't be tracked down by the guards, if they dared to come after them. She wasn't sure that they would.

The plan was to journey north for a few moonbeats, then turn due west and simply keep flying until they met Forever Beach. According to the map she had retrieved from Gola's wall, it would be a long stretch of coast to search. But she would recognize the Dragon's beach from Ondelle's memory. She recalled the large plateau at the foot of the mountains and the distance from it to the V-shaped stones.

The trees opened up a bit, allowing them to fly for brief moments of time, but they still kept close to one another, for the forest was writhing with movement and teeming with sound. Snorts, growls, and screeches followed them as they moved farther and farther away from The Shift.

A loud hum stopped them mid-wingstroke.

"Sliverleaves!" called Jarlath, dropping to the ground.

"I don't think so," said Brigitta, doing the same. She shaded her globelight and squinted into the trees.

When the hum had ceased, she turned back to Jarlath. His body shook as he gripped an old frore dagger that she had never seen before. She held her globelight to his face and stared at him for a moment, his eyes harder and colder than they had been earlier that night, almost menacing.

Before she could ask him about the dagger, a swarm of hairy black beetles shot into her light, startling them both. Brigitta dropped her globelight half, and the beetles immediately descended in a thrumming mass, enveloping the light.

In the abrupt darkness, Jarlath retrieved his own globelight half and set it to a low, warm glow. "Shoo!" he called, kicking and stomping at the beetles.

His foot landed on one with a sickly crunch. All at once, the beetles stopped shaking and humming and looked up at him. Dozens of angry beetle heads cocked, waiting for him to make another move. Then they looked up at the other globelight half shining in his hand.

"Oh, no you don't." Brigitta snatched the globelight from Jarlath and snuffed it out. The world went black and there was a flurry of little wingbeats and prickly beetle legs on Brigitta's face and arms. She shrieked and brushed them away. A moonsbreath later and they were gone.

Both she and Jarlath stood breathing quietly for a few moments, listening to the hum and scuttle as the beetle swarm moved on. When she was sure they were alone again, she relit Jarlath's globelight half and aimed it at the ground. Her half was gone.

"Bog buggers!" she swore. "Not one night in the forest and I've already lost half a globelight."

"We won't need it," Jarlath assured her. "After tonight, we'll travel by day."

All the menace she had detected in him had disappeared, and the glint in his eyes had returned. She had to be careful, she thought, the Dark Forest was full of tricks. She didn't doubt it could turn them against each other if they didn't watch out.

They stumbled on, and it wasn't long before they found a modest hollow in a tree. Brigitta managed a decent wall of dustmist, with a bit of firepepper for extra measure, to conceal the hole in the tree. They snuggled into their blankets, and before long Jarlath was fast asleep.

Of course, she thought, this was nothing to him. He'd slept in worse conditions. Much worse. This fact didn't comfort her, though, and all the tumbling thoughts and foggy memories and conflicting emotions, both hers and Ondelle's, nagged at her as she listened to the throaty sounds of the Dark Forest beasts.

Chapter Six

Ondelle stumbled into the cottage as Fernatta of Gyllenhale opened the door.

"Ondelle!" Fernatta cried, helping her old friend into her gathering room, which doubled as her classroom, and into her high-backed storytelling chair. "Sit here. I'll fetch you some tea."

When Fernatta returned with a mug, Ondelle was leaning back, eyes closed, looking less like a High Priestess and more like a frightened old woman.

"I cannot . . ." Ondelle began. She opened her black moon eyes, watery with pain. "I cannot hold this Water energy any longer, Ferna. It is taking my strength, and I am using up the Dragon's Gift in order to conceal it. It must be released."

Ferna placed the mug in Ondelle's hands and pulled up an old mushroom chair beside her. She dropped into it with a heavy sigh. "I know, I know . . . and I feel terrible for saying such a thing, but I wish I didn't."

Ondelle placed a hand on the sturdy Earth Faerie's shoulder. "I am so sorry to burden you with all of this. But I trust you more than any other faerie in the forest."

Fernatta placed her own hand over Ondelle's. "I left Elderhood all those seasons ago to avoid these sort of things. I *impart* knowledge through my Life Task. Keeping secrets is counter to my nature. It pains me to do so."

"Sometimes we must do the uncomfortable, and absorb the pain, to maintain peace and balance in the forest."

"Uncomfortable is one thing," Fernatta pointed out. "Hiding the truth is another. How do you think Hrathgar's village-nest would feel knowing we banished the innocent and good in her just because we didn't know how to deal with the bad?"

"And you would prefer they share your suffering?"

"I . . ." Fernatta started, then dropped her hands into her lap and shook her head.

"It was a long time ago, Ferna."

"I still live with our decision every day."

Ondelle, too, often thought of the good Hrathgar, alone with her dark self up on Dead Mountain. She wondered if the two Hrathgars were still alive at all. She thought of Hrathgar's family and friends and neighbors busy at the marketplace or preparing for the next festival, going about their daily lives. The only decisions they had to make were which color featherpaints to swap for their bundle of reeds or how much candleweb spinning to do in exchange for a basket of seasoned gundlebeans.

None of them had any idea how Ondelle had been tortured over the past several seasons with the task of marking, no, *condemning*, another faerie to her fate. She was about to create a lonely life for some young faerie. A life of making the same hard decisions Ondelle had made, of seeing the world without innocence.

"No one else knows of my energy's origin," explained Ondelle. "Who else can I turn to? I just need assistance in this endeavor, a confidant."

"Endeavor?" Fernatta said. "That makes it sound like nothing at all."

"If it helps any, I've decided to transfer only the Water," said Ondelle, staring out Fernatta's window into the trees. "I will not subject the child to unnecessary turmoil. She will have enough burden soon enough."

"But what of your instructions?"

"I will release the other elements when the time is right."

Fernatta stood up and paced the room. After a while, she paused.

"I'm not sure how I feel about that," she finally said. "On the one hand, the child will live a more normal life, and you will live a longer one. But in the end, won't she require these gifts? I love you as a sister, Ondelle, but I cannot sacrifice my nephew's child's safety for you."

Ondelle stood and made her way to her friend. She took her hands in her own and gazed into her face, rounded over the years, but with the same kind eyes of her youth.

"I will keep watch over her," said Ondelle. "I will check in with her through our shared connection. I will protect her as I live, and when I no longer live, I will protect her even then."

"I have to ask," said Fernatta, "is this merely your personal fears speaking? We both know what would happen if you sacrificed one of your own elements, let alone both."

"Honestly," admitted Ondelle, "I am no longer sure." She smiled a sad, ironic smile. "But if you do not trust my instinct in this, tell me now, and I will bestow all three elements at once."

"And leave me to watch over and protect the child?" asked Fernatta. She let go of Ondelle's hands and moved to the window. Outside, the Gray Months' melancholy hues were surrendering to the Grow Months' brighter ones. "I don't think I could make such a decision."

Brigitta and Jarlath woke early and had a quiet breakfast of dried berries and honeyroll while still stuffed inside their tree. They didn't want to waste time cooking anything. Afterward, Brigitta gathered the firepepper and dustmist and she and Jarlath were on their way.

The forest was as she remembered: strange wet moss choked the trees, ivy thorns pointed out menacingly, and sour Dark Forest smells poisoned all spirit. But it was a little less frightening than the first time she had left her forest. Perhaps it was because she was prepared and had more tricks up her sleeve, perhaps it was because it was her own choice this time, or perhaps it was because she was with a dependable friend.

She would not drop her guard, however, she told herself as they flew, hiked, pushed, and climbed over the branches and brush all morning. She admired Jarlath's ability to focus. He did not fill the air with unnecessary chatter, or even speak when one of them helped the other through a narrow space or lifted brambles out of the way. They worked well together with Brigitta's sense of direction and Jarlath's vigilance.

His silent trust was a relief, as she was in no mood to discuss the guilt she felt around her secrets, the growing strength of Ondelle's memories, or her new knowledge of her Auntie's part in her destiny. Instead, she concentrated on moving forward, creating a rhythm and breathing to it. Determined not to stop until lunch. There was nothing she could do but continue with her plan.

Hypnotized by her own motion, she moved onward as if through a passageway that had been cut through the trees just for her. At first she thought it was merely directional instinct, but after several moonbeats, she realized the forest was actually tunneling around them. Walls of thick trunks, branches, vines, and leaves had slowly formed on either side as they traveled. Even the ground was swimming with ivies. She hovered in the air, looking back at the way they came, and forward again at where they were headed.

"What's wrong?" asked Jarlath, doing the same. "Oh."

"I don't like this," said Brigitta. "I feel like we're being wrapped up in a—"

The word "cocoon" sat on her tongue like a spoiled gundlebean. Minq had assured her the carnivorous caterpillars kept to their nests in the northeastern side of the forest. But what if he were wrong, she wondered as she scanned the tunnel for sticky caterpillar threads. What if things had changed in the Dark Forest since he had left?

No silk strands stretched across the branches, which was a relief, but as Brigitta pulled back a giant leaf to reveal a tangle of impenetrable forest, a horrible knot formed in her stomach. There was no way out save forward . . . or backward. And if anything like a carnivorous caterpillar did come through the forested tunnel after them, they would be trapped.

"Jarlath," she whispered, "listen."

He wrinkled his face in concentration. "I don't hear anything."

"Exactly," she said, "nothing. Nothing at all."

She couldn't really see the forest closing in on them, but she sensed it. In tiny, incremental shudderings, it was squeezing them in.

"We should turn back," she said, gesturing behind them. Nothing but forest tunnel as far as the eye could see. "Let's find another way."

They fluttered back, retracing their wing-beats, traveling slightly faster. Again, Brigitta felt the forest squeeze.

"Calmly, breathe," she said. "Don't let it know you're afraid."

"Don't let what know I'm afraid?" asked Jarlath. "And who says I'm afraid?" He forced a laugh to demonstrate just how not afraid he was.

As they flew, it was impossible to deny that the twisted forest tunnel was growing narrower. Finally, Brigitta stopped again. "No, no, we're going the wrong way. We must have gotten turned around."

"This is the way we came," Jarlath insisted. "I swear it."

"I can't feel the direction any longer," said Brigitta, trying to keep the panic out of her voice. "Let's go up."

As they looked up, they instantly knew that was not an option. The top, sides, and floor of the forest were the same wall of impenetrable greens, reds, and browns, of prickles and burrs, of bark and branch. There was no sky, no ground, no sound.

Until.

From far down the tunnel of forest, the vines shook, the branches trembled, and the tunnel began closing in.

"Come on!" Brigitta screamed and grabbed Jarlath's hand. There was no room to fly, so she trudged through the forest's tentacles, pushing and grunting and thrusting her way forward, dragging Jarlath after her.

"It's swallowing us up!" she shrieked, pulling his hand, which suddenly felt much too rough and bony. She squeezed around only to face a solid wall of forest. She was holding on to the end of a tree branch.

"Jarlath!" she called as the forest closed in around her. "Jarlath!

She kicked and screamed, tore at the trees until her fingers were cut and bleeding. She did not dare sit down for fear the forest would close around her and she'd suffocate.

For the Great Moon, cried a voice inside her head, *use what you know!*

She didn't know if it was Ondelle's voice or her own or a combination of the two, but it stopped her struggling.

At least breathe, she thought, and then said it out loud. "Breathe."

In, out went Brigitta's breath. In, out sighed the forest.

"Okay."

The air was dark and bitter and heavy. She did her best to concentrate, to balance all her energy by conjuring images of something powerful and steady. Silver scales came to mind, swimming back and forth, back and forth, in a warm current. She held the image until she was collected and focused enough and then sent out a tentative mind mist, seeping in through the slivers of space in the twisted mass of forest encasing her. Slowly, through the tiny spaces, her mind mist drifted, on and on, on and on.

There was no end.

Just as she was about to break the mind-mist connection, she sensed the trees loosening up, like untying a knot. She drew her mind mist back as the loosening approached. And then she could hear the unraveling, gaining momentum, twirling toward her.

A moonsbreath later, the forest opened up and she was looking through the barky, leafy tunnel into a flowered meadow. Before the rift could close again, she quickly stepped through. As she did, a vine snagged on the scepter secured to her back and yanked it from her shoulders. She spun around, reaching into the trees, but the scepter had vanished, and the forest threw up its massive wall once again.

"No!" she cried, pulling her hands away, but not before several thorns snagged her fingers and a branch sliced into her arm.

"No! No!" she shrieked at the wall and then collapsed to the ground in despair. How could she have let this happen?

She sat there for a moment feeling sorry for herself before turning to face the meadow. It was abnormally sunny, and she had to shield her eyes from the sudden brightness. She stood, squinting into the harsh light, as she gaped at her surroundings.

"Impossible."

She was standing in the lyllium field outside of Tiragarrow.

"Impossible," she repeated, whirling around and around.

It was exactly like the field outside of Tiragarrow. It even sounded like the lyllium field she used to lie in practically every day. It had the same buzzing, chirping noises, and the same dragonfly wing flutters. But there was no actual movement. Just the sound of movement. And this field was bordered by a most unwelcome forest. A thick and spiny thing.

"Jarlath?" she called as she stumbled through the meadow. The shape of it was just as her lyllium field. The breadth and pattern of flowers the same. She stomped on the ground and reached down to touch it. It was dry and hard and rocky. It should not have bore any lylliums at all.

When she straightened back up, a winged figure was sitting in the middle of the field. It didn't seem to be moving, so she tentatively flitted toward it. It was definitely faerie-sized, but she couldn't tell the color of its wings. Or its hair. Or detect any of its other features. It was like she forgot what it looked like even though it was right in front of her. Even as she grew closer, she knew she could see it, but nothing specific about it registered in her mind.

When she was but moments away, she called out again, "Jarlath?"

The beast, definitely a faerie, stood and faced her.

Its features were her own.

Tall and lanky, with olive skin and auburn hair split into two haphazard hairtails on either side of its head, it wore a green tunic and carried a brown pack on its back.

Brigitta's hands flew to her face, and she landed roughly in the meadow, staring at the Brigitta before her. She wasn't sure if she should be afraid or not. She had spent so much time speaking to herself in her Thought Mirror, she was used to being scrutinized by her own image. Was this creature some kind of wild Thought Mirror?

"Are you me?" she asked.

"Jarlath?" the other Brigitta squawked and cocked her head.

"Uh, definitely not," said Brigitta, backing away.

"Jarlath?" it squawked again, then awkwardly chomped its lips as if it were using a mouth it wasn't used to owning. It hopped up and down a few times, trying out its legs as well. It wiggled its fingers and cried out in glee.

Assuming it wasn't going to attack her, Brigitta put her hands on her hips. "Who are you? What happened to Jarlath?"

Her strange twin cocked its head in the other direction until it was parallel with the earth. It blinked at Brigitta with its eyes one above the other.

"Yeah," said Brigitta, backing away. "I can see you're not going to be any help."

The beast straightened its head, blinked a few more times, but remained where it was. Frustrated, Brigitta screwed up her face and stuck out her tongue at it. The beast stuck out its own tongue, long and purple, like a worm.

"Ewwwww." Brigitta shrank away.

It hopped up and down more adamantly, squawking like a fat bird calling to its mate. Brigitta glanced around the field to see who or what it was calling to. When she turned back around, the odd beast was directly in front of her, staring. She leapt back, still unsure whether the thing was dangerous or simply annoying.

As slowly and calmly as possible, Brigitta stretched out a tentacle of Water energy to see if she could empath its thoughts. Its mental walls were strangely solid for something that appeared to be a complete idiot. Then, its body parts began to flicker; one moment its arm was an arm, and the next moment she could see the forest behind it.

"What are you?" Brigitta demanded.

"Are you," it repeated, this time sounding a bit more like a faerie girl and not as much a clueless bird. Its face moved through a series of other faces: her Momma, Ondelle, Auntie Ferna, Fozk—as if trying them all on for size. Then it went back to her own face and squawked happily, flapping its arms.

Was it stealing images from her mind? She backed through the field. Even if it wasn't dangerous, it was a horrible thing, and it wasn't getting her get any closer to figuring out where she was, what had happened to Jarlath, or how to get the scepter back.

"Well, nice to have met you," said Brigitta finally, eyeing her strange doppelganger. "I hereby dub this Oddtwin Meadow. And if you aren't going to help me, Oddtwin, I'll just be on my way."

She moved closer to the edge of the meadow, and the Brigitta beast moved with her, keeping perfect pace.

"You're worse than my little sister," Brigitta joked nervously. For a moonsbreath, the oddtwin's face was that of Himalette's. Then it was back to her own.

"Stop that," Brigitta insisted as she scurried away.

"Stop that," the oddtwin repeated, following her.

Brigitta stopped, and the beast stopped. Then, it began to convulse. For a moment, it shook so hard it was completely blurred, and Brigitta couldn't tell one body part from the other. When it stopped shaking, it had four arms and four legs. It scrunched up its face, grunted, and a loud popping sound filled the air as a second beast burst from the first.

Two hopping, squawking Brigittas now stood in front of her.

"That can't be good," she said.

The two beasts hopped toward her and cocked their heads. Their movements reminded her of Roucho, her Poppa's featherless delivery bird, and suddenly a shower of broodnuts fell from the sky.

"Ow," said Brigitta as one cracked on her head.

"Ow," said the oddtwins.

Brigitta reached down and picked up one of the nuts. It certainly looked just like a broodnut. She cracked it open and a black beetle flew out, like the ones that had stolen her globelight. It dove at her face, and she frantically waved it away.

The other two Brigittas began to convulse.

"Nice oddtwins," she said, slowly moving away from them. "Good oddtwins."

She was now backed up against the forest wall. As she felt her way along the branches and trunks and ivies and leaves for an entrance of any kind, the beasts started to shake so violently it seemed the earth would open up beneath them. And again when they stopped there were twice as many arms and legs than there should have been.

"That's enough, really," said Brigitta. "I get it, you like to imitate things."

Again there were popping sounds and a moment later, two more Brigittas flew out. This time, they landed on all fours and hissed up at her.

"Bog buggers," Brigitta swore as she moved faster along the forest wall, pushing and shoving to no avail. She turned and flew, searching and searching for some way inside.

Pop! Pop! Pop! Pop! She glanced back in time to see eight Brigittas trailing her, some flying, some crawling, some hopping.

Her heart pounded as she picked up speed. Pop! Pop! Pop! Pop!

There was no way back into the forest. The only way to escape was up. She hovered in the air as dozens of oddtwins scurried toward her.

Pop! Pop! Pop! Pop!

Risking the winds, she fluttered higher and was immediately catapulted back into the wall of trees, grazing her cheek with a sharp branch. Warm blood trickled down her face as she untangled herself.

Pop! Pop! Pop! Pop!

There were now over a hundred beasts after her, but a moonsbreath away.

"Stop!" she called and threw her hands in the air. To her surprise, the creatures stopped mid-flight, mid-hop, mid-slither.

As they all stared at her, little gashes grew across their right cheeks, and blood began to drip from them. Only the blood was black instead of red. Brigitta wiped the blood from her own cheek and examined her hand. Red.

If this meadow somehow manifested things from her own life, maybe she could manifest something on purpose. Something useful. Something to help her escape.

But the meadow kept getting things wrong, so it had to be something simple. Something nonliving . . .

She glanced up. She needed something to help her navigate the winds.

When she looked back down, all the oddtwin eyes were still on her, studying her. She took a deep breath, filling herself all the way to her belly. With every bit of concentration she had, she released her breath and visualized a *wind-winder*. She felt the soft white cords of it, woven from sun-bleached reeds from the marsh farm. Another breath and she visualized each perfectly spellcast square of it. One more and she encased this vision in a cocoon of air, protecting it. She felt its lightness, its balance, and opened her eyes.

Every oddtwin cocked its head at her.

And then.

All at once, they started to convulse.

"Oh, hagworms," she swore. "Bog bugging hagworms."

These things were going to double and double until she suffocated underneath them. She turned and flitted along the trees. There had to be a way out. There had to be a vulnerable patch of forest somewhere. And then she saw it, up ahead, hanging from a branch: a wind-winder.

She squealed, flew as fast as she could, and snatched up the net, kissing it with a grateful smack, just as the field exploded in multiplying oddtwins. She flew straight into the center of the meadow, with oddtwins close behind. As she flew she loosened and expanded one of the wind-winder's squares and tucked herself inside, buffeting on the wind. The net wobbled while she spread it out in a globe shape. She'd never actually used one before, only watched as the Perimeter Guards practiced.

Hands slightly apart, palms facing each other, she quickly brewed up a patch of balanced air. It was like blowing glass, only without the glass, just the shape of the air. The first one slipped through her fingers, and she gathered it back up. Once it was steady, she slipped it into one of the net holes.

Below her, the lyllium field was completely covered with oddtwins, crawling and slithering around each other like a nest of bugs. A few dozen flew in circles about their heads and cawed up at her as she formed two more patches of air. But she was still flying too low to go over the forest, so she beat her wings, grunting her way higher against the heavy dark forest air.

She filled two more net holes, but still couldn't get control of the wind-winder and was hurtled toward the trees by a sudden gust. Thrusting both hands up, she created two air pockets, one in each hand, and lay them in place just before she collided with the thorny branches. The wind-winder kicked in and the gust was absorbed into the net.

She filled the remaining net holes and fluttered away from the trees. Below her, oddtwins tried to give chase, but the winds were too strong. She wobbled around until she got her balance. It was tricky, and physically exhausting, to fly, concentrate, and keep each net hole filled with conjured air. But still, she managed to get herself higher than the trees and make her way over the forest, hoping she could find Jarlath within the thickness of it.

Encased in her wind-winder, she fluttered along the border of the field, seeing nothing but twisted trees, trees, and more trees. She widened her route and went around again, and again, refilling each net hole as her air pockets dissolved. But she couldn't maintain this forever, she was already more than tired, and there was no place to land. Either she would have to risk crash landing in an impenetrable forest, or go back to the lyllium field and face the horde of bizarre Brigittas.

Three air pockets collapsed at once, sending the wind-winder eastward. Brigitta molded the air between her hands once more as she drifted farther away from the meadow. She backstroked her wings, trying to gain purchase, until movement caught her eye. She shifted direction and fluttered toward the motion.

Sitting among the trees was what appeared to be a massive nest. Beasts scuttled along its sides like giant hairy ants, carrying various items in their pincher mouths: branches, fruit, and other bugs. In the middle of the nest stood Jarlath. And in his hands was the scepter.

He didn't see Brigitta above him at first. Balancing in the mess, he carefully poked the scepter into the nest as he eyed the buggy beasts scurrying about their tasks.

"Jarlath!" Brigitta called from above. "Oh, thank the Dragon!"

Jarlath looked up eagerly, but the rest of him stayed completely still. "Don't thank it yet," he said carefully. "And watch out. You do not want to get stung by one of those guys."

As if to demonstrate, a furry little black beast climbed up the inside of the nest on eight spindly legs. When it reached the top, one of the enormous ant-like creatures slashed at it with its rear end, barely breaking ranks, and the little beast tumbled back down into the nest, landed against some debris, and did not get back up.

"I'll lower myself slowly and you get into the net. Just pull evenly on two connecting sides of a square."

"Gotcha," said Jarlath, keeping watch on the beasts circling the nest. His expression grew puzzled. "Where did you get that thing?"

Brigitta maneuvered herself directly over Jarlath and, with careful wing flutters, descended straight down. "Long story," she said.

As Jarlath reached for the net, he pulled too harshly and disturbed two air pockets. The wind-winder tumbled away, and Jarlath held on as they slid toward the side of the nest. Above them, the beasts stopped their scuttling and peered over the edge, antennae circling in the air.

"Get in!" Brigitta screamed, and Jarlath opened the square enough to crawl inside. They tried to coordinate their flying, but it was too cramped for both of them to fully open their wings.

The beasts began scurrying down the sides of the nest.

"Grab my waist from behind," instructed Brigitta, "and beat your wings in exactly the same rhythm as mine."

Jarlath did so and Brigitta swung them up, patching the air pockets in the net as they climbed, higher and higher, out of the reach of the bugs.

"Now you can thank the Dragon," called Jarlath, his heart pounding behind her.

"Not until we find somewhere to land," she said. "You scout, I need to concentrate on keeping this thing in the air."

They drifted northwestward. It was easier to fly with both their weight and wings working together, but still exhausting for Brigitta's mind. She needed to rest soon or they would certainly crash.

Four air pockets dissolved at once.

"Jarlath!" Brigitta called as they slipped in the air.

"We have to go north," he said.

"North?"

"Toward the mountains," he affirmed. "It's the quickest way out of the forest."

She conjured more air pockets to replace the ruined ones, but they were weaker. "We'll have to fly lower," she said, "or the wind will destroy all my work."

They descended and headed north, Brigitta's strength dwindling until she could no longer conjure any new air pockets. The remaining ones in the net holes would have to hold until they could land.

"Up ahead!" called Jarlath. "I see a plateau!"

Brigitta squinted into the horizon and indeed there was a plateau, which would make for an easy landing, if they could reach it before the wind-winder collapsed.

"Hold on," she said, more to herself than Jarlath.

From behind her, she felt Jarlath shake his body as if to restart it for the final stretch. He tightened his grip on her waist and beat his wings with hers. Together they flew, as steadily as they could, toward the plateau. But, one by one, the air pockets gave way, and the wind-winder grew more and more unstable. They tossed and twisted toward the cliff, the last few air pockets dissolved, and they spun backward into the side of the plateau.

They hit hard, Jarlath taking the brunt of it. He let go of Brigitta's waist and they both grabbed for something, anything, on the steep plateau to steady themselves. Jarlath found a handhold and reached for Brigitta. Together they stretched one of the wind-winder squares open and helped each other out. As they shook themselves free, the contraption flew from their hands like a frightened bird.

Brigitta looked up to the top of the plateau. "It's not so far!" she shouted above the wind. "We can do it!"

Jarlath nodded, his face scratched and smudged with dirt. Then he grinned. "Yeah, we've been in worse situations!"

It was true, and suddenly, they burst into laughter. The kind that was part relief and part disbelief. They caught their breaths and examined the dark forest spread beneath them. The hissing, writhing, reeking dark forest was not so menacing from above.

"You first!" Jarlath gestured upward.

They half-scrabbled, half-flew, fighting the wind up the side of the plateau, and pulled themselves over the top, falling to the ground between two tall stones. They lay face-down in the dry scrub, breeze chilling their skin, arms and legs and minds numb.

Brigitta turned her head so that she and Jarlath were facing each other, a few pokey reeds tickling her neck. "Wanna camp here for the night?"

"I thought you'd never ask."

With great effort, they hauled themselves up and were met by hundreds of standing stones, like giant haphazard teeth bursting from the earth. After rewrapping and attaching the scepter to Brigitta's back, they walked carefully among and around the stones, a few dozen hands tall, half as wide, but not very thick. Brigitta grabbed the edge of one of them and tried to shake the thing. It didn't budge.

"What do you suppose these are?" asked Jarlath, circling another.

"I don't know," said Brigitta, brushing at the stone's sandy roughness with her palm. "But they'll protect us from the wind."

"Do you think this is natural or faerie-crafted?"

"I'm not sure," said Brigitta. "They do feel sacred, but kind of . . . dead?" She walked all the way around one, contemplating its uses.

Jarlath pushed at another one with both hands, then leaned into it with his shoulder. "They seem sturdy enough."

Brigitta walked around the object again, fingers lingering on the stone. "There's an echo of faerie energy here. Like a place that has been swept, but some dust lingers."

She rounded the corner, faced him again, and grinned. "As long as those oddtwins can't reach us up here."

"What are oddtwins?" asked Jarlath.

"Well, that's what I call them."

They fluttered and roamed through the numerous standing stones while Brigitta related her story of the lyllium field and the strange mimicking beasts that multiplied like firesparks. As they moved farther into the seemingly endless stretch of stones, everything else disappeared from view, and their voices dulled as if entering a cave.

When she finished the part about visualizing the wind-winder into being, she asked, "So, how did you end up in that awful nest?"

"When we were separated by the forest," began Jarlath, "it basically swallowed me up and spat me back out in there." He held up his arms and examined the tree-branch and thorn scratches, now sealed with dry blood. "I was terrified; I thought I had landed in some giant bird's nest." He shivered. "Thank Faweh it was only deadly poisondarters."

"Yeah," laughed Brigitta, "thank Faweh."

"Still," Jarlath continued, "I couldn't fly out! I kept getting blown toward the sides of the nest."

"What about the scepter?" asked Brigitta. She stepped around a standing stone and froze.

"Oh, I found it lying next to me. I was trying to dig my way—" Jarlath ran into Brigitta. He peered around her.

They had come to the end of the plateau.

Below them, a raggedy carpet of forest transitioned into a long stretch of flat, golden land. Above the stretch of gold, a vast and endless world of shifting blackness met the sinister clouds and sky in a distance so far away it seemed impossible.

Brigitta's hands went instinctively to her chest for her hourglass and instead found Gola's lifeless moonstones. Tears sprung to her eyes as she clasped them to her heart, holding Gola close.

"The Sea of Tzajeek," she said.

Chapter Seven

"Whatever you are planning, I won't let you do it," said Elder Ondelle, sitting down on Second Apprentice Hrathgar's bed.

"Hmmm," said Hrathgar, dropping into a chair in front of her Thought Mirror, "I don't recall you ever having stopped me from doing anything before."

"I will go to the Elders," said Ondelle.

"Really? Run to the other Elders for help?" Hrathgar laughed and turned to the mirror, studying the contours of her face. "And I always thought you were the strong one."

"Asking for assistance is not a weakness."

"Maybe not," said Hrathgar, "but being disloyal to your friends is."

"You were the one who left us, Gar," Ondelle pointed out. "For a long time. And yes, if it comes to the good of one friend and the good of the whole forest," Ondelle caught Hrathgar's eyes in the mirror, "then my duty lies with the forest."

The eyes reflected in the Thought Mirror glanced toward Ondelle, startling her. Something flickered behind those eyes, something frightened. Something trapped inside that couldn't escape.

Hrathgar quickly turned away from her mirror to face Elder Ondelle. Her eyes now mimicked the cruelty in her smile.

Ondelle stood. "What have you done with her!" she demanded.

"Whatever do you mean?" asked Hrathgar.

"You are not Hrathgar!"

Hrathgar waved Ondelle off. "Don't be silly, of course I am.

I've changed, is all. I know things. I've been places no White Forest faerie has ever been before."

As Hrathgar spoke, she rubbed at something underneath her tunic. She slid it out and dangled it on its strap in front of her own face, admiring it. "I have more knowledge, more power. I will not be an Apprentice for long."

Ondelle gazed at the stone, drawn into it. Before she could stop herself, she reached over and touched it. Images swarmed her mind: *her hands on a young blue Water Faerie's face, a woman with skin like a tree, a circular vibrating ring, thought-looping across the arena to a sprite* . . . and in a moonsbreath the images scattered.

"Anything interesting?" Hrathgar smirked as she tucked the stone back into her tunic. She leaned closer to the shaking Ondelle. "Perhaps you saw your own woeful end?"

"No . . . no . . ." stammered Ondelle, backing toward the door. "I saw yours."

It was Hrathgar's turn to be shocked. She caught herself and began to laugh.

"A girl," said Ondelle, more to herself than to Hrathgar. "I sent a young girl . . . "

She fumbled for the door. As she yanked it open, Hrathgar called after her. "I look forward to meeting her some day!"

Ondelle slammed the door and leaned against it, Hrathgar's laughter vibrating through it from behind her. The air felt thin; she couldn't breathe. Her hands flew to her throat. She looked up and around frantically, trying to find someone who wasn't there. Gasping.

Brigitta snapped awake. Jarlath was leaning over her, snarling, hands around her throat. A moonsbreath later, he pulled his hands away, and stared at her, dazed.

She sat up, choking fresh air into her lungs. "Jarlath! What in Faweh?!"

"Are you all right?" he asked, blinking in confusion. "You cried out in your sleep."

"You were trying to strangle me!" she accused, rubbing at her sore neck.

"What?" He shook his head vehemently. "Why would I do that? You were having a nightmare or something. You cried out. I just joggled your shoulders to wake you up."

Brigitta leaned back on her elbows and stared at him. He looked back at her, eyes only full of concern. Had she been having a bad dream? Why would he have been choking her? It didn't make any sense.

But it wasn't a dream.

She sat up again and hugged her knees to her chest. "I was having one of Ondelle's memories."

"In your sleep?"

"Yes, you know that happens."

Jarlath twisted around and sat cross-legged in front of her, pondering this. "Then how do you know they're not dreams?"

"I just do," she said defensively.

He nodded agreement, but there was hesitation in his motion.

"Well, it *was* a little different this time," she admitted. "Ondelle and Hrathgar had a fight and Ondelle started choking. Then, it was like she was looking for someone. And I had the strangest feeling it was me."

"You see?" he said, visibly relieved. "A bad dream." He lay back down with his arms under his head. "Maybe all your own memories and emotions are getting mixed up with them?"

Brigitta only shook her head. It was not a dream. She could tell the difference. She knew that memory was of the night Hrathgar tried to steal the power of the Hourglass. Ondelle had warned the other Elders. Hrathgar was overtaken by her evil side, then was split in two, and her two selves were banished to Dead Mountain.

Was Ondelle trying to warn Brigitta, too?

"My neck," she said, rotating it around. "It hurts."

"You probably strained it getting up to the plateau," Jarlath said, "or using that wind-winder."

"I guess," she said. She didn't want to talk about it any more. Something wasn't right.

"I'll take watch now," she told him. "Your turn to get some rest."

The sky was already lightening by the time Jarlath's breath turned to the deep and rhythmic cadence of sleep. Brigitta ventured closer to the edge of the plateau, leaning up against one of the stony pillars and gazing across the black sea as it licked the sand. A faint rushing sound glided through the air and she grew excited by the prospect of touching that water.

She flew back to where her traveling companion slept curled beneath a petrified pillar, and her heart trembled as she watched him sleep. If anything were wrong with him . . . if he wasn't the real Jarlath . . .

Had he been replaced by some oddtwin? No, she thought, those things couldn't string two words together on their own, let alone have a conversation. But she could still feel his hands around her neck and see the maniacal look in his eyes. And she couldn't shake the image of Hrathgar, terrified, in the Thought Mirror.

What was it if it wasn't something that happened back in that bug nest? How long had he been acting strange? Did it have something to do with losing touch with the Ancients, or, and she shuddered to even think of this, had he been duping her the whole time, working for Croilus and spying on the White Forest? Her gut told her, no, it couldn't be. It was something else.

And she didn't feel safe any more.

There was a little *blurping* sensation inside her mind, as if a bubble had popped in her head. She kneeled down and put her hands on the ground to steady herself.

Hello, a soft voice intruded. A voice she didn't recognize, but which sounded as if shaped from her own thoughts.

"Hello?" she called out loud.

Hello, the voice inside her head said again, accompanied by movement behind one of the stones at the edge of the plateau.

Brigitta picked herself back up and crept around the stones to find a beast huddled against one of them. Its skin was so light it glowed, and so thin she could see veins and organs within and a dark shape reverberating in its chest. Its eyes were bulgy black, like large wet pebbles, and its nose resembled a snake's, just two small pits in the center of its face. There were two slits in each side of its head instead of ears, and the skin over its lips was swollen and bluish, though its mouth was shaped much like her own. For clothing it wore only short trousers made of rough green plants.

It shivered as it held up its hands, palms forward, five webbed fingers on each.

I being Narru, it said without moving its mouth. *You hearing me?*

She nodded as the beast tottered forward into the gathering light, and she decided it was a male beast. He steadied himself against the closest standing stone.

"What do you want?" asked Brigitta.

Want? he asked, pulling his hand away and sifting through the grains of sand that had come loose in it. When he looked back to her face, he blinked a few times, lids closing sideways across his eyes, like curtains. He seemed quite young. She had no idea how young, he just had a childlike energy about him, curious and frightened.

"Where are you from?" she asked, more gently this time.

He smiled. *Pariglenn, Flota of the Saari. Having you knowing of this place and Saari?*

She couldn't have heard that right. "Pariglenn?" she asked. But as soon as the word left her lips, she recognized some of the Saarin's features from the mural at Croilus when they had found the Purview. The mural of the World Sages. This boy was from one of the ancient civilizations.

"But that's across . . ." She gestured out to the sea. "How in the Dragon's name did you get here?"

He gestured wide with his arms. *Going through a great—*

His face registered shock and pain and he fell forward to the ground. Behind him stood Jarlath with the scepter.

"Jarlath!" Brigitta cried, rushing to him and grabbing the scepter from his hands.

He grinned at her. "I knew that thing would come in handy!"

"What have you done!" She kneeled down to Narru and felt his head. There was a nasty bump on the base of his skull.

"What do you mean?" said Jarlath. "I was keeping this thing from attacking you."

"He wasn't attacking me," she said. "We were having a conversation."

"I hate to break it to you," said Jarlath, "but you were talking to yourself. You were not having a conversation."

"He was talking to me in my mind," she explained.

"Would you listen to yourself?" he cried.

"I know what I heard."

"And you can trust anything you hear in the Dark Forest?"

"This is different," she insisted. "Don't you remember his kind from the mural at Croilus?"

Jarlath's hands went to his head and he groaned. "For Faweh's sake, Brigitta, what is wrong with you?"

"What's wrong with you?" she retorted. She bent over to look into Narru's unblinking eyes. They had a thick film over them that she hadn't noticed before.

"He was putting some kind of spell on you," continued Jarlath in a gentler tone.

With her pinky finger, Brigitta gently touched the Saarin boy's cheek. It, too, had a thick, transparent layer over the skin.

Jarlath pulled her back. "You'd better not get too close."

"Stop it, Jarlath, he's not going to hurt me."

"You're right, he's not." Jarlath pushed Brigitta aside and, using his hands and feet, rolled the strange beast toward the edge of the plateau.

"What are you doing?" Brigitta fluttered over to Jarlath and yanked on his arm. Without the protection of the stones, the wind whipped at her wings as she struggled to pull him back.

"What does it look like I'm doing?" said Jarlath with a shove. "Getting rid of the ugly thing."

"You can't do that!" she cried. "He hasn't done anything wrong!"

She pulled harder on Jarlath's arm until he turned and snarled at her. "Do you want my help getting to your Dragon or not?"

She let go of his arm and stepped back. "Jarlath, please!" she begged him.

"You are so naïve. No wonder your forest is in danger." He turned back to the mysterious boy from Pariglenn and gave one final shove with his hands.

The Saarin fell over the side and Brigitta dove after him, getting under his body and catching him. He was heavier than he looked, dense with muscles, and she plummeted several wing-lengths until she could catch her balance. She fluttered frantically in the gusts of wind as she climbed back up. Jarlath simply stood on the edge of the cliff, arms crossed, scowling at her.

With a heave, she pushed the boy back up over the top of the plateau, his limbs flopping like dead fish. As his body fell over, something on his right hand caught her eye.

"Let's see if you can do that again," said Jarlath, sticking his foot on Narru's stomach.

"Wait! Look!" Brigitta held up the Saarin's hand. On his two middle fingers were matching rings, identical to the ones the Nhords had used to get through their Purview to find Brigitta in the Valley of Noe.

"Oh." Jarlath's expression softened, and then his shoulders slumped as, all at once, the anger drained from his body. He looked down at his feet as if the anger were puddled there.

"I'm sorry." He looked back up, dark hair whipping across his face. His deep blue eyes had regained their usual warmth. "I guess . . . I'm a little rash sometimes. I was just trying to protect you."

The Saarin moaned and shifted himself into a sitting position. His curtain eyelids opened as his hand went to the back of his neck. Thick lips pouted beneath his confused expression. Much *unfriendly*.

Brigitta helped the boy up and led him back to the protection of the stones. Jarlath followed in silence.

"Narru, this is Jarlath," she said, holding her hands out between them. "He can't hear you in his mind, so he thought you were going to hurt me."

The Saarin stared intently at Jarlath with his moist eyes. Jarlath shifted uncomfortably. *You being right. He having no hearing.*

"Well," said Brigitta as Jarlath and the Saarin regarded each other. "Maybe we should have some breakfast?"

Narru slipped behind one of the giant sand teeth and pulled forth a knapsack. It was brimming with dried fruits and salted tubers the likes of which Brigitta had never seen, even in the lushest White Forest farms. They were bright and fragrant, incongruous with the hazy morning above and threatening forest below.

At first, Jarlath wouldn't eat any of the Saarin's food. But, not wanting to appear rude or distrustful, Brigitta took one bite of everything Narru offered, and several bites of something he called lingomana, which had a crisp, tangy outer peel and a sweet pulpy inside. Her delighted sighs finally convinced Jarlath to taste it.

My sharing, your sharing? asked the Saarin in Brigitta's mind.

"Oh," she said, laughing, "you want to try something of mine?"

The Saarin nodded happily and Brigitta dug out some honeyroll for him. He crumbled it up in his fingers, enjoying its texture before filling his mouth with it. If he could have gone cross-eyed, Brigitta was sure he would have from sheer pleasure.

"This is all very nice," grumbled Jarlath. "But don't we have an important mission?"

He was right, of course. It had just been nice for Brigitta to forget herself for a while in Narru's cheerful energy. "Narru," she started, placing a hand on his, "we need to know where you got those rings."

"Puh," he said out loud and nodded. He popped his lips a few more times and felt them with his fingers.

My Foundings, he said, *having ring guarding*. Brigitta repeated what he said to Jarlath.

"Foundings?" he asked.

You not having? the Saarin said. *The ones of your keeping. Protecting and feeding, knowledge giving.*

"You mean parents?" asked Brigitta. "Our parents raise us, take care of us."

Sure, yes, making like that. Gatamuel and Sarilla. He having ring gifting and he giving mate Sarilla ring gifting. Now I having ring gifting. One for me, one for my mate giving.

"I see," said Brigitta, not bothering to translate for Jarlath, who was losing his patience beside her. "But do you know where the rings come from originally?"

Saari tellings of ring giftings from faeries.

"Yes!" Brigitta cried, wanting to hug the young Saarin.

"What?" demanded Jarlath. "What did he say?"

"Just a moment," Brigitta told Jarlath. "Narru, did a little fuzzy light come to you and did you go through a Purview to get here? A large round metal structure?"

The Saarin grinned wide with his bubbly lips. *Five sun risings past, floating light coming and playing with my thinking. Light helping me searching for Blood Seed. Making of Pariglenn. Heart of land.*

Little floating light coming to right Saarin. Narru patted his chest proudly. *No Saarin land walking like me. I practicing in light and dark, land walking.*

In the growing daylight, Brigitta translated as the Saarin explained that Flota of the Saari was his home, a series of floating and ever-changing islands off the eastern coast of Pariglenn. Ever since the Great World Cry had overrun Pariglenn with the element of Earth, the Saari spent the majority of their time in the ocean, as the land on Pariglenn was so fertile that everything grew faster than the residents could cope with. All of the beasts on Pariglenn itself either flew or dug and were constantly on the move.

Staying on land, being still, and you being buried, said Narru.

The small moving islands prevented the vegetation from growing too quickly, but also kept the communal Saari vigilant, as they were always adjusting to the rearrangement of their neighbors. The motion of the waves and tides were incorporated into all aspects of their lives. They were so accustomed to the movement of the water, however, that they were susceptible to "land sickness."

Not I, Narru said, eyes shining with pride, *I practicing land walking in secret. I going ashore and climbing trees.* He held up a webbed foot and extended some claws from each toe, grinning. *Much sharp from tree-climbing.*

Since the first time he had heard the tales from his *ersafounding*, his grandmother, Brigitta deduced, the young Saarin had been obsessed with finding the ancient Blood Seed, the "heart of land" as he called it, from which all roots on the continent supposedly began. The myth was that whoever found the origin of the roots would have the power to transport himself across Faweh. He felt a calling to find this Blood Seed, and his preoccupation with it made the other Saarin "concerning" for him.

"I know the feeling," muttered Brigitta.

Little floating guiding me to Blood Seed. Making purpose. Much meaning to me. So much, looking for origin even in dreamings.

It took Narru three suns to reach the center of Pariglenn, only stopping for brief naps in the trees, fearful he would be suffocated by the overgrowth if he slept too long. When he reached the center of the continent he found what looked like a red barren hill, but on closer inspection, discovered it was a mound of thin roots, so tightly interwoven he could climb them. And when he did, he was met by a round, silver structure engulfed in the roots. The whisper light slipped through it, and it began to hum and twist, loosening itself. The roots dropped away to reveal silver carvings shifting around the ring. He followed the whisper light through and landed on the plateau.

When he finished his story, he smiled. *Little floating making mind knowings.* He pointed to Brigitta. *I knowing being with you.*

Excited by the similarities, Brigitta related her experiences with the Purview in Noe and the Nhords, who came from the northern continent of Araglenn.

"Jarlath, Narru!" she exclaimed. "There must be a Purview on each continent. That's how everyone else came to visit the faeries in Noe. I bet there's two more to be opened, one on Carraiglenn and one on Storlglenn!"

"So what if they're all opened?" asked Jarlath, crossing his arms in front of him. "How does that help us right now?"

"I don't know," she admitted, "but I know someone who will." She turned to her new friend. "Narru, how would you like to come with us to find the Eternal Dragon?"

As Brigitta and Jarlath packed up their belongings, the Saarin chipped away at the top of the plateau, and then buried the cores, seeds, and stems of his food.

"I don't think anything will grow up here," Brigitta told him.

Not doing for growing, he answered, *doing for feeding. Land hungry.*

"Oh, well," she shrugged, "I guess if that keeps it from eating us . . ."

"Hey," asked Jarlath from around one of the stones, "have you seen my knife?"

"Where did you leave it?" asked Brigitta, wrapping up the scepter once again and strapping it to her back.

Jarlath got down on his hands and knees and wiped at the ground. "I didn't leave it anywhere; it was around my leg!"

"Maybe it fell off somewhere?" she asked.

"You've been with me all morning, you know I haven't been anywhere." He stood back up and paced around the standing stones until he came back and faced the Saarin.

"You!" he accused. "Open up your bag!"

"Jarlath!" Brigitta scolded him.

Narru gazed up from where he squatted on the ground, and Jarlath kicked a fruit core out of his hands, sending it flying off the cliff.

"Open your bag!"

Narru gestured at his bag and Jarlath ripped through it, pulling out a water canteen, more fruits, berries, nuts, and tubers. No knife. Jarlath stood there and scowled, breathing heavy through his teeth, nostrils flaring, as if he were about to charge.

"Jarlath," said Brigitta with all the calm she could muster, "maybe you should sit down for a while?"

Without warning, he lunged at her. But before he could reach her, he froze, his eyelids fluttered, and he fell to the ground.

The Saarin's bulgy eyes bulged even more. *You powerful telling at doing,* he said in awe.

"That wasn't me," she said, rushing to Jarlath's side. She felt his face and neck; he was alive and breathing. "I have no idea what just happened. But it's not the first time he's acted so strange. I'm really worried. Something's been wrong with him for a while."

I sensing your mistrusting. The Saarin lifted a flap on his leafy pants and revealed the frore dagger embedded flat against his skin, as if in clay. He peeled the knife off, leaving a dagger-shaped impression on his thigh, which he rubbed to reform the skin.

Maybe you should keeping. He handed the knife to Brigitta.

Against her better judgment, and everything she had promised herself she wouldn't do, Brigitta settled her breathing and sent a mind mist out to empath Jarlath's thoughts. What she felt was a dark barrier, and something confused and frantic behind it. Like the real Jarlath was trapped beyond her reach.

Then, she sensed that he sensed her, on the other side of the barrier. Just like when Ondelle had sensed Hrathgar's good inside the mirrored eyes of Hrathgar Evil. Brigitta sent tendrils of mind mist to search for a way inside, but there was no way to get through.

When she pulled away she realized the morning had passed and they were still on the plateau. She had no idea what to do. Some spell had been cast on Jarlath and she didn't even know when it had happened, how it had happened, or who had cast it. She had to get him back home to the Elders as soon as possible. One of them might know what to do.

But as she gazed out to the sea, so close now, the thought of turning back dissolved into grief. "Oh, Jarlath," she murmured at the expanse of water.

Before they had crossed The Shift, he had made her promise that she would go on no matter what. "You knew something was wrong, didn't you? You made me promise because you knew." She almost laughed, thinking about how furious he would be if she ignored her promise. She sniffed before she even realized tears were falling down her cheeks.

When she turned back around, Narru was wiping Jarlath's face of dust so tenderly it gave her a kind of hope. There was something comforting about the Saarin, like there had been something comforting about Abdira and Uwain. Like they were all connected. Like they were meant to find each other.

"Narru," she said, "I don't think he's coming out of this spell. Not without help from someone who knows more magic than I do."

Finding this helping now?

"I'm going to leave him here," she said, attempting to sound braver than she felt, "and come back for him later."

I helping, said the Saarin. *Leaving of foods and water in case waking.*

"Good idea." Brigitta looked around and picked up a chalky black rock. "I'll leave a message, too."

They moved Jarlath behind one of the thicker standing stones to protect him from the wind and bundled him in a blanket. Brigitta set up a dustmist camouflage for good measure and on the stone in front of him scratched with a rock:

WAIT HERE

KEEPING MY PROMISE

BACK SOON

"I'm sure he'll be fine," she said, choking back further tears. She leaned down and kissed the top of his head. "Come on, Narru, before I change my mind."

The young Saarin was right about his adaptation to land. A tremendous climber, he was limber and lithe, using the extended claws on his fingers and toes to dig into the rock face. Still, it was terribly windy and slow going. Brigitta flew next to him in case he should lose his footing, which he did several times, but the mind-connection between them made her anticipate each fall, and she caught him after he had barely left the rock. By the time they hit the forest floor beneath the plateau, it was well into the afternoon.

Odd, said the Saarin, once they had rested for a bit. *Land being so still and quiet.*

"Quiet?" asked Brigitta, shivering as she listened to the thrum and hum of the dark forest beasts and bugs. "Hardly. Listen to all those things."

Not beasts, land itself. Not earth growing like Pariglenn. He put his hand to the ground, like feeling for a heartbeat, and smiled.

"Maybe some day I'll take a trip to Pariglenn, and you can show me where you live."

Yes! The Saarin stood back up. *Shall we seeing Dragon now?*

Narru sprung along on the backs of his feet, almost like a frog, as Brigitta hiked and trudged and flew through the thick forest. Traveling with Narru reminded her of her journey to Dead Mountain with Himalette. Curious and excited, Narru didn't seem to realize how dangerous the forest could be.

"Narru," asked Brigitta, "do you have giant caterpillars on Pariglenn? Or giant frogs? Or giant beasts of any kind?"

Saari giants of Pariglenn, he answered. *Many giant beasts swimming in far out deep water. Only small beasts living on earth land. Much too quick earth land. All beasts swallowing up unless moving.*

"Swallowed up?" said Brigitta, and the Saarin nodded. "Perhaps I wouldn't like it then."

The woods were dense, the thorns sharp, sticky webs and spittle caught on their hands and faces and Brigitta's hair, but they still managed a steady pace. They grew quiet, saving their energy for moving through the forest, until the trees began to thin and a new sound, a muffled and gusty roar, filled the air.

"Shhh, what's that?" asked Brigitta. She hovered in the air and listened to the rhythmic rumbling beyond the trees.

Narru leaped up and down with his hands in the air. "Puh!" He popped his thick lips together. "Puh! Puh!" He pointed ahead of them excitedly.

The waving, his words reverberated in Brigitta's mind, *sea calling.*

Narru raced ahead of her, through the last of the trees, and she pushed herself to keep up with him. The roaring grew louder, the air colder, and the forest broke away.

They were met with a stretch of blustering sands that extended north and south into the distance until devoured by rocky mountains that shot into the sky, impaling the large grumbling clouds overhead.

Not being in sea since five sun risings! said Narru, and he leapt through the spinning sand dervishes, scattering pebbles and shells with his long feet.

"Narru, no!" Brigitta fluttered after him, squinting as the sands pelted her face. "Wait!"

Ignoring her calls, Narru splashed into the dark waters and disappeared.

"Narru!" she called again as she reached the water's edge. "Narru!" she cried desperately.

She landed in the wet sand, away from the wind-blown grains. The sea that she had thought was completely black was nothing of the sort. It was dark blue, darker than Jarlath's eyes, with grayish foam that rode the crests of the waves and sinister shadowy plants that stole what little light filtered down from the skies. She could see nothing past them, had no idea what might lie underneath.

"Bog buggers." Brigitta paced back and forth, dodging the water as it lapped the shore. She leaned down and stuck her hand in a small wave as it approached and the icy coldness of it shocked her.

If Narru hadn't been drowned by the sea's weeds, he had certainly frozen to death. Or been eaten by something. Whatever lived in the sea.

Her mission suddenly returned to mind. The Eternal Dragon!

She ripped the scepter from her back, conjuring Ondelle's memory. She had to summon the cliffs. Flitting back over the whirling sands, she buzzed up the beach where she thought the rocks should be. Sure enough, there they were, just like they had been in Ondelle's memory.

She felt vindicated and relieved. The Elders were wrong. It was not simply a matter of exhaustion and grief. She would summon the cliffs and the Dragon, and the Dragon would save Narru and Jarlath and the White Forest!

Her heart pounded as she approached the V-shaped stones. Like she remembered, they were about three hands high and flat on the top, like long narrow platforms.

She unwrapped the scepter and lifted it over her head, bringing it down hard into the sand, which accepted it easily. And then the sand took hold, like a baby's mouth around its thumb. She let go, and the scepter stood there on its own between the rocks.

She fluttered back toward the beach and waited for the rumbling to begin.

A little sand storm licked at her wings.

The waves crashed and rolled onto the shore.

The stones were still.

"Come on!" yelled Brigitta. "I did what I was supposed to do!"

Nothing. The stones remained exactly as they were, and a moment later, the scepter spat itself out into the sand.

Perhaps she hadn't shoved it into the sand hard enough. She flew back up to the rocks, picked up the scepter, and thrust it back in.

The rocks were still. A moment later, and the sand spat the scepter out once again.

Brigitta! came Narru's voice in her mind.

She whipped around to face the water just as the little Saarin leapt from the sea and bounded up the beach toward her, panic on his face. *Coming, coming up to beach!*

"Narru!" Brigitta cried. "Thank the Moons, I thought you were gone."

When he reached her, he grabbed her arms with his slick wet hands, claws extended, snagging her skin. *Coming up to beach! Many not-beings!*

"Ow!" she cried, and as she pulled away from him she saw something emerging from the water.

She and Narru leapt over the two platform rocks and squished themselves as flat as possible. Brigitta eased up to the space between them and peered through. More than one something was emerging from the sea. A whole flock of colorless winged somethings advanced together, as if to a piece of music only they could hear. Dozens and dozens and dozens of them appeared, lining up in formation along the shore. Amassing like shadowflies on a honeyed branch.

Faeries, Brigitta realized. Faeries larger than Brigitta had ever seen. Lifeless, yet somehow moving. Enchanted dead. As they emerged, each found a position on the shore and stopped, face forward, expressionless and waiting.

It took almost a moonbeat for all of them to gather on the shore, and once they had, they shuffled to part in the middle. A shimmering bubble rose from the sea and floated up the beach, landing between the parted faeries.

The bubble popped.

Brigitta's world wobbled around her, and she had to sink her hands into the sand to steady herself. For standing on the beach, in one of his ridiculous purple robes, was Croilus of Noe.

Chapter Eight

The Dragon sped past Ondelle in a silver streak, and the water around her cleared. In front of her was another bubble, just like her own, and a young faerie was trapped inside. She had dual elements, Water and Earth, and looked eerily familiar, but larger than any young White Forest faerie would be. Her eyes were closed, and her face relaxed, as if enjoying a gentle dream. Most definitely alive, she breathed long, slow breaths, but beyond that, Ondelle had no idea what state she was in or how long she had been that way.

The Eternal Dragon sped by again, this time clearing the waters farther behind the encapsulated faerie. Beyond her stood row upon row of colorless faeries without bubbles. Ghostly things, although not translucent; solid and organic, like living statues.

The Dragon circled around the rows of faeries and headed back toward Ondelle. She caught Its eyes and was instantly lost in their abyss. For a moonsbreath, it felt as if her mind were about to leave her body. It was so frightening, yet so exhilarating, that when the Dragon turned away, disconnecting her from Its powerful gaze, she slumped to the ground.

When she arose, there was a new orb upon her scepter. Still in a daze, it took a moment before she realized what the Dragon had done. The orb was beautiful, sparkling like a newborn star. It was her destiny; it was her charge.

"Welcome," spoke the faerie in the bubble.

Transfixed by the Dragon's Gift, Ondelle had not noticed the faerie awaken. With her eyes open, she no longer appeared so young. Deep and bright crystal blue, they held both innocence and wisdom. Joy and pain.

"I am Ondelle of the White Forest." Ondelle bowed, not sure what was custom when an elemental faerie met an Ancient for the first time.

"I am Narine of Noe," the Ancient said. "Please, stand for your knowing."

The High Priestess straightened up, ready to receive, her scepter grasped with both hands. Narine fluttered toward her until their two bubbles touched. She spread her hands forward and the bubbles mingled, then merged. A warm vent of air wafted into Ondelle's watery cocoon and Narine took hold of the orb.

A sudden burst of energies and images flooded Ondelle's being until Narine placed a hand on her arm, and they subsided into a gentler flow. Still, they were such disconnected thoughts and feelings and memories and dreams that she could not make any sense of them.

"Do not try to sort them as they come, nor force a meaning," said Narine. "It takes its own time for a body to figure out how to live with its knowing."

Ondelle nodded as Narine pulled her hands away. Her skin grew cold without the Ancient faerie's touch. Narine then pressed her hands upon her own chest and belly. They settled and her body quivered a bit. Her hands appeared to sink into herself, reaching inside to extract a nebulous entity.

She slowly moved the entity through her bubble, and it pulsed in the air like a heartbeat. She held it up to Ondelle; it was her Water energy.

Ondelle gasped. She had no idea elements could be extracted from living faeries, only ascended during dispersements. Did this mean Narine was no longer alive? And how could she be anyway, it now dawned on Ondelle, after one thousand season cycles?

Narine released the element to Ondelle, who took it in her own hands. She couldn't exactly touch it; she more held the air around it as it swirled and beat in front of her.

"This you are to give when the time is right," said Narine. "As my energies were given to you before you were born, so you will pass your three on to a new faerie for the future of Faweh. Above all, these energies must be protected. They are the last of their kind."

While the Water energy seeped into Ondelle's being through the palms of her hands, Narine pulled her bubble away and they became two again. The Ancient faerie girl drifted back to her original spot on the ocean floor, and then took root, with the haunting formation of Ancient faeries behind her.

"But," Ondelle called to Narine as the energy dissipated into her being, "how am I to give it and to whom?"

"You will know when the time is right," said Narine. Now bonded solely with her Earth energy, she appeared smaller and more fragile and somehow, farther away. "And when the time is right, you will know."

Brigitta opened her eyes, shook her head, and shivered in the cold dark air. She lifted her face, neck throbbing, and a layer of sand stuck to it. Wiping it with her hand, she tried to recall where she was and the last thing that had happened before—

"Narine!" She bolted upright and spied over the rocks in front of her to the beach beyond.

Then she remembered the last thing she had witnessed before being assailed by Ondelle's memory: Croilus and a force of entranced Ancients. But why would the Ancients obey him? What had he done to them and how had he done it?

She recalled the bubble Croilus had been encased in, just like the one in Ondelle's memory. Did that mean Croilus had been visited by the Dragon? Had Croilus called up the rocks on the beach?

She looked down to the space between the rocks, hoping it could tell her something. But the hole she had made earlier that day was already refilled with sand.

Croilus left Noe with Mabbe's scepter; it had allowed him to travel through the Purview. Perhaps Croilus had known exactly what he was doing and where he was going. Perhaps his plan had always been to get Mabbe's scepter renewed by the Eternal Dragon.

Did that mean Croilus now had the power of Blue Spell?

Had the Eternal Dragon made a mistake?

Brigitta?

"Narru!" She twisted around and saw the Saarin scrambling down from a tree in the forest.

Thinking you disappearing like Jarlath, he said, shaking with relief. *Thinking I being alone.*

A wave of pity washed over her. The poor stranger had discovered much about the outside world in a short amount of time. What she had discovered a few season cycles ago: the world was not a safe place.

She was very glad to see him, but troubled by the memories now crowding her head. She didn't even know where to start.

"Narru," she said urgently. "What happened? Tell me everything."

Man faerie flying with not-living faeries. He pointed toward the mountains. *All going away.*

"How long ago?"

Long as your sleeping.

"The man faerie in the purple robe," she tried again as gently as possible, "did he have a scepter with him?" She held up her own. "Like this one?"

Oh, yes, having like that. He nodded.

Something else occurred to her. "All those faeries were colorless, right? Like spirits?"

Narru nodded. *Not-living.*

"There wasn't a young girl faerie with bright blue eyes and silvery hair and green wings?"

No faerie as her I seeing.

Brigitta leapt up and grabbed her scepter. "We have to find her." She turned to the Saarin, who blinked his sideways eyelids at her. "You have to find her."

❦❦

Without a bubble encasing from the Eternal Dragon, it would be impossible for Brigitta to find Narine in the bone-chilling water. It would be too dark and murky to see, even with a globelight, let alone breathe. Narru, on the other hand, was built to swim in the ocean.

She described what she could from Ondelle's memory of her visit with Narine and asked Narru if he thought he could communicate with her.

Yes, this I believing. He nodded emphatically. *And when you speaking in mind body with me, we speaking to Narine.*

"Wait, you mean I can empath your mind and speak with her through you?" she asked.

Yes, you speaking with Jarlath in earth body. Speaking with Saarin in mind body.

"Narru, I can't understand half of what you say, but I think you're making complete sense."

The day had grown dim and windy. They trudged back down to the shore, holding their arms across their faces to protect against the pelting sands. A gust came off the water, yanking at Brigitta's wings, so she turned and walked backward, throwing them wide so that they wrapped around her, keeping the sands away. As she pushed her way to the shore, she studied the mountains to the north and the long plateau where Jarlath was hidden.

"Narru," she said, "Croilus went that way?"

Yes.

A heavy pang of guilt shot through her heart. "Hold on, Jarlath," she said.

She hoped for his sake they could find Narine. Imagine, she thought, Narine herself! Friend to Gola, daughter of the High Sage. Certainly she would know how to help them.

As the sand storms dissipated, and the beach transitioned into lapping waves, Brigitta turned back around and sat upon a small log, calling for Narru to stop. She removed the remaining globelight half from her pack, lighting it up to demonstrate, then breaking it into smaller slices and handing one to him.

He shook his head, amused. *Saarin own light making.*

"If you say so," she said. He waited as she stuck the slivers of light into the sand, little crescent moons glowing up at them. Then she closed her eyes and misted her mind out, tentatively reaching for his, as unfamiliar and awkward as a first kiss.

When she reached his mind, she allowed a few drops of Water energy to trickle into the space behind his eyes, and they settled there, almost as if sitting down in a chair that had been pulled out just for her.

This is how you all communicate, she said as it dawned on her. *By visiting each other's minds.* It made good sense for creatures whose homes were always shifting on the sea.

She sensed his mind assent without any words. It was obvious Narru was adept in this giving and receiving of "mind body" talking. It must be instinctual to the Saari. Effortless, like breathing.

Amazing, she said, her own thoughts reverberating in his mind.

Opening your eyes, he said.

She did, and she could somehow see him and the ocean beyond at the same time she could see her own self through his eyes. He viewed the world in what she could only describe as a tender light. His eyes took in far more detail and depth and color than a faerie's eyes did.

All right, she thought inside his mind, *I'm ready.*

Through the Saarin's eyes she dove into the water. It was murky, but he was built to move and live in it. His body emitted a glow that extended evenly through the gloom. She felt no shock of coldness, no fear of drowning, no sting when the salty wetness hit.

He was skilled at holding her mind with his, even more so than Ondelle had ever been. It felt like he was holding the "hand" of her mind, keeping her there. He propelled himself forward with powerful webbed feet, breathing through the slits in the side of his head. Traversing the sands, back and forth, they dropped farther and farther away from the beach. He swam one direction, then the other, methodically searching until finally he paused and shook his head.

No breath holding, he thought to Brigitta, *dizzy making.*

Brigitta almost laughed. She hadn't realized she'd been holding her breath. She exhaled and counted off in rhythm, like a lullaby, and the Saarin swam to it, comforted by her sing-song voice. Below them, shelled beasts scuttled across the sea floor, and in front of them, strands of mottled greenery stretched up, reaching for light, as tiny critters hid within.

He turned left and swam for a stretch, and then right. A large shape appeared, glinting in the dark water. As he swam toward it, Narine's figure came into view, encased in exactly the same manner as Brigitta had seen in Ondelle's memory.

Narru swam to within arm's length of Narine's sweet face. Even though her eyes were closed and her body still, Brigitta could tell Narine lived. Somehow, she had been protected all these season cycles, frozen in time, never aging like Mabbe had.

Hello? Narru called tentatively and poked at the bubble. *Are you awaking?*

The faerie inside shuddered, took a deep breath, and blinked open her eyes. Brigitta was shocked to see that they were now crystal white. Her shocked expression was mirrored on Narine's face, whose mouth dropped open when she found Narru in front of her. She placed her hand against her encasing.

"You're not—" She stumbled for the words. "Are you from . . . from . . . Pariglenn?"

Yes, Brigitta's mind reverberated his answer. *Narru from Flota of Saari. And being with me faerie Brigitta from the Forest of White.*

Speaking in Narru's mind body, Brigitta added. *I'm on the beach.*

Narine's eyes couldn't get any wider. "You'll have to pardon me, I have no concept of time any longer." She broke into a wide grin. "Nevertheless, how joyous this occasion!"

She moved forward and threw her arms toward Narru's head.

Her bubble expanded to include him, and Brigitta could feel the comfort of its warmth.

Narine's grin quickly faded. "Where are the rest?"

What do you mean? said Brigitta.

"I sense only my Air and Water."

That's me, said Brigitta. *Ondelle gifted me with your Water before I was born, then later, she gave me her Air.*

"What of her Fire?" asked Narine, now looking more than concerned. "And what of the Earth I gave to Croilus to take back to the White Forest? Where are those?"

Brigitta's heart dropped to her stomach.

Croilus isn't from the White Forest, she said. She could feel herself tensing up in Narru's mind body, and him struggling to keep her there.

"But I thought with the Saarin here . . ." Narine struggled to locate the question. "So, you have not come to disperse us? Faweh is not balanced?"

What? Of course not, said Brigitta, *that's why we've come to you.*

It was several moonsbreaths before Narine spoke. And even then, she took Brigitta by surprise by easing herself down on the ocean floor with an, "Oh."

What do you mean, Oh? Panic rose in Brigitta's chest.

Slowing breathing, Narru thought to her. *Calming thoughts.*

She tried to calm herself, but she could not believe this was Narine, the Ancient faerie from Noe. And now that she was just sitting there on the ocean floor, stripped of all her elements, she didn't seem any wiser than Brigitta herself. Even after all this time, Brigitta thought dejectedly, she was still just a girl.

You're supposed to be the one with all the answers, Brigitta accused.

"He had the Dragon's Gift in his scepter . . ." Narine stared off into the darkness of ocean. "He said he would take my Earth energy to the White Forest."

To steal your other energies! Brigitta exclaimed, her mind dizzy, her connection to the Saarin slipping away. She refocused herself on Narine. *He had no destiny markings, no element of his own!*

"That had been foreseen for the White Forest faeries. I assumed he had come just in time." She looked back up at Narru. "Who is this Croilus faerie?"

He's from Noe, said Brigitta. *He's a descendant of Mabbe. He tried to overthrow her.*

"What?" Narine sat up.

That's whose scepter he had, continued Brigitta. *That's how he tricked you.*

"That's not possible!" Narine stood, eyes wild. "Mabbe would have to be—"

One thousand season cycles old, confirmed Brigitta. *I met her myself. She was but skin held in place by magic. She's gone now, swallowed up by the River That Runs Backwards.*

"Oh, Great Moon." Narine trembled as she placed her hands on Narru's shoulders and looked into his eyes, searching for her faerie kin sitting alone on the beach. "I have given myself away: my elements, my knowings. But this was orchestrated a long time ago, you understand, by consensus of the Ancients. And now . . ." She closed her eyes and emitted a pained laugh. "This is how I'll spend the rest of Faweh's seasons. That was the risk we took all those moons ago."

Not understanding, Narru spoke up. *What this meaning?*

Narine opened her eyes and let go of his shoulders. "The Dragon gave Croilus his gift, and I've bestowed mine. That's the end of it. The knowings are spent, the elements released." Narine's encasing slipped from around Narru and the cocoon of warmth vanished with it.

No! said Brigitta sternly, startling both Narine and the Saarin. *I have not lost Ondelle and my friends and my family for Croilus to win. For the White Forest to be destroyed. I will get your Earth, and I will take back the Dragon's Gift.*

"But how?" asked Narine.

I don't know, but I will do it or die trying. What choice do I have?

I doing with Brigitta, the Saarin said, placing his palm against his chest.

Narine took a deep breath and nodded. "I have nothing left to gift you," she finally said. "I have no energy left for transference and no recollection of the knowings. As the last of them was given, so they were forgotten. I may appear solid, but truly I am an echo of myself."

What do you mean? asked Brigitta.

"I mean," said Narine, "my own destiny has been served. I can tell you pieces from my life, but forgetting is all I have left to do. I'm sure what happened to Mabbe was horrifying . . . Ancients weren't meant to live this long. It was a great sacrifice to cast the spell that kept me here."

She shook her head sadly. "I was hoping to be released to the ethers rather than sit on the bottom of the sea in perpetual ignorance."

Recalling some bit of her past, she abruptly pivoted to search the waters around her. "And soon the Dragon will claim what's left of my memories." She returned her attention to Narru and attempted a smile, but Brigitta could see she was truly frightened. "My gift back to It."

Then tell me what you do know, said Brigitta, *and I will do all I can to make things right.*

"I can tell you that all my energies will be attracted to each other," she began, "especially now that they are all released. You will sense the others as you approach, as they will sense you. They were meant to find each other again.

"I wish I could tell you what was in the knowing I gave to Croilus." She searched the waters again. "It will settle itself in him in a matter of moons, depending upon how much his body fights it. There are ways of provoking him so that the knowledge never completely settles. I do know the last of the Blue Spell will be useless to him unless it does."

Then we will have to make sure it never does.

A vast shadowy movement shifted behind her in the distance. Narine's body jerked, and for a moment her expression was blank.

She shook herself back to attention. "Never does what?"

Faerie girl mind-body slipping, informed Narru.

Brigitta focused all her energy on staying connected with Narine. *How do I provoke someone to keep him from a knowing?*

"Give him something to be unsettled about. A potent dilemma."

What about all the Ancients? Where have they gone?

"The Ancients . . ." said Narine, turning all the way around in a circle, noticing their absence for the first time. "Oh."

Man faerie leaving with non-living faeries, said Narru, gesturing toward the shore. *Going to mountains.*

They were somehow under his control, added Brigitta.

Narine opened her mouth to speak, but the dark movement returned, zigzagging in their direction. Her eyes glazed over. "I—I don't know."

Can we stop Croilus from controlling the Ancients? asked Brigitta.

"If they are connected, and he is killed," Narine said slowly, sifting through her broken memories, "they will be destroyed along with him."

As if being doused by cold water, Narine grew suddenly lucid. "Destroyed, Brigitta, not dispersed. The fifth element lost forever."

Then what do we do?

"You could still balance Faweh—" she started.

The dark shape grew closer, and her voice drifted away again.

" . . . even if it is too late for us . . ."

The shape swam into view: a silver- and green-scaled mountain of a beast.

" . . . maybe that would be enough to appease the Dragon . . ."

Brigitta? called Narru nervously, backing away from Narine.

How do we balance Faweh? Brigitta asked, urging him to stay.

"How?"

The beast tunneled into a mass of sea weeds, Its tail flicking through the water behind it.

Narine's eyes glazed over for a second time. "Birds," she said in a faraway voice. "I remember great white birds."

Not remembering long, said Narru as they watched the Ancient girl struggling to piece a memory together. *No sense making.*

"No," Narine said, voice fading, "the birds are important."

A sudden shift in the water thrust the Saarin backward, and he grabbed hold of two long rubbery plants to keep from floating away.

"You should go," Narine murmured and closed her eyes.

Narru clawed at the sandy floor with his feet, pushing away from Narine.

Calmly, so I can stay with you, said Brigitta. *It's all right, Narru. All right being for you,* he thought, *sitting on beach.*

She concentrated on staying with the Saarin, comforting his mind. The shape wound its way around within the sea weeds, and Narru twisted in the water, trying to keep an eye on it. She could feel his heart pounding, his panicked breath, and then, their connection ceased.

Alone on the beach in the dark and cold, Brigitta stood up from the log, jolted into her surroundings. On the shore, Narru rushed from the water and scurried on all fours, backward, like an upside-down spider. As she hurried to assist him, a monstrous head burst up from the sea on a neck of bright silvery-green scales. Long and slender, the neck stretched up and up, towering over them.

Brigitta grabbed Narru by the shoulders and they stumbled back as the beast's eyes opened, pulling them into Its limitlessness. Frozen in place on the beach, Brigitta and Narru held onto each other, thoughts scattered and useless.

The Eternal Dragon gave a great snort, and then opened Its mouth and inhaled.

Every last bit of warmth, every last bit of color, every last bit of light trembled and loosened and crackled until it all broke away and was inhaled through that awesome mouth. For a moonsbreath, Brigitta could see and feel nothing, as if floating in a void. And then, it all snapped back into place and the Dragon was gone but for a large round ripple on the surface of the water.

Brigitta and Narru sat clutching each other in the wet sand, speechless.

Dragon giving warning? the Saarin finally spoke, voice trembling.

"I don't know what that was," said Brigitta, unable to let go of Narru, "except another sign that we are on our own."

After they picked themselves up and dusted off the combination of sand and mud, they made their way wordlessly back up the beach toward the forest. Brigitta had no idea which was less dangerous at night, forest or beach, but she did not want the color sucked from her world again, let alone all her memories. She was done with Forever Beach.

They moved along the edge of the forest until they came across a portion of wood that had been wrenched away. A stray piece of purple fabric waved from a broken branch, and Brigitta plucked it off.

"Croilus . . ." she whispered, holding Narru back as she scanned the trees. "I don't feel anything. Narine said I would." She pulled at Narru. "Come on, there's nothing for us here."

As they traveled toward the plateau, she hoped upon hope that Jarlath was all right. She thought about the Ancient voices, the ones Mabbe had forbade the Noe faeries listen to. Croilus had listened to them and they had driven him mad and then brought him here. The Ancients had wanted all of Narine's elements to be united in one faerie with the last of the Dragon's Gift, so they could finally be dispersed when Faweh was balanced.

She doubted Croilus had such unselfish plans.

A wet blast of sand from the beach startled Brigitta from her thoughts. The plateau loomed in front of her. Night had cloaked them in with no stars to lead the way. It was either fortunate or unfortunate that the Saarin's skin glowed.

"Is there any way to turn yourself down a little?" asked Brigitta, looking up to the top of the plateau, which seemed higher and farther away than it had earlier that day.

Narru examined his hands and feet and smiled. *I being good lighting.*

"Yeah, but right now you need to be good hiding." She removed an extra tunic from her pack. "Put this on, and use the hood."

With her tunic on, he looked like an old faerie woman. Splashes of brightness shone from his fingers and toes as he grappled with the rocks. He and Brigitta used all their strength to fight the current of air as they ascended. She sent the Saarin scrambling ahead in case he lost his footing. But he didn't fall this time, and she silently thanked the Great Moon, as she doubted she had the energy to catch him.

A few moonbeats later, and they pulled themselves over the edge of the plateau, scurrying behind one of the great standing stones to get out of the wind.

"Do you remember where we left Jarlath?" Brigitta whispered, unsure of why she felt the need to do so.

Leaving him here, Narru said, pointing to the stone next to them.

"Here, but—" Brigitta twisted around. Sure enough, her scrawled message was still on the stone and scattered footprints marked the ground.

And then she felt it, a pulling, a longing. A part of her wandering lost.

Brigitta. Narru yanked on her tunic sleeve.

A few wingbeats away, Jarlath stood leaning against the side of one of the great rocks. He appeared winded, confused, but otherwise unharmed.

"Jarlath!" Brigitta called and fluttered toward him.

He stared, almost past her, as she approached. And just before she reached him, several other figures appeared around him, large and ghostly.

The enchanted Ancients.

They took up the space on either side of him as Brigitta dropped to the ground, and when she wheeled around, more landed behind her, closing her and Narru up in the circle.

"How lovely to see you again, Brigitta of the White Forest."

Croilus stepped out from behind them and flashed his sickly smile. "I believe you have something for me?"

As the Ancients herded Brigitta and Narru together, moving as one entity, she scanned their faces. They looked bewildered, as if not understanding why their bodies were doing what they were doing.

"Narine's energy!" cried Brigitta. "It belongs with me." She held up her hands as they closed in. "Ancients, can't you feel it? I am your kin!"

"They can't feel anything any longer!" Croilus's self-congratulatory laughter filled the air. "Not if I don't let them."

The old Noe faeries stopped moving and stared not at, but through Brigitta and Narru, who pressed his trembling body against her, fingers clawing her shoulder. A few of the Ancients parted and Croilus was there, angular face flushed with victory, scepter in hand.

"They are my servants," he said smugly. He tapped the closest one, a stout male with a beard that tapered to a point just below his chin. "Bags of skin held up by my goodwill."

Brigitta forced herself to look at the Ancient. Everything about him was colorless, probably lost to the Dragon Itself over time. His wings were longer than Brigitta was tall, but empty of life, and there was no hint of crystal or sparkle in his eyes. Croilus was right; there was no Ethereal energy among them. No energy of any kind . . . except . . .

She snapped her attention back to Croilus. Yes, Narine's stolen Earth energy flickered beyond her reach. Unsettled, the energy flustered inside him. Beads of sweat formed on his forehead even though it was chilly on the plateau. She met his eyes. A fleeting frantic look came over him until he blinked it away and scowled.

He's frightened, Brigitta thought to Narru.

Emboldened, she straightened up, remembering Narine's advice. "They won't harm me," Brigitta said to Croilus, "and you cannot control them."

As she said this, she felt him falter, and a tension released from the throng of Ancients. They were like puppets, but Croilus didn't own them as well as he wanted her to believe. The knowing had not settled in him.

She leered at the old Watcher, mustering all the conviction she could. "They will turn on you when they realize the evil in your heart."

He panicked and swung around maniacally, and the Ancients tumbled away. "Get her energy!" he cried. They stood there, looking at him almost curiously. He spun around, focused himself on Jarlath, and repeated his command. "Bring it to me!"

Jarlath broke away and streamed toward Brigitta with a battle cry, slamming into her and knocking her backwards. She stumbled to the edge of the plateau, and as she regained her balance, Jarlath leaped through the air and landed on top of her, pinning her to the ground. She struggled to loosen her wings from beneath her.

"Jarlath!" she cried, pushing at his chest. "It's me, Brigitta!"

A moonsbreath later, Narru rushed at Jarlath, but he deflected the Saarin with a well-placed kick, and Narru tumbled back into one of the standing stones. Jarlath lifted a rock from the ground and brought it up over his head as Croilus shrieked with glee.

Brigitta softened her voice and attempted a futile mind mist. "I know you are in there, Jarlath. And I know you'd never hurt me."

She stared into the frightening dark-blueness of Jarlath's eyes as he held the rock above his head, arms quivering with indecision.

"Jarlath," she whispered, "please, no."

With an anguished cry, he brought the stone down on the thin upper bone of Brigitta's left wing, and she both felt and heard it crack. She screamed in pain, writhing underneath him. He lifted the stone again, this time aiming for her skull, his face contorted, eyes wild.

A gust of wind streamed up from behind him, the stone flew out of his hands and sailed over the edge of the plateau. He twisted away and Brigitta shoved him off of her, the top of her left wing hanging useless.

She tried to stand, but was too dizzy with pain. It pounded

around her injury like a separate heartbeat. Another gust swept Jarlath off his feet, and he struggled in the current of air to regain his stability. In a frenzied struggle with an invisible foe, Jarlath managed to swing himself out of the wind, and he collapsed to the ground huffing and puffing for breath.

Brigitta followed the wind as it retreated to its source. Hovering next to a crumbling stone was High Priest Fozk of Fhorsa. He turned his attention to Croilus and the Ancients as she fought to stay conscious. Two ropes of air twisted out of Fozk's hands like snakes and wrapped themselves around Croilus's body.

Don't kill him! thought Brigitta frantically as the world faded away. *You'll kill the Ancients!*

Chapter Nine

Ondelle brushed her long black hair in her mirror. Her Thought Mirror. She held her image's gaze and numbed her mind, muddying her thoughts so she wouldn't have to listen to them.

Her image stopped brushing and dropped her hand into her lap. "Really, Ondelle?" she said from the mirror. "You think you can hide your own thoughts from yourself?"

Ondelle set her brush on the table below the mirror and folded her hands. "Sometimes it is best to be without thought."

"You were destined as a sacrifice," her image blurted.

"We are all destined to sacrifice ourselves in one way or another," she responded.

"She won't be strong enough with just the one element," Ondelle's image accused, then leaned toward her. "You are disobeying the Ancients and the Dragon Itself!"

Ondelle stood up and slammed her hand down on the table. "She's a child! And I was charged to protect her! What would you have me do, leave her all alone with enough power to destroy herself?"

"You managed as a deodyte."

"She will have an acceptance I never had. She will gain the trust of her forest."

"You cannot control her destiny, Ondelle," the image said quietly, playing with the brush in her lap.

They sat there in the silence of that truth.

The image spoke again. "Just be certain your motives are not self-serving."

Ondelle sat back down at her mirror. "I will protect her as necessary and bestow the gifts when it is time." She grabbed the edges of the mirror and spoke into her own black moon eyes. "But I will not allow her to be feared and abandoned by her own kin."

Brigitta! a voice called inside her head, and then her body was hefted up, weight tugging on either side of her.

"Brigitta!" a familiar voice cried close to her ears.

Minq!

Startled awake, Brigitta struggled to stand, turning to hug her friend.

"Oh, Minq, I'm so glad to see you!" she cried, grabbing his face and kissing him on the nose.

"No time!" He pulled at her.

It took a moment for her to get her bearings as Minq tugged at her from one side and Narru from the other.

In front of them, Fozk stood with his noose of air extended and loosened. It surrounded Croilus as he swirled his scepter wildly to keep it at bay. The airy ring twisted in on itself, knotting up and bursting apart. The Ancients whirled around, tumbling through the gusts of air that ricocheted off the standing stones. One shot of air struck Fozk, forcing him to the ground.

As Croilus and the Ancients retreated through the stones, the air continued to swirl about them, like water through channels in a river. Fozk's hair and tunic flapped wildly in the windstorm as he rose, lifted up his arms, and gathered the Air energy, shaping it into one large mass.

But something had tampered with it, expanding its force, and there was too much energy for Fozk to contain. The wind grew wilder, the stone in front of Brigitta cracked, and pieces of it pelted her body and face and injured wing.

"I can't hold it for long," cried Fozk, opening his arms to encompass more.

She looked to where Jarlath had been blown away from her. He sat on his knees, hugging himself and shaking in the windstorm. Brigitta held out her hand. "Jarlath, come with us."

He scowled at her, stood up on wobbly legs, and followed Croilus and the Ancients through the stones.

"No!" she cried and stumbled after him.

Another stone cracked and a large chunk of it slammed into the ground. She leapt to avoid it and a surge of pain ran from her broken wing to the center of her back.

Narru pulled her by the arm. *Too dangerous. Death making.*

"Jarlath!" Brigitta screamed, yanking herself away from Narru despite the pain.

"We must leave at once!" shouted Fozk. "We are no match for the stones!"

She turned to Fozk, wild-haired and wild-eyed, and felt the icy dagger of destiny. This moment, she had been here before.

When she had touched Gola's moonstone before leaving for Noe, Brigitta had been assaulted by visions. Crossroads, Gola had called them, marking decisions she would have to make. One of them presented itself now. But Brigitta had only seen the crossroad, not the decision itself, and she had no idea what to do.

"Brigitta!" Minq pleaded with her. He held onto the edge of a cracking stone with his hands and both ears.

When she looked back, Jarlath had disappeared. The world crumbled around her. Tears streaming down her face, she let Narru guide her to Fozk and Minq. With a snapping of his wrists, the High Priest released the Air energy he had managed to harness and formed a buffer of wind leading down the side of the plateau. Fragments of stone pelted them as they descended over the edge, Fozk carrying Brigitta in his arms, and Minq and Narru eyeing each other as they clambered down side-by-side.

Hunched over a log, Brigitta cried into her arms as Fozk set her wing, and Minq and Narru warmed dinner on the fire. They had made camp in a small clearing the High Priest had declared "safe enough" after he wove some dustmist and firepepper through the air.

No anger pricked at Brigitta that Minq had told the Elders where she had gone. She was too crushed about Jarlath. He would never have left her like that; she didn't care what she had promised.

"It was wrong to leave," she said through her tears.

"Puh," sounded the Saarin with a pop of his lips. *We Saari saying thing never wrong being, just other being.*

Brigitta lifted her head. "That's easy for you to say."

He stared at her, flames mirrored in his moist eyes. *I having no way home,* he pointed out. *Being that wrong?*

"I don't know." She crumpled back down again. "Maybe. How do you know *you* were the one supposed to follow the whisper light into the Purview?"

I being here, he said, *that how I knowing.*

Fozk paused in his task. "Are you going to share Narru's thoughts?"

"He doesn't hold my sense of despair," she said.

Fozk nodded and lifted his hands to create little airy cushions around the branch he had used to set her wing. He was gifted with the element of Air, yet she had never sought him out as a mentor, thinking he was somewhat fragile. Under his healing touch, however, she now realized his energy was simply lightly balanced, nimble, utilizing a quiet core strength. She considered what she knew of him: a gifted mind mister, more focused than the average Air Faerie, and a master of empathing.

Which meant, since he wasn't following her conversation with Narru, that the High Priest hadn't snuck into Narru's mind, nor hers for that matter. She twisted around, even though it pained her to do so, and looked into his sky-bright eyes, barely bluer than the pale skin and white hair around them.

"Thank you."

"You won't be able to fly for some time," he said, finishing the cushion and testing its strength. He moved to the fire to warm his hands. "When we get back, Adaire will tend to you. She is a more talented healer than I."

"I'm not going home," said Brigitta. "Not while Jarlath is still out there."

"You'd risk both your lives with only half your strength," said Fozk.

She was about to argue when Minq cut in, "You in no shape." He shook his head, ears flopping over his shoulders.

She knew they were right, deep down she knew, but she had to do something. She couldn't just leave Jarlath with Croilus. Back at the plateau, she had let him go because she had no choice. How could that have been a choice? Her wing was broken; she couldn't fly after them in the windstorm with the stones crashing all around. No, that wasn't the crossroads she had visualized through Gola's moonstone. The choice was much deeper, much more sinister than that. It wasn't just about Jarlath.

"High Priest Fozk," she said, closing her eyes and swallowing at the lump in her throat, "I have to tell you something. I have to tell you several somethings. And you have to believe them all."

Fozk pulled out a blanket and handed it to Brigitta, then spread one on the ground for himself. "I'm listening," he said, and gestured for Minq and Narru to dish out the meal, a broodnut mash mixed with some of the Saarin's tropical salts and dried seaweeds.

"I'm not crazy," Brigitta started, taking the proffered bowl from Minq's ear.

"I don't recall ever saying that you were," replied Fozk.

Brigitta didn't know where to start. If Fozk had gone to the Eternal Dragon like he should have after Ondelle died, none of this would have happened. Croilus wouldn't have a charged scepter or Narine's Earth energy. But no one, not even her, had known what Croilus was up to, so she couldn't exactly blame the High Priest for that.

"Croilus has the last of the Dragon's Gift in his scepter," she said. "He can call forth Blue Spell if his knowing takes hold. If his body can figure out how to live with it."

Fozk's expression remained still as Minq and Narru gathered closer.

"Go on," said Fozk.

"The High Sage's daughter, Narine, held back her elements when the rest of the Ancients transferred them to the White Forest faeries after the Great World Cry. When Faweh was ready to be rebalanced, her elements were to be united again in one faerie who would use the last of Dragon's Gift to lead the Ancients back to Noe to be properly dispersed. But Croilus isn't interested in dispersing Ancients with Blue Spell. He wants to control them for some horrible purpose."

She recalled the rhyme in the first Chronicler's book. A White Forest faerie would *travel back to times of old to make the balance right again.*

Something nagged at her. Something was missing. She couldn't figure out how everything was connected so the balance would return. The whisper light led them to Noe before the last of the Dragon's Gift was given. So that meant they had to balance Faweh *before* dispersing the Ancients. But maybe Ondelle had messed everything up by not gifting her Narine's Air and Fire energy when she was supposed to. And where was Narine's Fire energy now?

Both Brigitta's head and wing ached, and her mouth was dry. As if reading this thought, Fozk opened his pack and pulled out a canteen. Brigitta took several gulps of pipberry-sweetened water before continuing.

"I don't know what's going to happen now," she said as her tears came again. "I don't know what Croilus will do with the last of the Blue Spell. Or how he'll use the Ancients."

She rifled through her belongings and found the useless scepter. She unraveled it from its bindings and stared into the crystal on the end. "How can Faweh ever be balanced now? Without uniting the elements, without Blue Spell ..."

She handed the staff over to Fozk. As he reached for it, something glinted inside of his tunic: his hourglass necklace.

". . . your necklace," she murmured.

He reached for it, as instinctively as she used to. The motion triggered a memory. One of her own memories this time.

"Ondelle's spell." She sat up straighter and pointed to his chest. "In the necklace! There's still some Blue Spell left!"

Over the next moonbeat, Brigitta related the story of how Ondelle had placed the whisper light into her hourglass for safekeeping and sealed it there with Blue Spell magic that would return Brigitta to the White Forest if Ondelle died in Noe.

The dark forest noises faded into the background, and time stood still as Fozk listened intently to Brigitta's tale. Minq and Narru huddled together by the fire, wide-eyed and silent.

"But Ondelle didn't die in Noe," Brigitta concluded. "That return spell she cast was never used. So, it's still in there, right?"

Fozk took the hourglass out from beneath his tunic, held it between his palms, and closed his eyes. The rest of them waited while the muffled rustles and howls outside their circle of protection returned to Brigitta's awareness once again.

She considered the dustmist and firepepper that temporarily kept the beasts at bay. It suddenly felt like weak defense. The wisest and most powerful White Forest faeries might survive in the Dark Forest, but what about everyone else? What about Himalette and her Momma and Poppa? What about little destinyless Duna and Tustin? Who among them could manage carnivorous caterpillars or devious oddtwins?

Fozk opened his eyes and studied the hourglass. He looked up and nodded. "It's quite shielded, but, yes, I believe it's still there."

"Do you think there's enough to renew the Hourglass?" Brigitta asked hopefully.

"I'm not sure," answered Fozk. "I don't know of an occasion in which Blue Spell was conjured for one spell and then redirected for use with another."

"But we can try, right?"

"With your help," he said. "The spell was intended for you, so only you can release it."

What being Hourglass? asked Narru.

She turned to the Saarin. "The Hourglass of Protection. It was a gift from the Ancients. It keeps our forest safe, but must be renewed each season cycle using Blue Spell."

If you renewing Hourglass, this lasting only one season cycle?

"Yes, it would be temporary, but it could afford us some time."

"If it works," added Fozk. He reached over and patted Minq on the shoulder, whose expression had grown grim.

No way making protection lasting longer? asked the Saarin.

"No," said Brigitta. "It only lasts one season cycle. We can't extend the protection any longer without more Blue Spell."

"Actually," said Fozk, "we can."

Brigitta perked up so quickly she startled Minq. She winced as she shifted her wing. "What do you mean?"

"There's a spell included in the original White Forest Chronicles by Chevalde of Noe to indefinitely extend the protection if necessary."

"How come we've never used that spell before?" asked Brigitta, incredulous.

"Because it completely shuts the White Forest off from the outside world," Fozk said. "Forever."

Even though Fozk had done a credible job of easing her pain, Brigitta's mind still kept her awake. She regretted declining the ceunias leaf Fozk had offered as she tossed and turned beneath her blanket, contemplating the choice that had to be made: risk the lives of every White Forest faerie, including her family, or shut Jarlath out of the White Forest forever.

And what about her friends in Noe? If their connection to the Ancients had been severed, they would be unable to disperse Nightwalkers or use the Purview. What if they, too, were somehow under Croilus's command? She shuddered at the thought.

Another thought struck her. She had no power in the White Forest. She wasn't even an Apprentice any longer. The Elders would decide what to do no matter what she had to say about it. Of course, she could refuse to release the Blue Spell to them, but what kind of selfish faerie would that make her?

Ondelle had protected Brigitta in her way, so that she would not become an outcast among her family and friends, but Brigitta had managed to make everyone distrust and resent her all on her own. Perhaps that was part of her destiny as well.

She sighed heavily, exhausted by her own mind.

"You awake." Minq's small, high voice reached out.

"Yeah."

She sat up on her elbows and searched for her friend in the darkness. He was lying near the edge of the clearing by her feet. His ears stretched up and batted at some branches above his head where the dustmist wall had thinned.

"I sorry, Briggy," he said. "No go as planned."

"Does anything ever?"

"You happy we come for you?" he asked.

She dropped her elbows and sank into her blanket. The word "happy" couldn't find any purchase in her thoughts.

Minq lay his ears back down. "Fozk already know, back at Hive. Minq no betray you."

This information did not surprise her, but she wondered at it nonetheless. If Fozk had known she was going to steal the scepter, why in Faweh hadn't he stopped her from doing it? She curled her blanket tighter around herself, as if that would protect her from all that lay ahead.

"I still yours?" Minq asked, voice cracking.

"Of course, Minq," she answered. "And I still yours."

She took another deep breath, filling her belly fuller and fuller with it until she was certain there was no space left in her entire being. And then, she called forth her Water energy, which filled the minute spaces, the cracks and crannies, until she was so full she was numb.

Chapter Ten

It was all Ondelle could do to keep her hands from shaking as she took the jar from Perimeter Guard Gaowen of Thachreek and held it up to her face. A little fuzzy yellow light pattered against the glass as if attempting to communicate.

"Thank you, Trease, Gaowen," she said. "Please wait here for further instructions."

Trease looked relieved to be rid of the tiny light, but Gaowen's eager face leaned closer, begging for more information.

Ondelle simply smiled at them both. "I will return soon."

After she left the gathering room, her knees went weak, and she stumbled down the corridor to her personal chambers. She closed her door, pressed herself up against it, and opened the lid of the jar. The little light blinked up at her. Carefully, she moved farther into the room and set the jar on her dresser, then sat down on her bed, hands in lap. Waiting, heart pounding.

It had been many season cycles since she had received a new piece of her knowing, a morsel that had been tucked away until triggered by the whisper light. Until the moment the two guards brought the light to her, she had been certain that all of Narine's knowing had been evoked. How had such a thing hidden itself so deep inside of her that she could not detect it?

As the light floated out of the jar and toward her face, a familiar energy filled the room.

Hello again, something chimed, not in her ear, but directly into her head. A tinkly, musical sound.

"Hello," Ondelle breathed.

The light dove and bumped up against her chin, her neck, and down her arm. Ondelle turned her right hand over so that the light rested in her palm. It gave off a blast of energy and she gasped.

Suddenly, she knew: she must travel to Noe and find the Purview.

And all of her, including the part that Brigitta housed, had to come with her. Narine's energies jostled for attention inside of her. They knew they were not long for this body, that she had been preparing to let them go. But first, she had to convince everyone in the White Forest that Brigitta was meant to be a trusted leader. That it was her destiny to be so.

The journey back to the White Forest was slow and steady, with Minq and Fozk taking turns assisting Brigitta, who could still not fly with her injured wing. The Saarin, rejuvenated from his reconnection with the ocean, easily kept up with them, though he grew more and more anxious the farther inland they traveled.

At one point they encountered a deep swamp with boggy waters that burned everyone's skin, and they had to trek around it. They wove their way, choking on its vile air, scorching their lungs as if inhaling firepepper.

They camped in a deserted cave the second night, throats too parched to speak, only to wake to the tiny tracks of beasts that had infiltrated the dustmist barrier. Later, they discovered the little beasts had made nests in their clothes and hair and the inside of Minq's ears. They were all covered in little red bites by late morning.

The following afternoon, they reentered the White Forest. They had barely stepped across The Shift when Roucho, Mousha's featherless delivery bird, descended and dropped a broodnut at their feet. Carved into the soft shell was a message. COME QUICK, JARLATH! ROANE IS NOT WELL.

The entire party hurried to Tiragarrow, Brigitta ignoring the pain and speeding herself along with wing thrusts despite Fozk's warning that she might cause permanent damage. She was frantic, because in all that had happened, she had completely forgotten about Roane. She had left his older brother, his only living relative, in the Dark Forest with Croilus. If she could not get Jarlath back safe and sound, she would never forgive herself.

It seemed as if everyone in the entire village-nest was nervously milling about outside her parents' cottage. As the High Priest approached, the Tiragarrow faeries parted, murmuring and pointing to the strange beast that had returned with them. Minq put an ear across Narru's shoulder protectively as they made their way through the crowd.

Brigitta burst into her parents' cottage, followed by Fozk and Minq, while the Saarin dallied at the door, overwhelmed by the sudden swarm of strangers.

"Where is he?" Brigitta cried into the empty gathering room. "Where's Roane?"

"Briggy!" Himalette streaked out of her bedroom and straight into Brigitta's stomach, sending her backwards into Fozk.

The shock to her injured wing forced tears to her eyes, and she tried to pull her frightened sister away, but Himalette held tight to Brigitta's waist, burying her face in her tunic.

"I was making his lunch," cried Himalette. "Momma and Poppa were with the Elders . . . his eyes, they went dark and he . . . he just stopped."

"Stopped what, dear?" asked Fozk, placing a hand on Himalette's head. She gave a heavy, sobby sigh and relaxed.

She pulled her face away from Brigitta's chest, now moistened with tears. "Just . . . stopped."

"What do you mean?" gasped Brigitta. "He's dead?"

"No, not dead. Just not moving." She sniffed and shook her head. "Nobody knows what to do."

"It's not just Roane," a voice called from Brigitta's bedroom.

A moment later Elder Adaire stepped into the gathering room, her tunic sleeves rolled up and her face lined with worry. "It's Thistle and Granae, too. A few suns ago, they all simply . . ." She gestured helplessly and stepped aside so Brigitta and Fozk could take a look at Roane, lying on top of the covers of Brigitta's bed, breathing, eyes open, but seeing nothing.

"Fozk," said Brigitta, grabbing hold of his arm. "It's like what happened to Jarlath. Croilus has done something to the Ancients." She gazed upon Roane's innocent face. "And they're all Watchers, half-bloodline descendents of the Ancients."

He nodded solemnly.

"Do you think they will turn violent, like Jarlath?" she whispered.

"I wish I knew," he said, and then he patted her arm. "Perhaps at this distance, or from within the White Forest, Croilus cannot have the same effect."

"In Noe, the others . . ." Her voice trailed off. If Devin and Zhay and Ferris were in the same condition, they would be unprotected. She hoped Fozk was right about the distance preventing Croilus from having any power over them. And she hoped that the Nhords were with them, too. Abdira and Uwain wouldn't let anything happen to her friends.

"Brigitta!" cried her Momma and Poppa as they raced through the house to their daughter.

She pulled herself away from her thoughts as they approached, and it was as if she were watching two strangers. Her journey to the Eternal Dragon and back, and Ondelle's memories of them as young parents, had colored her feelings toward them. They looked so fragile and naïve to her now.

Her expression must have worried them, for they both slowed down and then stopped shy of any embrace.

"Fozk?" asked Pippet, grasping Mousha's hand without taking her eyes off her daughter. "Is she all right?"

"Her wing is badly injured," Fozk replied, "and the boy Jarlath was unable to return with us."

They carefully folded Brigitta into their arms, stroking her hair and rubbing her back. No, she thought, she was not *all right*. She didn't know what she was, but she felt strange, as if being pulled elsewhere. And even though her heart ached for the two faeries holding her, a part of her wanted to be pulled away.

Brigitta sat quietly in the meeting with the Elders and High Priest Fozk, watching the proceedings, detached, just a cloud observing the forest. Perhaps it was a way of protecting herself from having to make too many difficult decisions. Maybe choices were less like crossroads and more like logs in a river clogging its course. If one could just make a choice, the other logs would unjam, and the way would be clear.

She recalled how the knowing triggered by the whisper light had made everything clear for Ondelle. Brigitta wished for that kind of clarity for herself, for it to appear like magic, telling her exactly what to do.

She pulled her attention back to the room. The Elders and High Priest were discussing Chevalde of Noe's Impenetrable Spell, to be performed during twin full moons, which would lock the forest in its protective shell forever.

Or until Faweh was balanced once again.

"Yes, we'd be safe inside," said Fozk, "but without the ability to disperse the spirits of the dead, we would only be extending our inevitable extinction."

It was true. Without the elements ascending and transforming, no new elemental faeries would be born. And since the Watchers, the only ones who could perform dispersements, were all debilitated, and possibly dangerous, in a hundred season cycles or so, all that would be left of Faweh's faeries would be their feral kin of Noe. Frightened shadows of what was once a grand civilization.

Would future visitors from afar stumble across the White Forest, a strange protected area haunted by undispersed spirits of the dead? Would these travelers study the spirits behind the field like thunderbugs under glass?

"I don't think the question is whether we perform the magic or not," said Hammus. "I think the question is when we do it."

"I say the next full moons," said Adaire with authority. "Who knows what this Croilus faerie will be capable of once his knowing settles."

"It is not *his* knowing," Dervia pointed out.

"It doesn't matter whose it was," countered Hammus. "We cannot have his Blue Spell magic wreaking havoc on our forest nor our families terrorized by spellbound Ancients."

"I agree," said Adaire. "Let us be safe."

"But think about what we're saying," said Dervia. "You're dooming our younger generation."

"They're doomed regardless!" shouted Hammus. He lowered his head in apology and took a breath before continuing. "I'm sorry … this is hard on us all."

Mora, the newest Elder, placed a hand over his, and they resumed their discussion in a more subdued tone.

A strange pulse of air filled the space, pressing in on Brigitta from every part of the room all at once, though the Elders didn't seem to feel it at all. They began to fade from Brigitta's sight, and she shook her head. They came into focus once again, but quickly disappeared, and then she was looking across a great expanse of rolling hills leading to a breathtaking high narrow mountain that twisted into the clouds.

A throng of Ancients flew silently toward it like ghosts, and she gazed upon them with a mixture of anxiety and elation. As they passed in front of her, Jarlath floated by, caught in their tide. The harsh sunlight formed a strange halo in the distance, and it appeared as if they were all floating toward a ring of fire.

"Brigitta?"

Her attention was jogged back into the Elder chambers, all faces turned toward her, curious and concerned.

"Are you all right?" asked Mora.

"I know where Croilus is heading," said Brigitta as it dawned on her. She could still taste the air, as if she had actually been standing there across from the great mountain. "I could see it!"

"Perhaps you are too exhausted for this right now." Dervia turned to the others. "We need to contemplate this further. It is not a decision we can—"

"No," said Brigitta, startling them all.

Everything had suddenly clicked into place. Seeing Jarlath and the Ancients in that fiery ring had reminded her of when they used the energy of dispersing nightwalkers in Noe to get through the Purview. All the pieces of Narine in those whisper lights had the same message for Ondelle and the Nhords and the Saarin: open the Purview.

"You must do it on the next full moons," she said.

Her certainty and depth of command caught them off guard.

"You have something to share with us, Brigitta?" asked Fozk.

"Yes." She stood up, smiling for the first time in moons. "Yes!"

The logjam had been removed, and the course was as clear as a Green Season sky. "You will close off the White Forest," she told them, "and when you do, I will be on the other side."

There were five Purviews, Brigitta reasoned, one on each continent. Three had already been opened: the one in Noe, the one Abdira and Uwain came through on Araglenn, and the one Narru had used on Pariglenn. There were two left and no guarantee, after almost one thousand season cycles, that anyone would be around to open them on Storlglenn and Carraiglenn. No guarantee there were ears to listen and eyes to see the whisper lights when they came. And no guarantee any ears or eyes belonged to beasts as loyal as the Nhords or as curious as the odd young Saarin.

"I'm the only one who can do it," she said. "I can find Jarlath *and* the whisper lights using Narine's energy."

The Elders looked unconvinced, though the expression on Fozk's face was harder to read.

"Narine couldn't remember what she had given away," she said to him. "She hid knowings inside the whisper lights. If we open all of the Purviews, we can unite Faweh."

"Brigitta," said Dervia, "there is no proof that this is the case."

"Travel back to times of old to make the balance right again," she said to Dervia. "We *all* have to travel back, someone from each civilization. And they each get there through a Purview."

The room grew silent but for Fozk's deep inhale. "Go on."

"I can help open the last two Purviews, balance Faweh, and break the Impenetrable Spell." As Brigitta spoke, she grew more confident and more excited. "I just need to find Croilus and get the scepter and Narine's Earth energy back before the knowing settles and he figures out how to use the last of the Blue Spell."

Before they could argue, she described what she had seen while connected to Narine's energy, the expanse of land and the great peak, and they referred to the map of Foraglenn left to them by the Ancients.

"Sage Peak," said Hammus, and the rest murmured.

"That would make sense," added High Priest Fozk.

"Why?" Brigitta peered down at the map. "What's so special about Sage Peak?"

"It's a sacred place," said Mora.

"A powerful place," said Dervia. "A place where the Ancient Sages used to connect to Faweh's energy. A place of clarity."

"It is written," added Adaire, "that its energy is so pure that every thought is magic."

"I wonder what he's up to?" asked Hammus.

"Nothing good, that's for sure," said Brigitta. "But if he's looking to connect to that pure energy, I'm sure he'll be disappointed."

"Why is that?" asked Dervia.

"Because nothing in Faweh is as it was before the Great World

Cry," said Brigitta. "Didn't Dead Mountain used to be some kind of Sage retreat and Noe Valley a place of peace?"

"Let's hope he does more harm to himself than others, then," said Hammus.

Now that Brigitta had a way to find Jarlath and clarity in balancing Faweh, a plan quickly hatched from within her, as if channeling it from Ondelle herself.

"Narru, Minq, and I can go to Sage Peak for Jarlath and Narine's Earth energy and the stolen scepter. Then we'll travel to Storlglenn, find the whisper light, open the Purview, and figure out a way to travel to Carraiglenn through it. There, we'll locate the final whisper light, open the final Purview, and use it to return to Noe where we can call the Ancients so they can be dispersed!"

"We'll have the scepter and the rings to get through the Purviews," Brigitta went on, practically giddy. "The Nhord rings and the Saarin's rings. We can do this!"

"But how will you rescue Jarlath?" asked Hammus. "Even without being under Croilus's spell, he may still be in a stupor like the other Watchers."

"Ondelle gave her Air energy to me," Brigitta explained. "If I can get to Narine's Earth energy before it settles in Croilus, I'm sure there's a way to give it to Jarlath. Then he'll be an Earth Faerie with an energy of his own. He won't need a connection to Ancient energy anymore!"

Hammus and Adaire shook their heads while the others contemplated this possibility.

"Crossing the water to Storlglenn, or any other continent for that matter, has never been attempted by any White Forest faerie," Mora pointed out.

"Neither had traveling to Noe," said Fozk, "before Ondelle and Brigitta left."

"Besides," said Brigitta, "I'll have Narru. He lives in the sea. He knows water like we know how to breathe."

"IF you can transfer Narine's Earth energy, IF you can steal the scepter back from Croilus, IF you can cross an ocean, IF you can find the whisper lights, IF you can open the Purviews . . ." Dervia threw up her arms. "Brigitta, that's a tremendous amount of *ifs*!"

"IF I don't succeed," Brigitta said, matching Dervia's intensity, "you will be no worse off in the White Forest."

"But you would be trapped out there forever," said Adaire, and Mora murmured agreement.

"We can't let you go," said Hammus.

"It is not your decision," said Fozk, surprising them all.

He addressed the Elders, but kept his gaze on Brigitta. "We should assume our headstrong Brigitta would leave regardless of whether she had our permission or not," he continued, something between sorrow and pride radiating from his bright eyes. "I'm sure you'll agree it is far better she go well-prepared and with our support."

Later that afternoon, while Fozk gathered ingredients the Elders believed she would need for her journey, Brigitta sat watching him inspect the plants in the Hive garden, an ample patch of fertile land behind the entrance mound.

The day was painfully beautiful, striking clear blue sky, faerie children playing in the festival grounds, the smells of lyllium and dragon flower and tingermint weaving up from the garden. On such a day, it would be easy for one to forget about everything outside the forest, like dismissing a dream. But not for Brigitta while Jarlath was still out there.

She thought of the journey back home and the time she'd lost, and hoped her new lessons with Fozk would help make up for it all.

"High Priest Fozk," she asked, "how do you keep yourself, well, all to yourself?"

"Do you mean am I not tempted to listen in on others' thoughts?"

"I would be."

"No, you would not," he said, bending to feel a starkiss blossom before pulling the plant out of the ground with a graceful twist of his wrist. "You cannot master empathing otherwise. The ability to know must be balanced with the need to know."

Brigitta contemplated this as he gathered more plants. If he didn't read minds, he certainly had remarkable intuition. Maybe it was because he didn't attempt to invade others' thoughts that their emotions simply presented themselves to him. She wondered about her own selfishness and if she would only master her talents when she started thinking beyond her own desires.

The High Priest dusted off his hands on his tunic, leaving smudges of dirt. She decided that she liked how he worked with his hands, that he enjoyed being intimate with the earth. No small task seemed beneath him.

"Funny how knowledge appears to us sometimes, though," he said, dropping a few new seeds in to take the plant's place and patting the dirt back down around it. "For instance, did you know that the last conversation left in someone's Thought Mirror can be retrieved before the new owner uses it?"

He looked up from his task, eyes smiling. "If the previous owner sets the intention for it to be heard, that is. It's not that hard to do."

They looked at each other with new understanding, and Brigitta wondered at the breadth of Ondelle's cleverness. She had left him something in her mirror. Knowledge about who Brigitta was, perhaps. About her destiny.

"This was much harder to learn," he said, gesturing to the garden. "Elder Dervia has the natural gift." He placed everything in a basket and turned toward the Hive.

"I have no patience with plants or animals," Brigitta said, hanging back, stalling for time, desperately wanting to know what message Ondelle had left for him. "Or faeries, really."

He chuckled, each sound a clear percussive beat. There was so much more to High Priest Fozk than she had ever given thought. And so much knowledge each High Priest or Priestess kept to themselves until the time was right.

Before entering the Hive, the High Priest pulled some ceunias root out of his basket and tossed it to Brigitta. "Give this to your mother in a tea before you give her the news."

When he had vanished into the Hive, Brigitta went to pick up Minq and Narru, waiting for her in the festival grounds with a group of children. She watched Minq from the shadow of the tree for a while before approaching. The faerie children loved him, loved wrapping themselves up in his ears, loved snuggling into his belly. It dawned on her that she had no idea how old Minq was, or how long he would live. She wasn't even sure he knew the answers to these things.

With him was Narru, who blushed shyly as the faerie children led him in a dance across the festival grounds. He had been accepted immediately among the young ones, even if the older faeries looked at him with suspicion. It was difficult not to trust him, though, with his large sideways blinking eyes and innocent smile.

Brigitta had brought seven beings home to the White Forest, and strange as it may seem, she felt closer to all of them than any White Forest faerie. Even her Momma and Poppa. No one cared for them as much as she did, and since she had brought them there, she felt that they were her responsibility. Losing Jarlath, she had failed them all.

After Adaire's skilled healing Brigitta had been instructed to keep off her tender wing for as long as possible, so Fozk had called on two Perimeter Guards' assistance to see to Brigitta's transportation. As they arrived, bronze brothers with magnificent purple wings, she slid aside the fabric of the carry-cart to make room for Narru. The large guards took flight, with Minq struggling to keep up from behind.

This being nice forest home, said Narru, who had been extremely quiet since entering the White Forest. *Not being like ocean, though.*

He put a hand to his forehead. *Stillness making land sickness.*

"We'll get you back to the ocean," she said, taking his other hand. It felt slick and cool against her own skin, with fingernails like tiny black pebbles. "I promise."

When they arrived in Tiragarrow, Pippet set up an enormous feast for Brigitta and her friends. Himalette was there, and Mousha, too, strangely not in his lab puzzling over smoking beakers. No one spoke of Roane or Thistle or Granae, all taken to the Hive for "safekeeping." Pippet laughed overtly at every little thing, not wanting to darken the mood.

After supper, Himalette was dismissed to visit a friend, and then Brigitta did as Fozk had said and made a tea from the ceunias root for her mother and father, using the excuse that it was a gift from the Elders, which they of course could not turn down. But the calming effects of the tea did not do much to dampen Pippet's howls when Brigitta told her of her plan to leave the forest. Mousha sank into his chair, deflated.

"No!" cried Pippet. "No, no! I will not have you leave us again!"

"Mother," Brigitta said, gathering her strength, "I'm going. I must."

"Then I'll come, too!" she cried. "You can't go alone!"

Mousha held Pippet back and hugged her tight.

"You know you can't, Momma," said Brigitta, choking back her own tears. "You have to stay here for Poppa and Himmy."

"Why you, Brigitta?" begged Pippet. "Why you?"

"Because I'm the only one who can," she said. "My destiny was determined the moment Ondelle made it so."

Mousha nodded, lips pulled so tight they trembled, as he rocked Pippet in his arms.

"We've been poring over seasons of texts," said Adaire the following afternoon in the library with Fozk, Adaire, Dervia, and Mora.

Brigitta tried her best to concentrate. Her mother's pain deeply disturbed her, she couldn't stop thinking about the Watchers in Noe, and Gola, the one she always turned to for advice, had completely disappeared. The purple-winged Perimeter Guard brothers had checked for her, but Gola's home was empty, and no one had seen her in many moons. If she hadn't completely rooted by now, she would be by the time Brigitta, Minq, and Narru returned.

If they returned.

She held one of the moonstones between her fingers, wondering about the missing stone. If Gola had taken it with her, was there a way for her to find it with these ones? Could they call to each other like Narine's energies or like Ondelle did with the hourglass necklace? But the moonstones did not hum full of potential energy. They were cool on her skin and empty.

"Brigitta, are you listening?" asked Adaire.

"Yes." Brigitta refocused her gaze. "Go on."

"We believe you are the only one who can unlock the Blue Spell from the hourglass," Dervia said. "We also believe we have a way to get the Earth energy into Jarlath."

"Transformation," said Adaire. "You will transform Croilus's and Jarlath's energies."

"No small feat, we realize," added Dervia. "But we believe it is possible thanks to Ondelle."

"Transformation," Brigitta murmured, mulling over the idea like sucking on a piece of hard candy. She shook her head. "Without the help of the Ancients, I am not particularly adept at transformation in the best of circumstances."

"Then you will learn," Fozk said. "And perhaps Ondelle's memories will serve to speed the process. We have little time before the full moons."

As they excused themselves to attend to their duties, Brigitta realized that was the first time any of them had acknowledged that Ondelle's memories were real.

Her lessons began immediately after their meeting, and when

Brigitta entered Adaire's practice chamber, two clay pots sat on the table, one red and one gold. Adaire explained that the more hollow or porous something was, the easier to work transference on it. She focused her energy and in a few moonsbreaths, proceeded to turn the red pot gold and the gold pot red.

"That's not exactly what you'll be doing to them, but it matters not. It starts with one empty space in mind. If you can master filling one empty space, you can master filling all empty spaces."

"Elder Adaire, I mean no disrespect," said Brigitta, "but I don't think Croilus and Jarlath will be sitting around like clay pots for me."

"What if you approached them while they were asleep?" a voice emerged from the wall. It was Lalam; he had been standing there so quietly she hadn't even noticed him. A talent of the Wisings was knowing how to blend into a room until their services were necessary.

He pulled into the light. Kind hazel eyes shone down at her. There was no hostility there, surprising considering how Brigitta had last left him in the thought-loop.

"Wising Lalam," said Adaire, not even fazed that he had been listening in.

Brigitta wondered for a moment how many times a Wising may have been in a room without her realizing it. That was a trick she definitely wanted to learn. She thought of anxious little Glennis of Easyl, Himmy's friend who had Wising Destiny Marks. She could not imagine poor Glennis trying to be that still.

"You have a talent for transformation," Adaire continued. "Perhaps you can train with Brigitta each morning before she leaves?"

"Perhaps I could train with Brigitta each morning after she leaves as well."

"That is not possible," said Adaire. "You know very well you would be unable to return to the White Forest if you left."

"Until Faweh is rebalanced, you mean."

It wasn't quite a challenge, but Brigitta noted a slight twinkle in Lalam's eyes, and she could tell Adaire did not want to admit she doubted Brigitta's success.

"Are you suggesting, then, that you accompany her?" asked Adaire.

"With your permission, of course."

Adaire sucked in a breath. No Wising had ever requested to leave the services of an Elder before. Not to Brigitta's knowledge, at least. Adaire's face turned a deeper shade of red before she blew her breath back out into the room.

"Speak with Fozk," was all she said.

Things were definitely other than normal in the White Forest. To Brigitta's surprise, Fozk approved of Lalam leaving the forest. The Wising sat quietly next to Narru and Minq, while the Elders and Fozk discussed this strategy.

"He has knowledge of Earth energy," Fozk pointed out to the Elders, "and is young and strong." He turned to Brigitta. "Do you have everything you need for all of you to make it through the Purviews?"

"Just," Brigitta replied. "We have four rings and the scepter. But if we can't get the scepter away from Croilus . . ."

"Then I guess we'd better get that scepter back," said Lalam.

"Then it is settled," said Fozk with finality, sending everyone away to prepare.

In the time she had left, Brigitta exercised her injured wing and completed what lessons she could with the Elders: weather manipulation and poison reduction from Dervia, healing and transformation from Adaire, smelting and quickening from Hammus, mind misting and empathing from Mora.

Narru himself got lessons in vocalization from Song Master Helvine so he could speak some of his thoughts, and Minq had some informal flying lessons from the purple-winged Perimeter Guard brothers.

The afternoon before they were set to leave, Brigitta and Minq, with the help of Glennis of Easyl, searched from Bobbercurxy to No Moon's Canyon for Gola the Drutan. They had no luck, as there were simply too many trees. To Brigitta's disappointment, the moonstones didn't lead her anywhere; they only kept her cool when she pressed them to her skin.

When it was apparent they were going to have to leave the forest without saying good-bye to their beloved Drutan, Brigitta and Minq sat on the edge of No Moon's Canyon and cried as Glennis expressed her sympathies to them.

"Glennis," Brigitta said when she finally ran out of tears, "promise me you'll come looking some times. Promise me if you find her you'll tell her I'm sorry . . . and . . . and . . . that I love her."

"If I find her," said Glennis carefully, placing a hand on Brigitta's shoulder, "I promise I will tell her."

Chapter Eleven

Ondelle wove her hands through the air in her practiced manner. She had performed the High Priestess's task of resetting the Hourglass of Protection dozens of times, and there was no reason for this time to be any different, but still, the spell must be cast precisely. She glanced at the Elders: Fozk, Hammus, Adaire, and Jorris each held their own miniature hourglasses. Each holding the space for the Dragon's Gift to do its work.

She closed her eyes in concentration. A moment later, something deep within her chest moved, like a sleeping animal stirring. Then the energy was pulled, nearly yanked forward. A small gasp escaped her lips as the energy was pulled toward the entryway and across the passage, into a fissure in the wall.

She felt it there, the connection, behind the wall. She opened her eyes.

Brigitta.

And something else. A call to action. Something part of her had been anticipating since she had entered Pippet's womb and transferred Narine's Water energy.

"Ondelle, are you well?" asked Elder Dervia.

"I just need some air," she said.

Fozk stepped up and held out his hands.

"No," laughed Ondelle, "the outside kind. You may all rest for a while. You've done well."

She made her way outside, heart pounding, and scanned the forest and festival grounds. The arena was bustling, the faeries happy, celebratory. She closed her eyes and reached out with Narine's energy. She did not like to spy on Brigitta this way, but this was bigger than either of them. This was their dual destiny unfolding. And for as long as she had been anticipating this moment, she felt completely unprepared. How could it be time? Brigitta was still a child.

She concentrated her energy in that spot deep within her chest. But instead of reaching outward, like one would do while mind-misting, she folded the energy inward, to the infinite side of herself. A moment later, and she was flying into the lyllium fields. Her heart broke as she, now seeing as Brigitta, flew low over the lylliums and touched the petals. An innocent gesture. The last she may ever perform.

Everything was about to change.

In the full two moons' light, Brigitta and her family, Lalam and his family, Minq, Perimeter Guards Reykia and Gaowen, Fozk, the Elders, and the Apprentices and Wisings, including Glennis, who would be moving into the Hive soon, stood before The Shift. Entering the Dark Forest at night was definitely not Brigitta's first choice, but the Impenetrable Spell had to be performed with the full moons' energy.

Brigitta hugged her parents fiercely, but as briefly as possible. They wore brave faces for Himalette's sake, but Brigitta could feel their sorrow to her core.

"I'll be back, Momma," Brigitta said with determination before turning to her father. "You know I will."

"And a grand celebration we will have," said her Poppa in a voice choked with heartache. He kissed the top of her head.

Himalette hugged her next and handed her a small package. "Open that when you miss me," she said glumly, wiping her sleeve across her sniffling nose.

"Guess it will never get opened, then," joked Brigitta.

Himalette tried to laugh, but the sound got stuck in her throat.

"Come here, you big lola," Brigitta said, hugging her sister and kissing her cheek.

Auntie Ferna finally approached, but instead of hugging her, she kneeled down and looked intently into Brigitta's eyes, studying what she found. Then, she leaned in close and whispered into her ear, "Remember, Ondelle is within you. Always."

Then, Brigitta pulled away and nodded to the Elders, who nodded in return. They, too, had their brave faces on.

It was the first time Brigitta had ever left the forest with complete Elder consent, and she was leaving more prepared than ever before, with treated blankets and reinforced tunics, dried foods, dense breads, herbs, dustmist, firepepper, two globelights, four canteens, a smelting stone, healing kit, a real wind-winder, and Jarlath's frore dagger—distributed among the travelers' packs. In addition, Lalam carried a personal spell pouch around his waist.

Narru blinked his sideways eyes and wiggled his lips, testing them. "Good-bye," he said, then smiled shyly and waved.

Mousha held onto Pippet and Himalette tightly, as Brigitta and her traveling party stepped through the invisible barrier in the center of The Shift. Fozk took one end of the hourglass, and she took the other, holding it perfectly centered in the protective field.

"If this doesn't work . . ." A joke halted on her tongue as Fozk's icy blue eyes bore down on her.

"May the wisdom of all faeries be with you."

She nodded and they both closed their eyes. Brigitta misted her mind through her own body, down her arm. She misted out from her fingertips, lightly holding the hourglass, and into the hourglass itself, sifting through the sands toward the center where the protective field began.

Just as they had practiced, she met Fozk's mind mist right in the middle of the hourglass. They coiled their mists together, mingling their Air energies, and she used her Water to slowly fill in the empty space. They didn't rush; they let the energies blend naturally until there was no distinction between them.

Now, Fozk's voice reverberated in her mind.

Together they coaxed the Blue Spell forward. Brigitta thought the magic would resist, as if being woken from a long sleep. Instead, it burst forth so forcefully she was nearly knocked off her feet.

Then, the four Elders were with them, calling forth the Impenetrable Spell. Calling and calling until it emerged, an unshakable force.

"No!" she heard her mother wail, and she let go of the hourglass and opened her eyes.

The Impenetrable Spell quickly spread like gathering thunderclouds over the forest, thickening into a solid shell. And just before the shield sealed itself for good, something burst through it and collapsed to the ground with a sharp cry.

Lalam and Brigitta rushed over to see what it was. A young faerie with deep yellow wings was lying in the dirt moat. She stood up and smiled a dizzy smile.

"Glennis!" Brigitta hollered, "get back across or you'll be stuck out here!"

They both looked to the newly encased White Forest. By the expressions on all the faces on the other side, Brigitta could tell that it was already too late.

She turned angrily back to Glennis. "What were you thinking! You knew that would happen!"

"You wouldn't have let me come if I'd asked," Glennis said, brushing herself off.

"Of course not!" said Brigitta. "You have no business being out here!"

"I've just as much business as you," said Glennis.

"You'll get yourself killed."

"That's my risk to take."

Brigitta balled her fists. "We don't have enough rings!"

"Rings?" asked Glennis as Minq and Narru joined them. "What rings?"

"Looks like our party has grown by one Wising," said Lalam, straightening Glennis's pack.

Muffled voices came from the other side of the protective shell. Brigitta held her hand up to it. It was still transparent, but now solid. Smooth and neutral, like a jar. On the other side, her tear-faced mother pressed her own hand against it as Himalette clung to her waist, and Auntie Ferna put her arms around Mousha.

The Elders and Fozk appeared to be in a heated discussion about Glennis, as their glances suggested, but there was nothing they could do. The White Forest was impenetrable, and if Brigitta and her companions ever wanted to get back in, they had to face the gargantuan task before them.

"What's done is done," Lalam said, turning to Brigitta. "We'll figure something out along the way."

Brigitta nodded, removed her pack, and yanked out the healing kit. She grabbed a mossleaf patch and slapped it over Glennis's mouth, whose eyes bugged out in surprise.

"You will be quiet, do as you're told, and keep up with the rest of us," said Brigitta.

Glennis nodded and straightened up.

"Don't think I won't leave you behind if I have to."

Minq threw Brigitta a questioning glance as she hefted her pack, but she was not going to be soft on Glennis, no matter what any of the others thought. The Dark Forest was a dangerous place, and Glennis had just complicated everything. Compromised it, even.

She set her face as stone cold as she could. She had to be decisive. She had to make choices and move forward. And she had to tear herself away or she would never be able to leave. With one last glance at her loved ones, she took off toward the Dark Forest. "Come on, then."

She fluttered over the expanse of shifting dirt toward the trees. Minq and Narru bounded after her on their agile legs, with Glennis and Lalam taking up the rear. They slipped into the Dark Forest, cutting off their view of their home and kin.

"You have to feel the spaces first in order to move what's not there into them," said Lalam, face half lit from the globelight tucked into the tree branches. "Like that children's game, Ten-Go-Ten. You know the one."

Sleepy-eyed, the remains of their dinner before them, Glennis, Minq, and Narru watched from a log, as Brigitta and Lalam practiced in the scant area secured with a firepepper and dustmist wall.

Brigitta hadn't played Ten-Go-Ten in season cycles, but she knew what he was talking about. The game was played with two-toned stones on a grid, ten squares up and ten squares across. The object was to have all your stones on the board with the same color showing, and all touching in some way: diagonally, up, down, or across. Once you placed a stone, you could flip it over in any direction into an empty space, or jump over another player, flipping their stone instead.

Lalam drew a Ten-Go-Ten board in the dirt. "Everything has space that can be filled. I see objects in transformation as rearranging material into those spaces."

"But I still don't understand how you get them to move in the first place, once you've found the empty spaces?" she asked. "Adaire said she sifts them."

"Everyone finds his or her own way," he said, placing six different colored pebbles into the playing grid and staring down into them. As they all observed, one of the pebbles slowly turned from black to green. "I use rooting. I surround matter with roots and everything outside the roots is usable space."

Brigitta hadn't spent enough time in Earth energy lessons to study rooting, an advanced technique in which one's thoughts stretched out into limitless roots, almost like spider webs, allowing the faerie to detect an object's shape with the mind.

Brigitta sat down on her blanket, exhausted. "I don't have time to master rooting."

Lalam shrugged. "It starts with one root."

"You've been hanging around Elders too long."

Dinner complete, Glennis stuck the mossleaf patch back over her mouth and began to clean up. As Glennis focused on her task, with not a hint of complaint, a brief stab of guilt pierced Brigitta's heart. Perhaps she'd been too rough on Glennis. After all, it was her destiny to serve.

"To serve the destiny that awaits," Brigitta murmured, suddenly missing the hulking Nhord couple she had befriended in Noe. She hoped they were looking over the Watchers. She hoped they were all safe.

She looked around at her odd assortment of companions as they got ready for bed: a young faerie barely older than Himalette, a long-eared hairless beast with removable wings, a land-locked sea creature child, and an Earth faerie man she had tricked into allowing her to steal the White Forest scepter. A faerie she now knew to be reasonably skilled at rooting and transformation.

"Lalam," she said, "about the night of the Masquerade . . ."

"The thought-loop?" He smirked at her while he unraveled his blanket.

"Yeah." She crossed her arms and eyed him suspiciously.

"It was impressive," he said, slipping into his bedroll. He pulled the blanket around himself snugly and closed his eyes. "I would have looped me first instead of the novice Wising. That way, you could have taken me by surprise."

It took no time at all for Lalam to fall to sleep. In the meantime, Brigitta tossed around trying to find the best position for her newly healed wing, wondering why he had allowed her to thought-loop him in the first place. What had he witnessed, over the seasons, from his silent, concealed spaces in the Hive?

The young Saarin was falling behind. Lalam and Brigitta stopped to inspect him, and his skin was peeling, displaying more of his blue web-like veins underneath.

Land sick, he murmured in Brigitta's mind.

Around them the forest was dense and prickly, no water in sight. She examined the clouds through the tree branches and briefly empathed them, but they were forming in quick whispering curls, not dense wet masses. They spun in the air, teasing her with their lack of rain-ness.

"We need you, Narru," said Brigitta. "We can't cross the ocean without you, so hold on."

Holding.

Minq wrapped an ear around his shoulders to steady him as they plodded after Brigitta, Lalam, and Glennis.

"We have to find him some water," Brigitta whispered to Lalam.

A moonbeat later and Narru collapsed. Brigitta and Lalam carried him over to a blackened stump. Brigitta sat down, holding Narru's head in her lap.

"Take this." She placed a canteen to his lips and managed to get a few capfuls into his mouth. While she helped him drink, she became aware of a distant rushing sound beneath the thrum of the forest.

"The River That Runs Backwards," she said, head perking up.

They carried him through the trees, pushing branches and webs out of his way, until they were close enough to gather the water drops misting in the air. They gave him more to drink and wet him down, but even as the water absorbed into his skin, he remained weak and nauseous.

"I don't understand what's happening," said Brigitta to Lalam and Glennis. "It's plenty wet here, but he's not getting any better."

"I don't think it's just the wetness, Brigitta," said Lalam, mixing a stomach-easing concoction. He broke open a leafy pouch and poured the sandy mix into his potion bowl. "From what you have told us of it, the ocean sounds like a very different world. His kind are not meant to stay on land for extended periods of time. This may be killing him."

"What are you saying?" Brigitta let Narru's head rest back in her lap, and she placed her hand over his burning forehead. "I must choose between saving Jarlath or saving Narru? I don't know how much time I have for either!"

"No, not choose," said Minq, twisting around a tree whose wetness he had been wiping off with his ears. He pulled his sopping ears to Brigitta and squeezed more water into her hands. "I take Narru ocean, you save Jarlath, meet for crossing."

"You mean we separate?" asked Brigitta, splashing the water over Narru's face.

"Only slow you down anyway," said Minq, wiggling his small wings. "This way we all have chance."

"I don't know, Minq," she said. "Just the two of you?" The last thing Brigitta wanted was to be separated from one more friend. It would ruin her if anything happened to either of them.

"I know Dark Forest," he said. "I know forest like inside of ear. And Saarin know ocean like skin on stomach."

"He makes good sense," said Lalam. "And I doubt Narru could scale Sage Peak."

"I . . . I . . ." Brigitta shook her head. She turned to Glennis. "What do you think?"

Glennis startled from where she sat, mossleaf patch still smeared over her mouth. She pulled it away slowly and grimaced as it pulled at her skin. She thought for a moment. "I agree with Lalam and Minq."

Brigitta let this information sink in. *Decisive,* she thought. *That's how to lead.* She looked at all their faces and then down at the dehydrated Saarin.

"All right." She turned to Minq and Lalam. "But where will we meet up again? We still have to decide the best place to cross."

She pulled a blanket over Narru as Lalam took out their map.

Brigitta had been using Ondelle's principle of approaching the unknown *one step at a time* to avoid getting overwhelmed. But there was no denying that sooner or later they were going to have to cross the ocean. The task seemed too distant, and unreal, seeing as finding Croilus and stealing the scepter and Earth energy was problematic enough. She knew nothing about Sage Peak's magic. Who were the last Ancients to meditate in its caverns, and what did they leave behind that Croilus could use against them?

Lalam, Minq, and Glennis grew quiet as they studied the map of Foraglenn, Glennis tapping a stick against a stone around the fire pit. Brigitta stared at the stick as it rapped out its rhythm. She followed it up Glennis's arm to the bright tunic she wore. She had seen it somewhere before.

"Glennis," Brigitta asked, "when did you get that tunic?"

Glennis looked down. "Oh, this? Just yesterday morning, as a matter of fact. Do you like it? It's for my Wising ceremony. Well, it *was* for my Wising ceremony. Look," Glennis pulled out a small durma, a ceremonial drum, "they gave me this, too. I mean, I know it won't really come in handy or anything, I just wanted something to remind me of home . . ."

Glennis's rambling faded into the background as Brigitta tried to access some memory of—*Glennis leaning over the side of a boat with yellow sails . . .* She instinctively reached for the hourglass around her neck, but instead, found Gola's moonstones.

That was it. The moonstone visions.

"We were on a boat," said Brigitta. "You and I were crossing the ocean on a boat."

"We were?" Glennis asked, putting her durma away. "When?"

"Lalam, where would we have gotten a boat on Foraglenn? We were in a boat, I swear it!" Brigitta was almost frantic, mind grasping at the image. She was speaking of it as if it had already happened, and that's what it felt like. A vague memory, difficult to hold on to, like smoke.

"All right, you were on a boat," he said. "But I have no idea where you would have found one large enough to cross an ocean."

Brigitta wracked her brain to no avail. She could not conjure more than the fleeting image of Glennis on board some unfamiliar vessel.

"Why don't we lay out our journey and go from there?" suggested Lalam.

They went back to studying the map. "Sage Peak first . . ." Brigitta murmured. "Then Storlglenn is this way, east . . . but our eastern coast looks too rugged. Perhaps there is easier access here, from Icecap Forest."

Narru squirmed in Brigitta's lap and moaned.

"Shhhh," she said. "You need rest."

"Mnuuuuh," he muttered, and then crawled into Brigitta's mind. *Icecap Forest*, he said. *Lodge of Eastern Months.*

"Lodge of Eastern Months." Brigitta looked up at her companions. "What's that?"

"No idea," said Lalam as Minq and Glennis shook their heads.

Stop on Trading Route, said the Saarin, *before Great World Cry.*

"Trading route? Is there a boat there?"

"Uhnnnngggg," nodded Narru. *Boats being in all sea lodges. All lands trading.*

"Narru," Brigitta said, "why didn't you tell us this before?"

Never saying boat needing before.

Brigitta, Lalam, Glennis, and Minq all studied the little patch labeled Icecap Forest on the map.

"Then that's where we'll meet," Brigitta said, decisively. "Four by land, two by sea."

Lalam, Glennis, and Narru had been warned numerous times from both Brigitta and Minq about the River That Runs Backwards. About its dizzying madness, about its powerful pull, about not getting too close. Seeing it for themselves was another matter, and even Glennis was speechless.

They held onto each other as they made their way, traversing its banks, looking for the best spot over which to fly.

When they arrived at a section that provided a high protection of cliff, Brigitta set up the wind-winder with Lalam's assistance so that it created a shell around Narru's body, leaving a cushion of air in every direction. He wouldn't be flying anywhere himself; the point was to hold him up and make him light so Minq could guide him along. They had no idea how long their spell would last. Brigitta hoped it was strong enough to get him all the way to the eastern shore of Foraglenn, but that was unlikely.

They huddled around him, each taking hold of the wind-winder, and flew as high as Minq was able with his weaker wings, before setting off over the river. The sound grew intense as they crossed overhead, no one speaking, no one daring to look down. It pulled at them, sending each one off in frightening gusts, but they held on.

When they dropped down on the other side, Brigitta hugged both Minq and Narru, using every bit of willpower to hold back her tears. "We'll see you in the Icecap Forest at the Lodge of Eastern Months."

She kissed Minq on top of his head between the ears. "Boat or no boat," she added.

"No worry," he said. "Take good care of Narru. Like brother."

"Wait a good five or six suns," she said, "and if we don't show, find some way to get him home."

"You show," he said.

A moonsbreath later and the two odd beasts were off, Minq pulling Narru by the hand, and Narru bobbing along in the wind-winder. Not long after, Brigitta, Lalam, and Glennis headed out in the direction of Sage Peak.

Brigitta silently flew up front, picking her way through the forest and keeping an eye on the leaves and branches to make sure they weren't tunneling around them like they had done to her and Jarlath. Glennis chatted away, asking Lalam all sorts of questions about the differences between Earth and Water magic and the pros and cons of being a Wising. Maybe she'd learn more out here from Lalam than from the Elders in the White Forest.

"Do you always like being a Wising?" Glennis asked.

"I am suited to it," he responded.

"What was the hardest thing to learn?"

"Patience."

Brigitta laughed. It would probably be the hardest thing for Glennis to learn as well. She broke through the next twist of trees and stopped. The other two halted behind her.

In front of them was the most enormous flower Brigitta had ever seen. Only, it didn't seem to be attached to any plant. It was just sitting in the middle of a clearing on the forest floor. It was inviting, large enough for all three of them to lie down and take a nap. Hundreds of orange stamens extended from the center, and layers and layers of bright yellow petals, like giant tongues, beckoned to be slid down.

"That looks like fun!" said Glennis. "I know we're in a hurry, but can we try it just once?"

In some part of her mind, Brigitta knew they shouldn't, but that thought was quickly buried under another thought that didn't see why not. What was one more moonbeat, after all? They could always cut their lunch short. Or have it now. Only she wasn't sure if it was lunchtime. She wasn't even sure how long she'd been standing there staring at the strange flower. Or if she was hungry.

"Lalam." She spun around to ask if he knew how long it had been since breakfast, but he was no longer behind her. Instead, he sat on the ground stroking the anther of a stamen that had extended itself from the flower's center. As it nuzzled against his hand, its pollen rubbed off, sending orange dust everywhere.

"It's very soft," he said, brushing it up and down, a trail of orange dust settling on his tunic and in his hair. "And look." He pulled down another tendril next to him. Suckered onto the end of it was a blue-feathered bird about the size of Brigitta's head with long, stiff yellow legs.

"Huh," was all she could think to say. "Why would a bird stick itself to a flower?"

"I don't know," said Lalam, now stroking the bird, "but it looks peaceful, doesn't it?"

She had to admit that it did look peaceful with its eyes staring open blankly. Nothing on its mind. "It's very good at being still, don't you think?"

Before he could answer, the plant moved its tentacle-like stamen and snatched the bird away. It disappeared somewhere beneath the flower.

They both laughed.

"I think we scared it away," said Lalam, going back to petting the anther.

"Silly bird," said Brigitta. She scratched her head. There was something she was supposed to be doing, but she couldn't remember what. Maybe she had already done it.

She looked up at Glennis, now scaling the giant flower to get to the highest petal.

"Oh, yes!" exclaimed Brigitta, the rest of the world dropping away. "We were going to slide down the petals!"

Chapter Twelve

O ndelle staggered through the sand and collapsed halfway up the beach. The forest beyond was so dark she couldn't distinguish the individual trees. She didn't like that absence of light, did not want to enter the forest, but she knew she had to get off the beach. A fierce sandstorm was brewing, and she could sense something monstrous emerging from the depths of the sea.

Breathless, she struggled to get up. What was wrong with her? She had a scepter fully renewed with the great Dragon's Gift! She lived with more than half of Narine's elemental energy inside of her. She had her knowing.

Narine's knowing.

A sharp pain stabbed Ondelle in the temples and she cried out. The knowing couldn't settle; she had to rid herself of any resistance. But first, she had to move away from the shore.

She managed to push herself up on her hands and knees, and she crawled over the beach, the wind whipping up and pelting her face with sand. She closed her eyes and kept crawling until her hands felt earth and leaves. She pulled herself to the closest tree and hauled herself up off the ground, wondering if she'd be able to fly.

The Standing Stones. That was the safest place for her. How did she know about them? As soon as she questioned her intuition another stab of pain shot through her head. Ah, that was it. Trust the knowing. It would not settle otherwise.

To the Stones then. Without further hesitation, she took to the air, flying north along the edge of the forest. Concentrating on each wingbeat helped ease the pain in her skull as she climbed her way to the plateau and the protection of the Stones. She now knew them to be the remains of a gathering place, and she couldn't help smiling at Narine's memory of the serene lookout over Forever Beach, young Faeries and Saarin and Chakau'un lazing in the shade of the Standing Stones as their parents meditated together.

The wind picked up, knocking the memory away, and her headache returned. It drove into her temples and she fell against one of the stones, collapsing to the ground.

"Let go," she said to herself, trembling. "Trust."

To fight the cold, she wove a pocket of air around herself and breathed the warmth of her Fire energy into it. Even this simple spell brought pain to her head, and she leaned back into the stone. If this was what it would feel like each time one of Narine's memories came to her through the knowing, she dreaded her journey back to the White Forest. If she could but calm her mind enough. She took a deep breath and allowed any resistance to ride out on her exhale.

The pain of the knowing engulfed her. This time, it wasn't in her head. It was someplace so deep inside of her that her entire being was swallowed in grief. This knowing, a laceration on her spirit she would never be able to heal.

"No," she said. "Oh, Great Moon, no."

Her trust had bought her the truth. She picked up her scepter, staring into the crystal with new awareness, trying to see that truth inside.

She now knew the truth of Blue Spell as this: that every time a White Forest faerie used its magic, she was transforming an Ancient's energy. The fifth element, Ether, had been bound to the Ancients, as the other four elements had been bound to the White Forest faeries by the Ancients to protect them against a world gone mad. The Eternal Dragon had fed on balanced elements, and with the addition of the fifth element, transformed this energy into Blue Spell as a form of release.

As White Forest faeries were dispersed, so their energy was cycled back to the next Elemental Faerie's life. But as the Ethereal energy was transformed through Blue Spell, it was scattered with each use. It did not cycle back. The Ancients had sacrificed their energies to appease the Dragon.

By keeping the White Forest safe, the Elemental Faeries had been destroying the Ancients.

Brigitta opened her eyes, dazed, but with a nagging sense of urgency, a sense that she was running out of time.

It also felt as if something were sniffing at her.

She sat up and wobbled. She was lying on the ground while hairy plant roots wriggled all around her like long worms. She screamed, and they zipped back underground.

How long had she been lying there? And where was there?

Oh, yes. She blinked at the giant flower in front of her. It wasn't as pretty as her vague memory of it was. As a matter of fact, it was looking less and less like a flower and more and more like an enormous stomach with tentacles.

"Lalam?" she called as she stood up, holding out her arms and flitting her wings for balance. "Glennis?"

She searched through the petals, which were definitely more like wide slick arms, until she came across Glennis, who was curled up inside one, the edges neatly folded around her.

"Get up!" she called in Glennis's ear and then shook her.

The young faerie opened her eyes, yawned, and stretched. "Good morning, Brigitta."

"It's not a good morning. It's not morning at all. We need to find Lalam and get out of here."

"What's the hurry?" asked Glennis, sleepy-eyed. She yawned again and smacked her lips. "You said I could slide down the petals."

"You've already slid down a dozen times. Now, come on!" Brigitta peeled the slick "petal" away and helped Glennis step out.

She wiped off her slimy hands on Glennis's tunic.

"I did?"

She leaned in closer to Glennis. "SNAP OUT OF IT!" she screamed.

Glennis shrieked and then laughed. Brigitta pulled her by the hand around to the other side of the stomach plant's gelatinous body.

"Oh, no," she cried, dropping Glennis's hand. Lalam was suspended upside down by two tentacles.

"Silly Lalam." Glennis pointed at the older Wising and laughed.

"Yeah, silly Lalam," said Brigitta. "I need to get him down. Stay there!"

She took a step toward him and the enormous stomach burbled. Underneath its bulgy center, a long mouth, if she could call it that, opened up, stretching the length of the beast. A dozen purplish tongues flicked in and out.

"Bog buggers," hissed Brigitta and screwed her eyes closed.

Transformation, transformation, she tried to concentrate, but it was no use. She couldn't even pull up the Ten-Go-Ten playing grid in her mind, let alone any rootings.

She opened her eyes just as the mouth exhaled a gust of rancid breath.

"Whew!" Glennis waved her hand in front of her nose.

"Get back," said Brigitta, pulling Jarlath's frore dagger out.

"Are you going to carve something?"

"Not exactly." Brigitta lifted it up over her head. "Glennis, listen carefully. When I say fly, you grab one side of Lalam and fly! Understand?"

"Gotcha."

"I'm serious."

"Seriously gotcha."

"I hope so." Brigitta plunged the knife forward, slashing through the tentacle. Lalam dropped to the ground with a thud, the end of the tendril writhing around on the ground next to him.

"OOOOOWWWWWWWRRRRRRRRRRRRRRR!" roared the mouth, tongues flicking violently in and out, roots ripping from the ground.

"Fly!" screamed Brigitta, grabbing Lalam's right arm and kicking the end of the tentacle away.

But Glennis just stood there staring at the stomach beast and scratching her head. "Have you ever seen anything like it?" she asked.

The beast suddenly stopped roaring and searched the ground with its remaining tentacles until it found its missing piece.

"Glennis!"

"What?" asked Glennis, turning to face Brigitta and Lalam. She put her hands on her hips. "What's wrong with him?"

The beast popped the piece into its mouth and then pressed its remaining tentacles against the ground. There was a terrible ripping sound as it pulled itself out of the earth. Glennis wobbled for a moment, then shook her head as if her ears were water-logged. She turned back around to see the tentacled stomach-mouth before them.

And she screamed.

"Fly!" Glennis shot toward Lalam and grabbed his left arm.

She and Brigitta flew into the air, dodging brambly branches, up and up until they were far out of tentacle reach. They dropped onto a thick limb and set Lalam down so they could catch their breaths.

"He's – heavier – than – he – looks," panted Glennis.

"I – know," panted Brigitta as she handed Glennis the knife. Glennis held onto it as Brigitta slapped Lalam lightly on the cheek. "We gotta wake him up."

"Uh, Brigitta," Glennis poked at her arm. "What's that thing doing?"

The stomach beast had turned over so that it now lay on its bulgy center with the mouth on top, and its tentacles waving in the air. It reminded Brigitta of when Himalette used to lie face down on one of her beany mushroom bags, her arms and legs not long enough to reach the ground.

"Looka my big stomach," she would laugh and pat the beany

bag. "My stomach is so big I can't reach the floor."

"I have no idea," Brigitta said to Glennis, shaking away the memory.

Lalam mumbled and they returned their attention to him, now nearly awake, and puzzled by his surroundings.

Before they could explain, there was a loud popping from below. The stomach creature was growing itself a new tentacle, each extension of flesh popping itself into place.

"Now that would be a useful skill," said Brigitta as the beast repaired its sliced appendage.

Once the tentacle was fully regrown, the stomach beast stretched all its limbs in turn. Then, it pulled back two tentacles, extending them through the trees behind it until Brigitta thought they would surely snap off. The bizarre beast had more stretch than festival taffy.

Finally, it let its tentacles go and they sprung forward, wrapping themselves around two tree branches, and using the momentum to propel itself forward.

"It's going to smash into the trees!" shouted Glennis as the stomach beast shot toward them.

It did not smash into the trees, however. Instead, it slipped impossibly through the branches and thorns and ivies, finding the exact shape to fit through every space, elongating itself and shrinking other parts. With its sheer enormousness, it should not have been able to do what it was doing. But there was no time to contemplate the logic of it.

"Fly!" they all called out and fled the tree.

Brigitta could feel the swoosh of air as one of the beast's tentacles flew by, wrapping itself around a tree in front of her, flinging itself in her direction.

"What is it?!" cried Glennis from below her.

Even if they had known, Lalam and Brigitta didn't have the breath to answer.

"Higher!" was all Lalam managed as he struggled to fit through the hanging foliage.

Something snagged Brigitta's ankle and pulled. She snatched

onto a vine and pounded her wings, but couldn't free her leg. A quick glance told her it was being gripped by one of the mouth's long purple tongues.

"No!" Glennis cried and threw the frore dagger at it, slicing the tongue away.

Released from its grip, Brigitta sped through the air and grabbed Glennis's hand, pulling her after Lalam through the trees.

"Nice shot," she said, glancing back after Jarlath's knife as it disappeared. No going back for it now.

They flew without direction, merely following the natural space of the forest. They flew with every ounce of energy, and the creature followed. It would fall behind, then disappear, and they would think that they had lost it, only for it to come flinging itself forward again.

Scratched and bruised, they continued, Lalam and Brigitta taking turns leading the way and assisting Glennis, who was all but spent. Eventually, Brigitta looked back to find her fluttering to the ground. "I just can't—" Glennis cried.

"Lalam," Brigitta called, gesturing him back.

"Scout ahead," he said, already descending. "I'll bring her along lower to the ground."

Brigitta hesitated, hovering and listening. "I think we may have lost it this time."

She closed her eyes and tried to calm her heart, but it was overloaded. There was no way she had the focus to mist her mind out in front of them. And yet, she could detect something different in the air ahead. Something in the sound of it.

Below her, Lalam was giving Glennis a drink from his canteen.

"I'll be right back," she told them.

She flew carefully through the trees, glancing down at her bug-stained and web-covered tunic. At least they had been flying too fast to get stung or bitten by anything.

The air was definitely changing. Getting bigger was the only way she could describe it. She could sense the space of it. She could sense where the density of the forest changed and the space of air began . . .

That was it! Feeling the space of air on such a grand scale, she suddenly understood what Lalam had attempted to explain to her about transformation on the Ten-Go-Ten grid. She could feel those spaces now. Large and small. In everything around her.

Transformation was all about space! And to Brigitta, that meant focusing on Air energy. For Lalam, it was about focusing on Earth energy. She felt the space in order to find the "not space," while Lalam had used rooting to feel the "not space" in order to find the space.

She closed her eyes and flew, laughing. She could feel all the space, and not space, around her. She could fly with her eyes closed knowing this. Trusting this space and not space. She could trust her Air energy; she knew what relaxing into trust felt like thanks to Ondelle. She couldn't wait to tell Lalam! Couldn't wait to—

Suddenly, there was no more not-space stretched before her. Only space.

And she opened her eyes.

Brigitta had never seen such an expanse of land before in her life. Not even The Shift was as vast as this. She hovered in the air at the very edge of a cliff on the eastern border of the Dark Forest. Stretching out for what looked like hundreds of moonbeats below her were a series of low dark hills to the north and south. To the east, the hills rolled like waves toward a steep mammoth mountain that twisted so high it disappeared into the clouds.

It was a bit windy, but nothing she couldn't navigate. Still, she secured herself between two rocks before peering over the side of the cliff, which dropped straight down. It was enough to make even the strongest flyer dizzy.

A scream sounded from the forest.

"Lalam! Glennis!" she called, cursing herself for getting distracted. "This way!"

A moment later and she could see them speeding toward her,

the ridiculously persistent stomach beast flinging itself through the trees after them. She could see the panic in both of their faces as they realized the forest ended and the world was about to drop out from under them.

"Go up!" she hollered, and they obeyed.

Before the creature could follow Lalam and Glennis up into the trees, Brigitta called to it. "Right here, you big blob!" She waved her arms and whistled. "Yeah, I'm talking to you!"

As the beast threw its tentacles out, grabbing two of the final forest trees, Brigitta dropped down the other side of the cliff. The creature flung itself forward, stretching past Brigitta, before realizing it had run out of forest. One of its tentacles slipped from the trunk, flailing through the air, but the other tentacle held, and the creature began to spring back.

"Oh, no you don't!" called Brigitta, peering up over the cliff. She focused on the space around the tree where the creature had taken hold. Then she felt for the space inside the tree itself, the minuscule pockets of emptiness there. Calling on all moisture in the surrounding air, Brigitta attempted to replace all the tree space with water, and disappear the tree's not-space into it.

But she couldn't do it, it wasn't transforming, and the beast retracted back toward her. She leapt out of the way as the creature slammed against the side of the cliff and dangled there by its one tentacle. It released a thunderous roar and began pulling itself up the cliff face.

Brigitta frantically tried to reconnect to the tree space, but couldn't find it in her panic. Above her, Lalam called out, and Brigitta felt his rooting through the not-space of treeness until it broke apart. A blink later and he had transformed the chunk of tree held onto by the beast, and it dissolved to dust and scattered to the winds. The top of the tree fell away, the beast's tentacle slipped, and the creature tumbled down through the air to the foothills below.

Brigitta didn't watch it land.

Lalam and Glennis glided down to meet her.

"Is it gone?" Glennis asked, face stained with tears and dirt. She had a nasty gash on her forehead, another on her upper arm, and blood dotted her ripped tunic.

Brigitta nodded and collapsed to her knees.

"I couldn't do it." She looked up at Lalam. "How in the world am I going to transform anything to save Jarlath if I can't even turn something as easy as a tree into water?"

"You'll get it," he said, flitting to the edge of the cliff and peering down.

Glennis followed along and he held up his hand. "You might not want to see this. I can vouch that that thing isn't coming after us again."

They made camp just inside the trees and considered their journey to Sage Mountain. Over a modest fire, they fried some meaty mushrooms and it reminded Brigitta of the night she had met the Nhords. How she had immediately trusted them, as she had immediately trusted Narru.

Were their counterparts waiting for her over on Storlglenn and Carraiglenn? She pictured the images in the room above the dome at Croilus where they had found the Purview. One representative from each continent had surrounded the empty chair where the High Sage should have been.

Glennis popped a hot mushroom into her mouth and sucked her breath in to cool it off. "Why not just go right over the hills?" she asked after chewing and swallowing. "They looked deserted to me."

"Don't let that fool you," Brigitta said, squinting into the darkness. There was no moonlight due to the cloud covering, so she couldn't even see the hills below. It appeared as if they were sitting at the end of the world.

And then, something shimmered in the distance, lighting up one of the hills. They all perked up as a swarm of something fluttered around and over the hills, silently skimming the surface.

"What is it?" asked Glennis.

"Dunno," said Brigitta wistfully, "but it's beautiful."

"Don't let that fool you," joked Glennis nervously.

Entranced by the movement, they all stared as the lights skimmed and turned, fluttered and dove. The flock disappeared from view, and the faeries held their breaths, not sure what to do. Suddenly, the lights shot up over the cliff and descended on them. Brigitta, Lalam, and Glennis leapt up as the swarm of lights buzzed around, moving as a single force, and then landed in a tree, covering each branch so that the tree lit up like a star.

Brigitta stepped a little closer and examined the lights. Tiny, winged, silver and white striped beasts no bigger than her thumbnail fluttered there, causing the tree to vibrate and hum. She let out her breath and they scattered, splitting their little tribe in two before swerving back together again and dropping over the side of the cliff.

Spellbound into silence, Brigitta stared after the little beasts until her heart stopped pounding, and then turned back to the others. Each had shimmering tears streaming down their cheeks, liquid silver. She touched her own wet cheeks, pulling away dabs of lustrous tears. In spite of them, they all smiled and quietly got ready for bed.

They tucked themselves in for the night with an unspoken agreement that they would figure everything out in the morning. She could sense the other two lying on their backs, as she was, eyes open, gazing into the trees, wishing that the fluttering lights would return. Even if it were only in their dreams.

A thought struck Brigitta. If she and Lalam and Glennis could be exiled from their forest, so could other beasts. Maybe that brilliant flock was also trying to find its way back home.

"One day we will have to tell this story," she said. "The White Forest Chroniclers will want to record the great tale of the faeries who saved Faweh."

Lalam and Glennis laughed.

"I'm not so good at writing things down, or telling stories," said Brigitta, turning onto her side. "Glennis, I hereby dub you the Chronicler of Our Journey."

"What do I have to do?" she asked, twisting around to face Brigitta, eyes eager.

"Well, first thing is you have to name those beautiful lost lights."

"That's easy," she said. "They're called illuminoops."

"Illuminoops," Brigitta repeated.

"Illuminoops," Lalam agreed.

The night grew quiet around them but for the occasional grunt, howl, or croak. As the other two fell into a rhythmic breathing, Brigitta concentrated on connecting with her Narine energy, collapsing it inward as Ondelle had done to find her.

She just wanted to see that Jarlath was all right. That he was still alive even if there was no way to get a message to him. She thought about the illuminoops, how they appeared so spontaneous, yet connected. A thousand individuals making one remarkable whole. More than anything right then, she wanted Jarlath to see them. To see that there was still beauty left in the world.

Inward she went, sinking deeper and deeper. And just before falling asleep, Brigitta began to sense subtle movements around her. She was suddenly surrounded by hundreds of Ancients lying inside a large cavern with a clear, pointed ceiling out through which she could see the stars.

Chapter Thirteen

Lalam closed the door to Ondelle's personal spell chamber. He placed a tray bearing a teapot and two small cups in front of her on her work desk, stepped back, and waited for further instruction. The tea was Ondelle's personal recipe, a combination of lyllium, ceunias, and sharmock with a hint of firepepper to keep it warm, though not enough to burn.

She was fond of Lalam. If she had borne children, she would have been proud to call someone like him her own. He was loyal, discreet, respectful, and willing. And, most fortunately, he was bound to Earth, the final element left for Narine to gift, and the one with which she had the least experience.

She set aside the map of Foraglenn she had been studying and poured tea for them both. When the cups were filled, she stood from her chair, gesturing for him to pick up his cup. They began their private ritual at once, locking eyes, inhaling and exhaling from their cores, then taking sips of tea. The comfort and warmth of it flooded her bloodstream. A perfect brew; Lalam was a good student.

They set down their cups and Ondelle moved closer, placing her hands on either side of his face. He stared back, impassive, clearing his mind of all thought.

"Ready?" she asked.

He nodded.

They relaxed and fell deeper into each other's eyes as she misted out to him, the minuscule spaces of his body now familiar to her. She could occupy them without much effort, distributing the infinitesimal pieces of herself into the spaces of his being.

With each breath, she found her way farther inside, and when she felt completely connected, in that same way she had been drawn into the Dragon's eyes, she breathed her Air energy into those spaces, so that his Earth and her Air were counterparts.

It was agonizing; it felt as if she were wrenching her very essence away. But she had learned to bear the ache.

She breathed again, closer and closer to losing her energy entirely to him, unsure if she could get it back if she did. And just as the last bit of Air was released, she immediately drew it all back, rehousing the energy within her own body and sealing it within.

They both staggered back, breaking their connection. He put a hand to his head, gasping.

"Well done," she murmured, picking up her cup of tea, hands trembling.

He steadied himself, stepped up to her desk for his own cup, and nodded. He sipped as she sipped, breathed as she breathed, until they were both calm again.

"How do you feel?" she asked.

"Tired," he said, "but less disoriented than before."

They finished their tea in silence and placed the cups back on the tray, which he picked up as he steeled himself to leave. When he reached for the door handle, he turned around.

"May I ask a question?"

She gestured for him to do so.

"After our sessions, I experience feelings that aren't my own,'" he confided. "Feelings that disappear with a night's sleep. Sometimes feelings for people I don't really know."

"That makes sense," replied Ondelle.

"Is there anything I should do about this?" he asked.

"Do what you are called to do," she said, turning back to the map on her desk. "Thank you, Lalam; you should rest now."

He left the room with the tray. Left Ondelle to contemplate her impending transformation. She had to get this right, she thought.

Her plan had to be perfect. If Narine's four energies were not reunited with the last of the Ethereal energy, there would be no more Blue Spell. Ever.

The air was growing thinner the farther they flew across the foothills, which they had discovered, upon trying to land on one, were actually deep sand dunes. It was unbearably hot, and before mid-morning, they were drenched in sweat and flying at half speed in order to keep up their strength. There was nowhere to land in the sands, no water or shade for protection, so they kept moving, limiting their speech.

Each in deep concentration, they made good time despite the lack of air, until at the final hill before the great mountain, the air disappeared altogether.

Brigitta was in front when it happened. The temperature dropped, and she plummeted to the sand, sinking to her elbows and knees. She tried to take a breath, but there was nothing to breathe.

Lalam started to ask what was wrong, when he hit the pocket of deadness and fell. He gestured for Glennis to stop where she was, grabbed Brigitta's arm, and dragged her back toward where Glennis hovered, gasping at the thin air.

They crawled, hands and legs sinking into the sand, which threatened to pull them under if they did not keep moving. Unable to breathe, Brigitta's heart pounded, and her eyes stung, as she struggled to get back.

When they hit air again, a relief even as thin as it was, Glennis held out her hands and helped them to steady themselves enough to flutter back up.

After her wings were steady, Brigitta inhaled enough to speak. "Croilus got across." She inhaled again. "So can we."

Lalam inhaled. "There's nothing . . . to breathe." He looked worriedly at Glennis. If she collapsed from lack of air, there was no way either of them could carry her.

"He got across," Brigitta said.

She took a gulp from her canteen and then rummaged through her pack. She removed an extra tunic, one of her blankets, and a serving bowl and dropped them into the sand, where they immediately began to sink. Lalam followed suit, dropping a tunic, a bowl, and a firestone. Glennis pulled out a blanket, her bowl, and her ceremonial drum. She paused before dropping the drum.

"I'll make you a new one," said Lalam.

Glennis nodded and dropped it among their other possessions. Brigitta's load felt minimally lighter, but perhaps it was enough to get her across.

"I'll go first," she said. "I know air."

Before they could argue with her, she took the deepest breath she could manage and struck out across the no-air, allowing her breath to fill every part of her body, and releasing it in a slow and steady stream. Focus was key, she told herself as she trudged through the sand. She mind-misted out a wingslength in front of her, no more than that for fear of using her energy up, and tested the space. Nothing, nothing, nothing. Eventually, she was going to need to inhale again.

Her heart began to pound in her chest.

You're not going to make it.

Glennis certainly won't make this.

Turn around!

He was there, she reminded herself. Croilus was there on the mountain with the Ancients; she had seen it the night before. If he had gotten across, so could she.

Just when she thought her lungs would burst for lack of breath, she felt it. Her mind mist detected the other side of the nothing and she stretched out, falling forward into the sand. Mouth full of grit, she had no breath to spit it out, so she ignored the sand on her tongue and crept on. At least she could breathe again.

Then, there was solid ground beneath her hands.

She spat and wiped her mouth. It felt so good she laughed out loud. There was grass, too, she realized as she stood up and waved back at Lalam and Glennis.

They had made it to Sage Mountain.

Lalam sent Glennis along first, and through Brigitta's encouraging she managed to get most of the way across before Brigitta had to venture back into the no-air and haul her forward. Lalam made it the fastest, and after he arrived, the three of them smiled relief. They could do this. They looked up the steep mountain, so tall it cut through the clouds.

"We need to get above them," Brigitta said, pointing up. "That's where he'll be."

As the day passed into night they took shelter under some fallen boulders that reminded Brigitta of the rebels' Gathering Place in Noe. *Secret Palace,* Brigitta imagined Thistle whispering, and she smiled.

"Glennis," she called as she held the dustmist in place for Lalam to spread the firepepper protection, "what shall we name those despicable sand hills?"

"How about the 'Despicable Sand Hills'?" said Glennis, and Lalam laughed.

They finished their task and settled on a cold meal rather than risk a fire in case Croilus had a lookout. Still, it was chilly, so Lalam and Brigitta set to warming the remaining firestone and it created a small amount of heat around which they gathered. With their combined energies and talents, their spells were getting almost routine.

Or was it that she felt more connected to him since remembering his and Ondelle's private transformation practice? His hazel eyes gazed in question as she stared at him. She hadn't told him of the memory and was curious as to how much he knew. But she also felt it an invasion of privacy, and if there were anything he wanted her to know, he would tell her. It was enough that Ondelle had trusted him.

The anxiety of being so close to Croilus made for a fitful night, and morning found them approaching the climb silently, saving their strength for what lay ahead. The air was still too thin to fly well, but breathable, and the sun glared down on them as they made their way up the mountain. But the higher they climbed, the cooler it became, until the discomfort of the chill replaced the discomfort of the heat. Brigitta wasn't sure which she disliked more.

She was about to break the monotony of the climb with this pronouncement when she saw the first white flake. As they progressed, more and more white flakes fluttered about.

"It's called cloud ice," said Lalam, holding out his hand. A flake landed there and melted into his palm. "I've been told each piece is unique."

Brigitta tilted her head up to let some land on her face. Dancing flakes of frozen water. Miniature worlds.

"I like it," she said.

"It's going to get cold," Lalam responded. "Everyone bundle up."

Wrapping their treated blankets around themselves, they flew and climbed some more. The cloud ice turned dense and then disappeared into a fog so thick the faeries had to hold hands to keep track of each other. Their wings grew heavier and heavier until they could no longer use them at all. Clinging to the side of the mountain, they found a trail leading across and up. With no choice but to proceed, they continued, placing one foot in front of the other, Lalam in the lead.

A strange windy echo sounded through the fog, and Lalam stopped, holding Brigitta back with his hands. He scooted forward, and she and Glennis followed, until they could see movement within the fog. When they got a bit closer, the fog in front of them was sucked away, as if inhaled through a giant mouth.

"Rock dragons!" Brigitta called, slipping on the path beneath her and stumbling backward into Glennis.

Lalam pushed them both into the face of the mountain and they all froze, waiting.

The fog breathed back out again. And in again. And out again.

"I don't think it's any kind of dragon," said Lalam. "I think it's the mountain itself."

As they moved closer they discovered he was right. The path they were on led straight into a cave in the side of the mountain, which continued to breathe in and out, whirling the fog on its breath.

"This is it," said Brigitta.

She turned to look at her companions, fog breathing in and out around them. Lalam, sun-burned and sand-blown. Glennis, dirt-smudged and skin-scraped.

"Hey, listen," she began, putting on a brave face. "You don't have to come any farther. I'm the one responsible for this."

"What do you mean?" asked Lalam.

"What do you mean, what do I mean?"

"I mean why do you think you are personally responsible for any of this?" he asked. "Destiny was set in motion the moment the Ancients initiated their plan."

Brigitta chewed on this. Why did she feel responsible? Why did she feel guilty for Lalam and Glennis deciding to come along? She thought of how Lalam had allowed her to take the scepter the night of the Masquerade, and how Glennis had thrown herself through the protective field as the Impenetrable Spell was cast.

"What he's saying," said Glennis, interrupting her thoughts, "is that this is bigger than you and you're being selfish hogging all the glory."

"Well, that's another way of putting it," said Lalam with a smirk.

"It's our destiny, too," said Glennis, placing a hand on Brigitta's shoulder.

Brigitta stared into the mountain's mouth, inhaling and exhaling its fog as it had probably done for thousands of seasons.

"Yes," she finally said, "you're right."

Lalam lit a globelight and they stepped inside.

After they moved away from the mouth of the cave, the passageway curved up and around, spiraling like the Hive. It was dark at first, but then it grew lighter and lighter until they didn't need the globelight any longer.

Windows of ice appeared in the cavern through which they could view the outside world. The faeries curved one way and saw the vast ocean to the east. They curved the other way and all was whirling white below. After a while, instead of forming frozen windows, the ice held things trapped inside. Once-living things. Flowers and beasts of all shapes and sizes, preserved in the walls of the mountain.

They slowed to examine each one: an immense purple-lipped, white-petaled flower, something that looked like a miniature warwump, a flock of illuminoops—all frozen in place.

When they rounded the next curve, a large golden-maned creature stood in front of them on hooved feet. He was dressed in a black robe and had a wispy golden beard and piercing yellow eyes. Close to him stood a large white bird, tall as his shoulder, with the same piercing yellow eyes.

"Chakau'un," said Brigitta, recognizing the hooved beast from the illustrations on the wall of the Purview room in Noe. "I remember . . . Ondelle's knowing . . ." She could see the Chakau'un relaxing around the Standing Stones with the Nhords and Ancients. They had been friends.

She placed her hand up against his cold prison. "He's from one of the five civilizations. Carraiglenn."

"When we arrive there," said Lalam, "we will let them know of this one."

Brigitta nodded, then shivered. "Let's keep moving."

The frozen creatures eventually disappeared, as did the icy windows to the world. They had to rely, once again, on the light from their globes. They resumed a steady, rhythmic pace as they climbed, silently, higher and higher, until Brigitta got the sensation that she had been climbing inside the mountain forever.

When an unmistakable voice shattered the silence, her blood turned colder than the air around her. She stopped dead in her tracks and looked intently at her companions.

Croilus, she mouthed, and their eyes widened.

All this time, all this way, all this imagining of how this encounter would go, and here it was in front of her. With every bit of energy she had, she slowed down her heart and mind. This was a place of clarity. She would find that clarity now.

She signaled to Lalam and pointed to her temple, holding his gaze and hoping he would understand. As she fell into his eyes, she summoned the connection Ondelle and he had shared, and she misted out to him, searching for those minuscule spaces the High Priestess had sought. His mind felt familiar. And comforting.

Can you hear me? she asked.

He smiled and nodded.

Glennis's lips trembled as she shifted her gaze back and forth between them. There was no way to explain to her what they had done, so she simply signaled for Glennis to stay behind them.

Slipping quietly up the passage, Brigitta in the lead, they curved one final time before the mountain opened up. She held out her arms and gestured not to make a sound.

The massive cavern before them grew narrower and narrower as it stretched up and up, the cap of it a coating of ice so sheer they could see the blue beyond it. At the very peak, the ice reversed direction and funneled all the way back down to the cavern floor. Drops of water slid down the stalactite, dripping off its point into a hole in the floor and disappearing without a sound.

Hundreds of Ancients huddled around the edges of the enormous space, Jarlath a spark of color among them, and Croilus circled the icicle, hand rubbing at his chin. He looked too sure of himself, Brigitta thought as he smiled. They were too late. But a moment later, he cringed and held his temples.

The knowing, it's not settled yet, Brigitta thought to Lalam in their mind-mist connection. *But what's he doing?*

Croilus kept circling the icy formation as he rubbed his temples. Whatever magic the stalactite held, whatever clarity he was searching for, he was obviously having difficulty making sense of it. It was not too late to stop him.

I'm not sure he even knows, Lalam thought back to Brigitta.

Glennis looked helplessly at the two of them, and Brigitta felt sorry about her lack of mind-mist training, but there was nothing to be done about it now. Maybe they should just send Glennis back to the tunnel entrance before she got hurt.

Brigitta was about to ask Lalam what he thought about this when a pressure formed in her gut. Something was pulling at her insides. Something wanted her to move into the open cavern, and she was having trouble resisting the urge.

Oh, no . . . the dry coldness pricked at her skin. *What have I done?*

Lalam spun to face her, and she grabbed his arm, yanking him back into the tunnel. As they reached Glennis, Croilus let out an amused laugh, its echo bouncing off the cavern walls. They turned to run, but a host of Ancients blocked their path to the tunnel. All eyes were upon them, but the Ancients didn't make a move.

"You may as well show yourself, Brigitta of the White Forest," he shouted. "You've come this far."

The three faeries looked to each other in silent question.

"We are three to his one," Lalam whispered. "And his mind is not well."

"What other choice do we have?" whispered Brigitta.

They took a collective breath and moved into the room, spreading themselves out a bit to cover more space. Brigitta eased her way toward Jarlath.

Croilus's head spasmed as he opened his arms wide. "Welcome to my new palace. I am renaming it Croilus Peak. What do you think?"

"It's a bit cold," said Brigitta, eyeing the Ancients. They didn't appear to be doing much of anything, let alone following any sort of orders from Croilus.

Croilus held up his scepter with one hand and leaned over to touch the stalactite with the other, rubbing his palm across its slick surface. The icy windows above them vibrated with a low harmonious hum.

"Didn't you think I could see through you as you see through me?" laughed Croilus, removing his hand. "Narine's energy binds us together."

She had no answer for him and cursed her over-confidence. It was an obvious conclusion that no one, not even High Priest Fozk, had come to.

"I didn't realize you were that stupid," Croilus said with a snort. "I've seen it all, you know. Your Elders, your friends, your family. Your *forest*."

"Yeah?" she asked, trying to contain the tremor in her voice. "Too bad you can't get inside."

"Who says I can't?"

Croilus wrapped his hand around the end of the stalactite, and the icy windows above them shook once more. The sound of it vibrated deep inside her; it touched her core. It was something beyond any magic she had ever experienced. Something so ancient she didn't even know its name.

She really was an idiot. She had no idea how the magic of Sage Peak functioned, only that it was beyond her grasp. Perhaps Croilus could harness it to enter the White Forest or even break the Impenetrable Spell. He held up the scepter and Brigitta could both feel and see the energy of the stalactite channel through his hand, across his body, down his other arm, and into the scepter where it burst forth into the room.

The Ancients jerked alert, honing in on Brigitta, Lalam, and Glennis. The three faeries backed up and turned to flee, but it was too late, they were surrounded. Brigitta tried to mind-mist, empath, anything to see if she could connect with them using Narine's energy, but it was no use. The three of them were yanked away from each other and held apart.

Croilus faltered once again, pulling his hand away from the stalactite to his head, and the Ancients faltered, too. But he recovered quickly, too quickly for them to escape. With a sneer, he pointed the scepter at Brigitta, and Jarlath sprung forward. He landed in front of her, all trace of the old Jarlath gone, and held a sharp stone to her throat.

"Oh, I love it when friends become enemies," sang Croilus. "It reminds me of my own departure from Mabbe."

"Please, Jarlath," said Brigitta, looking as deeply into him as she could. "Please. You know me."

Focus on Croilus, she heard Lalam in her mind. *Keep him unsettled; he controls the rest.*

She turned toward Croilus as he approached. "I will enjoy ripping those Air and Water energies from you," he said.

"You mean Narine's Air and Water?"

His eyes flickered. "They are no longer hers!" he shouted, heading back for the stalactite.

He can't do it on his own, thought Brigitta to Lalam. *He needs the clarity from Sage Peak.*

Croilus hissed and Jarlath grabbed Brigitta by the shoulders.

"You can take them from me," said Brigitta as matter-of-factly as she could, "but it won't make any difference. It's too late."

The Ancients fumbled around her, and Jarlath loosened his grip. She strode toward Croilus as if she already had the upper hand.

"What do you mean?" demanded Croilus, removing his hand from the stalactite.

"Her Fire energy is gone. You can't generate any more Blue Spell."

"You lie! And after I take yours, I will find it." He pointed the scepter at her. "Imagine, with my Ancient warriors, I will be the most powerful faerie who has ever lived!"

"Ondelle destroyed Narine's Fire Energy when she died." She knocked his scepter out of her way. "Once you use your Blue Spell up, it's gone forever."

The Ancients stood down; Glennis and Lalam were released.

It's working, Lalam assured her from across the room. *He's losing his confidence.*

"No!" Croilus spun around, addressing the Ancients.

"They can't help you," Brigitta said. "They already gave their energies up to protect the White Forest."

He looked up at the stalactite in desperation.

"Good luck ruling Faweh from in here," she said sweetly, stepping closer.

His eyes bugged for a moment, then he grabbed his temples and released an anguished cry. While he was impaired, Brigitta reached for the stalactite. An icy shock shot from her hand to her heart, and she doubled over. Gritting her teeth, she looked up into the stalactite as if it were a living being. She imagined its spaces widening and its not-spaces melting into them. With a quick twist of her wrist, she broke off its tip.

The ceiling of ice cracked and rumbled above them.

"What have you done!" cried Croilus.

Before she could answer, pieces of ice started collapsing around them. With a roar, Croilus launched himself at Brigitta, struggling to get the stalactite tip back from her. She held it away from him as Lalam and Glennis pushed their way through the Ancients.

With a hand on his chest, she held him back while she gripped the icy staff, her warm fingers melting into it. But he was stronger than she. He reached past her and took hold of it, grinning his sickly grin. Brigitta grew weak and dizzy, her energies pulling at her insides from where her fingers gripped the ice below his.

Somehow, she realized, Croilus was using his own Narine energy to draw hers into the stalactite. Even that mere tip harnessed enough power from Sage Peak.

And she was holding it, too.

With a burst of clarity, she gripped the ice harder and locked eyes with Croilus. "Two can play that game," she growled, and dove into herself like plummeting off of Precipice Falls.

She retreated so far it felt like she had left the world. Then she was inside of the stalactite tip, swimming in the spaces between the not-spaces. Feeling, as Ondelle had, her own self divided up, distributing the infinitesimal pieces of herself within the ice.

And once she was there, she called to Narine's Earth energy to occupy the spaces with her.

To transform them.

Come with us, Brigitta said to it. *Come.*

And it did.

As Narine's Earth energy filled the spaces, Croilus's grip loosened, and Brigitta slipped back into her own skin, sealing the Earth energy into the stalactite tip.

Croilus screamed in anguish as he lost his grip. The Ancients dropped to the ground around Glennis and Lalam, and Brigitta pushed Croilus out of the way.

The ceiling shuddered and a block of ice fell to the floor, cutting Brigitta off from the entrance to the cavern.

"Go on!" she shouted and waved for Lalam and Glennis to escape. She turned to find another way out, perhaps up. But as she was searching, Jarlath tackled her from the side. She screamed at him as they struggled. "Jarlath, it's me!"

A chunk fell from the ceiling onto Brigitta's head, knocking her down. Jarlath seized the opportunity to leap on top of her and get his hands around her neck.

She gripped the icicle as her breath was squeezed from her. She kicked and bucked, trying to get Jarlath off of her. With the last of her strength, she thrust the icicle into Jarlath's neck and held it there as he howled in pain.

Dizzy and gasping for air, she tried to conjure the transformation spell, feeling the empty spaces within Jarlath, and the not-spaces of Narine's energy. As she felt the space and not-space, Jarlath's emptiness began to fill.

But it was all too much. She couldn't maintain her concentration; she had so little strength left. She lost her grip on the stalactite tip and her hand fell to the ground. The last thing she saw before she blacked out was Jarlath's distressed expression as blood-stained water seeped from the icicle's wound in his neck.

Chapter Fourteen

Ondelle was weak. She had never felt so weak in all her life. Weak and half missing. What was happening?

Oh, yes, she was dying.

She opened her eyelids, heavy as they were. Gola, the old Drutan, her trusted friend, stood in front of her with a pair of tired Eyes perched on her shoulder.

Ondelle placed a hand on her barky arm. "We are near our departure."

"Yes."

She summoned what was left of her energy and gripped her friend. "I need you to do something as I go," she whispered hoarsely. "It will be our final task."

Ondelle paused to cough and Gola waited until she could breathe again. She motioned for something to drink and the Drutan placed her knotty hand behind Ondelle's neck, lifted her forward, and put a leafed cup to her mouth.

"My Fire," she said after her parchedness had subsided. "Narine's Fire," she continued as Gola eased her back down to the pillow. "You must keep it safe."

Without question, the old Drutan nodded. "How shall I keep it?"

Ondelle closed her eyes again. "I need something non-living. Porous. Not a spell seed."

Immediately, Gola lifted her moonstones from beneath her tunic and gazed upon them through the Eyes. "One last service to the faeries?" she asked them.

She lifted the cord upon which they hung over her head and untied the knot, slipping the end moonstone from the strap and placing it on the bedside table. She hung the four remaining moonstones on her mantel.

Ondelle opened her eyes, heaved herself onto her side, and managed the smallest of smiles.

"Of course," she said as Gola returned to her bedside and held up the stone.

Ondelle gazed at it, preparing it as she prepared herself. She dove inside it and discovered its spaces so welcoming it was tempting to release her Fire into it right then and there. But there were good-byes to make, and she did not want to leave her journey incomplete. Instead, she focused on burnishing its pores with gentle tongues of Fire energy. The stone slowly transformed, as if taking a long breath, opening itself up to receive.

A knock at the door pulled her from her trance, and she fell back onto the pillow.

"May we come in?" called Dervia from outside.

"After it is done, hide it within you," Ondelle whispered as Gola pocketed the stone. "No one must know. For Brigitta's protection. She and it will find each other when they are ready."

"Brigitta!" Lalam cried, startling her awake. Chunks of ice surrounded them and more plummeted from the walls of the cavern.

"Jarlath!" she cried, sitting up, dizzy and sore, her wing paining.

"We've got him." Lalam helped her to her feet. "Come on."

They stumbled over and around the fallen sheets of ice as the cavern continued to shake. Ahead of them, just inside the mouth of the tunnel, Glennis dragged Jarlath on a blanket. She stopped, her face pooled in sweat.

Brigitta dropped to her knees in front of Jarlath and placed her hand against his cheek. Narine's energy was there; she could feel it coursing through him. Her body began to heave, sobs of joy.

"We left the icicle tip in his neck," said Lalam, pointing to the thick bandage around it. "We didn't know what would happen if we removed it."

"What of Croilus?" asked Brigitta, looking around. "And all the Ancients?"

"They disappeared," said Lalam, picking up the other side of the blanket.

"Disappeared?" asked Brigitta as she stood up again.

"Through the space under the stalactite."

"And Lalam held your spell in place!" added Glennis as they sped through the passageway.

"You made it so easy," he said, smiling down at her. "Ondelle would be proud."

Although Brigitta was relieved they had retaken Narine's Earth energy, it left her no way to find Croilus, she thought as they descended the mountain. She wondered what would befall the Watcher. He couldn't control the Ancients forever with what was left of the scepter's Blue Spell. And without Narine's energies, he couldn't generate any more.

Narine's energies.

All that remained was her Fire. And thanks to Gola and Ondelle, the wisest beings Brigitta had ever known, it was now safely hidden inside the Impenetrable Spell. Ondelle had been right to keep it safe until it was time. Until Brigitta, and the rest of Faweh, was ready.

Perhaps all there was to do then was to ignite the remaining Purviews.

The Purviews. She looked at her companions as they dragged Jarlath along the path and thought about the four rings in the pouch around her belt. She had not recovered the scepter. She did not have enough rings to get everyone through.

First things first. She looked down on Jarlath's pale face. One thing at a time.

After a night at the base of the northern side of Sage Peak, Narine's Earth energy had still not settled in Jarlath. It exhausted Brigitta with its restlessness. In such proximity, she was constantly drawn to the energy, a missing piece of herself. But it also felt like an invasion of Jarlath's privacy when she allowed herself to be drawn in.

Instead, she concentrated on simply keeping him alive. The cold and the loss of blood were making it difficult for him to heal. The lack of food and water didn't help, and who knew if Croilus's spells would have a lasting effect on him. Brigitta dripped water on his lips and rubbed his throat, hoping she could coax him into drinking it. Food was out of the question.

They traveled slowly over the course of the next sun, northeast toward Icecap Forest, with Jarlath wrapped in blankets held between two of them at a time. The sand hills were petrified on this side of the mountain, and the group traveled cautiously over the coarse ground. They carried Jarlath in short shifts, took a little food and drink, and numbed their minds to anything beyond their immediate task.

That night, by the fire in a cave, Brigitta confessed her fears to Glennis and Lalam. "If he dies, it's my fault." She hadn't cried in many moonbeats. She was beyond tears.

"If he dies," said Lalam, "it is Croilus's doing."

"It was my idea to steal Fozk's scepter and leave the White Forest."

"And where would he be now if you had left him in Noe?"

Brigitta put her head in her hands.

"There is no moving backward."

"Ondelle used to say something similar," said Brigitta.

Glennis moved beside her and put her arm around her. "He won't die," she said.

Brigitta looked into Glennis's gold-flecked eyes and realized it had been a long time since she had been annoyed with her.

"I'm sorry about the mosspatch," said Brigitta.

Glennis shrugged. "I deserved it. I would have mosspatched me, too."

That night, Brigitta dreamt of the illuminoops. She dreamt she was with Jarlath in the lyllium field as the bright little flock flew back and forth, circling the two moons.

He turned to Brigitta. "Thank you."

"For what?" she asked, but he just smiled and turned back to the tiny silver and white striped lights.

She moved closer to him, taking his arm in hers, and together they followed the illuminoops as they danced across the sky.

"Brigitta," said Jarlath hoarsely.

As she turned to face him, the world was swept away. She woke up to the sound of him coughing.

"Jarlath!" she whispered fiercely, tumbling from her blanket and rushing to his side. She fell into him and held him tightly, crying and crying until she realized he was convulsing. "Oh, Great Moon, I'm so sorry."

She pulled away, and he coughed a few more times and then grinned. "Always trying to kill me, aren't you?"

She fetched a cup of water and handed it to him, but he was too weak to hold himself up and drink, so she propped her pack behind him and led the cup to his lips. He grabbed her by the wrist and looked intently at her, the deep, deep blue of his eyes calling. Narine's energy was strong between them. He felt it, too, she could tell.

"Thank you," he said, just like in her dream.

The energy continued to flow between them. It was almost like looking into herself.

"Uh, Brigitta," said Jarlath, "this is kind of weird."

"Yeah."

He let go of her wrist and they both laughed nervously.

"You'll get used to it," she said, busying herself finding him something to eat. "Having an energy bound to you, I mean."

He held up his hands and examined them, as if they would look different somehow.

She fed him and told him of their adventures, he doubting some of the heroics, until the morning light came and Lalam and Glennis awoke. Breakfast was a celebration.

They could move faster across the foothills, but Jarlath still required many breaks. He would also stop for no reason at all, it seemed, as he searched for something inside himself that he wasn't ready to share. Brigitta did her best to be patient with him. After all, he had been more than patient with her over the past season.

She hung back, not just to give him his space, but because the closeness of the energy was too much for her. She also knew that the Earth energy Jarlath had been given was not exactly the long-lost kin he had been waiting for but didn't know it. It was probably more like a brother he never knew he had and didn't quite trust.

It was odd that Brigitta never would have pegged Jarlath for an Earth Faerie, but there was a certain suitedness about it. He was more contemplative than she remembered, his body more solid. And, now that she thought about it, he had spent countless quiet hours with Gola studying herbal arts.

Lalam started teaching him what it meant to be an Earth Faerie, but also said it would be for Jarlath to figure out. There was no way to explain how each energy was bound to any other faerie.

"It would be like you trying to experience what it's like to be me," he said. "Or I you."

After one particularly long break, Jarlath returned from a meditation with a smile on his face. "I feel stronger today," he said. "More settled."

He still wore the bloody bandage on his neck, but he didn't seem to be in any pain. The color had certainly returned to his skin, and his eyes sparkled as he took in the view. The solid dunes had broken up into a chunky scree that led all the way down to the forest below.

"This reminds me of the petrified bowl in Noe," said Brigitta as she kicked at the ground, "this rocky stuff."

"Yeah," Jarlath said, then got that contemplative look on his face again. "But I can also remember it differently."

"What do you mean?" asked Glennis as she dug out some

cookware and herbs.

"I mean," he said, "I can remember it as Narine remembered it."

"What?" Brigitta exclaimed, grabbing his arm, ignoring the pulse of energy between them. "How?"

"Narine's energy, I guess," he said. "Pieces of her memories are landing."

"Wait, do you think you received any of her knowing through the transformation?" Brigitta asked.

"Maybe," said Jarlath. "It was all mixed up inside of Croilus, her energy and her knowing." Jarlath turned to them and pulled the bandage from his neck. He wet the injury with his canteen water and wiped the dried blood away. Underneath was a star-shaped scar.

Brigitta reached up and touched the scar in awe, and Jarlath shivered. "The icicle worked kind of like a frore dagger," she said. "Only . . . prettier."

"I don't know how much of her memories I've got," he said, fingering the mark himself, "but they're filling me up."

"That will come in handy," said Lalam. He glanced across the scree to the horizon, and the ocean that waited for them there. "We're going to need all the help we can get."

Brigitta let go of Jarlath's arm. If he had enough of Narine's memories inside of him, surely they could figure out how to get through the Purviews, balance Faweh, and get home. Everyone must have been thinking the same thing, as they all suddenly smiled and a lightness of spirit settled on the group.

Jarlath's eyes twinkled even more and the familiar smirk returned to his lips. "And, boy, have I got things to tell you."

Lalam started a fire, and they huddled close as the sun descended and the two moons perched themselves above the forest. After they had eaten, and the gundlebean stew had begun to digest, Brigitta, Lalam, and Glennis sat expectantly, all eyes on Jarlath.

"It might take a while," he warned, poking at the fire with a stick.

"We've got time," Brigitta replied, pulling a blanket around her shoulders, and settling in for the night.

White Forest Lexicon

Blood Seed
The narratives around the Blood Seed are as old as the **Saari** civilization. They believe it is the heart of their land, and that it pumps energy through its roots. It was a very big deal when, thousands of seasons ago, they decided to place the Purview, a gift from the Ancient Faeries of Noe, on their sacred Blood Seed mound, a fertile hill made almost entirely of roots. They thought the Blood Seed energy would both feed the Purview and prevent anything harmful from coming through.

Over the seasons, the stories have reshaped themselves to incorporate the Purview as part of the Seed. It is said the heart has been sick ever since the Great World Cry. To honor the mother Blood Seed, each floating island of the new civilization carries a small red stone buried in its center. It is believed when Faweh is balanced again, these stones will grow roots and anchor the islands. (see also **Pariglenn** and **Flota of the Saari**)

blossom bells
Hanging chimes, shaped like flower buds, that can either be struck lightly for a quick, clear note or rubbed with a finger for a longer, deeper one. Striking different parts of the "bud" elicits a different sound, so there are many combinations of notes that can be played even on a small set of blossom bells.

Brigitta "of the White Forest" / "of Tiragarrow"
Faeries are generally called by their given name and village-nest of birth. Sometimes faeries change this reference if they have lived in a different village-nest for a long time, or even if they simply feel a kinship to an area. If they are referred to as "of the White Forest," as an Elder might be, it is to indicate they are in service to the whole forest. When Brigitta was called "Brigitta of the White Forest" by Fozk of Fhorsa, it was his way of showing respect and acknowledging her as part of the Center Realm community.

broodnut

Its "shell" is soft and thin, so that when carved into, the red meat of it is exposed. Named "broodnut" because love-sick faeries use it to carve messages to their heartthrobs. Also sometimes used in faerie games because it is light and soft. The meat of it is plain, but when cooked and spiced makes a great party snack. Broodnut trees grow best in the forest between the Earth and Water Realms near Green Lake.

bubblebug

Entertaining little winged bugs that skitter themselves across the top of still water and call to each other by popping the bubbles they create. They blow into the wetness with their long noses, gather up a stock of bubbles, dance around them with their tiny legs, popping as they go. Kids love to watch them and listen to them, but they are generally too fast to catch.

cloud ice

What we call snowflakes.

dusk owl

The largest bird in the White Forest, although there are only a few dozen in existence. Its coloring is so like the light at dusk, that no matter what the season, for a brief moment in time each day, the owl is completely camouflaged to the world. Its cry is a high-pitched breathy hoot. The White Forest sprites have been known to fly with the dusk owls that frequent their uul tree.

dustmist

A diverse and useful tool (created most often by a talented Air Faerie) used to spread spells, aromas, sounds, or any other light item through the air or to make it stick or stay in one place. Can also be used to conceal things. With a great deal of practice, one can learn to send messages using dustmist. Mothers can use it leave lullabies in the air above their babies. Festival grounds can be sprinkled with dustmist to keep sparkles or musical notes in the air.

Eternal Dragon (Tzajeek)

Most faeries in the White Forest only think of Tzajeek as a mythical creature from ancient times. In reality, the **Eternal Dragon** is as old as

Faweh itself. A winged sea-serpent with the ability to absorb, transform, and redistribute elements, Tzajeek is the only one of its kind. Its origin is unknown.

Tzajeek is neither good nor evil; It simply is. It originally fed on and redistributed the fifth element (as Blue Spell), visiting the Ancients through Lake Indago each season. After the Great World Cry, when the Lake disappeared and the Dragon's cycle disturbed, the Ancients sacrificed their basic elements to the lesser faeries and their fifth elements to the Dragon, which became a vessel to deliver Blue Spell to the White Forest faeries. It was a way to satiate the Dragon as well as distribute such power slowly and methodically over time. Eventually, the fifth element, and therefore Blue Spell, was bound to run out. The Ancients trusted the world would be rebalanced by then, and they would be properly dispersed.

firepepper
A Fire Faerie specialty. Fine, treated granules used to make something hot to touch. Firepepper can really burn, so it's not often used full-strength. More generally it is diluted and used in anything you'd want warm, like a compress, blanket, or water to bathe in. Some Master Gardeners use it to keep little beasties from getting into their gardens. Could be used to play practical jokes, but that would be mean.

Flota of the Saari
After the Great World Cry wreaked elemental chaos all over Faweh, the **Saari** of **Pariglenn** were forced to relocate to the water due to the land's over-fertility. They constructed island villages out of "planxis" (a combination of seaweed, earth, and salts), ever-changing with the tides, in order to avoid the strangling overgrowth. **(See also Saari)**

founding / ersafounding / erdafounding
Foundings are what the Saari call their parents, and ersafoundings and erdafoundings are what they call their foundings' foundings, meaning their grandmothers and grandfathers. The term "founding" is used because the Saari females all give birth at the same time annually in communal ponds to tadpole-like beings. When the babies are ready for the world, they simply crawl out of the pond and "find" an adult Saarin to care for them. There is no way to tell if the Saarin they find is actually a biological parent, but that doesn't seem to matter to them.

frore dagger
An ice-cold dagger that immediately heals the cut it makes. Originally used by the Ancients on anything that needed to be trimmed. For instance, if a tree had a sick limb, it could be cut off with a frore dagger and not leave a wound. A frore dagger can still be fatal if it strikes the right organs, as when Queen Mabbe used one on High Priestess Ondelle in Noe.

hands (as in "12 hands deep")
Faeries literally use the width of their hands to measure things, though the proper measurement of a "hand" is about two ½ inches. If you wanted to call someone small you might say, "You couldn't even measure with her!"

illuminoops
When Glennis named the fluttery flock of bright little silver and white creatures, she wasn't too far off. To the Ancient faeries, they were known as *luminamins*, but that name is long forgotten. They only live on Foraglenn, but their habitat was destroyed in the Great World Cry. The flock Brigitta and her friends witness is a collection of lost luminamins, continually searching for others like themselves to lead them home. Their deep longing for a place to call home can bring even the grouchiest of beasts to silver-hued tears.

lingomana
One of the many fantastic fruits available on Pariglenn, with a crisp, tangy outer peel and a sweet pulpy inside. Fruits and tubers are the only things the Saari eat from the mainland, because they are easily accessible from the shore. They simply swim up and harvest them. Their floating islands aren't very fertile, but the Saari are able to gather sea plants, extract salt from the water, and collect spices from the sea life. The Saari are vegetarians.

Lodge of Eastern Months
Like the faeries have their "season cycles" and the Nhords have their "sand cycles," the Saari have their directional cycle: Northern, Southern, Western, and Eastern. They are tremendous gatherers. Of all the old civilizations, they were the first to explore the other continents

because of this gathering instinct. They would make great pilgrimages to the other continents for seasonal items, often trading with the inhabitants. When they traveled east, they took lodging on Foraglenn at Icecap Forest. When they went west, they might stay on Storlglenn or Carraiglenn. North was Araglenn and south was the Valley of Noe. After the Great World Cry, the ocean was far too rough for travel, and the sea life too vicious, so the lodges were abandoned.

Masquerade / Festival of the Moons

The Masquerade, which takes place during the Festival of Moons, is exactly that, a costumed dance. But as Brigitta said, historically there's more to it. When the faeries originally came to the White Forest, all of their celebrations held more symbolism, because they were celebrating in gratitude for the generosity of the Ancients, for the protection of the forest, and for having each other when the rest of the world had lost so many. The fact that they had reasonable seasons that transitioned into each other because of the protection of the forest, was indeed something to celebrate. But as with the rest of the holidays, the celebration continues out of habit, even if the original meaning behind it has been forgotten.

moonbeat moths

An invention of Brigitta's Poppa. The moths glow and change color every moonbeat (which is about 15 minutes), so not only are they pretty, you can keep track of time with them. At night, at least. They don't glow in the daytime.

"mind body" speaking

What the Saari have developed over time is similar to faerie empathing. The Saari didn't always communicate this way, although they have always had some empathic abilities, which were mostly used for foundings to keep track of their young. After the Great World Cry, every beast had to adapt to new environments. The Saari grew ever more suited to life in the ocean, and "mind body" speaking is part of this evolution.

Moonsrise Ridge

Located in the northwestern part of the White Forest, Moonsrise Ridge is the highest land form in the faerie realm. It is a crescent-shaped ridge, rising like a scree-filled wave from the west and dropping into a sheer cliff face. The ends of the crescent rise from the forest floor so gradually one could easily walk up the ridge.

mossleaf patch
Basically a faerie bandage. The size of the leaf is the size of the bandage. One side has a treated moss that not only makes it stick to the skin, but speeds the healing as well. The treatment is harmless when placed on non-wounded skin.

oddtwins
These creatures, who are a phenomenon of the elemental chaos, did not exist before the Great World Cry. Brigitta is the first one to encounter them who actually has the ability to name them, so we'll call them oddtwins. They are not exactly real, but not exactly imaginary either. They are manifestations of projected energy. This chaotic energy creates from any consciousness it comes in contact with. Brigitta uses this energy, without exactly knowing how, to create the wind-winder for her escape.

Pariglenn (and the continents of Faweh)
The Saari's floating islands are located in a large bay off the northeast coast of Pariglenn, west of **Foraglenn** (where Brigitta lives). Pariglenn is the smallest continent on Faweh. The Saari were its major civilization before the Great World Cry made the land too fertile for them to inhabit. If one could spend some time there without becoming rooted to it, they would discover a tremendous diversity of flora and quick moving fauna. Faweh's three remaining continents are **Araglenn** (where the Nhords are from), **Carraiglenn**, and **Storlglenn**.

pebblenotes (see also song flight)
Small stones that vibrate with sound. They can be used for all kinds of things, from scoring original music to teaching songs to young faeries. They are spellcast to ring with a note fed to it either via voice or instrument, then suspended in the air and directed into song. (see also **song flight**)

poisondarters

Say you took an ant and multiplied its size several times. Then you added long, coarse, dark hairs and a pincher mouth that could slice through tree bark. Oh, and a deadly stinger on its rear end. That would be a poisondarter. Luckily, there are only a dozen or so nests of them on the entire continent of Foraglenn, as they too often fight amongst themselves and the fights result in less poisondarters. Also, they are not really hunters and do not stray far from their nests. They simply wait for other beasts to accidentally fly or crawl by. They also like to steal things from birds to line their own nests.

rainbow lizards

So called for their colorful stripes, which run in rings down the length of their body, including across their tongues. Faerie children love to catch them because when provoked they will spit different colors. Faerie parents hate them because the colored spit can stain. Artists have used rainbow lizard spittle for festive projects, though it's a tough material to work with. The colors don't mix well and it can be a bit sticky. Plus, who wants a breath lantern decorated with lizard spit?

rooting

As with mind-misting and empathing and transformation, there is a basic concept to rooting, but how it is applied is personal and each faerie finds his or her own rooting process. It's a technique used more often by Earth Faeries and involves stretching one's thoughts out and around matter like very thin roots (vein-like, really). From there, faeries can detect the attributes of the matter, its weak points, its density, how much water it could hold, etc. Rooting may also be used as the first step in transformation.

Sage Peak

As with most significant locales on Foraglenn (the Standing Stones, Dead Mountain, etc), before the Great World Cry, Sage Peak served a much different purpose. Its substantial height, funnel shape, and location near the heart of the continent produced a certain resonance found nowhere else in the world. Up there, the mind became so clear that a visitor could examine each of her thoughts like a physical entity, could even remove the thought from her head to contemplate it from all angles. But seeing one's own thoughts can be immensely disturbing, so only those who could deal with that sort of clarity would make the journey. In particular, new Sages to the World Council would visit before taking their posts.

The mountain rises steeply until it comes to a point and then turns in on itself to form an icy stalactite, which has been around for as long as the mountain. In the past, the rhythmic dripping was used for meditation. After the GWC, the clarity hid away in the stalactite, forming a very powerful magical hold on the peak itself.

Saari (singular Saarin)

The Saari of Pariglenn developed as one of the five major civilizations of Faweh, and they were the first to join the Ancients of Noe in creating the World Council of Sages. Next to the Ancient Faeries, they were the most industrious society at the time of the Great World Cry. Before the GWC, they even had several ships, being master navigators, gatherers, and traders (they preferred sailing the oceans to using the Purview).

After the disruption of the elements, however, when they were forced to move off the coast of Pariglenn to their mobile islands, they gave up world exploration. Over time, their physical features adjusted to ocean life: their fingers and toes grew webbed, their skin water-proof and luminescent, and their language transformed into telepathic "**mind body speaking.**" (See also Flota of the Saari)

Singing Caves

There are plenty of interesting places to visit in the White Forest, and each elemental realm contains unique features. In the northeast corner of the Earth Realm, for instance, lies a particular patch of rocky land so perfectly suited to playing with the breezes that gaping holes in the earth can swallow the air and blow it back out, forming soft low notes. Each cavern emits a different sound, and it often seems like the caves actually know how to sing in harmony with each other. A lovely spot for a stroll at night.

song flight

A special kind of song that is directed while suspended in the air, usually using pebblenotes, but one could also use sound bubbles or marbles or any other kind of note that can be hung in the air. **(see also pebblenotes)**

smelting stones

Brigitta gets a few lessons in "smelting" by Hammus and brings a smelting stone with her on her journey to Sage Peak. Smelting is heating something up to extract parts of it that can be used in various capacities: healing potions, food preparation, clothing, arts and crafts, etc.

Standing Stones

As Brigitta pointed out to Ondelle while they were in Noe, the Ancients didn't have very creative names for places, and they tended to simply name things for what they were (their logic being that all beasts would then understand to what it was they were referring). So, the standing stones found by Brigitta and Jarlath were indeed called the Standing Stones. And they weren't so much a sacred place as a place of leisure. There were so many stones upon the plateau, each with slightly different characteristics, that one could find the perfect combination of sun, shadow, temperature, sound, or soundlessness to match one's mood. One could sunbathe, read, meditate, practice a song in a lovely echoing spot, or simply take a nap.

"stomach beast"

Just like the oddtwins, the strange stomach beast that Lalam, Brigitta, and Glennis encounter in the forest is simply an anomaly. No one will probably ever know how it came to be, other than a product of the Great World Cry's elemental chaos. It is one of a kind, eats pretty much anything, and has the ability to entice any living creature to come to it. It is also exceedingly elastic.

thought-looping

Definitely an advanced technique, as with anything that manipulates thoughts. Minds are messy places and no two are alike. Generally, you take something someone said or thought and loop it around in order to give them a singular focus. You can loop one or more being's thoughts, but the more minds involved, the harder it is to make it stick. If someone said, "Good-bye," and another someone said, "See you tomorrow," you could fix that loop because it's logical. Thought-loops eventually slip away as other thoughts sneak in. Manipulating thoughts so that someone actually performs an action is much more difficult, especially if that action is counter to their nature. As a meditative practice, one could loop her own thoughts.

whisper light (Narine's)
It is true that whisper lights in general are just playful (or pesky) little plants that grow in fields, like the one outside of Gola's tree-home in the Dark Forest, and whisper the nonsense of subconscious thoughts to anyone nearby. These whisper lights were discovered by Gola and Narine when they were hiding out during the Great World Cry. Narine later made a pact with Gola, and hid "knowings" inside of whisper lights to be released to each continent when the time was right, so that the five civilizations would seek each other out through the Purviews.

wind-winder
Not all faeries are strong flyers. Air Faeries tend to be the fastest and most dynamic flyers, while Earth Faeries are slower, but steady. Wings can also be broken, torn, or injured and sometimes never completely repaired. The wind-winder was invented by an Air Faerie Inventor named Holt, and it took him a very long time to figure it out. The faerie using it must be adept at conjuring pockets of air in order to use it. Once each hole in the net-like structure is filled, the faerie is completely buoyant, growing less so as each air pocket ruptures. The better the faerie at conjuring the pockets of air, the more stable the wind-winder.

Coming Summer 2015
Faerie Tales from the White Forest
Book Four

The story that started it all . . .

Narine of Noe

While on a visit to Dragon Mountain, young Narine, daughter to the High Sage of Noe, witnesses the lonely miracle of a Drutan's birth. Called back home from her retreat due to political tensions in Noe, Narine spends her days distracted and haunted by her memory of the Drutan's cries.

Soon after her return home, though, Narine witnesses the four World Sages casting bad magic, and her father is caught in the crossfire. All of Faweh turns to elemental chaos, and the Ancients must decide quickly how to save their lesser faerie kin from a world gone mad.

An elaborate plan is hatched, and Narine's place in the plan is instrumental. But, she risks it all to travel back to Dragon Mountain in order to rescue the lonely newborn Drutan left to the elements that have grown unruly after this Great World Cry.

About the Author

Award-winning author, spokenword artist, and educator Danika Dinsmore teaches creative writing and world building to writers of all ages. When not in British Columbia with her husband and their big-boned feline, Freddy Suave, she takes her Imaginary Worlds program on the road to schools, conferences, and festivals across North America.

You can find Danika on her website: danikadinsmore.com or on Twitter @danika_dinsmore.

Made in the USA
Charleston, SC
02 May 2016